W9-CAL-686

ROGUE STAR

Michael Flynn

A Tom Doherty Associates Book
New York

This is a work of fiction. All the characters and events portrayed in this book are either products of the author's imagination or are used fictitiously.

ROGUE STAR

Copyright © 1998 by Michael Flynn

Edited by David G. Hartwell

A Tor Book
Published by Tom Doherty Associates, Inc.
175 Fifth Avenue
New York, NY 10010

Tor Books on the World Wide Web:
http://www.tor.com

Tor® is a registered trademark of Tom Doherty Associates, Inc.

ISBN: 0-812-54299-1
Library of Congress Card Catalog Number: 97-29835

First edition: April 1998
First mass market edition: April 1999

Printed in the United States of America

0 9 8 7 6 5 4 3 2 1

Noelle Nieves Flynn

ROGUE STAR

Characters

FarTrip

Forest Calhoun, command pilot
Mikhail Krasnarov, engineer and copilot
Ignacio "Nacho" Mendes, geologist

The van Huytens

Silverpond

Mariesa van Huyten, chairman of Van Huyten Industries
Harriet Gorley van Huyten, Mariesa's mother
Wayne Coper, Mariesa's neighbor and sometime lover
Barry Fast, Mariesa's ex-husband, a schoolmaster
Ed Sykes, butler at Silverpond

The Cousins

Christiaan van Huyten V, president of Argonaut Research Laboratories
    and Mariesa's older cousin
Brittany van Huyten Armitage, Chris's sister
Wilhemina van Huyten, everyone's great aunt
Norbert Wainwright van Huyten, Mariesa's second cousin
Beatrice van Huyten, Mariesa's aunt
Pauline van Huyten, Beatrice's daughter

Van Huyten Industries

John E. Redmond, Chief Legal Officer, VHI
Khan Gagrat, Chief Financial Officer, VHI
Zhou Hui, Mariesa's personal assistant and bodyguard
Charlie Jim Ffolkes, Mariesa's pilot
Keith McReynolds, former CFO and family friend (dead)
Will "Werewolf" Gregorson, president of Werewolf Electronics
"Fluffy" Gregorson, his wife, an artist
Belinda Karr, senior principal, Mentor Academies
Dolores Pitchlynn, president of Pegasus Aerospace, LEO Board
Steve Matthias, president of Thor Machine Tools
Correy Wilcox, president of Gaea Biotech
Wallace Coyle, president of Aurora Ballistic Transport
João Pessoa, president of Daedelus Aerospace, Brazil
Heinz Ruger, president of Ruger AG, LEO Board
Hamilton Pye, president of Ossa & Pelion Heavy Construction, LEO
   Board

The Peoples' Crusades

Roberta Carson, aka "Styx," or "Styxy," a poet and progressive and
   once one of Belinda's Kids
Phil Albright, head of the Peoples' Crusades
Simon Fell, Phil's right hand, leader of the Direct Action Faction

The Cadre

Dottie Wheeler
Melanie Kaufmann
Isaac Kohl
Ellis Harwood
Darren Winslow
Suletha ad-Din
Fred, a camera doid
Marti, a soundboard tech

Belinda's Kids

Chase Coughlin, Plank pilot wih Pegasus Aerospace Lines
S. James ("Jimmy") Poole, computer security consultant
Leilah Frazetti, Waldo operator on LEO
Tanuja ("Tani") Pandya, novelist
Leland ("Hobie") Hobart, superconductor chemist, creator of
    hobartium
Jenny Ribbon, teacher and caregiver

The Heights

José Eduardo Gonsalves y Mercado, "Flaco," Green Crew rigger-
    candidate
Serafina Cruz, his wife
Felipa Cruz, Serafina's mother
Clotario, Flaco's best friend still alive
Felix Mercado, Flaco's father
Mama Mercado, Flaco's mother

LEO Construction

Uncle Waldo

Red Crew

Wesley Bensalem, "The Rector," Red Crew site boss
Morris "Meat" Tucker, Red Crew rigging boss, one of Belinda's Kids
Rhys Pilov, lead rigger, Flaco's mentor

Green Crew

Tonio Portales, welder-candidate, Flaco's *pana*
Sepp Bauer, welder-candidate, Flaco's *pana*
Henry ("Tiny") Littlebear, welder-candidate

Bird Winfrey, NDT-candidate
Rosita Winfrey, his wife
Red Hawkins, rigger-candidate
Ivan Selodkin, rigger-candidate
Wendy McKenna, electrician-candidate
Delight Jackson, NDT-candidate
King Boudreaux, rigger-candidate
Hirao Murasaki, rigger-candidate

Gold Crew

DeWitt Christensen, Gold Crew site boss
Isaac McDonald, "Izzy Mac," Gold Crew rigging boss
Jimmy Schorr, lead rigger
Gennady Belislav, lead rigger
Taras Kutuzov, Gold Crew welding boss
Adrian Whitlauer, Gold Crew mechanics boss
Nigel Long, NDT technician
Conchita Ferrer, electrican
Kiril Korloff, welder
Grigor Dazhvilli, electrician

LEO Grays

Bolislav Drozd, control tech
Marshall, a medical doctor

SSTO pilots

Edmund "Ned" DuBois, "The Man Who," chief pilot for Daedelus,
    former SSTO test cadre
Gregor Levkin, "The Human Moon," former SSTO test cadre
Valery Volkov, "Johnny Danger," Aurora pilot, former SSTO test
    cadre

Yekaterina (Katya) Volkov, "The Ice Angel," Aurora pilot, former
  SSTO test cadre

The Government

J. Clement Donaldson, president of the U.S., recently reelected
Valerie Kloch, Secretary of Transportation
General Salvaggio, in charge of Special Projects
Capt. John Duckworth, Project Steel Rain
Maj. Lane Chamberlain, Project Lucifer

Other Players

Ed Wilson, an entrepeneur, president of Wilson Enterprises
Cyrus Attwood, owner of Klondike-American and other interests
Edward Bullock, Attwood's nephew and heir
Vanessa Bullock, his wife
Bernie Lefkowitz, scientist with FarTrip organization
Ernie Steubesand, a beachfront property-owner

Acknowledgments

I would like to thank Dr. Eleanor Helin of JPL, discoverer of 1991JW (and many other Near Earth Objects) for the particulars on the size and orbit of this particular NEO. I have dug it out a little, made it somewhat longer to compensate, and given it an oddball geography, all in the name of Art. There may come a time when we owe a lot more to Dr. Helin and her fellow skywatchers than a bit of background for a novel; but in all honesty, I hope we never do. Keep watching the skies.

Additional thanks to Dr. Geoff Landis, who has written extensively on the use of beamed microwave power for spacecraft and on the "incremental" approach to building solar power satellites. He also provided the dates and timing for the FarTrip mission and articles on the use of modified Shuttle external tanks for space station modules.

Greg Bennett provided information on welding in space. He is also president of the Lunar Resources Company, a private venture planning a mining colony on the Moon. The Artemis Project is a registered trademark of the Lunar Resources Company, and "Artemis Mines" is mentioned in the text with their approval. Visit them at http://www.asi.org. Also: a tip of my hat to brother Pat who found me a dummy zip code.

While this book was in production, a *Soyuz* supply capsule collided with the *Mir* space station and breached the *Kristal* module. Thus do events overtake "near future SF." Fortunately, in *Firestar, Mir* was "completely refurbished." Thus do novelists try to stay one step ahead.

Our lives are all collisions:
Rogue bodies meeting,
Impacting and rebounding,
And departing in directions
New and unexpected . . .
—Roberta Carson
The Ricochets of Life

Prologue:

Forrest Calhoun had expected many things of deep space. He had expected that it would be dark and cold and bright and hot and endless and confined. He had expected that the Earth and the Moon would become distant pearls on the velvet night behind him. He had expected loneliness and fear and boredom. But he had not expected that it would smell like someone's old gym socks.

Deep Space vessel *Gene Bullard* was a closed system. The air was scrubbed and recirculated, even replenished now and then from the fuel cells; but odors did linger in spite of everything: the memories of meals cooked, or of sweat expended; the tang of metal, the pungency of plastic; soap, deodorant, machine oil, the electric scent of wires running hot; the superclean, high-tech honey pot guaran*teed* never to whiff like a Port-a-John. All of it blended into a sour, nameless aroma that he never quite got used to.

Not that *Bullard* lacked sanitary facilities. She pushed a modified *Salyut* on her prow that had all the conveniences of home, except elbow room and a blue sky. The water was recovered, too; but in zero-g you could never luxuriate in a needle spray or even *think* about a soak in a steaming tub; and after two months living elbow to eyebrow, a fellow grew powerful tolerant of another man's stink, and downright thoughtful about a sip of water.

The control deck was a tight, cozy jumble: a triangle of seats, forward and "sunroof" viewports, a wraparound panel with heads-up monitors and readouts, storage lockers on every bulkhead. Room to float around a bit, but hardly "palatial."

Sometimes, during the long watch in the small hours of the ship's day, when Krasnarov and Mendes were sleeping, Forrest would jack his earclip into the comm circuit and listen to the whispers of distant Earth: the far-off chatter between Mir and LEO and Space Traffic Control; snippets of ship-to-ship chitchat on the orbital trade; occasionally, the warbles and "frying bacon" of data links and message packets downloading from Earth into *Bullard*'s computers; beneath it all, the hiss of the sun and the hum of Jupiter. Such "sounds" filled the emptiness outside, accentuated it; and made it emptier still.

The computer honked like an old-time jalopy horn, while the icon of a bowl antenna rotated in three axes. Numbers scrolled. A panel light switched from amber to green; another went red. Forrest came to attention. "Data link to Helios Light established at oh-two hundred Zulu, three July, two-thousand-ought-nine," he announced for the cockpit recorder. "On-board power hand-off to fuel cells. Data dump commencing." The on-board A/S logged everything automatically—and in triplicate, no less—but everyone had to pretend that humans were a vital link in the chain.

Glyphs and symbols danced across the screen. Ship's log, diagnostics, maintenance "squawk" list, sensor data, enroute observations and science experiments—digitized, condensed, packeted, and encrypted—and squirted to eager electronic ears hundreds of kiloklicks down-system.

Just in case we don't make it back personal . . .

Forrest pushed the thought away. They were a long way from help, and walking a tightrope the width of a calculation. Wouldn't take much to tumble off into Forever. The microwave power beam from Helios Light. The on-board fuel cells. The water regen. The precision of burn calculations. The uncounted welds and relays and connections and lines of programming code that made up a ship. Millions of things had to work, and work together, and work all the time. All the mission plans read how the crew would make it back alive, but Forrest hadn't any illusions when he signed the articles. During training, they had rehearsed every possible contingency and covered every plausible scenario; so they had a game plan for everything except reality—which never did go according to plan.

The counter display announced <243 blocks encrypted. Estimated transmission time, 13 min.> Forrest covered a yawn with his hand and watched the display. The <243> changed to <242>, then to <241> as the blocks spooled. Helios would "echo" the hash code to confirm receipt; and if the bounceback failed to match they'd have to do the whole thing over.

Damn, if I know when I've had more fun. . . .

Forrest was grateful for any break in the monotony, but it was a helluva thing when *this* was what you looked forward to. On the Earth-to-orbit traffic, there was always something happening. Preflight checklist, lift-off, rendezvous, mating or deployment, refueling, de-orbit, atmosphere braking, max-Q, rotation maneuver, descent and landing. A fellow could keep himself tolerably busy most times; and more often than not feel like a one-armed man juggling bobcats. Now, here he was *on the cutting edge*—the first human venture into translunar space—and all he could do was go along for the ride. He longed for a break in the by-the-numbers, in-the-groove, wake-me-when-we-get-there routine.

Funny, how dull the cutting edge could be.

A sudden commotion arose from the passageway that led through *Bullard*'s noselock into *Salyut*. Forrest glanced at the console clock. If Mike Krasnarov was coming aft to take the con, he was awful early.

But it was Ignacio Mendes that popped like a gob of chewing tobacco from the opening between the two pilot couches. The geologist cartwheeled across the flight deck and caromed off the aft bulkhead.

"Nacho, old son," said Forrest, watching the man bounce, "what the hell you doing up?"

For just an instant, he glimpsed a look of utter terror on the Brazilian's face. Then Iron Mike Krasnarov glided out of the passageway and snagged Nacho on the rebound, smooth as ol' Shaq in his glory days. The two men grappled and spun in the air together like ice dancers before coming to rest with one of Krasnarov's hands holding a stanchion and the other, Nacho's neck.

"Hey!" said Forrest, unsnapping his harness and kicking loose from his seat. "What the hell?"

Krasnarov shook the smaller man like a rag doll. "He snores in his sleep!" he bellowed. "For two months I have listened, but no more!" Then, before Forrest could move, Krasnarov hit the emergency evacuation button.

Explosive bolts blew and the outer hatchway sailed into the void like God's own Frisbee. Cabin air whistled after it. Alarms shrieked. Pressure dropped. Forrest's nose and ears began to bleed and frost condensed on bulkheads and coverplates. Krasnarov gripped Nacho by the collar and the belt and heaved him out into the starry night. The geologist spun into the darkness, and Krasnarov clapped the dirt from his hands. "Now, I get quiet!"

"Without air to carry the sound," Forrest observed, "I'd say it'll get *real* quiet."

Krasnarov hovered unaffected by the outrushing torrent. The air hurled note papers, a laptop, a data recorder past him, but his hair and his tight-fitting T-shirt and shorts were unruffled. He pointed an angry finger at Forrest. "And you are next, you black bastard!"

The gale snatched Forrest and hurled him through the gaping hatchway. He grabbed the rim and stopped himself with his body dangling over an endless pit. Methodically, Krasnarov ground his heel into Forrest's clutching fingers. One by one they lost their hold and Forrest fell outbound forever and ever and—

He awoke with a quick intake of breath.

The cabin was quiet, save for the constant murmur of the

equipment and the hammering of his own heart. Forrest closed his eyes and blew out his breath. *Hell of a dream . . .* A quick glance around the flight deck reassured him that there was nothing so monumentally stupid as a big red button to blow the hatch off. He laughed at himself and shook his head. Reality and fantasy were still jumbled together in his mind. *One hell of a dream.*

The computer console blinked: <Transmission successful. Handshake 02:38:14 Zulu.> The clock read <02:51>.

"Ship's 1——" He stopped, wet his throat, and started over. "Ship's log. Forrest Calhoun, Command Pilot. Successful handshake with Helios Light at oh-two-thirty-eight." When the next download came, someone would probably notice the delay between task completion and log entry. But, shoot, what could they do about it? Fire him? "Beam hand-off to power receptors at . . ." Checking another log. ". . . oh-two-forty. Footprint overstepping PV array twenty-one percent." His eyes glanced from readout to readout, taking in the ship's status. "Density down to one-third Earth-orbit nominal. Close log."

"Acknowledged," murmured the computer's husky contralto.

"I love you, too," said Forrest Calhoun, and almost meant it.

Mike Krasnarov—creased and tucked and combed as always—emerged from the passageway at precisely 03:55 to stand his watch. Krasnarov had a forehead so high that it plowed halfway through his hair to the back of his head. His brow was furrowed like the south forty; and the corners of his mouth were hidden by two thick, mustaches. His chin was gunmetal blue and gleamed like a well-polished fitting. The Russian shaved every day, but never once had Forrest seen him get down to anything pink. Back in the old flight test days, the ground crew had dubbed him "Senhor Machine," and Mikhail Krasnarov had accepted that appellation with pride. It was only fitting that his chiseled features had the color and sharpness of machine tools. During his off-watch, Forrest imagined, Krasnarov slept packed in comsoline.

Krasnarov saluted. "I relieve you, sir."

Forrest waved two fingers in the air near his forehead. "I am relieved," he said, and let Mike figure that one out. At what point did formality and ceremony cross the line from *esprit de corps* to *esprit de* Mickey Mouse? After two months in the Big Empty, even the jokes grew cold and stale. Forrest unbuckled and pushed himself up from the seat. "Weekly download went without a hitch," he said as they traded places with the thoughtless ease of practice.

"Power?" asked Krasnarov, just like he couldn't read the displays himself. He had to play the Change-of-Watch Briefing Game.

"The Lighthouse is still holding to schedule, but the beam's getting weaker. We'll be on fuel cells full time, soon enough."

Krasnarov rubbed one hand with the other. "Has Pod Number Seven responded yet?"

Forrest shook his head. "Negative. We might as well give up on it. Earth doesn't have a radar lock and it ain't answering our love calls."

Krasnarov pursed his lips. "She carries what? Fuel?"

Forrest didn't bother with the manifest. "Fuel," he agreed. "But we're fat there. We rendezvous with Pod Number Eleven in another eight days; and Number Three will be waiting for us by the time we reach the Rock. Both of those carry fuel."

"Not a critical loss, then," Krasnarov agreed. He buckled himself into the command chair and ran his hands along the control panels. He always did that, Forrest thought. Like a goddamn pianist playing a goddamn scale.

Krasnarov logged on and the computer went "oogah." Krasnarov scowled and Forrest suppressed a grin.

He and Krasnarov had rubbed against the grain ever since that sun-drenched afternoon in the hotel bar in Fortaleza when the flight test cadre met for the first time. Lord, what a crew that had been! Bobbi McFeeley and Gregor Levkin and good ol' Ned DuBois. Later, Bat da Silva and the Volkovs. Ego City. But Forrest had never had a smack of trouble with any of them, except for Iron Mike Krasnarov. Mr. Perfect.

Forrest would never have considered "Senhor Machine" a compliment.

"Oh," he added casually as he pushed off toward the nose tunnel. "Almost forgot. Just routine stuff on the bounceback. Magazines. Newspapers. Software upgrade . . ."

Krasnarov shrugged. UN Deep Space Command might never speak to them again and it would be all the same to the Iron Mike. Forrest tried again.

"No official communiqués."

Another shrug.

"Which means still no word on the Big Question," Forrest continued.

Krasnarov studied the dials. "And what is Big Question?"

He hated it when Krasnarov played coy. It was like an elephant going tippy-toe. "You know damn well. Who sets foot on the Rock first?"

Krasnarov sighed and turned his seat. "That is a question of interest only to showboats."

Forrest put on his best look of injured innocence. "You think I'm a showboat?"

Krasnarov snorted and did not answer.

"Okay, maybe so. I won't deny it. But it seems to me I recall a certain Russian—who we won't embarrass by naming out loud—who snuck aboard *Nesterov* on what was supposed to be an *unmanned* test."

"That was not for glory," Krasnarov explained, as if to a child.

"Yeah, yeah." Through the viewports, Forrest could read the large block letters on the forward hull spelling out the ship's name and RS-number; beyond that, the nested cylinders of *Salyut*; and beyond *that*—Nothing, stretching on forever. "You saved the flight and maybe the whole damn program. Going down in the history books was the last thing on your mind."

"And maybe," Krasnarov said, "Japanese are already being first. So what matter?"

Forrest shook his head. "Unmanned probes don't count. Even if they did reach the Rock last December, no one cares. There's a lot of symbolism in being first to do something new."

"On that, we agree," said Krasnarov. "But symbolism comes from deeds, not from gestures."

Forrest nodded as if he and Mike had not had this discussion a dozen times already. After two months, there wasn't a whole lot that hadn't been said twelve times over. He turned away from his contemplation of the viewports. "It ought to be someone with lots of EVA experience."

The Russian looked back sharply. "Meaning you?"

Forrest spread his hands. "Okay," he said. "Maybe it's time a black man took the first step."

"Or perhaps only a man with suitable gravity for the role . . ."

"Sorry, no gravity out here. Hey! That means we can't even flip a coin to decide. . . ."

Not even the hint of a smile. "We are the vanguard of humanity," the Russian chided him. "The man who represents us ought to be worthy of the role."

No mistaking who he thought was "worthy," either. Forrest took hold of the hatch rim, ready to push himself toward *Salyut.* "I guess, if the decision was easy, they would've decided before we left—and given us a memorable one-liner to utter spontaneously when the moment comes."

"It is a month yet before we arrive," Krasnarov reminded him. "Instructions may yet come. If not . . ." A nonchalant shrug and a lack of eye contact. "You are captain. You decide."

Forrest studied him for a moment before he spoke. "Tell me something, Mike . . ." *Do you resent being second-in-command, and second to a black man at that?* No, that was a question he never asked, and rarely ever thought. Besides, scuttlebutt had it that Ned DuBois had been first choice and had turned down the command. "Tell me something, Mike . . . Do I snore?"

Krasnarov gave him a puzzled look. Then he shook his head. "Not that I have noticed."

Salyut consisted of two four-meter cylinders joined by a conical frustum and capped by an observation blister. The smaller cylinder, just shy of three meters wide, was mated to *Bullard*'s nose collar and contained a μCD library, an exercise machine, and other "recreational aids." The magnetic chessboard had been left in mid-game—Krasnarov was playing with himself again—and Forrest moved a piece at random as he swam by.

The larger module, four meters wide, was the living quarters, with food and other stores, sanitary facilities, tethered sleeping bags, sensors, computer terminals, plant trays, and scientific equipment crammed everywhere they might fit, and a few places they didn't. Forrest paused just long enough to make sure that Nacho Mendes was sleeping the sleep of the innocent before entering the observation blister. Funny what dreams could do to you. You had to wonder if there was some sort of truth in them, and afterward you could never quite get them out of your mind.

The forwardmost module of *Salyut,* another frustum, was capped by a hemispherical nose of syndiotactic polypropylene. SPP was a clear, superhard metallocene plastic of the new "designer molecule" sort. Forrest settled his moccasins onto the Velcro pads and pressed the code sequence on the control pad. The protective shield dilated and uncountable stars spattered an endless night.

Pressed forward in the blister like he was, Forrest seemed to be floating among them. They were above him and below him and around him. Millions, billions, trillions . . . Might as well be "one, two, three, many. . . ." At some point, enumeration lost all meaning. The familiar constellations were lost in a sea of suns.

A man in his position, he couldn't help but be a role

model. He told himself that his burning ache to be first on the Rock grew out of that knowledge; that it was because thousands of kids, from Bed-Stuy to South Central, would be inspired by what he did, and personal glory did not enter into it. It was a seductive argument. A flattering one. It was a better image to look at while he shaved. Sometimes he admired Ned DuBois his uncomplicated swagger.

Let's face it, Forrest. Every step you've ever taken has been in Ned's shadow. A good man, a good friend; but always he was there ahead of you. Until now.

Forrest Calhoun, Mikhail Krasnarov, Ignacio Mendes. A black man, a white man, a "Latino." First world, second world, third world. *Let's not pretend there was no thought to symbolism in the planning of this mission.* How far did the symbolism go? To the choice of captain? Not the best; just a convenient token in the Game of Posing. He didn't buy that; he didn't want to buy that. He was good, and he knew it. But the thought was always there, niggling at him like a stone in his shoe.

There was no sense of motion against the starry backdrop. Forrest felt, as he always did up here, that he was going nowhere; that *Bullard* had somehow stopped dead in space.

He tried to find 1991JW. It would be moving retrograde now, as FarTrip closed in from its faster, more sunward orbit. A chunk of primordial planet-stuff too small to be worth a name, its only redeeming feature being an orbit that brought it close enough to visit. The instruments all said it was out there, though. Somewhere—he put a forefinger against the viewport—there.

Whoever touches it first. . . .

Sitting here in *Bullard-Salyut*'s forwardmost module, Forrest Calhoun was, by a few meters, farther from Earth than any other man. Destined to go farther still.

1.

House Call

Steel Dawn—from Vulcan's Forge out of Sunburst—measured herself against the rolling meadow, her legs stretching and her hooves rapping the hard-packed trail with each stride. Mariesa van Huyten clapped her knees tight around the filly's barrel, holding her seat easily on the trim English saddle. Her body flowed with the horse's pistonlike movements, seeking that mystic oneness of steed and rider. Grasses and stubble whisked against her kneeboots and jodhpurs, and the musty odor of mown hay and sassafras enveloped her like a mist.

The trail wound through the grasses toward the copse of trees at the base of Skunktown Mountain and Mariesa felt the filly's muscles bunch beneath her, anticipating the leap over Runamuck Creek. When Steel jumped, Mariesa's heart leapt with her. Small wonder that the ancients had given their horses wings!

Her cell phone signaled at the rise of the leap, nearly breaking her concentration, so that she came down hard in the saddle when Steel hit the farther bank. Cell–phone calls did not impress Steel, who had more visceral concerns, but Mariesa pulled up on the reins. Steel resisted, trying to take the bit in her teeth.

Yes, I'd just as soon keep playing, too. And the call might be nothing more than Harriet summoning her to dinner.

Still . . . She played the reins, guiding her mount up the rising ground at the base of the ridge. Steel, taking the ascent, slowed to a canter, then to a walk. Finally, the filly whickered, shook her head, and bent to take some succulent morsel from the surrounding bushes.

Mariesa dismounted and walked a few steps to take the kinks out. Her thighs felt like iron bands; her seat, like concrete. *The penalties of not riding more often.* Harriet was right: she spent too much of her life behind a desk. *Riding a tiger,* she thought with amusement. She doffed her cap and ran her left hand through tawny, shoulder-length hair before tugging it back in place.

The entire estate spread out below her like a tabletop miniature. A toy house, plaster hills, shrubs made of lichen and toothpicks. A red-brick, neocolonial building perched atop a series of carefully landscaped mounds in the bowl valley at the base of the ridge. Silverpond was not the largest of her estates, but she had grown up here and she held it most dear. On the far side, trim, manicured lawn spread like an apron, enclosing the reflective pond that gave the estate its name, giving way slowly to a carpet of wild grasses and country flowers, and approaching finally the line of birch and hemlock that blocked the view of the wrought iron entry gate at Old Coppice Lane. Facing her, an ornamental garden and hedge-maze created geometric patterns of color and shape. There was movement among the rows of flowers: Harriet, her mother, tending to her roses, followed by the patient, ever-suffering Miss Whitmore.

Mariesa pulled her cell phone from her belt pouch and thumbed *return call.* She put her left hand at the small of her back and stretched. It felt good to stand upright.

"Yes, Sykes," she said when the butler had answered. "What is it?"

"You have a call from the White House, miss; from the president's appointments secretary."

Business or social, she wondered. "Very well. I'll return the call when I can use a secure line. Say, twenty minutes."

"I took the liberty of so informing the caller."

"Sykes, you are a marvel."

She shut off her phone and returned it to its pouch. "Come on, Steel," she said, "time to go home. Make heap big smoke with White Father."

Steel had moved off a few paces and was contentedly cropping the grass near the foot trail that led to the top of Skunktown. There was a gazebo up there, and a spectacular view, but Mariesa spared the trail no more than a glance. She had not made that hike in nearly two years, not since the divorce.

The south wall of the sitting room at Silverpond consisted of tall, leaded-glass windows running from ceiling to floor, providing a light excellent for an afternoon of reading or working; and, given its location at the far end of the L-turn in the main first-floor hallway, a perfect refuge for solitary relaxation. Mariesa could work on her scrapbooks in quiet and without casual interruptions.

The thick, black pages, with the photographs and clippings arranged neatly upon them, contrasted with the antique ivory of the reading table and matching rail-backed chairs. Newspaper and magazine articles, courtesy of the clipping service she employed, were stacked neatly by her left hand; an opened pot of mucilage paste and a brush applicator, sat ready by her right.

Directly in front of her, against the east wall, was a sideboard with a rack of decanters and glasses. To her left, a long disused fireplace and, on the mantelpiece above it, a clock of superbly awful design: a gold-and-white filigree of leaves, a horizontal pendulum, a bell jar enclosing everything. Just the sort of rococo extravagance that appealed to Harriet. Above the clock, a trio of wedding photographs graced the wall.

Turning the scrapbook to a blank page, she aligned the photograph of Tani Pandya along the faint silver gridlines, squaring it just so.

The chime of the clock on the mantelpiece distracted her, and she listened to the muted sound of the ticking for a moment, then realized that she had been tapping her foot in time to it for some while.

She tsk'ed impatiently and turned her attention back to the scrapbook. She dabbed the back of the photograph with paste and pressed it into the book, holding it firm until the glue had set. Of all the children from that first year at Witherspoon, Tani had been one of the last to blossom; but now the *New York Times* was praising her first novel, *Taj Mahal,* as "the definitive statement of the new immigrant experience."

Mariesa stretched her arms straight forward and flexed the fingers; then she stood and paced around the room a few steps to relax. Sitting too long on seats meant for the eye and not for the rear. "Not for the butt," Barry would have said. "Not for the ass," Ned DuBois would have said. She wondered briefly how Ned was getting along these days. About Barry, she no longer gave a damn.

Aside from that wretched clock, the house was deathly silent. Sykes must be below stairs—ready if he was called upon, but otherwise relaxed with a quiet drink and a slushy novel. Mother was still out in the garden with Miss Whitmore. The other servants had left for the day. At any rate, they were not stomping about the south wing of Silverpond.

Her pacing brought her abruptly face to face with the triangle of wedding photographs above the mantel. Gramper and Mathilde, looking proper beyond their years, held pride of place: he with his slicked down hair and she with her flapper's curl and a cloud of white, Belgian lace surrounding her dark, round, It-girl countenance. Grandmother seemed a little bewildered, as if not quite sure what had happened to her. Grandfather, Willem Riesse van Huyten, wore a morning suit and a curious smile of triumph that lifted the ends of his black, pencil-thin mustache like the wings of a bird in flight.

In later years, she remembered, he had let the mustaches grow into long, white, drooping things. They used to tickle when he kissed her.

The second photograph was of Piet and Harriet. Harriet,

with a long, full, "Andrews Sisters" hairstyle, looked stunning in a flowing ivory gown that swirled around her feet like the foam of the sea. Harriet looked determined. Piet looked sober, for once.

The third photograph was of herself and Barry Fast. She considered it in silence for a moment, then reached out and took hold of the frame. Honestly. She did not know why she left it there. *Obsolete documents are to be promptly removed from all points of issue.* That was corporate policy, was it not? It was not as though she wanted to be reminded of him. Two years had not dulled the hurt, and every time she looked on his picture the pain stabbed her. And yet, she could not deny that he had happened, or pretend that five years of her life meant nothing. And removing the photograph would spoil the triangular symmetry of the display.

She had worn her hair shorter then: tight tresses, almost like a cap. And she wore a smile curiously similar to Gramper's. Nowadays, the hair was longer and grayer, and the smile less frequent.

Harriet entered the room, tugging at her gardening gloves, and Mariesa turned hastily from the array of wedding pictures and pretended to regard the clock, instead.

Harriet wore denim bib coveralls grass-stained at the knees. A smudge of dirt accented her right cheek. Her hair was a pure white that she no longer pretended to tint. She walked slowly to the liquor cabinet and sideboard, favoring her left leg.

"Mother," said Mariesa, "where is your cane?"

"I don't need it," Harriet answered. She laid her gloves on the sideboard and filled a glass with sherry from a crystal decanter. "The roses are not doing well," she said. "Too much chill in the air for July. I doubt I shall exhibit this year."

"I'm sorry to hear that, Mother. I know how much your roses mean to you. Have you had any luck with your new hybrid?" Mariesa edged swiftly away from the mantel until she stood once more by her seat at the table.

Harriet turned from the sideboard, double took when she

saw that Mariesa had moved, and shook her head. "No luck." She took a sip of her wine and paused for a moment with her eyes closed. "Ah, that is warming."

Harriet complained of the chill more and more often these days. Granted, it had been a cool year—those volcanoes in Japan—but not excessively so. Yet, Harriet had worn a sweater outdoors for nearly the entire summer. It bothered Mariesa in a way she could not quite fathom.

"What did the president want?" Harriet asked.

"Oh, who knows. A special seat at FarTrip Communications when the expedition arrives, I suppose. I'm to meet with him next week."

Harriet swallowed her wine. "I don't like that fellow. I never have. He doesn't understand money."

Mariesa smiled. "You mean his family hasn't had it for the necessary four generations?"

Harriet sniffed. "Your basic *nouveau* is too pushy. Breeding and manners come from stewardship, not from accumulation."

Mariesa had her own reservations about J. Clement Donaldson, but they regarded defects in his character, not in his financial history. She resumed her seat and took the next clipping off the pile, an account of a speech that Azim Thomas had given at a South Bronx high school graduation. Harriet watched while she pasted and mounted the clipping.

"I see you are still keeping up those scrapbooks," she said.

Mariesa pondered the comment, examining it for booby traps and hidden meanings, contemplating possible replies. "I promised Belinda," she said finally.

"Ah, yes," Harriet said noncommittally. "Dr. Karr."

"We both thought I ought to maintain some involvement in the educational thread of Project Prometheus. Belinda sends me dossiers each year of the most promising students in her academies. Those from Witherspoon and Pitcher, since North Orange is so close by."

"So you keep a scrapbook."

Mariesa's eyes dropped to the black, rough-textured page.

"Belinda thought it important that I think of the children as individuals."

"Belinda knows best, I suppose." Harriet finished her sherry in one convulsive swallow.

"The scrapbook was my idea. These children were in that first Witherspoon class Mentor graduated after receiving the state charter." *Children?* Where had the years gone? They were children no longer, but in their midtwenties—an age of immortality and possibilities. A space pilot, a computer consultant, a novelist, a chemist, a Marine Corps hero, a rigging supervisor on the LEO construction project . . .

A poet.

She flipped the pages backward until she came to a photograph of Roberta Carson—Styx, as she used to call herself. The picture was from the cover of her most recent poetry collection. Posed as *Mona Lisa,* wearing not a secret and provocative smile, but a manic, leering grin. A lovely young woman resisting the notion of her beauty. Half the poems in her last collection were thinly veiled attacks on VHI and the "brainwashing" at Mentor Academies. Mariesa touched the picture with a fingertip. *She used to come to Silverpond to be alone and to think. She used to look to me for guidance.* Silverpond had been the young girl's refuge. Mariesa could remember nights of companionable silence: herself, pressed to her telescope in the rooftop observatory; Styx, pouring earnest words and images into her tattered, black journal, sometimes reading her words aloud. Now, it was not so much the poems that hurt than that it was Styx who wrote them.

"They are my children," Mariesa said softly.

A clatter of glass. Mariesa looked up to see that Harriet had dropped her wine glass while replacing it on the sideboard. "Your children," she said, not turning. She picked up the glass and held it to the light, inspecting it.

"In a sense I have 'adopted' them. They are the 'odd ducklings' in Mentor's program. 'Rogue bodies,' whose orbits are off the ecliptic . . ." She paused when she saw that Harriet was not listening.

"The glass is chipped," her mother said, setting it aside. "Now Sykes shall have to discard it." She heaved a sigh and looked down, her hands resting on the handles of the sideboard, her back to Mariesa. There was silence.

"I always wanted grandchildren, you know," Harriet said after a time.

Softly, Mariesa replied. "Yes, I know." Remembering the blood and the pain and the weeks in intensive care.

Harriet stepped to the mantel and adjusted the wedding picture of Mariesa and Barry, which was hanging slightly askew. She stepped back and looked at the picture, hands on hip. "Sometimes," she said, "I miss that man."

"Mother, you astonish me! All you ever did was snipe at him."

"Yes, but after five years, I grew used to having him about."

Mariesa looked at the picture again. *Yes,* she thought. *So did I.* But she did not say it aloud.

Sometimes she wondered. If little William had lived—if the baby had not died within her—would Barry still be here, with his cocky smile and his ready wit, with his tender caresses and—yes—his steadfast support? Was it the child that drove her into the frantic isolation of her work and he into drink and the arms of another? Or was that only something that would have happened—that had been happening imperceptibly, all along?

Pres. J. Clement Donaldson was a good-looking man, but then television had assured a long succession of such men in office: cap-toothed, blown-dry, and photogenic as a bald eagle in flight. His hair swept like wings across both sides of a high brow. A touch of gray at the temples for the appearance of dignity and a touch of the dye bottle everywhere else for the appearance of youth. Appearance was all. He could exude calm dignity as easily as folksy charm. His smile when he greeted Mariesa was perfect, and the grip of his hand struck just the right balance between firm and limp.

This was a man who shook a great many hands—and who smiled to order.

None of which necessarily made him a bad man, Mariesa reminded herself as she followed him through the White House. As chairman of Van Huyten Industries, she had met her share of presidents. The amiable but iron-willed Reagan; the eager, if unfocused, Clinton. Bush, the apparatchik with no vision whatever. Even (when she had been young and new to her position) James Earl Carter. Of them all she had found only in Jim Champion a man she had genuinely liked. Regarding Donaldson, she had yet to form an opinion; which, considering the man had held office for going on five years, was rather an accomplishment on his part. There had been a Teflon president and a Velcro president. Now there was a Rorschach president.

Donaldson had dressed casually in tan slacks and a red pullover sweater. He wore slippers on his feet. It was Saturday, he said. His day-almost-off. He led her on a meandering and apparently impromptu tour of the building, showing her sights that she had seen many times already. Pacing them at a discrete distance, an Air Force warrant officer carried a locked briefcase. Mariesa wondered if they still called it "the football" and whether its continual presence was now a sort of ritual, like the Mace and Scepter that accompanied the English king.

"This old house has lots of history," Donaldson said while they paused in the East Room. "Yessir, a lot of history." A trivial statement, so obvious that Mariesa saw no point in responding other than with an interested look. "Did you know Abigail Adams used to hang the family laundry in this room?" He looked pointedly around the elegantly appointed ballroom and laughed. "The family laundry," he said again with a shake of the head. "Then Lincoln quartered troops here during the Civil War. And Theodore Roosevelt's children used it as a roller rink." Another chuckle as Mariesa dutifully followed him across the parquet hardwood. The bright polish reflected them both, as if they were walking on glass. "I think the old place misses children most of all. This is a house of middle-aged men. TR and JFK were the exceptions. Usually, by the time a man is seasoned enough to live here, his children are teenagers; or grown and gone.''

Mariesa had visited the White House before. She had slept in the Lincoln bedroom during Jim Champion's term. She had wondered then what it was like to live in a monument.

On the far side of the ballroom, Donaldson paused in front of the Gilbert Stuart painting of George Washington and shoved his hands into his slacks. ''This painting,'' he said, ''is the only item that survives from the original White House, the one the British burned in 1814. It's the only furnishing that has been here throughout the building's history. Sometimes . . .'' Donaldson's voice died and he stared into the painting's solemn face, seemingly oblivious to Mariesa. When he spoke again, it was almost to himself. ''Sometimes, when I look at him, I wonder if I'm worthy to live here.''

Mariesa often wondered that herself, and so did 42 percent of the country. However, it was a nice performance all around. Mariesa did not for one minute believe that the mini-tour had been on the spur of the moment, or that Donaldson's commentary had been anything but scripted, rehearsed, and meant for her ears.

Donaldson escorted her to the Green Room, a small parlor paneled with dark wallpaper and decorated in the Federal style: elegant, but spare. Above the fireplace mantle hung a portrait of Benjamin Franklin in his sixties—a younger man than the image the public most revered. On a side table sat a game board with smooth, round, black and white stones arranged in intricate patterns.

Valerie Kloch, the Secretary of Transportation, sat in a high-backed Heppelwhite chair, one of three grouped around a circular coffee table. She rose as Mariesa entered and extended her hand. They both pretended delight at meeting once again.

Mariesa accepted the seat that the president held out for her and settled in with a renewed sense of caution. She found a place for her purse on the floor beside the chair and positioned it carefully. She wondered why the president had asked her here. You never knew with this one. It might be nothing more than to wangle a seat at FarTrip Communications Center when the *Bullard* rendezvoused next month. Donaldson liked to be seen at important events. He liked to pose. He just didn't like to make decisions.

Maybe that was the secret of his success. Decisions always made someone mad. He had won his second term by a comfortable margin, but less so because the voters liked him than because they had no particular cause to dislike him. A careful man, and a lucky one, he had avoided both sexual scandal and economic recession by following the same simple rule: Keep Your Hands Off.

In response to some unseen signal, a White House steward entered with a silver tray bearing a tea service and British "biscuits." The young Filipino placed the tray on the coffee table, bowed politely, and departed. President Donaldson bent forward and lifted the teapot. "May I?" he asked.

"An honor," said Mariesa.

"The tea service," said Donaldson conversationally as he poured, "was a gift from the Russian people as a tribute to the new era of cooperation between us."

"It's very fine work," Mariesa said, accepting her cup.

"Did you notice," Donaldson went on as he serviced Valerie Kloch, "that the samovar is chased silver and bears the three national symbols? The bald eagle of America, the double-headed eagle of the Russias, and the globe-and-stars of Brazil. A fruitful partnership, and one due in no small measure to yourself."

"It was not entirely my doing," Mariesa demurred.

"Don't be modest," Donaldson insisted. He set the teapot aside and settled back in his chair, holding his own cup in one hand and his saucer in the other. "Your single stage to orbit vehicles . . . Ballistic transportation here on

Earth . . . Satellite repair . . . It's no secret that one of my predecessors was—how should we put it?—less than enthusiastic about the program? At least in the beginning, you had to work without the support of your own government."

More like with my own government's obstruction. "Some of his advisors," Mariesa allowed, "were not convinced of the program's value." A polite way of saying hostile; and hostile for an odd potpourri of reasons. On the one hand, an antitechnology, antibig business bias; on the other hand, the protection of established, big business interests against upstart competition. And mixed in there, she had to admit, a genuine skepticism that had almost proved right. What made political bedfellows strange was that they snuggled together because they wanted to screw somebody *not* in the bed with them. Worst of the lot to Mariesa's thinking were those mercenaries who had infested the White House in those days, and who had used the controversy as a way to extort Mariesa's political support for the president's reelection. She could respect an opponent, but not an opportunist. Opponents, at least, were believers.

Donaldson was a different kettle of fish entirely. While not supportive, as Champion had been, neither was he obstructive. When it came to outer space, he was King Log—and Mariesa was content that he remain so. Yet, she ought not to forget that many of the party stalwarts that Donaldson depended on had served that previous administration, and a sizable percentage still maintained their dark, ideological suspicions.

"Well," said Donaldson with a wan smile, "history has the final say, doesn't it? An idea may work out better than it sounded at first. Or it may ultimately fail even after an initial success." He glanced briefly at Secretary Kloch.

Someone's been whispering in his ear, Mariesa thought. But who? And what had they whispered? "A new business venture is always a risk," she said cautiously. "That's why it's best if the risk is limited. If a VHI venture fails, only VHI suffers. If a government venture fails, the entire country suffers."

Donaldson nodded slowly. "Maybe, though some would argue the point. You've heard the joke, I'm sure. 'When VHI catches cold, half the country sneezes.' What about your stockholders? Your employees? Suppliers who depend upon your companies' purchases? They suffer the consequences, too, without agreeing to the risk. Furthermore"— he set his saucer on the table and his tea-cup upon it; though he had not, Mariesa noted, drunk more than a sip or two— "as you have admitted, your success was not entirely your doing. You built on taxpayer-funded technology. And the public has the same right to a return on their investment as your private stockholders."

"What exactly do you mean, Mr. President?" Mariesa now set her own teacup on the table. Kloch had not even picked hers up, but sat stiffly in her chair with her fingertips to her lips and her hands folded as if in prayer, regarding Mariesa with still eyes.

Donaldson exchanged another glance with Secretary Kloch. "Valerie," he explained, "has some misgivings about the Shuttle external tank program that VHI and NASA worked out. She feels that NASA ought to receive a higher fee for delivering the tanks to your orbital construction site."

"Does she?" Mariesa turned her attention to the secretary of transportation. From the twist of the woman's mouth, she, too, had noticed Donaldson's sudden switch to third person. The problem with being a man who avoided personal responsibility was that it irritated your allies more than your enemies. "I thought an eight percent markup generous. Few private companies can boast such a profit margin."

"What you pay NASA for the tanks," said Kloch, speaking for the first time, "does not come close to covering their cost, and you know it."

"Valerie, the Shuttle used to jettison the ET and let it burn up in the atmosphere. Now, with an extra twenty seconds' boost, NASA releases the tank into orbit so LEO can rendezvous, attach boosters, and take it up to the construction site. LEO pays NASA the cost of the extra fuel and the extra depreciation on the Shuttle main engines, plus a fair profit; and assumes the risk of lifting the tank to its final orbit. NASA thought it was a good deal.''

"You mean a sweetheart deal. Unfortunately, the *former* NASA administrator had some far-out notions and allowed his imagination to outstrip his common sense. He approved ventures because he thought they were 'neat,' without any thought for the cost to taxpayers.''

"There is no cost to the taxpayer. If the LEO Consortium did not pay NASA to discard the ETs in orbit, NASA would discard them in the atmosphere—and the taxpayer would receive *nothing*.''

"NASA can secure more favorable terms elsewhere.'' That was delivered with a small smile of triumph.

Mariesa drew back. "Really. From whom?'' Only LEO and Mir were using ETs; and the Mir refurbishment did not plan on using more than the two already called for. Wilson Enterprises and the other players were either partners in the LEO Consortium or they were waiting on the sidelines to see how the venture panned out.

"I shouldn't need to keep you informed of developments in your own markets, Mariesa,'' said Kloch. "But Pac-Orbita has expressed some interest.''

The keidenran. The collapse of the Japanese "bubble economy'' in the late nineties had sent the whole world reeling into the "Christmas Recession,'' and the Japanese national economy was still running behind the recovery curve. "If they are pricing external tanks,'' Mariesa said, "it is to bid the price up and slow LEO's construction, not to build their own station.''

"So you say.''

"See here, Valerie . . .''

The secretary of transportation put her hands on her knees and leaned forward. "No, *you* see here. My department is responsible for commercial space transportation under 49 USC 35. I intend for the taxpayer to receive the greatest return possible. It's one thing for entrepreneurs to explore new technologies and take on new risks. That's what you people do best. You are the 'scouts', and scouts have been traditionally less disciplined. But once proven, the new technology needs to be properly regulated, to protect the public interest. Need I remind you that the Office of the Secretary has the responsibility to approve each and every NGO-launched space mission?''

NGO, or Non-Government Organization, was Beltway-speak for "everything else in the universe." "That provision of the act was rescinded by President Champion," she pointed out. Not that Kloch needed reminding.

"By executive order," the secretary said. "It could be restored the same way."

Mariesa turned to President Donaldson, who dropped his gaze and looked uncomfortable. "We hope such a step will prove unnecessary," he murmured. "To clear each launch through the Office of the Secretary . . . Well, that could cause traffic delays and might complicate launch schedules."

Might complicate . . . It would bring both the suborbital and the far more precarious orbital trades to a screeching halt. Especially if Valerie exercised her discretionary powers to selectively delay launches by people she did not like. The secretary of transportation had traditionally been one of the least powerful posts in the government. Now, thanks to the space trade, it was potentially one of the more powerful; and Valerie Kloch had not scrambled her way up from Port Authority commissioner to mayor to Cabinet to see such a potential go to waste. It was an open secret that she wanted NASA moved under her department and turned into something like a national flag carrier. Mariesa studied Kloch's face, looking for a clue, and saw . . .

Hope and triumph?

No, not quite. There was a certain wariness around the eyes. Hope, then; but not triumph. Valerie Kloch did not quite have Donaldson onboard.

Donaldson hated to make decisions. Mariesa had thought she would never have been glad of that fact; and even now she was only cautious. Donaldson's indecisiveness usually meant he was pulled in more than one direction, and Mariesa did not yet know what that other direction might be.

An awkward silence grew between them, until Donaldson, laughing with forced cheerfulness, clapped his hands together and rubbed them. "Well, we needn't make a decision right away. The price structure for delivering the external tanks to LEO needs to be revisited, that's all; but I don't know that selling ETs to the Japs is such a good idea, either. It might make more sense to shut the Shuttle program down entirely. Shuttles are far too expensive compared to Planks, rams, or even Black Horses."

"The Shuttle did deliver the entire *Salyut* module to FarTrip in one flight," Mariesa reminded him. "Nothing else can lift the *size* of a Shuttle payload." *A few more flights. Then you can shut it down.* Eight more tanks recovered to orbit and LEO could finish its station. But Mariesa did not voice the comment. Valerie had been right in one thing. It *was* costing the taxpayer money. Not the extra reaction mass to boost the tank to orbit, but the cost of operating the Shuttle, period. NASA had always flown at a huge loss. To encourage the government to keep them flying so LEO could pick up a few discarded components might be considered by some as more than just disingenuous.

"Oh, yes," Donaldson said, "there are quite a few options to be studied. It would be a mistake to act hastily." Valerie Kloch shot him a guarded look. The secretary wasn't getting what she had expected from this meeting. Ordinarily, that might have cheered Mariesa, except that Mariesa wasn't sure if *she* was getting what she wanted, either. King Log might just be a whole lot cleverer than he seemed.

Donaldson leaned forward and picked up his teacup. "I understand that FarTrip will reach its destination soon."

"August 23rd," Mariesa said, following his lead onto a new subject. That would be thirty-seven years, almost to the day, since she had seen the Firestar cross the heavens above the Grand Tetons and she had awakened to the threat of asteroid impacts. Sometimes, remembering how young that high school senior had been—she had been skipped two grades in elementary—she felt immeasurably old. Too many years had gone by; not enough years were left. The first orbital station was *still* unfinished, and the gigawatt power satellites were *still* paper models undergoing failure modes and effects analysis. And asteroids *still* whipped across the lip of Earth's gravity well every month. Sooner or later, one would curl in and strike. Another Tunguska— only striking Manhattan or Rome instead of the Siberian wilderness. Or striking the ocean and sending a giant tidal wave to scour the shorelines. Or another like the one that had made Meteor Crater in Arizona.

Or another Chicxulub. Another dinosaur-killer.

And we might never even see it coming.

"I suppose you will be having a big celebration," Donaldson said, hinting not too subtly for the expected invitation. Valerie Kloch rose.

"Clement, I have some business to attend to over on Seventh Street. The impact statement for the Allentown Ballistic Port is waiting for my review." She was obviously disappointed at the turn the meeting had taken. The president rose to show her out and Mariesa stood, too, waiting awkwardly by her chair until Donaldson had returned. *Okay,* she thought. *You've shown me the stick. Where's the carrot?* And what did he want her to do?

The president smiled apologetically when he returned. "I'm afraid Valerie has very strong feelings on your use of the external tanks." He paused by the game board and studied it, rubbing his cheek.

"Not *my* use, Mr. President; but the LEO Consortium. Some of VHI's companies are members of the consortium. That is all."

Donaldson looked over in her direction and his smile broadened. "Oh, don't try to fool a fooler," he said. "I put together any number of stockholder alliances in my time as a Street-walker." He selected a black stone from a ceramic bowl and placed it on the game board. "That was my strong suit, you know," he said as he rejoined her. "Building coalitions. I've studied the structure of your consortium closely and found it . . . fascinating. The VHI bloc is not a majority, not even the largest bloc of voting stock; but no other likely coalition can assemble a majority without VHI's shares.''

Mariesa retrieved her own tea and sipped it. It had gone cold in the mean time. ''Really?'' she said. She set her cup down again without asking for its replacement.

Donaldson chuckled. The folksy, down-home stump politician—and never mind the Bahamas tan or the Wall Street power broker in the twinkling eyes. Oh yes, a man who put off decisions; but not a stupid man. ''Look at the Congress these days and you'll see what I mean. What's the breakdown in the house?'' His uncertainty was rhetorical, meant to draw her in. Mariesa was confident he knew to the member how many seats each party held, and how tightly.

''There is a roughly equal split,'' she told him, ''between the Democrats and the Republicans.''

Donaldson nodded, as if she had passed her orals. ''That's right. One hundred ninety-two elephants and one hundred eighty-nine donkeys. So it looks like the Big Two have nearly equal power, while Liberty with thirty-six and American with eighteen are out of the loop, right?'' Donaldson leaned forward and wagged an admonishing finger back and forth. ''But reality is more subtle. The Liberty Party swings as much power in the House as the Democrats or the Republicans, while the American Party is zippo, nada, zero. And do you know why?''

Mariesa smiled harmlessly. *Teach your mother to suck eggs.* Balancing stockholder blocs was something she had picked up at Gramper's knee.

''Why?'' she asked.

''Because to build a winning coalition, to harvest that all-important fifty-percent-plus-one, the others *must* have Liberty on board. Unless the Democrats and Republicans join together. But they have too many hatchets to bury just for the dubious pleasure of freezing out Liberty. Since Liberty usually lines up with the Republicans on economic issues and with the Democrats on social ones, it's *their* agenda that gets a majority, more often than not.''

"Not always.''

Donaldson shrugged. "So, who gets 'always'? You compromise on some things to win on others. It's a matter of choosing your battles. That's why MacRobb can be so holier-than-thou. He doesn't need to compromise on anything because no one *needs* the American Party to build a winning coalition. Even if he does the old give-and-take and joins up with one of the Big Two, he just shifts the margin of defeat or victory. He can't change one into the other.'' Donaldson waved a hand. "The point I'm making is that an apparently small shareholder can actually be the keystone player. And you have positioned VHI in just such a way within LEO's board.''

"Mr. President, even if what you say is true . . .''

Donaldson interrupted her, spreading his hands out wide, palms up.

"Don't get me wrong. I admire the artistry. And as I started to say earlier, I see more value in providing LEO with the tanks it needs than Secretary Kloch does.''

Mariesa waited for a long, cautious moment. "You do,'' she said, not making it a question. *Here it comes,*

Donaldson bobbed his head. "Certainly, certainly. There are more important issues to deal with than who gets paid how much for a used fuel tank. For one thing, the American people are fed up with the barbarism in the Balkans. Massacres. Shelling of civilians. Concentration camps. Ethnic cleansing. They feel it is time to *act!*'' A slice of the hand through the air, like a tomahawk chop. "It's time to put a stop to it.''

"How do you propose to do that, Mr. President? Negotiations only work when both sides *want* to find a solution. The Great Balkan War has been growing for years. And the Non-Intervention Act means you can't send in troops.''

"Congress should keep its nose out of foreign policy,'' Donaldson snapped. Mariesa noticed that his smile became fixed when he was opposed. "But there is a way to intervene with no risk at all to American boys and girls. I play at *go,* you know . . .'' A wave of the hand toward the sparely elegant game set. ''It's the Oriental equivalent to chess; but while chess reflects crude Western values of maneuver, thrust, and attack, *go* reflects Oriental values of patience and position. It is a subtle game. Stone placements of no apparent value can become strategic time bombs as the play proceeds. I've been reading the old SDI study papers. LEO is the high ground, always prized by the military. Tremendous advantage of position.'' He leaned forward enthusiastically. ''We can drop kinetic weapons from there— nonnuclear, you see, but awesome energy. We can wipe out armored columns or warships with not much more than lumps of metal. Crowbars with just enough brains to recognize a target from the air.''

Donaldson waited for her response, a pleasant, almost pleased grin on his face, as if he had discovered sex for the first time and did not yet suspect that others already knew. Mariesa found her voice after a long struggle. Good God, the man was serious!

''That sounds like . . . a major intervention.''

''But it's not,'' he crowed triumphantly. . ''That's the beauty of it. Once the combatants realize that their position is untenable, they'll come to the negotiating table, where I can offer our services as a disinterested broker. Naturally, the weapons must be in place for the move to be credible; but they'll never be used. And once the crisis is past, they'll be removed.''

At least until the next crisis. Cross your heart, no foolin'. The problem was, it would set a precedent. ''LEO is designed as a commercial venture,'' she said. ''The board would rather avoid military or political entanglements.''

''The people want an end to the atrocities in the Balkans. The Greek navy's bombardment of Izmir was bad enough; but the Turkish siege of Salonika is pure camera-fodder. And now that Romanian forces have been committed south to support the Serbs—this is confidential, you understand—

the Hungarian army is concentrating on the Romanian border.''

"I agree, Mr. President, that the situation is distressing, but I fail to see how it is the business of the United States in general—or of LEO in particular—to correct it.''

A touch of color suffused Donaldson's neck. "Damn it, woman! People are dying!" The smile broadened until it seemed painted on. There was something very odd about a man who could talk about people dying with a smile on his face, even a phony smile.

"Congress will not allow the staging of weapons in—"

"*I* am the commander in chief under the Constitution, not Congress. And I can swing Congress, if I need to. Those Republicans who are not rabid isolationists and those Democrats who are not brainless pacifists . . ." He leaned forward with his arms on his knees. "Plus Liberty," he added distinctly.

Ah . . . "The Liberty Party platform explicitly forbids such foreign adventures."

Donaldson smiled in irritation, as if he could not understand the relevance of a party platform to practical men and women. "They are worse isolationists than the 'Washingtonian' Republicans. But they might listen to their major backers."

"And might I point out that, whatever the United States Congress does or does not decide, LEO is an international venture? Even if *I* agreed to use the station as a platform for orbital weapons, and even if I could get VHI's board to agree, I doubt that Matsushita or Deutsches Bundesbank would go along. As for Energia . . . The Russians, if anything, favor the Orthodox side and would regard any intervention as anti-Serbian."

"They sat still for the Skopje mission," Donaldson reminded her.

"The Russians had already tried to stop the Serbs from attacking the UN peacekeepers. They wanted to punish the Serbs for not obeying Mother Russia as much as they wanted to pull the blue helmets out of harm's way. That doesn't mean they'll tolerate wider involvement by the West.''

The president sat back in his Heppelwhite chair and placed his hands together under his chin. "I hear you. But foreign policy is still my bailiwick, I believe. I value your opinion, as I would that of any well-informed business-woman—but on business more than on politics. We have already agreed that VHI is the key player on the LEO board. If need be, you can force the issue. Otherwise..." He shrugged. "You still need additional tanks to finish the sta-tion.''

Mariesa sat very still. This was far too decisive to be a Donaldson initiative. Someone else had sold him on inter-vention in the Balkans—and specifically on intervention using space-based weapons. Mariesa did not object to space-based weapons in principle, but they no more belonged on LEO than antiaircraft batteries belonged in shopping malls.

"I will have to think about it," Mariesa said, rising from her chair. "And discuss it with my people."

Donaldson rose with her and extended his hand. "I quite understand." If this man understood anything, it was not deciding things right away.

When Mariesa reached the door, Donaldson spoke again.

"I hope you decide quickly. Every day you delay, thousands more will die.''

Mariesa gave him a bleak look, wondering if he realized that that would be the case in any event.

Flying north out of National in VHI's executive jet, Mariesa reviewed her meeting with the president, jotting notes on her cliputer for later discussion with her staff. She had re-corded the meeting, of course. The rodney was as small as magnetic spin transistors could make them, and that was very small indeed. As small as the clasp on her purse.

She glanced out the window on her left. The clouds on the horizon glowed fiery red, as if ignited from within. A wretched thing, to keep surreptitious recordings. But that sort of precaution was as routine as it was necessary in this age of dubbing and morphing. She could not imagine that Donaldson had failed to make his own recording.

After she had finished, Mariesa removed the earclip and sat for a while twirling the stylus between her thumb and forefinger while she studied her notes. This was Donaldson's secret, then. He avoided decisions by forcing others to make them. She would have to revise her opinion of the man.

Did Donaldson really think that U.S. ground troops could be kept out of it once he had struck from the safety of outer space? Both sides had to stand down for the gambit to work; and both sides were people who revered their holy martyrs. She did not believe for a moment that a mere threat would work. You have to show the cards to take the pot, Ned DuBois had once said. And once you were a player, you would get sucked in deeper and deeper. Probably the Navy, at first. Greek or Turkish gunboats—or both!—would attack the Mediterranean Fleet. A decade of defense cutbacks made the fleet a tempting target. Was it a paper tiger or not? After that, no country that remembered Pearl Harbor could avoid the slippery slope of involvement.

If I refuse to cooperate, I am not responsible for the deaths in the Balkans. Donaldson cannot make it so. The Serbs were responsible. And the Croats. And the Greeks and Turks and Macedonians and Albanians and Romanians and Bulgarians and Bosnians. Now, maybe, even the Hungarians. And only God knew what the sides were. Maybe there were no sides. Maybe there were only a dozen one-on-one conflicts sharing the same pool of combatants. There were some fronts where the Greeks and Bulgarians fought side by side against the Turks, and others where they fought each other over Macedonia. Only the Slovenes, sitting in their mountains under an iron umbrella of Italian jets, had avoided being sucked into the spreading madness; and if anyone had noticed that the price was to become little more than an Italian province, they were far too polite to say so aloud. Slovenia and the Dalmatian coast had once been Venetian possessions, and who knew what wild, irredentist dreams were mulled in the corridors of Rome?

"Charlie Jim," she said, and her pilot turned his broad, flat face in her direction, looking through the open door from the pilot's cabin.

"Yes, ma'am?"

"What do you think of the Balkan problem?" she asked him.

The pilot grinned and shook his head so that the two thick braids by each ear danced. "Not much."

Meaning that he had a low opinion or that he hardly ever thought about it? Or both. Charlie Jim lived an uncomplicated life in which beer, airplanes, and women figured prominently, but that did not mean he was uninformed. "What do you think we should do about it?"

"You 'n'me? Leave 'em alone." He grinned again and turned his attention back to his flying. "You mean the whole damn U.S.A." he said over his shoulder, "I say stomp 'em flat or leave 'em be."

"I see. And what about the space enterprises? The Planks, Wilson's ram accelerators, FarTrip, and all the rest? What do you think of that?"

Charlie Jim did not answer immediately. The *Pathfinder* sailed up the Northeast Corridor in the growing dusk while, below them, Wilmington drifted behind and the lights of Philadelphia appeared on the horizon ahead. Mariesa could see Charlie Jim studying her reflection in the windshield of the plane. Their two faces seemed to hover like wraiths in the night sky outside. A curious illusion.

"Used to be," the pilot said at last, "when a young man wanted a name he'd go off with maybe a few friends on the red-stick path. Take a few scalps, maybe steal a woman or some horses. Just so he could say he done something big." Charlie Jim jerked his head to the purple heavens. "Found something big to do, where you don't have to scalp no one."

"Building space stations," she said.

"More 'n that," he said.

"What, then?"

Another silence, longer this time, before Charlie Jim replied. And when he did, it seemed on another topic. "You know when you *hattak tohbi* came with your horses, we didn't have a word for 'em. For the horses, I mean. So folks scratched their heads and thought about it and then took two other words—*issi,* which meant 'deer,' and *ubah,* which meant 'big'—and they put 'em together and made a new word: *'subah,* which meant 'a deer, only bigger.' "

Mariesa laughed and Charlie Jim turned around again in his seat and gave her a steady, dead-serious look.

"What you want to do," he said. "Ain't no word for that, either."

Mariesa summoned Prometheus to meet at VHI headquarters early the following week. They gathered in the boardroom, around the long teakwood table and under the ruff-collared, beaver-hatted gaze of old Henryk van Huyten, who hung at his place of honor above the door. The portrait, by Pieter Lastmann, always faced the chairman's seat. That had been one of Gramper's rules when he had run VHI, and Mariesa had maintained the tradition. A reminder of the generations watching her.

Mariesa sat flanked by John E. Redman, her chief legal officer, and Khan Gagrat, her chief financial officer. The CFO shaved his head and wore a hoop earring in his right ear—an unnerving sight at accounting conventions. At the far end of the table, directly under the portrait, sat her cousin, Christiaan van Huyten, president of Argonaut Research Laboratories. He was deep in conversation with Steve Matthias, Prometheus program manager and president of Thor Machine Tools. Chris listened intently while Steve talked, nodding from time to time with the gravest expression. Tall and angular, Chris bore more of the van Huyten features than Mariesa did.

"I shall have to revise my opinion of Donaldson," Mariesa told John E. while they waited for the others to take their seats. Everyone always took the same seats, she noted; just like in a schoolroom.

"I always told you," John E. replied in his soft, Virginia horse-country accents, "that you underestimated him." Redman's hair, which he wore collar-length, was swept back in the modern style and shot through with gray.

"First he showed me he had the power and the authority to—No. *First* he showed me he was a humble human being trying to measure up to his predecessors. Then he showed me he had the power and the authority to stop the construction of LEO by loosening Valerie's leash and reneging on the ET deal. Then he pointed out that he needed the Liberty Party to forswear itself to get congressional backing for his plan—"

"Thinking whoever pays the piper calls the tune," said John E. with a smile.

"I pay Liberty pipers because I like the tunes they choose to play. There's a difference. Anson and Jenny and the others listen to what I have to say, but it's *their* party. *Then* Donaldson pointed out the pivotal seats VHI holds on the LEO board . . ."

"A pivot you carefully placed," the lawyer reminded her. She sighed. "That doesn't mean I can move the world."

"Life would be much easier, if you could," Khan remarked.

"Easier for the rest of you."

One by one, the other presidents took their seats. Profane, bushy-haired and barrel-chested Will Gregorson, founder of Werewolf Electronics, grumbled preoccupied greetings as he made his way around the table. João Pessoa, from Daedelus Aerospace, looking haggard after the long flight up from Brazil, received a curt nod from Dolores Pitchlynn, who headed arch-rival Pegasus Aerospace. Gaea Biotech's Correy Wilcox slapped Steve Matthias on the back as he entered and pumped the man's hand in a fine simulation of friendship. Wallace Coyle, president of Aurora Ballistic Transport, was a chocolate teddy bear and probably the only man in the room who did not have a rival—or even an outright enemy—sitting somewhere around the table.

A curious mix, thought Mariesa, not for the first time. *Gender aside, you cannot exactly call us "a band of brothers."* Her coalition. Presidents she had appointed. Presidents she had bought with their companies. Companies she owned, companies that other van Huytens owned. Companies the VHI Trust owned or held a controlling interest in. As Donaldson had so artfully pointed out, companies that jumped when she said frog. Employees, allies, and mercenaries; a volatile mixture. And yet together they had brought about the dawn of a new era. Some for career advancement, some for the potential profit. Some for the glory of touching the stars.

And some, like herself, because they feared the stars might one day touch them.

"Where's Belinda?" Mariesa asked. The president of Mentor Academies had not appeared yet.

"Belinda is ill," John E. said. "Nothing serious. She had Onwuka call and make her excuses."

Mariesa nodded. "Very well." Then, in a slightly louder voice, she said, "People? We may as well get started."

It was uncanny. It always startled her that, when she spoke up, others fell silent. It was power, of a sort; but it meant you had to fill the silence with words worth hearing.

"I take it you have all had time to read the summary I sent you. I need hardly remind you of its confidential nature. We must decide among ourselves what position to take to LEO's board, if Donaldson presses his request."

"Shouldn't Heinz Ruger and Hamilton Pye be here?" asked Dolores. Dolores held a seat on the LEO board, courtesy of the shares owned by her Pegasus Space Lines subsidiary. Ruger AG and Ossa & Pelion Heavy Construction were the other two VHI members of LEO.

"I asked Heinz to sound out our European partners, under the rose. And Ham pleaded pressure of work. They're lifting Number Four Tank this week."

"I wish he was here," complained Steve Matthias. "If

anyone knows whether we can complete LEO without all the tanks, it's Ham Pye."

"I think we'd need a major reconfiguration," said Chris van Huyten. "We can't spin the pinwheel if the number of tanks on the spokes are unequal. And we need two tanks on each arm if we want to rent out Mars-level pseudogravity to the UN's Project Ares. That means back to design FMEA. Six months to a year's delay while we work up new drawings and plans."

"What makes you think we won't get the last few tanks?" asked Correy.

Gregorson rumbled before he spoke and ran a thick-fingered hand through the bushy mane that surrounded his face. "Werewolf" Gregorson, others called him, and so he had named his company. Mariesa had kept the name—and the man—when she had brought him out of the jaws of creditors. He was a brilliant engineer, but numbers became slipperier for him when they had dollar signs in front. "I don't know what that man has in mind," he said in his deep bass. "I don't think 'Brilliant Pebbles' is ready for deployment, regardless what state LEO is in."

Dolores Pitchlynn rubbed her two hands against each other once or twice. "Could be it is, or could be it isn't."

Mariesa looked at her. "Do you know something, Dolores?"

The older woman shook her head. She had dark skin, tanned almost to leather, and hair bleached nearly white by the desert sun. She was not so much an unfriendly woman as one distant and hard to know. Her face seldom betrayed emotion. It might have been carved from the flint of the Mogollon Rim. "I have contacts here and there in DOD and TMDO, and sometimes you hear things. You know how it is. Somebody knows something and can't tell you, but they're just bursting with it. So you hear a little bit here and a little bit there and you put them together."

"God help us," said Steve Matthias. "That's all we need is to turn LEO into Darth Vader's Death Star."

"Don't blow it out of proportion," Correy said. "Donaldson just wants to use LEO for staging, right? So what's the big deal? I always thought a nonnuclear defensive shield was a good idea, anyway. Maybe this way we get a big infusion of American cash. Think what that would do to fund the rest of Prometheus.''

"Damn it, Correy,'' said Steve, "Prometheus wasn't organized for that purpose.''

"Were you there?''

A quiet, deadly reminder to Steve that Correy *had* been there—one of Prometheus's four original members. Steve, who had virtually blackmailed himself onboard, looked grim but made no answer.

"People,'' Mariesa said before the uncomfortable silence could become something else. "Let's line our ducks up, shall we? We need to reach a consensus on a number of issues and we need data on others before we can make any decisions.'' She nodded to her assistant, Zhou Hui, who sat unobtrusively at a side table near the bookcases. Hui activated her laptop and picked up her stylus, writing "Issues'' on the compad. Mariesa knew without turning that the wall screen behind her displayed the handwriting as printed text. Compad input screens found scrawls hard to read, so schools were teaching Spencerian and Copperplate once again. "Cultivating a good hand'' had become important. The revival of a nineteenth-century art by twenty-first-century technology amused Mariesa, on those occasions when she was in the mood to be amused.

"Seems to me,'' drawled John E., "that the biggest issue is our partners on LEO. Whatever the decision is, Motorola and the others have a stake in it.''

"I have a feeling,'' Werewolf said, "that that man''— he meant Donaldson; Mariesa could recall few occasions when Donaldson's name had sullied Will Gregorson's lips— "that man will certainly call in Motorola, Boeing-McDonnell, and the others for the same heart-to-heart talk he had with Mariesa. If he hasn't already.''

"Maybe he already has,'' Dolores said. "I received a very guarded phone call from Pete over at MacDac last

Thursday. It didn't make any sense at the time, but now I wonder.''

"We have *international* partners, too," John E. reminded them. "Even if all the American members agree, what will the Germans or the Japanese say?"

"Or the Russians," said Wallace.

"Or," said João Pessoa with a pointed smile, "the Brazilians."

"That's why I asked Heinz Ruger to make some inquires," Mariesa told the group.

"Does the government plan to pay us an adequate fee for the use of the facilities?" Khan asked.

"Bean counters," said Werewolf, to no one in particular.

Khan shrugged. "Military activity on LEO will decrease its usefulness and attractiveness as a business and industrial park. That constitutes a 'taking' under the law, and we are entitled to compensation. The *Third* Amendment may come into play, too."

"Could Donaldson argue 'national security' and exercise eminent domain over the American-owned portion of the assets?" asked Dolores.

Matthias rolled his eyes. "Oh, great. And everyone else would sit still for that."

"The legal justification is slim," John E. said slowly.

"I don't think he would go that far," said Wallace. "He isn't stupid."

Gregorson snorted. "Optimist. Besides, what makes you think he's the one actually calling the shot?"

"Yes," said Mariesa. "I wondered myself if the actual objective was to intervene in the Balkans or to intervene in the construction of LEO. We still have enemies in the administration."

"Bring back Champion," said Correy, pumping a fist in the air. The others chuckled.

"What is it, João?"

The president of Daedelus rubbed his nose. "Find out if the weapon system is ready. If it is, your Donaldson may be serious. If not, it may be, like you say, a ploy by some of his advisors to stir up trouble on the LEO board.''

Correy grunted and waved a hand around the table. ''Look what it's accomplished so far.''

The chuckles this time were nervous.

When the meeting had broken up and the others had departed, Mariesa sat alone in the board room. The bustle of activity in the outer office came as an indistinct hubbub through the heavy doors. She sat with her hands balled on the tabletop and stared into a worried countenance reflected in the polish. A lee shore, Daddy would have said. Shoal waters. Piet had loved sailing and had loved taking risks. He would take his ketch close-hauled to the coastline, daring the wind to shift and help the waves push him onto the rocks. Harriet, who knew nothing of sailing, would complain about the sun or the rocking motion. Young Mariesa, who did, would hold her breath until Piet brought the ship onto the opposite tack and cut into the open sea.

Mariesa contemplated the action list on her compad screen, where Zhou Hui had captured the give-and-take in neatly tabulated notes. She could remember when Prometheus had been a much simpler matter: plots and plans and secret meetings. The old hand-and-fireball logo. She could remember even when Prometheus was nothing but a wild-eyed notion that she and Correy and Wallace and dear old Keith McReynolds used to kick around this very table. Sometimes, at still moments like this one, she could hear the buzz of their voices. Worried, intrigued, thoughtful, playing with the notion, poking it with a stick to see if it would stir.

What would an asteroid do to the Earth if it ever struck?
A lot.
What can we do about it?
Not a damn thing.
What could we do about it?
Go somewhere else.
Swat it aside.
And so Prometheus had been born—of Wallace's fasci-

nation and Correy's cold calculation and Mariesa's trembling, barely reined terror. And Keith. She had never learned what had convinced and motivated that gentle old man.

She pushed back in her chair, tilting in a deliberately confident pose, and challenged old Henryk eye-to-eye. *It's not your call, you old pirate.* Henryk would never have started Prometheus; he only approved of sure things: like the Spanish Treasure Fleet off Cuba. Though Gramper, who resembled the founder in more ways than the set of a cheekbone, had pointed out that the Treasure Fleet had been no sure thing, either. Still, take a hardheaded, practical man like Henryk—or like Gramper or cousin Chris or most of her presidents—and dangle a nice ROI on a stick out in front of them and they would take a few steps to grasp it. And a few more, and before they were quite aware of it, they could tiptoe their way into Low Earth Orbit.

Chris, Werewolf, Dolores, João . . . Each member of her alliance had a reason for joining Prometheus. Telecommunications. Satellite repair. Ballistic transport. Solar power. Exotic materials. To Belinda, the whole project was secondary to her desire to inspire her students. All important. All worthy. But none of it mattered next to the possibility that the sky might really fall someday.

The others knew of Mariesa's interest in asteroids—she kept an observatory on the roof of her home and was active in SkyWatch, so it was no big secret—but only the inner circle and John E. knew that she had intended Prometheus from the start as a weapon to defend the Earth; and not even they knew what terror motivated her. Only two people had ever been that deep inside her.

She could send Dolores and Chris sniffing around Theater Missile Defense Organization. Someone else could bump heads with Ham over at Ossa & Pelion and decide whether Donaldson's scheme was even doable, given the current status of the station. Heinz could sound out Rukhavishnikov at Energia. But a group that size, while fine for spinning ideas and carrying out tasks, could not decide when to eat lunch, let alone a course of action. Only the pilot, feeling each tug of the sail, each pitch of the deck, could sense the right moment to put the helm hard alee. In the end, the decision would be hers and hers alone. Something she would carry with her for the rest of her life. And with Keith dead and Barry gone, there was no one at all with whom to share the agony of that choice.

2.

Collision Course

Roberta Carson rode the escalator up from the Potomac Avenue Metrorail station, still as a statue while other, more eager commuters clambered past her. The package under her left arm seemed to grow heavier as she ascended, as if from some perverse sort of gravitational theory. Bad news increased in weight the closer you got to its destination. She repositioned the tattered, bulky manila envelope, clamped it tighter with her elbow. Phil was not going to like the news. He was expecting it, but he was not going to like it.

But he knows better than to blame the messenger . . .

As the escalator neared street level it left the sheltering overhang and she began to feel rain. Roberta tugged the hood of her poncho up over her head. Silly, to dig a hole in the ground without a roof covering it; but it had probably looked real stupy on the architect's rendering. She had never seen an architect's drawing yet where the weather was bad. Maybe architects lived in a different universe.

Once at street level, Roberta stepped aside from the flow of pedestrians and looked around to get her bearings. This was one of those multistreet intersections with which Washington abounded. Even when you lived here, you sometimes had to check your directions. The late afternoon sky was clouded over, the position of the sun uncertain. The rain gave everything a shiny black appearance, transforming the asphalt and brick to diamond and glass in which blurred reflections ran like watercolors in a world turned upside down.

Fitting, she thought. Even if you had spent a year helping to invert it yourself.

A change in the wind blew a sheet of rain into her face and Roberta ducked her head and dashed across Pennsylvania Avenue onto Thirteenth—in this quarter of the capital, a quiet side street of three-story row houses set behind gates and postage stamp front yards. A single building occupied the entire block, sliced like a loaf of bread into town homes one room wide. One of them was hers. On the other side of Thirteenth, from the anonymous shadows of black, hooded jackets, a cluster of men watched her progress. A neighborhood in transition between decent and dangerous, but not yet quite sure which direction the transition would take. But, as Phil had told her, in this day and age to deliberately live farther than walking distance from a mass transit stop was an act of criminal irresponsibility. It was when decent folk stayed put and *refused* to yield that neighborhoods were saved.

Meanwhile, she kept her doors locked and she didn't leave anything valuable where it could be seen through the windows.

The porch light came on automatically when she opened the iron gate at the sidewalk. The door had a Facemaker "Doorwarden," but Roberta preferred the old, dependable magstrip readers. She did not trust the Doorwarden's advertised ability to detect and reject disguises. But before she could swipe her keycard through the slot, Phil Albright opened the door.

"Raining hard?" he asked as she scampered inside.

It was a silly question. One glance out the window, or a moment's silence given to the drumming on the porch roof would have answered it. But what he meant to ask was whether she was soaked. He was asking after her and not the weather. Roberta tossed him the manila envelope and he caught it underarmed in both hands. "It's not that far a walk," she said, answering indirectly his indirect question. She tugged her poncho over her head and hung it on the hook behind the front door. Then she pried her sneaks off without unlacing them and stepped into her house shoes. Her socks and the lower legs of her jeans were still damp, but it didn't bother her enough to change.

Phil inspected the bulging envelope, wrapped in cellophane to protect it from the rain. After a year of opening and closing, of papers removed and replaced and added, it had grown rather decrepit. Somehow or other, Roberta had never gotten around to finding a new envelope.

Phil Albright was an older man, just into his fifties, old enough to be Roberta's father if you went by calendars. He was short—five-six—shorter even than Roberta, and his dark eyebrows ran nearly together over his nose, giving him a glowering appearance even in his cheerier moods.

He made no move to unwrap the envelope. "Did it check out?" was all he asked.

Roberta didn't answer him. "I need a drink," she said, but that was answer enough.

"Christ." Phil seemed to sag and Roberta wanted to run to him and hold him up with her own arms because if Phil Albright fell the world would fall with him. He was destined, Roberta thought, to save that world, if an ungrateful world did not destroy him first. He dropped onto the sofa, tossing the envelope aside on the cushion, and rubbed his face with his hands. "Christ," he said again.

Roberta sat beside him with her legs tucked under her. She put an arm on his shoulders. "You can't let this beat you," she said, giving him a gentle shake. "It's not like we didn't expect it. It's just the last little piece of the puzzle."

Phil sat quietly for a moment. Then he said, "Simon Fell and I started the Peoples' Crusades together. We've been friends since . . . God. Since college. He was at Penn and I was at Princeton and we formed the Ivy Creepers, a guerrilla theater group. We used to stage demonstrations—Ah, that doesn't matter any more. It's just that I *know* Simon. We believe in the same goals. I thought we believed in the same means.''

The Peoples' Crusades boasted tens of thousands of paid-up, card-carrying members, coast to coast, in city and town; and behind them, hundreds of thousands of casual supporters. The Crusades—Phil had chosen the plural deliberately—fought child abuse, battering, pollution, poverty and homelessness, unfair labor practices, racism and sexism. It was a bastion of decency in a world that no longer cared.

Roberta touched his hair where it curled on the back of his head. "What will you do, Phil?"

He sighed. "What can I do? He's got to go. He took money from the enemy. Your research proved that. Those receipts and travel vouchers and phone records—him and Cyrus Attwood . . .'' He waved his hand vaguely in the direction of the rain-damp package. "There was no way Simon could not have known. He just thought that it didn't matter where the money came from. He thought you could kiss the devil and not get dirty.''

"It was nine years ago, Phil. It doesn't matter any more.''

Phil made fists with both hands and struck himself on the knees. "Goddamn it, that's not the point! It matters to *me*. And you know what the worst part is?''

She said no, even though she knew. Even though Phil had been agonizing over this for nearly a year while each bit and piece of evidence was tracked down and verified, and the Truth crept closer and closer, like some rough beast. He had to purge the Crusades of Simon and his supporters. Roberta saw that as clearly as Phil did. But if he hadn't *agonized* over the decision, he would not have been fit to lead the movement.

"Simon let himself be used,'' Phil said. "A cat's-paw so Attwood could score off Van Huyten Industries. What happens if *that* gets out? What price is the purity of the Cause? Kiss donations and memberships good-bye, just for starters; and depending on how the dice roll in the next Congress, maybe even investigations into *all* our finances. No, Simon has to go.''

"So," said Roberta withdrawing her hand from him at last. He hadn't even noticed her touch. "She wins."

He looked at her. He looked like hell. "No one wins, Carson."

Roberta shook her head. "Mariesa van Huyten wins. She splits the Crusades. Why do you think she had her dirty tricks people spend years piecing that evidence together?" She pointed to the tattered envelope with her head. "Why do you think she gave it to me?"

His smile was free of humor. "And why do you think you and I have spent the last year verifying each document in there? Mariesa and I have butted heads too many times in the past for me to take that bombshell at face value. And"—his lips twisted in that quirky grin of his—"you were her fair-haired girl, back in high school."

Morticia, the other kids had called her. The Girl in Black. "Styx," she had called herself. From coal-black lipstick to spiderweb stockings. She had been many things, then; but never fair. "I was naive and gullible." She had followed after the Rich Lady like a baby duckling. Had gone to that mansion of hers time and again when Life with Mother proved too much. "Until I found out how she was using the school to brainwash us. To make us good little soldiers for her conquest of the universe."

"The Good Little Soldiers." That had been one of her best poems. It had been her heart poured out in meters and rhymes. *The New Yorker* had published it, her first breakout from the small press ghetto.

> *Open up your skull, dear child,*
> *And let us stuff it full . . .*

"She's a champion manipulator," Phil agreed. "She doesn't see people, only resources she can use, or not use."

"Which really makes me wonder, Phil."

"What?"

"How is she using *us?* Why *did* she give me this evidence? She could have released it to her tame media outlets.

She owns Heimdall and *The American Argus.* Instead, she gave you a chance to take care of things privately.''

Phil smiled and took her hand in his. ''You think she's manipulating us somehow.''

''She isn't as crude as Cyrus Attwood.''

Phil released her hand and stood up. He walked to the front window and looked outside at the pattering rain. He stuffed his hands in his pockets. ''When I was younger,'' he said, ''I used to think there were Good Guys and Bad Guys, and you could always tell them apart. Later, after I'd been out here awhile, I learned better. There are Good Guys and Not So Good Guys; and Bad Guys and Not So Bad Guys. Mariesa . . . Most of what she stands for, I oppose. Big, grand ideas. A huge, hungry, wasteful society that eats worlds and craps pollution; that constantly wants and wants and wants, and never gives. But she stands by that honestly, and—sometimes—we even see eye to eye. I've never been able to figure out where she fits on my scale.''

''She doesn't,'' Roberta told him; and he turned and gave her a questioning look. ''She's not anywhere on your scale, Phil. She's something from outside Good or Bad. She just Is. Like a force of nature.''

Phil didn't waste any time. He had spent a year verifying the information van Huyten had passed on to him; but once he was sure it was true and not some elaborate trick, he confronted Simon with the evidence the very next day. Tucked into a corner of Phil's office at People's Crusades headquarters, perched on an uncomfortable plastic chair recycled form some school cafeteria, Roberta watched in misery while something she loved was rent in two.

The office was furnished with Spartan simplicity, reflecting Phil's self-effacing personality. A pair of battered vertical files, an old wooden desk, a corkboard thick with newspaper clippings. Photographs on the walls with Rubin, Alinksy, Nader, and other progressives shaking Phil's hand, the only concession in the room to a cult of personality. Phil himself sat behind his big wooden desk with his elbows propped up and his hands balled under his chin, staring past Simon to the far wall and the door with the frosted glass panel. Periodically, he closed his eyes, as if weary. Not watching Simon; just waiting.

Simon sat opposite Phil, drawn up a little awkwardly because there was no kneehole on that side of the desk. The incriminating papers were stacked in front of him, and he read through them methodically. Initially, Roberta had seen surprise on Simon's face. His normally calm, sharp features had widened momentarily; but, after the first sheet or two, they had closed up again and he paged through the rest of the material as calmly as if he had been reading a pop magazine. He examined each page carefully; and, once or twice, shook his head slightly while a grudging smile broke the composure of his face. Through it all, he said not a word. If there was any indication at all of his emotional state, it was the dull, red flush on his neck, behind the ear.

When Simon had turned the last page over, he squared up the stack; and Phil, as if the move had been a signal, shook himself and looked directly at Simon for the first time.

"Well?" he said.

Simon spoke. "Where did you get these?"

An interesting first question, Roberta thought. Not *What's this all about?* Or *What the hell is this crap?* There was no point to feigning ignorance.

"That's not important," Phil said.

"Like hell!" Simon's chin jutted out. "There's no way you could have gotten this material legally. It's a blatant invasion of privacy!"

Phil sighed and unballed his hands. "Then, you don't deny the evidence?"

"Evidence?" Simon swatted the papers with the back of his fingers. "This wouldn't stand up in court for a New York minute. The judge would throw it out, and he wouldn't even need a lawyer to tell him to do it."

"You seem to be implying that there will be a trial of some sort . . ."

Simon hesitated and his eyes narrowed. He ran a hand through his thick, blond hair. "What do you want?" he asked finally.

Phil sighed. "I want a lot of things. I want to hear you say you did it. I want to know *why* you did it. But most of all, I want to save the Peoples' Crusades."

"That's what we both want," Simon said quietly.

"Then this shouldn't take long."

The silence stretched out while Phil and Simon stared at each other. Simon licked his lips and glanced toward Roberta. "What's she doing here?"

"She did the legwork for me," Phil said, "verifying that . . . information."

Simon turned away after the first, brief look and Roberta let the breath drain out of her, grateful that Phil hadn't revealed her true role. That she had brought it from Mariesa van Huyten all tied up in a pretty pink bow. That she had *caused* this confrontation. She didn't know if she could look Simon in the face if he knew that.

She and Simon had worked together on a dozen crusades in the two years she had been at the headquarters, and she had grown to admire his canny practicality. If Phil was the visionary, the one who thought the great thoughts and spoke the words that shimmered in the air, Simon was the master tactician. He could visualize what was needed to carry out a crusade: from strategic planning down to the mobilization of crusaders and their allies and the resources they would need. "Phil's Right Arm," and partaking something of the nature of Phil; but more than (as some cattier Crusaders smirked) a glove with Phil's hand inside. He cared about the same things, though his concern was edged with anger more than empathy. Simon's problem, Phil had confessed to her during one of their off-hours meetings, was that he hated the landlord more than he loved the tenant.

"So it's come to this," Simon said. "Spying on us like a goddamn, jackbooted FBI fascist. I'm really pissed."

Phil ignored the thrust. "Why did you take Cyrus Attwood's money?"

"Are you running the Crusades as some little right-wing dictatorship, now? Or have you just signed on at the CIA?"

Phil insisted. *"Why did you take Cyrus Attwood's money?"*

Simon threw his hands up and sank back in his chair. "Phil, I will take money from Satan himself if it helps the Cause. You know that. We've done it before. Who do you think sent those anonymous checks? I never saw you hesitate before depositing them."

"You never saw me jump when Attwood said 'frog,' either."

This time Simon did flush. "That's not the way it was! The ram accelerator that Wilson Enterprises was building down in Ecuador . . . we thought it was a cannon like the Iraqis tried to build that one time, maybe even an atomic cannon. *You* thought so, too—"

"Because that's what Attwood told us. And we *were* planning a Crusade against it," Phil reminded him.

"Marching back and forth and waving signs in front of the Ecuadorian Embassy!" The scorn in Simon's voice was evident. He leaned forward and used his forefinger like a rapier. "The kind of people who'd build an atomic super-cannon aren't the kind who'd be impressed because a bunch of middle-class college kids had some time on their hands. They're the kind who—"

"—would plan and execute a deadly missile attack on their enemies?"

Simon struck Phil's desk with his fist. "Sometimes direct action is the only answer!"

Roberta spoke up. "That depends on the question, doesn't it?"

Simon turned and blinked several times, as if the response had come from an unexpected quarter. "Clever wordplay, poet," he said, after a pause. "Does it mean anything?"

"You were answering the wrong question," she said. "The ram was being built to orbit satellites and supply pods on the cheap, not as a comic book superweapon. Attwood lied. He hired you to wreck it because Wilson was going to launch refueling pods for van Huyten's test flight and he wanted that test flight to fail."

"The potential for mass destruction still exists," Simon insisted, "no matter what Wilson says his intentions were. We acted in good faith. And besides . . . disrupting corporate exploitation of space was a good idea, too. It still is."

"Cyrus Attwood certainly seemed to think so," Roberta said. It was an odd feeling, arguing with Simon. Oh, they had argued often enough during planning sessions, debating the pros and cons of some tactic; but this was . . . different. Not the zing of rational bullets, but the carpet bombing of emotion. Yet she had the odd feeling that Simon's scorn and anger was all crust; and that deeper inside he harbored other feelings. He was . . . happy, somehow. Relieved, perhaps, at being found out.

Simon cut the air with his hand. "Attwood had his agenda. We had ours. What difference does it make? There'll always be a capitalist to sell us the rope."

"You insist on missing the point, Simon," Phil said quietly.

Simon turned and faced Phil. "Okay, what's the point?"

"People were killed."

Simon's lips parted, but no words came forth. "Yeah," he said after a moment and his eyes would not meet Phil's. "Yeah. That was damn bad luck. Poor Henry. And now Cynthia's wasting away in some damn Andean prison. . . ."

"Let's not forget the Indios Henry hired; and the workman on the pipeline and the two security guards."

"Okay!" Simon stood up and his chair rolled across the room and bumped into the filing cabinet in the corner by the door. "Okay! It was a bad idea, and it was botched. Is that what you want to hear?"

Phil Albright sighed and shook his head. "You can't imagine how little I want to hear that." He leaned forward over his desk. "Simon, if I countenance that action, how are we different from the monsters who bomb clinics and shoot doctors?"

"We only planned to wreck the equipment. It was the

property we were after, not the people. Okay, the workman was killed; but that was an accident. No one else would have been hurt if ten Boom hadn't sent his company goons chasing after Henry. It was *his* fault that Henry and the others died; but corporate stooges always value property more than human life. They *killed* people just because some goddamn *property* got busted up.''

"It's the public, Simon. The dangers inherent in super-cannons . . . Whether private corporations ought to exploit outer space . . . Or whether our people or Rick ten Boom's security guards were actually responsible for the deaths . . . The public doesn't analyze that deeply. All they'll see is that Attwood hired the People's Crusades to conduct some industrial sabotage for him and some innocent people got killed.''

"Innocent . . . ? The security guards?" Simon paced the room like a caged tiger. "But, Phil, it was what—eight, nine years ago. We disavowed Henry and Cynthia when it happened and it all blew over. Why bring it up again?"

Phil sighed and looked down at the pile of bank statements and correspondence. "Because there's no statute of limitations on stupidity." He pointed to the paperwork. "If this information leaks out, the Crusades will look like prize dupes at best, and hired mercenaries at worst.''

"Why should it leak, Phil?"

"Because, despite what you may think, I don't spy on my associates. This little package was gift-wrapped and dropped on me out of the blue. *Someone else* has this data; so whether it leaks or not is outside of my control. If Wilson . . . or van Huyten . . . get wind of it, they may blow the whistle just to strike back at Attwood; and never mind that we get mowed down in the crossfire. So, I have to make sure that if or when that happens, the Crusades will have acted on this information *before* it became public knowledge.''

"If the media carries it.''

"Oh, they will. The *Argus* will put it on their home page and hyperlink it to everything from the market report to the

comics. Progressive newsnets would rather downplay it—
the old why-rake-up-ancient-history spin—but they'll carry
it, too. *Someone* will break the story and everyone will be
afraid it will be someone *else*. We can count on friendly
spin, but not on silence.''

Simon rubbed his hands together, and made a ball of his
fists. He looked at Phil. ''What sort of action do you have
in mind? Resurrect the dead? You're a good man, Phil, and
you're on the side of the angels, but I don't think you're
up to that one.''

''No, Simon. We already told the public that Henry and
Cynthia were acting from misplaced zeal, without any authority from the Crusades. This data''—a wave of the hand
at the packet—''shoots a great big hole in that story. The
action was clearly authorized by you.''

''So the line has to be that I acted without knowing what
Henry actually planned to do.''

Phil shook his head. ''Poor Henry. He's dead, so he can
shoulder all the blame.''

''It's for the good of the Cause. We both know Henry
would go along.''

''It's not good enough, Simon. You knew he bought the
Stingers. *You signed the fucking check!*'' Phil spread the
papers across the desk with a swipe of his hand, and Roberta
shrank in her chair from the unwonted anger. ''You can't
pretend you didn't know.''

''I told you. It was a screwup. It was unintentional.''

''Great. And what do we say the next time a polluter uses
that as a defense? God damn it, this is a war. The Light
against the Dark. And in any battle, the high ground is the
edge. The Establishment has a lot of weaponry that we can't
match, from dollars in their coffers to Congress in their
pocket, but *we occupied the moral high ground*. Nonvio-
lence! The public interest! The underdog victim! *We wore
the armor of righteousness!* And in one hasty, ill-considered
moment, you lost us all of that. Because if there is one thing
Attwood is not, it is an underdog; and if he has any interests,
they are not the public's. And an attack with Stinger mis-

siles on a ram accelerator may be a lot of different things, but nonviolent isn't one of them.''

Phil's words moved Roberta profoundly and she took her lip in her teeth; but Simon only said quietly. ''What do you want me to do?''

Phil hesitated a moment; then said, ''You'll have to resign.''

''This will split the movement.''

''Better that than destroy it.''

''Jesus Christ, Phil. We've been in this together since day one.''

''You and Felix Lara and whoever else was in on this . . . caper.''

''What is this, a purge?''

''We disavowed Henry and Cynthia on your advice. We let them hang out there to dry. For the good of the Cause, you said. Well, now it's your turn. Damn it, Simon, I'm not enjoying this either. You lied. To me.''

''You're damn right I did! And I'd do it again. For the good of the Cause. Because if anyone ever asks you what you knew and when you knew it, you're clean.''

''Well, thanks a whole hell of a lot.''

Simon flushed deep red, but before he could say anything, Roberta jumped from her seat before she could stop herself. ''Stop it! You two have been friends longer than I've been alive. It shouldn't end like this!''

Phil shook his head and gave her a devastated look. ''It couldn't end any other way.''

Later, that night, when her town house had grown quiet, Roberta lay alone in her bed and tried to imagine what she had to do. That she had to do something was clear; but what that something was she did not yet comprehend. Mariesa van Huyten would haunt her life forever unless she was exorcised.

She and Phil had gone out to eat after the confrontation with Simon. They had gone to a wonderful Chinese restaurant around the corner where the staff knew them and gave them special treatment. Over the Lo Mein and Happy Family she had tried—again—to convince Phil to run for office, maybe even for president. After a long succession of "pragmatists" and outright reactionaries, the country needed someone with a vision. Someone who could galvanize the conscience of the nation and aim them toward a proper future.

Someone who stood on "the moral high ground."

Phil had laughed, but she knew he was flattered by her admiration. *Which party would nominate me?* he had asked. I don't fit into any of their neat little boxes. The Republicans think a sustainable economy would cut profits; and the Americans think it would cut jobs. The Liberty Party can't see that letting property rights and the market set things straight is too damn slow, too damn little, and too damn late. The Democrats all spout my ideas, but to them it's just patronage—departments to expand and favors to dispense and "vote for us or kiss those favors good-bye."

Cut across the lines, she had argued. Cut across the lines. Republicans who favor small business over big business. Americans more concerned about workplace safety than immigrants and imports. Frustrated Democrats who value goals more than programs. Liberties who see that private action and public action are *both* necessary to secure the individual's rights. You can bring them together, Phil. (She had reached across the table and taken his hand and he had not pulled away.) Not through quid pro quo; not by you-scratch-my-back support among cliques with widely different goals; but by standing together on common ground.

If there is a common ground, he had said.

If anyone can find it, Phil, it's you.

With that wry, little boy's smile: *It sounds like* you're *the one who should run for office.*

She had walked with him to the Metrorail station and waited with him on the platform until the orange train had taken him away. Then she let the blue train carry her in the other direction, back to her own place. He had forgotten to return the magcard to her town house. She wondered if that had been oversight or foresight.

She always kept her bedroom dark, but enough streetlight seeped in through the drapes and curtains to pick out the shapes of furniture and clothing. Roberta wondered if Phil knew she was ready for him. He was a wise man and knew a lot of things, but he might not know that. She drew her knees up and pushed one of her pillows between them. That was the difference between boys and men, she thought. Boys her age—twenty-six—thought only about screwing. They were dicks with legs and a smooth pickup line; except when they didn't have the smooth line. But *men* had goals beyond which bed they were going to sleep in. *Men* had passions whose gland was the brain.

She would have to do something for Phil, something that would make up for the damage that she had caused. Something that would strike at Mariesa van Huyten for setting the whole thing in motion and causing Roberta Carson to *hurt* Phil Albright.

Something personal.

Business and technology? She would cede those fields. She was not so foolish as to think she would best the Rich Lady on her home ground. Nor was she so foolish as to think her poetry was more than an irritation. Her editors were already complaining that polemic made poor art. She would not blunt her talent using it like an axe to hack at her opponents. There were more notes than one she needed to sing.

But something. Some manila envelope she could hand over one day with the information that would discredit van Huyten for good and all; that would do to Mariesa's precious program what Mariesa had done to Phil's.

Thank you. She could hear Phil whisper in her ear, feel his gratitude on her lips, between her legs.

She didn't know what that information was, but she thought she knew where she could find the head of the trail that led there.

3.

Gideon

Flaco had known that it would be bad, but he had no idea
how bad it would be until Serafina called him by every
name he had.

"José Eduardo Gonsalves y Mercado! You cannot be serious!"

Flaco leaned against the frame of the open window and
stared at the snarling traffic on Fort Washington Avenue,
four stories below. At the grimy sidewalks, at the tight-
packed throng of people passing one another in rigid isolation. At the dealers and the hookers and the hustlers
hanging on the street corner—the corner of "Powder and
Pussy"—waiting for the cars from the 'burbs to come and
deal. He would give anything to leave this place and find
Serafina a home somewhere bright and green, where flowers
grew. The sun was still high and the breeze that rippled the
dingy white curtains of the apartment brought no relief from
the July heat.

Flaco shrugged and stepped into the kitchenette of their
two-room flat. He pulled a six pack of El Presidente from
the refrigerator, snapped one can out of its ring and tossed
it to Serafina. He took another one for himself and rubbed
it across his forehead and the side of his face. The icy con-
densation on the can let him forget for the moment how hot
it was in the city. Even the sleeveless undershirt he wore

did not help. "It is a wonderful opportunity," he said.

"An opportunity to kill yourself!" Serafina shook her fist at Flaco. The fist holding the can. It would be a bad thing, Flaco thought, to be near that can when it finally opened. He popped his tab one-handed with his thumb, and poured half the contents down his throat. Then he put the can to his forehead again and rolled it back and forth. Serafina could not understand how important this opportunity was.

"The company will take good care of us," he told her.

"The company cares only about the money!" she said.

"Righteous beans," he said, switching to English. It was not so grand a language as Spanish, but it did have its own peculiar charms. "They spend all that money training us," he continued in the same tongue. "They gonna take real good care of us when we're upstairs." He ought to speak English more often. It would be important when they made the final selections. They wouldn't take anyone along who couldn't talk to his crewmates.

"You're crazy, Flaco. My mother always told me never marry a Dominican. They're all crazy."

Flaco reached out and grabbed Serafina by the waist and held her tight against him. "That's why we come after you Boricua girls. You drive us crazy."

"Flaco . . ." She pushed against his embrace, but not too hard. He was a skinny man, but wiry, with arms as strong as cable. "You work as a rigger, you had to be strong." And there were worse places for Serafina to be than in her husband's arms.

"I told you all about the hazard pay and the bonus. No place to spend money in orbit, so you and me, we have a good pile when I come back. Enough maybe to buy us a nice house." Telling her about the hazard pay, that had been his mistake. Hazard pay meant hazard. Well, rigging was always dangerous, if you didn't know what you were doing. Be some special dangers up in space, Tucker had told him. Yeah. So, they wouldn't need people like Flaco, then. "Be plenty money," he told her as he insinuated his free hand between them, rubbing it over the hard, flat surface of her belly—not yet swelling with his son. "Set little 'Memo' up in style!"

"I wish you wouldn't call him that . . ."

"What, you want me to call him 'Billy'?" He used an exaggerated Anglo accent, with its flat, funny vowels.

"Mmm," she said, pressing against him. "You're still crazy." But she said that while she kissed him.

His fingertips found the waist of her jeans and he pushed them inside. Serafina squeeked . . . and pulled the tab on her beer can.

The spray spattered them both with the ice-cold liquid. It drenched the white undershirt he wore. Serafina laughed and danced away and Flaco chased after her. She ran behind the sofa and they faked left and faked right, and then Flaco leaped over the back of the sofa. She whooped and dodged him.

He cornered her finally in the bedroom, but they had both known when they started that he would.

Ossa & Pelion Heavy Construction held its qualifying trials at Pegasus Field, several miles south of Phoenix, Arizona. The company shuttle bus from Sky Harbor rolled through a different country than the one Flaco knew. He had never seen so much empty space, or so few people. It gave him the shivers. A dull-colored bird burst from the roadside brush and darted across the highway in front of the bus. The driver said it was a roadrunner and one of the other men on board said, "Beep-beep!" The way the driver laughed, Flaco figured he'd heard that one already.

The Pegasus complex was a half dozen low-profile adobe-tech buildings set in an arch around a broad landing field. The airport shuttle dropped Flaco and two other men at the administration building in the center, where they stood with their duffel bags in the hot, desert wind, wondering where to go next. A large bronze of a winged horse reared above the main doors directly in front of them. Through the gap between the admin building and the next one to the left, Flaco could see spaceships squatting on the field. Three of them were the small ballistic ships that flew Earth-to-Earth, but the big one with the scorch marks was an orbiter.

Flaco stopped a man in brown coveralls who seemed to know where he was going, and asked him where the riggers who wanted to work on the space station were supposed to meet. The man gave them directions and Flaco thanked him. As they set off, one of Flaco's companions spoke.

"Do you know who that was, *'mano?*" Tonio Portales was a thickset Miami Cuban who had joined Flaco's flight in St. Louis.

"Who?"

"That dude you stopped for directions. His name tag . . . That was Ned DuBois."

Flaco shifted his duffel bag to his shoulder for an easier grip. "DuBois? Wasn't he the man who—"

"Yeah," said Tonio. "He was 'The Man Who.' First dude ever took one of those Plank ships up into space."

Flaco grunted. "He still flying? I was just a kid back then."

"You chust ein kid now." Sepp Bauer, Flaco's other companion, had joined them at the Pegasus shuttle stop in Phoenix Sky Harbor. He had come from some place called Karlsruhe by way of JFK and spoke an English so badly accented that Flaco could barely understand him.

"I mean that was, what, nine years ago, right? I was only thirteen. In middle school. They showed it on a big screen in assembly."

"Yeah," said Tonio. "Remember how somebody blew up the big cannon, so the fuel pod got cracked and went into the wrong orbit? And then they thought his copilot was lost in space after the pod blew, but DuBois found him anyway?" Tonio shook his head. "Oh, man, I'd love to do something *cholo* like that."

Sepp grunted. "Zo, you hope *mine* tether breaks zo you can rescue?" He glowered dangerously.

Flaco watched Tonio puzzle out the syntax and then give Sepp a fearful look. "No, I would never . . ." the Cuban managed to say just before the big German burst out laughing.

They found the check-in table just inside the entrance to the second building. Flaco showed the first woman his driver's license and she gave him a name badge with his O&P company photograph already on it. The others had to look into a doid and have their image scanned onto a card. Their pixures—''pixel pictures''—looked as bad as anything ever captured on film. The second woman checked his plane ticket against a computer screen and gave him a chit that he could use for reimbursement later. The third woman gave him a folder stuffed with all sorts of documents.

"There are forms in here for you to fill out," the third woman explained. "O&P employment form. Government tax forms. This"—she pulled one out and showed it to him—"is an application for a green card. Because this phase of the construction is being managed out of Phoenix, an American work permit will be required."

Flaco grunted. "No necessito una tarjeta verde." His parents had brought him to the States from the Republic when he was eight, but he didn't see why he had to explain himself to anyone, least of all to a down-your-nose *'chicana.* Boricuas and Cubans were enough to put up with.

The woman looked doubtful, but shrugged. "Your packet also includes today's agenda,*'mano,*" she continued, "plus a map of that part of the facility you are allowed into . . ."

"And tomorrow's agenda?" he asked.

A wintery smile, all the colder for the desert heat he had just been in. "You will be given that *if* you are invited back."

Flaco saw what she meant when he entered the auditorium where the opening meeting was to be held. It was laid out like a movie theater, with a stage and a screen up front and rows of seats on risers. There were easily two hundred men in the room. Some pasty-faced Anglos, but mostly a mixture of bronze and ebony. Young, strong, and immortal. Thin, burly, bearded, clean-shaven. A handful of women, each the target of a dozen men. Flaco was surprised that so many had volunteered their personal time just for the chance to be picked for one of the fifty slots.

Eh, por que no? The pay was generous, and later you could point to the sky and tell your grandchildren that you had built a star. It would be a thing to be proud of.

The men sat scattered around the auditorium, some chatting in groups, twisting around in their seats and leaning over the backs, or standing in the aisles, or lounging against the wall under the projection booth, chattering in a hodge-podge of languages that blended into an unintelligible buzz. Most of them sat alone, slouched in the padded seats with their arms folded, waiting for something to happen. A few were sleeping.

There was a group of ten men—mostly chunky, mostly blond and pale-eyed—who clumped together and talked among themselves in a gargling language that Flaco guessed was Russian. He knew the consortium that was building the station included Russians—and Brazilians, Germans, and Japanese, as well—and he wondered if there were some sort of quota system in place: so many welders or pipe fitters from each nationality. Flaco wouldn't mind losing his slot to a better rigger—well, not too much—but it would not be right to lose it to a lesser man just because the lesser man held the right passport.

Tonio caught up with him and, a few moments later, Sepp. The German was frowning over his packet of forms. Tonio pointed. "I see three seats," he said and started down the aisle. Flaco and Sepp followed him. *Funny*, thought Flaco, *how three men who have just met can become partners*. He wondered how many of the other chatting groups were like his own: friends who were also strangers.

The first speaker was a suit, so Flaco gave him a special sort of attention. The suits would not make the decisions that mattered (unless there really were quotas to be juggled), but the suits usually knew all about "purpose and scope." Some guys didn't care about that. As long as you did what the crew boss told you and you got paid on time, what did it matter? But a man who knew *what* he was building and *why* did a better job building it, and that might matter when they picked the crew.

The video they showed on the pixwall was beautiful, backed by lively, inspiring music and narrated by a voice overlaid with lots of authoritative bass. Flaco would have sworn the space station was the real thing, if he hadn't known the "real thing" was still unfinished. And maybe parts of the video were real. Who knew? That movie last year where the star had OD'ed in the middle of filming . . . You could hardly tell which scenes had the live actor and which the morphed reconstructions.

The video started with a view of a Space Shuttle launch while the Voice explained how the external tanks were once jettisoned to burn up over the Indian Ocean. ". . . But Ourkind soon found a use for these enormous containers. A frugal sense of recycling, plus a dream . . ."

Animation, Flaco decided as the camera "followed" the Shuttle all the way into orbit itself. Space launches were cheaper than they used to be, but they still wouldn't have had a "camera ship" flying side-by-side with the Shuttle, would they? Flaco held his breath when the background faded to the black of space. The pixwall was a maxscreen wraparound, so it was almost like wearing a virtchhat, which was almost, like, for real.

"Now, when the Shuttle is finished with the external tank, NASA drops it off in orbit for pickup." The video showed a smiling Shuttle pilot waving through his front viewport to a crew of space-suited figures wearing the LEO "Roaring Lion" icon.

"Our guys," the Voice continued in a folksy tone, "attach the booster rockets, just as the great Forrest Calhoun and Ned DuBois did when they salvaged the very first external tank in 2007—after a programming error accidentally put it into orbit."

Flaco flexed his hands and studied the action intently. Animation or actual film, *that* was a rigging job. He nudged

Tonio with his elbow and jerked his head at the screen.
Tonio grinned and nodded. Yeah, they teach us the proper
method, you bet, but it couldn't be too hard if a couple
amateurs done it first.

"LEO brings these tanks up to the construction site at
orbit 6900/o/o/x/x, where they are now being configured
into a new space station . . ." Now Flaco was certain the
video was morphed. He watched men stringing cables and
nudging the huge tanks into line, head to tail to form the
hub shaft, fitting the others in pairs around it to form the
pinwheel, ready now for the welders, pipe fitters, and other
trades. Construction wasn't anywhere near that stage yet.
". . . Each tank provides over two-and-a-half kilosteres of
living space. That's ninety *thousand* cubic feet. Enough cubic for a hundred people to live and work comfortably.
More, if they're friendly . . ."

People living in cast-off containers sounded a lot like a
shantytown to Flaco, and some of the newsnets were calling
it just that. But none of those newsers were hiring riggers,
and something cheap-but-real beat a deluxe daydream any
day.

When the rah-rah and the flag-waving were done—and
they really did wave flags: full of stars, stripes, double-
headed eagles, rising suns, and all sorts of stuff to celebrate
the international nature of the job—the suits handed things
over to the hard hats, who gave a series of briefings a whole
lot more practical and a whole lot less inspiring. The
morgue shot of the Brazilian welder whose hardsuit had
ruptured sent a dozen of the men out of the auditorium. One
of the external tank modules would be named *Anselmo Takeuchi* in his honor, they announced. Cold comfort to his
family, but a grander monument than most construction
workers ever got. Flaco hoped they wouldn't have to name
all the tanks, but figured there'd be more than one placard
welded in place before completion.

A good thing indeed that Serafina was not here. . . .

One of the men they introduced was Morris Tucker, who
would boss one of the rigging crews. Tucker stood and nod-

ded to the assembly, but didn't speak; but then he never had been a man of words. Flaco had worked with Tucker on a couple of groundside O&P jobs. He figured "Meat" would be a tough boss, but fair; and hoped he would draw the man's crew after he was picked.

After the introductions, O&P marched them through a battery of medical and psychological examinations. Flaco's original application had included a complete physical exam, but LEO was taking nothing for granted. Doctors and nurses in white coats poked him and prodded him and extracted fluids by a variety of means, and they looked into places that he wouldn't even let Serafina look.

In one room they put him in a virtchhat and all of a sudden he was standing on a girder a long ways up in the air. He had to "walk" to the other end. When he glanced "down," people and cars were so small they looked like pepper on a tablecloth. When they told him to walk back again, the ground was so far down that airplanes flew below him.

He hated the pencil and paper tests most of all. A lot of the questions didn't make any sense. *Which would you rather be: a ballet dancer or a hockey player?* What did that have to do with rigging a job? Ballet dancers were all swish, but hockey players were dumber than a stone. So, which was the right answer for getting the job? I'd rather be dumb or swish? Psycho-testing. See if you're a psycho. He wondered if the tests were really any good.

"They don't want the best welders," a burly, copper-skinned man told him while they both waited on a cold, wooden bench to be called into still another examining room. "They want the toughest welders."

"No importa," Flaco told him. "I'm a rigger."

The other man laughed. "Riggers, too," he said. "You can be the goddamnedest rigger on the face of the Earth. But you won't be on the face of the Earth. They'd rather have a second rater who doesn't get seasick than a top-notch guy who pukes in his space suit. Hope you're not scared of heights!" He laughed again. "They'd rather have a guy who can think cool when it hits the fan than one who follows the practice to the letter—and then cites the paragraph number that proves he did everything right, after everything turned out wrong."

Flaco grunted. "Sounds like they want me, then."

The man chuckled and stuck out his hand. "Henry Littlebear, upstate New York."

"Eddie Mercado, Washington Heights. Folks call me 'Flaco.'" They shook hands. Littlebear was bigger than any man he'd care to argue with, and nearly bigger than any two. "What brought you here?"

"Same thing as most, I expect. Pay. Adventure. The chance to drop a gob of spit a real long ways. I hope you don't enjoy the weed too much, Flaco."

It wasn't anyone's business what he ate, drank, or smoked, so he made no comment. Littlebear tilted his hand up to his mouth, with his thumb mimicking a spout. "And you better not love the firewater too much. See, my wife, she's a med tech, so I know what some of these tests they're running are for. 'Weeding out the weed,' so to speak."

Flaco scowled at him. "What are you talking about, *tonto?*"

Littlebear grunted. "Unh! *Keemo sabe*. They no want-um potheads or alkies." Then, dropping the act. "Or folks with vacuum cleaners for noses."

Now Flaco grunted. He hadn't meant *tonto* in that way, but explaining would not have improved things, and Littlebear seemed to have taken it good-naturedly. Flaco was silent for a moment. Made sense, what Littlebear said. It would cost O&P a bundle to lift a man to orbit and keep him there. They wouldn't want drugs or alcohol to screw up his judgment. "Your wife ever tell you how long afterwards they can tell? I mean, if it was just a little bit?"

Littlebear grinned. "Nerve-wracking, ain't it?" He leaned against the plaster wall behind the bench and rubbed his hands together. "Wish I had me a drink to get me through this."

Flaco gave him a suspicious look, but the man was just grinning.

At five o'clock, the shuttle buses lined up in front of the building to take them to the hotels Pegasus had booked. Flaco stood in line with the rest and waited his turn to board. His hand stole to his breast pocket once or twice and patted the folded-up receipt that nestled there. Good for one more day, so either he had passed the tests or it took time to get all the results back. Not all the men in line wore the same grin he had. Some looked dejected; some, relieved. A few had an uncertain look, as if wondering what they had gotten themselves into.

A group of Pegasus employees had gathered in front of the administration building to watch. Civilian dress for the most part, though a handful wore colored coveralls. The pilot, DuBois, lounged against the cement column at the foot of the building's entrance ramp, talking to a younger man with red coveralls and punk hair. Morris Tucker joined them and traded fives with the slacker. Noticing Flaco at the bus stop, Tucker waved. "Hey, Flaco!"

Flaco returned the greeting, and the man in line behind him said, "Looks like you got yourself some grease."

Flaco shrugged. "Seen Tucker around. It don' mean nothing, 'cause he don' make the pick."

"Yeah, well, having friends never hurts. Be a shame if someone got a slot outta special favors."

Flaco turned and looked the man in the eye. "You know, 'mano, is a good thing you are already so ugly."

The other man was heavyset and wore a big, curly beard. Intricate tattoos of eagles and hawks twisted up both his arms. His eyes narrowed, and he twined his fingers through his beard. "How come?"

" 'Cause then when I rearrange your face, it won' make so much difference."

A couple of the men in line laughed. Sepp Bauer slipped

back a few spaces and stood next to Flaco with his arms folded. The bearded man grunted and his lips broke into a grin. "Well, Pancho, like the poet says, 'A man's reach should exceed his grasp.' " He offered his hand. "Name's Bird. Bird Winfrey."

Flaco hesitated only a moment, but there was no point in pushing things any further. Besides, they were about to board the bus and it would be a long ride into town. "Flaco," he said. "I'm a rigger. What's your game?"

"NDT technician. You guys put it all together; then I find all your screwups and make you do it over."

"Not me, *'mano*. You go talk to the welders, like Sepp here, or 'Tiny' Littlebear."

"Takes all kinds, 'Slim,' " the man agreed, now all amiability. "Takes all kinds."

Flaco had never expected Ossa & Pelion to put them up at a Hyatt, so he was not surprised when the bus turned down Van Buren Street instead, and drove between rows of broken, flickering neon signs advertising hourly rates. Some of the men—the foreigners, mostly—muttered comments about saving money at their expense; but Flaco lived in Washington Heights, so this part of Phoenix actually looked a little upscale to him. Still, nothing prepared him for the New Kon Tiki. With its facade of bamboo and rattan and the tiki masks flanking the doorways, it was about as unlikely a sight to find in the southwestern desert as he could imagine. Still, it had a bar; so, after dumping his gear in his room, he headed there.

The Aku-Aku Room was dark, with spotlights flashing off a faceted globe in the ceiling. In the back corner, a fountain dribbled into a pool in front of a plaster Easter Island statue and a pixwall that showed swaying palm trees and waves breaking on a lazy beach. The color was a little dull and some of the pixels had gone dark, so the effect was like looking through a dirty window. Booths separated by wicker partitions lined the left wall; and a bar with tall, bamboo-and-canvas stools stood on the right. The floor space between was packed with tables, just barely enough room between them for a skinny man like Flaco to squeeze through.

The waitresses wore grass skirts, halter tops, and sandals and did the hula when they walked through the room. The barman wore a grass skirt, too; but he was big enough that it didn't look like anyone was going to mention it. The decor was all Pacific Islands, except the CD-juke, which was wailing *a capella* "goofball" music with a Mexican beat.

A half dozen women in spike heels and heavy makeup were making the rounds, wearing skirts so short it was hard to see why they'd bothered. They cruised from table to table, chatting up the guys, touching them, sometimes letting themselves be touched. Bird had cornered one by the waterfall and negotiations were in process. A blonde with short-cropped hair draped one arm around the shoulders of a Russian rigger named Selodkin and leaned over the table so the man's companions could get a good look at her wares.

"Like flies around honey," said one of the grass-skirted waitresses near Flaco. She held a tray of drinks balanced on her hand. Flaco stepped out of her way.

"Which is which?" he asked.

She looked at him and brushed a dark curl off her forehead with her free hand. She hadn't spoken to him in particular. She had just voiced her thoughts. "Could work it either way, I guess." She jerked her head at the prostitute leaving with Bird Winfrey. "Never seen so many in here. Word musta got around that you guys were coming." She moved off with the drink tray, her grass skirt rustling as she rolled her hips.

Flaco didn't know if the disapproval he had heard in her voice was for the immorality or the competition. The waitress was plain-featured, with black shoulder-length hair and a face that had put on a lot of miles in a very few years, but who knew? She might be selling more than drinks, herself; and, as for quality, in that line of work the customers seldom dickered past price and delivery.

The bar was beginning to fill up with construction workers, so Flaco searched for a seat. He saw Henry Littlebear sitting on a bar stool that didn't look strong enough to support one of his legs. Littlebear had a schooner in front of him and he raised it to Flaco in salute.

Flaco found Tonio and a woman holding down a booth near the back and he slid in across from them. "*Hola!* How'd you beat me down here? All I did was go in my room and toss my bag on the bed. Here you have a beer already."

"There you go, you dumb Dominican. Wasting time on nonessentials." Tonio kicked his duffel bag, which was sitting under the table. "I came straight here. I can unpack later. This here's Lucia." Tonio wiggled a thumb at the woman. Dusky, with a white, uneven smile; a blouse so tight and cut so low that if she hiccupped she would pop out onto the table.

"I'm Eddie," he said.

"Hi, Eddie," she answered in a throaty, professional voice. "I have a friend, if you want . . ."

"I'm married," Flaco said. The woman gave him a look that went, like, "so what?" But Flaco didn't feel like explaining himself to a stranger.

"Just more for the rest of us," Tonio said, squeezing Lucia on the thigh. The woman laughed and wriggled provocatively, but her smile stopped at the eyes, which were devoid of anything but patience. Flaco looked away. Years ago, when he and Chino and Diego had decided it was time for them to be men, they had gone to one of the women on St. Nicholas. He had seen that look then, in the back of Chino's old Pontiac, and had vowed then that he would never again be with a woman whose soul was somewhere else.

The waitress who served them was the same one who had spoken to him earlier. Flaco figured the odds were against the Aku-Aku Room carrying *El Presidente*, so he settled for *Tecate*. The waitress took his order and Tonio's reorder, but pointedly ignored Tonio's companion. If either Tonio or Lucia noticed, they didn't care.

Sepp found them an hour and several drinks later. Tonio was in the middle of a long and improbable tale of immigrant smuggling in south Florida. If half what Tonio said was true, there wasn't a Haitian left anywhere on Hispaniola. Thanks to him, they were all in Miami or New York. Lucia pretended to listen and looked at her watch from time to time. When you worked piece rate, you didn't have a lot of time to spare for social chitchat. Sepp was a sudden blond presence by their booth.

"Dare you are!" he said, as if they had been hiding from him. Flaco slid over to make room and Sepp squeezed in beside him. Sepp looked around the lounge and put two fingers in his mouth and whistled. He made a bottle of his fist and poked his thumb at the table in front of him. Then he settled into the seat and grinned. "Now ve see vat disguises for beer in deese place." His gaze cruised over Lucia, moored on her breasts. "Hellow, Schatz'," he said, using the same smile.

Lucia batted her eyes. "Hello, Dutch." She moistened her lipstick with her tongue and shifted her posture to display herself better. Tonio scowled and pushed her.

"You're with me," he said.

She shrugged him off. "Whenever you're ready, *hermano*."

Tonio lifted his schooner. "*Momento*. I'm drinking with my compadres."

"What took you so long?" Flaco asked Sepp as the waitress dropped a bottle of Budweiser on the table without even pausing to see if that was what he wanted. Sepp twisted the cap off the bottle and took a swallow. He put the bottle down again with a shake of his head.

"In Bavaria, it vould be illegal to label diss 'beer.'" He threw one arm across the back of the padded bench where they sat. "It did not take zo long. I unpack, hang my clothes in proper order, arrange the drawers, stow my traffling pack . . ."

Flaco and Tonio looked at each other and laughed. Sepp listened to them for a moment, then shrugged. "On de space station zuch neatness vill matter."

Flaco stopped laughing.

Who knew when the testing really stopped?

Flaco could not sleep. During the night, it was said, the Arizona desert grew bitter cold; but here in Phoenix the empty night sky served only to release the heat pent up in the concrete and asphalt, so that the sweltering warmth that surrounded him seemed to ooze from the ground rather than from the scorching sky. The air-conditioning at the New Kon Tiki labored in vain.

He sat up in bed and stared at the glowing digital display of his travel alarm. Two o'clock? He would be in fine shape for tomorrow's—today's—competition! He didn't have to be better than everyone to win a slot on this crew, but he did have to be better than a great many someones. He sighed and laid his head down on his pillow.

Only to be snatched upright by a metallic crash outside his window, followed by a shouted curse. Flaco rolled out of bed and strode to the window, where he stood to the side and lifted a gentle edge of the curtain. That was a move that Diego had never learned. When there are noises in the night, you do not go and stand directly in front of a window.

Funny. He hadn't thought of Diego—or Chino and the others—in a great many years. Some things were best not thought of. The nighttime streets. The women and the product and the thick blocks of cash that bought both. The trembling eager high that was half adrenaline, half product. The sound of a lone car racing by, the sight of a dark alley mouth, the distant, toy pop-pop sound of a deal gone bad. The wary, *live* feeling on the edge.

In the alleyway three stories below, he saw the shape of a woman slowly rise to her feet beside the hotel kitchen loading dock. The streetlights at the end of the block created knives of light and shadow from the angles of the buildings; and the woman, partly in and partly out of the shadows, seemed unreal. A ghost of pale, disconnected legs and arms.

She brushed herself—futilely, considering the kitchen waste and the pools of fetid water that spattered the pavement. She whipped an arm up in a gesture of contempt, but whether at a particular person or window, or just at the building itself, Flaco could not tell. She turned on her heel—and nearly tumbled to her hands and knees again. She bent and held both hands against her thigh.

Flaco wondered if he should call someone or go down to her. Her long thighs seemed to run up forever, ducking only at the last minute behind the cover of her meager skirt. Watching her, he felt his desire swell. In this heat, skimpy dress only made sense, and he could not tell in this light or from this angle if the woman was one of the waitresses, one of the hookers, or even an ordinary citizen out walking in nighttime alleys for reasons of her own. Undoubtedly one of the women who had gone off with Bird or the Russians or the others, and who had found things a little rougher than expected. Reluctantly, he watched her limp out of sight before letting the curtain fall and slipping back into his own bed. He thought of the woman's thigh as he lay there and how it had seemed to glow from the distant streetlight.

On the third day, Flaco and the other riggers were taken to Pegasus Hanger Number Two for their practicals. The hanger, twenty stories tall, loomed over the rest of the complex just off the far right end of the horseshoe. Massive, square, and metallic, it was the only structure on the grounds that made no concession to adobe or the Southwest.

The orbital ship that Flaco had noticed on Monday had been brought inside. The ship's dingy, scorched-grey fuselage had been partly disassembled. One panel still in place near the nose bore the large block numbers "RS64" and the name *Harriet Quimby*. The orbiter—they were called Planks for some reason—was two hundred feet tall, with a shell made largely of titanium-sheathed smoke. "Solid smoke" was light—"structural aerogel," they called it; but it could be difficult to handle because of its very lightness. The size of smoked structural pieces could fool you into thinking they were heavier than they were, and you wound up moving them a little too fast and a little too hard. Not that that would damage the smoke, but it would sure as hell damage anyone in the way of it. By volume, smoke was mostly air, but it was strong, like honeycomb, and could withstand extreme loads and stresses. They were even starting to build cars with it—it was light enough to get fabulous gas mileage, but strong enough that it wouldn't crumple in an accident. Flaco had handled the material occasionally in construction work. The Wilson Tower in St. Louis had smoked its upper stories to gain height without putting a lot of weight on the load-bearing beams.

A crew of men and women in grease-stained red coveralls stood by and watched the riggers. "You dudes are crazy," one of the Pegasus mechanics shouted. "Me, I'm keeping both my feet on the dirt."

"Never said I wasn't crazy," Flaco told him. The man laughed and shook his head.

Three other men, olive-skinned with trim mustaches, stood a little apart from the mechanics, drinking thick coffee out of Styrofoam cups and talking to one another in Portuguese. The Pegasus people seemed to ignore them. These men wore brown coveralls, and their patches featured a winged sun rather than a winged stallion.

A third group, dressed in O&P blue with two stacked triangles on their badges, watched from a walkway a hundred feet overhead. Flaco recognized Meat Tucker, and figured the men with him were the other rigging crew bosses and their superintendent. Flaco rubbed the palms of his hands against his own denim coveralls and hitched his tool belt and harness a little higher. He'd had people watch him work before, but never so many and never with so much depending on it.

"Wonder how many of us will be left after today," Tonio whispered to him. "Figure they want to cut as many as they can before spending money on weightless and orbital training.''

"Don't forget to cup the water in your hand," Flaco advised him.

"What?"

"Judge Gideon, in the Bible," he said absently, while he scanned the setup. "He tested thirty thousand volunteers and picked three hundred of them." Tonio grunted, but made no reply.

There were two overhead cranes on traverse beams with blocks and tackle dangling from them. No, three, and the third one *way* up there was a pivot crane with an operator's booth. Did O&P expect them to be operatives as well as riggers? Probably. LEO would never lift featherbed. There'd be multitasking, for sure, on this contract.

A fiftyish man wearing a white hard hat and a long dust coat was waiting for them. He had a cliputer tucked under one arm. "Gentlemen," he said (and inevitably some wit in the back of the group said, "Who came in?" White Hat ignored the comment.) "I am your examiner. I have your work orders right here." He flourished the cliputer. "The O&P crew chiefs up there on the balcony will observe and judge your work and will advise me, but I will have the final downcheck. There are no appeals from my decision." He turned and pointed toward the partly disassembled Plank with the cliputer. "Your assignments are to prepare this equipment for its regularly scheduled preventive maintenance check. The Pegasus crew is on hand to assist you in tasks outside the rigging craft boundaries."

Flaco pursed his lips in a silent whistle. Van Huyten Industries was famous for its never-waste-a-mission frugality, so why not use the practicals to get some real work done? But that meant there was more riding on this test than just his own performance. The *Harriet Quimby's* performance on its next flight could also depend on him. He wondered if that extra pressure was deliberate. LEO's multinational investment was in the billions and the consortium meant to recover those expenses. There would be conflicting priorities for flawless work *and* for cutting costs and maintaining the schedule—with the workers caught in between, as usual. So, this trial might be more than to test their rigging skills. It might be to see how they would react to stress.

They tested in groups of five, while the others waited in the maintenance conference room. Those who went out did not come back, and Flaco pondered that while he sat and read a very old magazine.

Flaco went out with the fourth group late in the morning. The examiner printed a work order from his cliputer and gave it to Flaco and Flaco read it carefully. His task was to remove module 477JJK(3) from the forward superstructure and move it to the electrical bay. The CAD print that came with the work order highlighted the module and showed the anchors where he could hook on with the overhead tackle. It didn't look like a hard job; not one that would separate the real men from the wannabes.

He had taken two steps toward the crane elevator when he noticed the date on the drawing. Revision D. December 20, 2005. Three and a half years old . . . He glanced at the *Harriet Quimby*. Could be the gal was that old. He didn't know one model from another, and Planks of one sort or another had been lifting for nine years now. But who was to say that there hadn't been retrofits? Flaco turned and faced the examiner.

"Hey, *'mano,*" he called, waving the print. "This the current rev?"

White Hat looked up from his cliputer and, without a change of expression, held out his hand. Flaco gave him the drawing and he looked at the drawing control block, then checked something in his database. "No," he said, wadding the print into a ball. "*Quimby*'s to Rev F." He touched a button on his cliputer and a new drawing emerged, which he handed to Flaco.

Three other men in Flaco's test group looked at their drawings, and two said, "Shit," and brought their sheets back to the examiner, too. That was when Flaco knew that this would be a different sort of test, and that he could take nothing for granted.

Harriet Quimby was tall enough that the five examinees could work independently at different tasks. Three of them, including Flaco, were on the upper levels. The other two, including the sole woman among the rigger-candidates, drew ground-level assignments.

Flaco and the two other men entered the bright orange elevator cage. Flaco pulled the gate shut and latched it, and a short, black man engaged the lift motors. As the cage rose, he stuck his hand out to Flaco.

"Thanks, dude," he said. "Never thought they'd give us bad prints for a test. Name's King Boudreaux, from N'awlins." He shook Flaco's hand like a pump handle.

"Eddie Mercado, Washington Heights. People call me Flaco." He studied the young man. Light tan. Only five-four; but with the shoulders of a weight lifter. Flaco lifted an eyebrow. "King?"

"Pa thought 'Martin' was a sissy name, and Ma was a Methodist and didn't care for 'Luther.' " He shook his head. "Thanks again. About the rev, I mean."

After King got off on 3-Level, the third man, who had remained silent, spoke. "Yer barmy, mate," he said. He possessed a fine, curly red beard, a respectable beer belly, and the shiniest head Flaco had ever seen. "If you'd kept yer fool yap shut, we'd have two less competitors to worry about now."

Flaco shrugged. "What if you'd had an obsolete drawing, too?"

The bearded man snorted. "Think I'm stupid? I checked mine, just like you did. Here's your stop, mate." He pulled the cage door open. "See you round."

"Yeah. You, too . . . ?" He let the sentence lift into a question.

"Red Hawkins. New South Wales." Hawkins's handshake was a single, hard squeeze.

A Pegasus electrician and a pipe fitter were waiting for Flaco when he crossed the catwalk from the crane tower to the ship. The pipe fitter shook his hand and said, "Good luck." They had their own drawings—wiring schematics and piping drawings, respectively—and the first thing Flaco did was check his drawings against theirs. Subassembly numbers and rev levels matched. "Okay," Flaco said. "Let's find this sucker." The two Pegasus mechanics knew where the module was located, but they were following his lead. They would not permit him to screw up the maintenance, though. Test or no test, the ship was signed over to their care. But Flaco also knew that if they did intervene, he would have failed the test.

"Goddamn!" The voice came from floor level and the pipe fitter smiled.

"Guess someone down there just matched his mechanicals against the P-and-Ws."

"You talk too much, Bob," the electrician said.

"Ah, no harm done, Bob. Eddie here already got past that one." Flaco looked at them.

"You both named Bob?"

Bob-the-pipe fitter grinned. "Life's a bitch, ain't it?"

Flaco located a module that looked like 477JJK(3). The drawing said the module ought to have an asset tag; but when Flaco finally located it—in a different position than the drawing had indicated—the asset number failed to match. He looked at Bob-the-pipe fitter.

"This puppy have a mate?"

"Could be," the pipe fitter allowed.

"Now, who's being cute," said Bob-the-electrician. "Port side," he told Flaco. "These are regulator valves for the oxidizer tanks. Each tank got a main and a spare. Sometimes they get switched. Like you rotate your tires."

Flaco dusted his hands off and rose to his feet. "Let's go find it."

"Who cares?" said Pipe Fitter Bob. "They both look the same, and they both gotta come out for PM. What difference does it make which comes out first?"

What difference, indeed? Yet Flaco could not shake the

feeling that he was still being tested. *The devil did tempt me, and I did eat . . .*

"Get behind me, Satan," he said. But he said it with a grin to take any sting out.

"Hunh, fussy, are we?"

"No," said Flaco, "but I am thinking that the last thing you ever want to do in space construction is disconnect the wrong module."

The actual rigging was straightforward. A third man waiting for them on the port side was introduced as the regular rigger on that job. Flaco asked him if his name was Bob, too, and he winced. "Jesus, no. Call me Jimmy."

The two Bobs disconnected the hydraulics and electricity and signed off on Flaco's work order; then Flaco unbolted the module from the superstructure, pulling in a guy wire from the number two traverse crane to hold the unit in place until he was ready to lift. Then he checked out the structural integrity of the module. The drawing showed the support points but Flaco was taking little for granted. Be a hell of a thing if the module fell into two halves when he lifted, with only one half fastened into the tackle. Even after he had ratcheted the chains and lifted the module out of place, he called the crane operator over the two-way and told him to hold while he checked the balance and the security of the rigging. When he was satisfied, he signaled the operator and gave the thumbs-to-the-ground signal.

"Not too bad," allowed Jimmy. "So far. You still gotta move it to the bay and unrig it."

Flaco stretched his arms back as far as he could and arched his back. "You gonna teach me to kiss girls, too?"

Jimmy shrugged. "You could find worse teachers . . ."

"Watch it, down below! Crane coming." Red Hawkins, on the ship's 1-Level, was bringing across the number one traverse. The two cranes moved on parallel tracks, number one being somewhat higher than the one Flaco was using. "Hold up a few minutes, Chico. I need the crane operator for a while."

''Name's Flaco,'' Flaco told him.

''Whatever.''

Flaco grinned and slid to the deck with his back against a bulkhead and his right leg dangling out the open side of the ship. ''This is the part I like best,'' he told Jimmy and the two Bobs. ''Goofin'.''

Jimmy leaned out the side and looked down, holding onto the cross brace over his head. ''You know,'' Flaco told him, ''that as soon as we get outside, we can clue in the afternoon group to these little tricks of yours.''

Bob-the-electrician smiled. ''So who uses the same tricks all the time?''

Flaco ran his hand along the inner skin of the vessel by his head. ''How come you guys aren't trying out for this job?''

Bob-the-electrician shrugged. Bob-the-pipe fitter said, ''I don't like the commute.'' Jimmy-the-rigger said, ''Been there. Done that.'' Flaco looked at him.

''You been up?''

''I'm on the Gold Crew. We lifted the first couple of ETs into 69-double-ought. But the law says no more than six months up and then you get six months down, minimum, between stints. So O&P and the other contractors rotate crews. Blue Crew is up there now. Red Crew goes up next. You're Green—if you make the cut. You'll double up with Red Crew for a while, until you learn the ropes.''

''Crane coming through!'' Red bellowed from above.

Jimmy looked up. ''Nose lock,'' he said.

''Real bitch,'' said Bob-the-pipe fitter.

The nose lock shifted in its tackle and Flaco pressed the red button on his two-way. ''Crane,'' he said. ''Load's coming loose!''

Jimmy cupped his hands around his mouth and hollered to the workers on the floor below to clear away. The nose lock swayed back and forth under the now motionless crane. Red's face appeared from the next level up. ''What the hell you playing at, Chico? You trying to screw me over?''

''The load's loose,'' Jimmy told him.

Red tossed his head in annoyance. "Shit." He spoke into his own two-way and the crane tracked back toward the ship. The nose lock turned and fell a few inches. Flaco made throat-cutting motions and Red stopped the crane.

"I can see underneath. A stay-bolt is working loose. Every time you move the load, it swings a little and pulls it out more."

"Double-shit gum. I leave it hanging and it will by-Our-Lady drop sooner or later." Red tugged at his beard. "How about I lower it real fast? I might get it to ground level before it comes loose."

Or you might not . . . But it was Red's call. "Try it," he said. "I'll watch from down here and tell Crane to stop if anything happens. Did you hear that, Crane?"

"Gotcha." Flaco was glad to see the crane operator was taking things so well. But then, why shouldn't he? It wasn't him being tested. Flaco ran a hand across his brow. It was one hell of a test.

The nose lock began to drop and almost immediately twisted out of true. "Stop the drop!" Flaco told the operator.

The entire rig was now level with where Flaco stood on the decking. He couldn't see the loose bolt any more. "King!" he called. "How's it look?"

"Bad," the Louisianan hollered from the next level down. "The one stay is out entirely. Putting a bad strain on the others. You got three lines and God holding it up."

God, Flaco felt, could be relied on, but he wasn't so sure of the other stays. "Okay." Flaco put the two-way to his face. "Crane, what do you have on the pivot arm up in the ceiling?"

"Hook and ball, why?"

"Run some tackle out there and swing it over. We can run a basket rig under the nose lock and lower it using both cranes."

"I don't know . . ."

"Do it!" Flaco had no authority to give the orders. But someone had to do something, fast. He looked to Jimmy, who scowled and nodded and leaned out of the ship to make a thumbs-up gesture to the control booth.

The echo of the motors tripping in the ceiling emphasized how silent the maintenance hanger had become. Flaco watched as several cables of chain tackle ran out the pivot arm, which then swung across the room until it could drop the line between the nose lock and the ship. Flaco guided the operator using the two-way until the ball-and-hook dangled just outside the ship.

Flaco swallowed and gave a nod to the three men with him. Then he clipped his safety line to a crossbar and, before he could remember what a fool he was, stepped across and into the curve of the hook.

It was a big hook, strong enough to hold more than a mere human—and a skinny one at that; but Flaco could not stand comfortably except on one foot. He clipped his second line to the lanyard on the hook cable. Jimmy unclipped the first line and it rolled up into its reel on Flaco's belt. Flaco wrapped his arm around the crane cable and gave him a nod, trying to look unconcerned. Jimmy gave him a salute. "See you in heaven."

The cable danced and swayed. Flaco looked up to see Red Hawkins clipping himself on farther up. "We both don't have to be out here," Flaco said.

"Fuck you, Chico. This is my job. They unhooked your load down below and brought number two crane over to the other side of my load. I'm going to transfer over. You bring the fly end of the tackle underneath and I'll run it up the other side. Then we'll do the same thing with the second strap. You got a problem with that, Chico?"

"No problem. Like you said, gringo. Your job."

"And don't you forget it."

Flaco waited until Red had secured himself on the other side of the nose lock, then gave the crane operator the go-ahead to lower them both. When they met underneath, Flaco handed Red the free end of one of the chains. He was acutely aware of the massive structure dangling over him. He could *feel* its weight curling the hairs on the back of his neck. He said, "It would be tragic if the rigging gave way now."

Red grunted and looked up. "Yeah, it'd be the end of a beautiful fucking friendship. But look again, Chico. It ain't the rigging giving way, it's the nose lock. Fucking corrosion is what it is." He fixed the end of the chain to his crane. "And damn me if I'll let you look good at my expense."

They finished the job without speaking. When the basket rig was secure—and they checked *that* six ways from Sunday—Red gave the signal to the crane operator to lower away on both cranes. The nose lock swung as the new lines took off some of the weight and its center of gravity shifted, but it reached the ground without further incident. The other candidates and the Pegasus people burst into applause as Flaco dropped off the hook onto the floor. Meat, up on the catwalk, gave him a thumbs-up. Red slid down a free chain from the traverse beam. He glowered at the nose lock while he tugged his heavy canvas gloves off. Flaco tucked his own gloves in his tool belt and offered his hand.

"Good work, man."

Red slapped his gloves against his left palm. He looked like he wanted to punch out the mechanism. "I always do good work, mate." He turned away without shaking and faced White Hat, who had come over and was squatting by the nose lock. One of the men in the brown coveralls was kneeling by his side, and they were conversing in low tones. "So, what's the verdict?" Red demanded.

The brown-coveralled man held up fingertips covered with rust. "It appears to be saltwater corrosion, but we cannot be sure yet."

"No, mate. I meant the goddamned test!"

White Hat looked up. "The results will be posted this evening," he said.

Flaco grabbed the the examiner's sleeve and tugged him around. "You crazy, *'mano!*" he shouted. "What kind of test was that? People could have been hurt; killed, maybe!" He threw his work order, his exam paper, to the ground. Red stepped away, as if to dissociate himself from the outburst. Tomorrow Flaco would curse himself for yelling at the examiner and blowing his chances for the job, but right now he didn't care.

White Hat flushed, and his ears grew a prominent red. He stood up and yanked his sleeve from Flaco's grasp. "Get a grip, kid," he said. "We don't play things that way. You may not be worth jack shit, but that nose lock is sure as hell valuable hardware."

Flaco stood back and his arms fell to his side. "It wasn't . . . ?"

"A test?" White Hat snorted. "Of course, it was. It just wasn't planned."

Flaco flew into JFK on US West. Serafina was waiting for him at the end of the concourse and nearly knocked him over when she jumped into his arms. They were standing in the middle of the flow of traffic, but Flaco didn't care. For every glower they got from an outta-my-way business-man they got five smiles from people who remembered what love had been like.

"Oh, Flaco, I missed you," she said between rapid-fire kisses.

"And I missed you," he said, lowering her to the floor.

"Ha," she tucked her arm through his and they made their way through the crowds toward the shuttle bus. "You out there in the sunny desert with all those Mexicana women to tease you . . ."

"I did not see one *'chicana* half so beautiful as you." And it was true. Others might argue that Serafina's nose was a little too big, or that her breasts were not, or that her legs were too short; but not Flaco. He could remember the women in the New Kon Tiki, their golden brown and tan skin, their easy availability; but worn, and old before their years, and none so fine on the eyes as Serafina. Serafina's love was free, and so he had paid for it the ultimate price: the rest of his life.

For dinner that evening, Flaco took Serafina to Mambi on Broadway. It was a warm night. A night that wanted walking. They strolled crosstown arm in arm, letting silence do for words. August 16 was only a week and a half off, and a festive mood was beginning to build in the neighborhood. There had been Dominicans on Manhattan since the late seventeen hundreds. Upper Broadway—here at the northern tip of Manhattan—was a Dominican Broadway; and the clubs and theaters that lined the street pulsed to the merengue. The breeze carried the rich odors of *sofrito* and *mangu* and thick *guisados*. The *panas* and their *bombias*—the young men and their women—were laughing and dancing in the street, holding impromptu parties on the corners, or eating their *mondongo* with beans and wet rice. Not that the anniversary of Trujillo's capture meant anything to them. It meant little enough to Flaco, despite the long, impassioned stories he had heard at his grandfather's knee. Mostly third and fourth generation in America, the brightly dressed young men and women bubbling on the street knew the day only as an excuse for *alegria*.

Flaco exchanged greetings with a dozen friends in the few short blocks. Half of them did not even know that Flaco had been gone. A carefree bunch, even when care was called for. Here and there in the crowd Flaco marked older men in their thirties with hooded, predatory eyes, and he hugged Serafina closer to him. Danger wore an older face than it once did. There was safety in crowds, but it was never entirely safe.

Serafina had been expecting some *mamita*'s with the greasy *pollo frito* piled in baskets, so when he led her to Mambi, she gasped and said, "Flaco! Can we afford this?"

Flaco grinned at the successful surprise. By midtown and downtown standards, Mambi was not terribly expensive; but they were so far up the island that you had to go a long way downtown just to reach uptown, and by the standards of the Gonsalves Mercado saving account, dining out was not a thing to be done lightly. "O&P paid us for the week of testing," he told her. "So now we can celebrate."

"Your coming home."

"That, too."

Serafina fell silent. She stared at the restaurant window. In her reflection, a small frown creased her brow and her fingers briefly caressed her stomach.

They both ordered the *costilla de cerdo con berenjena* that Mambi was famous for. Flaco ordered a wine. It was not so proud a wine as to have a year on it, but it did not come in a returnable bottle, either. He lifted his glass to Serafina and said, "To us. You an' me an' little Memo." Serafina smiled and touched her glass to his.

"The trials went very well, I think," he said after he had swallowed and set his wine down. "Met some good men. And a few assholes, too. They told me helping out your crewmates, regardless, counted for a lot of points." He grinned. Serafina took a bite of her eggplant.

"This is very good," she said and developed an interest in her meal. "Mama came over while you were away. We bought a crib for Memo. And some clothes. Oh, Flaco! They were so tiny, I just wanted to cry."

There was no telling with women how they would react. Flaco smiled and tried to look confident. "Everything will be all right. You'll see." Sometimes, the thought of being a father terrified him. A helpless child, trusting him utterly, following after him. . . . He would have to provide for the little one. He didn't know if he was ready for the responsibility. He didn't know if he could lead the boy anywhere it would be worth his while to follow. Grow up, be a rigger like your *papita?* Or a waiter, like your *abuelito?* But ready or not, here it came. His hands trembled and he cut firmly into his pork rib with his knife. Did Serafina feel the same doubts as he did? It would never do to show his uncertainty to her. She depended on him to be the strong one. "The money I make on this job," he told her, "we set Memo up right."

Serafina's fork clattered on her plate. Flaco looked up. "What's wrong?"

"You are not going back, are you?"

"Of course, I am. I passed the trials. I told you, didn't

I?'' Or had the subject never come up in the joy of reunion? Had he known somehow to avoid it?

"Flaco, you will die up there!" A few heads turned in the restaurant, then just as quickly looked away. Young people spoke of dying too often. The reason was well known, and a reason best not known. Flaco wanted to leap up and tell them they were wrong; that Diego's death had turned him from that forever. He was a man of the construction now, a rigger. A life that was not so exciting and paid not so well, but which might last long enough to see your sons and your grandsons. No one shot you through your window at night because you were rigging on the wrong street corner.

But his quarrel was not with these strangers. Flaco's grip tightened on his fork and he stabbed his pork rib hard enough to send it off the plate. He had dreamed of this weekend as a happy one of laughter and lovemaking, never giving a thought to Sunday afternoon and the long flight back to Phoenix. "I will not die," he said. Death was something that happened—to quiet old men or to flamboyant young ones; but those who might have wanted to see Flaco dead were themselves no longer quick.

"Hundreds of men have worked up there," he assured her. "Very few have been hurt, even in small things." He did not mention Anselmo Takeuchi and how the blood had flowed from the eyes and mouth of his exploding body. His was not an error Flaco would ever make.

"What if you are not here for little Memo? How will your son and I survive without you?" Serafina twisted the napkin in her hands. Her eyes brimmed with tears. Pregnancy always made women more emotional.

"You'll be provided for. The benefits are generous."

She pushed away from the table and jumped to her feet. "You are cruel, Flaco! What will I do for comfort in the night with nothing but money for your bones?" She fled without waiting for his reply. Another woman in the restaurant raised her voice.

"You tell him, sister! They can't treat us that way no

more.'' She favored Flaco with a glare. Some of the men laughed and made motions with their hands or arms. ''Show her who the boss is.'' ''Stick it to her; that's what she wants.'' An elderly couple by the window, their lips pressed tight in distaste, bent over their *guisado*. Flaco pulled a couple of presidents from his wallet and threw them on the table without waiting to see what the bill was.

At the door, a solitary old man with his napkin tucked in at his neck stopped Flaco with a hand on his sleeve. ''It will be all right, young man,'' he croaked in a voice harsh with cigarettes. ''It is love that makes them mad. She would not hurt so much if she did not love you.''

Flaco was not such a fool as to chase after Serafina. She had not run from him in order for him to catch her. Not this time. The thought of her alone on the nighttime streets worried him, but it was not as though Boricua girls grew up any less savvy than Dominicans. She would go either to their apartment or to her *mamita*. He would find her. They would ''rendezvous,'' ''match orbits,'' like the newspeople on TV were saying about the spaceship and the asteroid, a little more than two weeks from now.

He looked up at the sky, but the city lights were too bright, and there was nothing up there but a grey, pale shroud.

The merengue was pounding in Ysidro's bar off Dyckman Street, but with more than a little of that Milwaukee ''goofball'' in the mix that the older *panas* found so irritating. Not the pure sound at all. Not Cibao; not even the southern style, with its log drums. But Flaco had come here for the drinks, not the music.

''Is it wrong of me to want to provide for her?'' he asked Clotario, his best friend among those still living. He stared into his tall, thin glass of *El Presidente*. ''Is it wrong of me to want to afford things for her?'' His voice was slurred from the drinking. He could hear the soft, slushing sound of it, but he didn't care.

"No," Clotario said. "Of course not. It is only that she will be lonely for you."

Flaco drank his beer, set the glass down hard on the table. "Seven months' training," he said. "Groundside and spaceside. But I'll be back before the child comes."

"A long time," said Clotario, "for a woman to be without a man inside her."

"She will not be the only one lonely," Flaco said with a twist to his lips.

Clotario nudged him. "Ah, but there will be women on the crew, no? Even in space they have the secretaries. And you yourself mentioned a few welders and technicians."

Flaco stiffened. "Serafina is the only one for me. I have given her my pledge."

Clotario laughed. "Oh, you are the righteous one, Flaco." He made a mock sign of the cross and kissed his fingers. "Your lady welders may be as attractive as their own welding tanks, but you will see. They will grow more beautiful as the months go by. Never will they be as lovely as your Serafina, who is the most desirable woman in all the Heights; but"—leaning toward Flaco—"they will be so much closer."

Flaco turned his attention back to his beer. "One voice inside me says, 'Flaco, stay with your woman and take care of her during her months.' But another says, 'Earn the money you will need to care for her forever.' How often do such opportunities come for men in the trades?"

"There are other trades," Clotario said casually. Flaco gave him a dead look, and he shrugged. "Then, if you wish, I can look after Serafina while you are gone."

Flaco stared at him through the gauze of alcohol. Saw the easy smile on his lips; heard the smooth assurance in his voice. Before he was quite aware that he was doing so, Flaco had sunk his fist in the pit of his friend's stomach.

Clotario fell gasping for breath, and Flaco found himself suddenly in the center of an open space, as the others in the bar made room. Ysidro reached under the bar and said, "Flaco, you and 'Tario take it outside." He made no other moves. Everyone stood very still. Flaco bent over the gasping Clotario.

"You do not touch my wife while I am gone."

Clotario lay with his knees tucked up, clenching his belly. "Flaco, I didn't . . . mean . . ."

"You will not allow anyone else to touch my wife when I am gone. If anyone does, I will kill him. I give my word on that. Do you understand?" Clotario nodded dumbly and Flaco bent lower, putting himself in the man's face. "I do not give my word lightly. I have done so only twice. Once when Diego died in my arms, and once when Serafina and I stood together before God. And you, Clotario, know how well I kept my word on that first occasion."

The voice whispered to him from the alleyway on Dyckman. "Flaco," it said. "Hey, Flaco."

It was the street talking to him, he thought. When he turned, he saw a woman standing there, looking tired, feigning interest. "Long time, Flaco," she said.

Flaco made to pass by. She stepped out and took him by the sleeve and pulled him into the alley. Flaco staggered after her, too woozy to resist. The alley was rank. The ancient bricks of the buildings were sweaty with runoff from the clogged rainspouts on their roofs. "What do you want, *bomba?*" he asked. But it was a stupid question, because he knew what she wanted. Her fingers told him.

"I need you, Flaco," she whispered in his ear. Her tongue licked him there, sending a thrill down his spine. "They tell me you were good. Fast and clever. You can help me." She wrapped her arms around his neck and pressed herself against him, but the notion gradually soaked through the alcoholic mist that it was all a ruse so she could whisper to him.

"Jaime, he beats me alla time if I don' make enough tricks."

"Leave him," Flaco said shortly and she laughed.

"Then who gives me powder? You could do that. You'd be nice to me. Nicer'n Jaime." She was drunk, too, Flaco realized, or high. He could have her here and in the morning she wouldn't even remember, and that would be like it never happened.

"I can be nice," he admitted.

"Jaime, he's getting a load tonight, from downtown. I know where he's gonna be. You're smart, they always said. You could nine Jaime and sell the shit and then you 'n' me, we'd be phat."

"How much shit?" he asked, because his tongue, awakened by alcohol, was living its own, dangerous life.

"Ten keys, at least," she told him. "Mexican pearls."

Flaco pursed his lips. He didn't know street for pearl these days, but five years ago ten keys would mean thirty kilobucks, as much as a six-month tour on LEO.

Thirty kilobucks of Mexican pearl could also get you nined, but death was on the station, too. A nasty, lonely death, either way. And if all he wanted was a place for Serafina and himself, here was a way that was faster and only a little riskier. He could use this woman—he didn't know her name, though she obviously remembered him—he could use this woman to take "Jaime"—a nobody, but somebody enough to cast pearls—and then cut her or keep her, as seemed best.

Serafina was in bed when Flaco finally returned home. She pretended to be asleep, but Flaco knew it was pretense from the stillness with which she lay. He stood in the bedroom doorway, bracing himself with one arm on the jamb against the swaying of the floor. The August night was too hot for sheets, too hot for nightgowns. Serafina lay beautifully uncovered, wearing only her white lace underwear. Flaco's breath came shorter.

He could have her. She probably wanted him to, or else why was she lying just so? He had never forced himself upon her. But he had never struck and threatened his *pana* before tonight, either. And if tonight was the time to rediscover the old Flaco, the Flaco of the careless streets, then perhaps it should be the whole man that was found.

But he turned away without disturbing her. The old Flaco was best left buried. He closed the bedroom door gently and found his way to the couch in the outer room, where he lay down carefully. A two-room, walk-up flat in upper Manhattan. It was little enough, but it was theirs. Their names were on the lease. But how he dreamed of escaping! A house, with trees, and a yard where Memo could run and play and grow tall and strong.

Sleep would not come. After a time, he rose from the sofa and walked softly to the open window. He sat on the sill, looking down at the nighttime. The crackling neon signs of the twenty-four-hour cafés; the blinking traffic lights at the corner; the furtive men and women conducting their business in shadowed doorways, in parked cars, among the children's playthings in the little park where the streets all came together. A black car rolled up Fort Washington Avenue, slowed at the intersection, and turned right. No one paid it any mind. Not the hustlers; not the hookers. Not the couple standing in the doorway to the transient hotel, whose rhythmic movements never missed a beat. Not the whiskered old man with the strap still around his arm, staring where the stars ought to have been, pulse thumping to a rhythm no one else could hear.

He wondered if the woman had been setting him up; if this Jaime was someone who had reason to remember old scores. Most likely, she had been tempting each man as he came and would continue to do so until either Jaime heard of it and nined her or someone took her up and got both of them killed. By turning her down, Flaco had undoubtedly condemned the next man along the street to a nasty death.

And yet, every man thought he had the eggs and the brains to carry off such a play.

Flaco turned away from the window. It was not Serafina he had to save. It was not Serafina he had to pull away from these streets. As long as he could hear their siren call, the old Flaco would never stay entirely dead.

Saturday was strained, and he and Serafina spent their time not in lovemaking, but in making arrangements to sublet the apartment. It made no sense for her to stay there alone all those months. She would move back with her *mamita;* he would put his things into storage. Flaco's parents would take care of the lease and keep an eye on things. When Flaco spoke to his father over the phone, *papita* gave no hint whether he thought Flaco wise or foolish; but that had been papa's way, as far back as Flaco could remember.

After that—after he had helped Serafina move back to her mother's place in Spanish Harlem—it made no sense to wait for Sunday evening. So, after one last night in their apartment, he turned the keys over to *papita* and caught an early morning flight back to Phoenix. For the first Sunday in the five long years since Diego went down, he missed Mass.

INTERLUDE:

Rock Concert

The radar display pinged at slow, deliberate intervals and a simulated woman's voice whispered closing distances in Forrest's earclip. "Relative velocity, twenty," murmured the A/S. Forrest sighed as he adjusted the burn, keeping his trajectory centered on the profile displayed on the pilot's pixcreen. The flight plan called for a hundred days to reach the Rock, forty days hanging around, and then another two hundred-odd days on the long orbit home. And the whole year long he would be listening to the goddamnedest sexy voice in the universe whispering in his ear.

Could be worse. Could be Krasnarov whispering in his ear. . . .

He could see the Rock through *Bullard*'s sunroof viewports: a motley of light and shadow difficult to make out against the starry backdrop. He couldn't decide if they were coming up underneath the asteroid or they were flying upside down as they approached it. Which way was up? Every which way . . . "Damn hard to see that mother," Forrest complained. "Even the sunlit side."

The Iron Mike sat in the Plank's copilot seat with his face pressed into the crosshaired, close-approach telescope calling off angular velocities while Forrest tickled the attitude jets. "Dark body," he commented without looking up.

"Just like my women," said Forrest. Krasnarov made a

face, but kept his eyes firmly on the telescope. Forrest wondered what the Russian did for amusement when the computer's contralto grew too much for him. *Close your eyes and think of Mother Russia. . . .*

Nacho Mendes made a noise halfway between a sigh and a grunt and Forrest grinned without turning around. With no specific duties during the close-approach maneuver, the geologist was playing TV producer, feeding digital video to Heimdall Communications back Earthside.

VHI had hoped to recover some of the expenses of the voyage by syndicating the whole thing as a TV show. Sensor doids strategically placed inside and outside the ship collected visual and other data. Why not use the images for entertainment?

Because there's nothing more boring than watching three guys cramped inside a tin can scratch themselves for a year. Forrest could have told them that from the get-go, but no one ever invited him into the rubber room where decisions like that got made. The departure from Mir got good ratings, and the first en route rendezvous with a ram pod two weeks later; but the other "episodes" bombed, and the Powers That Be finally decided to wait for close approach and touchdown and run a two-part special instead.

Maybe they teamed me and Mikey because they hoped personality conflict would enliven the show.

"Two echoes on the forward," he alerted Krasnarov. "Something else out there. Does mama bear have a cub?" The discovery that some asteroids had their own personal moonlets had caused quite a sensation among the stargazers some years back, but Forrest's concern was more practical. Even with low relative closing velocities, he'd rather not bump into any loose change if he could help it.

"Supply pods identified," Krasnarov announced. "Three of them."

Forrest glanced at the radar. "Acknowledged." The second echo had already resolved into three distinct points. No interference with his approach, but he noted from the Doppler that one pod was slowly falling astern of the asteroid.

Have to go rope that dogie first. Behind him, he heard Nacho's whispered commentary on the ship-to-Earth feed.

Forrest wondered how many folks on Earth were actually watching the show, given the gut-wrenching thrill of a barely visible rock growing slowly larger on their TV screens. Probably half the audience was hoping for an attitude jet to get stuck, like on Gemini Eight, so FarTrip would go smashing into the asteroid and brighten their otherwise drab lives with a bit of death and destruction.

Forrest adjusted the aim on the external searchlights to heighten the visual contrast on the asteroid.

A long, narrow ovoid, nearly black. About five hundred meters long, according to the range finder. Pitted and pocked with countless craters. A hole on the end facing them. A big hole. Like God had played through and taken a divot.

"A very odd shape," Nacho said, as the ship closed in and the perspective shifted. Whether he spoke for the Earth audience or for the crew, Forrest did not know. "The Rock appears to be bilobal. One portion is long and thin; the other, smaller and more ovoid. From this angle, it looks like a large, legless grasshopper. Set the laser spectrophotometer, Captain," Nacho requested. "I want to get a second composition reading. From the smaller lobe, this time."

"Location selected," said Krasnarov from his station. "Entered into targeting computer."

"Set phasers on stun," Forrest agreed. Krasnarov raised his head from his eyepiece and gave him an irritated look. Forrest energized the laser.

You couldn't see the beam. That had disappointed Forrest during the practice drills in Earth orbit. Too many sci-fi movie ray guns had led him to expect light sabers slashing the night. A small region of the brighter lobe began to vaporize. "Spectrum reading captured," Krasnarov announced.

"Our analysis of the earlier vapor sample," Nacho told the Earthside audience, "showed the larger body to be mostly iron and nickel, with some silicates and lighter met-

als. The smaller body"—he paused while the data rolled up
on his side screen—"is primarily silicates of various sorts.
There is evidence of aluminum and magnesium in the spec-
tra . . ."

Forrest grunted to himself. So, the Rock was made up of
rock. If that constituted a Big Surprise, geologists should
get out of the house more often.

"The difference in appearance and composition," Nacho
continued, his voice rising a notch, "suggest that the two
lobes were originally separate bodies, fused in a collision.
This opens up many exciting possibilities for planetary science."

Forrest imagined the Earth audience pinned to their seat
by that one. *Hear that, Mabel? Might could be two asteroids
hit each other!* Okay, give Nacho his due. It probably was
exciting. It was just a real special kind of excitement.

"Something reflective," announced Krasnarov. "Bright
flash, north edge. One hundred meters from the left."

"Yeah, I saw it," Forrest said. He stopped the traverse
on the searchlight and brought it back on target. "Computer," he said. "Searchlight. Maintain fix absolute reference. End instruction." He released the control button and
let the A/S take over. Artificial Stupid neural nets were dedicated to particular tasks. This one would keep the searchlights aimed despite the motions of the ship and the target.
"Nacho, can you put a doid on that sucker? Max mag."

"*Sim.* Number Two doid on the main screen."

"Seven hundred meters," the computer told him. "Closing velocity, ten."

Forrest fantasized that it was the asteroid itself speaking
to him; that the Rock was a woman waiting for him, urging
him closer. A dark body, scarred by an uncaring universe,
and not very reflective. Yeah, he had rendezvoused with
plenty of those. Never a landing, though. Never a home
port . . .

"*Sancta Maria!*" said Mendes. "What is that thing?"

Forrest glanced at the pixcreen above the forward viewports. *A gleaming metallic monster looming over a black,*

craggy horizon . . . Skin glittering gold and silver in the ship's searchlight . . . Thin, spiderlike antennae . . . Two black, triangular patches that stared unblinking at the approaching ship like empty eye sockets. . . .

But that's impossible, Forrest thought. *Nothing can live in the vacuum of space.* He checked his close-approach radar again. "Parallax. Whatever that thing is, it's not on the asteroid, but behind it."

"Another ship?" asked Nacho.

Whatever it was, they'd be making its acquaintance shortly. One thing about ballistics: it was damn hard to change your mind about where you wanted to go once you were on your way. Forrest's hand shook as he made his next course adjustment. *Me? First Contact? Little green men in a spaceship . . . I'm not ready for it. The* world *isn't ready for it.* Krasnarov sang out his angular motions, calm and clear and business-as-usual. His face, when he raised his head from the viewfinder for a brief study of the monitor, expressed interest and little more. But were the lips pressed a little tighter, the eyes a micron narrower? Were the gears shifting deep in the bowels of Senhor Machine?

"I am putting on my data glove to study the image," he heard Nacho announce. "Computer. Pixcreen A. Display scale." A linear scale appeared in the corner of the screen and a virtual cartoon hand nudged it over by the silver creature.

Three meters wide.

Really *little* green men. . . .

It looked bigger at first because the asteroid's horizon is closer than we're used to.

Nacho double-clicked on the image and the edges shimmered. A CAD program took it and reduced it to finite elements, leaving only a stick figure of the vessel, truncated where the asteroid had blocked the view. The image rotated and turned. Then, in dizzying succession, a variety of designs were superimposed. Within seconds, the A/S had found a match in the μCD library. Krasnarov burst out laughing.

"It's the Japanese probe," said Nacho. His voice was flat. Disappointed? Relieved? Forrest twisted around and looked at the Brazilian, but the man's broad face was a foreign language that Forrest could not read. Forrest settled back into his harness and laughed.

"For a moment there, I thought . . ."

Krasnarov looked at him. "Thought what?"

"Nothing." Forrest concentrated again on his steering. "Braking burn. Five seconds." Too much lollygagging. They were off the rendezvous profile. But who would have thought that, after losing contact so soon after departure, the Japanese probe would still arrive successfully at the Rock? It must have been holding station since last Christmas, waiting for instructions that never came.

Jesus H. Christ spent forty days and nights fasting and meditating in the wilderness, and in the end had a vision of his True Name and the course his life would take. FarTrip was scheduled for its own forty-day layover in the planetary wilderness, and if they would not exactly meditate, they would at least study on the situation, and the freeze-dried, dehydrated, squeeze-it-from-the-tube, microwaved goop that comprised their meals would do for fasting until the real thing came along. But when Forrest pointed out the parallels to his crewmates later that day all he got on the bounceback was a blank look from Krasnarov and a nervous laugh from Nacho.

Forrest ordered everyone to rest up for the upcoming "morning." There was a lot on the menu. Set the anchor bolts and the tether for *Salyut*. Conduct an initial survey and lay out an isometric grid on the surface. Erect the on-site powerplant and align its solar antennae. Undock *Bullard* from *Salyut* and collect the three supply pods that were coorbiting with the asteroid. A busy time indeed, and no time to waste.

"Beginning nitrogen purge," Forrest announced formally and for the record. "Switching over to pure oh-two and ramping cabin pressure down to seventy kilopascals." That was Stage I. Stage II would be thirty kilopascals, the same as suit pressure. He snapped over the lock on the air mixture controls with a flourish. "The 'No Smoking' sign is lit!" he declared.

Krasnarov grunted. Now that the Earthside transmission was finished, he saw no reason to play Mr. Congeniality. "It is no joke," he said. "Ship air and suit air must be equalized, or we risk the bends. Your Shuttle astronauts spent two hour prebreathing pure oxygen to purge the nitrogen from their blood, but are too many EVA scheduled for this mission."

"Well, gee, Mike," Forrest said, "I didn't know that. Thanks for sharing it with us." Krasnarov pressed his lips together. Nacho looked from one to the other, but said nothing. "But I wasn't just wise-cracking about no smoking," Forrest went on. "As long as we're explaining the obvious to each other, let's not forget what a pure oxy environment did for Grissom, Chaffee, and White. If a fire does break out we can snuff it by popping the airlocks, but that'll be a real bummer if we aren't wearing suits when it happens." Once again his dream of the month before flashed through his mind. Sucked out of the can and falling into Forever . . . Plastic fittings and fiber optics reduced the risk of sparks, and most of the fabrics were resistant to oxygen impregnation and the pressure was being reduced . . . Still, you could never be too careful.

"It would be better," Nacho said, "if our suit air could be Earth normal."

"Sure would be, son," Forrest agreed. "If you want to try bending your arms and legs against a hundred kilopascals instead of thirty—plus strapping a couple nitrogen tanks on your LSS backpack."

After the other two had retired to *Salyut,* Forrest violated his own order about getting rest and spent the next several hours in *Bullard* monitoring the relative motion of FarTrip and the Rock. The Rock was a little booger, but it did have gravity. And any two bodies in the universe attracted each other, excepting only himself and Mike Krasnarov.

They were all as skittish as a preacher's kid in a barrel-house. Even the Iron Mike. Taking refuge in trivial lectures and wishful thinking and—be honest, Forrest!—silly wise-cracks. They should give each other a little more space. Though . . . Forrest looked out the forward viewport, past the long axis of the asteroid to the starry void beyond. It wasn't as if there was any shortage of *that*. Starting tomorrow, they would really begin to feel how far away from everything they were.

Forrest was still buckled into the command chair four hours later when Mike Krasnarov rose unbidden from the transfer tunnel. He didn't say anything, but hovered beside Forrest like the ghost of Christmas Yet to Come. Forrest unbuckled and floated free of the seat and Krasnarov took his place, running his fingers along the control panel as usual. "Keeping station?" he asked, as Forrest inserted himself into the passageway. Forrest nodded and departed.

Instead of going to his bunk, Forrest propelled himself through *Salyut* to the forward blister. 1991JW, craggy, ragged, broken, and pocked, filled the window with a jumble of light and shadow. Not a very big world. Not glamorous, like Mars or Venus or the Moon. No one had ever gazed on it in the evening sky and dreamed dreams. Yet it was the only world Jimbo Calhoun's little boy was ever going to get.

Sensing motion, he turned and saw Nacho Mendes hovering behind him. "I thought I ordered you to get some rest," he growled.

"I couldn't sleep."

"Oh, the three of us, we'll be in fine shape come morning . . ."

"I've dreamed of this all my life. Ever since I was a child . . ."

"Did you? For me, it was the piloting. Forrest Calhoun, Rocket Jockey. Hey, look, Nach' . . . About what I said earlier . . . I'm sorry I was so sarcastic. But when Mike gets on his high horse, it just rubs me wrong, is all."

Nacho said nothing for a while. "You've known each other a long time," he said at last.

"Nah, it just *seems* like a long time." Then he thought about it and shrugged. "Yeah, I guess we have. Since the old flight test days on Fernando de Noronha, ten, eleven years ago."

"They tell stories about him. About you."

"Legends in our own time. That's us."

"There was the St. Petersburg suborbital. You and he were copilots for that."

"Yeah, and the two of us were booked to take the old *Bessie Coleman* up to orbit. Except Levkin boogered the stew at Claudio's, so he and Ned got the first orbital flight instead. Yeah, there was a lot of pranking back then." One time he had dumped a trash can on the simulator cabin while Krasnarov had been inside training. But Levkin had crossed the line. "Remind me sometime to tell you what Tabasco sauce in a space suit's Urine Collection Device feels like."

"Didn't Mike go aboard an unmanned test launch?"

"The first one. *Nesterov.* We were all damn tired by then of all the sims. You know? And there were some glitches in the remotes, but I think he just wanted to be the first to fly the bird. We all did—"

"Where is he now?"

"Who, Mike?" Now there was a dumb question! "He's back in *Bullard* watching that things don't go bump in the night."

"Are you sure?"

Now wasn't that a helluva thought? Mike sneaking over to the Rock just to be the first to touch it? It would have been unthinkable in the old by-the-book, good-team-player days of a generation ago; but there was a different breed of cat flying today. An eye on the risk. More willing to defy authority. Plus an authority more willing to tolerate defiance—provided it succeeded.

A helluva thought. They were all here to do a job, but you couldn't help but think of the glory. Or that folks back home might have certain expectations. VHI probably lusted after the mining rights, and might have a claim if a VHI employee first set foot over there. But, hell, Russia and Energia had claims, too. And Brazil. And the UN itself. Even Wilson Enterprises, whose ram accelerators and supply pods had made the mission thinkable.

He shook his head. Too complicated for Jimbo Calhoun's little boy.

"Krasnarov won't prank," he decided. "He's too methodical, too *planned*, to go EVA without a lifeguard. Not with six hours left on the nitrogen purge. 'No mistakes' is his personal motto. He snuck onboard *Nesterov* because he *knew* the test would fail without a human hand. When ole Mikey weighs the pros and cons in that precision balance of a brain, the chances have to get better, not worse, before he'll pull a hack."

Senhor Machine.

Forrest almost wished that Krasnarov *would* try a stunt. Something crazy. Something human.

He rubbed his face with both hands. Should have sent a shrink along. Or done a better job picking the crew. Not that they weren't the best, but maybe they should have given less attention to expertise and more to personality when they did the old eeny-meeny. Maybe they should have tapped three more congenial souls. Though the three nominees could harmonize like the Boys' Choir of Harlem and after ninety-nine days vacuum-packed together, they'd still be almighty testy by the end of it.

"Someone has to be first," said Nacho.

"If VHI or the UN Deep Space Command has a preference, they've been almighty sly about telling us." Either they didn't care—hard to believe—or they couldn't get their corporate and political act together—much easier to believe. They would probably be debating the damnfool question for five days after it ceased to matter.

Maybe he should cast lots. Or download a request for instructions.

Nuts. It's your call. You're the captain of this little joy ride; not VHI, not the UN Deep Space Command. He conjured his father in his mind. A big man, with hands the size of footballs. A cotton farmer with white sharecroppers when for a black man in East Texas that had still been a defiant act. *What should I do, Pa?*

Pa's rolling bass wasn't there to answer. It hadn't been for too many years. Pa wouldn't see his son on the TV or feel his heart swell watching him. Of all the things Forrest wanted that he couldn't have—and there were many—that was the one he wanted the most.

The initial touchdown would be televised; and, if not quite the whole wide world would be watching, at least a significant fraction would be. There was something deeply symbolic about tomorrow. Something almost ceremonial. It would make a difference what he decided. And not only to himself.

So what would his old buddy, Ned DuBois, have done?

Screw it. Ned would be over on the Rock already, waving to the cameras. Showboat? Hell, when they painted the big, red letters on the paddlewheel housing they spelled out SS *Ned DuBois.* The very day FarTrip cast off for deep space, Ned DuBois and his sidekick, Chase, had taken a Plank all the way to the Moon, just for the hell of it. Low Earth Orbit was "halfway to anywhere." All the pilots on the orbital trade had talked about trying it some day; but old Ned, he was more doing than talking.

And yet Showboat Ned had given up a sure seat on this expedition. Because he wouldn't leave his wife and daughter for a year? Or because he thought Forrest deserved the slot? Only fair. Maybe Ned hadn't spiced Claudio's *feijoada,* but he'd sure as hell flown into the history books sitting in Forrest's seat.

One of the great things about free fall was that you could fall asleep anywhere, in any position. You didn't have to lie down—in fact, you couldn't lie down if you tried . . . Forrest awoke the next morning still floating in the observation blister with his slippers still fastened on the stick-fabric mat. Poking his head into the crew quarters, he saw

Ignacio Mendes, already dressed and groomed, with his hair slicked down and his ducktail tied up in the back with a green ribbon. Nacho floated near his bunk with his head bowed over clasped hands and his eyes closed tight. Of the three of them, Nacho had the least experience in space. Two years of training, along with the other geologist-candidates; but he did not have the long familiarity that Forrest and Mike had.

A long way from home, and that first step is a doozy . . .

Nacho made the sign of the cross and kissed his fingers. He opened his eyes and started when he saw Forrest.

"Don't let it bother you, son. 'His eye is on the sparrow.' Remember your training. Keep your wits about you and your friends close by." Forrest grinned. "Or maybe it was the other way around."

Nacho attempted an answering smile, but gave it up. "Senhor Machine is already suiting up," he said, pointing aft with his thumb.

"That's Mikey. The early bird does get the worm. Why don't you hustle yourself back there and see if there're any night crawlers left. Tell Mike to check all your seals and safeties." He clapped Nacho on the shoulder and sent him aft with a push to his butt.

Isaac Newton sent Forrest coasting back into the blister. He stopped his motion with automatic touches to stanchions and bulkheads. For a few moments longer, he gazed over his shoulder at the Rock. Finally, he kicked away. There never had been but one decision he could make, and damn Ned DuBois anyway.

The Plank's normal cargo bay just aft of the control cabin had been reconfigured for FarTrip into an all-purpose space, with personal stowage, ship's supplies, spare parts, tooling, and even a few compact fabricating machines, neatly folded away into lockers and bins, courtesy of Boeing Space Outfitters. The Boeing folks had cut their teeth packing for the Shuttle back in the old days, and they liked to say they could stow an elephant in a handbag if they could only figure out where the folds were.

Forrest battened the manlock to the control deck and turned to face the others. The Iron Mike looked faintly absurd in a suit striped like a barber pole, though it was no less absurd than Nacho's polka dots or Forrest's own checkerboard. Someone in the rubber room had decided that visibility was more important than dignity.

"Time to make it happen," he said.

"Well?" said the Russian. He was rubbing the antifog compound on the inside of his helmet visor. "Have you decided who will be first? The rest of us have work to do." Forrest's suit, hanging in its rack against the aft bulkhead, gave the impression of a fourth crewmember, stoically waiting instructions. It returned a look as blank as Krasnarov's. Forrest noted that Old Fuss and Feathers had already hooked up the electrical harness to Forrest's hard torso, too. The "Snoopy cap" floated in the air above it, giving the impression that an invisible man wore the suit. Forrest saw the drink bag and food bar were in their holders inside his helmet and the mission checklist attached to the torso's left wrist. *Busybody,* he thought. *Always double-checking everyone else. Sorry, Charlie, but they named* me *El Jefe.*

"In a minute," Forrest told him. "Where's my long johns."

Officially, the NASA-developed "long johns" were called the Liquid Cooling and Ventilation Garment. Bureaucrats had such a way with words. They couldn't come right out and say "space suit." They had to say "Extravehicular Maneuvering Unit" and then call it an EMU for short. You could carry on an entire conversation with those guys and never once use anything but an acronym. No wonder they had managed to make space flight boring.

Forrest zipped up the front of the Spandex garment and flexed his muscles. "I feel like a comic book character," he said. "Someone paint a big F on my chest."

Krasnarov spoke aside to Nacho. "For once, he is accurate."

The lower torso was a single garment that included boots and a ring bearing at the waist. Once he had pulled it on—an interesting feat in zero-g, but Forrest had done it often enough—he crouched under the upper torso and slid arms first into the hard shell. His arms moved easily into the sleeves and his head out the neck hole. Forrest waited until Krasnarov unsnapped the torso from the rack, then he fastened the waist seal and hauled in his Snoopy cap and put it on. He checked all his seals and then Krasnarov checked them all again.

Forrest eyed his ship's clock.

"Almost showtime," he announced. "The datalink is locked onto Helios Light and the pickups are all aligned. You know your marks." Forrest positioned his earclip and throatmike and switched to the Heimdall network frequency. "We're ready up here," he announced. A glance took in his two companions. Both nodded. Krasnarov impatiently; Nacho nervously.

Forrest waited for the bounceback. *One potato, two potato* . . . When it finally came, he heard a smooth, synthetic voice saying, ". . . commercial ends in fifteen, fourteen . . ." Forrest grunted and checked the time on his "heads-up" visor screen. He had to assume that the Heimdall techs were savvy enough to take the speed-of-light lag into account. If he started when the countdown reached zero, his commentary would reach Earth just as the commercial actually ended, and Heimdall could "go live" at just the right moment.

Of course, some numb-nut would be sure to complain to the FCC about false advertising. What "live from 1991JW" meant when the images were nearly a minute old was enough to delight a Jesuit.

"Okay, guys," he said, cutting Heimdall out of the listen-in for a moment. "Here's the way it's going down." He liked that expression. Going down. The big cargo lock faced the asteroid, which made that direction officially "down." Not so's you'd notice; but sometimes, if he was real still and used a lot of imagination, Forrest thought he could feel the Rock's infinitesimal tug. He explained how they would carry out the initial task.

Krasnarov shook his head. "Still showboat," he conceded, "but a better show."

Forrest cut Heimdall back in just as the countdown reached zero. "Greetings again from the Rock," he said, facing the onboard doid. He gave his very best down-home, aw-shucks, brave-in-the-face-of-danger smile. He assumed that Krasnarov, floating on his left, looked suitably heroic; and that Nacho at least looked willing. "Like we told you yesterday when we did the parallel parking, the Rock isn't exactly the sort of place where you can land a spaceship—especially one like FarTrip, which isn't designed to land anywhere. There's not a whole lot of level real estate over there. And it's not very attractive—gravitationally or beauty-wise." He grinned at his own joke. "In fact, we won't be *on* the asteroid so much as *at* it."

Forrest had decided with the very first broadcast that "folksy" was best. It was the way he was born and raised and, as Krasnarov liked to point out, he didn't do "dignified" very well. And he was, after all, dressed like a damn checkerboard.

"Our first order of business is to run a tether from *Salyut* to the Rock. This will not only keep our Home Away from Home from drifting off station—um, out of position; but it will help our crew move back and forth by sliding along the cable. The task will require all three of us to EVAde." He turned to Krasnarov and Mendes. "Ready?" His two crewmates nodded. "All right. Helmets on."

Like three conquerors crowning themselves kings. . . . Well, they were, weren't they? They seated their helmets and gloves and sealed them. Each seal required three independent motions. You couldn't open them by accident. Forrest and Krasnarov checked each other's seals, then they both checked Nacho's. When Forrest was satisfied he switched to suit frequency, but left Heimdall in the listen-only loop. "Let's do it."

They filed through the air lock one at a time. Krasnarov

first, Forrest last. When he got outside, the others were waiting by the air lock, gripping the handholds. Krasnarov had already unshipped the tether reel and was holding the gleaming clasp. Forrest made patting motions around his space suit. "Hey, I hope one of you guys remembered to bring the house keys with you . . ." Nacho laughed. Krasnarov said, "My suit leakage rate is below point-three kilopascals."

No sense of humor, Forrest decided. The only time Krasnarov would ever wear a silly grin would be when he died and the muscles all relaxed. "Sure, Mike," he said. "Nacho, check your delta-p." The suits were made of impervious neoprene and Kevlar and polyurethane-coated nylon and all what have you. Not exactly cheesecloth, but there was always some leakage.

Forrest pulled himself via the handholds and footholds to the outside equipment locker, where the piton driver was located. It didn't make sense to store bulky outside gear inside the ship. He stuck his feet into the footrests underneath the locker and twisted the latch with the t-bar on his equipment belt.

The problem with working in space, as Cernan had discovered to his peril, was that there was no damned leverage. No gravity to makes things stop once you made them go. When he twisted the t-bar key, the key tried to twist him, too. Without the footholds, he would have gone into a spin.

The piton driver was a smooth, light cylinder with a handle and trigger. Forrest checked to see that it was fully pressurized, but he did not load a piton into it yet. He clipped it to his belt tether, closed the locker hatch, and twisted it shut.

"Calhoun, have you tested your propulsion unit?"

Krasnarov must have Alzheimer's disease, Forrest decided. He kept forgetting who the captain was. Forrest would have to set him straight after they were off the air.

He pushed away from the Plank and gave a short burst on his suit jets that sent him coasting back toward where the others waited. The suit propulsion units, or "spews," were arranged so he could move in any direction, and were controlled by an A/S to prevent tumbling. A braking burst brought him to a stop by the air lock.

"Everything seems to be working," he said casually. "Got the tether; got the driver. We all set?"

You couldn't see heads nod through the darkened visors, but nobody said wait-a-minute-we-forgot-something. Forrest pointed to the Rock, two hundred feet "below" them. "You've got the landmarks fixed, right?" Meaning the area of the asteroid's surface within view of the outside doids. Wouldn't do to put on a show, if the action happened off-stage. "Nacho, you hang on to the tether. Mike'll be right behind you. Don't worry. It's just like jumping off a twenty-story building."

Nacho didn't answer for a moment. Then he said, "Just like practice."

"All right. On my signal. Three. Two. One. Go!"

The three of them started toward the asteroid. Mike un-reeled the tether behind him while he guided Nacho, who, Forrest noted, was using his spew after all. *Just hope he knows how to brake.* He switched Heimdall out of the circuit for a moment and beeped Krasnarov. "Soft landings," he said.

"I am watching him," the Russian replied.

He could feel the slight push of the compressed gas thrusters, but it hardly felt like motion. It was the Rock that seemed to approach them. A black slug of iron and nickel pocked with ancient craters. Forrest kept the smooth area they had selected as a landing zone centered on his faceplate target array and the spew's A/S nudged him sideways just a little.

If any of them touched ground before the others, they'd need the slo-mo instant replay to prove it. There was some dust, the debris of millions of microscopic impacts from interplanetary pebbles; but not enough, Forrest noted with a pang, to leave footprints in.

Nacho dropped to his knees and tested the ground with his thumper. He pointed and fired a burst of florescent orange paint from his finger gun to mark a place. "Here," he said. "There are no fractures to weaken it."

Forrest loaded a piton into the driver and pulled the hammer back. He placed the muzzle in the center of Nacho's target and pulled the trigger.

The bolt shot home and if the asteroid could have rung from the impact, it would have tolled like a cathedral bell. Forrest felt a momentary vibration through his boots before the recoil lifted him into the air. But he had been expecting that and used his spew to bring himself back down.

Krasnarov stepped in with the fly end of the tether and snapped the buckle through the eye bolt that Forrest had seated.

The whole operation had taken place in the space of three heartbeats. Find a spot; drive it home; snap it on. In the pause that followed, the three of them faced one another and, without a word spoken, exchanged a high five. That had not been planned. It was a spontaneous gesture that even the Iron Mike indulged; because, by God, they had just Done Something Right. Who was first? *We* were first, and what had to be done, we did together. If Mariesa van Huyten or anybody else back home had been looking for symbolism, they didn't have to look any further than that.

And then Forrest spoke the first words uttered by any human being on a body in translunar space. He had never been one with ready words, except for a joke and a bit of easy banter, and making memorable speeches about mankind's destiny was not his style. He had decided against making a speech for that very reason. Let the commentators and the other important people back home handle the ringing pronouncements. Yet, what he said did ring—with the sound of a bolt driving home. He turned to the others in his crew.

"Let's get to work."

4.

Waking the Dead

August came and, with it, the long-awaited FarTrip rendezvous. Mariesa repaired to her lodge in the mountains high above Jackson Hole far from the cameras and publicity. The lodge, made of wood logs and looking very primitive from the outside, sat on the lip of a broad, semicircular cup—a "cirque"—where ancient glaciers had taken a bite from the mountainside. Antelope brush and mountain rose clothed the sharp, stone-littered slope below.

Wayne Coper came over from his own lodge on the other side of the cirque and they swam together in her swimming pool. Afterwards, leaning on the rail that enclosed the hardwood deck behind the lodge, they enjoyed the view. The planking beneath them was stained from the water that drained from their bathing suits and ran down their legs. A brisk swim always invigorated and, at that altitude, the dry air and the unfiltered sun quickly dried things. Through the thick stands of lodgepole pine and Engleman's spruce far below, Mariesa caught glimpses of the waters of Jackson Lake glittering like sequins in the sunlight.

"So," said Wayne, "you won't be watching this asteroid thing from Brussels or Johnson? Why not? It's your baby, right?"

"It is past time," she told him, "that the public stops associating my name with every space venture. I wasn't the only player, even in the beginning. Granted, VHI companies provided the Plank, the beamed power, and one crew member to FarTrip; but Wilson Enterprises provided the supply pods, Energia supplied the *Salyut* and another crew member, NASA lifted the *Salyut* into orbit. . . . I could go on. The enterprise must become the common property of all mankind, if it's to thrive.''

And besides, though she did not mention the thought aloud, she had no desire to watch the inevitable preening of Donaldson and others whose only contribution to the effort had been to refrain from strangling it.

''We're going to watch it from up here, on my pixwall. Special feed. You can come, if you want.''

He flashed her an ironic smile. ''Will Harriet be there?''

''Oh, dear Lord, no. I believe it is Budapest this season.''

''Then I may come after all.'' The wind tousled his gold-gray hair and he brushed back the curls with his hand. Wayne was a husky man her own age, broad-shouldered and ready with a smile. His arms and legs were covered with light curls that glistened with beads of water and his chest was lightly matted with hairs evident only to the touch. ''Buff,'' they used to say.

''The conclusions she would leap to . . .'' Rubbing his chest with the backs of her knuckles.

''Does she know I have a lodge up here now? You haven't told her, have you?''

''Not a word. Remember how she used to throw us together when we were in school?''

''Oh, Mom and Dad were in on the cabal, too. It would have been socially perfect. A merger of the Copers and the van Huytens. They did everything but strip us naked and lock us in a bedroom together . . .''

Mariesa laughed. ''Too direct for Harriet. She prefers a well-laid scheme. They all must have been terribly crushed when we broke up.''

''*I* was terribly crushed. I didn't understand why. I was in love with you.''

''You only thought you were. It was just hormones.''

A vagrant breeze off the snowcap above the lodge twisted down the mountainside and touched her with its cool breath. Mariesa felt the goose bumps rise on her arms and legs. She must have shivered, because Wayne put his arm around her shoulders. She did not object, and he left it there. "Nothing wrong with hormones," he reflected. "But, yeah. I saw years ago that it would never have worked out. You would have been 'my first wife' instead of my . . ."

Instead of a reliable friend, a useful neighbor, and an undemanding, if occasional, lover.

"My guests will be arriving shortly," Mariesa said, gauging the time by the sun.

"Ah," he said. He stroked her shoulder softly with his hand, then released her. "Cobb and his staff must be on their way up from the village, then."

She turned and faced him, and played her nails along his arm. "Not until I call him."

Wayne was never pushy, but he recognized the signals. It was funny, she thought, as his arms enfolded her. Sex had never been a consuming interest in her life. She had indulged out of curiosity when she was young; and out of love (or the appearance of love) when she was older; but she had never indulged solely for recreation. Yet lying with Wayne on a pool towel on the redwood decking meant no more to her—or to him—than playing tennis. Neither love nor curiosity entered into it. It was just something good friends sometimes did together—like playing tennis. She could still count the men she had had on the fingers of one hand. Her cousin Brittany needed a spreadsheet.

"What's funny?" Wayne asked. His hands stroked her back gently, unfastening her swimsuit top so smoothly that she was barely aware it had been done.

"Nothing," she said. Spreadsheet, indeed.

The Werewolf could not abide being in the same room with an electronic device without tinkering with it. Even after the technician declared that the pixwall was tuned into the satellite feed and that the color and everything else was nominal, Will Gregorson insisted on adjusting it himself. He scowled at the screen while he touched miniature knobs with blunt, clumsy-looking fingers. He opened the panel on the side of the wall and adjusted settings that Mariesa had not even known existed. He even interfaced a keyboard and dealt directly with the programming for individual pixels.

When he was done, he backed away from the equipment and glowered at it.

"That looks much better, Will," Mariesa said, although she could see no appreciable difference.

"It will have to do," Werewolf allowed.

He was a hard man to please. Steve Matthias had once accused him of being a perfectionist, and the 'Wolf had demanded to know if that meant Steve was "an imperfectionist." Steve, who juggled Prometheus's multiple, interfacing projects, and so was intolerant of anything that caused schedule delays, responded, "The Perfect Is the Enemy of the Excellent." The two of them might have consumed the entire meeting in Dueling Clichés had Mariesa not put a stop to it.

"The blue is still a little off," Werewolf said.

"It's fine, Will," his wife told him. Gregorson's wife matched his broad build, but was light-complexioned where he was dark and as pleasant as he was gruff. She went by the unlikely name of Fluffy. "Subtleties of color are wasted when you're doiding an asteroid." Fluffy Gregorson was a well-known painter, though under a more Bohemian *nom de art*. "Will is always after me," she confided to Mariesa, "to do pixel-painting. He claims it's a new form of art, but of course it's only an extreme form of pointillism."

"Do you license your works to be digitized?" Mariesa asked.

Fluffy looked at the floor-to-ceiling, wall-to-wall, thin-film screen and shook her head. "Only for small screens. I don't do murals."

"I have several landscapes in the wall's memory," Mariesa said. "Sometimes I have the wall display the Grand Canyon or the Hudson Valley, or *Mare Tranquilitatis*. Usually I just relay the outside view. It gives one the illusion of sitting out of doors. Let me show you."

Mariesa touched the keypad to demonstrate, and the satellite feed test pattern gave way to a panorama of the Grand Tetons. The Eagle Nest, Bivouac Peak, Mount Moran . . . Stubborn snow clung to the niches and creases of their upper flanks, resisting the August sun. In the foreground was the rough-hewn wooden deck that ran around three sides of the lodge; and, standing on the deck enjoying the view, was Belinda Karr.

Belinda was a short, stocky woman of athletic build. Aggressively gray-haired, early sixties, approaching retirement—if retirement had been a word in her vocabulary— she walked with the energy of a wound spring, barely slowed by her years. *Mens sana in corpore sano* . . . Once, years ago, she had shown Mariesa an Olympic bronze medal she had won with the U.S. field hockey team.

Turning, Belinda faced the lodge, and seemed to look directly at Mariesa. An illusion, Mariesa knew. From the porch, the outside wall looked like perfectly ordinary wooden timbers. The doid pickups were barely noticeable, even if you looked for them. Still, Mariesa nearly raised her hand in greeting before she remembered that she was looking at an image, and the image was only one-way. She excused herself from Fluffy and hurried to the front door where she took a light sweater from the peg hanger there and flung it over her shoulders. August was high summer, but at this altitude summer was an academic concept.

Belinda had stepped off the porch to the hardpan that encircled the lodge. Small stones ranging from fist-size down to pebbles littered the yard, a reminder that tons of ice had once slid down this very mountainside to engulf the plains below. Only a few tufts of hardy, high-altitude grasses poked through the gravel. Belinda had crouched to pick up one of the rocks when Mariesa caught up with her.

"Are my rocks that interesting?"

"Hello, Riesey." Belinda did not rise immediately. She studied the stone she had picked up and turned it over in her hand. "I remember reading one time that these mountains were a seabed eons ago; and this"—she tossed the lichen-spotted rock to the ground—"was once the muck at the bottom. Sometimes you see fossils, if you look closely enough. Like me."

"You're hardly a fossil."

Belinda tried to rise but stumbled, and Mariesa clutched her by the forearm and helped the other woman to her feet. Belinda wore a green-and-white checked flannel shirt with the sleeves rolled up to her elbows. Her hand was warm and dry; her grip on Mariesa's arm was firm. Her nails, pared like a man's, were polished with a clear lacquer. *I have no patience for nail care*, she had told Mariesa once. *There are more important things to worry over than a broken cuticle.*

"And hardly facile, too." Belinda brushed the knees of her baggy jeans. "I must be getting old," she explained.

"Tosh. If your mind is young, the body will follow along."

"These are young mountains," Belinda said, dusting her hands, "as mountains go. The wind and rain haven't quite worn them down to nubs, like the hills where you come from. Yet they're immeasurably old. It makes me feel young just to contemplate them."

"Belinda," Mariesa said in sudden alarm, "why did you go into the hospital?"

Belinda squeezed her arm. "Don't worry, Riesey. I'm not Keith. I won't go away without telling you first." Mariesa began to walk slowly back toward the lodge and Belinda kept a hand on her arm as they walked. The memory of Keith's death could still seize her by the throat.

"It was such a shock," Mariesa said. "One minute we were talking; the next, he . . . wasn't there any more. My friends die, and my enemies won't."

A few steps went by in silence, then Belinda said, "They told me it was exhaustion."

The way she said it you would have thought she'd been told the cruddy uglies. "You ought to take things easier."

Belinda gave her an amused look. "Excellent advice, considering the source."

Mariesa laughed. "Yes, we'll both drop in harness, won't we?"

"Mentor's at a critical juncture," Belinda told her. As senior principal, Belinda oversaw the private and charter schools that were part of VHI's Service Industries Division. "We may have to close our Indianapolis practices. The city schools have improved to the point where our quality is no longer a selling point."

"The hazard of setting an example is that others copy you. What options do you have?"

"We could niche ourselves, the way some hardware stores and booksellers do when the superstores move in. Adapt or die."

"Yes. Circumstances change. It's the only constant. I was . . ." She hesitated momentarily. "I was thinking about Barry recently."

Belinda paused on the bottom step of the porch and spoke without turning. "Were you?"

"Yes. I was wondering how he was getting on since . . . You know."

Belinda faced her. "I'm surprised you care. Considering."

"I meant professionally. He was one of your best principal teachers."

"He was competent."

"Please, Belinda. I know you never liked him personally, but—"

"All right, he was the second coming of Socrates, if you like. As far as I know he's still running that private teaching practice you set up for him in North Orange. And as far as I know, he's still making a go of it."

"There were a lot of things," Mariesa told her, "that we never got straight between us."

Belinda tugged her hand from Mariesa's elbow. "There are a lot of things," she replied, "that you never got straight with a lot of people."

"You mean about asteroids." Belinda said nothing, and silence formed between them.

"Among other things," Belinda said at last.

Mariesa said, "You know I dislike talking about my feelings. My . . . fears. I know that was unfashionable once, but personal reticence is 'in' nowadays. By not 'sharing my feelings,' I was simply ahead of my time."

"It's not that, Riesey. Or it's not only that." Belinda turned and walked slowly up the steps to the lodge. Mariesa had never seen her use a stair rail for support before.

Reality fails as art because it is badly scripted; but Heimdall Communications used time delay to juggle and select from the views downloading from FarTrip. Sometimes, in the video style of the "Naughty Oughts," the screen juggled views from the ship and all three crew-member helmets all at once, in a kaleidoscopic variety of magnifications, overlays, and montages that Mariesa found hard to follow.

The asteroid gleamed an iron black-and-white under the ship's floodlights, and the derelict Japanese probe hovered in the background, sparkling in subdued colors, partly eclipsed by the rock. Sitting on the couch watching the life-sized images on the broad pixwall, Mariesa felt as if she were aboard FarTrip herself, observing Calhoun, Krasnarov, and Mendes through a portal on their ship or sometimes through their own helmets. Wearing a virtchhat, she thought, you could imagine you were there yourself.

Calhoun's choreographed landing surprised her. She had expected the command pilot to place the first footstep himself. The man had an ego as big as Ned DuBois's and an even greater flair for showmanship. Well, she herself had argued at the planning sessions that the crew be given as much autonomy as possible, and that Mission Control limit itself to advice and support. Let the men and women in the field make the tactical decisions, she had said. The day of centralized direction was over.

Forrest Calhoun's words—*"Let's get to work"*—had a better ring, she thought, than any of the pretentious speeches that had been proposed. Full of bold thoughts and grandiose words, they lacked the simple sincerity of Calhoun's matter-of-fact statement. She made a mental note for Gene Forney to play it up in Heimdall's newsscrolls and downloads. *Let's get to work.* As good a motto as any for the new millennium.

Werewolf Gregorson, sitting on her right on the long sofa, bobbed his head toward the pixwall, where the three men had scattered to various tasks. An inset image showed a commercial—what most households were receiving at this point. "Dolores thought if Calhoun was first, Pegasus would have a claim on the asteroid. I bet she's frosted."

"Dolores is too impressed with symbolism," Mariesa said. "Ability, not ceremony, will determine who receives the mining rights."

"No one can 'own' an asteroid," said Belinda, who sat on Mariesa's left. Werewolf leaned forward and looked at her across Mariesa. "Maybe not; but if Dolores claimed it, who would come out and jump her claim?"

"This year? No one. Next year? No bet."

"The number of companies with extraterrestrial mining capabilities," Mariesa said dryly, "is somewhat limited. For now."

Werewolf hunched forward and tugged at his beard. "Krasnarov is supposed to put up the power plant next," he said. "Did you want to watch or—" He paused as Cobb passed by, offering a tray of sweets. Hiram Cobb was the lodge's caretaker and doubled as butler whenever she held affairs at the place.

Mariesa selected a sweetmeat from the tray. "Or what?" she asked.

Gregorson glanced at his wife, sitting on his other side and leaned closer toward Mariesa. "Or discuss that man's threat," he said lowly.

"Donaldson."

"Who else is threatening us?"

"Today or this week?"

Werewolf glowered. "You know what I mean."

"It's a wicked notion." Belinda's voice was steel. "I don't know why the board didn't reject it out of hand."

"There were some arguments in its favor," Mariesa said.

"Hmph. And I bet I know whose. Weapons of mass destruction in orbit? It dirties the dream. It puts blood on our hands."

"Only if Donaldson gets to use them. He may use them only as a threat, or Congress may tie his hands."

"He may not ask Congress," Werewolf said. "The Constitution clearly gives *Congress* the authority to make war, but the precedents for unilateral presidential action are so ingrained by now that that particular genie may never be stuffed back into its bottle."

"Donaldson doesn't wash his hands without getting consensus," said Mariesa. "He spreads the decision out. It's his way of not accepting blame."

"A wonderful leader we selected for ourselves," said Gregorson. Mariesa turned to him.

"Will, we have to deal with him, one way or another. Don't let your dislike of the man color your evaluation of the situation. The threat to Aurora and Pegasus are genuine . . ."

"If he lets Kloch invoke Chapter 35," Belinda said, "or withholds the external tanks, take it public. LEO is popular. You can round up enough votes in Congress to overrule him, if you work at it."

"That means getting political."

"Riesey, there's mud 'behind the scenes,' too."

"I will keep that advice in mind."

Belinda crossed her arms and slumped in her chair. "A schoolteacher's advice. I can just hear what Dolores and some of the others would say about that."

"We have to consider what is best for the business, Belinda."

"Best in the *long* run, Riesey; not only what's best in the short run. There's a moral issue involved."

Werewolf grumbled, as he did so often when he was about to disagree. "Don't be so sure all the morality's on one side, Belinda. Putting those weapons in orbit could end the Balkan War—or prevent future wars. That goes into the moral balance pan, too.''

Mariesa gave him a curious look. ''I thought you were against the proposal.''

He shook his head. ''Not in principle. Like I said, you can make a case for it. My problem isn't with the plan, but the planner.''

''With Donaldson.''

''Yes. If it's going to be done, secretly and unilaterally is a crappy way to do it: it seems calculated to maximize negative publicity. What if the objective is to disrupt the LEO board with internal squabbles? What if the weapons plan is only a means to that end?''

''I don't believe that Donaldson is that subtle.''

''No. *He* isn't. But was this his idea in the first place? It strikes me as too damn bold to've hatched from that particular egg.''

''Who would've put him up to it?'' Belinda asked.

Mariesa thought about it. ''Cyrus Attwood, for one,'' she said. ''The technophobe faction at Peoples' Crusades, for another. In short, opponents who want to preserve the *status quo*; and opponents who want to turn back the clock to the *status quo ante*.''

Werewolf held up three fingers. ''There's a third faction, Mariesa. Not opponents, but competitors—who only want to hold us back while *they* steal a march.''

''Like Pac-Orbita, you mean.''

Werewolf shrugged. ''They aren't opposed to the race; just to us winning it.''

''You haven't narrowed things down much,'' Mariesa said wryly.

''As far as I'm concerned,'' Belinda said, ''it doesn't matter. Who cares what the ends are if the means themselves are wicked?''

Mariesa shook her head. ''There are no simple answers.''

''Sometimes there are, Riesey, if you ask the right question. If you don't cloud the issues. Too much sophistication can look remarkably like naïveté.''

After the crowded boisterousness of the lodge in Wyoming, Silverpond seemed like an abandoned city. She and Harriet seldom encountered one another, save at meals. *It is too large a building,* Mariesa thought, *to be so empty.* But that reminded her of the husband who was no longer present and the son who never had been. She took shelter, as she so often did, in the Roost—her office and her refuge. The small, close room had been built in what had been the attic and provided a panoramic view of Wessex County from its dormer window. Her rooftop observatory was close by. There were times when she spent most of her day up here alone. The staff would not come unless summoned, and Harriet had never bothered.

Mariesa opened a file on her home computer and labeled it *Donaldson—Pro and Con.* In the *Pro* column, she wrote: *Avoid de facto shutdown of Aurora, via Chapter 35.* And: *Assure availability of external tanks to complete LEO.* And: *Additional funding in compensation.* After a few moments of thought, she added: *End Balkan War????* She jabbed the question mark button several times because she was not entirely sure that the move really would accomplish that.

In the *Con* column, she wrote: *May cause dissension on LEO board.* And, because she respected Belinda, *Morally wrong?*

The central column, she reserved for questions of fact: *Donaldson's real objective? Donaldson the Prime Mover? SDI weapons operational? Russians, Japanese, etc.? If yes, can I "deliver"? If no, will Donaldson carry out his threats? Can LEO be completed if Donaldson does stop ETs?* She looked at the list she had created.

Too may questions. Not enough answers. Donaldson would not wait forever, and after a while delay became ''no'' by default. She cupped her chin in her hands and contemplated the array, but wisdom would not come. She wished she had Gregorson's moral ''balance scales.'' She could weight each argument based on its impact and its likelihood and drop them all onto one pan or the other to see which way the balance tilted. But life was never that easy. Justice carried scales . . . but wore a blindfold.

A decision required a decision statement. What did *she,* Mariesa Gorley van Huyten, want out of this? She inserted a new row at the head of the table and typed: *Protect the Earth from Asteroid Strikes.* A wry smile crossed her lips as she typed. Ultimate paranoia or ultimate practicality? You could read the statement both ways.

Protect the Earth from Asteroid Strikes. That was *her* purpose, regardless what Donaldson intended. Regardless what the Prometheus Steering Committee or the LEO board intended. She would take either side of Donaldson's plan if it furthered that objective. But which option would do that? Would a "yes" accelerate the completion of a protective shield by forestalling the threatened roadblocks? Or would "yes" delay it by disrupting the construction of LEO?

She stood up. There were no answers. There were no nice moral equations. There were other players, with other values, playing other games. You could weigh each possibility, assess the likelihood of each scenario, and still the decision was never automatic. She went to the dormer window and gazed outside.

It was a cloudy night. The sky was a roof. First Watchung Mountain was a wall—a long, sharp ridge that ran out of sight in both directions, its summer greenery dimmed by the pallid light. To the west, cornfields undulated in the winds; to the east, a dingy pall hung over North Orange. A dreary vista without the sun to light it. She wished it would rain. There were pleasures in watching the rain.

The intercom chimed.

"Yes, Sykes?" She spoke without turning. The room was empty; she was talking to the air. Sometimes it bothered her when she could not see the person she was talking to.

"A message from Mister Forney, miss."

"At Heimdall? What is it? Has something happened with FarTrip?"

"No, miss." The speaker relayed Sykes's voice with superb fidelity. He *sounded* as if he were in the room with her. The cruel illusion of telepresence. You could forget how alone you were. "Mister Forney has faxed a wire service story to your attention. Cyrus Attwood—"

"Oh, dear Lord," she asked bitterly. "What has that bastard done now?"

"Died, miss."

The news jarred her like the stroke of a bell. She wasn't sure why. Not surprise, exactly. Attwood was at an age when death was a likely line item on his daily to-do list. Nor was it sorrow. He had done everything in his power to stop Prometheus. He had instigated government harassment by an earlier administration. He had forced the shutdown of the Arizona laser and its removal to Ecuador. He had publicly campaigned against the SSTOs. He had sent a man with a knife to threaten her.

And he had suborned murderous activities: Heitor Carneiro, Daedalus's deputy flight director, had sabotaged the first orbital test flight; a renegade pair of Phil Albright's Crusaders had attacked Wilson's Antisana ram; and the mysterious outlaw hacker, "Crackman," had planted a logic bomb in the *flocker* software. Close calls and more luck than anyone deserved. Ned DuBois had had the orbital flight software double-checked on no more than a hunch; and Jimmy Poole had code-danced while *flocker* was running in real time and defused the logic bomb before the rescue ships would have collided at Skopje. And ten Boom had managed to launch the vital fuel pod just moments before the missile struck the ram. Good luck all around, if you didn't count the bodies on the ground at the ram site.

Either Attwood was literally insane—and we shoot mad dogs, don't we?—or he had simply refused to know what measures his bought agents resorted to. And that, too, was an insanity.

No, she felt neither surprise nor sorrow. Only—a massive oppression had been lifted from her without warning. She felt disoriented, as if a shackle she had been pulling against in vain had been abruptly loosed.

"Yes," she said. "Thank you, Sykes, for passing that on."

Mariesa lowered herself into her chair by the computer desk. A padded, tall-backed contour seat, it fit her body like a glove. She swung back and forth in it, kicking her feet. A smile played around her lips. This was the first positive contribution Cyrus Attwood had ever made.

A dim shadow appeared on her desk and she spun in her seat to face the window. A break in the clouds had appeared and, through it, a slice of the setting sun.

She attended the funeral, of course.

It was the mannerly thing to do. Enemies or no, she and Cyrus had been long acquaintances. They had moved in the same circles; knew the same people; attended the same charities and galas. And if the Attwood fortune was smaller than the van Huyten, and its concentration diluted among a wider range of heirs, it was nonetheless one of respectable size and of even greater antiquity.

And besides, she needed to satisfy herself that the devil was really dead.

The viewing and the services were scheduled at St. John the Divine on Manhattan Island, so it was a simple matter for Charlie Jim to fly her to the helipad along the Hudson River, where one of Laurence Sprague's drivers met her with a limousine. Harriet went with her, of course. She had flown back from Budapest just for this. After all, she had known Attwood, too, in her social circle.

Traffic slowed to a crawl near the north end of Central Park, then to a halt as the limo turned onto Amsterdam Avenue. The street was a-sea with yellow taxicabs and darkly tinted limos, all converging on the cathedral.

"Such a crowd," Harriet marveled.

"Cyrus's death is rather popular."

Harriet pursed her lips. "Such talk. *Nil nisi bonum*, you know."

Do not speak ill of the dead . . . Why not? Did death bring virtue in its wake? "Don't worry, Mother. I shall behave myself once we are inside."

"I know the man was a boor, but one performs one's social duties."

"He was worse than boorish, Mother."

"Because you and he did not see eye to eye? Hardly grounds for such hostility. After all, you and I do not see eye to eye, either, on some subjects."

Conversations with Harriet were battles. Sentences were salvos. Her remark was light-hearted, but it was a challenge as well.

"You and I are not enemies, Mother . . ." Though she had been. In some things. And had proven infuriatingly right in the end. ". . . and you have not hired killers when we have disagreed."

Harriet tsk'ed. In a life of hyperbole, truth could go unrecognized.

On the way into the church, she overheard one of the on-air personalities speaking. ". . . a voice of caution in the new, uncertain era of change . . ." There was no camera, only a cameraman wearing a doid on his headband. The on-air could have worn it himself, using a throatmike for the commentary, except the cameramen had a union and the personality would not have been on-view in millions of homes.

Cyrus had been High Church, of course. Not that he had been a believer—Mariesa doubted he believed in anything beyond his own privilege—but, thoroughly Establishment, thoroughly conventional, and thoroughly Anglo-Saxon, it was inconceivable that he could grace any church but Episcopal. There had been an Attwood on the *Mayflower*. A distant, collateral relative, not an ancestor, she remembered him saying at one of Harriet's parties, years ago. That God-shouting, Low-Church Puritan hippy was the black sheep of an otherwise respected and conventional family. He had made that joke to a doyen of the Mayflower Society, at that.

Funny, that she should remember the man laughing and cracking disrespectful humor.

After the services, a church usher sought her out and invited her to meet privately with Edward Bullock, Attwood's nephew, and heir to the bulk of his holdings. The Attwoods had been childless, and Bullock had been like a son to the couple, or so the story went. Mariesa followed the usher to the sacristy off one side of the high altar. She glanced at the Crucified One as she passed through the sanctuary, a tortured body writhing on a cross. Would the church have been less successful, she wondered, if its founder had not sacrificed himself for the sake of its future? Her own church was a Reformed one, and preferred an unadorned cross. A reminder of the sacrifice, but without the agony and pain.

Bullock waited alone in the sacristy. He was a thin, delicately featured man of thirty-five. He dressed well, in clothing of a conservative cut, with a discreet mourning band barely visible against the black fabric of his sleeve. His lips were full and red and protruded just a little. Quite attractive, if you went for the pretty-boy-pouting type. He stopped his pacing when he saw Mariesa and crossed his arms.

"So," he said after a moment's regard, "you are 'Lilith.'"

"I beg your pardon?" There would be no handshakes, she saw.

"That's what Uncle called you. 'Lilith.' The mythical temptress who preceded Eve in the Garden. Sometimes he called you 'the Serpent.' I'm sure you had your pet names for him, as well."

The Devil . . . "Our goals differed."

Bullock laughed. "He hated everything you stood for: instability, ruination."

"Progress," said Mariesa. "New frontiers."

More secret amusement on his pouting lips. "I believe I said as much. Billions in sunk costs—zeroed out, virtually overnight. Five-year plans made worthless by unplanned and unregulated developments ... You may call it 'progress.' He called it 'instability.' ''

"And you?"

He shrugged. "A stable, well-managed State is best for everyone. It keeps a rein on ruinous competition and assures that markets are rationally allocated. It protects us from inequitable foreign competition. It allows us to work cooperatively toward the common good, and provides a safety net against bankruptcy and failure."

She crossed her arms impatiently. "Did you really ask me here to lecture me on Italian fascism?"

"In a moment," he said. He studied her with a look that bordered on insolence. "You're an anarchist," he said. "An economic anarchist. 'Every man for himself, and the devil take the hindmost.' People could not possibly be happy in your wilderness of boom and bust."

"But they would be free to *pursue* happiness, and that is all that was ever promised."

The young man waved a hand in airy dismissal. "My uncle had a vision—of a safe, well-tended Garden of Earthly Delights. Where the lion could lie down with the lamb ..."

"As indeed they can. Though only the lion rises back up."

He paused again. Not a man accustomed to being interrupted, Mariesa saw, wishing he would get to the point. "You're a cynical woman. He told me that, and I can see now that he was right. You were the serpent in his garden. Well, he is vexed no more." Bullock turned to face the sacristy door, which stood open to the altar. Attwood's casket rested on its bier. A berobed priest read words from a book while he shook an aspergum over it. Six pallbearers waited by. Two other nephews, three older men—cousins or business associates, likely—and a teenager with his hair swept back in the popular "oughty" bird-wing style. Bullock's son, she had been told.

"He's at rest now," she heard Bullock say. " 'Where the

serpent stingeth not, nor harsh words pierce. Where cool waters refresheth the brow.' ''

Mariesa glanced at him and saw eyes blurred with water. Wherever Cyrus Attwood was now, she was reasonably sure ''cool waters'' was not a geographical feature. She said nothing, and Bullock straightened the jacket of his mourning suit. ''We will be driving to the cemetery directly,'' he said. ''Strictly family and friends.'' He turned away from the door—and turned back for just a moment. ''He was a good man. I will miss him. I'm sure that your conflict with him shortened his days.''

And finally that proved too much for her to take. ''A good man?'' she said before she could stop herself. ''Blackmail? Sabotage? Murder? A peculiar definition of 'good.' ''

The tight, moist smile on Bullock's lips quivered for a moment. ''Oh, he *tried* blackmail—against my advice—but your Barry Fast wouldn't cooperate. Stuck up for you quite strongly; not that it did him any good in the end. And I'll admit that Uncle did engage in industrial pranking . . .''

''Pranking? A fine word for *sabotage*. What about the people he had killed!''

Bullock turned skeptical eyes on her. ''Had people killed? Uncle Cy?''

''I guess he forgot to tell you about that part. He bribed an employee of mine to sabotage the first orbital Plank mission. He hired an outlaw hacker to sabotage the Skopje rescue in ought-seven. We only avoided midair collisions by a hair's breadth. And your uncle financed the missile attack on the Antisana ram, where several people *were* killed.''

''Oh, come now. You don't expect me to believe that, do you? Yes, he did pay your man, Carneiro, to bugger that test flight. I'll admit that. But he never expected the dago would stoop to murder. We were sitting together in the Union Club when we heard, and Uncle was *appalled* by what almost happened. Appalled. He was forced to rely on unreliable agents.''

''Not appalled enough to desist. Maybe the realization

that he could order life and death got to him. Maybe he discovered it was a rush.''

''That's whack. We're evidently talking about two different people.''

''Yes. Perhaps we are. If he was . . . ill, he could have shown a different face to you than he did to me.''

''I've heard quite enough of your baseless accusations. . . . We are ready to leave, so I must make this shorter than I had planned. The reason I sent for you . . . Did you know it's against the law for an American company to sell products in Third World countries if they would violate health, safety, or environmental regulations in this country?''

There were few better ways to prevent such countries from developing . . . But Mariesa said nothing. She regretted now having argued with him. Whatever sort of man Cyrus Attwood had been, Bullock had loved him; and the funeral service was hardly the venue at which to parade his crimes. Yet it galled her to hear him praised, even by his family.

''Our lawyers will go to court next month to get an injunction against atmospheric beaming of microwaves, on health and environmental grounds.''

Which would shut down the power to several hundred satellites, including the LEO construction site . . . ''You can't be serious,'' she said. ''You're not just attacking VHI, but Motorola, Boeing-Mac-Dac, and others as well. Including the governments of Kenya and Ecuador.''

Bullock shrugged. ''They should be more careful of the company they keep. And as for 'the wogs,' we'll goad some UN commission into action. All we need are plausible scare stories and gullible reporters.'' He turned toward the doorway to the altar. The priest saw him step forward and nodded to the pallbearers, who hefted the casket and prepared for the recessional.

Mariesa could not understand Bullock. He was a young man, her junior by a decade. The young were supposed to embrace the future; not the past, not the status quo. Yet his opposition was adamant, even hysterical. Why make enemies of third parties? It was unreasonable. Yet personal animus might easily outweigh reason.

"One question," she said as he stepped out of the sacristy.

He looked at her over his shoulder. "Be quick."

"Why did you tell me what you plan to do? It gives me time to prepare a defense."

"This is my uncle's funeral," he said. "I didn't want you to enjoy yourself too much."

Harriet was waiting for her by the vestibule: a rock in the stream of people leaving the cathedral. When Mariesa rejoined her and they walked out together to where they would meet the limo, Harriet said, "You were closeted with him quite a long while. I heard some whispered comment on it in the pews."

"They were impatient to leave. We delayed things."

"Mr. Bullock cuts a rather handsome figure, does he not? Granted, he is young, but . . ."

Harriet could never stop handicapping potential husbands. Bullock was already married, but that was a mere technicality in a day when spouses had become disposable commodities.

Mariesa spun and looked up the central aisle of the now-deserted church, at the crucifix that hung above the altar. "Now why would he do that?" she asked. "He could have gone along with what they wanted. Why did he have to sacrifice himself?"

Harriet's face looked puzzled and shocked. "You are not talking about Jesus Christ, are you?"

Mariesa shook her head and turned away from the altar. A sardonic smile curled her lips.

"Hardly."

The subdivision was called Schooner Lake. The carved wood sign at the entrance bore a fully dressed Yankee Clipper riding the winds, and the street signs were topped with a miniature replica of the same ship. Everything was done

up in beige and blue and pseudonautical motifs. The streets
were named Hawser Lane and Fo'c'sle Circle and Bowsprit
Drive. Even the decorative banners some of the residents
flew toed the thematic line. They sported ships, anchors, sea
birds, lighthouses. Never mind that a clipper ship was not
a schooner; or that the pond that lay at the center of the
ring of townhouses would hardly support a rowboat, let
alone anything dressed in sail. There was no end to the
creativity of developers. Nor much beginning.

Mariesa pulled into a cul-de-sac off Topgallant Road and
parked her Ford Skyline in a space marked VISITORS. The
other cars were mostly midsized models, a scattering of utility vehicles and sports cars. A Mercedes or two. This was
a middle-class development, but decidedly upscale. The
people who lived here had money, or expected to.

Across the parking lot, a young boy tossed pebbles at a
second-floor window. Mariesa paused after locking her car
and watched in puzzlement. Whatever was the boy up to?
Finally, someone opened the window and exchanged a few
words with the pebble-tosser. Then, a second boy climbed
out the window and shimmied down the drainpipe. Mariesa
caught her breath until he was safely on the ground and the
two had run off together, then she shook her head and went
in search of the address she had been given.

Number 1227 was the end unit on the building. It had a
door knocker in the shape of an old sea-dog captain. Surely
the covenants did not require anything so outré! A glance
revealed that the other doors in the building indeed bore
plain brass knockers. Gingerly, she reached out and lifted
the pipe jutting from the grinning face.

"Avast!" cried a computer voice from the speaker grill.

Which was why she was laughing when Barry Fast answered the door.

If he was surprised to see her, he gave no sign. He grinned
that amused grin of his and took her hand just like they
were old friends. His touch was polite, but familiar as he
led her to a sparely furnished living room. A compact brick

fireplace on the outer wall, flanked by two windows; a long, gray sofa that was soft and comfortable when she sat in it; a "tower of power" in the corner with μCD-ROM player, amplifier, hard drive, and other equipment Mariesa did not immediately recognize. On the desk beside the tower was a wide-screen monitor and a laser writer. The corners of the room were occupied by red clay pots brimming with tall, leafy plants. There were no other chairs. The only place Barry could sit was at the desk across the room or on the sofa beside her.

He remained standing.

"Can I get you anything?" he said. "A Manhattan?"

"No. No, thank you." She was nervous being here. There were years between them. Years of intimacy. Years of estrangement. She was not sure why she had come.

"Some ice water, maybe?"

"Yes. Fine." If she had determined to be a ·guest, she could not deny him the duties of host. Barry ducked into a kitchen alcove on the other side of the work desk. Beyond that was a dining room with a dark wood table with a floral spray centerpiece and table settings for four. It did not looked much used. The other room visible from where she sat was lined with bookshelves and had a sliding glass door that led onto a patio deck. "The reason I was laughing," she said, "was your door knocker . . ."

His head appeared for a moment, a flash of teeth. "Oh, God, yes. It's awful, isn't it." Then, continuing from the alcove: "But it's 'nautical,' like the rules say; and the board couldn't find anything in the covenants that forbade it."

"Still finding ways to thumb your nose at the rules, are you?"

"I don't like being fenced in by other people's notions."

"Were you the one who changed the Fo'c'sle Circle street sign to Fo'c'sle C'cle?"

He laughed. "No, but I wish I were."

"You haven't changed."

A moment of silence before he reappeared with her ice water in one hand and an amber drink in the other. "In some ways,'' he said. Mariesa glanced at his drink as she took her glass, but she said nothing. How did the joke go?

You drive me to drink.

That's not a drive; it's a putt.

''How have you been getting on, Barry? You look well.''

He took a long swallow. ''Well enough. I think I may have a life again. Why are you here?''

She hesitated. ''I don't know yet. It's . . . It has been years.''

''Two. And never a word from you that wasn't filtered through a lawyer. Now you show up on my doorstep.''

''You would not have wanted to hear the unfiltered words.''

He finished the drink, looked at the empty glass. Then he turned his stare on her. ''But I did need to hear them. I *wanted* to hear them. You should have screamed. Ranted. Pounded on me with your fists. You should have asked, 'Why?' and rejected all my answers. Do you know why?''

She shook her head.

''Because it would have showed that what I did meant something to you. But you took it so damned coldly, like you take everything else in life but your precious project . . . Like you were just looking for an excuse to dump me.''

Her water glass was sweating, making her hands cold and wet. ''I don't remember it that way.'' She remembered running, crying, through the woods. Barry had called her ''cold'' that last afternoon; on the bench atop Skunktown Mountain, when he had shown her those awful photographs. ''I felt betrayed. It hurt.''

''Did I ever mean anything to you? Or was I just something to throw in Harriet's face?''

''That is a terrible question!''

''Not half as terrible as that I need to ask it.''

She looked around for a table, found one beside the sofa, and set her water glass on a black slate coaster. She would not meet his eyes. ''You meant something,'' she said softly.

''What did you say?''

''I said, you did mean something to me.''

"Did. But not any more."

There was no way she could pretend. She would be another person than she was today if he had not been in her life. Maybe better, maybe worse. Happier, or not so happy. There was no way to tell who she might have been. A stranger, someone different. Because she had known Barry. That could not be meaningless. "You still do, but not the same something."

"Fair enough." He turned his glass one way, then the other. He upended it and let the last few drops trickle down his throat. "How have . . . your projects been going?"

"Oh, you know. A dozen pots, all boiling at once. And a dozen hands trying to upend them."

He grunted. "I read in the paper where Cyrus Attwood died. That's one less lunatic to worry about."

"I'm afraid I may only have traded an old enemy for a young one."

"I wasn't sorry to see the last of him. It was because of him that you and I—"

She stiffened. "Let's not rewrite history," she said sharply. "Or shoot a dead messenger, even so wretched a messenger as Cyrus. All he did was have you photographed while you . . . did it . . . with that woman. It was the doing that mattered. It would have mattered even if I had never learned."

He closed his eyes. "I'm not proud of it. But it wasn't as simple as you make it out."

"Try to simplify it for me, Barry. I'm a 'real smart chick.' "

"Damn it." He turned on his heel and vanished into the kitchen alcove once more. When he reappeared, his glass had been refilled. "What possible difference can it make now?"

"Do you still drink?" she asked.

He looked from her to the glass in his hand and back. "Are you still frigid?"

She rose from the sofa. "How dare you!" And yet, if anyone deserved to ask the question, it was Barry; and if anyone deserved even part of an answer, he did. There was more than one hand that had arranged the poses and pressed the shutter on that camera. She was not entirely blameless. She turned away from him, because she could not look at him; and after a few moments she spoke. "I will not pour out rationalizations about Gramper or Harriet or Piet; but the van Huytens have always favored reserve. I could never 'let it all hang out.' But I am trying to learn to be more . . . spontancous."

Barry laughed and she turned, red-faced, to look at him. "I can just imagine the twelve-step program," he said. I'll bet you tackle it with the same single-minded intensity you bring to everything else. Schedules. Practice exercises. Development program. Test flights . . ."

"That is quite enough—"

"But, Riesey, that's the same old same old. Still the lean mean thinking machine. You obsess. But 'obsess won't make the heart grow fonder.' Practiced passion isn't the answer. Your problem is you magnify everything, from lovemaking to asteroids, and then go overboard. You used to wake up in the middle of the night with that horrible dream and"—he paused and studied her, sudden concern in his eye—"and you still do, don't you?" She wouldn't answer, but felt her lips harden against each other. Who was he to feel concern for her? He nodded. "You're a fanatic. You're obsessed with the asteroid threat."

"But I am right," she whispered.

"Sure. I know it. So what? That doesn't make you not obsessed."

She turned to gather her purse. "This is not going well, is it?"

"I don't even know what 'this' is. Why *did* you come to see me?" He took another long swallow.

"It doesn't matter."

"You came all the way from Silverpond to Berwick Township to talk about everything and say nothing and it doesn't matter. Right."

She held her purse against herself. "It is a long drive. May I impose . . . ?"

"Oh, yeah. Sure." He waved a hand. "Through the rec room." He turned away and stared out the window.

Mariesa left him and used the facilities briskly. She only wanted to be away from here. It had been a mistake to come. She paused while washing her hands and looked into the mirror, surprised at the distraught face she saw there. *It was he who had kept the mistress,* she reminded herself. And he probably would have done so regardless how passionate she had been. She could have moaned and groaned and ground her hips like a harlot, and he still would have wriggled inside that schoolteacher's skirts. He was the sort of man who fell into things too easily.

Returning through the rec room, she noticed the photographs and paintings that Barry had hung there. One was a reproduction of the Karen Chong painting of the experimental Plank *Nesterov* lifting from Fernando de Noronha in a tower of flame. Another was a photograph of Barry surrounded by the "Student Marketplace" students—Leilah, Chase, Tani, and the others, with Grantland de Young, who had been Witherspoon's building manager back then. A third was of Ned DuBois, posing with Barry and herself. She had the same photograph; and only now did she realize that it was Ned and her in the foreground and Barry a little bit behind. A fourth was a painting of a night scene on a desert mesa. A pencil-thin beam of light pierced the sky from the great microwave laser in the center of the scene. Among the watching figures she could mark Werewolf, who had built it, and her cousin Chris, who had designed it; and the Air Force general in his wool flight jacket; and there, at the edge of the circle of light, half in the shadow, Barry Fast, with one hand on the shoulder of a young hard hat. None of this would have happened, the painter was saying, without the teachers.

Barry had been a teacher. Until his marriage had made it pointless.

"Karen Chong painted that one, too," said Barry. Mariesa turned and saw that he had joined her. "That's supposed to be Meat Tucker in the hard hat."

"I've never seen it."

"Chris commissioned it and gave it to me. That was . . . That was good of him."

"Chris is a good man."

Barry nodded at the painting. "That was the night of the first test, when we beamed electrical power to the *Gene Bullard*'s solar panels. The night the baby—"

Mariesa's hand went to her womb. "I remember. Sometimes, almost, I forget."

"Yeah." He stepped away. "Well. I won't keep you."

"I came to thank you," she said.

He stopped and his eyes narrowed. "What?"

"The reason I came to see you. I came to thank you."

"Thank me? For what?"

She continued looking at the painting. It was done up in shades of blue and violet and the night sky above the figures was impossibly starry. The white of the tracer beam blended into the river of the Milky Way. "When Cyrus tried to blackmail you with those photographs, and you refused to cooperate. You could have gone along with his scheme, and maybe those pictures would have been destroyed and maybe I would never have seen them."

"And maybe Attwood would be trustworthy."

"Oh, he kept his word when he gave it. That was the funny thing about him. It was a mad vision, but he believed in it. So, tell me, Barry, why you let yourself be crucified."

"This is going to sound hokey."

"Try me."

"I believed in what you were trying to do." She turned to face him and he quickly averted his gaze. "Oh, not the killer asteroid stuff," he continued, waving his hand, "but getting people to look up again. I saw the hope it gave those kids. You made the future something they could build; not something they had to endure. I wouldn't have a hand in smothering that."

"So you sacrificed yourself for my vision . . ."

"I wouldn't call it that. I thought I could weasel out of it somehow. I guess some ways I was just as crazy as Attwood. Only, old Cyrus . . . He told me he'd show you those pictures and you'd see what kind of man I was. But he forgot one thing."

"What was that?"

"He had to show them to me, first; and *I* saw what kind of man I was."

Saturday midafternoon traffic on the Gray Horse Pike was light. Mariesa picked a lane and stuck with it, driving a little bit faster than the pack. When she came up behind a car, she swung out into the far lane and around the obstacle. Putting miles between herself and Barry.

It was hard to say just how or when Barry had entered her life. The Mentor conference in the summer of '99? But he was just a face then, a charmingly cynical teacher she had chanced to encounter. The meeting at Silverpond when they had screened the Institute nominees? The time she had invited him to stay for dinner when his car died? You couldn't pin it down exactly. It had crept up on her, like a thief in the night.

Now it looked like she would have as much problem pinning down his exit. He would fade out, just as he had faded in. Someday, someone would say, hey, remember old Barry Fast? And she, depending on who she had become and the mood she was in, would dredge up the good times or the bad from the silt of her memory and play remember when.

It was up to her what she chose to remember.

Along with the paintings and photographs Barry had chosen to display in his home Mariesa had noticed two other things. From where she had stood in the rec room she could see into the kitchen alcove, where a bottle of amber liquid stood on the counter beside the refrigerator. The label read APPLE JUICE. The second thing, on the other wall, beside the dining room, hung a portrait photograph of herself. A three-quarter profile, taken in the light blue Herrera gown with a simple choker of pearls around her throat, prettied up in the flattering way portraitists often did.

Barry had kept that photograph, and it hung framed and mounted in the town house he had bought in the settlement after the divorce.

5.

Departure

Roberta Carson watched the landing on the asteroid because everyone else at Crusades headquarters was watching and probably just about every place in the whole country you couldn't not watch it, so what the hell. You could admire the adventure. You could admire the heroism. You could even admire the theater. It was something the whole wide world had done together—from the high-tech, lab-coated Westerners to the Kenyans who serviced the Kilimanjaro laser—and if Mariesa van Huyten had her great long finger stirring this pot, too, she had not been the only cook. And that liberated Styx to enjoy the show, at least a little.

Crusades headquarters had once been a grocery store, and a honking big front window gave a panoramic view of row houses and store fronts, a mixed residential/commercial Washington neighborhood, neither upscale nor slum. The domes and monuments of Government City were out of sight on the other side of the building. A large circular table littered with papers and forms and magazines and this morning's bagels-and-coffee dominated the center of the room. The cadre sat on folding chairs, bunched together on one side of the table so they could all get a good view of the television bracketed to the wall, where the astronauts capered in the awesome night.

"A lot of money," said Dottie Wheeler, "just to watch three guys drive a spike into the ground."

"But consider what 'ground' that spike was driven into," Isaac Kohl replied.

"*I* think it was inspiring," Melanie Kaufmann said.

The cadre was a smaller group than it had been a month ago. Simon Fell was gone. So were Felix Lara and the others in the Direct Action Faction. Roberta did not approve of what Simon had done, but the Crusades would miss his organizing hand. Sloppiness was slowly creeping into their daily operations. Mailings were going out late; phone calls and E-mail were not promptly returned. No one wanted to sit at the receptionist's desk.

Dottie shook her head. She was a slim woman in her midthirties with short-cropped red hair and a preference for baggy sweaters. "The money spent on that circus could have been spent here on Earth."

"Where do you think it was spent?" Isaac asked.

"And it added a lot to the economies of places like Kenya and Brazil," Melanie said.

Roberta picked up a tray carton and began gathering up the trash from the table. She collected the aluminum cans first, sloshing them to make sure they were empty and carting them to the big blue recycle tub.

"Distorting the economies, you mean." Fiftyish Ellis Harwood was broad shouldered and favored twill jackets in houndstooth patterns. He taught political science at the university and was a fellow at several prestigious think tanks, so his intellectual credentials were firm; but he looked like a retired football player. He had, in fact, played college football "back when it was a sport and not a business," and liked to preach what he called a "muscular progressivism." *Why does our side get all the wimps?* he liked to ask. He leaned forward on his arms and shook a finger, as if he were conducting a seminar. "The world can't afford for everyone to live a wasteful Western lifestyle. We don't do those people a service by seducing them from their traditional ways of life with Western toys."

"That's right," said Dottie.

"I agree that we have to think smaller and stop wasting resources so much," Isaac said, "but it's new technology that will let us do that."

"That Hollywood production—" Harwood gestured to the television—"was hardly an example of thinking small."

"And now they've gone and ruined the ecology of that asteroid, too," said Dottie. "Big Industry isn't satisfied ruining just one planet."

Harwood twisted in his chair. "What do you think, Bertie?"

Roberta detested the nickname "Bertie," but she never made an issue of it. Isaac was "Ike" and Melanie was "Mel," just like Dottie was "Dottie." It was Ellis's way of being friendly, and never mind that *he* picked the nicknames. He could intimidate you with that booming voice and his air of absolute certainty. It was easier just to let it go.

"Yes," said Melanie. "And what does Phil think?"

Roberta started filling the box with the little tubs of Philadelphia Cream Cheese and the wrappers and paper sacks that the bagels had come in. The knives she clattered into her ceramic mug. "Why don't you ask him?" she said.

"Oh," said Melanie with airy dismissal, "I thought you might know."

"He ought to say something," said Dottie. "We need direction on this. The Crusades ought to speak with a single voice."

Roberta glanced at the office door. Usually Phil left it open so anyone could drop in any time and talk to him. Sometimes, though, he needed his privacy, or he was on the phone. "We don't have to speak out on everything," Roberta said. "If we never stop talking, people will eventually stop listening."

"That's their problem," said Dottie.

"No." Harwood nodded thoughtfully. "Bertie's right. What we choose to say should be well-timed and important enough to get attention. We don't want to sound like constant nags and whiners.''

''And we don't want to stand across the path of history yelling, Stop!'' Isaac said. ''That's what conservatives do. 'Progress' is the root of progress-ivism. We just want to make sure that the progress is in the right direction; that it's spiritually uplifting, inclusive, prudent, and fair.''

Roberta left them and carried the carton into the kitchenette in the rear of the building, where she set the mug and the silverware in the sink while she dumped the trash into the bin. She picked up the mug and rinsed it out. Isaac Kohl entered with his own mug and refilled it from the percolator. A laser-printed sign above the percolator read BE SURE TO UNPLUG AT THE END OF THE DAY. Someone else had written by hand underneath: BUT ONLY IF YOUR PARTNER AGREES.

Isaac spoke while he filled his cup. ''Did you catch what Dottie said? 'Ruin the ecology of the asteroid'?'' He shook his head.

Roberta shrugged. Sure, it was a herbie thing to say. Did Dottie even know what an asteroid was? Or an ''ecology''? ''Not everyone can be fully informed on every issue. Her heart's in the right place.''

''Meaning she dislikes van Huyten almost as much as you do. Me, I can take her or leave her alone.''

''Who, Dottie or the Rich Lady?''

''Both. Systems are the enemy, not people. If half of what Dottie says is nonsense, I just listen to the other half.''

Roberta shook out her mug and dried it with a towel. She hung it on the pegboard on the kitchen wall. ''How do you know which is which?''

Isaac blew on his coffee and took a cautious sip. He made a face. ''That's awful. Someone should clean the pot.'' He cradled the mug in his hand. ''You and I have something in common,'' he said. ''The others like to make Big Statements, but you and I are fact-oriented. We want data. I didn't go to a Mentor school like you did, but at least you can thank your 'Rich Lady' for that much.''

Roberta wiped her hands. She didn't think she and Isaac had all that much in common. "It really used to bug Simon," she remembered. "Asking for the facts. I think it bugs Dottie and Ellis, too."

"Ellis thinks you're questioning his expertise when you do that. Dottie thinks it means you don't believe."

"It's not a question of 'belief.' We're not a church. We're not preaching a religion."

"Some of us are," Isaac said. "*That's* what bugs *me*. I joined the Crusades to help solve problems, not to sing progressive hymns and speak in humanist tongues."

"It's a weak sort of belief that dreads the facts." She could feel a poem start to form in the back of her mind. Belief and fact and acceptance and proof and how it all jumbled together in the mind. She hoped she would not forget the images before she had a chance to jot a reminder in her notebook.

Isaac's coffee had cooled and he took a swallow and shuddered. "I think that was Simon's problem," he said as he poured the rest of the contents down the sink. "I don't think he was a believer at all. I think he *expected* the data to contradict us, so he never wanted to look. Me, I'm more optimistic. I think the more data we have the more it'll support our positions."

"Which makes you a believer, too," Roberta pointed out. Isaac laughed.

"Yeah. 'Everyone has to believe in something. I believe I'll have another drink.' "

"W. C. Fields." Roberta identified the quote. With Isaac you always had to play one-up. He wanted to be an alpha male, but hovered somewhere around omicron.

"You have your gurus; I have mine." Then on a more serious note, he added, "Phil does need to take a stronger hand, now that Simon's gone. Or he needs to appoint a new chief of staff."

"Why are you telling me?"

Isaac shrugged.

"We're not dating," Roberta insisted.

"Okay, you're his confidential assistant and you go out on meetings. Look, it doesn't bother me. Phil's not my type." He grinned.

People who made a point of saying how unbothered they were were usually the most bothered of all. Roberta wondered if the others had any inkling what those meetings had involved. That she had been the bearer of the tidings that swept Simon Fell out of power and crippled the Crusades. That she and Phil had met and talked and agonized over what to do with the information as they carefully verified each and every item. And that personal feelings, no matter how intense, had never once intruded on the business at hand.

She knocked on the office door and opened it just enough to stick her head inside. Phil Albright was on the telephone. He covered the mouthpiece and looked up. "What is it, Roberta?"

"Do you have a few minutes, Phil?"

"I'll call you back," Phil said and hung up. "Have a seat." He gestured at the half dozen mismatched chairs scattered about the office. "You look upset."

Phil was perceptive, always alert to the feelings of others. Roberta rolled one of the wheeled chairs to the side of the desk, next to the old wooden file cabinet, and sat uneasily on the padded seat. Phil waited, his head cocked like a bird's. His dark features focused on her; his soft, kindly eyes studied her. His hair looked like steel wool, but it was soft to the touch. Roberta kept her hands firmly in her lap. "The Cadre was discussing the asteroid landing," she said.

"I was watching in here while I made some calls. Impressive."

"Some of them feel we should have taken a stance on it."

When Phil smiled, the brightness of his teeth offset the dark brows that knit together over his forehead. "I'll bet I can name names," he said.

"I told them we didn't have to take a stance on everything."

"That's right. We don't. Too much economic power flowing into too few corporate hands. People being left behind by the new technologies. Launch pollution upsetting the atmospheric chemistry. There are plenty of things to be concerned about, but the asteroid expedition—in and of itself—isn't one of them. Besides . . ." And again that ivory smile lightened his face. "Maybe the world needed to feel good about something."

"I think the Cadre needs to hear *you* say that."

"If you think it will help. . . ."

"And that's another problem, Phil. Now that Simon's gone, you need someone who can keep the Cadre focused. Either you need to get more 'hands-on' or you need to get more hands on."

Phil looked confused for a moment before he chuckled. "Cleverly phrased. How would you like the job? Chief of staff. Get a 'hand on' the office."

"Me?" *Long nights spent in policy discussions, working out strategies, making plans. Working closely together. Late night dinners in half-empty restaurants.* "I'm not an organizer, Phil. I work in words and ideas. And—"

"And what?"

"And if you did name me as new chief of staff, some tongues out there would really start wagging."

His eyebrows arched. "Really? Why?"

Sometimes she did wish he would come down from his mountain. He was a visionary and needed far vistas, but sometimes a man ought to be able to see what was right in front of him. "They think . . . Some of them . . . Maybe all of them . . . That you and I . . . That we . . ." She stopped in confusion.

"I thought you worked with words. . . ." But his smile took the barb out of the comment. He meant it as a gentle jibe. Roberta let out her breath.

"They think that you and I are seeing each other."

His thick eyebrows curled around a frown. "That we

see . . . ? But . . . Oh.'' He looked at her, and it seemed as if he looked at her with new eyes. She saw how they focused this time not on her face alone. "Do they have some . . . reason . . . for thinking that?''

Did he mean had she *given* them a reason? Roberta straightened in the chair and felt how it tilted back on its springs. Should she have worn a skirt for once, or a better blouse? If today was the day that Phil finally saw her, there should be something more fetching for him to look at. Phil was not so shallow as to be impressed by the accidents of physiology, but how you presented what you did have spoke to how you perceived yourself. Appearances weren't everything, but they weren't nothing, either.

"Only that you and I spent a lot of time together while we were investigating van Huyten's allegations against Simon.''

"And against Attwood. Let's not recall the puppet and forget the puppeteer.''

"Well, some of them interpreted that as something more . . . personal.''

"I . . . see.'' Phil folded his hands under his chin and brooded into a space a little in front of him. After a moment he raised his eyes and looked at her. "As long as you and I didn't misinterpret, we're okay. Are you all right with that?''

It struck her suddenly what his concern was. She might have taken it as personal, too, and considered it sexual harassment. It was all she could do to keep expression from her face. Surprise or laughter would be wrong. Was that why he had never hinted at any interest? Was he so sensitive that he would not risk giving offense? "Of course,'' she said. "It was a sorry business, but it had to be done, and done confidentially. The fewer who knew, the better.''

"Yes. Well.'' Phil gathered some of the papers on his desk and shuffled them together. "Staff meeting this afternoon, right? We're filing a lawsuit against that nursing home chain. And we're starting an investigation of those orphanages in the Midwest. Environmental study on that maglev train proposal. What else is on the agenda?''

"I'll have the list on your desk by eleven," she said, rising from the chair.

"Thank you." The phone rang and he picked it up. "Yes, Hannah? . . . All right. I'll take it."

Roberta edged toward the door. As she reached it, Phil cupped the mouthpiece again and said, "Roberta?"

"What?" Her hand was on the knob. She was almost out of the office.

"Would it have bothered you if it *had* been personal?"

"No," she said, and she was out the door before it mattered.

North Orange looked cleaner, somehow; and she couldn't put her finger on why it did.

Roberta cruised slowly down Queen Anne Boulevard looking for the address she'd been given. The Queenie. The Queen. Annie's BVD. When she'd been in high school, at Witherspoon on the north side, downtown was the Place You Didn't Go. During the day, most of the stores were closed up, and those that weren't sold gimcrack, tawdry goods. During the night, unattractiveness segued into danger. A brisker business went down along with the sun. Pushers and hookers hawked their wares with quiet signs and nods or with blatant displays. Come and get it. Come and get it. I got what you want. And if I don't, you don't know what you want. The cops could only nibble at the edges. The NO-men ruled. They sold protection, fixed prices, took their cut. Kept the Island Nation and the Lords of Victory at bay. They were a government, of sorts. It was NO-man's-land.

Roberta hadn't visited North Orange since the time she had come home from Europe to find her mother had died; and if the city was no longer sliding downhill, it was because it had hit the bottom a long time ago. There was no one left here she could call a friend. Most of the kids in her school had scattered to the winds after graduation, but she hadn't known any of them even then.

It was still midafternoon, but the street corners were already filling with idlers—waiting for the night shift. The skillets lounged in airways and squatted on stoops and watched with lazy eyes as Roberta drove past. Go home, white bread, 'fore it gets night. You too white; you shine in the dark. What in the name of heaven had persuaded Barry Fast to start a school down here?

A whole block of gutted buildings that had once filled the corner of Queen Anne and New Berwick were gone, the blackened studs and shattered windows razed at last sometime during the last two years. The wreckage had been something of a landmark, a way to give directions. *Turn right at the corner where the gas line exploded.* Maybe that was why downtown looked cleaner. There was less of it.

She found Discovery School in an old three-story walk-up in the middle of Justin, a residential street only a few blocks east from the abscess of the Queenie. Ragged and weary-looking, the row houses promised what her own neighborhood in Washington might someday become. But there were flowerpots in some of the windows, with bright pink and white blossoms, and a fresh coat of paint on most of the doors. Mothers, too many too young for the role, sat on the stoops of the buildings and chatted. Two or three were sweeping their porches. A few cracks of hope in the pavement of life. A promise that someday a flower might push through.

The sign was nothing spectacular. DISCOVERY SCHOOL in block letters. No bright colors; no decorative balloons. No one down here would have been fooled. "Fast and Morgenthaler, Principal Teachers." Hunh. Of all the teachers Roberta had had, dorky Mizz Morgenthaler was the last one she would have thought to find in a clinging-by-the-fingernails charter school in the heart of NO-man's-land.

Roberta eased the dilapidated Neon into a parking place near the school. She didn't own a car herself, and knew better than to rent anything good-looking for a trip this bad-looking. Two vain attempts to hire a taxi to take her downtown had been enough to send her to Rent-a-Wreck. She pushed the NeverLost console under the dash. The satellite locator system hadn't worked the whole trip from the rental lot, but she saw no reason to leave it out where it could be seen.

A woman leaned on her broom and stared at Roberta as she locked the car. "Hey," she called, "that my 'Dul's parking space. He back from work at six."

Roberta wanted to answer *has it got his name on it?* But hell, how many of these woman had a man who came *home* from work at sundown? "I'll be gone by then," she said. "I'm just visiting the school to talk to Mr. Fast."

The woman grunted. "You gone teach there?"

An odd question to ask. "No."

The woman gave a swipe with her broom at the porch stoop. "Then we don't need you down here."

A half dozen other women nearby were listening to the exchange with faces expressing a wide range of disinterest. "I'm sorry," said Roberta.

"Yeah." The woman resumed sweeping. "We all are."

Roberta thought she should say something, anything. But the only thing she could think of—how clean you keep this block—sounded so horribly patronizing that the words would gag in her throat. So she said nothing and climbed the steps to the Discovery School.

Inside the front door, in what must have once been an entry foyer when the house had been a home, a woman sat behind a desk. In feature and clothing, she was indistinguishable from the women on the block outside, except that over her shift she wore a bright green vest bearing an emblem that must have been the school's logo. She looked at Roberta with wary cheerfulness. "Can I help you?" she said. She looked like she meant it but wasn't sure she ought to. The nameplate on the desk read MRS. MOLAND.

Sing-song voices drifted from the rooms down the hallway. She could hear a faint chorus of laughter from the second floor. "I'd like to see Mr. Fast. My name's Roberta Carson. I used to be one of his students, years ago."

The woman at the desk said, "Can I see some ID?"

Surprised by the request, Roberta fumbled in her purse, finally coming up with her DC driver's license. "How's this?" she asked.

"We have to ask," the woman said absently while she studied the document.

"I know how it is."

The woman looked her in the eye as she handed the license back. "But we know how it's gonna be." She consulted a hand-written ledger. "Mr. Fast is teaching until four. You could wait in the library, if you wish, Ms. Carson. Second door on the right."

"Call me Roberta."

Severely: "At Discovery, we address each other formally."

So listen to Miss Priss . . . "Oh. Well, thank you, Mrs. Moland." She turned away, but there must have been something in the tone of her voice because the receptionist spoke sharply.

"You don't like it, do you? Think I'm a tight-ass, right?"

Roberta shrugged and turned. "I grew up in a more casual decade."

"Well, things be differ'nt now. And maybe you been dissed as much as black women been dissed in raps and movies and out there on that street—" an arm jabbed toward the front door—"maybe you appreciate a little common politeness a whole lot more."

Feeling rebuked, Roberta found her way to the library. The room looked as if it had been a library originally— maybe the only room in the house still fulfilling its original function. Dark, wooden bookcases were built into the walls from floor to ceiling. The center of the room was occupied by weenie tables and chairs.

Grade school. She'd forgotten how little weenies were.

There were no children present for the moment; only the librarian, a bald, heavyset black man with a gold hoop earring in his left ear who sat behind a desk. "You Ms. Carson?" he said. "Mrs. Moland says you were coming." His accent was Islands all the way down to his shoes.

"Tracking me? You don't trust folks much, do you?"

The bald man laughed and didn't bother to answer. Roberta drifted over to the bulletin board. Colored foil letters ran across the top:

> *Know How It's Going to Be!*
> *—Alonzo Sulbertson*

Must be the school motto. About as inspiring as any motto managed to be. She wondered who Sulbertson was and why they picked the line. What did it even *mean?* There was a row of photographs underneath. Grinning little boys and girls, mostly black but with a sprinkling of brown and white. The first was a chubby boy in a striped shirt standing in front of a charred house.

DOBIE WESTON, CLASS OF 2010

Dobie was reading in his bedroom one night when he saw flames in his neighbor's house. He called 911 and told them what was happening and where the address was. Then he got his mother and the two of them went next door and rang the bell until they woke up the neighbors. Because of his quick thinking, Dobie saved three people, including a baby, plus their pet dog.

The other photographs were similar, though none of the stories underneath were quite as dramatic as Dobie's. Three girls who had visited a lonely old woman every week until she died . . . Another girl who had gotten a scholarship . . .

What is this, a new kind of honor roll?

"Styx!"

Now, there was a name from the past! Roberta turned to see Barry Fast in the doorway. "Styx's dead," she told him.

"I keep her in a box and only haul her out for special occasions."

Fast wore a grin as wide as his face; as cheerful-looking as ever; but his eyes looked old. There were wrinkles in their corners. If those were crows' feet, it must have been a crow the size of Rodan; and while there were no white streaks in his hair, there was less of it all around and it was definitely a shade or two lighter than she remembered.

Well, being married to Mariesa van Huyten must put a lot of years on a guy.

Roberta took the hand he offered. Over his shoulder, she saw children lining up in the hallway, single file, under the direction of older children wearing white Sam Browne belts and a serious mien. Some of the weenies wore the same green vests over their clothing that the receptionist had; others had stuffed theirs in their backpacks. Someone rang a great big honker of a handbell and the line of students began to file out.

"Uniforms?" she asked, tracing a vest over her blouse. Fast shrugged.

"Sort of. The vests help promote a sense of community here at Discovery; but we make them easy to take off, so the kids don't get in trouble on the street."

She followed him to one of the reading tables and they found a couple of adult-sized chairs and pulled them up. "Why would they get in trouble?" she asked.

"It makes them a target. There's still an element in the neighborhood that thinks study and hard work is 'acting white.' There was a fight over in the public school last year. A couple of Haitian kids were beaten because they were getting good grades."

"God, I remember that happening when I was a kid," Roberta said. "Some things never change."

"Oh, they change," he said with a sigh. "It just takes a long time. If I didn't believe that, I would have given this up years ago."

"I heard you did. Give up teaching, I mean." If Styx was going to unravel Mariesa van Huyten, she had to start with the one loose thread that dangled from that knot—Barry Fast.

Fast shook his head. "For a while. Given the circumstances."

"*She* made you."

Fast didn't bother to ask which "she" Roberta meant. "No, not really. But if you're married to the woman who owns the corporation that owns your company, it does put a strain on the chain of command." His smile was rueful; his gaze, inward.

The silence was only momentary, and when Fast spoke again it was to ask her what she had been doing with herself, so they talked about poetry and Prague and the Peoples' Crusades. And old times at Witherspoon and whatever happened to who. Fast filled her in on several of her classmates, and Styx pretended like she was actually interested.

She kept looking for a way to wrench the conversation back to van Huyten without being real obvious that that was why she had come in the first place, but Fast was maddeningly conversational. He described how his school worked: the use of neighborhood talent for everything from playground proctor to handyman to teacher; the normal school "boot camp" for volunteer teachers; the three master teachers who mentored the apprentices and journeymen; and on and on and on while the afternoon grew dim and the librarian packed up and said a cheery good-bye and she was going to have to leave soon without getting one single lead on the Rich Lady when all of a sudden her name dropped right into the discussion.

"Mariesa provided the seed money for the school's endowment," Fast said. "We supplement it with annual pledge drives and corporate donations. Put most of it in equity funds, so we get a steady return. Right now, we plow it back; but in another couple years it should be ready for harvesting and we can loosen the belts here, a little."

"Ms. van Huyten funded the school? I didn't think she was interested in the inner city."

Fast shrugged. "Oh, she had to start somewhere, and

places like Witherspoon made the most sense. I didn't see it myself, at first. But like Belinda used to say, 'You can't do everything at once, so you have to do something first.' *Then* grow the program into the tougher jobs. Besides, Mariesa wants to save the world, and these kids are part of it.''

Roberta shook her head. ''To make us all good space cadets, so we'd support her corporate programs and make her lots of money. Let's not call that 'saving the world.' ''

Fast looked at her. ''I don't think you're being entirely fair.''

''She was just using us.''

''At least that means she thought you were useful.''

Roberta stood up and stepped away from the table. She looked at the rows and rows of books. That was how you told a good school from a poor one. They had lots of books. There was even a pair of desktop computers and a rack of old-style CD ROMs. Maybe the only ones in NO-man's land. ''That isn't funny,'' she said. ''You don't *use* people!''

Fast waved a hand at her. ''Oh, sit down. Of course you use people. Didn't you ever call a plumber?''

''When you call a plumber, the plumber is doing what she *wants* to do. 'Using' is when you trick someone else into wanting *your* goal.''

Fast sighed. ''Have it your way. We've both had our problems with Mariesa van Huyten, but ... At least grant her better motives.''

''To save the world,'' Roberta said grandly with a sweep of her arm.

Fast was silent for a while, tapping his finger on the table while he regarded her. He leaned back and the seat creaked alarmingly under his weight. Finally, when he spoke, it was on a different subject. ''Did you watch the broadcast from the asteroid?''

The topic of his ex-wife had become difficult, so he was dropping it. Her trip up here had been a waste after all. ''Sure,'' she said, wondering how to bring the conversation to a graceful close. ''I guess everybody did.''

"Did you know that the asteroid's orbit crosses the Earth's orbit?"

Puzzled, she said, "Yeah. That's why they were able to go there."

Fast shook his head. "No. That's why we *had* to go there. At least, why *Mariesa* felt we had to go. There are lots of asteroids like Calhoun's Rock. Maybe tens of thousands; and we don't know where they all are. Someday, one could hit the Earth. Heck, we get a couple tons of gravel every year from little-bitty asteroids that break up in the atmosphere. Sooner or later, something a lot bigger will come along. Maybe not a 'dinosaur-killer,' or a 'continent buster'; but maybe a 'city-smasher.' So when I say she wants to save the world . . ."

Roberta could not keep her mouth from dropping open. "You mean it literally . . ." She mulled that one over; shook her head. "What are the odds?"

Barry flipped his hand. "About like winning all fifty state lotteries in one year." He smiled with half his face.

"And she thinks that risk—"

"No," said Barry. "She *feels* that risk. It gives her nightmares. Some of her advisors agree that it's a potential problem, and that an impact like that would have a serious . . . uh, impact. They don't feel her urgency, is all."

"Then she's overreacting to a minor risk . . ."

"A lot of people think steps ought to be taken. She just gives it a higher priority than most. Besides, you work for the Peoples' Crusades, so you should know all about overreacting to minor risks."

"That's not fair, Mr. Fast; and you know it. The Crusades are working for a better world."

"And so is she. Look, it's personal and I wouldn't have said anything; except . . . Well, she talked about you often."

"I'll bet."

"And she reads your poetry."

Styx sank slowly back into her chair. "She reads my poems . . . ?"

"As of two years ago." Dryly: "I can't answer for more recently."

Roberta shook her head. "She just wants to find out what I'm writing about her."

"Have it your way. I just wanted you to know she admires you, and you have her motives pegged all wrong. What she did with the schools wasn't out of greed for money. Just cut her some slack, is all I ask."

Roberta stood again and looked at her watch. "Did she cut you any slack?" she asked. She had no idea what the divorce had been about. But she figured on what she knew about Barry Fast that the initiative had to have been the Rich Lady's. A bleak look came over his face and he stared toward the far wall of the library.

"She doesn't even cut herself any."

Fast showed her to the front door and saw her out. The sun had gone behind the buildings and the streetlights along Justin had come on. Well, about two-thirds of them. A battered brown sedan cruised slowly up the street. Roberta hoped it wasn't " 'Dul" come looking for his parking place. She pulled her jacket together at the collar and started down the stairs. Once inside her rental car, she locked it and sat quietly for a moment before she inserted her card and looked into the Facemaker "Thief-Be-Gone."

So the Rich Lady was afraid of asteroids. Maybe even a phobia. Was that why she spent all those hours up in that rooftop observatory of hers? Asteroids hitting the earth? It sounded a little loony to Roberta. Something maybe you *thought* about, but not something you *worried* about. She filed the information away. She wasn't sure if she had a handle she could use, but it was the first chink in the Rich Lady's armor that she had ever found.

'00 Reunion Committee
Witherspoon High School
400 Thicket Lane
North Orange, NJ. 07056

4 September 2009

Dear Member of the Witherspoon Class of
Double Naught:

As you probably realize, we didn't get to
hold a proper Fifth Year Reunion. What with
the recession and all, no one ever got around to
organizing one. But we say, Better Late Than
Never! Our class has had more than its share of
success stories: a congressman, a breakthrough
novelist, a scientist, a world-renowned poet, a
space pilot, a famous computer consultant, even
the Hero of Skopje! We were the class that was
Born to Fail. We put the "Naughty" in the
"Naughty Oughts." Come and help us rub the
world's noses in it! Renew old friendships and
have a fun evening of dinner and dance.

Place: Wessex County Country Club
(Take the Gray Horse to Old Morris Road
exit. Three miles west, on the left.)
Date: Saturday, 14 November 2009
RSVP: Above address
See you there!
Greg Prescott, *Class President*
Karen Chong, *Reunion Committee*

The letter irritated Styx, coming as it did a week after
her visit to Discovery School. Barry Fast had dredged up
old memories of Witherspoon. Shadow pictures of half-

forgotten faces. Tall, awkwardly skinny, shaven-sided, earring-dangling Chase Coughlin whispering his lust into her ear. Fat, nerdy Jimmy Poole saving the seat beside him on the bus in case Styx ever lost her mind and sat there. Bubble-headed Leilah Frazetti and her equally bubble-headed quarterback dildo, Greg, laughing at her when they thought she couldn't hear, because she chose to dress differently than the "socials." Dim-bulb jocks and cold-eyed sociopaths and self-absorbed teenaged narcissists and faded nonentities whose lives had never touched hers at all and whose names she could barely remember.

Renew old friendships . . . ?

She had never been friends with any of them. She had known few of them in school and none of them thereafter and, since graduation, had spoken only with Tani Pandya. Styx had never been close to anyone, not even to Beth, her mother—who had died unremarked while her daughter had been discovering the New Art on the banks of the Vltava. *World-renowned poet?* How dare they brag on her as if she were a part of them? What had they ever done? She didn't need them to admire her; she didn't need them *to read her poems!*

That night she went out to the liquor store on Potomac Avenue and brought home a bottle of Stolychnaya vodka and drank enough of it that she could not remember drinking the rest, and she had not done that since the year she shook the Wessex County dust from the soles of her Doc Marten boots.

It was the vodka that dreamed it up, and the hangover that entered the E-dress. In a more sober and reflective mood, she would never have done it; never have even considered it. But a "famous computer consultant" might find things that a "world-renowned poet," flailing about on her own, never could.

She hooked the Blue Line to L'Enfant Plaza, where she could use the bank of public picture phones, and found a booth that was reasonably clean and not too badly damaged.

Once locked into the privacy of the peephone, she called up the Crypt and found the public encryption key for Poole sEcurity Consultants.

The screen blinked <dialing>, <waiting>, <connecting>. Why did computer geeks think people wanted to know all that? Just put the call through . . .

The screen clarified when Poole sEcurity Consultants locked in its private key and decrypted the signal. Roberta found herself looking at an image of . . . Herself.

"Poole sEcurity Consultants," the image said—in her voice! "How may I direct your call?"

No, not quite herself. The receptionist wore her hair shoulder-length, and her voice was huskier. She wore a clothing style that Roberta would never consider long enough to reject, cut low enough to reveal a far more robust physique.

That little weenie . . . How long did he have to hunt to find a receptionist that was her near-double? And what did that tell her about S. James Poole? She nearly hung up then, but the receptionist repeated her request and Roberta said, "Let me speak to the head weenie."

The other woman was unflappable. If she had remarked Styx's resemblance to herself, she gave no sign of it. "Do you wish to speak to our Mister Poole?" When Roberta agreed, the screen blanked momentarily and was replaced by an image of Jimmy Poole.

She would have recognized him instantly. He had always been fat and the evidence was that despite his wealth and fame he had not blown it all on a Nordic Trak. The last nine years had tightened his face a little around the eyes. They had lost their gee-whiz, whiny stare and gained a squint of crafty suspicion.

And irritation. Poole scowled at his screen, muttered something under his breath and reached out to touch a button invisible under his visual field. The picture phone flipped back to the receptionist, who smiled and said, "Poole sEcurity Consultants. How may I direct your call?" And then, a moment later, flipped back to Poole, whose look of irritation had been replaced by one of surprise.

"It's you," he said.

That was when Roberta realized that the receptionist had been a computer morph. That S. James Poole, computer security expert, had scanned a photograph of Roberta Carson—it was not hard to find a book jacket bearing her likeness—dressed it differently, *given it bigger tits!* and a sexy voice. Roberta leaned close to the screen.

"Have you read up on the copyright laws regarding unauthorized use of another person's likeness?"

Poole blinked several times and he smiled a quirky half smile. His fingers played just out of sight below the screen and two inset windows opened above and to either side of him. Smaller versions of the receptionist . . . No, one of the receptionist and one of herself in realtime.

"Do you really think she looks like you?" Poole asked. He brought the two images together and superimposed one on the other. Green and red highlighted the differences: a taller brow, a wider nose, deeper cheeks . . . "There are measurable deltas in the twelfth, twenty-second, thirty-first and thirty-fourth eigenfaces. In a court of law, this would constitute evidence of 'no-malice' mistaken identity."

"But—"

". . . And would fall just outside the closure of the set of faces constituting 'a person's likeness,' defined as 'those facial compositions recognized as identical by face-recognition security algorithms.' Who do you think wrote the code for those algorithms? Next question?"

Poole's smile was so smug that, for just a moment, Styx understood why Chase Coughlin used to weal on the little herbie. It took a conscious effort to remind herself that she had called him with a purpose. She rubbed her forehead trying to will away the vodka headache. If she was smart, she would hang up now.

She looked at Poole, who was waiting with ill-concealed impatience. She could probably get him on harassment. The "reasonable woman" standard didn't give shit about eigenfaces or recognition algorithms. She hated the way he had taken her likeness and toyed with it to please his adolescent male fantasies, manipulating her image the same way that Mariesa van Huyten had tried to manipulate her mind. Symbolically, it gave him power over her, and autonomy was something that Roberta Carson would never cede.

"I need to get information on someone," she said cautiously. Though if an encrypted line into Poole Consultants was not secure there was no security anywhere.

"A datassembly," he said, as if she had flunked a vocabulary test.

She showed her teeth to the camera. *You'll get yours later,* she telepathed. *These teeth are made for biting.* "Yes, of course. A datassembly." Another thing she hated was the way geekdom created neologisms out of perfectly acceptable English vocabulary. A race between the jargon-defined cognoscenti and the great unwashed masses who insisted on picking up the terminology and using it. Positive feedback. The more the public learned, the greater the need for the next level of stupefying in-speak. A comic poem began forming in the back of her head. "It will be very difficult. The person I want the information on—"

"The target."

"The, uh, target will be protected by very good security, both personal and corporate. Getting the inf—datassembly, you may need to, uh, bend the rules a little."

Poole blinked three times and reached out to another unseen control. The screen blanked and came back, this time with a red-and-white striped border with *Poole sEcurity* repeated in black block letters in the margins. "Okay, Styxy. Spill it. You're inside my pentagram now and it's my nickel. First rule is never say *anything* inside a public key laager. Government has keyword search routines and miniCray crypt-robbers that can bleach even the blackest code. Encrypted conversations on public nets draw their attention. The pretext being that's how the Lords of Drug communicate. Right now, I'm code dancing. My system has co-opted your pee-phone's pea-brain and is shuffling codes at both ends faster than crypt-robbers can break them. That will last as long as it takes the government's Artificial Stupid to realize there is a major serious black hole in its information feeding trough and start marshaling resources to this nexus. So speak, Styxy. And make it good.''

Roberta took a deep breath and, with it, the plunge. ''I want to get the goods on Mariesa van Huyten and VHI.''

''What goods is that?''

''How would I know? That's why I need you.

''You want an outlaw hack.''

''Not necessarily, but I'm fishing around. I can't predict what information will be useful, or what you might have to do to get it. Some of it may be illegal.''

A shrug. ''So what's your point?''

Roberta thought S. James Poole had become a computer security expert the way Willie Sutton had become a bank security expert. There had been stories in the newsmags a few years ago. Allegations. ''Proofs'' later shown to be ''forgeries'' followed by unsubtle hints at libel suits. And the story dropped right off the public's right-to-know viewscreen. Nothing to the accusations? Or had countermeasures been taken? ''Can you do it?'' she asked.

Another shrug. '' 'Can you' is the wrong question.''

''*Will* you do it?''

''I didn't think the Peep Crew went in for this sort of fun. Isn't 'privacy' one of your hot buttons?''

''Peep Crew?''

An impatient cough. ''Peoples' Crusades. You're one of. the Cadre, aren't you? And the crew has been looking for a good baseball bat to whack VHI with.''

''I'm not doing this for the Crusades. Phil doesn't know anything.''

''You can say that again. Good old plausible deniability, right? Wink-wink. Nudge-nudge.''

Roberta kept a tight rein on her temper. What sort of world were they creating when people like her had to cozy up to amoral slugs like Jimmy Poole to get what they needed? It was more than a question of information haves and have-nots. It was the creation of new kinds of sin. "It's not like that."

"Sure. You guys are out to save the world. You are the Holy and Righteous, predestined for salvation. But you're not, you know."

Dryly. "I guess an appeal to Crusades's idealism is not the answer to the 'will you' question."

"Even when you have the right idea, you dramatize and exaggerate so much you wind up discrediting your own causes. Mostly it's just posturing and making speeches. You've been crusading for how long on homelessness? And you've not built one stick of affordable housing yourselves."

"Neither have you," she pointed out.

"Sure. But I don't claim to be Doing Good for anyone but myself."

"I see you learned the van Huyten lesson plan real well."

"Don't project, Styxy. I learned *that* lesson long before Mentor came on the scene. The taunts and the jibes and the snickers. . . . You, of all people, ought to know what it was like to be smart in a school full of dummies. That's one of the reasons I used to like you. You had a brain, and you weren't afraid to show it."

Oh God, I'm the secret love of his life. There couldn't be a God; not if he allowed *that* to happen. "What about stopping VHI from accumulating so much power that we'll all have to jump when she says frog? Or before one of their grandiose plans goes seriously bad."

"You're still pressing the wrong buttons, Styxy. 'This, too, shall pass.' Once upon a time, Howard Johnsons was the biggest restaurant chain in the world. Where are they now? McDonalds and Burger King ate their lunch. Or, remember Microsoft? I got no beans for *or* against VHI. You've been hanging out so much with the 'crew' that you've mistaken agreement for proof. I'm not afraid of the same bogeymen you are."

"Then you need to be better informed about the wider world."

"You mean outside Herbie City? Insult me all you want. It's a novel way to convince me to risk prison to help you out."

There was a moment of silence while that sank in. Poole hadn't spoken like one who regarded that possibility as a likely one; but it was, after all, what she was asking of him. "What about money?" she asked at last.

"For an open-ended outlaw hack? You can't afford it. Your boss might, but you say 'he doesn't know.' "

"Phil isn't rich. He lives frugally and simply."

"In a luxurious town home in one of Washington's tonier neighborhoods."

"That belongs to his sister. He just stays there when he's in town."

"Far be it from me to puncture any fantasy balloons. You're trying to convince me; not vice versa. The clock is still running. I may have to cut you off."

"Okay. No more guessing. What will it take?"

The image of Poole tugged on its lower lip. Its eyes danced around the margins of the screen. Fingers twitched and the screen blanked and reopened. "I've bought us some more time," he said. More lip tugging. More silence. Just before Roberta would have screamed out loud, Poole spoke. His eyes looked everywhere except at her. "Sex," he said.

"What?" Not sure she had heard him properly.

"Sex," he said again. "That's my price."

"With me?"

Hopeful sheep's eyes found her. "Would you?"

Gaah . . . Ice formed between her thighs. Never. Not even if it meant never getting her revenge on the Rich Lady. She would never let that pallid, dickless slug inside her. Her skin crawled just imagining his touch. "No," she said.

He nodded as if expecting the answer. "Then find me someone else."

"Find you someone else?"

"Yes."

"*Pimp* for you?"

His eyes wandered away again, looking here, there. Not

checking readouts on his console, she realized. Just avoiding eye contact. "I just want to know what it feels like," he said. "I want to know why everyone seems so obsessed with it. I'm twenty-four years old and I'm still a virgin."

For which millions of women go to bed each night happy . . . "Hell, Jimmy, that can be fixed for $50 on Queenie's BVD." And if Jimmy was two years younger than she was, he must have been skipped a couple grades in school, which might explain a lot. That was easier on the teachers than dealing with a child genius in their classes. No wonder Jimmy was a social abortion. Or would he have been that way anyway?

"You don't understand," Poole said. "I want a woman to *want* me."

"*That* costs $100."

"Then you won't have a hard time meeting my price. Don't call me again on a public line on this matter. If we need to talk, call here and ask for Tulio Gucci, and I'll set up some smoke and mirrors." And with that, the screen went dark.

Roberta slumped in the padded seat and blew hard. Her head still throbbed from last night's fellatio with the Stoly. Goddamned stupid stunt. She wasn't sure why she had done that, because all she had to show for it was a head God was using for batting practice; a mouth like the bottom of a bird cage; and judgment so badly impaired that she had called Jimmy Poole for help and halfway promised to be his pimp.

I want the woman to want me. Styx wondered if there was any price that could purchase that unlikely commodity. But it needn't be the real thing. Jimmy dealt with simulations all day long. One more simulation wouldn't matter.

Someone banged on the door to the peephone booth, which meant the call-in-progress light had gone off, triggering the instantaneous impatience of the modern age. Roberta punched the open button and was barely able to squeeze out against the fiftyish woman pushing in.

"Excuuuuse me," Styx said with exaggerated sarcasm.

"*I* wasn't hogging the booth," the woman replied.

Snotty Boomers. They thought the world owed them its gratitude just for existing. What do we want? You name it! When do we want it? NOW! Peace or stock options or access to a peephone. The object didn't matter, only the wanting did. Styx smiled wolfishly at the woman. "Have a nice day," she said in as syrupy a voice as she could muster.

She floated with the flow down the escalator to the Metro Blue Line. Yeah, give her Jimmy Poole's honest geek any day. Jimmy Poole and Roberta Carson—and Chase Coughlin and the others, too—might live on different planets from each other, but at least they were all in the same universe.

That fake receptionist . . . A faux-Roberta, morphed just enough to be legal, not enough to be unrecognizable; probably used by Jimmy to enhance his wet dreams. The Ugly Duckling adopted, not by a Swan but by the Toad Prince. Sleeping Beauty awakened by the French kiss of Jo-jo the Dog-faced Boy . . .

She had thought that morphograph gave Jimmy some unspecified power over her, but she realized now that *she* was the one with the power. Her charms—such as they were—had ensorceled his mind. *His* will was impaired by thoughts of her; not vice versa. So the only question was whether or not *she* would find a woman that would let Jimmy fuck her. A tasteless business; but if that's what it took, that's what it took. No excuses. No fear.

There was one out there. Women came in all shapes and sizes and bent of mind. Out of nearly three hundred million Americans there was bound to be one woman who would find Jimmy attractive. Probably not two, but surely one. And the only other question was how long and how hot the shower would have to be afterwards.

In a sudden, quirky thought, Roberta wondered if she had conversed with the real Poole at all or with another construct like the receptionist. Could an A/S be flexible enough to handle the sort of meandering conversation she had just had? A/S wasn't a topic she kept up on, but she could imagine an eerie sort of future in which simulacra kept up the appearance of personal intercourse in a world from which all humanity had fled.

6.

Friends in High Places

Sometimes the choices were easy. The weights of good
and evil sat in different pans, and you could reject the one
and embrace the other, as Flaco had done years before when
he left the streets for Serafina. But at other times, good and
bad were commingled. All during the groundside preparation—the physical testing, the schematics and plans, the
treadmills and puke machines, the "vomit comet," everything building up for the grand day when the Green Crew
would go up—all during that mind-numbing, body-
wrenching month, the image of Serafina hovered before
him, drawing him on to provide for her, holding him back
to be with her. Twice he nearly resigned, to seek other jobs
closer to the Heights. But always there was the pay scale,
plus the hazard pay and the completion bonus, and the vision of the ranch house with the aluminum siding and the
tall, shady trees beneath which he and little Guilliemo
would play baseball together. No grimy, concrete street,
with its siren call, ready with its sweet, sexy legs or tight
snake's eyes to swallow him and Serafina and Memo whole
along every dream he had ever had.

He wrote to Serafina at her mother's address, telling her
all was well, telling her about Tonio and Sepp and Henry
Littlebear and Ivan Selodkin and the other men he had met.
About the hijinks and the nervous anticipation. He left out

the parts about the safety drills or the occasional arguments or a fight he nearly had with Red Hawkins. Such details would only confuse her. He told her he would be home for the Christmas feast after the three-month training, and again in May, after the second three months; so he would be back in time for Memo's birth, and you couldn't ask for any better schedule than that.

Serafina wrote back: a careful, proper letter wishing him well and saying nothing of her fears, asking only that he be careful for the sake of his unborn child. Flaco could imagine her mother leaning over her shoulder as she wrote, telling her what words to use, sucking all the blood out of it. Felipa Cruz had never approved of her daughter wedding ''that Dominican,'' perhaps with sufficient cause at the time, and she still kept a falcon's eye on Serafina's happiness.

When the day came for the trip to LEO, Flaco waited with the others in the administration building while a self-propelled tug pulled the *Harriet Quimby* to the center of Pegasus Field. Flaco stood with his hands jammed in his pockets in front of the pixwall, watching the ship's progress. It was a long wall and the view was panoramic. An early morning launch, with the sky still a very deep blue, but a bright rose tinting the ship and the hangar building in the foreground. Had the thick, blast-shielded wall had windows instead of outside doid pickups, this was the scene one would see; but somehow the pixview lacked the immediateness of a window. It was more like watching a video than watching reality.

Tonio Portales, the Cuban, stood by Flaco's side, also watching the ship move across the landing field. He bounced a little on the balls of his feet; small movements, so that he seemed to be vibrating, like a spring. Impatient, or nervous, or both. Flaco kept his arms tightly crossed over his chest. ''Some final exam, eh, Tonio?''

. ''What do you mean, Flaco?''

Flaco nodded toward the view. ''We fixed her up. The rigging, the welding, the electrical. Now we get to ride in her. I sure hope you weld a tight seam.''

"Don't you worry about that." Bird Winfrey had come up behind them. His fingers were entangled in his long, wiry beard, twisting and flexing as if they had flown into it and gotten trapped. The tatoos on his bulging arms flapped their wings as his muscles tensed and untensed. "You don't worry," he said again, "because I personally checked each weld he made."

Tonio faced him. "I don't need no NDT tech second-guessing my work," he said with a belligerence made slightly comic by his stature. He had to look up to see the Bird's beard. Winfrey didn't bother responding to the challenge.

"Never dreamed I'd fly into space wearing T-shirts and jeans," he said. "Always wanted me a Buck Rogers suit." He sucked his breath in and blew it out again. "Here comes the bus. Last chance to back out."

The pixwall showed the approaching bus: white with a red, winged stallion painted on its side. Flaco looked at Winfrey. "Who's backing out?"

The Bird shrugged. "Look around you. Supposed to be fifty men in Green Crew, twenty-five in this lift. So we're down to what, twenty? Guess some of the guys gave some serious thought to what they were getting into and found that deep down inside they didn't have the sand for it."

"I'm not backing out," Flaco told him. Winfrey shrugged again.

"Hope springs eternal," he said. He glanced at Tonio. "How about you, Pedro?"

The Cuban made a sudden move, but Flaco had been waiting for it and his hand clamped tight around Tonio's forearm. Winfrey laughed. Tonio tugged his arm from Flaco's grip. "I can take care of myself," the Cuban said.

"You go right on thinking that, little man," said Bird.

"Let it go, Tonio," Flaco said. "We're all nervous about the lift, and we each work it off in different ways."

"Ece pato es lleno de mierda."

"Let that be his problem, not yours."

Tonio grunted and turned on his heel. The waiting area

was filled with rows of low-slung chairs where most of the men were waiting. Some, like Littlebear, were reading magazines; others were squirming or pacing or cracking their knuckles. Still others were napping in a show of unconcern. A few had been watching Bird and Tonio quarrel. Sepp Bauer was sitting rock-still, looking straight ahead. Not reading or napping or watching anything in particular. It was a disconcerting habit he had; almost as if, having no immediate tasks at hand, he simply turned himself off.

Noticing the direction of Flaco's gaze, Winfrey said, "Naw. Ol' Fritz, there, he'd be the last one to back out. Don't know if he doesn't know enough to be scared or he knows enough he isn't."

"His name isn't Fritz," Flaco said.

"Whatever you say. But what's in a name? 'A rose by any other name would smell as sweet.' "

"Then you don't mind if I call you *un mamao pendejo jualabiche?*"

Bird threw up his head and brayed. "*Hell, no,*" he said in a Mexican-accented Spanish. "*I been called worse 'n that.*"

The loudspeaker interrupted them. "Attention in the lounge," said a synthetically smooth voice, neither male nor female. "*Harriet Quimby* is ready for boarding. Please line up at the gate with your identification and wait for the door to open."

Bird chuckled as the others filed by. "*Harriet*'s ready for boarding," he repeated. "A lady is always ready to be boarded. Isn't that right, Wendy?"

Wendy McKenna was an electrician, one of only a half-dozen women in Green Crew. She barely glanced at the NDT tech as she passed by. "Up yours, Winfrey," she said. Winfrey nudged Flaco.

"After three months upstairs, we may be glad to get that much action."

Flaco turned away and fetched his carry-on bag from the seat beside Sepp. He kicked Bauer's shoes, and the German looked at him. "We're boarding." Sepp grunted and rose to his full height, arched his back with his arms stretched overhead. "Gut. I wass about to get bored."

Flaco took his place in line behind Sepp and Tonio and waited patiently while the men at the front of the line looked into the Facemaker, which confirmed their appearance against the version coded on their magstrip cards and the master in the A/S ROM. All three had to agree, and it would be easier to get plastic surgery than to change the master dataface. Red Hawkins contrived to give the recognition algorithm a problem, as the light reflecting off his bald head confused the doid. Winfrey, who had come into line behind Flaco, called out, "Grow some hair, fer Crissake!" Hawkins flipped the Bird the bird.

"You come up here, mate, and I'll rip a wig right off your chin."

"Quiet down," said the gatekeeper.

Flaco slung his carry-on over his shoulder. Next three months was beginning to look like a real long shift.

Harriet Quimby's passenger bay was oval in cross section with the seats arrayed in two concentric circles facing inboard. A ladder ran up from a hatchway in the center of the floor to another in the ceiling. *Decks,* not floors and ceilings. Flaco supposed he would have to learn the terminology. A few seconds' misunderstanding might be critical.

He found himself a seat in the outer circle, next to a napping, broad-shouldered Negro garbed in a gray coverall jumpsuit. The seats were angled way back, so that Flaco was lying as much as sitting. There were about a dozen men and women on board wearing 'suits of various colors and designs. Veterans, Flaco figured, running errands or returning from R and R. One man's suit had BOEING-MCDONNELL stenciled on the back; another's read ЕНЕРГИЯ НПО Flaco studied the man in gray beside him, whose 'suit bore a shoulder patch with a silhouette of an ancient galley. The Negro opened his eyes and Flaco, caught in the act of scrutinizing him, flushed and faced forward.

There was a distant boom and the ship reverberated to it. Flaco sucked in his breath. The Negro chuckled. "That's nothing but the main cargo hatch closing up. Trust me. When the torch lights, you'll know it."

Flaco tried to look unconcerned. "Yeah, well. This is my first time."

"Sure it is. My first time, I near jumped out of the seat when the hatch closed." He chuckled again. " 'Course, I rode in a cargo module, so it wasn't near so comfortable as this." He glanced at the digital clock on the wall. "Ten, fifteen minutes now, tops."

"I'm not sure I ought to be doing this . . ."

The gray-suited man rubbed his cheek. "Be a little tough changing your mind, if you wait much longer."

"No . . . I don't mean I'm scared or nothing. I'm not scared of anything . . ."

"No? You ought to be."

"Just I don't like leaving my *bomba.* I know I'm doing the right thing. And I'll be home before the baby is born. But I just feel bad about bein' away, you know."

The other nodded slowly. "I do know. My dad used to be away for months at a time when he was with the peace-keepers. Mom would get awful worried, especially when the news went bad. But you don't do anyone favors by taking Easy Street. Mom used to tell me—'cause sometimes when I was a kid, I'd feel it real bad he wasn't home. She said, 'It's who he is, Leland. If he stayed put here and drove a cab or worked the line . . . well, I'd have him more, but I wouldn't have *him.*' Smart lady, Mom."

"Yeah." Flaco rubbed his hands together, felt how moist the palms were. "I hope Serafina feels the same way about me . . ."

"Serafina. That's a pretty name."

"She's an angel. I—"

The call came from the hatch in the center of the deck. "Listen up, dust bunnies, 'cause I'm only gonna say this once. It's your neck, not mine." The head that emerged from the hatchway was close-cropped on top and shaven on the sides. The body that followed wore a red Pegasus jump-suit with the flying stallion logo and the name Coughlin sewn above the right breast. His sleeves bore four white bands at the cuff. *This guy is our pilot?* Flaco wasn't sure he wanted to trust his fate to a man little older than himself.

"First off," Coughlin said, "welcome aboard Pegasus Aerospace Flight 89S, Phoenix to LEO, with a stopover at Mir. If your travel plans do not include Low Earth Orbit, they shortly will—unless you get your ass off my ship. I'll tell you what I just told your friends on the lower deck. First, stow all your carry-ons in one of the secured lockers. I see a bag on the deck there, bunny. Stow it, now. Trust me. You don't want any loose objects flying across this cabin when we accelerate. Second, you wearing any ear-rings, especially big dangly ones, take 'em off, now . . ."

A few men unfastened their ear ornaments. Wendy, who hadn't worn any, smirked. One man with shocked black hair and a pointed face stuck his chin out. "Howcum?" he asked. "You have something against guys wearing jew-elry?"

Coughlin flicked his own earlobe. "See me groundside, bunny. I got better than you'll ever. But we max five g's going up; and if I had anything dangling by a wire from my lobes that suddenly weighed five times what it should, I'd turn damn thoughtful. Same goes for any pens, keys, or combs or anything else you got in your pockets. If you don't want a big honking bruise on your chest—or anywhere else—take 'em out and put 'em in the compartment under your armrest."

There was a flurry of movement while the Green Crew emptied their pockets. The men in the coveralls grinned and shook their heads. "What do you think, otter?" one said to another. "Just dust," was the answer.

"Your harness," continued Coughlin, "is a five-point harness. It ain't too hard to fasten and unfasten; and if you can't figure out how, you have probably just made a bad career move. When the lift starts, lie flat in your frame with your arms on the padded armrests. Do NOT try to move.

Especially do not try to scratch yourself. Wheezer Hottlemeyer did that on his first lift, and now we call him 'Squeeky.' Four: none of you is sitting near an emergency exit, because there ain't no emergency exits. If the profile is good, you don't need 'em; and if we smooch, they wouldn't help anyhow. One toot on the horn means one minute to lift. Three toots means the torch is lit. Any questions?'' His attitude said he didn't expect or want any.

"Friendly guy," Flaco whispered to his seatmate. "He'd make a great stewie." The pilot may have heard him because he turned suddenly in Flaco's direction.

But what he did was he traded fives with the black man. "Hey, Hobie!"

"Hey, Chase!"

"Heading back to Kristal?"

" 'Nother run of experiments. Screening design. Doping the lattice to see if we can get better ductility without losing conductivity.''

"Whatever turns you on, otter. Me, I gotta herd these dust bunnies over to LEO. Maybe I'll see you next run.''

"Say yo to Meat for me.''

"Word.'' The pilot skinnied up the ladder to the flight deck and the internal hatches banged closed one by one. Sealed in for sure, now. Flaco turned to the man called Hobie. "You guys know Meat Tucker, the rigger boss?''

The black man nodded and adjusted his harness. "Chase, Meat 'n' me went to school together.''

"Small world," said Flaco.

The man chuckled. "You should see how small it looks from orbit.''

Physical discomfort Flaco could deal with it. He was no stranger to it. The brutal, crushing acceleration reminded him of the time a wall had collapsed on him at a construction site in Queens and he had lain flat on his face with a course of bricks for a blanket. And the weightlessness that followed brought nausea and disorientation with it, but he had been drunk often enough to recognize those sensations, too. Mental discomfort was another matter. The pixcreens on the cabin wall relayed a view of the Earth falling away beneath them. Any second thoughts now were better left unthought.

Quimby rendezvoused with Mir on her first orbit and Hobie and one of the Russians shouldered their gear and kicked off toward the ladder, sailing through the air like a couple of fish. Up and down had been scrambled and Flaco no longer could tell the deck from the overhead without first checking where the couches were. A curious thing: the compartment seemed larger than it had on the ground.

The pixview showed an asymmetrical Tinkertoy assembly of modules, dominated by two large external Shuttle tanks on one side. Satellite repair garages, Hobie told him. The Argonaut scientist shook Flaco's hand before departing. "I gotta go see they don't bogie my equipment when they unload the cargo. Good luck on LEO."

"Yeah. You, too. Good luck on your experiments, whatever they are."

Hobie laughed. "When I understand the process, I'll be the first to let you know. But I'll let you in on something. LEO makes a full circuit in just under two hours. And your girl lives in, what did you say, New York? So eleven times a day you'll be closer to her than you were in Phoenix."

Afterward, Flaco hovered by the pixscreen and pretended to watch the unloading. Then two men and a woman boarded the *Quimby*, stowed their carry-ons and buckled themselves into some empty seats. Coughlin spoke over the intercom and announced a departure window in twenty minutes, "so all you bunnies better get fastened." The woman from Mir made a buck-toothed rabbit face at them.

The bunny business was beginning to wear a little thin on Flaco. He already knew he was a novice. He didn't need to be constantly reminded of the fact.

Or did he? His lack of experience might be something he could forget far sooner than he ought to, so the constant reminders might have a purpose. Flaco pulled himself back to his seat using his hands and the backs of the couches.

The Boeing-McDonnell man said to no one in particular, "I thought bunnies were supposed to hop." Flaco ignored him. He had watched the more experienced men kick off and sail through the cabin, touching down on their destination like ballet dancers, but Flaco thought it looked too easy to be that easy and would rather someone else crack his head by pushing off too hard. He buckled himself in and waited with his eyes closed for the next departure. What Hobie had told him helped a little. LEO was three hundred miles up and that wasn't very far away from Serafina at all.

But half the time he'd be all the way round on the other side of the world.

Coughlin let them see LEO as he made his approach by slaving the forward doid pickups to the pixcreens in the passenger cabins. Flaco saw an array of gossamer girders enclosing the work site, illuminating the space with floodlights, holding things in place with stay lines. Structures like those would collapse if they were built on Earth; but up here, they did not fight gravity. To one side, in what Flaco took for the marshalling yards, were three Shuttle external tanks, one partly disassembled, together with a dozen ram pods and what must be the leftover parts from other ETs. Flaco counted three LOX tanks and one intertank. Nearby, a stripped-down Plank orbited as a yard engine.

In the center of all this was the station itself.

Three ETs had been disassembled and reconfigured with the hydrogen tanks linked nose-to-tail. Two of the intertanks had been used to create pressurized transfer tunnels linking them, so that the whole looked like a single, long cylinder with rounded ends. The forward tank bore an array of antennae and other equipment: a solar power receiver and a heat radiator, both temporary. That was construction headquarters, according to the prelift briefing. The "bunkhouse" was the one just behind it. Flaco studied it carefully. It would be his home for the next two months. The dull, rusty color made it nearly invisible, despite the bright floodlights attached to the free-floating structures. A reflective coating was being applied by robots crawling around the outer skin, but only a small part of the tank was covered as yet.

The third tank in line, the warehouse, was also being used as a dock, so the approaches had been kept clear. The *Quimby* maneuvered as it closed orbits. Since the A/S that controlled the pixview kept the image rock steady, the transient accelerations Flaco felt in his ears—forward, back, up, down, left, right in a confusing jumble—argued with the lack of movement his eyes saw on the screen.

It was an argument his stomach lost.

"Ah, sweet Jaysus," said someone in a broad brogue, "the sweet parfume of bunny spew. Use the by-Our-Lady blow bags, will ye?"

Flaco clenched his jaws shut and looked around, gratified to see he was not the only one among the newcomers to boot his lunch.

Their entry into Port LEO was greeted with a tumultuous welcome by the Red Crew, who surrounded the Greens as they entered the warehouse from the smaller, ten-foot entry bay, pumped hands and pummeled backs, until the whole crowd of them were floating this way and that inside the tank. One of the Reds took Flaco's carry-on from him.

"Here, let me help vit dat, bunny. You must be tired from your trips."

"Wot'd he bring?" asked a companion. The first man zipped open the bag. Flaco said, "Hey!" and made a grab for it that his welcomer easily evaded. Flaco suddenly found himself floundering without support, far from any wall.

"Looks like cookies," said the first man, lifting a sealed plastic bag.

"My wife baked those for me," Flaco said.

"Och, and a fine cook I'm sure she is. What else did she give you?" A third man took the bag and reached inside. "This isn't beer, is it? Sure, that'd be contraband. Ah, no. Fruit punch." He turned to his companion and smacked his lips. "I haven't tasted fruit punch in donkey's years."

"*Gott sei dank,*" said the first man.

"Lookee here. Beef jerky . . ."

"That's mine," said Flaco.

A fourth man slapped Flaco on the back. "Welcome to ziggy. We're the Welcome Wagon, except we work it the other way." When Flaco turned back from this distraction, there was no sign of the first man or of his carry-on.

"Hey! Where did that *hijo de zorra* take my gear?"

"Vere does the time go?" the first man said, looking at his watch. "Back on duty, everyone."

In a chorus of "Good luck" and "Look me up when you settle in," the Reds disengaged from the Greens and—Flaco did not see how they did this—were soon sailing down the length of the bay toward the manlock at the far end.

Flaco looked around at his companions, most of whom wore the same dazed look he did. They were in a large cylindrical bay twenty-seven feet across and fifty deep. Big white numbers painted on bulkheads read 1-B and 1-C. Ahead was a bulkhead with an opening in the center which Flaco suspected would lead to 1-D. Bins of various sizes, stencilled with number codes, lined the walls, arcing overhead and underfoot. Between every third file of bins, recessed lights encircled the bay. Most of the Greens were drifting in midair, some spinning slowly; nearly all bereft of their satchels. Flaco saw that Henry Littlebear and Sepp Bauer had retained their bags, but then the man would be hard to find who could pry something from their grasp did they not wish it.

"What do you think, otter?"

Flaco tried to turn and see who had spoken, something he found extraordinarily hard to do. He felt like he had that time Serafina had dragged him ice skating at Rockefeller Center. There was nothing he could get a purchase on.

"Looks like a bunny raid to me," said a second voice.

"Good thing we waited before disembarking. Could've got mistaken for dust bunnies, you and me."

Bodies began to sail past Flaco—the company men who had been aboard the *Harriet Quimby*. They floated gracefully, like scuba divers, though without flapping their arms or legs. "Yo!" called Tonio. "How do we get out of this?"

One of the . . . otters . . . reached out and grabbed a spar of the dunnage that lined the walls. It brought him to a halt and spun him around so his feet found another spar and he was facing them. "Dunno, dusty; but I'd vacate this section if I were you. They take it to vacuum when they unload the big stuff. Easier to bring cargo in through the space doors than through the locks. Besides, Uncle Waldo expects you to report in, up in the bunkhouse, so don't hang around here any longer than you have to." With that, he flexed his legs and shot off after his companions.

For a moment, nobody spoke. Then a chorus of voices all broke out at once. "Who does he . . . ?" "How we gonna . . . ?" "That son of a . . ." "*Vacuum?*"

The main question in Flaco's mind was who was Uncle Waldo? The one thing he knew for certain was that O&P had spent too damn much money to train and lift them just to lose them to a hazing ritual. So either someone would come and fetch them after letting them flounder a bit more, or they were expected to work their own way out.

Flaco twisted his neck to see what he could see.

What he saw was that Red Hawkins had managed to keep a grip on a spar at the far end of the entry space, just before the second ring frame and the rows of bins that lined the midsection. Red was smirking at the rest of them, but Flaco noted that he kept an iron grip on the spar and his carry-on was nowhere to be seen. "Hey, Red," Flaco called him.

"You know what, Chico? You look goddamn funny hanging like that."

"Reach out and grab Lou's hand."

"What for, mate? He's not my type."

"Because then Lou can grab Wendy's hand and Wendy can grab—who is that?—Ivan; and we can make a chain and pull everyone over to where they can get a grip."

Red laughed. "Why should I do that?"

"Two reasons, *colorado*. One is someday you may need one of us to pull you out of a bad spot . . ."

"Not likely, mate."

"And number two. I don't think the testing is done yet."

Red scratched his chin thoughtfully. "If this is a test, then why should I help you? Four of us were smart enough not to get yanked out into midair. So we go on forward; we win the race."

"You sure about that?"

Red's eyes narrowed and he pursed his lips. After a moment's contemplation, he said, "You may have a point, Chico."

"Goddamn it, Baldy," said Bird Winfrey. "Just do it." Flaco saw that the others hadn't waited for Flaco and Red to come to a resolution, but had formed chains linking to each of the other three men who had kept anchored. One by one, those farthest out were pulling themselves in on human ropes.

Red said, "Much as I like the sight of you guys hanging out there . . ." He extended a hand.

Flaco was the last one in. When he found a hold on the struts of the storage bin, he nodded to Red. "Thanks, *'mano*."

The Australian was unimpressed. "You better be right, because you and me will be the last ones into the bunkhouse now." He turned away from Flaco and pulled himself arm over arm along the crisscrossed bars of the stowage bins.

Flaco looked back over his shoulder before following and was surprised to see the pilot, Chase Coughlin, hanging in the manlock from 1-A, the "back porch," with an older, short-cropped man in Ossa & Pelion blue-and-black. The O&P man said nothing, but he held a cliputer in his left hand. Coughlin grinned and made what would have been a thumbs-up sign if he hadn't been upside down to Flaco.

The orientation was held in the bunkhouse, which occupied two entire bays of the Number Two tank. Here the walls were lined, not with lockers and bins, but with cubicles, each of which was open toward the center. Each cubicle contained an e-set and a v-hat and two personal lockers. In one, a Red crewman was rolling a sleeping bag into one of the lockers. Flaco eyed the cubicles with suspicion. Storage lockers for people . . .

He also noticed that the bays had been rigged out with ropes in an apparently chaotic fashion, but whether the space was always dressed this way or it had been done as a concession to the "bunnies" in Green Crew, Flaco did not know. He found himself a position where he could wind his arm around one of the ropes and noticed that, while the Green Crew tried with some success to align themselves toward a common "floor," the handful of Red Crew men who joined them floated any which way. Flaco wondered if he could ever get used to that. Here and there, free-floating mobile units the size of a soccer ball hovered in the bay. Their spherical skins were knobby with fixtures, lenses, and air jets.

The briefing was conducted by the same iron-haired man who had watched from the manlock. Wesley Bensalem was one of the four rotating project managers overseeing LEO. He was a solidly compact man, muscular and tight-faced, with hair cut forward over his brow, like a Roman emperor's. He gave the standard welcome-aboard speech, introduced the crew bosses, gave out billets and assignments, and laid down the rules and regulations. "We run a strict site here," he announced. "There will be no epithets or slurs. Keep your speech civil and polite. There are too many of us in too small a volume. If someone feels they need a little space, give it to them. This is no place for claustrophobes or agoraphobes, but you might notice that up here we don't have anything *but* claustros and agoras." There were a few uncertain laughs. Bensalem smiled—perhaps because so few had understood his jest. "What I mean is: all our space is either cramped inside these cans, or runs off to infinity in every direction. Nothing in between. It can get to anyone after a while. So be aware of that and cut your on-site coworkers a break. Second, you will consume nothing that alters your mind or your senses or your coordination. No alcohol or other drugs. Foul or offensive language warrants a fine, but drugs are grounds for immediate dismissal. And if the infraction is serious enough, we might not wait for the next Plank before we dismiss you.'' There was more nervous laughter, but Flaco noticed that none of the Red Crew joined in. They looked like a down-right grim lot. Flaco thought he might turn pretty grim himself after a couple of months under Bensalem.

''As for fighting and sex, I will not tolerate anything that interferes with the construction schedule. If you feel you just have got to have it out, and I'm talking about fighting now''—this time the laughter was full and genuine and Bensalem responded with a thin, tight smile—''bring it up with the crew bosses and we will arrange a formal fight— a duel, if you will—under carefully supervised conditions. As for sex—''

''Carefully supervised conditions! Right-o, mate.'' More laughter, which Bensalem waited out.

''I can't keep two consenting adults from consenting to whatever they damn well please. Just remember this. No one *owns* a woman. There is an on-site sex ratio of six-point-eight to one, so you will act with unfailing respect and you will always obtain permission beforehand. Force will be met with immediate and summary justice, but 'personal precautions' are your own responsibility. Any woman who becomes pregnant will be sent groundside and dismissed. Any man she names will likewise be sent groundside and his wages garnisheed for child care. Likewise, if any communicable disease is contracted. Personally''—and here he smiled coldly—''I recommend abstinence.''

This was greeted with a few boos and catcalls. ''I don't wonder he does,'' Tonio said *soto voce*. ''It don't look like he's checked the oil in a lot of years.''

Flaco shrugged. ''*No importa*. I will not betray Serafina.''

Sepp Bauer clapped him on the back, which sent him into a mild spin. ''Dot's gut,'' the German said. ''De ratio is now six-point-seffen to one.''

After the orientation there was a luncheon, consisting of Green Crew's ''confiscated'' food items. Most of it, Flaco learned, had been in unsuitable containers, anyway. He studied the drinking bulb he had been given and turned to Tonio.

"It has been a long time," he said in Spanish, "since I sucked on a baby's bottle."

Tonio was already at work. "Pretend it is a woman's nipple. Your experience should be more recent." He laughed.

Flaco looked around the crowded bay. "We are supposed to find our mentors an' become acquainted," he said in English.

Tonio shrugged. "There is always time for that. Where have they to go?" He regarded the bulb with a sigh. "Fruit punch," he said. "Who would try to smuggle fruit punch on board when the world is full of more interesting beverages?"

Flaco didn't answer him. "My mentor is a Russian named Pilov, but I don't know how to recognize him."

"Use statistics," Sepp suggested. "Move at random through the party and eventually you will find him. Probability is one-over-e."

"Or find *her*," said Tonio with a knowing look. "Perhaps you will be the lucky one-in-seven."

Flaco released his hold on the netting and kicked off gently from the wall. He sailed toward the other side of the bay where he saw a small knot of Reds. Head first. Halfway there, he gave thought to the coming impact and tried to execute the flip-over maneuver he had seen the more experienced hands perform so they would land on their feet. He couldn't quite bring it off, however, and wound up colliding sideways with the storage cabinets, netting, and two of the Reds.

"What was that?" he heard one of the Reds ask as he straightened Flaco out.

"Bunny hop," said the other.

"Aren't they cute when they do that?"

"Excuse me," Flaco said. "I'm looking for a rigger named Pilov, supposed to be my OJT instructor."

The first Red said, "That a fact?" He turned to his companion. "You wanna talk to this bunny, Rhys?"

"It's a dirty job, but someone's gotta do it, and I drew the short straw." With that, the first man kicked off, leaving Flaco with Pilov. Flaco searched for something to say.

"Your name is Rhys Pilov?" he said finally.

"Yeah. My da was an émigré Russian sailor and Ma was Welsh. And one or the both of them had a warped sense of humor." He smiled well enough, but there was an edge to his words. "Everyone gets one free laugh at my name. Second one costs. A lot."

Flaco knew when to change the subject. "The project boss, he soun' like a hard man."

"They call him the Rector," said a new voice. Flaco turned, but all he saw was one of the mobile spheres hovering nearby. He looked around for who had spoken, but no one was paying him any attention.

"Who said that?" he asked.

"Uncle Waldo," Rhys explained. He pointed to the sphere. Flaco looked again at the mobile.

"Welcome aboard," said the sphere.

Flaco turned to Pilov. "What is it, an A/S?"

Pilov wagged a thumb at the mobile. "It's not polite to talk in front of them as if they weren't there."

"Who are you calling an Artificial Stupid, bunny? I'm as human as you are."

A light dawned. Flaco pointed a finger. "You're virtchin'."

A pause; then. "Give the man a prize. But I'm telepresent, not virtching. The difference with teeping is that you guys claim to be the real world. Though you couldn't prove it by me."

"And they call you Uncle Waldo? Why?"

Another pause. "There's a whole crew of us, but there's no way for you on-sites to tell which of us is running what mobile or sessile. It saves time to call us all 'Uncle Waldo' than to find out who's on which channel."

"Paint a face on it?" suggested Pilov with the air of repeating a long-stale joke.

"What's a sessile?" asked Flaco.

"Hah-hah," said Uncle Waldo. Then, a moment later: "A sessile is a unit that can't move around. If I switch channels, I can be somewhere else—"

"—the public address system, for example—" said a voice in a speaker near Flaco's head.

"—but it bothers you bonebags if we do that too much," the sphere finished. "We can even virtch and hang out in the data-stacks. Anywhere, as long as it's in the network."

"You're not on-site yourself?"

"Nah," Pilov told him. "He's down below, along with all the other virtchuous types."

"There are some tasks that need to be done," Waldo said, "that don't pay the freight to lift a bonebag. Clerical, administrative, routine . . . Management'd teep the whole project if they could, but some work needs real-time reaction. When the time lag on the bounceback doesn't matter, they off-load the work onto a telecommuter."

"The time lag . . ."

Pause. "Speed of light transmission from the station down to the dustball and back. Depends on line-of-sight or how many relays have to hand it off. It's why I don't answer right away."

"Oh. I thought . . ."

"That I was a little slow, right? Yeah. A lot of people get that impression. They can't help it. It's subconscious. But I wanted to work on this space station more than anything I ever wanted in my life."

"But not enough to come up personally?" said Flaco.

The pause this time was longer than the bounceback could account for. Finally, the sphere said, "Look, bunny, you don't know me. There could be a lot of reasons I don't lift. I might be paraplegic. I might be bedridden. Or have a phobia about flying. I might have a two year old in the house here with me that I can't leave for six fucking months at a time. I might be in witness protection. You're an on-site mobile and I'm an off-site, but we're both working the project. Understood?"

"I didn't mean it that—" But the mobile shot away with a blast of compressed air that stung Flaco's face. Rhys shook his head.

"You shouldn't get Uncle Waldo mad at you," he said. "He's everywhere." He tugged on his lip as he looked after the departed sphere. "I wish he wouldn't talk that way, though."

"What way?" Flaco asked. He hadn't meant to suggest that the off-sites were more timid . . .

" 'Dustball,' " said Rhys. " 'Bunny.' You can't exactly say Waldo is a bunny; but he's not exactly an otter, either. He shouldn't come on talking like one. He hasn't earned it."

Flaco spent the first day in suit drill. There had been suit training at Pegasus Field, but it was a different matter without gravity. In fact, Flaco found everything a lot more difficult than he had expected. Rhys showed him how to sign out the equipment from the lockers in Number Three module. The stockroom clerk was Uncle Waldo, but evidently a different handler than the one Flaco had spoken to at the party, because he gave no sign of recognition.

His first trip outside, under Rhys's supervision, was a short one. When Flaco stepped out of the manlock, he held his breath and listened for the whistle of air that would tell him something was not sealed right. He had checked everything and, more importantly, Rhys had checked everything; but you couldn't *not* think about the possibility.

He hovered over a vast chasm, but felt no fear of falling. Up and down were missing. Earth was "down" in some sense; but when he managed to twist and bring the planet into view, he found that it was "above" him. *I'm flying above the world upside down,* he thought. He stared at the sparkling white and blue of the Earth, trying to make out the shapes of the land, to see if he was over New York or not; but the angle of view was too strange and, after a moment, he gave it up.

Rhys drilled him on suit control. When Flaco tried the

suit attitude jets, he fired too long and flew out to nearly the full length of his tether before he found the brake controls on the reel. Rhys told him what a fool he was because, if he hadn't been tethered, he'd be sailing off into the Big Empty right now; and while Flaco himself could be easily replaced, the rigger's suit was expensive.

Then they clipped a line to the cable running over to the Number Four tank, which was scheduled to be brought into the configuration next. "As long as I gotta wet-nurse you," Rhys told him, "we might as well get some real work done."

There were some Red Crew riggers on the tank attaching the omnidirectional rocket motors that would nudge the vessel into configuration. An electrician was on-site to make the connections and set the logics. He had Wendy McKenna in tow. Uncle Waldo was present, too: a larger, more rugged unit than the mobiles inside the station. He had a detachable trailer that carried the tooling and equipment the job needed. Uncle was the surveyor, supervising the positioning of the motors.

Rhys didn't let Flaco do anything except some of the manhandling required to position the motors to Uncle's satisfaction. Under normal circumstances, Flaco would have resented being relegated to an apprentice's task—he was a goddamn journeyman, thank you very much—but these were not normal circumstances, and Rhys had the power to downcheck his OJT rating. So Flaco swallowed his pride and did as he was told. The work was monotonous and repetitious—you mount one motor, you've mounted them all—and it was easy to forget that you were working in space. And that was the one thing you must never forget.

He also discovered how tiring zero-g vacuum work was. Everything that was moved had to be stopped; every motion had to be countered. Tools did not stay where you put them. Unless you were very, very careful when you let them go, you always gave them some residual velocity. Then you had to haul them back on their tethers—or you cursed yourself for not snapping the tether in place. Though he had not done much physical labor, Flaco found himself panting long before the end of the shift and his visor was steaming up from his breath. He was afraid his physical weakness would score against him, but Rhys said all bunnies were that way at first and that was why each one had a babysitter.

Afterwards, he hauled himself wearily down the guide wire to the bunkhouse. When he got there, he could tell which Green Crew members had been outside and which had not by counting the number of bodies racked out in their cubicles. *"¡Hola, panas!"* Flaco said when he spotted Sepp and Tonio among the other bunnies. Sepp was practicing laps across the twenty-five-foot interior of the bunkhouse, kicking off, twisting, and touching down on the far side, then sailing back while Tonio watched.

Each cubicle was a five-by-seven-foot box containing two color-coded storage lockers, a miniature A/V entertainment set, and a tethered sleeping bag that could be rolled up and stowed away. Eleven bunks, set head-to-toe, formed a ring around the interior hull, so that, lying in one, you had the disconcerting sight of other sleepers looking up at you. Eight such rings lined the walls of the two aft bays of Number Two Tank. It was not the most spacious accommodation that Flaco had ever had, but he had been packed into construction trailers that were a lot worse. The common space made up for things. Being in free fall, the entire volume— nearly 1,600 cubic feet—was available.

Flaco could not drop into his sack. He had to *pull* himself in. Up here, you even had to work at relaxing! It was all he could do to unzip his coverall. When he bent to tug his feet out, he found himself slowly spinning—the ice dancer effect, Rhys had called it. Flaco straightened out and the spinning stopped. At this rate, he would wear himself out trying to get to sleep . . .

Tonio pulled himself over to Flaco's bunk. "Oh, my poor Flaco," he said. "Never have you been more aptly named."

Flaco gave him the fig. "You look like you had an easy day of it," he said. "Relaxing inside in your shirtsleeves."

"He wishes he had shirtsleeves," said Sepp, touching

down beside Flaco. "Tonio learned a valuable lesson, today." He grinned at the Cuban and kicked off again. Flaco looked at Tonio, who looked resigned and held up an arm with an angry red scar along the back of the forearm.

"*¡Ay-yi!*" said Flaco. "What happened?"

The Cuban shrugged. "Molten metal does not flow properly here. And my clamshell was not tight."

"We were told so at Pegasus," Sepp said, making a brief stop on his lap. Tonio watched him go.

"I wish he would stop doing that. At Pegasus, he would jog every morning. Remember? At least that was outside and not inside our dormitory." He regarded his burn and touched it gently. "It is one thing for a man to tell you about something; another to experience it. It was very odd, my Flaco, to watch the metal and the gasses misbehave so."

Sepp touched down again. "The Bird rejected two of Tonio's welds."

"Did he?" Flaco said with sympathy.

"The X ray showed bubbles and voids," said Sepp, kicking off again.

"It's a common problem in zero-g welding," Tonio said. "So Antonov told me." Tonio ran a hand through his hair. "There were many such rejects today. It is a matter of learning the practice properly. I only wish a different NDT tech had checked my welds."

"Why is that?" Flaco asked.

"Because when I saw him again, the Bird had two skull-and-crossbones stenciled on his X-ray camera. I think he enjoys rejecting the work of others, Flaco."

"Ah, a critic, then."

"If I could have understood my 'mentor' better, these mistakes would not have happened. But he is Russian and barely able to speak the English . . ."

"All of the welding masters are Russian," said Sepp. This time when he alighted, he grabbed hold of the partition between Flaco's bunk and the next one over and planted Velcro slippers on the Stay-put pad. "This is exhilarated. Is that the right word? One flies like the eagle!"

"Or at least like the flamingo," said Tonio. "You are an unlikely eagle, my friend."

Sepp grinned. "So long as I make no more 'bunny hops,'" he said.

"Bunnies," said Tonio, with a shake of the head. "My instructor was as young as I am, yet he treated me like a child."

"Mine vass *younger* den I," said Sepp.

"Ah, but you are an old man beside us. Nearly thirty."

"Space makes you older," said Flaco. "I am twenty-two and Rhys is twenty-four; but in space you learn the care and caution of an old man, and so you become older than your years. Or you die and never become older at all."

Sepp grunted and looked around the bunkhouse. "I wonder how many of us will die?" he said in a conversational tone. He might have wondered about the weather.

"None of us," said Flaco, "if we look out for one another." He held out his hand and the other two grabbed it. Tonio chuckled.

"That is very careful and cautious of you, Flaco. You are aging before my very eyes." He pointed directly overhead. "My bunk is on the other side. It will be an odd thing, looking up from my bed to look down on yours. Do not play with yourself tonight, Flaco, lest your manhood fly across the room like a missile and strike me in the face."

Flaco laughed and gave Tonio a shove with his foot. Then he pulled himself into the sleeping bag without waiting to see if the push sent the Cuban all the way across or not.

INTERLUDE:

"Before the Hills in Order Stood . . ."

Forrest Calhoun inserted a doid stake into the socket he had just driven into the rock. A twist locked the stake in place and activated the doid on its tip. Small solar panels opened like a flower in bloom, and a pop-up window appeared in the upper-right corner of his visor with the doid's array number and a hash of gray static. Forrest jiggled the stake's laser and it searched back and forth until it found another stake in the network and established a handshake. The neural net A/S aboard *Bullard* integrated the signals into the rest of the array and the static in the popper reconfigured into a color close-up of Forrest himself. He grinned and crouched just a little so that he was looking directly into the pickup.

His helmet screen displayed a miniature Forrest, visor darkened against the sun, suit a ridiculous checkerboard of visibility, a backdrop of black rocks and blacker sky. *Damn. I'm really here.* The thought never ceased to astonish him. Jimbo Calhoun's little boy had come so far up in the world that he couldn't get any more "up" without using another world.

Forrest gathered his piton driver and and a clutch of sockets and doid stakes and moved on to the next location. Nacho had marked it with fluorescent orange. He found it on top of the long, low ridge he had dubbed the Great Wall of

China. Good view. A doid up there could monitor a fair chunk of real estate. Forrest jumped to the top of the ridge.

It took an effort to keep his feet planted. "Walking on air," he told himself, "if there was air to walk on." Gravity was weak on the Rock—not so much a force as a whimsical suggestion—and the hang time was enough to make every hotdog in the NBA explode with envy. By the same token, it was easy to get carried away and actually leap off the Rock entirely. Nacho had done that once already. Hell, a good sneeze would be enough for an orbital launch.

After planting another stake, he told the A/S to give him an overview of the coverage. The popper was replaced with a map of the asteroid's Dayside, overlaid with the grid that Nacho had surveyed during the first two days. About two-third's of the grid was colored in, indicating that one or more doids had a view of them. Blinking dots located him and his two companions. Mike was up at "Cabeza City" on the Headrock, setting up the power plant. Nacho was working his way down the "Big Rock Candy Mountains" toward the west end of the main body.

Forrest cleared his visor. Eyeballing down the long axis, he could make out the strobes from Nacho's suit. The little guy was hammering away like ol' John Henry, whacking and labelling specimens of surface rocks from a representative sample of grid elements. A second, smaller, and more difficult sample of subsurface rocks would be taken later. Forrest watched the geologist for a while. The Rock wasn't so big that that you couldn't see most of it from just one spot, but it was easy to wander out of sight—into a crater or over the astonishingly close horizon. Once the network of digital cameras was complete, the entire surface would be under surveilance. Until then, standing orders were: Always Stay in Sight.

"Calhoun." Krasnarov's voice on the suit comm interrupted Forrest's thoughts. "Your assistance is required."

Forrest sighed. One of his jobs was to assist the engineer "when needed"; but just once—just *once*—he would like to hear Krasnarov say, *I need your help.*

"On my way." Forrest bounded in long steps over the ragged surface of the asteroid. As he moved east, he had the faint and probably imaginary feeling that he was not only losing weight, but going uphill. Forrest weighed six grams at "Anchorhead." Because of the Rock's peculiar shape, he weighed five times less than that at "Cabeza City." On a sphere like the Earth, the center of gravity was always straight down, but on this celestial knockwurst, it could be behind you, too . . .

With every leap, Forrest studied the ground ahead with his shoulder lights. You had to watch your landings. The rock was rough and dark, and gleamed like knives where the sun struck it. There had never been wind or rain to dull those ragged edges. The lack of air set light and shadow all a-jumble—brightness punctuated by abrupt, hard shadows where ancient meteor impacts had created a miniature geography of ridges and basins. Even on Dayside there were scraps of night.

Krasnarov had the antenna mast assembled and laid out on the surface with its base near a socket bolted into the rock. The engineer's main project was to test the feasibility of generating power and smelting ore on-site, and Step One was to plug into the sun. Without rotation or atmosphere to screw things up, Krasnarov's solar array could harvest thirty-six kilowatt-hours per square meter all year long.

"Whatcha need?" Forrest asked.

"A fulcrum," Krasnarov said. "You stay here and make sure the mast goes into the socket while I raise the structure."

"You're the engineer," Forrest said genially; and if Krasnarov took that as a reminder of who was the *captain,* that was his problem.

When the Russian reached the far end of the mast, he raised it in an apparent display of superhuman strength. "Are you ready, Calhoun?"

Forrest knelt and grabbed the lower end of the mast. "Roger-dodger, you old codger."

"What?"

"Go ahead."

Krasnarov walked forward, angling the structure above his head. Forrest guided the butt end into the anchor socket and provided some additional leverage to help the engineer. On Earth, such an effort would have been unthinkable. Even on the moon, you'd have to think more than twice. But here, Krasnarov actually had to take care not to toss the whole structure off into space.

When the "flag raising" was done and the anchor bolts were driven home, Krasnarov inspected everything and made small adjustments to the guys aligning the structure. Finally, when he had satisfied whatever internal standard obsessed him, the Russian stood back and put his hands on his hips. "It's good," he decided.

"That's what God said on the sixth day," Forrest said. Krasnarov looked at him, though through the sun-darkened visor Forrest could see no hint of a face, let alone of an expression. If he thought the comparison fitting, he did not say.

"It is an accomplishment," the Russian said after a few moments of silence. "Or the first step toward an accomplishment. On-site power generation is something humanity has never done before in space. There is nothing amiss in taking pride in such an accomplishment."

"Hell, Mike. If we stop and pat ourselves on the back every time we do something no one else has done before, we'll break our fool arms."

Okay, so it wasn't the funniest line Forrest had ever delivered, but Mike could at least have groaned. Instead, he said, "After raising the mast, a few moments' rest is called for. If I choose to use those moments to reflect on humanity's accomplishments and you use them to make jokes, the time is not wasted in either case."

Though there was no mistaking which case the engineer regarded as a better way not to waste time . . . But then Mike saw nothing funny in the odd grasshopper shape of the asteroid, nor in the fanciful names Forrest had given some of the grid elements.

"I have a thought, Captain," Krasnarov said.

"Good. There's another accomplishment to take pride in." Krasnarov, he had noted, was unfailingly correct. The man never called the mission commander "Calhoun", and never called the engineer's assistant "captain." Either Krasnarov thought Forrest was two different people, or Krasnarov himself was two different people.

The Russian turned and indicated the Japanese probe that hovered on the horizon like a man peeping over a fence. "The robot reached its destination and has maintained its station since December. I think its onboard systems are working, and only the comm link is bad. If so, we may be able to repair it."

"Or it may be deader than a doornail ... Yeah, that's good thinking, Mike. I'll contact Deep Space and see what Pac-Orbita has to say."

"I could use my upcoming rest period to inspect the mechanism. There may be an obvious malf—a bent strut or a disconnected cable—something easily fixed."

"You'll use your rest period to rest."

"I will be resting. It is only a short stroll over there. I will play tourist."

If Forrest didn't know that Mike Krasnarov was humor-challenged, he would have thought the Russian had his tongue deeper in his cheek than a chipmunk. "Can't stop a man from sight-seeing," Forrest agreed.

"Good." Krasnarov turned aside and picked up a parabolic dish, which he hooked to a cable dangling from the top of the mast. "Now, I have work to finish. And this is *your* scheduled rest period."

How Mike had gotten the conviction that Forrest needed these constant reminders, Forrest didn't know, but he had long ceased responding to the not-so-subtle subtext.

If Krasnarov annoyed Forrest because he took things too seriously, Nacho annoyed him by not taking them seriously enough. Each day, the geologist's explorations took him farther west along the Dayside, closer to the enormous crater on the back end, until the inevitable happened. The A/S belched like a ship's foghorn and the Voice said, "Personnel approaching edge of visual field."

Forrest was floating high above the world, off-loading a ram pod that he had brought in with *Bullard*. He checked the terrain map on his visor display and saw that the "personnel" in question was Nacho. Any farther, and he would be out of sight of everyone, including the A/S. Forrest cussed under his breath. The geologist knew the rules as well as the next guy. Not that there were that many "next guys" around here.

He opened the command link to Mendes's suit. "Nacho, old buddy, where you headed?"

"I finished today's specimen collection, so I thought I'd inspect the Cave and see how to include it in my sampling. It is the secondmost interesting feature on the planetoid."

Forrest didn't think that wasn't saying much. But then, Nacho had different interests than Forrest did. Nacho could no more *not* poke his nose into that crater than Mike Krasnarov could break into spontaneous tap dancing. And Nacho had a point. Since no one expected the hole in the tail end of the asteroid, it hadn't been included in any of their work assignments. Well, that was why you sent people instead of robots.

"Okay," he said, "but wait until I get there. Remember the line-of-sight rule."

"I will only be inside for a few moments."

"That's what the salesman told the waitress. You wait. That's a direct order." He dogged the supply hatch on the ram pod—not that he expected burglars, but things had a way of drifting off if you didn't watch them—and rode the tether down to the supply cache by Anchorhead, where he picked up a doid stake. Then he spewed toward the back end of the Rock. It was faster than playing frog through the Big Rock Candy Mountains between Anchorhead and Pancake Flats. When he touched down again he found Nacho waiting by the lip of the crater at the west end of the asteroid.

Nacho called it "the Cave." Forrest called it "the Anus."

Mike Krasnarov called it "the crater at the west end of the asteroid."

"I didn't think it would matter," Nacho said as Forrest set a new doid stake in place and turned the power on. One of the solar collector petals stuck and did not unfold until Forrest tapped it with his forefinger. The "flower" not only collected power to operate the stake and the laser links to the rest of the network, but shaded the doids just below it so they would not be blinded by direct sunlight.

"Rules always matter," came Krasnarov's voice over the suit link. Forrest frowned. The Russian should be too busy to eavesdrop; but when he raised the doid view of Cabeza City on his visor screen popper, he saw that the other was indeed working on the power plant.

"This rule has a reason," Forrest said. "The surveilance system still has blind spots—and your Cave is one of them. If anything happened while you were inside, Mike and I wouldn't even know about it until it was maybe too late."

"What could happen?"

"Son, if I knew that I wouldn't worry so much."

The geologist didn't make a further issue of it. He was wrong and he knew it. Nacho was okay, but his attitude toward rules was the mirror image of Krasnarov's. *So, on the average, we're reasonable . . .*

Nacho guided himself around the lip of the crater and inside. Forrest followed, keeping one eye on the doid view of Krasnarov at Cabeza City, another eye on the view from his latest stake, and the third eye on where he and Nacho were going. They wouldn't be too far in, he noted, before they were off the grid again. The doids could see a fair distance, but they couldn't see around corners.

Forrest switched his receiver to monitor the geologist's notebook.

"—complete absence of a crater wall or evidence of ejecta elsewhere on the Rock. But gravity is so weak that most of the debris is thrown entirely off the body, where it co-orbits. Crater appears to be deeper than first thought. Sunlight blocked from more than the first twenty meters, so the bottom—that is, the far end—is obscured in shadows. Note: lighting needed inside the Cave to explore deeper. Unusual—perhaps unprecedented—for a crater to be deeper than it is wide. Feeble gravity . . . Maybe melted rock from the original impact froze before it could sag into a cup.''

As they moved farther into the Cave, they passed from light to shadow and the views on Forrest's helmet snapped off abruptly. Space was all blacks and whites. There was no dimming out. No twilight. He and Nacho played their suitlights off the dark walls. The rock face resembled dirty Styrofoam, smooth but pockmarked. It curved away from under their feet and closed in again over their heads. Forrest ran one of his lights around the circumference. It was hard to judge distance without any landmarks; but the Cave still looked as wide as it had at the mouth—about ten meters. The asteroid's center of mass lay ahead of them, so walking into the Anus had the slight feel of walking straight downhill.

Which meant walking out would be walking uphill.

''This is far enough in for now,'' Forrest announced.

The Brazilian protested. ''We haven't reached the far end yet.'' His lights probed down the hole, failed to find its bottom.

''We're already farther in than I'd like to be without full lighting. We've both put in a full day's work already and I'd rather not have to climb out of here on my spare oxy tank. How much can you really learn by shining your suitlight around at random? Wait'll we develop a game plan and get some floods in here.''

Mendes took a few more steps and swept his beam through the darkness ahead. He sighed and turned back. ''You're right.''

''I don't have to be right. I'm captain, remember? That wasn't a suggestion.''

Mendes did not turn around. ''Then, would you *like* a suggestion?''

Forrest hesitated only a moment. "Go ahead."

"Don't remind us so often that you are the captain. We haven't forgotten."

"I was joshing."

"It may be a cultural thing. I don't always know when you're joking."

"*Et tu*, Nacho?"

"Let's sit and rest awhile."

"I lost the doid view from Cabeza City when we entered the Anus. I won't know if Mike gets into trouble."

"Forrest, of the three of us, who is the least likely to get into trouble? And the rules say we should rest every so often. Low gravity work is more tiring than it appears, and—"

"All right. All right. We'll rest a few minutes." Forrest waited for the Brazilian to rejoin him.

"A fascinating body," Nacho said.

"That's what my last girlfriend told me."

The geologist ignored the remark. "I mean, in the first place it is a Swanwick body—a smaller asteroid fused to a larger one. But then, to find this Cave . . . The striker would have had to come directly out of the west, unless the Rock has shifted orientation since then."

"In the same orbit?" Forrest pursed his lips. "Not if it was traveling fast enough to burrow *this* hole. Its greater velocity would have put it higher above the sun." Forrest had played chaser and target on enough orbital rendezvous to have the velocity/altitude duality sink into his bones. Move faster equals climb higher equals fall behind. "Must have been crossing orbits."

Nacho sounded doubtful. "Then the striker would have hit at an angle, and the Rock is not spinning."

"Maybe it used to spin and the striker is what stopped its clock. You'll know more when you locate the remnants down at the bottom. Riddle me this, though. How come the walls in here are so smooth compared to the surface?"

He saw Nacho's glove rub the rock under them. "If I had to guess—and I do—I would say that the molten rock from the impact froze in place. Since then, it has not weathered.''

Forrest looked at him. ''Weathered . . . ?''

The Brazilian chuckled. '' 'Steel Rain,' '' he said, quoting the popular song title. ''Micrometeor 'rain' weathers these bodies all the time. One of the moonrocks—from Apollo 11—had an impact crater on it two microns wide. The mark of a 'snowflake' travelling *very* fast. Celestial erosion. The Cave is shielded from the 'rain,' but . . .'' Nacho's lights traversed the cave wall. ''Yes. You see those pockmarks? Those are small impact craters. And there. That is a sizable one. Do you see it? Probably an object the size of a grapefruit, one whose angle of entry was shallow enough to carry it this far in before striking the wall.''

''That cave mouth is a mighty small bull's-eye, son. Even for grapefruits.''

''Ah, but many eons of opportunity, Forrest.''

Forrest grunted. He ran his light under their feet, tracing the path of their footprints in the faint dust created by microstrikes. No one had ever made footprints here until this moment. Not since . . . Not since the crater was first formed, but when was that? ''Will this hole eventually fill up with 'rain'?''

''Eventually,'' Nacho said with sardonic humor. ''Or the Rock may be . . . pummeled? Yes, pummeled into a sphere. Each strike knocks pieces loose, and any debris that is not entirely ejected settles toward the center of mass.'' He pointed inward, toward the midpoint of the asteroid. ''It may take billions of years—and a large collision will probably destroy the Rock long before—but the cosmos will try to 'knead' the Rock into a proper spherical shape.''

''You mean a ball of rubble?''

''No. Sintering would fuse it into a solid object. Over time.''

''Hunh. I guess the unchanging face of deep space ain't so unchanging.''

''No, it isn't. Split Rock, in the Moon's Taurus-Littrow Valley, was knocked loose from the southern massif by a meteor two hundred million years ago and tumbled to the valley floor. Oh, there is change, *senhor;* but don't hold your breath waiting for it. These features may last for millions, for tens of millions of years.''

'' 'Before the hills in order stood/Or Earth received its frame . . .' ''

"Excuse me?"

Forrest scraped the ground with his boot. "An old hymn Ma used to sing." There was a line in the rock there, a score that ran off straight as a rule. He scuffed it some more. "Lookee here." He followed it with his searchlight. It seemed to corkscrew around the inside surface of the Cave.

Nacho knelt and touched it with his gauntlet. "It looks like the track of a small object that entered the Cave and skimmed around the wall instead of impacting." The geologist played his lights on the score line and bent closer. Then he studied the unscored rock.

In the circle of light, Forrest saw several other gouges running parallel to the first. "Must have been a whole meteor *shower,*" he commented. *Talk about "Steel Rain"* . . . "I'd've hated to be inside this barrel when that load of buckshot blew in." Come to think of it, he'd've hated to be inside with just one rock bouncing around off the walls— snowflake *or* grapefruit. The chance of something finding that portal during the few minutes they were down in here were mighty slim, but he couldn't stop himself from glancing toward the mouth of the Cave.

And his heart nearly stopped when he saw two lights coming straight toward him.

"Jesus!" he said.

"No," said Krasnarov's voice over the intersuit channel. "Only me."

"What the hell are you doing here?" He was angry with Krasnarov for having scared him.

"I discovered that I was not under safety observation, as required by your procedures. You have been out of contact longer than the allowed maximum. Had anything happened, the A/S would have been unable to . . ." He paused and looked around. Forrest could hear his grunt of surprise.

Listen to Mr. Rule Book . . . Forrest had been a civilian test pilot, but he had run into plenty of military Johnnies back in the old days who walked around with a rule book stuck up their ass. "What can I say, Mike, but 'oops.'"

"Out here, 'oops' might be the last thing you say."

Forrest had no retort to that one, since Mike was dead right. "Let's blow this joint. Nacho? Let's go." The Cave was a larger stucture than they had thought at first. It certainly warranted a major rev to the work plan, which they would discuss during the end-of-shift debriefing aboard *Salyut*. He wondered how a meteor could have driven so deep without cracking the Rock into itty-bitty pieces. Maybe the headrock was the perpetrator, and it had bored all the way through and popped out the other side before coming to a stop. He laughed. *That* scenario probably violated a whole lot of physics.

"Come on, Nacho. I said, let's go."

The geologist was hunkered down over the groove in the cave wall. He turned to face them. As his visor came into line with Forrest's suit searchlights, it automatically darkened; but before it turned black, Forrest glimpsed a badly puzzled face.

"Something is wrong," he said.

"What?" Krasnarov said, "What do you mean?"

"The Cave. It is too cylindrical. It has been bothering me since we entered. Craters are almost always hemispherical sections."

Forrest shrugged. "So, this one is different. You said the light gravity . . ."

"And when I look closer, the rock does not appear to have melted and refrozen. There should be bubbles from the oxygen and other gasses that boiled out. Forrest . . . Captain. I do not think this is a natural formation."

Krasnarov said, "Ridiculous!"

"This is not an impact crater, but a bore; and these grooves are the markings of some sort of excavation."

"An excavation," Krasnarov said. "By whom? When? For what purpose?"

"I don't know," the geologist said. "You want answers, and all I have are questions. Whoever . . . Whatever dug this tunnel, it was a very long time ago."

" 'Before the hills in order stood . . .' " Forrest whispered. He played his light around the walls. Could it be true? *Could it?*

"Your conjecture is absurd, Mendes," Krasnarov insisted. "If you do not understand how an impact could have made this cavity, the deficiency may be in your understanding, not in the cavity. There is some natural explanation. If the interior of the Rock was of a different, more volatile material, it might have vaporized when struck, leaving this shell behind."

"Now who is absurd, *Engineer?*"

Krasnarov shrugged off the reminder of expertise. "And your knowledge is based on a sample of . . . how many asteroids?"

"Plus the study of a great many meteorites!"

"All of which were superheated passing through the Earth's atmosphere; so if they contained such material, it was gone before whatever fragments were left touched ground. A volatile inner core might explain why the Tunguska Object exploded."

"I am *certain*—"

Forrest grunted and intervened before the argument could go further. "So was the preacher, Nacho; but do you have anything resembling *proof*?"

Nacho remained firm. "I know it!"

Forrest considered that. The idea that this hole had been dug out by unknown beings unknown millenia ago for purpose or purposes unknown was . . . Exciting. Intriguing. Daunting. But just a *trifle* unsubstantiated. This was neither the time nor the place for an extended discussion. "Okay," said Forrest, "we'll work up a plan of study. From here on everybody keep an eye out for anything unusual. But we don't tell Deep Space yet. I don't want this expedition to look foolish in front of the whole world, just because we saw something we wanted to see."

Nacho turned abruptly and bounced past them. Forrest and Mike followed, but not too closely. Leave the little geologist his space. He was too excited now to listen. Wait awhile and the man's easy-going personality would reassert itself. Then they could discuss the hypothesis more objectively.

Krasnarov spoke over the engineering channel. "A word, Captain."

Forrest took the cue and cut Nacho out. He turned to face the engineer. "What?"

"Dr. Mendes is overwrought."

"Yeah. Well. 'It's been a hard day's night.' "

"He may need rest. His work has required more physical exertion than yours, or even mine. As you said, he saw what he wanted to see."

"I'll consider your advice, Mike."

"Good." Krasnarov broke contact and leapt like a gazelle after Mendes. Forrest watched the Russian pause in the circular mouth of the Cave to gaze momentarily at the starry void beyond. Mighty Mishka, Explorer of Worlds. But not so mighty if someone else had pithed an asteroid millions of years before his ancestors had even swung down from the trees. If Nacho had seen what he wanted to see, then Iron Mike Krasnarov had not seen what he did not want to see.

So, on the average . . . Forrest turned and looked down the gun-barrel length of the crater. The borehole. On the average, what in hell *had* they seen?

Themselves, maybe.

7.

Fish in a Barrel

Stepping into Gaea Biotech's New Orleans facility was like stepping out of doors. The reception area was an atrium, filled with miniature trees and colorful flowers and infused with delicious fruity fragrances and the earthy smell of loam and peat. A skylight prism scattered the sunlight and lent everything a soft, unearthly hue. Away from the window, a fountain bubbled into a *faux* pond full of water lillies, hyacinths, and darting goldfish. *A forest glade,* Mariesa thought as she and Zhou Hui stepped inside. Rustic, wooden chairs and a table with the usual technical journals were tucked into one corner. A cardinal on the branch of a dwarf sycamore cocked its head at them before flitting to a more remote perch.

The receptionist was a live human being—a welcome touch in a world where visitors often confronted only a telephone and a plant directory. "May I help you?" The young woman who stepped into the "glade" had broad features and straight black hair. She dressed casually and carried a brown-and-black house cat tucked in her arms. To all appearances, she was just out strolling in the woods. Mariesa had to look carefully before she marked the earclip and the thin-filament, fiber-op throat mike.

Mariesa took the offered hand. "I'm Mary Gorley," she said—the name she used when she wished to be incognito.

"From Corporate. I'm here to see Correy Wilcox and Wallace Coyle. This is Zhou Hui, my assistant."

Hui bobbed her head in acknowledgement and adjusted the lightly tinted, wire-frame glasses she wore. Her diminutive stature and delicate features gave the illusion of utter fragility, and the computer that hung from her right shoulder might have weighed nearly as much as she did. But the fragility was a lie. Hui knew martial arts for which Mariesa did not even know the name, and there was not an object in the room that she could not use as a weapon.

. The receptionist spoke *sotto voce* and then listened for a moment before nodding. "Mr. Coyle has already arrived and is waiting for you on the jump pad."

"The jump pad?" Mariesa finally spotted the receptionist's desk, artfully hidden among the foliage. The sight of the monitors, keyboards, and disk drives were a relief, in a way. Correy ran an interesting shop, but Mariesa had not thought the receptionist spent all her time smelling the roses and waiting for visitors.

"Dr. Wilcox has 'gone fishing.' "

From her expression, Mariesa took the phrase to be a common jest at Gaea. "Very well. Do I need to sign in somewhere?"

"No. Your name and voice-print were recorded and time-stamped. Ms. . . . Zhou, is it? Would you mind repeating your name and affiliation for the computer?"

"Certainly," Hui said, enunciating clearly. "Zhou Hui. VHI Corporate. Was that sufficient?" Hui's smile reduced half the human race to jelly, but the receptionist was in the wrong half.

"Thank you, very much. Do you need an escort to the jump pad?"

"No, thank you," said Mariesa. "I know the way."

The receptionist shook hands with them again and hoped they would enjoy their visit before she vanished like a wood nymph. On their way through the inner doors, Mariesa said, "I like Correy's 'log-in' procedure. We should consider using it at corporate headquarters."

Zhou Hui, who wore her own earclip and throatmike, nodded. "I have already whispered into the system here and downloaded the relevant file into a viral quarantine drive at Wessex, along with a note to the staff there."

"Excellent, Ms. Zhou. You always anticipate my needs."

"Having the corporate override password helps." Hui cocked her head and listened to her earclip. "The word is going out over Gaea's intranet that Chairman van Huyten is on-site."

Mariesa sighed ruefully. She hated being fussed over. "The receptionist recognized me."

"No, the voice recognition A/S had your voiceprint on file and flagged it."

Mariesa sighed and shook her head. "It's getting harder and harder to be sneaky, these days."

The jump jet on the roof was a Daedalus *Flying Carpet,* an executive model. Mariesa found Wallace Coyle standing beside it, chatting with the pilot. Wallace was smooth-featured and overweight in a pleasant sort of way. Like so many others that Mariesa knew, he smiled a great deal; but on Wallace it was always genuine. She squeezed his hand warmly.

"Wallace, how have you and Georgia been? How's Aurora Ballistic doing these days?"

The chubby black man grinned. "Fine and fine, as if you didn't know."

"Actually, I'm afraid Prometheus has grown too big for me to keep abreast of all the details."

"Not like the old days, hey?" Wallace stood aside to let her board the jet. Mariesa paused and looked at the pilot.

"I take it we are flying out to Gaea's fish farm . . . ?"

The pilot nodded and touched the bill of her cap. "Yes, ma'am. Triton 3. Dr. Wilcox jumped out this morning for a meeting with project management. It's not very far."

"No, of course not." Mariesa climbed aboard. The *Flying Carpet* model was a typical commuter jump jet. Twelve rows of seat, two on one side, one on the other. Not much more that a flying toothpaste tube. She found herself an aisle seat about halfway back and Wallace placed himself across the aisle from her. Zhou Hui took a seat in the front row, giving them some privacy.

After they were fastened in, the louvres on either side of the fuselage opened and Mariesa glanced out the window into the twin nacelles on the fan deck. The fan blades, covered with thousands of microscopic flaps, looked almost like feathers. While she watched, the lifters spun up and vanished into a curiously undulating blur. Microprocessors in each shafthead adjusted the MEMS flaps, continually altering the blade shape to compensate for turbulence. Hushprops, they were called. Mariesa could remember how noisy the first experimental jump jets had been.

The hum increased and the hoverjet rose slowly from the roof. Mariesa turned toward the aisle to avoid the view, and gripped the armrests firmly with both hands.

"I suppose you already heard," Wallace said casually, as if he did not notice how the plane wobbled as it rose. "Sky Watch found another NEO. Passed within two hundred kiloklicks of Earth last week."

The pilot chose that moment to phase over to horizontal flight. Jumpers always dipped a little when they traded off the lift from the fans to the wing surfaces, producing a momentary, giddy feeling of weightlessness. Mariesa sucked in her breath and her grip on the armrests grew tighter.

But the feeling in her stomach did not go away even after the flight stabilized. Another Near Earth Object? There were too many already! The sky was filled with grapeshot. "Details?" She whispered, so as to not distract Hui, who was chatting with the copilot.

"Asteroid 2009PB. Pasadena found it two days ago. I read the notice in SkyWatch's newsgroup. You didn't see it?"

"I have not had much net time lately. You say it passed us a *week* ago?"

Wallace nodded. "Hard to spot those suckers." His grin seemed wildly inappropriate. Did he not realize what he had said? That the blow could have fallen without warning? Mariesa sat back in her seat and took deep breaths.

"How . . . large was it?" she managed.

"JPL estimates ten to fifteen meters on the long axis. Don't worry, Mariesa, it would have broken up and burned in the atmosphere . . ."

Don't worry, he said. She would have the nightmare again tonight. She always had the nightmare when she learned of another NEO.

"Is something wrong?" Wallace asked.

The nightmare was always the same. It varied only in the exact point at which she awoke. "No. No. Only . . . you know how I feel about the subject." Wallace did not know a tenth of how she felt. She had kept her terror locked away, and only Keith and Barry had been given the key. "The Tunguska Object burned up in the atmosphere, too," she reminded him, "but with enough explosive force to flatten an area the size of New York City." Her whisper must have grown strident, because Hui glanced briefly her way.

"I know, Mariesa," Wallace said quietly. "I know. That's why we started Prometheus, remember?"

Mariesa forced herself to relax, forced herself to ignore the adrenaline rush. She took a deep breath, knowing how irrational her fear was, yet unable to quiet it. She gave Wallace a grateful smile. Wallace, at least, recognized the danger; even if he did take things too calmly.

It was ironic, when you came down to it, that the media called her the Moon Lady when she felt so little interest in space flight itself. SSTOs, solar power satellites, power beaming . . . Certainly, she could appreciate the intrinsic worth of such projects—their potential had drawn in the hard-nosed likes of Chris, Dolores, Heinz—but they were only a means to an end. If she had an obsession, it was not with "exploring space."

"The reason behind the reasons," Keith had called it, though Keith, like others, thought space flight worthwhile for its own sake, too. "I just cannot help but wonder," she said to Wallace, "what if, when *it* comes, Prometheus is still unfinished?"

No need to explain what *it* was. "We will know 'neither the day nor the hour,' " Wallace told her. "All we can do is keep our lamps lit, our eyes on the night, and our hope in the hollow of His hands. And our powder dry. But, remember," Wallace added, "nothing is likely to come our way for thousands of years."

Mariesa straightened in her seat and looked resolutely forward. She deliberately untensed her hands from the seat. "Yes. Silly to worry so much."

Triton Number Three, anchored to the sea floor five miles off the Louisiana coast, was a wagon wheel afloat in the water—a wagon wheel that covered five acres. Barrel cages, two hundred feet long and forty-five feet in diameter, jutted spokelike from the central concrete and steel platform hub. The SPP dome and steel tubing flashed against the waves while the pilot circled. An ocean-thermal pylon beside the central hub marked the power plant. Tritons Numbers One and Two had been built around old oil rigs. This was the first station designed from scratch strictly for mariculture.

The jump jet switched to VTOL mode and hovered over the top-deck bull's-eye, cutting off Mariesa's view. The plane settled like a leaf. Men rushed from shelters along the margin of the deck to secure the plane with cables. Only then did Mariesa release her breath . . . and the seat's armrests. Flying had always made her nervous, but lately it seemed to be growing worse.

Correy Wilcox was waiting for them on the deck when they climbed out. He wore a bright green windbreaker emblazoned with the Gaea double helix. The sea breeze blew strong and cold, whipping Mariesa's clothing like a line of pennants. The wind was hard enough to rip the words from her lips and fling them to sea—to light on puzzled ears in Biloxi, she fancied. Zhou Hui held onto the railing of the jet's stairs. The wind seemed strong enough to blow her away. "Let's get below!" Correy's shout came to her ears as a whisper. She followed Correy to the control tower at the northwest corner of the deck, where gangways led up to the tower and down to the lower decks. The interior was painted in cheerful greens and yellows.

Out of the wind now, Mariesa paused for breath. "How can the Gulf be so cold in August?" asked Mariesa.

Correy shook his head. "There's a tropical storm brewing. It always seems colder in a blow. When it's calm, you can get a damn fine tan."

Mariesa, who preferred tans acquired on beaches of fine, white sand, nodded without speaking. She could not imagine sunbathing on the jump deck of a mariculture station. "We could have met in your offices in New Orleans," she said.

Correy shrugged as he shucked off his windbreaker. "Ah, you know how it is. A problem blows up and no one can handle it except the top boss. Then, when you get there, everything's No Big Deal, because no one wants to look incompetent. Arnaud should've handled it himself; but I didn't know that when I left, so . . . Here we are." His two aides vanished belowdecks. "And besides," he added when they were out of earshot, "it's less likely that anyone is listening."

Mariesa glanced at Hui, who had pulled her earclip and throatmike from her computer satchel and plugged in. Hui shook her head, a brief movement, but one that Correy caught. He grinned.

"How small does Werewolf make his mops, these days?"

Hui held up her left hand. "Do you like my ring?" she asked.

Correy took her hand and studied the stone. He shook his head. "Will stuffed a mop *and* a microprocessor into *that?* I'm impressed."

"You ought to be," Mariesa said. "There is a radio link to Hui's portable in there, too."

Correy shook his head again. "I never understood the fuss that Chris and Will made over magswitches and spin transistors. Guess that shows why I'm not in electronics.''

"Magtronics, they're calling it nowadays," Wallace said. "I just bought one of those new Kiwi desktops from Lobster Mag-Tron? Has the power of an old-time Cray. Next year it'll be half the price and half the size; but, hey! I gotta be me.''

The meeting room on C-Deck was hexagonal with a matching table in its center. The middle of the table was a sprit level with crosshairs. "So I can tell when the discussions are on the level," Correy joked when he pointed it out to them. Each of the walls was pixied, relaying end-on views of the six barrel cages. Five of the barrels teemed with fish streaming toward them on one side and away on the other. The door through which they had entered was centered on the empty one. "Clever," said Wallace, stepping closer. "Is this real time, or a recording?''

"Real time. Arnaud just harvested a quarter million pounds of redfish out of Number Three spoke. He's going to seed it with cod fingerlings from the clone vats down in 'the sphere.' See that central pipe that goes down the long axis? That dispenses high-protein food pellets eighty times a day.''

"Why cod?" asked Wallace. "Do they grow fast?''

"Not particularly," Correy admitted. "Redfish mature to market size in twelve to eighteen months, and mahi-mahi grows to five pounds in only five months. Those are our biggest moneymakers. Still, there's always a market for the traditional cod, and wild supplies have been spotty ever since the Marine Mammal Protection Act.''

Hui had been setting up her equipment. She glanced at Correy. "Really? Why?''

Correy spread his hands. "Without the annual cull, the harp seal population exploded. Along with other predators. Pretty much depleted the fisheries off the Labrador coast over the next decade, which then led to the seal population itself crashing a few years later. Classic lynx-and-hare process; any competent ecologist could have predicted it.''

"I thought it was overfishing that did it," Hui said.

Correy laughed. "Oh, that, too. It got so bad in the Banks that if you cast your net in the water you'd haul in four Japanese and a Norwegian for every cod. Yeah, that old camel was carrying a lot of straws."

"Do you have any problems with predators here in the Gulf?" Wallace asked.

"I'll show you the trophy room after the meeting. This place is Fiddler's Green for top feeders. All that prey out there, swimming around . . . The sharks are brutal, but dumber'n a stone. The mammals, though . . . they're pretty sharp. We had a sea lion once come right up to a spoke on Number Two—that's the one off Santa Teresa in California—and *suck* fish right out through the netting. No fooling. Just like through a sieve; redfish puree. That was before we installed the fiberglass 'pike wall' and trained the dolphins to act as guard dogs."

Mariesa seated herself at the table and waited patiently for Correy and Wallace to finish playing tour guide and tourist. She watched the mahi-mahi in the wall directly opposite her seat race toward her, turn sharply just before they seemed about to smash into the meeting room itself, then race away. Around and around in such a hurry, but never getting anywhere. Well, it wasn't as if a fish ever had an appointment to keep; still, she sometimes felt the same sense of going around in circles herself.

Wallace got her attention. "Did you know Correy powers this place through ocean thermal?" he asked. "Uses the temperature difference between the surface water and the deeps to run a turbine. You see, the ammonia boils at surface . . ."

"I know, Wallace." Mariesa sought to keep the impatience from showing, and failed. "The basic technology was proven out eighty years ago. Can we get down to business?"

Wallace and Correy exchanged glances. Then Wallace eased into the seat by Mariesa's left and Correy took the one directly opposite, consciously or not, placing distance between them. Correy twined his fingers together and stretched his arms, not quite cracking his knuckles; then he rested them on the table.

"All right, Mariesa. It's been a long day for me. What was it you wanted to talk about?"

"The Donaldson Initiative."

Correy nodded, unsurprised. "Yeah, I thought so. Have you decided which way you want to go?"

Mariesa shook her head. "I'm still sounding out the options and listening to arguments. I believe that both of you are in favor of it."

Correy sat back and threw an arm over the seat back. "Do you?" He was dressed casually, in an open-necked sports shirt. His broad face sported a ruddy hue that was not quite a tan and not quite a burn. With his easy grin and his light athletic build, he might have been a professional golfer or, given the background of the pixwalls, a sports fisherman. "I thought you heard all this back in July."

"The situation is dynamic. Besides, I want to see each of you individually—" a nod to Wallace—"or nearly so."

"Divide and conquer, eh?"

"You really ought to shed that cynicism of yours, Correy. It is hardly charming."

"But useful. I've been called a lot of things. 'Profitable.' Never 'charming.' "

"Correy," said Wallace Coyle, "we're the inner circle. You, me, and Mariesa. We're the only ones who understand the real purpose of Prometheus; so we're the only ones who can give her advice informed by our fifty-year horizon and ultimate goal."

"More than fifty, if you work the probabilities. But . . ." He held his hands up, palms out. "I know. I know. The Mississippi had two consecutive 'hundred-years' floods not very long ago. Probabilities are only meaningful *a priori*. *A postiori* . . . well, *a postiori* means you get it in the butt."

"SkyWatch discovered a new NEO last week," Wallace contributed.

Correy chuckled. "That's a funny phrase. 'A new NEO . . .' Yeah, I heard about that. Small potato, though."

"Small potatoes mean big potatoes, Correy," Mariesa insisted. "The big ones are just less frequent. Earth took three 'big' hits during the twentieth century: Tunguska in 1908, the Amazon around 1930, and Siberia in 1947. They found more than a hundred tons of debris on that last one. *And those are only the ones we know about.* 'If it wasn't seen, it didn't happen.' Three-quarters of this planet is ocean. Who knows how many strikes there were that no one witnessed? The Micronesia Bolide in February '94 was one hundred kilotons—about five Hiroshimas on the city-killer scale—and all the people on the ground saw was a flash in the sky 'brighter than the Sun.' Had that bolide been a little bigger or been traveling a little faster—"

"But it wasn't and it wasn't. Don't get me wrong, Mariesa. I'm with you. The threat is real, and worth acting on. But we won't convince people by spinning scare stories and hypotheticals."

Mariesa forced herself to remain calm. It always happened this way. She always became a little too agitated when the subject turned to meteors. *Correy's right,* she told herself. *It's a low probability.* But another part of her mind—the one that had seen that streak of light in the sky so many years ago—whispered subversively, *but it could be tomorrow* . . . "Very well, Correy. What is your point?"

The president of Gaea studied his hands. "First of all, I *don't* support Donaldson's initiative."

"Eh? But I thought . . ."

"I don't oppose it, either. It's a nonissue. I don't think he can pull it off. Too many frogs have to jump, and not all of them want him to kiss them. I do think we can *use* him for our own purposes. Mariesa, you've always made an issue about 'not being ready when the time comes.' Well, here's a way to get something in place right now."

"Donaldson plans to dump scrap metal on the Balkans. How does that help us?"

"Simple. Your cooperation comes at a price. Do you remember those battlefield lasers? The ones they didn't use in the Gulf War?"

"Sure," said Wallace with the enthusiasm of a techno-junkie. "Stand-off weapons. Fry a tank at fifty miles. So what? We're not in this to fight Donaldson's war for him."

"Think it through, guys," Correy pleaded. "Why were we planning solar power satellites in the next decade? Now, me, I'd just as soon *not* burn coal in the atmosphere—the gasses are radioactive and the ash is a carcinogen with a 'half-life' of infinity. So I say moving power gen up into orbit is a good idea anyhow. But the spin-off is those power lasers can raster an approaching object into fragments. So, here's your chance. Get one of those DoD battle lasers installed on LEO. It's smaller than the gigawatt jobs we have on the drawing boards, but little rocks are more likely than big ones. We can practice on little guys that would burn up in the atmosphere anyway—like that Micronesia hit you mentioned. We get to develop targeting and control software, test concept outside computer sims, and between times."—he shrugged—"we can sell beamed power to Artemis Mines."

"On the moon." Wallace whistled. "That's slick."

Mariesa pursed her lips and willed her heart to stop fluttering so. "These lasers are existing technology?" Correy nodded, but Mariesa determined to have Dolores check it out. One always heard stories about secret weapons held in waiting; but they might be nothing more than stories. "Will Gregorson is dead set against the whole plan," she mused aloud. "He detests Donaldson, but this might be just the thing to get him aboard."

"*If* we go along with the president," Correy added.

"Yes. Though if we don't, he can make our lives legally miserable."

Correy shook his head. "I don't think he can pull that off, either."

"It's been done before. Or have you forgotten the early days already?"

"That was then; this is now. Too many people in too many countries have a finger in the pie now. Corporations, governments, international agencies . . . It's not just you any more—''

"It never was 'just me.' ''

"—Donaldson would have to take on a lot of comers. Including people within his own administration. *I* think he's bluffing. He's a lot of things, from stock swindler to weathervane, but he's not a kamikaze."

"Unless''—and Wallace's voice drew her attention to him—"unless whoever is pulling Donaldson's strings doesn't mind sacrificing his puppet."

Mariesa folded her arms. *Donaldson thinks he can use us, and Correy thinks we can use Donaldson.* But problems arose when puppets had minds of their own. Strings had two ends, and a lot depended on who yanked the hardest.

Somehow it seemed right that she spoke to Dolores Pitchlynn over a video link. The woman had a distance to her, a remoteness very much like the southwestern desert she called home. Grand and impressive from a distance; dry, hard and eroded from up close. Even face-to-face, Dolores radiated an aloofness. Even when she smiled. *Especially* when she smiled. Mariesa had never heard her crack a joke. It seemed odd that, of all her Steering Committee, she felt closest to and most distant from the two women. Mariesa could (and had) confided secrets to Belinda Karr—late at night, huddled together on the balcony outside the rooftop observatory at Silverpond, with the distant stars cold upon them. But she could no more imagine confiding in Dolores Pitchlynn than in the wind-carved, sandstone pillars that overlooked the woman's Fork-U Ranch.

Reach out and touch someone, the old commercial had said. But you could reach out ungodly far and never touch Dolores Pitchlynn. There was something relativistic about her—she seemed to recede the faster you approached.

Well, the path to success had never been smoothed before her. Not by accommodating laws; not by fortunate inheritance. She had clawed her way to the top at a time when, for a woman, genuine claws had been needed. If the price paid included a little warmth, it was a price many had paid in those days. And there was the one consolation: Dolores Pitchlynn never had to wonder whether winning meant the game was rigged.

"Are you certain of the information, Dolores?" Mariesa asked the hard-edged visage on her screen.

Pitchlynn nodded imperceptibly. "As much as I can be. No one would speak openly, of course. 'Need-to-Know' and all that. They take their oaths and clearances seriously. But my people scenario'ed possibilities, and identified a number of activities that would have to see daylight if a project of that sort was running dark. The usual things. Certain materials suddenly hard to get, or their prices bid up. Scientific papers on certain topics drying up. A shift in the proportion of open NSF grants to classified ones. Probable players ordering suspicious quantities of likely components—and ordering to 'mil-spec' rather than 'best commercial practice.' Maybe it's two-plus-two equals five, but all that must add up to *something*."

"I see. And you think it's—"

"Brilliant Pebbles, or something like it."

"Then Donaldson is serious."

"Or he's putting on one hell of a show."

"In secret? Is he that clever, to put up a Potemkin Village that no one was supposed to notice?"

"Oh, I don't doubt he knows we would check things out for ourselves. It's dark; but it's not black. He could anticipate that we'd look for the sort of intelligence I've mentioned. But the signs point to activity that predates your meeting with him. Some of it even started during the Champion administration."

Mariesa leaned back in her seat. Her office was a somber one, dominated by heavy, dark woods and solid furniture; browns and blacks interrupted by sprays of flowers cut daily from the corporate greenhouses. The walls were decorated by photographs of the Plank tests and the LEO construction, and by fanciful paintings of *faits* yet to be *accompli*. Hard-edged techno-painting. Dolores's tanned face, on the monitor in the wall, coordinated well with the decor. "What's your opinion?" she asked the woman, though she felt certain what the answer would be.

"You mean, should we accept the proposal? Definitely. A lot of government money is flowing by underground right now. I don't see why we shouldn't dip into the stream."

"Subcontract on some TMDO projects?"

"Why not?"

"I would just as soon not become dependent on a cash flow that can dry up with the next Congress. It's like the pusher says: The first hit is free, but after that, you're hooked."

"Picking up some low-lying fruit won't warp our cash flow."

Mariesa did not care to debate the issue with Dolores. The older woman knew her own mind and knew how to navigate through dark Pentagon waters. Maybe she could kiss the toad and not get warts. After all, it was not as though the government had no legitimate economic role. It was only that it was too easy to grow dependent on it. It was *easier* to cut a cost-plus or a fixed-fee contract than to grapple with the give-and-take of the marketplace. There were contractors who, during the Cold War, had forgotten how to compete. They became expert at stroking procurement officers and lobbying congressfolk, but they thought that profit was something you *negotiated*. "Perhaps," Mariesa said, conceding the point. Short of the Van Huyten Trust forcing Dolores out of Pegasus, there was little she could do if the other woman ceased to be a loyal ally. Loyalty, like profits, was earned—and paid back with interest.

The limousine rolled east along Interstate 80, through the shear cut in Passaic Mountain, where the highway dropped suddenly toward the coastal plain. The sides of the cut had been raw rock decades ago, when the road was put in. Now the granite and schist was softened by the grasses and flowers and, yes, even trees that sprouted from unlikely nooks and ledges and cracks.

What will happen to all the trees, Gramper? she had asked back then when, catching a glimpse of behemoth machines from the windows of Gramper's car, the earth had been all red and raw and muddy from the recent rains.

They'll grow back, Riesey, Gramper had comforted her. *Nature is resilient. She survives because she adapts.* And he had looked at her gravely, with eyes both sad and serious. His beard had not yet become the white and whispy thing of his last years, though it was already shot through with gray. *Remember that, Riesey, if you want to survive. It's a lesson* some *have never learned.*

Yes, Gramper. She had been too young to fully understand him. She was not sure she fully understood him now. She had only known, with a feeling mixed of expectation and uncertainty, that they were going to visit Daddy, and that Gramper was sad.

Sykes, his light brown hair already thinning, had been the driver then. He took Gramper's car around a bend in the old, two-lane county road and the nascent superhighway ducked from sight behind them; and so young Riesey, twisting in her seat to watch the earth-eating monsters, missed the first glimpse of the sanitorium that the gently curving road brought into view.

"Astral projection?"

John E. Redman's drawl brought her back to Laurence's limo and the hum of tires on the paving. She stared out at the passing roadside. These superhighways were once intrusions, now they were simply part of the landscape. A lesson there, but what? That "Earth abides," or that you can grow used to anything? "I'm sorry, John E. What did you say?"

"You seemed miles away."

"Not miles," she said. "Years."

"Ah. I thought you were trying astral projection to get to Washington faster."

She craned her neck to see the hillside on the right as they passed it, but there was no sign of the sanitorium. Perhaps it was gone. Perhaps it never had been visible from the highway. She could see the county road, looking oddly antique through the tinted glass. Virtually unused, now. A lone pickup truck, its color muted by the window tint, wound across the shoulder of the hill. "Who is ever in a hurry to get to Washington?"

The lawyer chuckled. "Oh, the old town has its uses. It lets us put all the lunatics in one spot, so we can keep an eye on them."

"You exaggerate. Most of them work quite hard at what we ask them to do. The problem is we ask them to do too much."

"Hunh. You're probably right. We always run to Daddy when we want something bright and shiny. But . . . have you reviewed your testimony?"

"I hate reading prepared statements. They seem so artificial."

John E. turned slightly in his seat so that he faced her. "To make the points we want to make to the committee, a 'spontaneous' speech would be even worse. We want to lay out the facts and figures on power beaming. You can't pretend to have those at your fingertips."

"And besides, it's a ritual."

John E. smiled. "And besides, it's a ritual." He opened the manila folder he had taken from his briefcase earlier and ran his finger down a list he had. "My staff estimates that just under half the committee is already favorable or inclined to be favorable to our position. Testimony from Wilson, Motorola, Comsat, and other players has some of the rest of the committee wavering. The State Department even sent one of their guys over to testify about the effect a ban would have on our relations with Ecuador, Brazil, and Kenya . . ."

"Then Donaldson isn't using this bill for leverage," she mused aloud.

"Hmm? No, of course not. He wants to use us, not block us. If the Atmospheric Protection Law passes, it takes his lever away. No, this is Bullock, pure and simple."

She sniffed. "Bullock is neither pure, nor simple."

"No, he likes to stay in the background and pull strings,

doesn't he? A lot like his uncle that way. He's lined up the most astonishing alliance the old town has seen in donkey's years. Environmentalists who are convinced that power beams somehow damage the atmosphere. Xenophobes who hate the idea of Latins and Africans cashing in—though they're too careful to say so out loud. It's all 'trade balance' and 'economic dependence on unstable Third World regimes.' MacRobb and the American Party are thick with *that* crowd. And then there are others—firms who drew the short straw in the new economic order and don't like it. They'll testify about 'unfair' competition.''

How did Phil Albright feel holding hands with MacRobb, she wondered? The American Party was ''the Party of the Working Man,'' but sometimes you had to lift the white sheets to see the union label. Phil must surely feel uncomfortable with his allies this time around. According to John E., Quinlan was ready to take the machininsts right out of the AFL/CIO unless the board stopped dithering and came out four-square against MacRobb—and the Teamsters were threatening to leave if it did.

''If you accept Donaldson's offer,'' John E. pointed out, ''he could squash Bullock for you.''

She raised her eyebrows. ''You think I should?''

He shrugged and returned his folder to the briefcase, closed it, and looked at her. ''I'm your lawyer, ma'am. I give advice. Whether you cooperate with Donaldson or not, I make sure it's legal.''

''But you have your opinions.''

''It would be malfeasance for me to advise you against VHI's best financial and legal interests. The incentives in this case are all economic; the objections are all philosophical. Personally . . .'' He hesitated, as if he had never before considered the possibility of a personal opinion. ''Personally, the less I see of government, the happier I am. Yes, I know, I know . . . You can't play a game without rules and referees. What I object to is when the referees start making coaching decisions, start calling the plays, start putting sandbags on the ankles of the better players. But intervention in the Balkan War . . . ? Foreign policy *is* a legitimate role for government. Donaldon's strategy may get him impeached when it comes out, or it may win him the Nobel Peace Prize. Or both. That's politics, and that's *his* problem. Our problem is, if we refuse, how badly can he hurt us? And if we go along, do we get just compensation for the loss of value in our properties—up to and including the possible breakup of the Consortium?''

She reached out and touched him on the arm. ''Do you think it would?''

He threw his hands out. ''What did Heinz Ruger say? The Germans would be happy to see Smokey the Bear stomp out that Balkan forest fire. And the Russian *government* would be just as happy—but can't say so because the opposition would eat their lunch come election time. Ivan supports the Orthodox on general principles, but would rather not get the Turks all excited. Johnny Turk would go through the Balkans like crap through a goose, pardon the expression, if Greece were knocked out; and there are all sorts of Russo-Turkish auld lang synes that we in the West never bothered to learn. Our Japanese and Brazilian partners have no interests in the Balkans, so they don't see any reason to risk diddly-squat over them. They'd be bent out of shape if we went along with Donaldson, but whether they'd break the Consortium would depend on the bottom line impact.''

''Our little 'family' would remain intact, then?''

''A bit more dysfunctional, but . . . probably. Tell me, Mariesa, where does Steve stand?''

She gave him a blank look and he scowled in irritation. ''Come on. I'm your lawyer, remember? That's like a priest, only we get paid more and we have more fun at night. I can read an appointment calendar. You've been making the rounds of the Prometheus Group. Are you buying or selling?''

''Neither. Just listening.''

''Hmm. A good beginning, anyway. Can I guess what you've been hearing? A few yeas; a few nays. Some lean one way, but can live with the other. And some—If I had to guess, I would guess Belinda, Steve, and João would have a real hard time swallowing a 'yes.' '' He leaned back in his seat and swiveled to face front again. "Dissension in the Consortium," he said over his shoulder, "is a possibility; but if I were you, I'd be more worried about your own Steering Committee."

The rain drummed on the roof of Silverpond, a steady, fierce, insistent beating. It was one of those dark, ominous Eastern rains, when stormclouds blackened the sky, making nightfall out of noon, flooding the underpasses and clogging the storm sewers, mocking umbrellas and windshield wipers. It was the kind of rain that tore and drove up *under* your clothes. Drops falling so hard and fast that they *hurt* when they hit, more like hail than the "quality of mercy." It lacked only the lightning and thunder to make it complete.

Inside the walls of Silverpond, inside her rooftop Roost, the howling outside and the buffeting of the rain and the wind on the windowpanes was like some monster kept at bay. It made the sprawling, nearly empty mansion seem suddenly close and cosy. It was a day that called for hot tea and a crackling fire . . . And a close friend. Downstairs, Mariesa imagined, Mummy huddled in the sitting room with her book of roses. And Sykes was doing whatever it was butlers did when unsummoned. Miss Whitmore was perhaps dusting in one of the unused rooms or, more likely, was diligently writing the romance novel that consumed her off-duty hours. The remainder of the staff was not resident, and Harriet had given them the day off, to stay at home during the storm.

"It's a foul day, Wallace," she told the image in her computer's popper window.

Wallace Coyle blinked and looked thoughtful. "Would it help," he asked, "if I told you it was bright and sunny here in St. Louis?"

"Not even a little bit."

"Well . . ."

"No, I take that back. This *is* the sort of storm where I'm glad to know a spot of sunshine exists somewhere."

"It's not mathematically possible for winds to be blowing at every spot on the Earth. Something topological about covering a billiard ball with hair—there has to be a bald spot." He rubbed a mocking hand across his receding hairline.

"You are a great comfort, Wallace."

He laughed. "Has that file converted yet?"

"Uh, I haven't been watching." She glanced at the main screen of her new Kiwi desktop. "Yes, it has. Oh, thank you, Wallace. I was afraid I would lose the entire database."

Wallace made a pouting face. "Nah, they're smarter than that nowadays. The Kiwi's *gothic* operating system is a new architecture, but its filters can translate nearly anything. You just have to know which collander to pour the database through."

"Nevertheless, I'm grateful. I was ready to reconnect my old system."

"Oh, don't do that, Mariesa. Major rule. Never look back."

Wallace logged off and the popper window vanished. Mariesa activated the microphone and spoke to the system. "Computer. *Skyrock.* Open."

The screen blinked and a color-coded view of the Inner System displayed instantly on the main screen. The planets out to the asteroid belt appeared as out-of-scale icons; the asteroids in her database, as blinking dots. Mariesa raised her eyebrows a fraction. Even in an age jaded by microsecond response times it was possible to be impressed. "Display," she said. "Accent. First object: *Harriet.* Second object: *Gidget.* Endlist. Run."

"Acknowledged," said the computer.

I'm talking to a machine, she thought. A lot of people had talked to their machines over the decades, sometimes in frustration; only now the machines were talking back. A/ S. Artificial Stupids. She hated the name, but it had caught on too well. Perhaps because the public was reluctant to come to grips with the other possibility. *Why search for artificial intelligence,* Chris had told her one time, years ago, *when what we need is the natural kind? Artificial stupid is easier, because we have more models to build on.*

The planets and asteroids began to swirl around the sun icon. Months, and then years ticked off on the clock in the popper. One of the asteroids had brightened and was leaving a fading dotted-line tail behind itself. That was Harriet, a Near Earth Object she had discovered two years ago. *Not too near, thank God.* She winced as, in forecast-year 2037, the asteroid brushed the Earth icon. An illusion caused by the deliberate mis-scaling; she had assured herself on *that* point. Drawn to scale, Earth would be a pinpoint, too. A second popper announced that Search Object Gigdet could not be located within the specified time frame.

No surprise, there. How many times had she run this particular recreation? A hundred? It had become very nearly ritual, but it was like a pulled tooth. You couldn't help poking your tongue into the hole. "Display. Pause. Timer. Reset. AD one-nine-nine-zero. January. One. Set." The display blinked and reconfigured. Again, Mariesa admired the speed. Her old system had needed nearly a full second to shift time frames. The asteroid labelled Harriet disappeared; one labelled Gidget appeared.

The display again ran forward, this time at a slower pace. The scenario displayed only verified sightings and interpolations between them. Chris had written the code himself and she had sharewared it with a dozen acquaintances in SkyWatch. As 1999 approached, Mariesa tensed and leaned forward.

Gidget swung around the sun toward its aphelion, slowing in response to Kepler's law. Then—in early 1999—it vanished. No physical sightings after that. She had 'inherited' Gidget through SkyWatch, but had been unable to relocate it in the spring of 2000. Some perturbation in the meanwhile had shifted it into a different orbit. A collision. A nudge from Papa Jove. Who knew? For a long time she had blamed her own calculations. Perhaps she should have put the photograph on milk cartons. *Have you seen this stone?*

When 2007 rolled around, Harriet appeared.

She watched it for a while in silence before breaking the run once more. "Reset. Start point. No change. Scenario B. Set. Run."

Gidget and Harriet were like Superman and Clark Kent. Never seen together. She waited, tapping a finger against the desktop, while the alternate scenario played itself out. This time, Gidget's position was extrapolated forward from its last known location and Harriet's, backward from its first.

It was eerie. As Gidget swung past aphelion, its path blended into Harriet's; and Harriet fell sunward.

They can't be the same asteroid. Asteroids don't change course like that.

Unless struck by another body.

Unless some new gravitational anomaly awaited discovery.

Unless . . .

Mariesa pondered, and not for the first time, the increasing frequency of NEO sightings. Partly, she knew, that was an artifact of the data. More people were looking, and the search methods were more sophisticated. At one time it had been practical only to search where the asteroids were in opposition, since they were at their brightest at that point in their orbits. But computer imaging had reached the state where objects in quadrature and even within the sun's glare could be detected. And charge-coupled devices using A/S neural nets had even automated the search process. So it was, as Glo and the others had told her, no surprise that the rate of discovery had increased. After all, a systematic search had been underway only in the last fifteen years.

And yet . . .

Mariesa sighed and logged off the program. The screen on her Kiwi went to idle and she rocked back in the contoured chair. Around her, the Roost was a dimly lit arrangement of shadows. She rubbed the bridge of her nose. It was too much. People were demanding too much. Sometimes she wished she hadn't been born the granddaughter of Willem van Huyten, with ancestors wrapped like a coil of chains around her waist and with an ungrateful world to save. Sometimes she wished only for quiet nights at her hobby and a not-too-demanding job during the day.

Or at least, someone to share the burden with. Like Keith McReynolds, or . . . The wind howled *whooo* and shutters banged stacatto against the outside wall. A wild night, but with the windows snugged up and the dome closed shut, and maybe some soft music and a glass of Bristol Creme . . . God, on nights like this she missed Barry most of all. He had been a kind and considerate man, never pushy. He had known how to listen. He had known how to please a woman.

Known too well, as it turned out.

A flash of bitterness almost too faint to hurt. Yet, his ghost continued to haunt Silverpond. There were times— odd distracted moments—when she expected to meet him coming out of the library or relaxing in the solarium.

She rose and walked across the room to stand in the doorway to the observatory. The big reflector rested, properly shrouded, in its horseshoe mount. An array of doids and CCDs and now-obsolete photographic equipment lined the cabinets on one wall. Her souvenir case, with its racks of meteorite fragments, sat against another. Framed photographs and pixures of stars and planets and galaxies dotted the room. One, a blowup from the Galileo probe, showed Shoemaker-Levy striking Jupiter like a jackhammer.

Styx used to come here, too. To stand on the balcony outside, or to sit alone in the dark, writing her poems with the sort of fierce intensity that only a teenager can muster. Sometimes, with great shyness, she would read them aloud to Mariesa. Almost, amid the shifting shadows of the darkened observatory, Mariesa could pick out the young girl's shape; but it was only the sweater she kept here against the chill of an evening's observations, hanging from the back of a swivel chair and fluttering ever-so-slightly from the air conditioner.

Mariesa turned away and reentered the Roost. Perhaps she ought to go downstairs and spend the evening with Mummy. It was little enough they had in common, but it was mostly harmless.

She shut down the Kiwi and headed for the elevator. One asteroid pair was curious. One suddenly vanishing Jekyll intersecting with one newly discovered Hyde could be a coincidence. But, thanks to Chris's software, SkyWatchers had now found seven such pairs, with intersection points dating from 1972. Other SkyWatchers were plumbing their databases, and more pairs would surely be found when the databases were pooled.

Seven pairs, so far.

All of the "Jekylls" were in the Belt; all the "Hydes" were NEOs.

8.

Trajectory

The bookstore was three stories tall, its walls and partitions racked thick with hardbacks and paperbacks, grouped by topic, arranged by author. Eye-catching covers faced out among the marching ranks of spines. The inevitable best-sellers and hype-books, the self-serving political memoirs, the celebrity books with their coy "written with" winks; the comic strips and cookbooks; the media tie-ins and the gaming tie-ins and the tie-in tie-ins. But also the anthropology and the history, and the great literature of a dozen countries in a dozen languages; gazeteers and atlases; scientific texts and books for the thoughtful lay public. There was the musky smell of fresh paper and ink. There were nooks with chairs and people reading; a room with children and the murmured magic of words.

It was, Roberta thought, heaven on Earth.

It was also something of a facade. The shelved books were all for show. Display copies: one per title; because book people needed something to fondle. They loved the browsing, the happy discovery of an unexpected title, the casual conversations—*Have you tried this one?* The chance glimpse of an eye-hooking cover. An experience still hard to duplicate on the Net. If you wanted a book, you put your order in at the desk and they would download it, hardcopy it, colorprint a cover, and bind it, all in less than an hour.

For the younger, more impatient crowd, a µCD disk to slip into their Bookman. It seemed a bittersweet, autumn sort of thing to Roberta. On the one hand, it meant that even midlist books were always available, and the blockbusters and media tie-ins did not muscle the originals and stand-alones off the shelves. But on the other hand, she could not help but think that this was the last fluorescence of the Bookstore, the flare of embers collapsing into a dying fire; and as search engines and spiders and virtchhats improved you could do all this at home, in a terrible, lonely approximation Almost Like the Real Thing.

She shuddered.

The manager had met her at the entrance and welcomed her to Denver. It was so good of Ms. Carson to read from and autograph her latest poetry collection. The store arranged these Meet the Author affairs on a regular basis and they were usually well-attended. Roberta followed after her, nodding, half-listening to the chatter, responding when a comment seemed called for. Roberta found self-promotion distasteful and grudged any time spent away from the Crusades; but Phil himself had insisted she make the book tour. The more she kept in the public eye, he said, the more meaningful her work on the Crusades would be. Part of her value to the Crusades was her prominence in the arts.

Phil had driven her to the airport himself and, just before the security checkpoint, in front of any number of people, had given her a brief embrace and wished her good luck.

Four days of cookie-cutter appearances at bookstores and on call-in radio stations had fatigued her. Fly in at night; check into the airport hotel; hope you connect in the lobby next morning (she had lost an hour and missed a radio show in Portland because her escort had gone to the wrong hotel); chat for a while with a host who—maybe—had actually read her book (and who once, in San Francisco, was actually an enthusiastic devotee of the New Art); drag her sorry butt over to the bookseller's and spend the afternoon and early evening reading selections and signing copies. Then dinner, always at a restaurant the locals thought was ''special.''

Afterward, racing to the airport to catch her evening flight, hoping that traffic or the weather would keep everything on schedule, because the whole thing was a juggling act and one delay or missed connection could drop balls all the way across the country. She knew it should be a rush for her, that the egoboo should keep her stoked and smoking; but honest-to-God, after a while all the bookstores looked the same and all the dinners tasted alike and she couldn't keep any one person's name attached to any particular face.

The manager led her to a nook where several rows of chairs had been set up in front of a table. About half the chairs were already occupied, which was a good sign, unless they all got up to leave when they saw this was not a rest spot. "We'll start the session at five-thirty," the manager told her. "Some people like to stop by after work, so we try to time these things to accommodate them."

"One for the road, eh?"

The manager chuckled. "It's Denver," she said by way of explanation. That was a constant, too. In every city, the booksellers told you how their town was especially bookish. Who knew? Maybe they were all right. Maybe a tube-weary world was changing for the better. "Would you like something to drink?" the manager said. "We have a refreshment bar with fruit juices, coffee, and tea. The other author is over there now. I'll bring her back so she can get ready and the two of you can meet."

What Styx wanted was a shot of vodka, but Roberta stuffed her back into her box before she could spoil the mood, and said, "Apple juice would be fine."

A few people checked their watches and left; a few more entered the nook and sat down. Two of them had copies of her latest collection; and another had a stack with every chapbook she had ever put out. *Hot damn. Groupies.* They always asked the damnedest questions. *What were you seeing in your inner eye when you wrote the line, "Moon-lit lake look; two lights too late . . . ?" What were the "two lights"?* And the obvious answer—she'd been playing around with sprung rhythm and the line had just *felt right*—

supplanted by the more polite it-gotta-be-read-in-context. And throw the question back on them. What does it mean to *you?* They liked it when you made them a part of the discussion, as if they themselves were a part of the meaning of the poem. And what the hell? In a way, they were. Everyone, in their heart, pondered a different moon-lit lake, for entirely different reasons.

The other author was Tani Pandya: Short and dusky, a rounded nose, straight hair parted in the middle, the look of baby fat that no number of years would ever quite burn off. The manager had barely opened her mouth to introduce them to each other when Tani said, "Roberta!" and rushed to embrace her.

Styx had never been one to endure embraces. Beth, her mother, had offered damn few for practice. Whatever demonstrativeness Elizabeth Carson might have possessed on that Wyoming commune where Styx had been conceived had long before dried up and blown away. But Roberta endured Tani's embrace and even tried, awkwardly, to return it. The store manager said, "Do you know each other?"

"We went to high school together!" Tani said.

That was near enough true that Roberta did not try to correct her. It would be too hard to explain. Did two people go to school "together" if they had hardly known each other? Or did they just attend the same school at the same time? Of all of them—the hood, Chase; the gang-banger, Azim; the bubble-headed bimbo, Leilah; the basket case, Jimmy; and all the others—Tanuja Pandya had had the most conventionally promising future—and had come very near losing it.

The reading went as well as readings generally did. Roberta's new collection was *The Early Years,* a set of poems she had written as a teenager and Emmett, her publisher, thought it might still appeal to the young adult market. Doggerel, mostly; but with some of the bite and the hurt of those days. On the cover, the "Y" in *Years* was cleverly distorted so that it might just as easily be a "T." Her later work was orders of magnitude more sophisticated, but also orders of magnitude more affected. Was it even possible to achieve one without the other? Was the artificiality of craft the price one paid for rising above the fumbling naïveté of youth? Or was the sophistication itself the price that was paid?

Tani's novel, *Taj Mahal,* had been favorably noticed by the New York critics. One of the big-name syndicated sysops had mentioned it, so now it was all the rage. Tani read a short passage in which a character named Spyder, a sensitive but troubled young girl, spent a night of terror amid the dark shapes and subtle sounds of a forested hillside only to find, in the morning, that she had been safe within the tame greenbelt of a comfortable subdivision, surrounded on all sides by middle-class homes. "Spyder" sounded suspiciously like young "Styx," though nothing of the sort had ever happened to her; and the more Roberta listened, the more she understood that Spyder was not Styx. There were pieces of Styx in there; but there were also pieces that were not Styx, and other pieces that she refused to believe could have been Styx. Art drew on life, but art was more than life. *Taj Mahal* was autobiographical, but it was still a fiction—a construct: built of facts, but fashioned into truths.

After the readings, after the inevitable dinner, Roberta and Tani found themselves at the Westin Hotel at Denver International Airport, with nothing to do until red-eye flights took them off in different directions. The airport had been built in the middle of nowhere, so many miles out of town that, at first, no one could return a rental car with a full tank of gas. Some clever people had built gas stations closer to the airport; some even cleverer people had started building a high-speed monorail from Union Station in downtown Denver out to the airport.

She and Tani installed themselves in the hotel lounge, "to talk over old times," as Tani put it; though Roberta wondered how they would fill the void after the first minute or two. Tani ordered a fruit juice and Roberta ordered a vodka tonic. Just one. That was her rule.

"So, are you going to the reunion?" Tani asked after the drinks had been delivered.

Roberta snorted. "Not even on a bet." She left her drink untouched for now. That was another of her rules. It was a question of showing who was master.

Tani looked genuinely surprised. "Really? Why not?"

"Going isn't the default setting. I don't need a reason *not* to go."

"But—"

"*You're* not going, are you?" She looked into Tani's eyes and saw perplexity. "You are!" But why would someone with Tani's sensitivity want to associate with that gang of mouth-breathers?

"I know Leilah won't be there, but—"

"But what?" Roberta leaned toward the other woman. It wasn't right to live a life constructed of illusion. "Listen, Tani, Leilah was never your big home skillet. She only let you hang with her crowd because *all* the beauty queens—" She stopped, suddenly appalled at the cruelty she was about to say.

But Tani was there already. "I wasn't some herbie from the swamps, Roberta," Tani said softly. "You're not puncturing any balloons. I was a plain, chubby girl. I still am. I know that. And Leilah thought she looked prettier if someone plain was standing beside her. But that was her own insecurity. Deep down, she never really believed she was beautiful."

"It wasn't that . . ." *I just don't want to be the kind of whack who would bring up something hurtful.*

"And it'll be stupy to see everyone again. Karen Chong will be there; and Dawash Patel and Jerry Goldfarb—"

The "brains." Styx hadn't flocked with the Brains. She hadn't flocked with anyone. It suddenly occurred to her that Tani *had* attended a different school than Styx. She had different memories altogether. "And Azim Thomas?" she asked, quietly discovering that she *was* the kind of whack who could dredge up hurtful things.

Tani's eyes dropped to the cover of her book. *Taj Mahal.* A convenience store in a strip mall, but surmounted by the glittering dome and spires of the world's most beautiful tomb. Windows plastered with advertising, community notices, lottery come-ons; worn automobiles parked around it; graffitti decking the brick side wall. It might have been any convenience store on any street corner in any town in America. But underneath, it was Pandya's In-and-Out at Maple Grove and Wessex in North Orange, New Jersey. Tani brushed the illustration with her thumb. "Azim didn't pull the trigger," she whispered. "In the end, he redeemed himself."

A war hero. The Congressional Medal of Honor. "No thanks to Mentor or to Mariesa van Huyten."

Tani looked up. "Is that all that matters to you?"

"And I'll bet Jenny Ribbon won't be there, either. Or Cheng-I Yeh, or any of the kids that Mentor failed; the ones who shattered and broke and fell between the cracks. Why should I go and celebrate with the winners and pretend that we were all successful because of *her* wonderful school reforms."

Tani's lips set. "Get real, Styx. Mentor was a symptom, not a cause. Change was in the air. Art changed. Poetry changed. Politics changed. . . . And schools changed, too. Private, public, *and* charter. Mentor was a little ahead of the curve, but a surfer doesn't create the wave. The kids changed the schools as much as the schools changed the kids. No, there are only two people that *I* credit with my success. One of them is *me,* and the other one is *you.*"

Roberta pulled back. "Me."

"I might still be behind the counter at the In-and-Out, living out my dead father's dream, if you hadn't stopped by."

Yeah, the place had been a tomb in more senses than one. Her father had been shot there, but it was Tani who'd been buried. "All I did was tell you that you were meant for more. Anyone could have said that."

"But you're the one who *did.* And, it *meant* something to me, because . . . You probably don't remember, but it stuck with me. Remember when Mrs. Conner asked each of us to name a role model in our lives, and you named your-self?''

Roberta laughed—a short, surprised sound. ''I did?''

''Word up, beanie. Mrs. Conner tried to get you to name someone famous, but you stood your ground. That's why it meant something to me when you came into the store that day. We have to be our own role models. We each have to live up to our own vision of ourself. No one else's. No politician or politician's other; no actor or athelete; no teacher or preacher. Not even Baba, himself. That's what 'Chandra' comes to realize in my book.''

''I don't think I was that reflective, not then. I just had an instinctive antipathy against fulfilling expectations.''

Tani shrugged and stirred her juice with her straw. ''It doesn't matter why you said it. Later, when you forced me to . . . to confront Azim . . . *That* did surprise me.''

''Surprised you . . . Why?''

''Because your independence has a dark side. In high school, you always acted like you didn't need anyone in the whole world.''

''I didn't.''

''That's a cruel delusion, and crueler if it was true.''

''Maybe I don't like other people to plan my life the way van Huyten tried to.''

''Oh, dear Krishna! Are you going to let Mariesa van Huyten run your life forever?''

Roberta leaned close, in Tani's face. ''She does not run my life!''

''She certainly does. Only it runs *away*.''

''I resent—''

''What's the mathematical inverse of a role model?''

Roberta seized her vodka and stood up. ''I don't need to sit here and listen to this.''

Tani looked at her fruit juice and pushed it aside. She rose, too. ''You do; but you won't.''

Roberta took her by the sleeve as she walked past. Other late-nighters in the lounge were looking at them. She could see the questions in some of the eyes. *Lizzie lovers' quar-*

rel? She could see speculation in others. Lone business travelers soaking up their gin and scouting their opportunities. "And who are you?" she asked Tani, "to tell me that?"

"I thought," Tani said, tugging her sleeve from Roberta's fingers, "that I could return the favor."

"One best-seller doesn't make you a guru."

Tani's arms dropped to her side. "Good-bye, Styx. I still hope I'll see you at the reunion."

"Don't hold your breath."

When she was alone, Roberta sat down again in the booth. The vinyl seat sighed and Roberta stared into the candle flickering behind its glass mantle. The dancing candlelight cast golden shadows in the booth. She tossed off her vodka tonic, placed the empty glass carefully on the white tablecloth. Across the lounge, a fiftyish businessman in a rumpled blue suit and loosened tie watched her over what must have been his fifth shot of the evening. He wasn't drunk, exactly, but he probably saw her through a buzz of expectation. Styx took over and Roberta leaned back against the padded bench and hiked her elbows up on the back of the seat. When the cocktail waitress floated by, Styx asked for another drink and drank it off briskly when it came. The third drink arrived without her asking and she avoided the eye contact that would have forced her to acknowledge the giver. She extended no overt invitations.

The buzz was on her, too, now. A feeling like being coated in glass, of being impervious and sealed off from the rest of the room. All her senses were numb. The world was odorless and tasteless and unable to touch her. All sight was distanced; all sound muted. She sat with her arms spread to push her chest out and waited for the Boomer businessman to get drunk enough to stagger across the room and suggest that his purchase of her drink entitled him to fuck her.

She waited for it so she could blister his tail. Ream him out a new one; maybe even call the airport cops in and file a harassment complaint—and how would he explain that one to his yesdear wife back in his high postage subdivision? At the very least, Styx would shoot him down so he'd streak like a flaming meteor across the sky. First-, second-, third-degree burns. Incinerating to ash and exploding into a blank and sterile crater.

The bookstore in Manhattan, the last stop on her tour, was altogether smaller and more intimate. It was situated on lower Broadway, just a mugger's dash from the Houston Station subway stop, on the border between the Village and the East Village, in a neighborhood that had once been hip, then not, and was becoming hip again. Alone of the stores Roberta had visited, it had no best-sellers, no coffee table books, no cute books, cookbooks or cat books; and certainly no comic books. Even its name, *Bring Home the Bacon,* was a delicious wink at the stock in trade and the sort of clientele it drew.

When she saw Phil slip quietly into the back of the oh-so-serious audience, she nearly stumbled over her lines. He flexed his umbrella once or twice and then stood unobtrusively beside the rack of French existentialists. Roberta bent over her booklet and continued reading, though she knew the lines by heart.

> "... If you listen hard, you hear the hush
> In fields where once we lay ..."

She closed the book to polite applause. The Serious Crowd never quite knew what to make of her. That she was one of the voices to come out of Prague during the Naughty Oughts marked her as the Jenuine Bean; but she questioned conventions, and no conventions are so hidebound as those of the avant-garde. Her frequent use of rhyme and formal structure bothered them. Yet, she was no more retro than the New Art novelists who had mined genre fiction and revitalized plot and pacing in the literary novel. Perhaps what bothered them the most was the way the New Art had achieved a niche in the popular world. Truck drivers and waitresses reading serious novels? It was like a close-knit club discovering that the guys down at the gas station knew the secret handshake.

After a few perfunctory closing remarks by the bookstore's owner, the group broke up for coffee and Roberta made her way to the back of the store, where Phil waited. "I'm sorry I missed most of it, Robbie," he said. "The storm blew a tree down across the tracks and the Metroliner was stuck in Philadelphia for nearly an hour. Did everything go okay?"

Roberta brushed the back of his hand with hers. "Sure, Phil. Did you want to stay for coffee?"

He looked at his watch. "It's a little late, but what about dinner?"

"I'm starved." From the murmurs she heard around her, her erstwhile audience was more impressed by her knowing Phil Albright than by her poetry. For a moment, the implicit sexism irritated her. Her merit, whatever it might be, did not depend on knowing powerful men. But that was their problem, not hers.

"How about the Wilmot Proviso?"

"Exclusive."

"Well . . ." And he grinned that shy, little-boy grin of his. "I'll buy. You've earned it."

At the door, he looked up at the black-gray roiling mass of cloud crossing over from Jersey. He popped open his bright yellow, "doorman"-style umbrella. "Better stick close to me or you'll get very wet. It's only two blocks—unless you'd rather cab it."

Roberta hunched close to him and took hold of the belt of his raincoat. "No, this is fine. I can tough it out. Just remember not to walk *too* fast."

"On my signal. Ready, one, two . . ."

On three, they dashed into the pelting rain. It was a big umbrella; it was a broad umbrella. But it did not protect them entirely. By the time they had ducked under the canopy at the Wilmot Proviso she was well and truly soaked. Her raincoat had protected her clothing for the most part, though collars and cuffs were sodden; but her hair was brown seaweed and her stockings were sponges that squelched with every step. "Oh, God," she said wringing her hair in her hands. "I must look like a drowned dog."

"No," Phil said. "Not really. Here." He pressed his handkerchief on her. She took it and wiped at her dripping hair.

"I look awful."

"No," Phil said again. "You look . . ." He hesitated and she looked at him. "You look . . . lovely."

"I never knew you could lie so easily, Phil."

He laughed and seemed to lean closer for a moment, as if wondering if he could kiss her.

Go ahead, she thought. *Make my day.*

Instead, he brushed her cheek with his hand. "You ought to get out of those clothes," he said. "You'll catch cold."

"You aren't exactly bone-dry yourself."

"Look. I booked us into the Beekman Tower for tonight. I had your editor, Emmett, send your luggage over there. I mean it wouldn't make sense to try to make it back to Washington this late. So, why don't we catch a cab and go up there and dry out? Then we can order room service; or if the rain lets up, maybe see what's in the neighborhood."

How many rooms did you book, Phil? One room or two?

The rain drummed on the canvas canopy. It cascaded off the flaps and down the aluminum supports. The doorman inside the restaurant watched them. He wasn't about to come outside until they gave some sign of being tipping customers. "Sure," she said when she felt her voice was in control. "Sure. I don't like eating fancy, anyway."

"Uh." Phil was all apologies. "You won't exactly be avoiding 'fancy' at the Beekman . . ."

"Well, hey, I guess I can suffer if you can."

The Metroliner sped down the Northeast Corridor Line at a steady clip, eating the miles between New York and Washington. The wheels kept up a steady, rhythmic clatter and the car swayed like a lullabye. Roberta sat in the window seat, half dozing, half dreaming while Phil worked on his laptop beside her. From time to time, they traded soft glances. Her arms and legs and body tingled, as if she glowed. *Turn out the lights,* she thought, *and you could read by the gleam of my soul.* Her journal was an arm's reach away, but she couldn't summon the energy to reach for it. But it was a good line to work from, and she would remember it.

Scenery whipped past the window, almost too fleeting to take in. Now, meadowlands and marshes—with sluggish streams meandering among grasses, cattails, and the odd radio tower or two. Now, blocks of burned-out, half-demolished warehouses and tenements. Pockets of dense forest, green leaves pale as September groped toward autumn—then, sudden platforms on which people huddled, heads turning to watch the express hurtle through. Sometimes, trains going north passed like a hammer a few inches away. Finally, farmlands set amid scrub and sandy soil. "Next stop, Philadelphia," the conductor announced as she passed through the car. She checked the ticket stubs on the seats where Phil and Roberta sat, noted the Washington destination, and passed on.

Phil, who had the seatback tray folded down and his laptop plugged into the Rail-Fone, glanced up as the conductor checked the tickets and, locking eyes momentarily with Roberta, smiled briefly and bent again over his work. Roberta turned again to face the window.

Now why on Earth should we feel shy with each other now? she wondered. After what we did last night . . . Action, reaction. Impact, then rebound. Newton's third law, or something like that. She could see his reflection even in the glare of the window. *He works too hard,* she thought, watching him. *He's always* on. He might not even know *how* to relax.

Unless I teach him.

Phil adjusted his reading glasses, scanned a page that had emerged from the miniprinter in his laptop, and scowled as he reread it. He handed the page to her and said, "Here.

What do you make of this?'' When Roberta took it from him, their fingers touched.

It was E-mail off the Net. A gibble-gabble of dates, times, routings, shunts, and nexi ran halfway down the page. Received from. Routed through. Netdresses. A Triple-A Triptik for the Interstate I-way. Then, finally, the message:

> To: PHILBRIGHT@PeopCru.Com
> From: A. Friend
> Subject: STAR WARS
> Message: IT LIVES

She laughed. ''There's more parsley than steak.''

His eyebrows arched the way they always did when he was puzzled by one of her images. ''Hm?''

She pointed to the routing. ''All this prelude—for a two-word message.''

His smile dimpled his cheeks. ''Yes, I see what you mean.'' He tapped the page with a fingernail. ''I'd bet anything this origin nexus is a public terminal, though.''

''Why?''

''I hear the sound of a whistle blowing.''

They said that Phil Albright and the Peoples' Crusades had sympathizers everywhere, but surely it was the Metroliner's approach to the Trenton Yards that caused the train's engineer to blow the whistle at just that moment. The coincidence was so unlikely and so absurd that Phil and Roberta looked at each other for a long moment with their lips pressed together before they both burst out in laughter. Heads turned in the car. Annoyed looks; puzzled looks. A few reciprocal smiles; though they could not have known the joke and must be only enjoying the sight of a happy couple.

When the chuckles had died away, Roberta said, ''I still don't get it. 'Star Wars lives.' Are they making a tenth movie—?''

Phil threw his head back and laughed again; then stopped when he saw she had not joined in. He laid a hand on her shoulder. "You really don't know, do you?"

"You're making fun of me."

He withdrew the hand. "Oh, no. No, believe me," he said, instantly contrite. "Never. It's just that I'm . . . grateful that you grew up not knowing. Things could have turned out very different." He fell silent for a moment; and when he spoke again, it was in a more serious voice. "Star Wars was a wild brainstorm that conservatives once had of putting weapons of mass destruction into space."

"What? But . . . Isn't that against the law?"

"Of course, but they were the sort who didn't let a few laws bother them. They found what they claimed was a 'loophole' in the law and said it was a *defensive* weapon, to stop incoming ballistic missiles."

"And it wasn't."

"It couldn't have been. Tens of thousands of components . . . And they would all have had to work perfectly the first time it was used. How likely is that? And even if it was reliable, all the Soviets had to do was throw together another couple hundred missiles and overwhelm it with sheer numbers. And, do you know what the irony is?"

"No. What?"

"The Soviet Union was on the rocks and ready to break up. Those old Cold Warriors *had* to know that. So who did they really plan to use it on?"

Roberta shivered at the thought of all that Death floating over her head. Rename the planet Damocles, because that'd be one world-class sword. "So what does the message mean?"

Phil frowned as he reread the printout for the nth time. "Congress killed the program during the Bush recession, and Clinton drove a stake through its heart. It stayed dead for a while, but Champion revived bits and pieces under the pretext of 'basic research.' I've been hearing whispers that Donaldson has gone even further and put systems into secret development and testing. I didn't really believe the rumors. Donaldson may not be the most active body ever to mildew in the White House, but I always thought he knew his center. This . . ." He turned the message over and creased it in half. "This, I'm afraid, is a whistle-blower. I think it means deployment."

Roberta looked up, but there was nothing there but the luggage rack. "It's not nuclear, is it?"

Phil shook his head. "Star Wars was a shopping cart full of goodies for the military-industrial complex. Who knows which system the president is activating?" He tucked the message into his shirt pocket, patted it as if to assure himself that it was there.

Roberta clenched her hands tight. "This means a Crusade. A big one."

Phil shook his head. "Not until I know for sure. I've been suckered once."

Phil was a great thinker, but he was not a decisive actor. He was better at *why* than he was at *who, where, when, and how.* "Simon would have acted."

Phil's shake was more emphatic. "And Simon was suckered twice. That second time could have sunk us. No. This could be a setup. It could be a misinterpretation. It could be a baseless rumor, passed along like a cold at a child-care center." He frowned and tugged at his lower lip. When he did that, his thick eyebrows came together over his brow and he looked dangerous and feral. The dimpled boy was swallowed up by the brooding hunter. "I contain multitudes," Whitman had said. And so did we all. Phil was a complex man, and as such, was many men. Full of humor, full of righteous anger, full of tenderness. A mind like a knife and a heart like a lion.

And he knew what he was talking about. "You're right, Phil. Crusaders wear the armor of truth, so we've got to polish our chain mail."

He looked at her and the thoughtful look dissolved into something else. He placed his hand on hers, covering it. With her right hand, she brushed at the dark hairs on the back of his. "I know you have a lot to do, Robbie," he said. "But could you take this on for me? Dig up a cuirass or two? And maybe a lance and a mace? You can co-opt Isaac. He's good with computers."

He only thought he was. We're talking White House here. This was something way too serious to trust to Isaac's Net-stincts. "I know someone better."

"One of us?"

"No, he's a mercenary."

"A mercenary?" Phil's brows knit in doubt. "Can you trust him?"

"What I can pay him, he'll stay bought."

"I don't want any leaks. Not until we're ready."

"I can handle it, Phil."

He pressed his lips together. After a moment, his head bobbed. "All right. Handle it how you want. I have faith in you. One thing I want to know most of all."

"What?"

"Donaldson shifts with the winds. I want to know who's blowing in his sails."

And in which direction is he sailing? Roberta thought. Who needed a missile defense in this day and age?

With all the slings and arrows that Earth was heir to, it was a wonder that the planet had not long ago cashed out and left the game. Man's inhumanity to man—and to nature—had burdened the world with so many ills that the patient seemed always in a terminal state.

At least, so it seemed to Roberta. But every now and then there was a crack of light, and that kept her going. Progressives did have victories. Hard fought, tentative, sometimes one step back for every two forward. The ozone layer was recovering. Childhood pregnancy was down two years running. The AIDs epidemic had petered out, and the gay community was breathing again, though softly. But the conference on global cooling had adjourned without a consensus; and there were still too many homeless, despite the boom; and the glass ceiling was stuck on seventy-five cents to the dollar.

So, when she arrived at Sea Isle City with the Crusaders

camera crew to doid the cleanup efforts, she was in a mood nicely balanced between hope and gloom. That the cleanup was already underway was good, but that oil spills still soiled beaches was not.

The town itself was built on the sort of narrow barrier island that attracted hurricanes the way trailer parks lured tornadoes. The buildings were the usual Jersey Shore ticky-tacky of rental cottages, seafood eateries, and saltwater taffy stands, permeated by the odor of brine and mist. Sand everywhere: in the streets, on the porches, in her shoes; even on the beach where it belonged; tracked by thousands of flip-flops on the feet of pudgy, dough-faced women and suburban doctors.

No one on the beach today, though. The residents lined the fences behind the dunes and the yellow POLICE LINE—DO NOT CROSS tape—those who were not on their knees thanking God (or Allah or Krishna) that it was already late September and the Season was over. It could have been worse. It could have been May.

The beach was a dull-brown, tarry mess, through which police, officials, Crusaders, and other volunteers slogged in high-top rubber boots. The regular media behind the fence line glared at Roberta when she led her crew down onto the slick-coated sand and showed her special pass to the thirtyish cop standing guard. Phil Albright's name opened a lot of doors.

The cop handed the papers back to her and said, "I usually warn people with beach passes not to leave any litter behind 'cause the fine is like a full ounce troy, you know? But, dude, what difference does it make now?"

"It always makes a difference," Roberta told him. "We can always not make it worse."

"Yeah." The cop turned his head and studied the beach. "Word."

Roberta found a hummock where her crew could set up, alternating between shots of the beach and shots of *The City of Mobile* awash almost to the deck-line on the rolling horizon. With magdoid viewers, you could even see part of the gash that had opened the tanker like a FedEx packet. Roberta handed the binoculars to the cameraman. "Max mag," she said. "Full enhance."

"Awesome," the man said, peering at the wreck.

As for the *Takehashi Maru*, they'd get no shots any time soon. Not without some very special equipment.

"How could two ships that big not see each other miles away and swerve?" That was Fred, the cameraman. He was fastening his doid band around his forehead as he scowled at the hulk on the horizon. From it, a fan of glistening black water spread across the waves, damping them, sloshing finally onto the beach at the feet of the knee-booted men and women with the shovels and sieves and high-pressure sprays. Fred sounded angry and bitter, and who could blame him?

But fair was fair. "There was a sea fog," Roberta told him. "And those ships can't turn on a dime."

"Then they should build 'em so they can."

Marti spread the legs of her soundboard and synthesizer and propped them into the fine, slithering sand—hot and dry, here, above the high tide line and the muck on the beach. Roberta longed to kick her shoes off and wriggle her toes in it. Marti activated the power cell· for the soundboard's A/S and let her earphones dangle from her neck. "I wonder which captain was drunk this time," she said.

"Both," said Fred. "One on sake; one on tequila."

Her support crew laughed, but Roberta thought any judgement was premature. No one knew why the freighter had hit the tanker, fog or no fog. Maybe no one would ever know; though public outrage would demand some plausible reason. Some why for the un-why-able. It would be hard to run a breathalyzer on the *Takehashi*'s captain. Initial reports had the man going down with his ship, a gesture that horrified her. What cruel sense of duty had driven him to embrace death? What cultural pathology had made it seem right? Yet compared to the weasely way so many others tried to avoid responsiblilty, she could not help think there was something admirable as well in the man's utter acceptance of it.

A cleanup volunteer stalked toward them, stabbing the ground with the shaft of his rake like the staff of some righteous prophet. A young man, maybe nineteen, with short-cropped hair and only a single stud piercing his ear. "Look at it!" he shouted when he was near enough. "Look at it!" Shaking his staff; shaking with rage. "This is a disaster! This beach will be dead for years, and does anyone even care? No, these things just keep getting worse and worse. They won't be happy until the whole world is covered with an oil slick. Hello?" He rapped the side of his head with his knuckles. "Wake up? Show the world what they did here." He stood vibrating on the knife edge between rage and sorrow, until sorrow won.

"Oh, God," the man said, as tears streamed down his cheeks. He brushed at them with a free hand, leaving black smears in their wake. "Oh, God, I didn't want to cry." Roberta put an arm around his shoulders.

"It's okay," she said. "That sight should make us all want to cry."

After a moment or two, the volunteer straightened and shook his hair from his face. He dabbed at his eyes, this time with the back of his hand, squared his shoulders, and looked directly at Fred, who, with his headband and virtch-goggles, was obviously the camera. "Just let the world know," he said. "Some people make the messes, and some people clean them up. We each have to decide for ourselves which one we want to be. I've made my choice. You make yours. But while you're thinking, we could use a few more willing hands down here."

As he walked back to rejoin his crew, Roberta said, "Did you get all that?"

"Tres bean, dude," said Fred.

"Most excellent," said Marti.

"Save the file. Then get me some establishing shots. Beach, volunteers, spectators, ships. You know what to do."

"No problemo." Fred looked around and Roberta flipped down her shades so she could see what the doids were collecting on her eyescreens. There was a moment of vertigo as the motion of the images Fred was collecting clashed with her inner ear. The sound from Marti's board was a cacophony of shrieking birds and slapping surf and chattering volunteers and rushing sea breezes. One by one, Marti identified them and tutored the A/S until the sounds muted. Using the soundboard, she could suppress or accentuate any of the sounds, depending on Roberta's needs. When Fred shot the greasy breakers, Marti fed them the sounds of waves on sand and of gulls crying out, while muting the conversations, the chunking of the shovels, and the hiss of the high-power sprays.

"He was good," Marti said. "The dude with the rake. He gave good bytes."

"What?" Roberta removed her earclip. "Oh. Sure. A little over the top, but . . ."

"Over the top? How?"

Roberta waved at the soiled beach. "Well, this isn't exactly the end of the world. Compared to some spills in the past, this is small potatoes. When I was a kid—"

"Whack enough. What do you want, dead sea lions?"

"No, but that's what I'm saying. It could have been worse. The tanker was double-hulled, so the spill was limited—"

"Sure. And now it's wallowing out there with water between the hulls, too heavy to tow—"

"—And the response team was in place within hours with proven means and equipment. The cleanup is already underway. Klondike-American is cooperating fully—"

"Because they know their ass would be sued if they stonewalled."

"I don't care *why* they do the right thing, as long as they do it."

Marti's face set into hard lines. "I *do* care why. If they only do the right thing because they're afraid of getting caught, what do they do when they think no one's looking?

That's why we need to control them. Otherwise, they'd go wild, polluting beaches all over the world, all because of their addiction to profits."

"All I'm saying," Roberta said soothingly, "is that we've had our share of successes. We ought to tell people."

"You got to be careful about doing that," her sound-mixer said. "People don't understand nuances—it's all or nothing with them. When you say 'it's not as bad as it could have been,' what they hear is, 'everything is fine.' "

"What's going on at the other end?" Fred asked before Roberta could respond. "They won't let our cleanup crew in."

Roberta shaded her eyes against the sun and peered at a knot of people gathered around the yellow tape at the far end of the beach. She didn't answer Marti. Verbal Ping-Pong was a loser's game, anyway. Besides, Marti had a point. *Crisis* mobilized people better than *misfortune*. But how often could you cry "wolf" for every fox and weasel before people began to discount what you said?

A strand of police tape had been drawn across the southern quarter of the beach. On the near side of the tape, a policeman faced a group of volunteers. On the other side were people in coveralls with tanks strapped to their backs. "There *is* a cleanup crew over there," she pointed out.

"Not," said Fred. "They're wearing some sort of corporate logo."

"So maybe it's a crew from Klondike-American. It's their oil, right? So they ought to help clean it up."

"Doid them," Marti said. Fred, who understood protocol, looked at Roberta, who nodded.

"Let's see what they're up to," she told the doider.

Fred climbed to the top of the dune to get a better view. Roberta plugged in her earclip and flipped her visors back down just as Fred zoomed in on the distant group. Roberta flew with the zoom, riding the wind. Figures became people.

Two men in suits and a third in flannel-and-windbreaker faced a group of volunteers at the tape line. Tall Suit was thin and lanky, well over six feet tall, with a countenance that Roberta found naggingly familiar. Short Suit was a broad-shouldered man with close-cropped blond hair and the ruddy look of those who played outdoors. *A sailor,* she thought for no apparent reason. Maybe someone from one of the ships? Yeah, with that fancy suit. Right.

Pixels popcorned around her peripheral vision as the doid's A/S erased intrusive foreground and replaced it with interpolated background. Slowly, the sense of *telescoping* faded. Then the soundboard washed out the intervening noise and Roberta was suddenly *there,* a telepresent ghost, hovering in the air just above and in front of the barricade tape.

"—my own property," the old man in the windbreaker said in a high-pitched, nasal voice. "I got a say in who—"

Marti's voice broke in. "*His* property. The beach ought to belong to all the people."

"Hush. I want to hear."

"—EPA permit." That was Tall Suit, showing a sheet of paper to the crew leader. "We're testing alternative cleanup methods here." Short Suit, shifting his feet impatiently, turned and signalled to the crew in the green coveralls, who began to spray something on the congealed goop at the high tide line. The policeman shrugged and the crew leader finally turned and waved his people back. The two suits watched them go.

"I swear, Chris," said Short Suit, "I think they resent the competition."

"No good deed goes unpunished," the tall man observed philosophically.

"Look at them. Steam cleaning with *detergent.* Busting their humps and for what? They'll just drive the gunk deeper into the soil, like they did in Alaska that time."

"Out of sight, out of mind. At least, they're reacting."

"Yeah. Activity matters, not accomplishment."

"They're doing the best they can, Correy. They just need better tools. That's why we're here. We still don't know how well these bugs of yours will perform outside the lab."

Roberta thought, *Bugs?* and Marti said, "They're damned gene-techers."

"Don't worry, Chris. They'll do the job."

The flannel-shirted property owner spoke up. "How long to eat up all the oil?"

Correy pursed his lips and scanned the beach. "I'd guess two days to get most of it; another week for the rest."

The old man made a face. "What stops 'em from going on and on until they eat up all the oil in the world? I don't want to be sued if this gets out of hand."

The short man laughed. "Their ancestors had a couple of eons to 'eat up all the oil' and they didn't manage it."

"I don't understand."

"What Correy means," the tall man explained, "is that his product is derived from naturally occuring bacteria. He didn't, ah, 'invent' oil-eaters. God did. Or Nature."

"Mr. Steubesand, ninety percent of the petroleum in the ocean got there naturally, through seeps and fissures. Millions of years of accumulated seepage. So where'd it all go?" Correy waved an arm at the sea. "What do you think this beach of yours would look like if there *weren't* oil-eating bacteria out there?" He reached into his jacket pocket and pulled out a folded sheet of paper, which he showed to the homeowner. "There's the specifications. A genetic recombination of three natural strains; designations ATCC30015, ATCC29347, and ATCC15075. They've been around since Mary milked the cows. Each one contained a plasmid degrading different hydrocarbons, so my people cocktailed 'em into a gryphon that can lunch on anything from hexadecane to two-methylnaphthalene—*and* do it faster than fifty grams per cubic meter per day, too. This is all in the EPA application and permit, Mister Steubesand."

The old man brushed the paper aside. "That's all lawyer-ese. Technical stuff. I can't make heads or tails of it. But I read stuff in the newspapers about mutations . . ."

"Oh, God," the ruddy man laughed as he stuffed the specs back in his pocket. "*They* can't make heads or tails out of the technical stuff, either. Their idea of mutants comes from Marvel Comics. These 'bugs' of mine are pampered laboratory pets. They need an oleophilic microemulsion—urea, laureth phosphate, and oleic acid—for fertilizer and surfactant. They can no more survive in the wild than a chihuahua.''

Flannel-shirt shook his head. ''I retired down here to enjoy the ocean. I pay my bills from beach fees and from renting out the ground floor of my cottage. This mess could bankrupt me.'' He looked out at the bleeding tanker. ''I wish I could sue those bastards.''

''Sorry,'' said the taller man dryly. ''The Clean Water Act prohibits private lawsuits. The government will negotiate a settlement, but it all goes into a special fund. We'll do the best job we can for you, Mr. Steubesand.''

The old man retreated to his cottage and Tall Suit turned to his companion. ''Wave action cleans up the residue?''

Short Suit crossed his arms and stared at the ocean. ''Wave action would clean this entire beach, if we let it. But it'd take longer than our normal attention span and kill next summer's tourism. Forty percent evaporates in the first forty-eight hours. Ninety to ninety-five percent of the remainder would get eaten anyway—by *Pseudomonas oleovorans* and my pets' other wild cousins. We're just helping the natural process along, so we don't have to wait two years.'' His mouth twisted. ''And lose the beach fees.''

''Don't be cynical, Correy. If the beach gets clean either way, why not minimize the time and the hurt? This way, we make money and Steubesand doesn't lose any.'' He lifted a pair of binocular doids to his eyes and studied the wallowing tanker. ''Bullock should be here,'' Chris said. ''It's his oil. How much profit would you say he lost today?''

''My heart bleeds for Eddie Bullock.''

Chris lowered his doids. ''He's going to take most of the heat for this. Never mind that it was his tanker that was hit.''

Correy grunted. ''And never mind that the freighter was diverted because of the backlog at Port Elizabeth. Or that the backlog was because the dredging hadn't been completed. And that the dredging hadn't been completed because the EPA sat on the silt samples until the permit expired—''

''How far back the daisy chain of cause-and-effect do you plan to go?''

''Until I get to someone I don't like. That's what makes this one so hard. Bullock. The EPA. The protesters who delayed the dredging. There's someone *I* don't like at every step.''

The tall man threw his head back and laughed. ''Correy, there's someone you don't like behind every bush and tree.'' He pulled the EPA permit from his jacket pocket and waved it at the other man. ''Who gave you the go-ahead for this trial?''

Grudgingly, ''The EPA. But that was because your cousin is kissy-face with Donaldson. Call me antisocial if you want, but you can't say Bullock and his allies are our friends. I bet it griped him good to hire us for this job.''

''So. He needed a quick cleanup; the EPA wanted a restricted test site; and we hold the patents. I can live with it if Bullock can.''

Correy studied the ocean, where a tugboat was hauling a chain of pontoon booms encircling the spill. ''Helicopters should be here in another five minutes to spray the slick. Personally, I think we should go with Elastol III when it's on the water like that. Gel the stuff, then peel it off with rollers. At least you get the oil back that way. Recycling. Frugal use. Isn't that where it's at?'' The tall man said nothing and, after a moment, the short man said in a different tone, ''Mariesa talk with you about the Donaldson business yet?''

Tall Suit jerked his head, and Roberta thought *The Rich Lady! That* was why the man had looked so naggingly familiar. A family resemblance. This Chris person must be a relative of some sort. A cousin, Correy had said. The Crusades probably had his name in the ''enemy'' file. Chris van Huyten? Yes. The research labs. Argonaut. But what was this business with Donaldson?

"She knows I don't approve."

"Listen, there are issues involved that you might not realize—"

"Have you mopped up?"

"Jesus, Chris. We're standing in the middle of an open beach. Who's listening?"

"Mop up first, then I'll tell you."

"You sound like Werewolf, now." The short man pressed the jewel on a ring he wore and touched a control on the earpiece of his goggles. "Scanning," he said in a sarcastic voice. Then, "Oh, shit." He turned and looked directly toward Roberta. "Countermeasures," he told his companion and did something else to his ring. Then the picture broke up and went dark.

"Fuck!" said Fred. He tore his doid set off at the same time Roberta flipped up her eyescreen visors. He threw it into the sand. "Fried," he said.

Marti played some buttons on her consoles, tried them again, then struck it with her fist. "We lost everything," she said. "That bastard found our frequency and virused us."

"He can't do that," Fred complained. "First Amendment."

"Why'd they do it?" asked Marti.

How'd they do it? was a better question, Roberta thought. That ring . . . She looked at their own generator, a clunky monstrosity the size of an automobile battery. There were, it seemed, gadgets not yet on the market. The rich and powerful had access to technologies off-limits to normal people.

"We better go back and tell Central," Marti said. "Gene-tampered bacteria being released in the open. God." She looked at Roberta. "You'll tell Phil personally, won't you?"

Roberta ignored the subtext. "As soon as I reach a phone."

"Good. They might have wiped out my hard drive, but

they can't brainwash my memories. At least not yet. We better watch out for cars trying to run us off the road on the way back to the office. There's no telling how far those people will go to protect their secrets.''

"Chill,'' Roberta said, unaccountably irritated. "The cop by the barrier tape knows what they're doing. So does the old guy in the cottage. *So does the EPA.* Not to mention a couple dozen worker bees and helicopter pilots. *It's not exactly a secret.*''

"But, then, why did they wipe my hard drive?''

"Maybe they don't like invasion of privacy any more than we would if they were listening to us.''

"That's different,'' said Marti.

Roberta turned and looked back. It was hard to make out against the afternoon sun, but it looked like the short man, Correy, was still watching them. Was he doiding and listening? Did he have paramikes? Roberta couldn't see anything like Marti's soundboard, but then she had never seen anything like the ring the ruddy man had used to fry their system.

It wasn't to whack the info they'd already collected, Roberta realized as her companions packed up their equipment and prepared to leave. Like she told her companions, they hadn't overheard anything they couldn't have learned elsewhere; and Chris van Huyten hadn't even thought about mopping until Correy changed the subject. No, it had been to prevent them from overhearing things yet to be said. And that meant things that were not yet public knowledge and for which VHI might not have "all the necessary permits.''

Something to do with Donaldson and Mariesa van Huyten.

Voices in the night. You would expect conspirators to meet under cover of darkness, in out-of-the-way corners. Either Jimmy Poole had a better grasp of these things or it was sheer bravado, but he always made contact during the busiest time of day. Maybe he was right when he said the best place to hide a conversation was in the buzz of a crowd, and the bigger the crowd, the better. And no crowd was bigger than the Internet at high noon. A million jostling conversations crisscrossing continents. If government know-bots were keywording the babble, they had their work cut out for them.

"You really think I can get laid if I go?"

"I can almost guarantee it. You know what sort of class-mates we had. How many do you think would hop in the sack with you if they knew you were rich?"

The face on the screen became cosmically innocent. "I'm not all that rich. And if I were, there are people I'd just as soon not know."

Roberta figured he meant the IRS, but that wasn't her problem. "Look, all you gotta do is go somewhere where they can dude you up. Top-of-the-line suit; nails buffed; hair cut and styled. Visit some high-class places so you can talk about them like you go there all the time. Read some news-papers so you're up on the latest stories—"

"I don't read papers; I surf the net. Infodensity is higher and you get the cross-talk buttoned into the hypertext."

"Okay. Whatever. The thing is, you need to be able to talk about shit besides computers."

A puzzled look followed by a nod, a realization that there might well *be* other shit. "And all this will get me a woman."

God help her, it would. Why did it make her ashamed to realize there were still women who wrapped their legs around power symbols? Was it instinct? Did men look for signs of fertility and women for signs of power because one carried the seed and the other supplied and defended the nest? Nuts. Biology wasn't destiny, and grabbing hold of someone protective wasn't security. That was dependence. She was her own protector.

"Yes," she said.

And—God help her—cleaned up and toilet trained, S. James Poole would be considered primo meat by half the women in America. So, did cleaning him up and training him in the social graces make her an accomplice before the fact? Or did it make her a rescuer of waifs, like that "Mother" Smythe in Pittsburgh she had heard about? "All you have to do, Jimmy, is act"—*not repulsive*—"halfway attractive." *Swave and debone-er* they used to say when she was a kid. She studied Poole's image. Suave and debonair, hunh? *To dream the impossible dream . . .*

"I couldn't think of any reason to go and meet with that gang of losers," Jimmy Poole said.

"Well, now you've got one."

"Then I don't really need your help to get laïd, do I?"

Meaning why should he help her now . . . Was the little weenie trying to wriggle out of his promise, or was he only playing head games? "Only if a boxer doesn't need his coach to win a bout."

Poole nodded, as if she had passed a test. "You'll come, too?" A plaintive tone. Was it only to have his "coach" nearby? Or was it to have Styx handy as a backup in case he struck out across the board?

"Yeah, I'll come," she said. "See all my bosom buddies from high school."

"I don't care about seeing the buddies," said Poole with a grotesque smirk on his lips. "As long as I get to see the bosoms."

INTERLUDE:

A Walk on the Wild Side

As August dropped dead and September rolled unstoppably toward October, work at the Rock fell into a routine. Krasnarov tended the power plant, maintained a livable environment, and ran experiments in power beaming. Forrest kept himself amused fetching supply pods as they swept near the Rock. He moved equipment, tracked inventories, juggled the work schedule, tended the shipboard hydroponics tanks, prepared reports for Earthside, and lent a helping hand to the others when they needed one. Nacho hopped from rock to rock like a billy goat, collected his samples, and continued searching—long after Forrest had shrugged off the possibility—for evidence that the Cave was not a natural feature.

There was danger in routine. You grew too accustomed to life at the edge of the envelope; you took it for granted. Hell, you'd play the damn xylophone on an alligator's teeth once you got used to the critter's smile. Routine drove out fear, which was not good; because fear could be your friend.

There was always more work than time to do it. The whole crew was workaholic and more than once Forrest had to shove some R&R down their collective throats. If that meant some tasks got scrubbed, too bad; because it also meant that no one zoned out at a critical moment.

The inside of the Cave was brightly lit now by an array

of "streetlamps" intended originally for Darkside operations. It was spliced into the doid network, too, courtesy of a set of fiber-ops that carried signals around the lip of the entrance and out onto the Dayside. The place possessed an odd sort of fascination for all of them and by some unspoken consensus they had begun to gather there at the end of each workday.

"The perfect place to wind down," Forrest said. "All the place needs is a bartender and a few gals from the office."

"And some atmosphere," Krasnarov said. The two of them sat together on a flattish sheet of rock that had broken from the cave wall. Nacho, a few hundred feet farther in, whacked away at a specimen he had chosen. Forrest could feel the impacts vibrating in the stone.

"All good taverns have atmosphere," Forrest agreed.

"No, what I meant was—"

"Oh, I know what you meant. I was joking."

"Hardly a surprise."

Maybe Mike was joshing, too; but Krasnarov had that way about him. Everything he said sounded harsh when he said it. Maybe it was his tone or his inflection; maybe it was a voice like two stones grinding against each other. "This wouldn't be a good location for a saloon, anyway," Forrest said. "Not enough drive-by traffic."

"Unless," Krasnarov said sardonically, "our little friend is correct."

"Two visits in who knows how many millenia? That's not exactly a rest stop on the New Jersey Turnpike." Forrest found a flake of rock that Nacho had broken off in an earlier sample. He picked it up in his gloves and turned it end over end. "You know Nacho works probably twice as hard as you or me."

"Granted," Krasnarov said. "Is why he may grow tired and lose judgment more readily."

"I didn't mean it that way, *tovarish*. I mean, it seems unfair; but this *is* a rock-hunting trip, after all, and Nach' there, he's our rock-hunter. In a way, he *is* FarTrip; and you and me, Mike, we're just the chauffeur and the building super.''

Krasnarov didn't chuckle. Instead, he answered stiffly, ''I am doing important work with the pilot plant.'' He waved a hand at the ranks of streetlamps. ''Who has illuminated this world?''

''I bet what you did is you said, 'Let there be light.' ''

''No, I activated the photovoltaic array. We are too far ahead of the Earth for the Helios laser to be of much use, so I focused it on the Sun. With no rotation and—''

Forrest would have rubbed his face with both hands if that face hadn't been encased behind an SPP visor. ''Jesus H., Mike. What am I going to do with you?''

Krasnarov answered with some testiness. ''English is not my mother tongue. Perhaps I speak more literally than you.''

''It makes you sound like a prick.''

''And you, like a clown.''

Forrest used his spew to navigate into the center of the tunnel. ''I know what I'm doing,'' he said.

''I did not say you were incompetent.''

''A clown, but a competent one. Yeah, thanks.'' Forrest released the flake gently and backed away carefully with a short burst that did not disturb it. He returned to the shelf where Krasnarov waited. ''How long do you think it'll stay there?'' he asked the Russian.

Krasnarov blinked at the fragment floating in the middle of the tunnel, then he glanced down the length. ''Perhaps a quarter hour. It is already moving.''

''Yeah, so I see. But it ain't in any hurry. Fascinating stuff, gravity, when you don't have too much of it. Can you imagine playing raquetball inside here?''

Nacho's polka-dotted suit approached them. Forrest said, ''You done for the day, boy? Time to punch out and hoist a few cold ones.'' The geologist unslung his sample bag and lobbed it. It described a lazy parabola. Nacho was hunkered with them before the sample bag reached the ground.

"Shoot," said Forrest, "you could play both sides of a raquetball game here."

"It is mostly the same materials I have been finding on the surface," Nacho reported. "Analysis may prove otherwise, but it looks like ilmenite and taenite."

Forrest snorted. "Hell, those sound like a couple of tribes out of the Bible. 'I rode out with the Taenites and we smote the Ilmenites, hip and thigh.' "

Nacho laughed. "I overheard what you were saying earlier," he added. "About this cavern. You may have the right idea. Not about making a neighborhood bar, but . . . Think about it. Seal this cavern up, fill it with atmosphere, and you have a sizable habitat. That may be what the Builders planned." Forrest could hear the capital-B in the man's voice.

"It may be what *we* plan," Krasnarov said. "When someday we move the Rock to Earth orbit."

Nacho started to reply, then shrugged.

"The deeper segments of this fissure," Krasnarov pointed out, "are clearly natural. They are jagged, filled with rubble; zig-zag, rather than straight. I think that when the Headrock struck, it cracked the main body. Then, by chance, another large object struck at the far end and entered the fissure, augering it out as it disintegrated."

"What are the odds of something like that—?" Nacho asked. Krasnarov interrupted him.

"Probably greater than that life would evolve from self-replicating clays, complexify into higher organisms, fly to the Rock, and argue about this fissure."

Forrest laughed and clapped Krasnarov on the shoulder. "Mike, don't let anybody but me ever tell you you don't have a sense of humor."

Nacho sighed and picked up his specimen bag. "The debate is fruitless. How soon can we melt and distill these samples?" he asked the engineer.

"The pilot smelter is still inoperable," Krasnarov told him. "You will have to settle for spectrographic analyses."

"You haven't located the malf?" Forrest asked him.

"I will."

"It's not top priority. Unless those samples you already smelted were atypical, we already have a good idea what the Rock is made of."

"The smelter tests are to evaluate the possibility of asteroid mining," Krasnarov reminded him.

"It's good rock," Nacho told him. "It assays seventy percent useable ores, like many meteorites found on Earth. Even with traditional methods, we could extract seventy million metric tons from this body. With high-tech methods . . ." He shrugged. "We filled several oxygen cylinders from the pulverized rock in the solar furnace—plus some condensed metallic vapors from the column takeoffs. Not quite 'Steel Rain,' but the next best thing. Steel Dew, perhaps."

Forrest chuckled. That the Rock was mostly iron and nickel did not exactly cause his jaw to drop; but the amount of oxygen locked up in feldspars and the like did startle him. "Rocks is rocks" had always been his attitude. Good for building walls or stunning rabbits, but he had never thought of them as *made* of anything—and had damn sure never thought of disassembling them! That a breathable atmosphere could be cooked out of the very ground beneath his feet was a surprising and oddly beautiful thought.

"There is aluminum, too," Krasnarov pointed out. "And an A1Ox engine achieves a specific impulse of 315 seconds at a chamber pressure of 3,000 psia. If we had such an engine, and if Dr. Mendes could locate enough aluminum-bearing rocks, and if we had the right equipment, we could refine an aluminum-oxygen monopropellant right here on the asteroid for our return trip."

"If? Hell, son, if we had a couple gals with us, we could throw a party."

"We could even use an iron-oxygen fuel," Krasnarov added as if Forrest had not spoken. "It has a weaker impulse, of course, but"—glancing around at their surroundings—"iron is rather more plentiful."

As the three of them left the Cave, Forrest wondered what

the next expedition would have on its menu—assuming there was a next expedition. A bigger mirror. A real smelter. A1Ox engines. Build a damned interplanetary fuel refinery. Hell, it *would* be like a rest stop on the New Jersey Turnpike. The asteroid had a synodic period of eighteen and a half Earth years; which meant FarTrip II would have plenty of planning time before the next close approach. It also meant the only way he'd ever see this place again would be on a pixwall in front of his rocking chair.

Still, it tickled him to think that the Rock was actually a big chunk of low-impulse, iron-oxy rocket fuel, and that, if you were sufficiently clever, you could—to stretch the point only a little—shove a match up the Anus and the Rock would putt-putt through the sky, consuming itself in the process.

Last out of the Cave, he paused and looked back into the brightly lit interior. Tiny suns blazed on their poles, scooping globes of light from the darkness. The farther sections, where the lights did not reach, were coal black. *Like looking down a gunbarrel.* And the lights were white-hot buckshot. He wondered just what the hell the Cave was. An odd natural feature? An unfinished habitat? A mine? There was a thought niggling in the back of his head, but it wouldn't come loose and, after a moment, he gave it up.

In mid-September they shifted operations to the Darkside.

Night lived on Darkside. The sun had not touched it for tens of thousands of years, perhaps for eons, and the shadows here were permanent. Forrest knew it was only his own imagination, but he thought that the sun's long absence had made the shadows blacker and more lasting than those on Dayside. Even with the floods from the repositioned *Salyut* and the network of "street lamps" spaced about the terrain, stubborn pools of blackness persisted in the nooks and crannies of the ragged terrain; and, although the shadows withdrew into the microcraters when you turned your suitlights on them, they oozed back out again as soon as your back was turned.

Forrest issued a warning about leaping into poorly lit areas—good advice in any strange town—and had to reinforce the warning after Nacho landed in a shadow-masked fissure, fell, and put a slow leak in his elbow joint. A good thing that Pod Four had included replacement suit components among its supplies or Nacho would have spent the rest of FarTrip on the inside looking out. It sobered the exuberant Brazilian, but only a little and only for a while. Forrest named the fissure the Chasm of Death. Later, Nacho found that it connected with the back end of the Cave. From the placement and appearance of the ejecta, he concluded that the Cave had been created first and then the Headrock had struck, cracking open the front end of the Rock.

Cracked clean through, like an egg. That meant no way they could shift the Rock into an Earth-bound orbit without it coming to pieces on them. The strap-on boosters recovered from Number Six Pod stayed in their cases. Too bad. The Rock would have made a honking big spaceship . . .

Forrest hated office work; but it had to be done, even up here. He had coopted *Salyut*'s smaller module for the project office for the duration. Reports, analyses, summaries for the Peanut Gallery back home, on-board inventories and readiness checks, suit maintenance, power usage, you name it, if a project manager had thought of it, there was a form to be filled out. That the forms were all virtual made no difference. Computers had not eliminated paperwork; they had only automated it. He was analyzing pod trajectories when Nacho's voice broke in on the all-suit circuit.

"Forrest, Mike, come here! Quickly!"

Forrest's head jerked up and he quickly scanned the monitors. Krasnarov was at the power plant trying to locate the smelter malf, or at least find out how to make the next smelter more robust. Nacho was farther west exploring the "Flatirons," a jumble of sheetlike rocks where, according to Nacho's theory, the region had sheared and folded up like an accordion when the Headrock struck the Body.

"Problem, Nacho, old buddy?" Forrest was already out of his sling and heading for the airlock.

"No emergency," Nacho said, "but you must see this yourselves." Like all of them, Forrest wore his "long johns" while he was in *Salyut,* and kept his suit plugged in and prepped. Too many comings and goings to waste time fussing with your wardrobe. Forrest suited up briskly, but not *too* quickly. *Festina lente*, Father John used to say back in high school. Make haste slowly. No point in creating an emergency when there wasn't one.

When he reached the Flatirons, he found Nacho crouched in front of one of the slabs, a six-foot-tall trapezoid improbably flat and smooth but pocked with a few microcraters. A relatively new formation, to judge by the sparse number of "raindrops." Krasnarov had preceded him and stood a little to the side.

Forrest watched Nacho play with a lamp, angling it this way and that. He switched to the engineering channel. "What's going on?" he asked Krasnarov.

"Nothing," said the Russian. "At best, an overactive imagination."

"Look here," Nacho said, backing away. "The angle is awkward. You may have to move the light to get a proper contrast."

Forrest took his place in front of the rock. "I don't see anything."

"Look lower. About a meter and a half off the ground."

Forrest went to one knee and adjusted the light. The rock here was crisscrossed with microfractures. Short lines running at different angles. The lines crisscrossed and connected with one another in several discrete clusters that resembled irregular snowflakes, like someone had whupped a windshield with a ball peen hammer. Is that what had excited Nacho? Some geological curiosity? "Well," said Forrest, "it ain't like I haven't seen any fractured rocks lately."

"Those are not fractures," Nacho said. "Only surface scratches."

Forrest tilted the light so he could judge the depth of the scores and saw that it was so. The lines were shallow. "I still don't get it," he said. "What's so special that you drag me away from the paperwork? Not that I'm ungrateful, mind you."

The silence grew, until Krasnarov said, "He thinks it is writing."

"Writing." Forrest looked from one to the other of his crewmates. Two darkened visors atop comically colored suits. Two faces dimly seen, both expressionless, yet both full of emotion. He looked back at the slab. "It doesn't look like writing."

"Neither does cuneiform," said Nacho, "if you're not familiar with it. Or Chinese ideographs. Or Gaelic ogham. I am no linguist—"

"Be it noted," Krasnarov said dryly.

"—But I am not blind, either! I think each of those four clusters is an ideogram of some sort."

Krasnarov laughed. "You think the Chinese have been here? Which China? Taiwan? Szechuan? The Guangdong Republic? What warlord could mount such an expedition?"

"I did not say it was Chinese!" Nacho snapped. Forrest rose and turned and stepped between them before they could take more than a single step toward each other.

"Chill," he said flatly.

They stood that way for a moment, frozen in place; then Nacho backed off. "You wanted proof, Captain?" he said. "Now you have it."

"Proof," Forrest said. Maybe. *If* this was alien writing. It might be just wishful thinking. One bald assertion "proved" by another assertion equally hairless. And who said aliens would have a written language anyway? They might be very different from humans. Communicate by flashing colors or by radio waves or something. He had read that once, years ago. Yet the hypothetical traits of imaginary aliens proved nothing one way or the other. Who was to say aliens could *not* have a written language, or be very much like people in every way that mattered?

He examined the rock face once more. If it wasn't writing, what was it? Evidence of space cats sharpening their claws? Maybe the Cave was their lair ... Maybe a bucket of gravel not traveling quite fast enough relative to the Rock to make more of an impression? That sounded more likely; but then, why only here, on this one section of one flatiron?

And if it was writing, who had written it, and when, and why? A visitor, obviously. Nothing living had ever or would ever call this Rock home. But, then, where had they come from? And why stop here when there were more interesting worlds nearby?

Forrest sighed. Too many questions; and not even the hope of an answer. There was no way to settle the issue. Not here. Not now. And not by the three of them. They would have to copy the material. Doid it and take it back with them—and become either the prophets of a new vision of the universe, or the grand prize winners in the laughing stock lottery.

Floodlights bathed them, casting their sudden shadows like spears against the rocks. Forrest jerked, and, when he turned, saw the Japanese probe idling above them, bathing the three of them in a pool of brilliance.

"I wish you hadn't fixed that mother, Mike" said Forrest. "I swear it. They're supposed to get clearance from Deep Space before repositioning, and that decision has to route through me."

"Pac-Orbita," said Krasnarov, "undoubtedly grew curious as to what we found so interesting." More dryly, he observed, "A curiosity I share with them."

"Nacho, shag on back to Home Depot and fetch us a doid to record this, ah, feature. Get a 24-D. Top resolution."

"Right." The Brazilian bounded north toward their supply cache. Forrest switched to the engineering circuit.

"All right, Mike. Spill it. At best, an overactive imagination, you said. What's 'at worst'?"

The engineer did not hesitate. "He may have scratched those patterns himself."

"Nacho?"

"You think he could not? He *wants* to find evidence that aliens were here. How badly does he want it?"

"Badly enough to fake it. Is that what you're trying to say? Why?"

"To convince us."

"But you're not convinced."

"No."

"I don't know," Forrest said. "You can carry skepticism too far, too. I once read how Thomas Jefferson heard about a meteorite found in New England, and he said it was easier to believe that a Yankee professor would lie than that stones fell from the sky."

Krasnarov snorted. "An extraordinary claim requires an extraordinary proof," he said. "Your Jefferson was right to be cautious."

"The Cave *is* unusual."

"Captain, I have been unable to ID the malf that shut down our pilot smelter. That does not mean I think aliens sabotaged it."

"I get your point. But those scratches do sorta look like writing, once you start thinking about it."

"Once you start thinking about it, anything may look like writing. People have read meaning into the casual fall of a shaman's bone throw. Into tea leaves in the dregs of a cup. The human imagination is a marvelous thing, Calhoun, capable of great creativity. It can find pattern where there is none." He paused, and his voice when he spoke again was more distant. "When I was a child, our family lived for a time in the taiga. You know what it is, the taiga? My father explored for LukOil. In the summers, I would walk into the woods and sit there with my back to a tall birch and listen to the rush of the wind through the trees. If I listened long enough, it would sound as if the trees were hissing in a strange, whispering tongue. Sometimes, I could almost make out the words. It was a pleasant fantasy for a young boy living in the wilderness; but Calhoun, never once did I believe those words were real or that the firs and the birches really spoke to me."

"Yeah," said Forrest. Fancy would never cloud reality in Krasnarov's world. It was hard enough to imagine a gangly young Krasnarov in knee pants hiking through the forest. To picture him communing with the trees staggered the imagination. "But, Mike," he said, "Nacho couldn't have scratched those patterns. There are micros that hit that slab *after* the scratches were made."

Krasnarov said nothing for a moment. Then he stepped up to the rock, nearly pushing Forrest aside, and peered at the markings. His glove reached out and touched them. "That could be faked," he said at last. "With enough skill."

"I don't think he was here long enough to do such a careful job."

Krasnarov kept looking back toward the scratches. "He may have been adding to it a little at a time over several days."

"Now who's abandoning Occam's razor? Look, maybe Nacho's seeing things; but then again, maybe he's actually seeing something. I don't know—and that may make me the smartest one here. All I'm saying, Mike, is don't *dismiss* the possibility just because it seems outlandish."

"That we find evidence of aliens on humanity's *very first* landfall beyond the moon?" His laugh was almost a bark. "What is the probability of that?"

Forrest shrugged. "I dunno, Mike; I ain't no statistician. But I'd guess it would depend on how much *other* evidence is floating around out here. On the moon, on Mars, on other rocks. Evidence might be as common as pennies on the sidewalk."

Krasnarov made no answer. He said, "Here comes Mendes with the doid. I had best get back to my smelter."

"Mike, if you can't pinpoint the malfunction by the end of shift, drop it and we'll reschedule your workload. It's getting to be an obsession with you."

"Yes. Perhaps we should all drop our obsessions." Krasnarov leaped off toward the Headrock, graceful as a ballet dancer.

* * *

When Forrest pulled himself out of the shower cubicle into *Salyut*'s main module, he saw Nacho Mendes perched in his sling by the geologist's station near the habitat's nose, bent intently over his keyboard. The 'fresher was just forward of the frustum between the smaller and larger modules, so Nacho was framed in the circular window of the open observation blister. The Brazilian wore only a tight pair of briefs. His skin bore a faint olive tint and his muscles were hard and wiry. He did not look up while Forrest pulled fresh underwear and a coverall from his locker. Forrest sniffed the clothing. "Fresh," these days, was a relative thing. If *Bullard-Salyut* had whiffed on the outbound leg, it must really be rank by now; though Forrest's nose had OD'd long since and he no longer particularly noticed.

"Fresher's all yours, Nacho," he announced. His skin tingled from the hot air blowers.

"In a moment." The geologist continued to type.

"No rush. It's the same old water. You know, I think I'm beginning to recognize some of the molecules, they've been around the loop so many times."

Nacho looked at him. "Another joke, right?"

"Right. And a particularly fine one, I might add. You know, after I teach you to recognize jokes, I think I'll teach you to laugh at them."

The geologist turned back to his typing. "I'm not in a laughing mood, right now, Captain."

"I'm captain, now, hunh?" Forrest looked back over his shoulder. The Iron Mike was not in *Salyut*, which meant he was over in *Bullard*, sulking in his tent. "Guess you're referring to my decision on what to include in the captain's log."

"What *not* to include."

"Mike didn't like my decision, either."

"I weep for him."

"Don't wax sarcastic, son. I don't plan on looking like a fool in front of the whole wide world. That's Ned Du-Bois's job. Union rules."

"We ought to tell Deep Space what we think those inscriptions are; not just put the data in the dump and flag it as 'possibly interesting.'"

"What *you* think they are . . . Mike didn't think we should include that data at all. Speaking of which, I need to read through both of your reports before I enclose them with the download." That was the part that really frosted Krasnarov. The captain's log, with the engineer's and geologist's reports, was supposed to supplement the data dump by highlighting major issues; but this week's major issue was not one that Forrest chose to highlight.

"I know I am right."

Forrest slipped into his coveralls, an awkward procedure in zero-g. Nacho could not help but know that he was the envy of every geologist on Earth and that everything he did would be reviewed and second-guessed and twisted by all the better-credentialed experts who had lusted for his berth aboard FarTrip. Favoritism, they said, because he was Brazilian. Scientists could be bitchy, despite all their vaunted objectivity. Yet Nacho was willing to take the chance of being mocked by his colleagues. Did that measure the depths of his conviction? Or the depths of his delusion?

"Maybe you are right. Maybe you are." Forrest paused with his coverall zipper half-pulled. "You know . . . I always thought if we ever did encounter another people, there would be no mistake about it. I mean, like we'd find a big, honking monolith buried on the Moon; or their spaceships would land in Washington, D.C., or we'd intercept a message between the stars. I never thought it would be 'maybe-this/maybe-that.' A collection of ambiguities. If there was more or better evidence, I wouldn't hesitate to tell Deep Space about it. But I'm the captain and I can't afford to look herbie. Black folks are allowed to do lots of things these days, but being as fallible as a white guy isn't one of them. I got an image to uphold."

"You might uphold that image better by taking a chance instead of playing it careful."

And why *was* he so hesitant? Because Mike had called

him "a clown" in the Cave last week? Who the hell was Krasnarov that his opinion should matter? Forrest tugged his zipper up, hard. "I know about taking chances," he said pointedly.

Nacho didn't reply. He ran a finger across the rim of his console. "Mine was supposed to be a life of leisure," he said finally. "My father owned factories, a rubber plantation. I had only to do nothing and comfort and wealth would be mine. Instead, I became a 'rock hound.' "

"Did you." It was a clipped comment, not a question at all. Nacho looked at him.

"My father argued with me, cajoled me, threatened me. Who would he pass the family holdings on to, if I would not shoulder the burden?"

Forrest placed a pair of slippers on a Velcro pad and pushed his feet into them. He was now anchored, like a seaweed to the ocean floor. He flexed his feet and pulled loose from the pad, floating into the center of the main module. "So why did you?" he asked.

Nacho hit a few final keys; then he unhooked his sling and floated free. He stretched and arched his back and turned to look out the observation blister. "All my life," he said, "I dreamed of going into space. I read science fiction, and I longed to make strange discoveries on alien worlds." He tugged on a cabinet latch and turned about like a porpoise, facing Forrest. "I was no jet pilot, but a geologist had once visited the moon and I thought that *this* would be the sort of man to make such discoveries. So as a child I collected rocks. I would come home covered with dirt." He shook his head. "My parents thought it a foolish and grubby hobby, but they indulged my whims. Only, no one was going to alien worlds any more, certainly no Brazilians. So I majored in business, as my father insisted— but I took the science electives because I could not bring myself to let go of the hope. Then, one day, my father told me something he had learned through his political connections. Brazil was building rocket ships in secret. Yankees and Russians were involved, but a Brazilian company, Daedelus, was prime contractor and Brazil was providing the facilities and a Brazilian was the prime pilot . . ."

"Yeah, Bat da Silva, he was one hot jock." He hadn't been prime, though. Krasnarov had. And Forrest had been Number Two; and Ned, Number Three; and somehow it was Ned who came up with the brass ring. But why ache over that now? There had been eight prime pilots. Let it go at that. He swam over to the dry soil trays where their shipboard garden grew.

"That night, on our estate," Nacho continued, "I looked at the sky with new eyes. It was possible now. It was possible. So I defied my father and changed my course of studies, all on the chance I would someday be eligible for a moon expedition."

"Talk about playing the long odds . . ." Forrest shook his head as he set up the zeolite monitor for a self-diagnostic. "Could be worse, though. You're a goddamned household name. World famous. What does your father say now?"

Nacho's face became unnaturally blank. "We have not spoken in years."

Forrest paused without striking the test button. "You mean he never even called to say congratulations or good luck, or even good-bye?"

Nacho shook his head. "I am still working *with my hands* on a job beneath my dignity. It does not matter to him that my work is on an island in the sky."

Forrest winced. "Jesus, that's cold." His own daddy, he was sure, would have burst with pride. It was funny how one man could see a step down where another saw a leap up. "I get your point, though."

"Do you?" Nacho pulled off his briefs and stuffed them in his storage locker. Then he kicked aft toward the 'fresher cubicle. Forrest moved aside to let him pass.

"Yeah. About taking chances and playing it safe."

Nacho paused with his hand on the 'fresher lid. "Forrest, I gave up everything—my family, my wealth, my own father—to walk on another world and discover wonderful things. This—here on the Rock—will be the only chance I will ever have. How would you feel, knowing some Earthside analyst will study those files and announce *his* discovery to the world?'' He slipped inside the cubicle and closed the lid before Forrest could answer.

''You so sure an Earthside analyst will discover any such thing?'' he asked the sealed 'fresher.

Bullard docked onto *Salyut* with a satisfying *clang*. The command cabin reverberated from the contact and a row of panel lights turned green. That meant all the docking prongs were engaged. The monitor displayed a three-dimensional transparent view of FarTrip.

''Docking successful, honey,'' said the A/S.

Forrest grinned. He couldn't wait until Mike discovered the latest mod to the A/S audio interface.

''P and W systems,'' Forrest said aloud, ''display.'' The diagram brightened with a network of red and yellow lines marking the hydraulic and electrical circuits. ''Connect.'' He heard the pebble clatter of relays and valves tripping. Tiny flashes flickered across the display, indicating the interfaces between *Bullard* and *Salyut* reconnecting for departure configuration. One light remained lit. A flashing label read RELAY STUCK and gave an asset location number.

Looks like a job for Super Mike. Forrest hit a few keys to flag the malf for engineering attention. It was a minor bogie, but departure was set for 2 October and time, tide, and Mother Newton waited for no one. He checked the doid views to see what Mr. Perfect was up to.

One of the three personnel monitors showed Forrest looking at himself in the monitors. He could see himself looking into another screen and in that one still another image. Like mirrors within mirrors.

The second monitor showed Nacho busy at Hopper Head Junction, the string of grid elements that marked the seam where the smaller body had sintered to the larger one. The geologist was checking the network of paired laser reflectors, one on each side of the fault, that would detect any differential motion between the two lobes of the asteroid. They had to be set carefully because, once FarTrip was gone, the system would have to monitor the asteroid's structural integrity without human maintenance. It was still not clear from the data that the two rocks were permanently joined. A good tug from a passing planet might yet yank them apart.

The third monitor showed Krasnarov inside a small, flat-bottomed crater near the power plant relay on the Chin. He was dancing.

Dancing?

Forrest frowned at the screen. The engineer was doing the ol' soft shoe, all right; sweeping one foot, then the other, back and forth in front of him, kicking up a cloud of dust around his ankles. Forrest had named that area the Chin, not only because of its location on the fancied grasshopper head, but also because it seemed to be the region most subject to micrometeor punches. The softer rock of the minor lobe had been reduced to powder in several places and the cups of most of the midsized craters had a fine coating on their bottoms.

The dust slowly settled to the ground under the Rock's feeble gravity. For the life of him, Forrest could not figure out what Krasnarov was up to. He watched the monitor for a moment longer, then opened the engineering channel.

"Mike, old buddy, what's with the Baryshnikov act?"

The figure on the screen froze. "Calhoun, is that you?"

"Well, now, Mike, who the hell else is there who can call you but me or Nacho? Unless Nacho is right after all." It was odd to talk to a man who was a miniature image on a doid monitor, especially one who was not facing the doid. It was like Gulliver talking to the Lilliputian king.

"Funny, Calhoun."

"Maybe we can get a dance troupe together, what do you think? 'Course, if the Rockettes ever did their kicks up here, their legs would reach escape velocity and never come down."

"Would you mind some advice, Calhoun?"

"Sure." Why fight the inevitable? Though whether he'd "mind" the advice was another story.

"If you are to be the captain of our venture, you ought to show more *gravitas*."

If you are to be the captain . . . The boy had evidently not been paying complete attention during crew assignment. "I already have gravity, Mike. Women tell me how attractive I am."

"*Gravitas* was the Roman virtue of seriousness—"

"I *know* what Goddamned *gravitas* is. I studied Latin in school." The nuns had had some mighty peculiar notions, Latin among them; but at least he'd gotten an education.

"Then perhaps you ought to exercise it more often." The TV image placed one foot carefully in the center of the crater and pressed down, withdrawing the foot just as carefully. "There," Krasnarov said, "something to remember us by."

Why you old glory hound . . . "Room there for two more footprints, son?" he asked dryly.

"One is sufficient," Krasnarov explained. "It is not my footprint; it is humanity's."

"Oh," said Forrest. "I would never dream of confusing the two."

If 2 October was the drop-dead date, the day they would say good-bye to the now-familiar terrain of the Rock, then the days leading up to it were the deathwatch. Certain equipment would be disassembled and brought back, other equipment would be left in place; still other equipment would be shut down and secured against a future visit. They went over the asteroid like a trio of nephews through the mansion of a late, rich uncle; but the work did not have the excitement—the *expectation*—of the initial exploration, nor the fascination of the later experiments and analyses. They knew the Rock now. They knew its secrets, or as many of them as it had chosen to divulge. The activity was a closing up, a winding down, an end. It called for different emotions.

As for any remaining secrets, it was like he had told Nacho. If you can't stand not knowing, stop asking questions. Maybe the clues would be cracked. Maybe some astrophysicist would prove that the Cave could not be natural. Maybe a clever cryptographer would calculate the probabilities and find that the Flatiron markings were almost certainly nonrandom. And maybe—most likely—the clues would go unsolved forever. Because the mystery was unsolvable, or because there never was a mystery in the first place. Those who wanted to believe would believe, and those who did not would keep saying "But . . ."

D-day. D for departure. Forrest waited at the base of the tether at Darkside Station for Nacho and Mike to finish their checklist and join him. Heimdall Communications was in the circuit, marking time until FarTrip was ready to drop the tether and depart. They would play downloads from onboard and rockside doids for the grand finale. A big production, all around. Forrest was impatient with such ceremonies. They always seemed contrived to him. He hated mouthing a prepared script, and he hated having to come up with spontaneous remarks; so either way it bugged him. While he waited, he carried on a desultory, time-delayed conversation with Dennis Tolliver at Heimdall.

Nacho's yellow polka-dotted suit appeared over the horizon from Dayside and a few moments later settled to the ground beside Forrest. "Everything is 'buttoned up' over there," he said.

"Good," said Forrest. He was getting nervous. He rubbed his hands together; but enclosed in fiberglass, ceramic, and composite like they were, it did not help. "I hope I can think of something to say to the People of Earth besides 'Let's blow this joint.' "

Nacho laughed. "Keep it simple. If they wanted flowery speeches, they would have sent an actor along."

Forrest scanned the horizon. "Where's Mike? Wasn't he with you?"

Nacho turned his suit toward the rim of miniature hills over which he had come. "He was right behind me."

"So, where'd he go? Computer. Location. Krasnarov. Locate." The pop-up window on his visor activated and a visual of the Rock appeared, overlaid by Nacho's grid. The image rotated a quarter turn and one of the elements flashed. A dot appeared inside it: Krasnarov's suit beacon. Before Forrest could say anything, the dot moved into the next grid element. "Where's that sumbitch going? Doesn't he know we have a show to do?" It wasn't like Senhor Machine to miss a schedule. Hell, you could use the man to calibrate a clock.

"Doidview. Krasnarov. Show."

No mistaking the red-and-white-striped suit that appeared in a second window. He was moving rapidly above the ground, using his spews. The view was from a groundside doid just east of the Flatirons and showed him approaching, then passing out of sight overhead. A new view, from another angle, replaced it.

"Don't worry, Forrest," said Dennis Tolliver's voice, hissing with distant static. "You'll think of something."

The comment puzzled Forrest for a moment, until he realized that the Earthside liaison was responding to an earlier remark. Quickly, Forrest cut Earth out of the circuit, as he and Nacho took off for the Flatirons to intercept Krasnarov. He didn't know what the Iron Mike was up to, but he was pretty sure he didn't want the whole world watching.

When they reached the Flatirons, Krasnarov was chopping away at the "inscription stone" with a rock hammer. Nacho cried out and landed close enough to Krasnarov to collide with him. The two of them staggered away from the stone like dancers whirling in each other's embrace. Really bad dancers, but they both managed to stay upright. Forrest landed more carefully, placing himself between the other two and the stone. He stooped and picked up the hammer that Krasnarov had dropped and opened the all-suit channel.

"Did you manage to catch him, Mike?" Forrest asked; and then before the engineer could answer, he added, "Ignacio, I've told you to watch your horizontal vector! If you'd fallen you might've cracked your faceplate. We've managed thirty-nine days on the Rock without a serious injury. I won't tolerate one on our last day here.''

Nacho started to say something, but Forrest overrode him. ''Yeah, I know. You were trying to stop Mike here from removing the stone. I agree with you; but that's no excuse for careless suithandling.'' Then he addressed the engineer. ''Mike, taking the stone back with us for the dirtside experts to study has its points. I'm sure we could find a place aboard *Bullard* to stow it. But I think the best thing to do is to leave it in place, so the next expedition can study it in context. What do you say?''

Both men were silent. They knew as well as he did that Krasnarov had been defacing the stone, not trying to remove it for transportation. You could tell by seeing where Mike had struck. His aim wasn't that bad. Time enough later to find out why. Meanwhile, by not taking official notice, he had given them both a way to back off. Mike had not deliberately defaced what might be an alien inscription. Nacho had not deliberately tackled Mike, endangering them both. Polite lies, but the homebound leg was more than two hundred days in a very small space; and sometimes the only way to live together was to smile and lie like hell.

''You are right,'' Krasnarov said at last. ''It should be left here for the next expedition.''

''Good.'' The next expedition would not be for another eighteen years, unless engine technology took a quantum leap in the meantime. Long enough to be forever. Forrest turned away and studied the markings. The damage was minimal. Krasnarov had not had enough time to accomplish anything. A few chips were gone from one of the ''ideograms,'' but they had doid records for the experts to study. If these were not alien inscriptions, taking the stone back would have been silly. If they were, it would have been sacrilegious. And as for obliterating them . . . Well, the same logic applied.

He started to turn away, froze, turned back and looked at the snowflake patterns with sudden certainty. ''Of course,'' he said aloud.

"Of course what?" asked Nacho. But Forrest did not answer him. He stepped toward the slab and raised the hammer and struck the rock with the pick side. Nacho gasped, but Forrest had struck well above the spot where the spiderweb patterns lay. Krasnarov said, "What are you doing?"

Three strikes and Forrest had made a crude "F." Three more and he had an "A." His blows did not go deep. The rock was hard and all he managed were superficial scores. But they would do. They would do for another million years. "FARTRIP," he spelled out, and "2009." He squared off the round letters.

Nacho said, "Yes. That's right."

He spelled out CALHOUN next. Every strike of the hammer seemed to bring him closer to whatever had carved the stone in eons past. Yes, I was here, too. I have stood where you once did. I have put my name on a rock in heaven. Alien creatures, perhaps. Too alien to understand; but in this one thing, brothers and sisters to every human who had ever stepped out into the dark beyond the campfire.

When he finished, he handed the hammer to Nacho and stepped aside. The geologist added MENDES underneath, making the D like a wedge and the S like a backward Z. Then Nacho stepped away and, with after a moment's hesitation, offered the pick hammer to Krasnarov.

But the Russian would not take it. "This is absurd," said the man who had planted a footprint in a dust-filled crater. "Showboating." He activated his spews and rose from the Rock like Christ ascending into heaven. "We have a schedule to keep."

Nacho watched him go, then he looked, first at the rock hammer in his hand, then at Forrest. "Give me that," Forrest said. Nacho handed him the tool and Forrest faced the slab once more. He carved Mike's name—using Cyrillic letters, as was only right. КРАСНАРОВ. Let future explorers stumble over the mixed alphabets. He wasn't doing this for them. He wasn't doing this for anyone. It was only the doing of it that mattered. Krasnarov could think his own thoughts, believe his own beliefs—because it didn't matter what he believed. It only mattered that he had come.

When he had finished, and before he turned away for the last time, Forrest Calhoun paused and laid the rock hammer at the base of the slab. You never knew. Whoever came along next might not have the right tools with them.

Only later did he learn that, having cut Heimdall out of the audio circuit, he had forgotten to cut them out of the video, and that, consequently, there was no need at all for any departing speeches. He had said everything worth saying with his hammer, and half the world had wept.

9.

Close Call

The Shuttle hydrogen tank was an ochre whale in an ocean of ink: massive and silent, drifting slowly off the "starboard bow" of LEO Station. Standing by his post at the D winch, Flaco watched the boosters that dotted the tank's hull fire in complex patterns, turning it and coaxing it ever closer. How could something so massive move so gracefully? And yet, it did. Cables like harpoon lines ran from the tank to the winches on the nose of LEO Station, where Flaco and the other trainees waited to reel it in. Oh, they had it lined and gaffed, all right!

Rigger-trainees and their mentors manned five of the six winches; the B winch was tended only by an "otter." At the last minute, Art Fitch had refused to EVAde, freezing in the airlock, staring into an infinity that had suddenly become "down" in his mind. He was being sent Earthside on the next bumboat. Flaco felt bad for the man, but it meant one less rigger jostling for the final cut.

Flaco was uncomfortably aware of his mentor, Rhys, hovering close by, watching him. The task was straightforward enough: Guide tank four into position and secure it. The tank had already been dressed out with attitude jets, a male docking collar, and a trio of alignment lasers. A Waldo-trained A/S neural net controlled the engines that nudged the massive vessel toward its assigned position. All the hu-

mans had to do was attach the cables and secure the tank
after it was docked. So it was not, except for the site conditions, the toughest job Flaco had ever rigged. Yet, he
could not shake the feeling that Rhys watched him intently
whenever his back was turned. Was he being trained or
tested? It was hard to tell, and that lack of assurance made
him uneasy. Yet, when he glanced over his shoulder at
Rhys, the man was studying the approaching tank.

Flaco felt itchy inside his rigger's hard-suit. He could not
get comfortable. He could not adjust his cap, or tug on his
pants, or hitch up his tool belt. All his accustomed gestures
and motions were impossible. When he shifted position, he
had to flex the balls of his feet just so, to break the magnetic
seal that held him to the skin of the Number Three tank.

In space, no one could see you fidget.

Fitch had been an amiable sort, with a great booming
voice and friendly smile. But it had not stopped him from
washing out. Nothing like that would happen to Eddie Mercado, Flaco vowed. He would make sure of that. He had
left Serafina to seize this opportunity. He had left her behind
when he ought to have stayed with her. To be sent home
now would be unbearable disgrace.

"Just take up the slack, bunny," Rhys warned him. "You
don't want to yank too hard."

The winches, like the attitude jets welded to the approaching tank, were A/S-controlled, and powered by Seebeck motors that ran off the temperature difference between
their sunlit and shaded plates. The winches kept a steady
tension on the approaching vessel, guiding it toward the
nose ring on Number Three. Flaco and the others were
standing by "just in case." Once the connection was made,
the riggers would secure the couplings, but that was 'pren-
tice work. How was he to impress his mentor with his skills,
if his skills were barely called for?

"The guidance jets will compensate if the winches pull
too hard," he said, a little truculently.

"Sure, and that's how we find out our jerry-rigged propulsion system has just that moment run out of fuel. Ever

see two tanks collide? Me neither, and I don't want to. Not
when I'm lead rigger on the job. Never assume anything
will compensate for carelessness.''

Flaco was not advocating carelessness. Sometimes it
seemed that Rhys enjoyed twisting his words; that there was
something more to it than the usual "bunny hugs." He
watched the approaching tank rise. "It ain't movin' so
fast."

"So. When you get back inside, check out 'momentum'
and 'kinetic energy' in the μCD library. Then come back
and tell me what else beside velocity is in the equation.
Ziggy ain't like Earth. In a collision, this vessel you're
standing on might crumple in slo-mo; but it will, by damn,
crumple. I don't think the sardines''—he stomped one magnetic boot on the hull—"would appreciate that."

Flaco could feel the metal skin vibrate through the soles
of his feet. His winch kicked in, pulled in a few inches—
centimeters, they said up here—a few centimeters of cable,
and waited.

"Rhys is right," said a voice on Flaco's earphones. "I
could upload the simulation onto your helmet's visor-
screen, if you like."

"Butt out, Waldo," said Rhys, and for once Flaco agreed
with the man. Uncle Waldo could be a real pain in the ass.
Granted, the telepresent workers were supposed to audit
critical activities and keep video records, but it always
seemed to Flaco as if they were eavesdropping.

"You see, Flaco," Rhys went on, "that tank there didn't
come with a ready-made guidance and propulsion system.
It's something we rigged just to ferry it into place. Now we
did the best we could—which is damn good—but it's not
exactly Mil-Spec work, and something could always go
wrong. That's why the Rector evacuated the forward bay."
Another kick of the foot. "And that's why we're out here
enjoying the night air. Robots, sure, they're as fine as can
be for routine tasks, but they have the devil's own time if
things go outside the envelope. That's why they're called

'artificial stupids.' Your job, dusty, is not to be the natural kind.''

Flaco swallowed his irritation. "Yessir." He wasn't entirely responsible for snubbing the tank. There were five other winches. But he didn't think Rhys would appreciate such fine distinctions. Besides, if the lines were not played just right, the tank could swing around on the cable ends like the Devil's bola. "Crack the whip" was no more desirable a game than "bumper cars" when the playtoys were this big.

The tank rotated clockwise, then counterclockwise, as its lasers sought the matching array on the forward face of Number Three tank. Flaco could feel his heart begin to race even as his winch took up more of the slack in his cable.

Maybe it was his notion that he was being tested, or maybe it was Rhys's warning about expecting the unexpected, but Flaco frowned as the tank continued to hunt back and forth. "Something's wrong," he said.

Rhys cut in on the all-suit channel. "Stepan, abort the approach."

A half-dozen thrusters on Number Four fired simultaneously, stopping all motion and spilling velocity. The tank came to a halt relative to LEO Station. "All right, bunny," Rhys said. "That decision just cost the consortium a couple of troy ounces of gold. Can you back it up with anything but rabbit fever?"

Sure, thought Flaco. *You would never have given that order just on my say-so. And that means you saw something, too.* Had this been planned as a way to test the trainees? He had enough experience with VHI's odd ways to wonder. "The A/S couldn't orient the tank," he said aloud. "It kept turning back and forth without locking on. My guess is something's not lined up right."

"Could be a lucky guess. Yeah, Rod, what is it?" Flaco did not hear the Canadian rigger's response, so it must have been on the "otter" channel. "I don't care if they're both placed to spec, Rod. Measure up the total variance and let me know ASAP. I have six otters out here wagging their tails.''

Flaco stepped forward to get a better view. The nose of the Number Three tank was shrouded by the Intertank, a cylinder that linked the LOX and LOH tanks in the normal Shuttle configuration. Here it was being used to join one LOH tank to another. Since Number Three was destined to be the center tank on the Hub structure when the station was complete, this particular Intertank had been modified in orbit with Kingsbury magnetic bearings. The spin decouplers would let Number Three roll like a barrel while the rest of the Hub stayed motionless. But ''spin-up'' was a long ways off, yet. A couple years, at least; after the Spokes had been assembled and attached.

Flaco saw McGibbon, the Canadian rigger, checking the targeting lasers set around the rim of the Intertank. Flaco could see now that Number Four was coming in off-center. A swarm of fireflies flickered in the beams of the worklights. But how could there be fireflies in space?

''Back off, Flaco,'' Rhys warned. ''Smack between is not the best place to stand during coupling.''

''McGibbon is out there,'' Flaco said, pointing to the bright orange suit dancing around the lasers.

''Sure, but Rod's an otter. He knows what he's doing.''

Flaco checked himself before he made a remark he might later regret. Rhys Pilov held Flaco's training card— figuratively, since it was a virtual card—and it was his prerogative to mark Flaco down for any reason, or even for no reason at all. If there was one man aboard LEO who could send Flaco back home in a New York minute, it was the Russo-Welsh senior rigger. Flaco did not much care for being so much in another man's grace.

They brought Number Four in the rest of the way by hand, using the winches and cables to line the tank up and then pull it forward until the the butt-end of the new tank nestled into the cup of the Intertank and the male and female docking collars almost kissed. Uncle Waldo calculated how each cable had to be played and how fast it was to be reeled in or let out. And if the mechanical guiderails they used to replace the defective lasers was just something they rigged up using struts from the parts bay; why, that was what riggers did. Rhys himself climbed inside the Intertank to check that the prongs had engaged properly. "Don't complete the engagement until I'm back outside," he warned them. Caught between the coupled hydrogen tanks and the Intertank shroud, Pilov would be entombed. Afterwards, a simple cough of the engines was enough to drive the docking hooks home and the new tank was locked onto the rest of the structure. Flaco made a few suggestions, but mostly he did as he was told; and when Rhys double-checked all his work, he held his pride cupped carefully in both his hands.

They reentered LEO through the main manlock in the admin module. This was an entrance that had been cut through the tank's skin about thirty-four feet from the nose, into 3-D just forward of the admin offices. Eventually, eight such portals would be cut: four to provide access to the Spokes and another four for possible expansion to an eight-spoke configuration. Meat Tucker, the rigging crew boss, was waiting for them when they desuited. He was twenty-seven, older than either Rhys or Flaco, and wore his ponytail rolled into a ball at the back of his head, where it was held in place by a burette shaped like a human bone. Stepan Korodin, the propulsion engineer who had been overseeing the A/S from inside, was with him. Like the other maintenance and utility workers on board, Stepan wore gray "roaring lion" coveralls. M&U ran the station while the Rector's crew built it.

"What was it, Rhys?" Meat asked.

Rhys carefully mopped the sweat from his forehead with an absorbent cloth and ran a hand through his hair. Flaco had been surprised on his first EVAsion at how much sweat a man could work up doing work that to an observer would appear superhuman and effortless. Well, the same could be said of ballet dancers, too. A man doing any kind of work . . . if it *looked* like work he was not doing it well. Rhys shook his head. "Not sure, Meat. Rod McGibbon checked the lasers and one of them is out of position relative to its mate, but nothing is ever one hundred percent in position. There was some reflective debris around the nose of Number Three. Might be coating from the painter Waldos working on the outside skin, or it might be welding dross from when they attached the mag bearings. Reflectance may have confused the tageting laser, or the range radar, or both. The whole approach looked off-centered to me."

Meat nodded. "Okay. Uncle Waldo is doing a FMEA. Once we've identified the cause-chain, I need you to work up a corrective action plan to avoid any repeats. We may not know everything, but we always have the right to get smarter."

"One week suit?"

"When's the next hub tank coupling?"

"Five weeks."

"Take your time, then; but have the plan operational before then. And, Rhys?"

The lead rigger paused before leaving the briefing room. "What?"

"Tell your boys to be careful. The next mistake might not be the sort we can learn from."

Rhys's lips thinned and he nodded. Flaco said, "What kind of mistake can't you learn from?"

Meat did not smile. "One that kills you."

"We haven't lost a rigger yet," Rhys pointed out. "And only one serious injury."

"You're forgetting Takeuchi."

"He was a welder, not a rigger."

"We're all one team, Pilov." A new voice. Flaco looked for the source and found Wesley Bensalem, the site manager, floating in the portal from the 3-C. His short, gray hair, combed forward, was not enough to cover his frown, and the lines in his forehead and the line of his mouth compressed his face like a vice. "Tucker, Pilov, Korodin. In my office. You, too, McGibbon." He paused and blinked, as if seeing the five Green Crew trainees for the first time, and asked, apparently as an afterthought, "How'd the training go?"

It wasn't clear who the question had been aimed at, and Meat and Rhys looked at each other before either answered. Rhys said, "They did okay."

Okay. Flaco clenched his fingers but held his peace. The job had not gone according to spec and they had improvised and it had worked. *Okay.*

"Mercado, here," Meat said, "saw that the tank wasn't locking on."

Rhys shrugged. "So did Fette and Caplan; not to mention all of the otters. And Caplan saw it before Mercado did."

"Yeah, but—"

"If you're going to give credit, Meat, give it to everyone."

In the momentary silence that followed, Flaco could hear the unspoken comment: *and not just to your friends.* For the first time since applying for the job, he wondered if knowing Meat on Earth would be a drawback rather than a benefit. Could that be why Rhys was so cool toward him? "Look, *'mano,*" he said to the lead rigger. "I didn' make any mistakes out there."

Pilov barely looked at him. "That isn't good enough."

If there was one thing his years on the street had taught him, it was never to show your heart to men who would cut it out. So he smiled and said, "Yeah. Sure. You're right." Someday, though, Rhys would eat those words. Someday, he would gag on them.

Before he left the briefing room, the Rector turned and looked at Flaco. Flaco traded him stare for stare. Then Bensalem grunted, fishtailed on a guidebar, and kicked out of the room.

"You shouldn't do that," said one of the Red Crew veterans, a man named Fahrlander.

"Do what?" Flaco asked.

"Let the Rector notice you." He shook his head. "It's not a wise thing."

"You tell 'im, otter," said another man. "You tell 'im."

* * *

Each LOH tank was divided into six bays, marked by the five major ring frames in the structure. The short, ten-foot bays at either end were devoted to storage and to the man-locks between tanks. Meat called them the "front and back porches." B-, C-, and D-bays were twenty feet each, E-bay, just aft of the front porch, was just under fifteen feet long.

The mess hall in 2-D was the strangest room Flaco had ever seen and even after a month in space he was still not entirely used to it. Granted, in microgravity you did not have to sit level on the floor, but it struck him as odd to find tables checkerboarding the entire volume, and people "sitting" at all angles. With a crew and a half on board, space was at a premium. In theory, thirty men and women could occupy the mess hall comfortably. In practice . . . Flaco sometimes found men doubled up, eating off both sides of the same table—though that was considered rude without extenuating circumstances. A system of nylon guidlines crisscrossed the bay. Even the Red Crew veterans used them, mostly for purchase and for changing directions. Delight Jackson compared them to the rigging on a sailing ship and had even given names to some of them.

When it was Flaco's turn at the meal dispenser, he ran his magcard through the slot and said, "Give me something tasty this time, Uncle." The food was free, a part of the contract, and you could have as much of it as you wanted; but free or not, usage had to be carefully monitored for inventory levels and resupply. It wasn't worthwhile to lift live personnel for that sort of work, so Uncle Waldo was in charge of inventory control, and everything had to be checked out or checked in or checked off.

A self-enclosed tray slid out of the slot and Flaco picked it up. He stuck his tray in one of the microwaves and waited. A sign read NO FOOD FIGHTS and WATCH YOUR CRUMBS. Flaco ignored the gob of mashed potato obscuring one of the FS.

"You say that all the time, Flaco," the speaker grille said after the usual delay. "Inventory's FIFO: first-in, first-out.

You get the next meal in the magazine, and that's it. Trust me, Flaco. None of the others are any better.''

It bothered Flaco that Uncle Waldo always knew who he was, but Flaco never knew Waldo's actual identity. He didn't even know if he was talking to a man or a woman, a black or a white. He scanned the mess hall for his friends. "What's your name?" he asked. He noticed Sepp at a table across the room and slightly above where Flaco hovered and waved to get the man's attention. Sepp did not respond, but that was typical of the man.

"Why do you care, bonebag?" the speaker asked. "The next time you come in here, someone else may be handling meals, and I'll be virtching somewhere in Accounting."

"Let's jus' say I wanna know who I'm talking to."

"Yer talking to yerself, mate," said Red Hawkins, who placed his own meal in an adjoining microwave. Flaco ignored him and waited to see if Uncle Waldo would answer. The microwave chimed and Flaco removed his meal. He lifted a corner of the lid and sniffed at the contents. Meat loaf, he thought. Macaroni and cheese. Something that looked like mashed potatoes only it was orange. Ay, for some *guisado* or some *costilla de cerdo!* Eat all you want, yes; but who would *want* to eat this all the time?

"My name is Leilah," the speaker said.

"You're a girl," Flaco said, surprised.

"Bloody good it does you," Red commented, "when you can't pork her from here."

"A woman," Leilah said.

"I've pleased a few women in my time," Red admitted. "You a looker, there, Sheilah?" He grinned into the doid beside the grille. "We need you up here. The women we got all look like Jones's last meal."

"You've pleased a few women, have you?" Leilah asked. "Then you must have dated an awful lot."

Red nodded, but with a profoundly puzzled look. Flaco didn't get it, either, at first; and when he did, he turned quickly away. "I'll catch you later, Leilah," he said, and then climbed monkeylike up the rigging to the table where his friends sat. Halfway up, he let himself laugh.

Sepp didn't react when Flaco perched beside him. He had that vacant look he sometimes wore, as if his thoughts had wandered and had forgotten to come home. Sepp was the only man Flaco knew who occupied his idle time with idleness. Tonio Portales, across the table from him, grinned.

"He is meditating again," Tonio said. "He is searching for the inner truth." The Cuban laughed and stirred the puree on his plate. "Have you met my compadre?" he asked with a nod to his right. "This is Tiny Littlebear, and he is one fine welder."

Flaco said, "We've met." He shook hands briefly with the big Mohawk. "Is this the welders' mess, then. Perhaps you do not wish to eat with a lowly rigger."

"Ah, Flaco," Tonio said, "we have pity on you. Eat." He waved a gracious hand over the table. "Here you see the three finest welders on all the station."

"Best among the bunnies, at any rate," Littlebear chuckled. Tonio's smile froze briefly.

"How long will they keep that up?" the Cuban asked. The words were light enough, but Flaco thought he heard some of the same edge he himself felt.

"Wit'out gravity," Sepp Bauer said, "they can keep it up indefinitely."

"The Sphinx has awoken!" Tonio exclaimed.

"Personally," said Littlebear, "it don't bother me none. I'm from the Rabbit Clan anyway. I'm used to it."

"A most prodigious bunny," Sepp said, eyeing the Indian's bulk; though he should have been the last to talk. Sitting between them as he was, Flaco was reminded of standing between the two external tanks the week before.

"Did you guys watch the show from the asteroid?" Flaco asked. "They put it on the pixcreen in the ready room while we were suiting up."

"Down in the barracks, too," Tonio said. "A few of the guys complained they couldn't see their regular shows, but most of us watched. Everybody cheered when the Negro captain carved their names in the stone."

'' *'Man,* that was something,'' Flaco said. ''All alone out there . . .''

''They should not haff done that,'' Sepp said with a shake of his head. ''Vandalism is what it was. Chust like graffiti.''

Flaco had grown up in Washington Heights. He had never seen a wall without graffiti. He shook his head. ''So, what's your point?''

Bird Winfrey passed by above them. He looked down, saw them, and grabbed a rope to stop. ''Hey, Pedro,'' he called to Tonio. ''Thought you'd like to know. I checked all your welds this shift and couldn't find a damn thing wrong with any of them.'' He waited a heartbeat before adding, ''And I looked God-awful hard.''

The Cuban tilted his head. ''I don' need you to tell me how good I am.''

''Not when you got yourself, right? Well, see you 'round.'' He kicked off on the guide line and sailed toward the crew quarters in the next bay aft.

Tonio watched him go. '''*Man,* I hate that Anglo.'' He looked at Flaco. ''You find that funny?''

Flaco had been reflecting that, with a name like Winfrey, Bird was one of the few Anglos he had ever met who really was an Anglo. ''Not me,'' he said.

''Bird doesn't bother me,'' said Littlebear. Tonio laughed at him.

''The Third Army wouldn't bother you, *amigo.*''

''He's a Non-Destructive Test technician,'' Tiny insisted, ''It's his *job* to radiograph our welds.''

''Yeah, but he *enjoys* it.''

''Ach,'' said Sepp suddenly, ''it is time for my shift. Are you coming, Tiny?'' There was no weight in space, but when the two welders had gone, the table felt distinctly less massive.

''Are you going, too?'' Flaco asked. Tonio shook his head.

''I just came off shift.''

''How does he do that?'' Flaco wondered. ''Sepp, I

mean. He didn't even look at his watch and there's no time-clock on the bulkhead he was facing.''

Tonio shrugged. ''A mystery. His mind holds mysterious powers.''

''There is no cause to mock him when he is not here.''

''I was not mocking him. Well, maybe a little. But the mind *does* hold mysterious powers. Yours, mine. Even our phlegmatic friend. It only takes some unloosening.''

''Meditation is too much work for me.''

''Perhaps with pearls.''

Flaco froze with his fork in midair. A dab of mashed pumpkin squash dislodged and floated in the air. Flaco quickly retrieved it before air currents could waft it away. ''That isn't funny,'' he said, and he swallowed the squash.

''Sometimes,'' Tonio said, ''when one cares about things too much, a little uncaring is good for the soul. It restores perspective. Sepp appears so relaxed at times that I wonder if it really might be Mexican pearl. He has that same look of peaceful contentment; the same air of not caring.''

''You don't think he—''

''What, *Herr Doktor* Health-food? *Meister* My-body-is-my-temple? No, but the chemical exists naturally in our brains. Perhaps his brain produces more than ours.''

''Good,'' Flaco said. ''I like Sepp, but too much pearl can be fatal.''

''How do you mean, Flaco? It's a natural substance. It does not addict. And under its influence, a man becomes passive, not violent.''

''It killed my best friend,'' Flaco insisted.

Tonio seemed genuinely puzzled. ''But how? Pearl is harmless.''

Flaco shook his head. ''But the lead is not.''

It was hell Outside. They drummed that into you from the first day of training. It was deadly cold and searing hot, and radiation poured off the sun like sleet. High vacuum could suck the air from your lungs or the blood right through your skin in a matter of seconds. There was nothing to grab hold of, no gravity, no air for a wing to bite. It was slipping on a banana peel forever and ever. Exploding heads were comic book stuff, but—like Bennett, the suit tech Gray, explained—put a hole in your suit as small as an eighth-inch and you had twenty seconds to get into pressure. At that point it was a coin toss whether your brain and nervous system had been irreparably damaged.

So nobody went Outside without careful thought and thorough preparation, and never, ever alone. But with all the focus on the dangers of EVAsion, it was all too easy to forget that Inside wasn't all that safe, either.

Number Four tank, now it had been joined to the station, needed dressing out. Its interior swarmed with riggers and electricians and pipe fitters and welders, all suited up because the bay had not been pressurized yet. Bundles of parts and prefabbed structures were secured in 4-E, which was serving as their marshalling yard. Plans and schematics were magged to bulkheads. Robots and Waldos darted on compressed-air jets or crawled along walls and struts. Bone-bags dodged and twisted among them, doing the work that demanded real-time reactions. The happy chaos of a construction site . . . in three dimensions.

The plans said that this bay was destined for dry-soil plants, so some joker had named it Iowa and the name seemed fated to stick. The plans indicated a total acreage in the zeolite trays of just over a quarter acre. Flaco was no farmer, but that didn't seem like much of a farm to him. It was about the lot size he was hoping to buy with his bonus money.

The project was multitracked, with several subtasks running concurrently, but the basic job at this stage was to install the utilities. The tank already contained considerable plumbing and circuitry for the original cryogenic pumping system, and the project engineers had used as much of this as they could; but more would be needed to adapt the space for more complex functions. Piping and pumps for hydraulics, and for air and waste; electrical and data bases, wiring and switches; data ports and power outlets; air scrubbers;

instrumentation to monitor pressure and temperature; and a host of other things you never much thought about until you had to provide them or die. There wouldn't be amber waves of grain waving around inside "Iowa" for a long time yet.

There were mandatory rest periods after each bout of strenuous activity, and Flaco used one of them to watch Tonio at work. Watching other people work always gave him pleasure.

The welder stood in a metal framework, with his feet planted firmly in a pair of stirrups. He held an electron gun in his right hand and a black box in his left. An umbilical connected the box and the gun. A clamshell with a port for the gun covered his work area to contain the gasses and molten metal.

"It's delicate work," Tonio told him without taking his attention from the dark glass window that let him see what he was doing inside the clamshell. "You have to make the metals flow together, to blend. So . . . I move the beam in small slow circles, so the weld looks like a row of coins. And you must be careful that gasses do not become trapped in the weld. That is a problem in zero gravity. So you see, my friend, this is not like rigging, where all you need are big muscles and small brains."

Flaco suppressed the urge to nudge his friend. Perhaps it was hard for others to see that mating structural members and walking the steel could be delicate work, too. He glanced up as a robot crawled past on the bulkhead above Tonio. The robot—or perhaps it was a Waldo—was laying down electrical conduit. Wendy McKenna was feeding a rainbow of wires into it from a set of spools. A second robot crawled after the first, squatting at intervals to weld brackets to hold the conduit in place. With each pause, a bright, actinic flash leaked around the edge of its skirt. Everyone called it "the farter."

There were eight lighted switches on the T-block in Tonio's left hand. These were for various power settings. Tonio's left thumb hovered over a ninth switch, which he called the kill switch.

"You need a sure touch, too," Tonio went on. "The UHT—that's the gun. They call it the Universal Hand Tool. The trigger, it has two positions. You pull it back to the first position, that's to weld or braze. You pull it back all the way, and that's for cutting. There!"

Tonio raised his helmet away from the view glass and removed the UHT from its port. "Let's see the Bird find anything wrong with that one." His helmet visor slowly lightened, revealing a grinning face.

"No importa," Flaco told him. "Bird, he's over on Number Five tank, checking for cracks and structural damage." The ETs took a lot of stress during launch, so each one was carefully tested before moving it into place. Also the skin had to be prepped to keep it from flaking and cluttering the orbit with nuisance debris. "I think McMaster is checking welds himself today. At least, I seen him around here."

"McMaster?" Tonio shook his head. "'*Mano* . . . He's good. He wrote the book on NDT." Then he grinned his cockeyed Cuban grin. "Maybe I'd rather have the Bird check me out, after all." He flipped a toggle switch on the handle of the gun, frowned, and carefully reset the toggle to the center position. "Number two cathode is out. I gotta tell Uncle Waldo. Middle slot is 'off,' but some of the guys just shove it all the way to the right, cause they know it's dead. Get a bad surprise if number two cathode starts working again . . ."

"Seems a bad design," Flaco offered. "The trigger. The toggle." Tonio shrugged.

"It's Russian. Or Ukrainian, or something. I guess they had to use stuff from different countries, so no one would feel offended. Like they bring us supplies on Protons and Ariane Sixes, and even on ram pods. Besides, the Russians invented space welding."

Flaco began to make some inconsequential remark—his break was about over—when the alarm honked on the all-suits channel. Someone shouted, "Loose steel!"

Flaco looked around in time to see a rod some fifteen feet long and as wide around as his face swinging across the bay. He registered, irrelevantly, that the shouter was wrong and the piece was made of aerogel, solid smoke, and—more relevantly—that its tip was coming directly toward his helmet. But the thought had no more formed than a hard shove to his back sent him sailing out into the bay.

Had there been air in the bay, he would have felt the breeze of the rod's passing. He turned and saw that Tonio had kicked out of his braces toward the arbitrary "ceiling" of the bay. The rod struck, denting the clamshell, bending the struts on the workstation, breaking the weld. Then it pogo'ed and the far end began to swing across the room like a scythe. He heard someone on the all-suit cry out, and another voice say, "But I only gave it a little push . . ."

Flaco reflected that bouncing like a Ping-Pong ball inside the bay while a fifteen-foot rod of structural smoke pogo'ed presented an interesting problem in probability. Not that math interested him in the least, but the solution in this case seemed to have some direct importance to him. He activated a suit macro and let the A/S play with his compressed air jets to stabilize his tumbling. Then he took manual control and set out to intercept the swinging end of the beam.

He reached it and took hold with both hands. The contact jarred him. *The baseball meets the bat . . .* He only hoped it did not tear a hole in his suit. He let the attitude jet A/S sense his speed and direction, then he told it to fire in the complementary direction.

Another body joined him. Red Hawkins. And he saw that others had grabbed the farther end, as well. And Rhys Pilov and Ivan Selodkin wrapped a loop of cable around the rod. And . . .

It was no longer a runaway.

Flaco's jets had cut out as soon as they had sensed zero velocity. Thank the Virgin for macros, Flaco thought. They freed you to think about *what* to do, not *how* to do it. He blew his breath out and closed his eyes briefly. Then he quickly checked his internal suit pressure on his heads-up visor display. Slightly below nominal, but in the operating range. He waited for a dozen heartbeats, but the reading did not change. He began to breathe again.

He had read somewhere that every species of mammal had the same lifespan, when time was measured in heartbeats. He was using up a lot of years right now.

"Well, mate," said Hawkins, looking at him across the rod, "I guess that's another rigger crossed off the list."

"Everybody makes mistakes," Flaco said.

"Not everybody makes excuses," Red answered. "That's wot'll do 'im in."

"You never made any excuses?"

Red smiled broadly. "Never had to."

Flaco found Tonio by the ruins of his work station. He looked up when Flaco touched him on the arm of his suit. He shook his head sadly and waved at the wreckage. "Best damn weld I ever made, Flaco. And the Bird never saw it. Now look at it."

"Hey, *hermano*," Flaco said, touching his helmet to Tonio's. "I want to thank you. For pushing me out of the way, I mean. If you hadn't been braced in those stirrups . . ."

"No importa," Tonio said. "Had to push you. You were blocking my escape."

"Yeah, well . . ."

"I know." The welder clapped two gauntleted hands together. " 'Bout now is when we all go down to the cantina and get drunk, except the damn Rector won't let us. How we supposed to deal with this?" He gestured toward the work station, but Flaco understood what he really meant. Smashed faceplate or torn suit or busted ribs and legs. It hadn't happened, but it might have; and it damn near had.

"Accidents happen. We just got to put it behind us."

Tonio shook his head again. "Best weld I ever made."

There was only one vantage point on LEO Station from which you could see the Earth, unless you suited up and went outside. And that was the viewport in the outer hatch of the personnel lock in Number One, the cargo bay where the bunnies had first floundered about more than a month ago. The other hatches, for whatever reason, faced outward. You could see the moon; you could see the stars; but you could not see your home. The doid views on the pixcreens in crew quarters did not count. That was looking at a pixure, not at the real thing.

Meat Tucker had told him that New York longitude would be underneath the station at oh-seven hundred, station time. High up to the north, since LEO was in nearly equatorial orbit. Flaco hoped it would not be overcast again. It would be night in New York, and the city would be glowing like a jewel. Serafina would be asleep in her mother's apartment, dreaming of him perhaps, as he also dreamed of her. He reached into his coverall pocket and pulled out the locket she had given him, flipping it open with his thumb.

Serafina gazed back at him. Her smooth, dusky, unblemished skin . . . The promise in the parting of her lips . . . The radiance of her eyes and teeth would put the lights of New York to shame. ¡Ay-yi! It would be another month before the trainee rotation sent his half of Green Crew back to Earth. Another month of aching. When he went groundside, he would take Serafina into her bedroom and scandalize her mother. They would not come out for a week. Maybe, two weeks. He would be down for another two months before they let him come back for the second half of the training.

If they asked him back for the second half.

I love you, Eddie. There will never be another man for me. He could see her face when she said that. Content, happy, filled up. He could see her hair spilled across the pillow; hear the whisper of her breath in his ear; taste her tongue inside his mouth; feel her skin blending into his. *Then, will you marry me?* he had asked. And Serafina had wrapped her limbs around him. *Oh. Yes. Oh. Flaco. Yes. Never leave me.*

No, bombita. Never.

And so what was he doing here a couple hundred miles up and a couple thousand south? He opened his eyes. City lights on the edge of utter black. That must be an ocean, he thought. The cities marking its shore were few and small.

He could not recognize the night coast under him. Perhaps it was Ecuador? The ocean was to the left of the coast, but he could not remember now which direction was north. He did not know if he had rotated in the weightlessness of the airlock. He did not know where Serafina lay tonight.

He had almost died. If Tonio hadn't pushed him, he might have floated there, paralyzed, while the swinging rod played baseball with his head.

That might have been best. Death and dismemberment benefits were generous; and he would never have to worry about raising little Guillermo. Never have to worry about disappointing him. A living father is fallible; a memory never made mistakes.

"She's awful purty," the voice behind him said. Flaco turned with a sudden jerk, snapping the locket case shut as he did.

"Who is?" The locket slid back into his pocket.

It was Wendy McKenna, the electrician, and one of only a handful of women on board. She was short, solidly built but with long, delicate fingers. Her hair was cropped short, not quite in a buzz. She filled her blue O&P coveralls very nicely. She pointed toward the viewport with her chin. "The Earth. Lady Terra."

"Oh. Yes," Flaco agreed, "very pretty." The manlock was big enough to accommodate two people wearing hardsuits. There was no reason Wendy could not pull herself in beside him with room to spare. Yet the space seemed all of a sudden very crowded.

"You can't even see it all," she said. "It's such a big world. People dirtside have no idea how big. I could spread my arms wide and not be able to span it." The airlock was not a place to spread one's arms, though she did. Flaco ducked, but their hips bumped together.

"I haven't seen you back here before," she said. " 'Flaco,' isn't it?"

"From Washington Heights," he said automatically and offered his hand. Her grip was firm and confident. "And you are . . . ?"

McKenna laughed. ''Try to tell me that there's one jack on this crew that doesn't know each woman by name, mass, and work schedule.''

''Well,'' Flaco admitted, ''it is a subject that comes up from time to time.''

She laughed, showing small, even teeth. ''I'll bet it does. I'll bet a lot comes up. You probably have ratings. 'She's a bow-wow.' 'That one's a submarine.' ''

Flaco felt a touch of red at the tips of his ears. ''Men sometimes talk that way, to make themselves feel more desirable.''

''Hey,'' Wendy laughed, swatting him backhanded on the arm. ''You ain't a-woofing. Some of the jacks up here got a lot of nerve calling any of *us* a dog.'' She looked him over. ''Not you, though, Flaco. You're buff. Good pects; tight buns. Bet you'd be dynamite between the sheets.''

His flush grew deeper; embarrassed not so much by her talk—though Serafina would never speak so crudely—as by the fact that her tight presence with him in the airlock was affecting him.

''Oh, look!'' she said. ''It's coming up!'' She meant the Sun, he thought. The darkness below them had lightened to gray and the eastern limb of the Earth had taken on an incandescent glow. McKenna's hand groped, found the control panel, and turned off the interior lights. The airlock fell into twilight, brightened only by the Earthglow streaming through the port. McKenna pressed closer toward the view and Flaco backed away to give her space, but she brushed up against him anyway. *It was her arm,* he thought, *that rubbed against me. Only her arm.*

The sun burst over the horizon and framed Wendy's face in an oval of golden light. Her delighted smile was a sunburst all its own. ''It's so beautiful,'' she said. ''So bright and sudden and glorious. It's like nothing you can see on Earth.''

''Yes,'' Flaco said. ''It's quite fine.''

She turned to face him, to press close against him. ''Have you ever made love in 'the dawn's early light'?'' she asked.

He could feel her curves pressing into him; feel himself responding. He took her by the shoulders and pushed her back and she turned her face, ready to be kissed. He saw that she had undone the top of her coverall, so that it was a cover-not-quite-all. He could reach in there; cup her, stroke her, pull the fastener farther down. He could . . .

. . . push himself away with too much force. Being smaller, Wendy sailed backward a little faster than he did and she struck her head on the rim of the viewport.

"Jesus H. Goddamn!" she said, grabbing her scalp. "What the hell's wrong with you?"

"I—I'm sorry," he stammered. And he saw within himself, to his horror, that he really was sorry. He had wanted this woman. He still wanted her. "I'm married," he offered as an explanation.

"So was my ex-husband and that didn't keep him from crawling inside half the panties in Fort Worth. What makes you so all-holy pure?"

Flaco shook his head, and sought refuge in words. "I keep my promises."

"Oh, listen to the prig. Let me out of here before I scream rape. I can't stand you people, think you're better than anyone else." She pushed past him roughly, shoving him and not caring how hard.

"I don't think that," he blurted out. His words stopped her at the inner hatchway. "That I'm better than you."

"No?" Her voice and gaze were skeptical.

"No." Flaco hesitated a long time before he went on, but McKenna waited. "There are more sins than lust," he said. "I have been guilty of far worse than lying with the wrong woman. It has been washed away by repentance, but I must watch always what I do and guard always how I feel. I even envy you. When you release yourself, you spread pleasure. If I do . . ." He shook his head. "The neighborhood where I grew up was not gentle."

McKenna snorted. "At least you don't claim to respect my 'honor.' Thank you for that much."

Flaco watched her retreat into the loading bay. He waited

quietly in the airlock, so they would not be seen leaving together. So that wagging tongues would not tell tales of what had not been.

But what might have been. A desirable woman. Direct and available; shaped to fit a man, and not interested in rigging any cables to hold him by. Never had the bonds of duty chafed so badly. Yet, if he were not true, then what could he be but false? And false to one meant ultimately false to all, for a man's soul was seamless. He would become something mean and contemptible, a betrayer of trust.

Two months was not a long time to be in space, not by current standards. It was just long enough to shake your ground legs and learn how to handle yourself, but not long enough to get cocky about it. The otters all said how it was too long to spend wiping bunny noses, but by then Flaco had learned to ignore their remarks. He knew phase-over was coming because the bumboats starting bringing up Gold Crew members and taking Red Crew down. Ossa & Pelion did not turn over the entire shift at once because continuity of the work required some overlap in personnel. Green Crew was an exception. They had been aboard primarily for training and final qualifications and the whole group would go down before the second lift came up for their round of training. Flaco could see the looks of joyous anticipation on the faces of Gold Crew.

No, not very long, at all. Yet long enough to build friendships, have a few fights, and a few laughs; long enough for a brush with death and a brush with lust and to stare into the rapturous infinity of stars. Long enough, that Rotation Day began to feel as much like "going away" as "going back."

It was because only two weeks remained that Flaco said nothing about Tonio's toothpaste. There was no point in creating an issue with so little time left.

"It's a pearl," Tonio said when Flaco caught him. "And so what?"

The sanitary facilities in Number One bay were small and

cramped; otherwise Flaco might not have noticed. You did not so much enter a shower as wear it. Step inside, seal it up, turn on the suction, and make sure your filters were in place. No one wanted loose water globules all over the station. Magdalena Würm had nearly drowned in the shower the first week because she hadn't used her nose filters properly. Inside the cylinder, the air became water-saturated and you had to wait for the suction and the blow-dry before you could remove the plugs. It was a mark of Magdalena's beauty that no one offered to help by zipping into the shower with her. Not until the eighth week on-board anyway, and even then it was Gladys Winchell who offered.

Some of the men had found the shower so irksome to use that they stopped using it; that is, until their close associates and neighbors forcibly reintroduced them. Even so, there was a marked preference for the slots just before or just after the time when the facilities were given over to the women. In between, they were nearly deserted. Line up a little early or hang in a little late and who knew how lucky you could get? Though usually the first women in were Millie Hess and the Untouchables: Two lizzies and three virgins; though, as Red Hawkins cracked, what difference did the motive make when the goods weren't on the market?

If, on the other hand, you wanted to be alone . . .

Tonio was hunched over the vacuum sink, playing with his toothpaste tube when Flaco emerged from the 'fresher cubicle. He was squeezing it with the cap on tight, working it with his thumbs, like there was something inside that he wanted to push out.

Which there was. Small, round and off-white, nearly invisible in the paste that covered it.

"Tonio!" Flaco said. "What are you doing? What is that?" But he had seen enough of them to know. They had littered the carpet by Diego's outstretched hand.

Tonio held his hand out. Three small spheres were embedded in the sticky white mass that covered his fingers. "Do you want one?" Flaco recoiled.

"No."

Tonio shrugged. "I offered," he said.

"It's wrong!"

"Flaco, we almost died," Tonio said.

"That was a month ago. You shrug it off. You get on with things."

"Sure, you're the Iron Man. Nothin' scares you. But I smelled the breath, *'mano*. I smelled the stinking breath and I felt the wings. I shit my pants, Flaco. You understand me? You understand what that means? I close my eyes and I see it all over again. I suck on these"—and he worked the pearl between his thumb and fingers—"and I don' care so much. You know? It's still there, but I don' care so much."

"You can talk to the counselor . . ."

"Sure, Uncle Waldo, he really knows what it's like up here, don't he? You go to a priest for sex counseling, too?"

Flaco played one fear against another. "The Rector could dump you out the airlock for having those."

But the Cuban only laughed. "He won' do that. That was just to scare us. Besides," he added, "I only suck when I'm off duty, so it don' affect my job performance none." He lifted the pearl, toothpaste and all, to his lips.

Flaco's hand closed on Tonio's wrist, holding it in a band of iron. Tonio didn't resist him. It was characteristic of pearlers that they became calm and pliant. No one had yet decided if that was a benefit of the drug or its price.

A long heartbeat went by before Tonio said quietly, "You gonna hold my hand for the next two weeks, *pana?*"

"I seen 'em, *'mano,*" Flaco said with his face pressed close to Tonio's. "I seen 'em on Dyckman and the Nick. You start out not caring about the big, scary things. Like death." *Like fatherhood,* a traitorous voice whispered in his mind. "But after a while, you stop caring about a lot of things, like shaving your beard, or trimming your 'stache. Or washing up. Or cleaning your clothes. Like zipping down before you go, or wiping your ass after. I seem 'em, Tonio. They're sitting there in their stinking pants on some old alley grate, staring at nothing at all. Maybe, sometimes, they eat; if someone tosses them some stale bread. You *afraid,* my friend? Be afraid of that."

He released Tonio's wrist and backed away. Tonio raised the hand slowly to his lips, and hesitated. He looked at Flaco with watery eyes. "It's just every couple days," he insisted. "Just enough to keep the edge off. I know some guys, they manage it. They control it. Not everyone's a bum, you know." Carefully, he placed the sphere under his tongue. His lips closed around his finger and he left it there while his eyes took on a dreamy look.

Flaco turned away, unwilling to watch; unwilling to participate even to that extent. He snatched his coverall from the magclasp by the sink and kicked off toward the manlock into the crew quarters. "Don't let no one else see you," he warned Tonio. "Not Sepp, not Tiny; 'specially not Red or Bird. You hear me, *cubano?*"

"You worry too much, Flaco. You care about too many things."

The Rector looked up when Flaco entered the project manager's bay. He and another man were hovering around an SPP cylinder in the center of the bay, discussing the 3-D projection inside. Meat Tucker and the pipe fitter supervisor were bowed over a computer screen on the other side. Most of the project's administration was conducted by Uncle Waldo, down below; but there were always decisions that could only be made on-site.

"All I know, Wes," the second man was saying, "is that the design change came down from high up. Higher than Hamilton Pye, if you ask me." He was a tall, thin man with a sunken face, a prominent chin, and an unruly mop of straw-colored hair. In the 3-D tank, Flaco saw a model of the station—but with a squat, silver cylinder attached to the Earthward side of the Number Four tank. "Ham says a Shuttle will bring it up, whole. We just have to attach it and create access from Number Four."

The Rector grunted. "What you mean 'we,' white man? Sounds like Gold Crew has the job." He scowled at the tank. "It spoils the center of mass," he said. "What happens when we put the spokes on and spin up? Sure, I know Number Four is decoupled, but . . ."

The tall man shook his head. "I don't like it. Hush-hush. Which means either government or big-time proprietary project. The drawings are Mil-Spec, so you tell me which."

The Rector glanced over and saw Flaco. He scowled and touched a panel. "What is it?" The second man ignored him and peered more closely at the projection. As the whirling plastic "leaves" inside the cylinder stopped spinning and the lasers stopped flickering, the image broke up and scattered. The Gold Crew boss shook his head.

"I—" Flaco swallowed. *I just caught my best friend sucking dope in the 'fresher cube.* How could you say something like that and not gag? How could you say it and remain a man? And yet, he owed the project his loyalty, too. What did you do when duty called two ways? "I—need to see Meat about running the manlock through to Number Four." The rigging boss at the other end of the bay looked up at the sound of his name.

The Rector waved an impatient hand and Flaco swam past him. It wasn't as if the manlock job didn't have plenty of questions, but he hoped he could think of one to ask that didn't make him look really stupid.

Only two more weeks.

He hoped he wasn't *acting* really stupid.

10.

Making the Deal

It was an elegant gathering and all the Best People were there. The hotel ballroom swarmed with highly placed dignitaries, with actors and athletes and singers, with the wealthy and connected, and the sons and daughters of the Old Families of four nations. They were chatting, renewing old acquaintances, seeing and being seen. Women elegantly coifed and displaying novel gowns, moved in a cloud of laces and silks, in rainbow hues and textures and cuts; decked in jewels retrieved from safe deposit to dazzle or beguile or incite envy. Three women wore gowns of MEMS fibers, with the microscopic levers flexing to display different patterns and colors in response to the wearers' whims and the preprogrammed microprocessor "sequins" their fingers toyed with. The men wore somber, contrasting black— punctuated occasionally by uniforms or by something California.

Young King William was splendid in a plain naval captain's uniform emblazoned with ribbons and medals and the sash of the Order of St. George. Beside him, Presidente Guiterrez sported a sash of red, white, and green and a sunburst medallion on his breast. President Donaldson and Canadian prime minister Folkestone, at the end of the reception line, seemed dowdy by comparison. On the wall behind them a tall banner proclaimed: NEO-ENCEPHALITIS: LET THIS LIFETIME BE ITS LAST!

As a high-ticket fund-raiser you couldn't ask for a better draw. At what other event of the season could one be seen with so many important and famous people? Although, to be fair, the cause was a worthy one, and to decline the invitation would have been insensitivity of the highest order. Mariesa had accepted, despite a dozen projects and a thousand everyday crises clamoring for her attention. But if she chafed at the hours lost forever in posing, they were at least hours posed in a good cause. The chamber music was a pleasant mix of light classical and contemporary; the hors d'oeuvres were tasty, and the mood was decidedly upbeat, despite the distressing *raison*. Perhaps Harriet was right, and she ought to budget some of her time toward relaxation. Even machines went down for preventive maintenance.

The media skittered through the crowd, doiding the famous and photogenic, recording their Concern for the evening news-bites or the infotainment celebrity shows—as if the ability to memorize and recite dialog on command made one an expert in epidemiology. Well, to be fair, neither did turning a profit or pulling in votes. The only opinions that did matter were not at the gala, but in a score of laboratories in four countries. Their sounds were seldom bitten. Genuine scientists always hedged, and the media craved buoyant optimism or croaking doom. Last month's oil spill on the Jersey Shore was a case in point. How did you handle a "bad-but-not-catastrophic" spill? How did you handle a "successful-with-some-glitches" cleanup?

Mariesa wound her way through the reception line. She offered condolences to the king—in whose country the epidemic had started—and to the president of Mexico, where the illness rate was highest. When she reached the end of the line, Donaldson sandwiched her hand with his own and murmured some pleasantries. Mariesa responded with some mindless platitude about better funding for encephalitis research. Donaldson shrugged sadly, as if to say money could not solve everything. When Mariesa made to move on, he held her firm and said in a low voice, "Have you come to a decision yet on my proposal?"

"No, sir. My staff is still evaluating."

"Caution is a virtue," he responded—and who would know better? "But the situation is growing toward crisis. Every day is a day lost and many more dead. Don't make me act without you."

Mariesa said something neutral and disengaged. The dignitaries were lined up behind a bullet-proof shield of SPP and the greeters filed through after passing a very polite but thorough security screen. None of the newsers could hear what was said behind the shield, but they certainly noticed that Donaldson spoke with Mariesa a bit longer than with any of the others. It was only later that she realized that, if anyone *had* overheard, it would have sounded as if Donaldson had asked her about funding some encephalitis-related project and that she was hesitant. King Log, he might be; but a clever sort of log, all in all.

Whoever arranged the banquet seating had mischief in his heart. When the reception was over and those who had paid the three ounces per plate flowed into the adjoining hall for the traditional rubber chicken, Mariesa discovered herself seated next to Phil Albright and across the round table from Edward Bullock. The idea that the seating was random was ludicrous.

The table seated six. Mariesa had been paired with her cousin, Norbert, a thin, angular man who seldom left Boston. Bullock had brought his wife, Vanessa, a retiring woman but beautifully dressed. On Phil Albright's left, completing the circle, sat Roberta Carson.

Mariesa glanced curiously at Albright, wondering why he had brought Styx with him. The campaign against neo-encephalitis was certainly one in which the Peoples' Crusades could join; but it was hardly one on which to hector Mariesa van Huyten. They were on the same side this time. VHI's Aesklepios division was among the companies searching for a cure. Could they possibly object to that?

The table was near the front of the hall, not the most prominent spot, but close by the dais. When the staff brought out the fruit cups, Mariesa happened to glance up and saw Donaldson watching her from the corner of his eye. She pretended not to notice and let her gaze travel on to King William and elsewhere. She recalled that the president was a *go* player and that *go* was a game of subtlety, position, and patience. She was being maneuvered; but how? And in which direction?

"It's a pity Aunt Harriet could not come," Norbert said. He had all of cousin Chris's features—the long nose, the dark eyes, the jutting chin, the lanky stature—but none of the sparkle and cheerful good humor that Christiaan cultivated. Norbert was a charcoal sketch of a man. He had always seemed to her the most remote and snobbish of her cousins. He was, in fact, more distant in blood. The son of Gramper's baby brother, Wilfrid, Norbert was younger than Mariesa's uncles and aunts, but older than her other cousins. He projected a staid, Olde New England correctness. Where Brittany's life was one of golf and parties and discreet, carefully planned affairs, Norbert Wainwright van Huyten's was one of concerts and literary guilds and earnest civic-improvement groups, though more because that was what one did than because of any heartfelt commitment.

"She wasn't feeling well," Mariesa said. "Her leg is bothering her again."

"Yes. Phlebitis, isn't it?" A dutiful question. Norbert neither liked nor disliked Mariesa's mother, but propriety required his concern. And who was to say that such social conventions were inferior to the brutal and cutting honesty that had been in vogue for so long?

"She'll feel better in a few days. It really distresses her to miss this affair."

"Sure," Styx interjected. "It's the social event of the season."

"You don't know her well enough to say that, Roberta." But it was near enough true that Mariesa raised no higher defense than that. Harriet meant well, nor did she stint on her donations. But to donate her *time* was a foreign concept. Without a social draw, such as this gala, it would never occur to her. Norbert, who knew only a little of the history between Mariesa and Roberta, frowned at the impertinence and kept silent.

"I'm surprised to see you here unescorted, Mariesa," Bullock said. "I heard you've been seeing your old flame. What is his name?"

"Wayne Coper," Norbert contributed. He shook his head and turned to Mariesa. "I remember Mom and Dad clucking over the way your parents kept throwing the two of you together. Like breeding horses," Dad used to say."

"It's nothing serious," Mariesa said. "We're just old friends."

"He played football, didn't he? Of course, I was only a boy then . . ."

"Can we drop the subject? A woman does not need a male escort to go places these days."

Norbert sniffed and turned to Vanessa Bullock, whose husband let a smug glance toward his wife play across his face for a moment before he bent into his fruit cup. Damn it all, why did so many feel that a woman without a man was incomplete? Phil Albright pursed his lips and thought a moment.

"Wayne Coper . . . Wayne Coper . . . He's a lawyer, isn't he? Yes, I know the man. He's done some excellent advocacy work for the Nature Preservation Society."

Mariesa turned to him. "I said can we drop Wayne? Who are *you* seeing these days, if you don't mind *my* asking?"

There was a moment of suspension, in which guilt and defiance played across Phil's features and he and Styx traded glances. Then Mariesa felt the surprise overwhelm her. *Oho! Phil hasn't brought his aide-de-camp. He's brought his date!*

Then: *Why, he's old enough to be her father!*

Then: *What business is it of mine?*

Mariesa put her half-eaten fruit cup aside for pick up. She had read most of the extensive file that Luanda Chisholm's security people kept on Phil Albright. She could think of nothing in it that impugned his private life. He lived "higher on the hog" than his public persona pretended—Thanks to his sister, Cookie, most of his properties were not *legally* his own. But Mariesa hardly considered that a character flaw. More importantly, there was no hint of a hidden cruel streak. He had been married once before, but the divorce was amicable and Zena Albright spoke well of her ex-husband even today.

And why am I so concerned? It wasn't as if she was Roberta's mother.

"Robbing the cradle, are we, Phil?" That was Bullock. Oddly, the question sounded more like envy than disapproval. Nudge-nudge, wink-wink, getting some firm, young flesh there, Phil? Mariesa felt her ear tips grow hot with embarrassment for Roberta.

Vanessa Bullock said, "The most stable couples are those who are closest in age." Mariesa heard the ironic twist she gave those words and wondered if there was a "sweet young thing" between the Bullocks.

Styx stuck her chin out. "I'm not a child. I'm twenty-six years old. King Willy is only twenty-seven."

"And 'Philly' is . . . ?" Bullock said.

Albright leaned back in his seat. His thick eyebrows always made him look ominous. When he failed to smile, he could look dangerous. "I stopped counting years when I learned the difference between age and maturity."

Touché, thought Mariesa and bent over her salad to hide her grin.

Norbert only shook his head. They were discussing the boundaries of a field on which he did not play. *The joys of love are overrated,* he had told Mariesa one time. *The pleasure is fleeting; the entanglements, messy; the posture, ridiculous.*

Bullock let Phil's remark pass. "I heard your old partner, Simon Fell, is wanted for questioning by the sheriff in Lafourche Parish."

Albright stabbed at his salad, lifted a forkful of greens. "Really."

"Yes, something about sabotage to a paper mill down there."

"*Your* paper mill," said Roberta. "One that was polluting Lake Salvador with chlorine."

Mariesa had no doubt that Bullock played loose when it came to chlorine waste. On the other hand, she had no doubt that the potential harm was exaggerated. Thousands of Peruvians had died of cholera when that country, mindful of EPA warnings about "chlorine pollution," had stopped chlorinating its drinking water. It was possible to go too far, whatever one's direction. However, since the barbs were flying between Bullock and the Crusades, she declined to step between them.

"Ah," Bullock nodded, "then you do know about it. Yet, you haven't said anything to distance yourself."

"I never distanced myself from Hurricane Dafydd—or a lot of things I had no responsibility for. I'd think *you* should be the last one to criticize sabotage," Albright added pointedly. "Or the excessive zeal that Simon sometimes shows."

"That old canard about my late uncle, I suppose." Bullock dropped Mariesa a significant look.

"Cyrus was hardly responsible," Vanessa Bullock interjected, "for the criminal behavior of his hirelings."

"His alleged hirelings," Bullock amended. "I might also add that, unless you can prove those assertions in court, anything more could lead to a libel suit."

"Eddie," said Phil Albright, " 'they ain't nobody here but us chickens.' "

And Norbert, thought Mariesa, *who is as righteous a prig as anyone I know.* A surreptitious look showed her cousin listening thoughtfully.

"All we know for certain, 'Philly,' " Edward Bullock said, "is that the incident you refer to was masterminded by *your* friend, Simon Fell, and carried out by *your* people."

"And paid by *yours*. I've seen the receipts."

Bullock's expression froze. "Have you? And what receipts are those?"

Albright did not answer him. "Henry and Cynthia were good people," he said heavily. "They just went too far. We disavowed them."

"But not your friend, Simon. Not then, and not now, for his latest act of sabotage."

"We . . . are no longer associates." Phil looked at Roberta, who said, "Phil didn't know about Simon's involvement until two months ago. As soon as he did, he . . ."

"Oh, it was heartbreaking, I'm sure," Bullock said. Roberta gave Mariesa a look of pure venom.

"Simon and I were like brothers," Albright said to no one in particular.

"More than brothers, I've always heard." Bullock speared a cherry with his fork and lifted it to his lips. "You met in a boys' boarding school, I believe?"

Phil Albright laughed. "Only someone like you could imagine that an innuendo like that would bother me."

Norbert dabbed his lips with his napkin and suddenly rose. "Excuse me," he said, "but I'm not feeling well."

Watching him go, Mariesa glimpsed a fleeting look on the face of President Donaldson and she realized that, if Donaldson knew about that package of information that Mariesa had passed on to Styx, he had a hook on all three players at this table: Edward Bullock, because his uncle had suborned sabotage and attempted murder; Phil Albright, because his chief assistant had acted as cat's-paw; and herself, for invasion of privacy and the withholding of evidence of a felony.

Strange bedfellows, indeed, the four of them. Donaldson, herself, Bullock, and Albright. For the first time, she wondered if the seating arrangement had been meant to maneuver someone else, and not her.

Not that it mattered. In any collision, both bodies traveled altered paths afterwards.

* * *

After the banquet had ended and most of the high-profile guests had departed, Mariesa visited the rest room to freshen up for the trip back to Silverpond. Charlie Jim would be waiting for her at the West Side heliport. While she was brushing her hair, one of the stall doors opened and, in the mirror, Mariesa saw Styx emerge.

Roberta froze when she noticed Mariesa; then, face set like granite, she strode to a wash basin several feet away and stuck her hands under the faucet. Water sprayed in the silence. Mariesa hesitated a moment, then spoke.

"Did you enjoy the gala, Roberta?"

"Oh, yeah." Styx shook her hands hard, glared at the towel dispenser—Mariesa could almost hear her thinking about the chlorine used to make the paper—and turned to the air dryer instead. The air jet howled when she stuck her hands under the sensor. "It was real fancy, all right. Too bad no one did anything like this when the disease *du jour* was AIDS. But then you and your buddy, Bullock, wouldn't have been caught dead at an AIDS benefit."

"How can you be so smugly certain of that, young lady?" she snapped. "Do you think that, because I hold one stance you dislike, I must hold all the others that you dislike? Don't you think people are a little more complex than that?"

Roberta looked startled for a moment, then shook her hands, and the drier slowly wound down. "Ten years, and I finally got you to lose your temper. I'm not sure exactly how, but it's nice to know it can be done."

It's because you're an ungrateful young woman . . . Carefully, Mariesa gathered in the threads of her temper. She wasn't sure herself why Roberta Carson was so able to get under her skin. "And Mr. Bullock is hardly my 'buddy.' "

"Yeah? From where I stand, I can't tell you two apart."

"Then perhaps you should stand somewhere else."

Roberta grunted. "Well, it's been real, Rich Lady. See ya on the Riv'."

"Wait."

The two of them stood very still and quiet for a moment. "What?"

"Phil Albright and you . . ."

"Is that any of your business?"

"No, but . . ."

"Then, shut up."

"I do not disapprove . . ."

"Jesus Christ, do you ever listen to yourself? Who writes your material? 'I do not disapprove . . .' Thank you so fucking much."

"Only one thing, Roberta, before you go."

And what on Earth held that girl back after such a parting line as that? "What?"

"I can see your mother in you."

"You leave my mother out of this. You never knew her."

"Everyone who has ever tried to get close to you, you have driven off. Don't do that to Phil."

Roberta strode to the door and stopped there. She turned. "How touching of you to care."

The rest room door was not designed to slam. There were pads and an air piston to cushion it. And yet, it slammed.

"A flying crow," said General Salvaggio, "always catches something."

Mariesa van Huyten accompanied the man down the musty, concrete corridor, matching him stride for stride. Airmen standing guard at doorways snapped to attention as they passed. Mariesa wondered if they were always so spit and polished or if they reserved the heel-clicking for visiting VIPs. Dolores Pitchlynn walked briskly on the general's right side. In their wake, a cloud of aides trailed with the purposefulness of those whose importance depended upon the rank of others. The air was cool and moist, but three hundred feet above their heads the alkaline deserts of West Texas baked in the sun.

"The problem," the general continued, "is to make sure it's the right something." He laughed at his joke and half the majors and colonels echoed him.

The hallway had been recently painted. Surely they had not done that just for her visit! But when she looked more closely, she could see how worn and tattered everything was. This base had been a command center, a hardened redoubt built "off the books" during the height of the Cold War, recycled now to other purposes. She didn't suppose she could fault the security arrangements, but the place could do with a little sprucing up.

The general paused at a final set of doors and distributed hairnets from a plastic bin. "This is where we apply the ablative coating to the aeroshell. Normally, you would need a filter mask, too; but we won't be in there that long. One thing . . ." He paused to emphasize the importance of his next statement. "Everyone in that room is cleared, but you will not ask questions or speak openly about the intended mission of this asset. Is that understood?"

Mariesa nodded. Dolores said, "Of course."

Zhou Hui said, "Shall I leave my equipment here?"

The general smiled as if to say that Zhou Hui was very well-equipped indeed. No one supposed her shoulder pouch contained all her "equipment." To leave all her electronic devices behind would very nearly require her to strip naked, and the general knew that as well as anyone. Maybe—from the way his eyes lingered—he was half-hoping for just that. Mariesa wondered if the general knew how easily he could lose his hand if it ever wound up somewhere where Hui did not want it.

"Officially, it's a Heckyll Mark II air-to-ground missile," one of the colonels told them on a cue from the general. He spoke as if each word had to be squeezed from the tube of his throat. Sometimes, if you held secrets long enough, you had to force them out. "The shell and its vanes are hardened, but entirely conventional and recognizably based on the Mark I prototypes. Guidance and optical target acquisition are the usual DOD ordnance A/S. The multilayer, peel-off ablative coating that lets the bird survive the plunge through Earth's atmosphere is what NASA uses for its recoverable satellite packages. All standard materiel, supplied aboveboard by contractors working on nominally different projects. It only comes together *here*. We assemble the components, apply the coating, download and calibrate the software, and tutor the neural net to recognize the appropriate visuals. The Crow can lock onto armor from any angle down to forty-five off the vertical.''

"What sort of explosive does it carry?" Mariesa asked. One of the captains, a man named Duckworth, snorted just softly enough to deny that he had.

"No explosives at all, ma'am," the colonel explained gently. "Dump a load of scrap metal from four hundred klicks, it's moving close to twenty-eight-hundred meeps— uh, meters per second—when it hits. That's just shy of two miles a second. Each kilo carries the energy of a train wreck—four million joules. Turns a tank into shredded wheat.''

His grin made Mariesa shudder. What it did to the crew inside the tank did not bear thinking about. She was no sentimentalist. War was war; and a bullet in the belly would not be a morally superior act. The men in the tanks were prepared to give what they ran the risk of getting; and the residents of the houses they shelled would not fare much better than shredded wheat themselves. The Balkan War was an ugly and gruesome business all around. The *Times* had characterized the ferocity of the fighting as "*a mortally wounded man crawling fifty miles for the chance to strangle an enemy on his deathbed.*" Perhaps Donaldson was right, and ending it with a hammer blow was better than letting it drag on and on and on.

If it worked. If it ended the fighting and did not simply add another combatant to the list.

"Are there any questions?"

From his attitude, the colonel expected none, certainly none from civilians, and absolutely none from a couple of "girl" civilians; so Mariesa let Dolores carry the ball. What sort of cross-range capability did it have? How easily could camouflage fool it? Did it need Brilliant Eyes for external targeting control? What about abort capability? Mariesa barely listened; though she enjoyed the colonel's expression. Dolores sometimes liked to show how connected she was, and Mariesa did not begrudge her rubbing the colonel's nose in the fact.

For herself, Mariesa cared less about the operational details of the weapon system than about its reality. And the way everyone was acting, it was very real indeed. Unless Donaldson was putting on a very elaborate show for her—and there were far too many players involved for that to be plausible—the president was dead serious about his proposal to end the Balkan War and he might even be right about it working.

For the laser demo, they went above, into the heart of the Staked Plains, where the sun was a molten, brass smear in the sky and heat rolled off the hardpan flats in nearly visible coils. The very air writhed, so that distant objects seemed to flicker and dance like candle flames, and pools of false water shimmered on the glaring, alkali beds. Nothing lived here but scrub—even cactus shunned it. Animal life kept sensibly under cover and ventured forth only at night. The Spaniards had crossed it—and had planted stakes to mark the scattered waterholes, topping some with the bleached skulls of horses or cows to warn of alkali-poison. Later, men with trail herds had followed the stakes toward the cool, green pastures of the Colorado country. A treacherous and deadly crossing. How many conquistadors and cowboys—or even Indians!—had left their bones to whiten here?

Mariesa viewed the scene with a certain amount of detachment from inside the cool comfort of the "Ike" command rover. The periscope doid relayed a full three-sixty view to her wraparound helmet. Wearing the virtchhat, Mariesa could imagine herself outside under the deadly sun—in a desert unaccountably air-conditioned and equipped with soft bucket seats.

The rover had perched on the edge of an arroyo, providing a panoramic view of the proving ground. Below, an old remote-driven Abrams M1A battle tank lumbered down the arroyo, trailing a cloud of dry, white dust in its wake. To the right, and nearly on the horizon, the laser installation was barely visible. At least fifty miles, Mariesa judged. And they wouldn't push the envelope for a VIP demo. Effective range might be limited only by line-of-sight and the curve of the Earth.

"Lucifer has been in our arsenal since the nineties," their Army escort announced, "But, never show everything you've got, right?"

"Then it's never been battle-tested?" Dolores asked. Mariesa flipped up her virtch-visor and the desert disappeared. The interior of the Ike was a compact mobile command center, with doidscreens on each bulkhead, satellite links for the up-and-down, and a squat, cylindrical 3-D map tank in the center surrounded by staff chairs and consoles. Both the map tank and the consoles were inactive for this exercise. A driver sat forward in a separate compartment, but he had left the hatch open. Dolores and Mariesa occupied the G2 and G3 seats while Major Chamberlain sat in the command chair. Zhou Hui had taken the starboard-side gunner's saddle. She did not wear a virtch helmet. She never cut herself off from her surroundings.

"Oh, it'll work." Major Chamberlain was a gray-haired careerist who seemed genuinely delighted to show them her toy. "I was on the development team, and the physics is sound. Everything else is deployment and tactics. Technology can't compensate for a battle manager who doesn't know *how* to apply a tool effectively. But the only way to get experience is to use it. . . ."

"I understand," said Mariesa. She did not for a moment believe that there was no tactical doctrine in-place for use of Lucifer.

"It works just like a supermarket scanner," the major rolled on. "Parallel beams in a crisscross pattern. . . . Except you wouldn't want to run a loaf of bread past this baby. Talk about *toast!* At close range, we've actually sliced and diced soft targets into itty-bitty pieces. But you asked for a hard target at a distance, and that old Abrams was destined for the salvage yard anyway.'' Major Chamberlain might be just the opposite of the closed-mouth Air Force colonel who had explained the Crows yesterday, but Mariesa noticed that she never mentioned anything beyond the basic briefing package. Ask her something sensitive, Mariesa suspected, and she would chatter so much you'd never realize you never got an answer. There was more than one way to keep your mouth shut.

"Tracking," the driver announced. "Locked on."

The major turned to them. "Ladies, don your virtchies."

Mariesa flipped her visor back down and the desert panorama reenveloped her. She knew she would see no beams of light, not even if it were night. The military hardly desired a weapon that announced its own location so dramatically. So she concentrated on the target, playing with the helmet controls until the tank filled her vision like Behemoth.

Even toothless as it was, it radiated implacable power as it progressed down the arroyo. When it reached the flats and turned into the open country, its gun muzzle tracked menacingly to and fro. "Firing," she heard the driver announce. The tank continued to lumber forward. At first, Mariesa could see no change. Looking closer, however, she noticed how antennae and small appurtenances had been sheared off and how the dust cloud kicked up by the treads glowed a soft pink.

Then, little by little, the tank began to die.

It was sad in a way. A tiger at bay; its immense strength useless against an enemy it could neither see nor fight. A bright jigsaw puzzle of lines appeared on the side armor, like someone had taken a bloody knife to it. Parts of the forward glacis—thicker plate armor—began to flush dully. A water tank on the side burst and steam erupted from it. Electrical wiring sparked and hydraulics ruptured, spewing black smoking oil. The driver's hatch lost its hinges and fell off to the side. A dull belch of smoke issued from under the turret and the cannon ceased to track. The barrel on the 120-mm gun fractured near the muzzle end and the flame suppresser dangled. Then the left tread snapped in two places and the tank abruptly slewed to one side, exposing its vulnerable rear deck to direct line-of-sight. A fine network of crosshatching appeared on the engine compartment of the now immobile target. "Cooking," the driver's voice observed for the benefit of the firebase.

Fuel ignited and the Abrams was instantly enveloped in an expanding ball of plasma. Mariesa stared as flames and greasy black smoke groped toward her, reaching out and seizing her . . .

. . . And she yanked the helmet off her head and gasped air. "Smoking," said the driver. "And goosed." He turned and grinned at her. "And if that sumbitch had been carrying M829E3 in her magazine," he said, "you would have really seen a cook-off." Mariesa sucked in a slow, cooling breath of recirculated air. One moment, the tank had been sitting in a faint cloud of vapor and steam and dust; the next, it was an inferno. The crew would never have known they were dead.

There were a million questions. How would Lucifer function in orbit, she wondered? Was it radiation-hardened? Vacuum and temperature resistant? No need to compensate for atmosphere turbulence; and no line-of-sight interruptions. But the intended target was a lot more implacable than an Abrams tank. No delicate electronics or mechanisms to disrupt. Only solid rock to fragment and vaporize—with the vapor jets deflecting the course. That meant target acquisition at extreme distances. What would Lucifer's effective range be without atmospheric attenuation or curvature to hobble it? *I want one of these to play with. . . .*

She wasn't looking for an end product, she reminded herself. As far as asteroid killers went, this was just something for test-of-concept. A test bed for software and tactics. Something to practice with. "Can it be converted to power transmission?" she asked. That was the sane reason for her interest in the laser. Very long distance power beaming. That was the reason practical, hardheaded, bottom-lined people like Chris and Dolores could buy into it. That the system could be grown into an asteroid defense was a spin-off she did not care to mention; sometimes not even in the privacy of her own thoughts.

The nudge, when it came, came from a totally unexpected direction.

Bernie Lefkowitz was one of Belinda's Kids. Not one Mariesa kept in her scrapbook, but part of the nearly face-less ranks that had come along following that turbulent in-augural year. He had graduated from a private Mentor practice in Washington State in 2002, and was a reception guest at Mariesa's clamshell house on the cliffs overlooking the Pacific Ocean. She remembered him, barely, as a bright mind trapped in a gawky body.

When he appeared at VHI headquarters unannounced and clearly agitated, Mariesa impulsively cleared an hour. When she heard what he came to say, she cleared another hour. And after that, the rest of the day was lost.

Zhou Hui showed the flustered young man into her office. He looked around the room. The "space" paintings—and the photographs that were slowly replacing them. The black calendar obelisk. The golden and blue flowers that bright-ened an office of dark woods. The long picture windows with the view of First Watchung Mountain. The Scrooge McDuck clock on the wall facing her desk caused him to double take, and he relaxed just a little bit.

The visitor's chair was ergonomically designed—though in a subtle fashion. Initially comfortable, it grew slowly more uncomfortable to the sitter. Mariesa wanted her visi-tors to feel at ease, but she did not want them going on and on. It would be hard to know if young Bernie was com-fortable or not, the way he continually shifted position and fingered his "dress" cap. Mariesa considered offering a drink—or perhaps a sedative—to calm him down. "So," she said, settling comfortably into her own chair. (It had no time limit on its comfort.) "What can I do for you, Bernie? 'World shaking,' I believe you told my assistant."

"Well, uh. I wanted to be sure you would listen to me."

By this time, Mariesa had his Mentor file on her heads-down desk screen. Graduated in '02 from Harris and Adelhardt in Seattle. Straight As—and, at a Mentor practice, that meant something. Postgraduation annotations mentioned a B.S. from MIT and a Ph.D. in physics from Berkeley, followed by a postdoctorate in planetology at FarTrip.

Her eyes barely dropped while she read. "Does this visit have something to do with FarTrip?"

Bernie dropped his cap and half-rose from the chair. "Did Dr. Marcel call you? What did he say?" He blinked rapidly several times. "No. How could he know I was coming here?" Then, looking at her: "You know I work there, right?"

"I take it you are calling on me out of channels," Mariesa said dryly. "I ought to remind you that I hold no official position in FarTrip or on the UN Deep-Space Commission."

"Sure, but everyone knows . . ." His voice faltered. "I shouldn't have come. I guess that's what you're trying to tell me. It was a whack. I'm sorry I bothered you." He started to rise, but Mariesa hushed him down.

"You're here. You might as well say what you came to say."

He lowered himself slowly. "Understand, it's not just me. There are about a dozen of us—and we're not all junior researchers. Dr. Golasiewski agrees with us; and so do Drs. Longo and Hutton. We *think* Dr. Blessing agrees, but he's afraid to say so openly because he doesn't want to hurt his reputation. But he hasn't dissed us, either, because if we're *not* whack, this could be the biggest thing that ever . . ." He ran down, looked at her hopelessly. "I'm not making any sense."

"It would help if you started at the beginning. *What* is it that you and Dr. Marcel disagree on?"

"Aliens, Ms. van Huyten. Aliens."

Of all the messages that he might have come bearing, that was the most unexpected. Images flashed before her. Soft-contoured, infantilized ETs; jagged, hard-edged conquering monsters. It took a moment before Mariesa could respond. "What on Earth are you talking about?"

"Not 'on Earth.' On Calhoun's Rock. Thousands of years ago. Maybe millions."

Mariesa made a steeple of her hands and tucked them under her chin. "I've seen no press releases," she said, "so would it be fair to conclude that you believe there is evidence and Dr. Marcel and the other senior researchers do not?"

Bernie Lefkowitz nodded vigorously. "They're long gone, but they were there."

It was such a startling assertion that she could conjure no reaction. "And your evidence is . . . ?"

"The tunnel the Away Team found in the west end of the Rock."

"The 'Away Team'?"

He flushed. "It's what we call the on-site crew. They're not the only ones exploring the Rock, or even the most important ones. *We're* exploring it, too, through their eyes and ears and hands."

"A 'tunnel,' you said. I thought it was a cave."

Bernie snorted derisively. "Paradigm trap. What could make a cave on an asteroid? Water erosion? Uplift and folding?"

"The model is that the asteroid formed around more volatile cometary matter. A 'jelly-filled donut,' I think I read. Then another asteroid struck and vaporized the volatiles. The crater left by the second asteroid and the cavity left by the comet-head combined to form a rough cylinder."

But Bernie would not be persuaded. "Then there should be some trace of volatile compounds in the walls of the 'Cave' and none have been found—"

"Yet. But the absence of evidence is not the evidence of absence."

"You sound like Dr. Marcel," her visitor said bitterly. "He wouldn't listen, either. He had to stuff everything into his old, accepted paradigm, like Ptolemy adding another epicycle."

"In any disagreement," Mariesa reminded him, "between a distinguished, elderly scientist and a Young Turk, it is not *necessarily* the distinguished elder scientist who is wrong."

"I *know* I'm right. I just want an opportunity to investigate the possibility."

What price "investigation," Mariesa wondered, if the conclusion is already "known?" Scientists were no different from the rest of humanity on that score. They sought out the evidence to support their intuition and left the demolition to others. If science was more objective than literature or religion, it was because the rules of evidence were stricter. She began to suspect that Bernie Lefkowitz had come to her with the idea of throwing Authority into the controversy, and she did not like it. That he was a Mentor graduate and ought to know better bothered her more.

"And you want me to *order* that you be given the opportunity? What makes you think I have the power to do that?"

Lefkowitz flushed. "No, nothing like that. Only. . . . Dr. Marcel insists that it's lack of funding that keeps us from pursuing, um, side issues. I thought, maybe. A special bequest. Allocated just for 'heterodox' investigations . . ."

"You want me to finance your hobby horse."

Bernie rose. "I guess I've wasted my time. And yours." He stooped to pick up his cap.

"Mr. Lefkowitz, I have not said yes or no. Leave your netdress with my assistant and I will get back to you. *After* I have received briefs from your colleagues arguing the case."

The young physicist nodded and turned to go, but he hesitated at the last moment. "One other thing. When Calhoun carved the names of the crew into the Rock . . . ?"

"Yes?"

"Why did he choose that particular spot? It was nowhere near where the ship was anchored. So why there, and not somewhere else?"

After he had gone, Mariesa sighed. Politics. It didn't matter where you looked. In parliaments, in boardrooms, in universities, in research labs. Politics was there, because people working together always had conflicts of interests; and politics was the juggling of interests.

She activated her terminal and logged onto the FarTrip node of the Infobahn. She spent the next hour examining views of the "Cave" that had been downloaded from the *Gene Bullard*'s computers and following the hyperlinks to on-site mineralogical analyses, data from the now-functional Japanese probe, and to textbooks and other related information.

She found nothing to either "confirm or deny" Lefkowitz's thesis. But, then, she was only an amateur with a passing knowledge of orbital mechanics, asteroid composition, and cratering. She did agree that the Cave required an explanation, but she was not convinced that an *alien ex machina* met the requirement.

Her surfing brought her to the famous sequence in which Forrest Calhoun had carved the expedition's names into the Rock. Let some carp—as they did—about defacing the work of God-Nature. Let others compare it to a dog marking a fire hydrant in a pathetic attempt to assert ownership of a world not of its making. Mariesa found it inspiring.

She studied the scene, rerunning it several times, trying to discover what Bernie was getting at. What had he meant when he said, *Why there?*

Mariesa froze the picture at the point where Calhoun stepped away and the recording doid gave a clear picture of the rocks. She flipped back and forth between that view and the earlier record of the pristine rock. The hyperlink let her do this easily. Back and forth, like the tachyscope she had once used to compare photographs of the sky. The slab with the names; without the names. With the names; without the names. The slab itself remained unchanged, except for a few stray marks that must have been slips of the hammer.

Calhoun had chosen this location because it was the only unblemished flat rock on the asteroid's face. That had to be it. The only defects were a few small microcraters and the three sets of complex fractures where something had struck a glancing blow. Calhoun had 'scribed a name above each one.

With the names; without the names.

It stole across her gradually. A frozen feeling that began in her bowels and worked its way up her torso and out her limbs. A numbness that narrowed her vision to the pixure of a slab of rock on another world. With the names; without the names.

No.

Both versions had names inscribed on them. One of them had two sets.

That was what Bernie had hinted at just before he left. Something that even he felt reluctant to say aloud. And *that* was why Calhoun had chosen just this spot to leave his memorial. A salute across a chasm of years.

But if aliens had been altering asteroids, and asteroids had been altering courses to bring themselves closer to Earth. . . .

The next day she booked time on the video comm link at Deep Space headquarters. The day after, she called Forrest Calhoun and spoke with him for half an hour. And the day after that, she called W. Clement Donaldson and agreed to supply a weapons platform in exchange for a functional battle laser of the Lucifer class.

11.

Perturbations

The first thing that happened when Roberta loaded the disc was that a big, golden badge appeared on the screen with an announcement that possession of the information on the disc constituted a felony. If he had nothing else, Jimmy Poole had a flair for melodrama.

The second thing that happened was that all her Web links shut down. *That* torqued her. It meant the weenie had slipped her a virus, which meant her virus sieve was not as good as she thought. And who knew what else Slick Jimmy had slicked into her system along with the Web disabler? When she rebooted, would all her confidential Crusades files bleed off into Jimmy Poole's data banks? You heard stories when you asked around. Nothing provable; but knowledge was power, and Jimmy was greedy in more ways than one. Just as well she had told Super Weenie to send his reports to her home and not to Crusades headquarters. If security had been breached, better here than there.

She studied the badge icon for a few moments. The first couple of packages from Poole sEcurity had been "clear view" datassemblies, and Jimmy had E-mailed them to her openly. If Jimmy didn't want any active links while *this* disc was readable, it must contain something more serious than media indices and newsgroup clippings. She clicked the decompressor, and a placard replaced the badge. It read, *Don't say I didn't warn you.*

Roberta hesitated. She was stepping over a line now, and she knew it; but it was only a small step—and one amply justified. Sometimes bending the rules was called for. The rich and powerful loopholed the rules all the time, and the poor and powerless had to use whatever measures came to hand, sniping with electronic rifles from behind virtual rocks and trees at the arrogant ranks of privilege. Roberta gathered her resolution like a cloak and double-clicked the placard.

A datalanche tumbled off the disc and buried her hard drive. Files mushroomed in her directory. Folders were created, opened, stuffed with documents, closed, labelled, and stacked on the desktop. Many folders. The Great Wall of Folders. Thank God for virtuality. That much actual paper would measurably deplete the nation's softwood forest reserves. Damn Jimmy, anyway.

The problem with keyword harvesting was that you pulled in a ton of chaff for every grain of wheat. Jimmy knew that, which made his smug innocence even more irritating. "You hired me to get the data," he told her after his first delivery. "Organizing and interpreting it is your job." Using word games to finesse his obligations probably struck Jimmy as the pinnacle of cleverness. *Hah, hah, I filled my end of the bargain. Not my fault if you can't make sense of it.*

Well, screw him. As long as he came through, she didn't care what he thought he was getting away with. And (fair was fair) until she knew what she was looking for, she couldn't tell Jimmy what was important and what wasn't. Better that he deliver a ton of hay than a handful. There was a better chance that it contained needles.

A few things she knew to look for. *Asteroids*—according to Barry Fast, a major phobia of van Huyten's. *Prometheus*—since it would do no good to strike anyplace but where the woman kept her heart. Any intersection with *Donaldson*—because she knew from the overheard conversation on the beach that something was going down between the Rich Lady and the president. And Roberta suspected that that something had to do with Star Wars.

The timing was right. Mariesa van Huyten had visited the White House in July. That was a public record from Jimmy's first package. Ostensibly, the purpose had been to invite the First Poser to the asteroid rendezvous ceremony. But then the Rich Lady herself had skipped the ceremony. So what was the real purpose of the meeting? It was shortly afterwards (according to "Deep Whistle's" third cryptic E-mail) that the president moved a secret Star Wars project to the front burner. Had van Huyten put him up to it? Maybe VHI stood to make big bucks building the weapons.

Roberta watched the directory imitate a fungus on the popper window. Reports, letters, memoranda, data bases. Jimmy had slipped his spiders and worms from the public net into the VHI system and from there into Silverpond itself, the Rich Lady's personal datachine. Any system that suckled on the Web could be entered, Jimmy had told her.

She hadn't approached him yet about mousing the White House for Phil. She suspected that might spook the weenie, or at least jack his price up. Jimmy talked like a cybertough, but he hadn't become successful by futtering the Big Boys. And if the collusion between Donaldson and van Huyten did involve "Deep Whistle's" warning, then her private probe into van Huyten's affairs just might forward her Crusaders project anyway. Two birds, one stone.

The file count on her screen had reached the thousands. And the little vise icon had only relaxed about halfway. She left her computer running and went out to the kitchen, where she rummaged herself a bottle of spring water from the Nifelheim magnetic refrigerator. ("Cold as 'Hel'" was their motto.) Totally ozone friendly, the 'fridge used no coolants at all—let alone the toxic and explosive replacements industry had tried to force on the public in place of CFCs. It kept things cold with magnets—something about the way the atoms in "memory alloys" lined up when a magnetic field was rapidly flipped on and off. Some of the Crusaders had worried about the effect of electromagnetic fields when the magnefridges first came on the market, but science had disproven that theory long ago and, as Phil pointed out, it didn't help their credibility to holler giddy-up to a dead horse.

She took a swig and stood by the rear windows over-looking her postage-stamp backyard. Twenty-five, maybe thirty feet from her back porch to the wooden fence at the alley. Fifteen feet from one neighbor's fence to the next. A big chunk of that was taken up by an old, one-car, wooden garage that she used for storage. Not much open space back there. Hardly enough to play checkers, let alone Frisbee. Not like the acres and acres behind Silverpond. No place to ride your horses or shoot your grouse. (There had been a shooting last year in the alleyway; though it was not a grouse that the emergency squad had lifted off the gravel.) Sparse, strawlike grass was vanishing under a light blanket of patchy snow, through which the slate flagstones leading to the alley gate, showed wet and black. *I'm dreaming of a white Thanksgiving . . .*

She took another drink. One time in high school, when she had taken refuge at Silverpond, she had pestered Mariesa van Huyten into going out into the snow with her. That had been a February, she remembered; a month more traditionally winterbound than November. Styx had made snow angels, flopping backwards into the soft, wet, scrunchy blanket that covered the mound on which the house was built, spreading her arms to make the wings. Van Huyten watched with an amused smile on her lips, as if she had never seen the game before; and for one weird moment Styx thought the Rich Lady would plop down and join her in the snow. Afterwards, van Huyten had bundled Styx up warm with a blanket and a cup of hot chocolate while Miss Whitmore cleaned and dried her clothes.

It was the strangest memory. She could see the whole scene. The Rich Lady sitting by the mantle piece under that *absolutely ridiculous* clock, her pale cheeks reddened just the slightest bit from the cold and the ozone-sharp air. Snow-reflected sunlight sifting through the floor-to-ceiling windows, lending everything a faerie, crystaline whiteness. Herself, on one of the pale antiqued chairs with a red-and-yellow blanket wrapped around her and the plain china mug steaming deliciously under her nose.

And how could you see *yourself* in a memory? It was as if she was having a retroactive out-of-body experience; as if Styx was another person entirely.

Come outside, Mother, and make snow angels!

A younger voice, that one. Eager and pleading. *Please . . . ?* But Beth, as always, too tired to play with her. And . . . running down a carton-crowded hallway into her room, past stacked, unopened boxes—residue from a larger house, now almost forgotten—and slamming the door behind her and throwing herself on the bed—

Spilt milk, Styxy, she told her former self. *Go back to sleep.*

The snow spread whitely, nowhere very thick. Just a light dusting, the Weather Channel had predicted. Gone by morning.

The datalanche would have been impossible to work without a keyword filter, and Isaac Kohl obliged her by building one, after she swore him to confidentiality and coopted him onto Phil's Star Wars project. Isaac installed the keywords. Strategic Defense Initiative. SDI. BMDO. Brilliant Pebbles. Brilliant Eyes. A dozen different weapons systems, some of them mutually exclusive! The other keywords—those relating to van Huyten—she installed herself. As Simon Fell had rightly pointed out, it might someday be important to say Phil never knew. If she'd had any doubts in that direction, Jimmy's little badge had dissuaded her.

Still, it was like pouring the Jersey Shore through a child's sand sifter. She let the system run all day while she worked at the Crusades, and at night she skimmed off the cream and read it.

A godawful load of dreck. Long, rambling, jargonesque, corporate newspeak. "Once the SOW has been set, a BOD will be delivered per the PERT . . ." Acronym city.

Responsibility-shunning passive voices. "It has been determined that . . ." (Stand up like a man, damnit. *Who* determined it?) Mind-numbing petty details. Every now and then—a diamond in the rough, something that looked interesting or that piqued her curiosity. Those she flagged and wrote on a sheet of butcher paper she had hung on the wall of her home office. Whenever she saw a connection, she drew a line between the items involved and gradually a web grew on her wall. By the third day, she was using different colors for highlight.

It meant long nights after longer days, broken only on those evenings when Phil came over. On those occasions, they went out to dinner and discussed strategies and tactics or just philosophy; and when they returned and went upstairs together, she kept her office door firmly closed.

The hardest part was acting at headquarters as if nothing special had grown between Phil and her. She wanted to shout it. She wanted to dance. Truth demanded the light, and what she shared with Phil was True. Instead, they behaved with perfect correctness. It was "Roberta" and "Phil" because they were coworkers in the struggle and it was first names all around, but the other things they called each other in private remained unspoken. When they sat around the bunched tables in what they laughingly called "the boardroom," Roberta made sure that she always sat at least two seats away from him. Melanie and Dottie would disapprove if they knew she was sleeping with Phil, though whether from feminist principles or personal jealousy would be hard to say—and only in the cartoon fantasies of the Right were those two motives contradictory. Ellis would disapprove, too; because he felt that personal emotions had no place on the barricades. Celibate for the cause, he liked to proclaim, and for him it might even have been true. Some of the others—Isaac Kohl, Darren Winslow, Suletha ad-Din—might not disapprove and might even have wished them well; but when you got right down to it, it just wasn't any of their damn business, was it? She and Phil were entitled to their privacy precisely because their lives were so public, but it still hurt to pretend among their friends. It felt like a lie.

"Next item," Phil said.

"The Jersey Shore oil spill," Roberta said. As office manager, she kept the agenda. If she had not exactly transformed the Cadre into a paragon of order, she had at least reduced the chaos that had consumed their meetings since Simon's departure. She had resurrected Simon's practice of reviewing the status of each Crusade at biweekly meetings. But some of the Cadre—Ellis, Dottie, and Isaac especially— had a tendency to go on and on, and she had a special signal that told Phil when it was time to rein things in. Simon used to do the reining-in himself, but it would be a long time before she had the sort of authority that Simon had wielded. That was less gender than it was seniority: most of the Cadre had been with Phil longer than she. Simon had controlled them because Simon's status had been unquestionable.

"Recommendation is to terminate the demonstrations," Roberta said. "The cleanup was successful. People see us still picketing and they see the beach all clean and they wonder what the hell we're doing."

"The beach only *looks* clean," Dottie argued. "I bet if we dug down and took samples, we'd find a residue that those damn bugs didn't eat."

"We raised that issue with the EPA and with New Jersey's DEPE," Isaac Kohl reported. "Gaea Biotech came back with a demand that samples be taken from the entire beach, not just from the part they worked on; so we dropped it. *I* think we ought to be trumpeting the whole thing as a success. Even if there is some residual pollution underground, the worst was cleaned up. The whole crisis was handled quickly, without muss or fuss. We ought to celebrate."

"Noted," said Roberta, jotting a few words in the margin.

"As long as we celebrate the right half," Dottie insisted.

"Our half of the beach looks just as clean as theirs. And *we* did it the right way: by mobilizing people who cared and putting our own time and sweat into the work. Celebrate *that*, not spraying artificial life-forms all over the sand."

"You're missing the point, Dottie," said Ellis. He leaned back in his chair and spread his arms. "You all are. The point isn't how well we clean up messes. It's that we *make* the messes in the first place. Would you congratulate a child who knocked over a glass of milk just because he mopped it up afterwards?"

"Well, yes," said Melanie. "Of course, you would."

"Okay, I picked a poor analogy," Ellis said cheerfully. "We wouldn't want to damage a child's self-esteem. But I don't think we have the same concern about Klondike-American." There was general laughter around the table. "Sure, our volunteers did heroic work cleaning that beach," Harwood continued, "but we need to remind the public that the original spill was wrong. Do you know what the worst aspect of those oil-eating bugs really is?" He didn't wait for an answer; he seldom did. "Not that they were released into the wild, but that *by making the cleanup easier, they make spills more forgivable.* 'Heading for a reef?' " he said in a mocking voice. " 'Not to worry. We'll just sprinkle the magic pixie dust and everything will be fine.' "

"I've captured your observation, Ellis," Roberta said. "We'll put it on the New Business agenda for the Friday strategy session."

Harwood paused with his arm still in the air. He looked at Phil. "We stop looking for ideas, Phil?" Albright shook his head.

"Of course not, Ellis," Phil said smoothly, "but this meeting is for status review, not for planning. We can't pursue every suggestion or we'd never get through the list. You remember how meetings used to drag on into the night."

Ellis Harwood, who was one of the major drags, shrugged. "I suppose some of us have better uses for our nights." He turned a smile on Roberta. "You certainly have put things on a more businesslike basis, Bertie.''

Roberta said, ''Thank you,'' even though she knew he had not meant that as a compliment. Ellis was an academic. For him, the debate was everything. But the Crusades had to *act*, and act *effectively,* achieving the most results for their meager resources. If that meant something like cost/benefit ratios and watching the bottom line, that was simply a fact of life. ''Nonprofits,'' they liked to say, but that wasn't quite true. If they failed to bring in more contributions, grants, dues, and donations than they spent on protecting and repairing America, the Crusades would simply fold—and then what? Who would ''tilt a lance for the defenseless'' then? Strictly speaking, the Crusades ran an eight percent profit margin—but the eight percent was ploughed back into good works, not stuffed into the pockets of capitalists or the obscene paychecks of managers. As Phil had explained to her, income was like energy in a biosystem. An organization had to make a profit to continue operations, just as an animal had to eat to live. But eating was not the purpose of life.

''Next item,'' said Phil.

''EarthSafe Solar,'' Roberta announced.

''Status?''

Isaac Kohl answered, since he was the designated champion for that Crusade. ''We ran our system test last week. Everything went great. With any luck, southern California should avoid blackouts next summer, and the number of brownouts should be way down.''

Harwood spoke up. ''I still say giving more energy to southern California is like giving a loaded gun to a child. We're still treating symptoms, Phil. We have to change the heart!'' He thumped himself on the chest with his fist. ''People have to *want* less. You don't help an addict by giving him more tobacco.''

''We know that, Ellis,'' Phil said. ''But we have to get from here to there. Remember what I've always said: When power is short, it won't be the powerful who go without.'' Roberta reflected that Ellis had twice now compared the American people to children.

Darren Winslow was new to the Cadre. He still raised his hand before he spoke. "Uh, we *have* taken adequate measures to protect the ecology . . . ?"

"The ecosystem," Isaac said. "Of course, we have. That was part of our mission. The PV farm was built on an especially barren stretch of desert. We did careful impact studies before we built, and the Nature Preservation Society will conduct independent environmental audits twice a year against the ISO 14000 standards." Isaac thumped his finger on the table as he made his points. With his thick, curly hair and black-rimmed glasses, Isaac definitely fell on the nerd side of the nerd-hunk axis, and the aggressiveness of his gestures always struck Roberta as a little absurd. The Mouse That Roared. "We wanted to make a major point with this enterprise and show Corporate America that you can be environmentaly responsible *and* profitable."

"Do you think it was wise to take such a chance?" asked Ellis.

Isaac smiled. "Why, Ellis? Don't you think it *is* possible?"

It wasn't easy to score off of Ellis Harwood, and it was uncommon enough that Ellis didn't like it when it happened. Roberta saw that in the tightening around his eyes and lips and in the pause before he found a response. "It's not that, Ike," he said. "It's that we lack experience in running a utility. EarthSafe could fail for a host of reasons that have nothing to do with responsible behavior. But would Joe Six-pack think that deeply?"

Ellis might like the sound of his own voice, Roberta thought; but that didn't make him stupid. She made her own marginal note: *Professional management? Ask Art Kondo.* She made the high sign to Phil Albright and Phil said, "Let's keep moving, people."

They were only three items into the list. Robert kept the sigh to herself. Maybe Simon Fell had gone too far, but he had been, by damn, a man of action among the academics.

* * *

There was always a lot of mail at the Crusades and someone had to sort it. There was the fan mail and the hate mail. There were suggestions from fanboy sideliners and skinny from whistleblowers. There were requests for information and cries for help. There were donations and dues and contributions. There were importunings and newspaper clippings and requests for interviews and I-net downloads, and every conceivable form of human hard copy communication. There were even advertisements, and come-ons for credit cards, and invitations to sign up for group health. *Dear Mr. Crusades* . . . one of them began. Sometimes they were good for a laugh.

Roberta usually did the mail. Sometimes Darren or Suletha helped. Less often, Melanie or Isaac. Scut-work. Boring. She had never seen Ellis or Dottie pick up a letter opener. But saving the world was not all big speeches or waving signs or pontificating for the True Believers. If the Crusades had any strength, it lay in its network of dedicated supporters and sympathizers. Snail-mail, E-mail, fax, website hits, b-board posts, and telephone calls were the channels that kept them in touch with that base. You couldn't let those channels get clogged. Response, even a form response, was more than a warm fuzzy; it kept people *out there* feeling a part of the Crusades. And every now and then, something valuable turned up. A warning. A clue. A pointing finger.

The electronic stuff could be keyword-and-context sorted by an Artificial Stupid, but the hard copy had to be opened and sorted by the natural kind. Tedious, but Roberta had worked out a system that let her machete the In stack. Donations, dues, and the like went into a basket for Melanie to log, bundle, and deposit. Hate mail, she put aside for the postal authorities. Ads, she trashed. Other letters, depending on subject matter, went to one of the Cadre. Solar to Isaac; battered women to Dottie; labor relations to Ellis; and so on. Sometimes, scanning too quickly, she made a mistake and gave a message to the wrong person; and that person would either trade off with the right one or toss it back on

Roberta's desk—depending on who was dissing whom, or who was on the rag that day.

A nice, fat check drawn on the Bank of Tokyo from Art Kondo, with another letter urging EarthSafe to look into copper indium diselinide PV cells. Roberta scribbled a note to Isaac—EarthSafe had its own bank account—and went on to the next item.

An offer to settle out of court on the crusade against discriminatory racial hiring at a franchise restaurant chain in Missouri and Arkansas. Excellent cooperation from the parent corporation, who had leaned heavily on the franchisee. *Good work,* she scribbled in the margin and handed it to Suletha when the woman passed by on her way to the coffeepot.

A hand-written letter in a naggingly familiar cursive. She glanced as usual at the body of the letter, to learn the topic.

. . . when she turned to talk to a friend, her waist-length hair became entangled on the mill shaft. The force yanked her head back and swung her in an arc to the other side of the machine, slammed her on the floor, and scalped her. Jesus, Phil, you should have seen her in the hospital. Preventive action would have been so simple! *Guard-rails, hair nets, even an (admittedly intrusive) company haircut policy . . . Felix plans to pay the plant a little "visit" . . .*

Working conditions. Labor relations. She started to write Ellis's name in the corner, but hesitated. Felix? Her eyes dropped to the signature.

Simon Fell.

No wonder the handwriting had seemed so familiar! She checked the salutation—*Dear Phil*—and the envelope—addressed to Phil at his sister's town home. It must have gotten mixed in with the office mail down at the post office. She read the rest of the letter.

. . . Felix plans to pay the plant a little "visit." After that they may be open to some reasonable settlement. Granted, the little hillbilly twit shares the blame—she should have been paying attention, and long hair in a factory is plain crazy—but the company bears a lot of the blame, too; and

now they're trying to stiff her on the workman's comp. Jesus, Phil, she was fucking scalped! *Pass this on to Colraine at* Baxter, Howe *and see if he'll take it on contingency. We owe him one.*

Roberta read the letter over once more. Then she folded it and placed it back inside its envelope. She took the envelope into Phil's office and placed it in his in-basket, where he would see it when he returned from his Los Angeles trip.

The table in the entrance hall of the Wessex County Country Club was filled with memorabilia of John Witherspoon High School. A yearbook. Copies of the school newspaper. Tickets stubs from the senior prom. (Who on earth had saved their ticket stubs, and *why?*) The program book for the class play. (*Forty-second Street*—and until she saw the booklet, Styx could not have named it.) Photographs of jocks doing jock stuff. The football team had been unbeaten senior year. Styx had barely been aware the football team existed.

"Roberta Carson! We're so happy you could make it!"

Oh, God. Cheerfulness. Roberta put on her number three smile and turned to the nearby registration table, where two strangers sat behind rows of name tags. She tried to read their own tags without seeming to. 'Tino Perez and Karen Chong-Godfrey. The former was angular, tan, and looked like he expected women to make appointments. Roberta accessed Styx's memory and there was no relic of Perez there. Chong-Godfrey was an earnest, Oriental face, the kind that always seemed wider than it was high. What was it about Chinese faces that they seemed eternally young until they became immortally old? She vaguely remembered Karen Chong (the "Godfrey" part must be matrimonial) as an aspiring painter and wondered if she had ever made it big. Karen handed her a name tag and a program book and Roberta mumbled thanks as she headed for the banquet room. How long before she could gracefully leave?

Hors-d'ouerves and appetizers and earnest clusters of young men and women. The solarium behind the banquet room was a-hum with conversation. About one-third of the faces seemed to teeter on the brink of terminal boredom, and Roberta assigned those tentatively to non-Witherspoon spouses, dragged to this little soiree to display as trophies.

Ouch. Chase Coughlin (that dick-head) still with the dangly earring and the shaven sidewalls. He was chatting easily, drink in hand, with two women Roberta did not recognize, rubbing them with his eyeballs; licking them with his smile. Still the old pelt-hunter; still the trouser snake. She wondered if he still practiced petty larceny and extortion. Not a single kid off the number nine bus had, in living memory, entered school with lunch money intact. They all became contributors to the Chase Coughlin Benevolent Society Loan Fund, which circulated at impressive interest rates. What is he now? Banker? Telephone solicitor? Advertising pitchman?

One time, at that big party that van Huyten threw for the high school kids, Chase had cornered her by the hedge maze in the backyard and, before she could do or say anything, had grabbed her. "Copped a feel," giggling grandparents liked to say, as if it were something innocent and playful. Maybe it was Chase's idea of dropping a subtle hint. If so, Styx's cryptic response had been Rosie Palm and her Five Sisters delivered at terminal velocity across the dental work.

She found her way to the cash bar and ordered up a vodka and ice. The barman—his badge named him Julio—raised an eyebrow and a half-smile, as if to say he knew what kind of woman drank her vodka neat, and implied without even a change of stance that he got off work at ten. Styx gave him an eyeball stroke, because he was no-fooling buff as shit, and stuffed a deuce into his tip cup.

Turning around, she noticed Greg Prescott at the other end of the solarium. Short-cut, straw-colored hair, with the indefinably flabby look of the ex-jock. If Chase had once assaulted her body, Greg had assaulted her soul—far more than once. All those oh-so-important, swaggering jocks and socials who had treated her like dirt. Prescott had a woman with him who smiled faintly and followed him as he circulated and glad-handed one and all. A wife, Roberta guessed.

Quarterback Greg used to boink Cheerleader Leilah on a regular basis—and three others more or less at random. Back seats, locker rooms, the Bunny Wunny Motel—even under the bleachers on the athletic field, if Jimmy Poole's school bus whispers could be credited. "A flute concerto," he had snickered. The difference between the Gregs and the Chases of the world, Roberta decided, was that Chase never acted like he was doing the girl the favor, and never pretended that anyone's pleasure but his own was foremost in his mind. There was at least a charming sort of honesty about that.

Roberta tried to fade into the background like always, but standing alone at a reception seemed to bother too many people. They swooped by and insisted on overcoming her "shyness," never dreaming it was distaste. A few of them—Roberta promptly forgot their names—went on about how they read all her poetry. That was like a big So What, but she couldn't help but feel flattered. One of the goals in the Prague Manifesto was to bring the New Art to the common people, and they didn't get more common than North Orange, New Jersey.

There was Azim Thomas, the "Hero of Skopje." He was wearing civilian clothes, but Roberta could see the oh-so-discreet lapel pin that represented the Congressional Medal of Honor. Well, Thomas had been a banger right up to the robbery and felony murder at Pandya's In-and-Out, after which he had disappeared for seven years. He'd found his niche, that was sure. The difference between packing nines for the Lords of Victory and toting rifles for the U.S. Marines was mainly one of legitimacy.

Roberta searched the room for Tani Pandya, but didn't see her. That girl better show up! It was half her fault that Roberta was here.

"Hello." It was another woman, also insulated from the crowd, cradling a half-empty glass of soda. "You're Styx, aren't you?"

"Roberta," she said. "I stopped being 'Styx' a long time ago." She was still there, though. Styx was. Sometimes she popped out of her box and whispered nasty thoughts.

The other woman chuckled. "I used to be someone else, too."

Roberta checked the name tag. Jenny Ribbon. She locked eyes with the woman. "You vanished," she said.

Another smile. "Half our class vanished. Azim. Leilah. You. Technically speaking, we shouldn't be here. We never actually graduated, you know."

That was what she remembered about Jenny Ribbon. Technicalities. One of the brains, like Tani and Karen Chong, but a brain with a secret weapon: her mother. If there was an advantage to be gained, if there was a loophole to be found, Mrs. Ribbon would find it. And swoop down on the school to wangle the angle, because winning on a technicality was still by-God winning.

Roberta took a swallow of her vodka and the icy electricity sent her mind back to the secret bottle she had kept in her dresser and that her mother had never found. That sudden moment of *deja vu* was why it was Styx who responded. "Why *did* you go milk carton?"

That was straight, blunt, direct. The true Styx approach. Poke at the sore and see if it still hurts.

"It's no secret. . . ."

"Everyone guessed. No one knew."

Jenny looked at her drink. "I wish this was something stronger. No . . ." She waved off Styx's offer to pour some of her vodka into the the glass. "No, I don't dare. I've been there and come back." She took a sip of the Seven-Up, though how that would steady her nerves, Roberta had not the slightest clue. "Look, I'll tell you how it was. You know how everyone went how lucky I was and I had everything? Well, everything was never enough. I was smart. I was a good swimmer. I danced decently. *But it was never good enough.* I always had to be first. Prima ballerina. Grand prize. First in the class. Once I placed second in the butterfly, and you would have thought I had floundered and splashed like a neo. Second to a girl who later won Olympic gold. But my mother took the ribbon and *threw it in the trash.''* This time she did take Roberta's drink and pour some of it into hers. A pretty weak mix, but it seemed to brace the woman. The ice rattled as she drank. "I would have done anything to please my mother. I used to argue with the teachers over every little quiz grade. A point here, a point there. Who knew what would make the difference when they later chose the valedictorian? One day, it hit me. Sooner or later, I *would* fail at something, and when I did I would have a ton of excuses and quibbles and . . . And I would *be* my mother.''

"Yeah," said Roberta. "Escape. I know about that."

Jenny drained her glass. "I shouldn't have done that. With your vodka, I mean. If you see me drinking anything strong later today, stop me. Okay?"

Roberta swallowed a mouthful of vodka. "Sure." She didn't ask why. "Where did you go?"

"I climbed out my bedroom window and Chase met me with his car. He dropped me at the train station, and I headed west. I wound up on the street in Pittsburgh with a bottle for my friend, and I was this close to whoring. But someone found me and put me in Pittsburgh's Hope . . ."

"The orphanage."

"The boarding school. Why shouldn't poor people have boarding schools, too?"

"Did you meet 'Mother Smythe' there?"

Jenny Ribbon laughed and leaned closer. "I *am* 'Mother Smythe,' " she said in a whisper. "I called myself Jenny Smythe for a while. After they dried me out and turned me 'round, I stayed to give back some of what I'd gotten." She straightened and swirled her empty glass until the ice clattered. "Paying forward, that's what we call it. Better than paying back. Some of the children that come to us . . . God. A few of them are on court orders, but mostly, the parents themselves bring them. Strung-out addicts. Abusive boyfriends. Drive-by shootings. They want to get their kids away from all that. Even the 'dicty moms. 'I'm no good for

her,' one mother told me, 'but I want her to have a chance.'
But they have to work with us, the parents do. We're not a
dumping ground. And little by little, 'one day at a time,'
we change the look in their eyes.'' Jenny looked past Roberta's shoulder—at what, Styx couldn't imagine. "God,
Roberta, you don't know what it means to restore someone's hope.''

Roberta wasn't too sure about hope, but she did know
what astonishment meant. That the school's most self-
centered princess had grown up into "Mother Smythe" was
far more astonishing than that Azim Thomas had become a
war hero. "Have you seen your parents since you've been
back?''

Jenny snorted. "God, no. What would we say to each
other? 'Hi, remember me? I'm the child you drove onto the
streets because you wouldn't accept less-than-perfect?' ''

"Yes," said Roberta seriously. "You *can* say that. You
can say anything. Apologize. Brag. Scream at them. But you
ought to say *some*thing.''

Jenny looked uncertain. "Why?''

"Because someday you won't be able to.''

When Jimmy Poole arrived, a wave of conversation
spread through the room, much as a toad arriving on a lily
pad would cause ripples in the pond. And Roberta had to
admit that the little weenie had duded up stoopid. His hair
was slicked back, raven-wing style, to reveal a skull-and-
bones earring. His wrist flashed gold and silver. His suit had
been tailored to fit—nothing off the rack would ever drape
that shape very well—and was cut in the kimonolike "ov-
erbreast" fashion popular these days in Rome and Singa-
pore. His shoes were mirrors. Roberta watched a dozen pairs
of eyes lock on and radar-track. Some envious—Jimmy was
by far the most financially successful member of the class—
but some speculative. Roberta prayed that there would be
one gold digger among the women. One classmate—or
classmate's spouse!—who would splork the weenie, who
would splork anything rich or famous. Because if Poole
drilled a dry hole tonight, he would claim Roberta for his

consolation prize. (Had she promised that? Had she failed *not* to promise that?) If she refused, Jimmy would stop mousing VHI for her. And if she didn't . . . Roberta shivered.

Let it be Greg Prescott's wife, she prayed. The woman had looked a little tucked in at the corners. A little extra-curricular ruffling of the sheets might be just what she needed.

She remembered Meat Tucker as a dim-bulb metal-head. He still had the long hair—bound up into a neat ponytail; but he wore a retro, knee-length black jacket over a pure white, tieless shirt buttoned to the throat. Used to be when "dressing up" meant no holes in your jeans. He walked a little oddly, as if he were trying—and failing—to toe-dance. A laughing voice over her shoulder said, "Looks like he doesn't have his land legs back yet."

Roberta turned to see who had spoken, and it was Chase Coughlin.

He focused on her and blinked. "Hey . . ." Uncertainty. The name tag eye-dance. "Roberta . . . *Styx?* What brings you back slumming?" A smile and a hand extended. Hey-how-are-you, just as if that same hand had not once squeezed her breasts. Roberta used a number two smile on him and wished for a moment that she still wore those metal-toed boots that had been so *in* back then.

Talk about asteroid impact. His two planets would go spinning off in different orbits.

"Curiosity," Roberta told him. "See if everyone's as herbie as I remember." Chase laughed and waved. "Hey, Meat. Look who's here."

"Since when you friends with Meat?" There had been a scene in school involving money owed, pushing and shoving, and a screwdriver yanked from a back pocket.

Chase shrugged. "That was then. This is now."

Tucker joined them, along with a short, wide black man that Roberta remembered as some kind of Jock God. "The Doorman," they had called him. "You remember Styx Carson," Chase said, "the poet-queen of the New Art?"

Roberta replayed the remark in her mind, looking for some hint of sarcasm, but found none. She shook hands with the others. "What you drinking, Styx?" Chase asked. She told him what and he disappeared with her empty glass.

"Still playing metal?" Roberta asked Meat. Why not be polite? Only friends and enemies deserved special treatment, and Meat and the Doorman were neither.

Tucker made a face. "Try getting anyone to listen to anything but goofball these days." He shoved two fingers into his throat and made gagging sounds. The Doorman chuckled. Roberta remembered him as a quiet boy who hardly ever spoke and stuttered when he did. He had won some sort of state championship · and Roberta suddenly wished she could remember what it was so she could mention it to him.

"Maybe Angel and Buck'll be here and we can get together, just for old times' sake." He studied the corner where the band would set up for dancing after dinner. "I hope they didn't book goof for tonight."

"I don't like your poems," the Doorman said.

The remark came out of nowhere. She had to play it back to be sure she heard right. She gave him a puzzled look. "I don't expect everyone does, but . . ."

"Oh, yeah, a lot of it's okay. I'm not much for poetry, but it's hard to avoid your stuff. 'Feet of clay; heart of claymore' is almost a cliché by now. I'm talking about the way you attack VHI."

"You mean I speak out about the way *she* manipulated us into—"

"Stuff it. Wasn't for Mentor, what would I be today?"

Which led to the fascinating question of what he actually was today.

"Hobie's a world-class scientist," said Chase, returning with a fresh glass of vodka for her. He handed it to her with a smile that said he wouldn't have any objection to sharing a hotel room with her tonight. But it was a friendly smile, almost a playful one. If it happens, it happens; but he wasn't pushing. He still had that high-energy intensity to him; but it was more focused now, more controlled. She realized suddenly that he had no recollection of having grabbed her snatch in high school. Chase existed only in the present tense.

And even back then, he had waited on a lonely side street to help a desperate girl run away.

"He discovered Hobart's Law," Meat contributed helpfully.

"And hobartium," added Chase. The Doorman, Hobart, rolled his eyes.

"That must be quite a lot of egoboo for you," Roberta said.

"I can't say it didn't tickle me," Hobie said, "but the boo came when everything clicked into place, not when Chris van Huyten named it. All I'm saying is that, w-wasn't for Mentor and all that, what would I be today but some washed up ex-NFL tackle and a special-hard question on sports trivia? So I don't 'pre-ciate it when you diss the people that helped me."

Somehow, she had thought of those barbed poems being aimed only at the Rich Lady. It had never occurred to her that they might prick others as well. Artists liked to talk about "touching" other people's lives, but the reality of it was messy. Sometimes you left a smudge on what you touched. She looked into the hardness of Hobart's eyes and saw that she had made an enemy of someone she hardly even knew, and that wasn't right. Enmity ought to be personal.

The others were still chatting around her.

"You down now?" Hobie asked Meat; and Meat said, "Yeah. Gold Crew's up. Spent three months hand-holding a bunch of bunnies, but I think they'll shape. What about you, otter? When you lift again?" Hobart named a date— up in February, down in March, up in April "for the big harvest" and down in May—and Chase said, "You're a regular Ping-Pong ball, Hobe. Ned DuBois himself is gonna fly that May lift, so be sure to genuflect when you climb aboard."

Roberta slipped away while they were talking. The Doorman was a big-time scientist. Chase was a space pilot. Meat Tucker was building a space station. All three of them sucked into Mariesa van Huyten's Grand Plan, and Hobie, at least, with his eyes open. She wondered how many others at the reception were fellow travellers, and how many, like herself and Tani Pandya, had escaped the flypaper.

For dinner, she sat with Tani and with Jimmy, Chase, Hobie, and a woman that Hobie had brought. It was an awkward meal. Hobie, Chase, and Hobie's fiancée formed a closed-loop conversational group. Jimmy talked too much; though at least he didn't embarrass himself. But it would have been awkward no matter who had been at the table.

After dinner, Karen Chong gave out gag awards. One of them, for who had come the farthest to be at the reunion, she declared a tie between Morris Tucker and Leland Hobart, who had both come down from Low Earth Orbit. Roberta, thinking about the others and who they were and what they had been, thought it ought to have been a multiway tie. A lot of them—Azim, Jenny, Chase, Tani, Jimmy, even herself—had come a long, long way to be here.

Styx had promised Jimmy he could score at the reunion, but she hadn't imagined Tani as the basket.

They stopped to say good-bye before they left. The band was still playing and Jimmy bounced a-rhythmically to the beat. He always did that when he was eager and impatient. Up and down on the balls of his feet. He was wound; he was *pumped*. He was, by God, going to get laid for the first time in his pathetic life. Tani seemed cheerful, too, but why on Earth would a sensitive, intelligent woman like Tani jump into bed with Jimmy Poole? She was no fame-and-wealth groupie. But maybe she didn't know what Jimmy had in mind. . . . He might have suggested a drive, a drink, a late-night movie, and Tani would have believed him. She was an innocent in many ways.

Roberta opened her mouth to say something, a warning, a prohibition; but the words gagged her. What could she say that did not make her a *pimp?* What sort of excuse was it to say, *I thought he'd pick someone else?*

Tani went out ahead and Jimmy lingered for a few moments. "Thanks, Styx," he said. "I owe you big time." He held out a plump, clammy hand, but Roberta would not take it.

"Don't hurt her."

He looked genuinely puzzled. "I didn't know it hurt."

"That's not what I meant. If Tani backs out at the last minute, you let her."

Jimmy laughed like a horse. "You set this up, you know. You're the one told me how to behave. I watched movies and I read books. I went to some high-class places, and I watched how people acted. I created a *new* Jimmy Poole. Rev 3.2. It was hard work. I deserve my reward."

Hard work learning how to act human.... "She's not a *reward.* She's a person."

"Yeah, Styxy. And so am I." Roberta had no answer to that and he turned toward the entrance hall, checked himself, and turned back. "But you know what else? I read Tani's book, and I'll bet anything you want to name that you haven't. I've been inside her head a little; and"—he flushed a deep red—"I liked what I saw. And tonight, I discovered something useful. This whole sex hack is easier if you *like* the person."

Roberta said. "Just remember. The show's not over. And I'll be talking with Tani afterwards. If I don't like what I hear . . . Well, I have those metal-toed boots in a closet someplace."

He looked back at her. "You think I'm stupid? I'll run Rev 3.2 as long as I have to." He grinned and tapped his skull. "It's all in the grayware. The brain is just a neural net, and I create A/S personas. Tonight's Jimmy Poole? Just a new persona."

"Personas," she spat. "Is there a *real* Jimmy Poole in there?"

"We all run personas when we interface with the world.

Difference between you and me, Styxy, is I know I'm doing it."

In the dark, it took a long time to find.

No one lit graveyards at night. And she wasn't really sure where the plot was. So she circled the cinder track, playing the headlights across the ranks of tombstones. The ones outside the circle looked newer and she concentrated on them. A couple of times, she parked the car with the engine running and the headlights on high and walked through the silent rows. When she found it at last, she repositioned the car so the lights were trained on it.

MARY ELIZABETH CARSON
1952–2005
MAY SHE REST IN PEACE

A standardized sentiment. The stones were probably carved with the expression already in place, wanting only names and dates. There were no flowers—what did dead people need with flowers, anyway?—but the grass had grown over the mound in a thick, soft carpet. Roberta crouched and plucked a stem from the ground. There were weeds. Dandelions and crabgrass. Did the dead gossip about each other's lawn care?

Bullshit. There wasn't anything under there but what four years of decay would leave.

"Hi, Beth," she said, "remember me? The girl you drove out of your home? I'm b$^{aa}_{aa}$ck." She laughed aloud in the still of the night, and sobered instantly at the awful sound it made. The place was unearthly quiet. The Gray Horse Pike was a pale ribbon across the north face of Skunktown Mountain. Headlights slipped along it like pearls on a string, but no sound reached the graveyard. Skunktown itself loomed high and black; blacker than the sky above it, where stars and the background glow from North Orange created a softer gray. Silverpond lay on the other side of that ridge. That was where Beth had driven her—frying pan to fire.

From someone who never seemed to care to someone who only seemed to care. She wondered if van Huyten was home tonight.

"I'm famous, Beth." Mother had never let her call her Beth. "I've made a mark. So I guess you can't tell me what a loser I am." No, be fair. She had never called her that. "In case you're wondering why it took me so long to come over to play . . . Well, I never had the time. Just like you never had the time for me." But in the cold, November silence she could hear how mean and self-pitying the words were. What had she expected of the woman? Roberta could see more clearly now, everything focused through the lens of time. The long hours and the long commute; bone-tired and irritable, but doing the job of two just so they could squeak by. The child hadn't seen it. She had judged Beth more harshly then. Still, Beth could have made an effort. She could have *pretended*. How tired and overworked did you have to be to be too tired to watch your daughter play in the snow?

"It was the best you could give her," Roberta told the grave, "but she didn't understand."

She was Roberta-the-child, impossibly eager, so easy to disappoint, who wanted nothing at all from the world but unconditional love.

Roberta lived life in segments, and with each segment a new person was born. Jimmy Poole had been right, but a little bit wrong, too. He could call them personas if he wanted; but they were lives, not masks. Each was a bubble, sealed off by some epochal event. Asteroids had struck her life from time to time. Roberta-the-child had died when Mark left and Beth morphed and they had moved into that awful tar-paper-and-shingle house out where the Pike crossed the old canal locks.

From the ashes of Roberta-the-child's funeral pyre had risen Styx; and, oh, what a piece of work she had been. Proud, independent, clear-headed; but angry and withdrawn, solitary and friendless, too. There were always prices paid. "You'll be glad to know I don't drink anymore. Hardly."

She wondered if Beth had ever twigged to the vodka. Maybe she should have left it out for Beth to find.

Styx had carved out her little niche and had flourished there until the Great Betrayal, when the Rich Lady had revealed her true colors. From that broken chrysallis had wriggled the bohemian New Art butterfly, grand proclaimer of the Prague Manifesto, casual lover of a dozen soulful men. "Did you ever read my poems?" she asked. Years ago, in Prague, she would not have cared one way or the other. Now, suddenly, it became important to know; and it was something she now never could possibly know. She could imagine Beth passing her chapbooks around the office saying, "That's my little girl." (Posing naked for the cover, but, still . . .) Stupifyingly bourgeois; and yet, it would have meant they'd touched.

No touching now.

She ran her hand across the grass, stroking it like fur. But the Prague scene fell apart in bickering and sniping and clique-making. Transplanted from Old World to New, the Poet had become the Activist and now the consort of the finest man on the face of the Earth. *Who's next?* asked Styx, whispering from her box. *And what rogue star will shatter your life this time?*

She stood up and smoothed her skirt. "I used to love you, Beth," she said. "And for a long time, I wanted to love you and you wouldn't let me. So I stopped. Now I want to again, but I can't." They were frozen in time, both of them. The cuts and the put-downs and the thousand petty defiances were all that were left, and there was nothing that would ever replace them. That was what death meant. Life was change.

She turned away from the grave. Double bullshit. She'd been wrong. There was a lot under there and it would stay there forever and it would rot.

INTERLUDE:

"Vanity of Vanities," Said the Preacher

Departure required only a brief burp from the main engines. It wasn't much of a burn, but then there wasn't much to burn loose from, either. For days afterwards, it seemed as if nothing had happened—the ship and the asteroid continued to coast in tandem—but in fact, they had been committed irrevocably to different paths; and, little by little, the Rock drifted behind. *Bullard* had slowed into a faster, more sunward orbit. For a long time, the Rock lingered in their rearview, chasing after them like an abandoned puppy after the family car.

One honking big puppy . . .

FarTrip and the Rock parted company for good soon after they crossed the Earth's orbit and swung outboard in early November, with the asteroid heading farther out, rising above the plane of the Earth's orbit, and slowing for aphelion later in the year. FarTrip's orbit had a tighter radius and less inclination and would hit its own aphelion a lot earlier. Soon they could no longer see the Rock without instruments. Nacho claimed he could spot it with the onboard telescope, but Forrest lost interest. He was not one to spend his life looking backwards.

With *Bullard* now to starward, Earth began catching up to them. That struck Forrest as the wrong way to run a rendezvous—the chaser *ought* to be below and behind, but who ever heard of a *planet* as the chaser? He was willing to go along with the gag, though. If the deep thinkers were right—and the computers agreed that they were—Earth and FarTrip would intersect on May 15, one day short of a year after the bon voyage party aboard Mir.

And if they were wrong . . .

This was the loneliest part of the voyage, a time that seemed to draw them naturally toward introspection. The Rock had gone into the outer darkness, and the Earth had not yet come into sight. The forward telescope—*Bullard* was facing "backwards" on its orbit—could pick out the Earth-Moon and resolve the bright spark into two miniature crescents; but with the laser footprint spread by the distance, communications were weak and uncertain. The three of them were the only fragment of humanity in this neck of the woods, and would be for a long time.

Seven and a half months on the Long Orbit. It didn't seem fair that it was longer than the outbound leg and the stopover put together. It was anticlimactic, like remaking *King Kong*, where you shoot the monkey in the first reel and spend the rest of the flick on the cleanup effort in the street down below.

The prompt chattered like a chimpanzee and Forrest made another entry in his personal log. The A/S voice announced in silky tones: "Approaching end of watch, darling."

"You tell 'em, honey." Forrest glanced at the clock. Almost midnight. The middle of the night out here in the middle of Night. He shut down his personal log and sealed it with his hardkey. That log would be a bestseller some day, no doubt about it; if only he could find the right co-author to knock it into shape. He pushed himself out of the command seat and floated to the forward viewports.

Sure is dark outside. Gonna be a cold and lonely Thanksgiving. And the only turkey onboard was Krasnarov.

Forrest kicked away from the viewport. Ah, hell. What did midnight mean on the Long Orbit? It was always midnight outside the viewports. He pulled himself into the tunnel that led to *Salyut*. Time to go fetch Mikey.

He wondered if things would seem less dreary if they had not left so much unresolved on the Rock. Outbound, you could savor anticipation, all the more exciting for being undefined. Now, all the mysteries were behind them, and they had learned all they would ever learn about them. Nacho and Mike could recycle their opinions as endlessly as the scrubber system recycled the air and water, but there would be no new data for a long, long while.

Forrest passed down the transfer tunnel between the three nested cryogenic hydrogen tanks, through the ship's nose-lock and into the frustum that he called "the foyer." It was just large enough for one man, and when *Salyut* was detached from *Bullard*, functioned as the habitat's airlock. He poked his head through the inner hatch and looked down the length of the vessel. The privacy curtain had been pulled aside, so he could see all the way to the nose. The smaller module was brightly lit and a chess problem was laid out on the magnetic board, but the main module beyond that was illuminated only by soft sleep-lights.

Mike Krasnarov was swimming laps.

Forrest watched him sail down the shaded length of *Salyut* into the observation blister, where he twisted and kicked off toward the rear. He arced gracefully past the tethered bag where Nacho slept, past the geologist's work station and the dry-soil racks, past the 'fresher and through the connecting frustum into the smaller module. He touched, as gently as a feather, on the game board and pivoted like a ballet dancer, his feet kissing the bulkhead by Forrest's head before a flex of the ankles sent him back again toward the bow. He gave no indication that he had noticed Forrest. Never a talkative man, Krasnarov had grown positively mute since leaving the Rock.

Why'd you do it, Mikey? Chipping away the marks on the Flatirons. If they really were alien inscriptions, it was sacrilege; and if they were not—as Krasnarov believed— why bother? There had to be a reason. Senhor Machine never did anything without a reason.

Forrest had asked—as command pilot, he had *demanded* an explanation—but the Russian had responded with only a dignified silence. He had absorbed Nacho's bitter accusations and Forrest's reprimand like he was flint himself, accepting the blows without any visible mark. In the end, Forrest had given up asking. Whatever motive had driven the Russian, it would surface in its own time, or not at all.

Three times Krasnarov made the circuit while Forrest watched, passing from light into shadow and back again. Straight up and down the center axis, touching only at each end to make his turn. There had been bets on the outbound leg about who would be first to accomplish that, but the competition had worn thin after a while. Trust the Iron Mike to keep at it and never mention it to anyone.

When Krasnarov touched down again by the hatchway, Forrest said, "Shift change, *amigo*. Front and center."

Senhor Machine reached out and grabbed hold of the handle to the collapsible exercise rack, turned and came to an easy rest with his feet planted on the bulkhead. Forrest pulled himself out of the hatchway and the Russian pushed himself into it. "Foolish exercise," he said, but Forrest didn't know if that meant swimming laps or standing watch. He only knew that, outbound, he had never had to fetch Krasnarov when his watch rolled 'round; and Krasnarov had never reported with less than cleaned-and-pressed precision.

After the engineer had gone, Forrest unlatched the excerchine and folded it out. He fastened the stays and set the mechanism for some upper body work. When he was seated he shoved his feet into the straps, gripped the handlebars, and began pumping. There was no pull-and-release here; he had to move the masses both directions. Pull-*and*-push. That was better for the muscles, anyway. You didn't stretch the fibers only in one direction.

He had just settled into the rhythm when Nacho spoke from his bag.

"He reminds me of a caged animal."

Forrest looked up. In the dimness of the main module the geologist's bright obsidian eyes gleamed. Forrest adjusted his sweatband with one hand. "He does, does he?"

"Back and forth. Back and forth. Like a tiger behind bars."

"You should be asleep this watch."

"Nearly every day now, just before his watch; or just after."

"Yeah, I've noticed," Forrest said.

Nacho unfastened the stick-strip on his bag and wriggled free. He pulled the flaps together, folded them, and stuffed the bag into its locker. The bag billowed, struggling against its fate. "He never used to do it," Nacho said, fastening the locker at last. "The pacing, I mean."

"Is that what you think it is? Pacing?"

Nacho straightened his singlet and shorts, pulled his moccasins off their fasteners. "You think he is exercising?"

"We're all a little impatient to get home."

Nacho shook his head. "I think he is troubled, not impatient."

Forrest stopped pumping. The masses on the exerchine continued on their tracks until they hit the stop blocks. "About what?"

Nacho shook his head again. "I have lost all respect for the man."

"Have you?" But what did the respect of Ignacio Mendes mean to a man like Krasnarov? Senhor Machine had never chased after approval or fame, only after accomplishment itself. Did Mr. Perfect need anyone's respect beside his own?

"He has changed," Nacho said.

Forrest rested his arms on the handlebars and turned his head over his shoulder, toward the rear of the vessel. "Yeah," he admitted. "He sure ain't the barrel of laughs he used to be."

Slowly, Earth gained on *Bullard*. Comm signals grew stronger, thanks to Mr. Square-of-the-Distance. Just before Christmas, the crew assembled on the command deck for a celebration. Forrest waited with three drinking bulbs in his hand while Krasnarov studied the comm monitors. The Russian scowled, rubbed his stubbled chin, entered a setting by hand. The comm warbled like a canary, then began to "fry bacon."

"Upload commencing, boys," murmured the A/S.

Finally, Krasnarov shrugged. "Helios beam density exceeds fifty percent of nominal."

Nacho whooped and Forrest sailed the drinking bulbs across the cabin. "Gentlemen," he said, "let us splice the mainbrace."

It was only a fruit juice, of course. No grog on this voyage. Alcohol was too easy an answer to fear and boredom, and an answer that was too easily wrong. Krasnarov tapped his bulb with a forefinger as it coasted to him, and it hung, spinning, in the air before him.

"An arbitrary distinction," he said. "Why fifty percent?"

"Why not?" Forrest responded. "We're getting enough beamed power now we can go to part-time on the fuel cells. The message uploads are getting clearer. You might say it marks our return to Earth's neighborhood. Or, to be precise, the Earth's neighborhood has returned to us."

Nacho chuckled. Krasnarov shrugged and snagged the bulb out of the air. He broke the tip off with one thumb. "*Nichevo*," he said and squirted the entire contents down his throat.

Somehow, when Forrest opened his eyes, he knew that he had awakened too early. Usually, he slept soundly until his internal clock woke him for his watch, but something had roused him this time. A sound. A motion. Considering the living conditions in *Salyut* you couldn't be too light a sleeper or you'd get no sleep at all.

Snugged up in his tethered sleeping bag like a damn Christmas stocking, Forrest looked around to see what had disturbed him. Subdued, green lamps picked anonymous shapes out of the darkness. Forrest had drawn the privacy curtain when he turned in, but now its free end waved in the air currents as if trying to elude the groping fingers of the magnets that normally held it in place. Turning his head the other way, he saw a figure crouched in the observation blister.

Krasnarov.

The Russian had his back to Forrest. He was hunkered down with his knees tucked up and his arms wrapped around his torso like a lover's embrace. With his black T-shirt and shorts, he seemed almost to blend into the splendor outside. He stayed there unmoving, anchored to the mat by his slippers, staring at the stars.

Or maybe sleeping, Forrest thought, because Krasnarov did not move for what seemed like a very long time. Then, abruptly, the Russian unfolded himself and launched a fist at the blister.

"Svolochi!" he said, *"Vy shchitaete Krasnarova durakom!"*

The blow struck with a dull thump. SPP was a very hard material, a metallocene plastic impervious to impacts a great deal harder than Krasnarov's fist. Yet Forrest could not help but flinch at the gesture.

Krasnarov turned from the blister, and Forrest snapped his eyes shut and feigned sleep. He felt, rather than saw, Krasnarov hover for a few moments by his sleeping bag. He could feel the heat of the man's body, hear his harsh breathing as he bent low over Forrest's face. Forrest resisted the impulse to turn in his sleep or to snore—or to open his eyes and go "boo!" which was even more tempting. A moment later, he heard the brushing sound of the curtain flaps parting and the snap of the magnets grabbing the free end.

Forrest lay awake, looking after the departed copilot and wondering. It had only been a glimpse, caught in the moment between Krasnarov's turn and Forrest's eyes snapping shut; but there was no doubt about the fierce anger that had burned on the Russian's face.

* * *

When Forrest took the watch a few hours later, Nacho told him to expect a download. "Deep Space called to make sure when you would be available," he explained. "The message will be encrypted, so you will need your dongle."

Forrest thanked him and did not address the obvious question in the Brazilian's eyes. *What's up, boss?* Forrest did not know himself. He fingered the hard slip of encoded plastic in his coverall pocket. Encrypted? Messages they'd had a-plenty. Earthside newsloads, personal E-mail, mission plans, software upgrades. Once, a set of blueprints when they'd had to machine a component from bar stock. But never before anything encrypted to a private key. He felt a sinking feeling in his heart. It was bad news, he was sure. His house had burned down. Someone he loved had died.

But his caller turned out to be none other than Mariesa van Huyten, herself. On video, too, he saw when he had inserted his dongle into the decrypter and the gray scale had coalesced into an image of the Deep Space communications room in Brussels. She was alone, which was unusual. At least, no one else was within range of the doid. In the background, Forrest saw the remnants of holiday decorations on the walls of the comm center. The image was washed out, the colors faded; and the picture fuzzed out now and then. They were still at the extreme range for Helios Light's targeting laser.

An alarm bell rang in Forrest's head. Big bucks. The chairwoman of Van Huyten Industries was not an official of FarTrip or UN Deep Space Command, so this was a private message, using bandwidth already committed somewhere else. Forrest wondered which facility had been switched to fuel cells so Helios could make this unscheduled narrowcast.

Back in the old days, van Huyten used to drop in on the secret test field from time to time. Forrest hadn't known her near as well as Ned DuBois, who had ways of meeting women denied to ordinary mortals, but she was no stranger. He hadn't seen her since the reception at her mansion when the FarTrip crew was named. Still, she looked older and more tired than Forrest remembered. Her face seemed worn and her eyes troubled. Unless that was the transmission quality. She was the richest woman in North America, or so they always said. What did she have to be worried about?

Van Huyten wasted no time in idle chitchat. "I have some questions, Captain, if you have the time."

Well, no. I was really, really *busy.* "Of course. What is it you want to know? Over."

"Can you hear me? Oh, dear. Is this going through?"

"Remember the time lag, ma'am. It takes awhile for your signal to reach us and for our bounceback." Forrest decided to stay mum until everything sorted out. This call was costing a pretty nickel, but it was her nickel and she had a lot of them.

Finally, he saw her flush, and she said, "Yes. Sorry. They explained the lag to me, but . . ." Her mouth turned up in a brief, whimsical smile. "This is not exactly a face-to-face conversation, is it?"

Forrest chuckled. No, it wasn't. He was talking to an image from the past. At this moment down on Earth, the woman herself was waiting patiently for the answer—before Forrest had even heard the question. Though what "at this moment" meant under the circumstances was a question to tickle a physicist's funny bone. This image was a digital recreation of van Huyten's face and voice, based on data from electronic sensors. He was not looking at a *real* image, nor hearing a *real* voice.

"I suppose that's why most of FarTrip's communications are one way," van Huyten continued. "Very well. This discussion will remain confidential. You will share it with no one else. Is that understood? I will wait for your answer."

"Sure," Forrest told the doid pickup. "Go ahead." He wondered what he looked like from the other end. Three guys batching it for seven months couldn't look too sharp by now. Even the Iron Mike had lost that fresh-out-of-the-box appearance.

The bounceback took a little longer than the speed of light could account for. Van Huyten looked like she was having second thoughts. Then she sighed and said, "Some of FarTrip's people have noticed something . . . well, 'intriguing' in your data. Perhaps you have noticed it as well. You recorded some odd features in grid element"—she paused and looked at a card in her hand—"Grid element Iota-Nu-37. Records I-N-slash-37-dash-120 through 159. Do you know the items I mean?"

Forrest did not even have to call up the master records list. She meant Nacho's "inscriptions." "Yes," Forrest said. "We call that grid element 'the Flatirons.' What about them? Over."

Another long silence while the woman seemed to make up her mind. "Some of FarTrip's analysts think those fracture patterns may not be natural." She stopped and Forrest waited to see if she had finished. He was about to respond, when she said. "You flagged those records as 'possibly interesting,' Captain. I thought . . . You three inspected the site personally . . . Perhaps, you also drew conclusions?" She acted like someone poking into a hole with a stick; not sure about what might crawl out, or that she would like it when it did.

This time there was a definite pause for a response. "There was some . . . discussion, ma'am," Forrest said. "Our geologist, Dr. Mendes, believes they were . . . um, alien inscriptions. Engineer Krasnarov disagrees. Over."

There. It had been said. But, hell, if some dirtside analysts had made the same guesses, he didn't see why Nacho should be deprived of the credit. Or the ridicule, depending on how things turned out.

"And what do *you* think, Captain Calhoun? Oh . . . Over."

"Me? I'm just a rocket jock. I know enough to know I don't know enough. That's why I left it off my report. I wanted to see if anyone else would reach Dr. Mendes's conclusion without being prompted." *There, that should take care of Nacho's priority.* "For what it's worth . . . I was skeptical at first. It could have been wishful thinking on Dr. Mendes's part. Now . . ." He hesitated for a long heartbeat. Then, with the feeling he was crawling out on a very thin limb a long ways above the ground, he said, "Now, I think the marks *were* an inscription. A sort of 'Kilroy was here.' Over."

The advantage of the time lag was that it gave you time to think about what to say next. The disadvantage was that it gave you time to think about what you had just said. The words were irrevocably on their way. No way to call them back.

Van Huyten's response, when it finally came, was oddly restrained. Forrest had expected either excitement or skepticism. Instead, her countenance barely flickered.

"I see," she said. "And so, you inscribed the names of your own crew . . . Very well. It's not an unreasonable supposition. Astonishing, but not entirely unreasonable. There are some researchers down here—a minority, to be sure—who share that opinion. The debate is quite lively. But . . . I must *know*. For other reasons. Was there *any* supporting evidence? Anything at all?"

She forgot to say "over," realized it, and threw it in while Forrest was already responding. Forrest sensed . . . Worry? Preoccupation? As if the possibility of ancient alien visitors was just one more straw on a weary camel's back. "Dr. Mendes thought the cavern was pretty peculiar. He thinks it's too cylindrical to be an impact crater and that some of the gouges and other interior marks indicate . . . excavations of some sort. He thinks it may be a mine, or a habitat that was never finished. About that theory, I am less convinced. It could also be, in Engineer Krasnarov's opinion, an unusual, but perfectly natural, formation. Nothing else; unless something's buried in the rubble underneath the Headrock. That was the only place we weren't able to search; not without a honking big crowbar. Over."

She smiled when the humor reached her. "But you did cover the entire surface and interior cave. You're certain. Over."

"Yes. The possibility was too enormous to ignore, so I directed a systematic search of the entire Rock. Nacho, Dr.

Mendes, took the back end and the cave. I took the center, and Engineer Krasnarov took the Headrock and the area immediately around it. None of us found anything else, ambiguous or not. Maybe Pac-Orbita can map the surface with that interplanetary *paparazzi* of theirs. The hi-rezz cameras might spot something we missed. Maybe something large scale. Over."

Van Huyten smiled. "Like a carving of a face?"

Forrest laughed. When it came to jokes, deep space communications was hell on your timing. "Yeah. Like that."

Van Huyten made some notes on her card. "There was some speculation on the cave among the staff; but, of course, everyone is being ultracautious. None of the data is absolutely unequivocal, is it?"

Forrest shook his head. "No, ma'am. Some scratches at the very borderline of what might be writing; a cavern that might be no more than a geological curiosity. Over."

"You are being cautious, too. I do not like equivocal answers, Captain Calhoun."

Forrest stiffened in his seat. "I'm trying to give you the facts, ma'am, without a lot of theorizing. It ain't me that's equivocating; it's the universe." He waited a beat before adding, "Over."

The lag crawled by and Mariesa van Huyten flushed a second time. "Oh, no. I was not chiding you, Captain Calhoun. Please accept my apology. I was only irritated because—you phrased it quite well—the universe is equivocating."

Forrest hesitated for a moment. "Now, would you answer a question of mine?"

Again, the hesitation was longer than the speed of light could account for. "If I can, Captain Calhoun," she answered.

"All right. You told me right up front that this was all confidential, right? But everybody here onboard knows about the Cave and the Flatirons; and from what you said, it's no big secret dirtside, either. So, just who am I keeping this secret from? Over."

It was hard to tell when his question reached her. Her face barely changed expression. It grew only a shade more wary. "Ah. Perhaps I was unclear, Captain. I asked you to keep the *discussion* confidential, not its subject matter. Do you understand? I would rather not have it bandied about that I had called you over this matter. There are . . . other issues, which need not concern you at this point."

Even Deep Space itself was out of that loop, he discovered when he asked. Deep games at high levels was not Forrest's natural habitat. What those "other issues" were he was just as happy not to know.

Afterwards, Forrest told Nacho and Mike that "some experts on Earth" had raised the same theories as Nacho, but he left out van Huyten's personal interest. The Brazilian took that as vindication, even though Forrest reminded him that it was a minority opinion. Nacho all but did an end zone dance right in Krasnarov's face, but the Russian reacted stoically. Rather than the denials or objections Forrest expected, Krasnarov made no response at all. He simply listened to the announcement, shrugged, and returned to his tasks. Nacho thought he was a sore loser; Forrest was not so sure.

An opportunity to speak to the Russian alone came after that same evening's meal. Forrest lingered, sorting the waste and utensils for recycling, until Nacho left to take the first watch. Krasnarov sat with his legs hooked around the retractable stay-bar and his arms planted on the fold-down table, scowling at the drinking bulb in his fist, and looking as if he wished it held vodka. Forrest found a dessert bar in the larder and perched across the table from Krasnarov. The dessert bar had no wrapper, but its amalgam of nuts, honey, grain, and carob was enclosed in a wax envelope guaran*teed* to be both edible and tasteless.

At least they got the tasteless part right; and come to think of it, the nut bar itself wasn't far behind in either category. But, hermetically sealed or not, what did you expect of year-old snack food?

"Can I have a few words with you, Mike?"

Krasnarov barely glanced at him. "Should you not be preparing for sleep? You have the middle watch tonight."

"We need to talk about your performance lately."

The engineer raised the bulb to his lips. "What does it matter?"

"Could matter a lot, old son. Something's been bugging you lately and it's affecting your job performance. You've been letting too many tasks slide. You're way behind on your checklist. You mind telling me what's eating you?"

"Yes." Krasnarov bent over the table. With his right forefinger he traced spiderweb patterns in the metallocene surface.

Forrest took a bite off his dessert bar. "Maybe you don't understand, *amigo*," he said when he had swallowed. "If you're falling behind, I may have to reassign some of your work to Nacho or myself."

That pricked the Russian where it hurt! Krasnarov's head snapped up and he gave Forrest a level stare. Finally, he sighed and said, *"Nichevo."*

"The hell it does matter—"

Krasnarov gave a harsh bark of a laugh. "You are funniest, Calhoun, when you jest unintentionally. 'It does not matter' because *nothing* matters any more. Or ever did."

Forrest shoved the stub of the nut bar in his mouth and bent forward over the table. "You want to let me in on the rationale for that little bit of Russian *angst*?"

"Perhaps, you are the wise one, after all. Perhaps japery is the only sane way to face the universe." Krasnarov turned and hurled his drinking bulb across the module, where it caromed from cabinet to bulkhead before being entrapped by the folds of the privacy curtain. Startled by the outburst, Forrest waited for Krasnarov to fill the silence that followed.

"Have you ever run?" the man asked finally. "In competition, I mean."

Forrest pulled back and shook his head. "A little track and field in college."

"How far behind in a race do you have to be before you give up?"

"Hell, ask me something hard. You *never* give up. Ever. If you find yourself behind, you just run a little faster, is all."

"And if the leader is in a race car and you are afoot? And the car is already halfway across the continent and you are still in your starting blocks? Do you still just 'run faster'?"

"What are you getting at?"

"How far behind must you be before your efforts become pathetic and foolish?"

"Suppose you tell me."

Krasnarov shook his head. "They make *all* our efforts look foolish."

"Who does?"

"They do!" A wave of the arm—pointing, but in every direction. "The aliens. Mendes's 'Visitors.' *Bozhe moi*, I wish I could get drunk."

Forrest straightened on his perch. "I thought you didn't—" He shook his head. "I don't understand."

"I have always seen the future as our destiny, as the country where we will spend our lives. And now, we find that others are already there. *The Promised Land is already occupied*. So what is left for us?"

"I . . . don't know. Join them?"

"Always the younger brother, eh, Calhoun? Well, it is a role that suits you. What is the point of effort if we are always the younger brother, walking in another's shadow?"

Unaccountably irritated, Forrest snapped, "We can still be the first humans."

Krasnarov laughed without humor. "Tell me, Calhoun . . . Who was the first Kenyan to fly the Atlantic solo? You cannot even be sure there has been one, can you? What could such a man look forward to? Building his monoplane, stoking it with petrol, taking off heavy into the wind, knowing that if he cannot reach airspeed his craft will become a fireball hot enough to melt steel. Flying half-blind through the driving rains over the empty ocean . . . And in the end his feat would mean *nothing*. Because others had done it decades before *and moved on*. Americans and Europeans make the crossing now for sport. We would follow his progress with amusement, with our rescue ships keeping pace, our commentators reporting on his position. The pilots of other planes would wave to him. The contrails of our jets would cross the sky far above him, passing him without even noticing. He could not possibly duplicate what your Lindbergh did. *We would make a mockery of his bravery and his dreams*. No, Calhoun, do not interrupt. With every kindness in the world, we would only show how empty and futile all his efforts were.''

Forrest shook his head. ''That's an awful lot of philosophy to read into some scratches on a rock.''

''Sometimes, Calhoun, I envy you your simplicity.''

''Yeah. ''Tis a joy to be simple.' But, Jesus, Mike, it's a little premature, isn't it? It might all be natural, like you said. Scratches on a rock . . . A hole in the ground . . .''

A great, gusting sigh. ''And footprints.''

The moment froze in Forrest's mind. Nothing moved. A crumb of carob hung in the air. The digital clock on the bulkhead blinked its meaningless time. The Russian's jaw muscles were bunched. You could have stripped cable in his teeth. ''What the hell you talking about?''

''There were footprints,'' he said.

''I don't remember any damn footprints, Mike, and I sure as hell wouldn't forget that! You jiving me or holding out?''

''It had to be done.'' Krasnarov's countenance was more wooden than usual. Yet, wood is living. It grows and twists and splits.

''What had to be done? Are you sure they were footprints? What did they look like?''

''I was looking for a suitable place to plant a footprint, symbolic of humanity's accomplishment,'' he said mechanically, as if replaying the scene in his mind. ''I found a small crater where sufficient dust had accumulated to leave a clear imprint. But closer inspection revealed two and part of a third print already there." He paused reflectively and his eyes focused inward.

"At first," he continued in a distant voice, "I thought one of us had made them. But they were cross-ribbed in a way that was different from our own boot soles. And they were smaller. The prints were wide, almost circular at one end and came to a blunt point at the other. Which was the front, and which the back, I could not guess. A few casual steps tracing a chord across the crater floor to be lost in the hard rock at either end. They were spaced close together, so the walker either had very short legs . . . Or he walked on three of them."

"Sweet Jesus . . . I've got to see them. What are the record numbers?"

"I made no record," Krasnarov said.

Forrest froze. "Why the bloody hell not?" he shouted. "Something like that—Jesus H. Christ!" He slammed his fist against the table and looked away. It was too late now to go back and doid them. Damn! How could Mike forget something like that? Maybe that explained his moping lately. He had made a mistake he couldn't undo. He glanced back at Krasnarov and caught a sudden, fleeting look, equal parts smugness and despair. "Why didn't you call me and Nacho over?"

"Preparing for departure, there was a lot to do."

"Well, son," Forrest said, letting the sarcasm show bluntly, "I think we could have postponed one or two action items for something like that . . . What about the Japanese probe? Can Pac-Orbita get a good camera angle on that crater?"

Krasnarov shook his head. "No. They are gone. I obliterated them—"

Forrest suddenly remembered the weird shuffling dance he had seen Krasnarov perform, sweeping his feet back and forth. Brushing out the footprints? And soon after—the next day—he had hopped over to the Flatirons to deface the inscriptions.

In the silence, the equipment muttered to itself. Forrest

leaned back and stared out the forward blister, visible over Krasnarov's shoulder. A billion stars twinkled there in the endless void. Unfathomably distant in time and space. If he had spoken to a Mariesa van Huyten who was minutes in the past, here he was looking at stars as they were hundreds, thousands, millions of years ago. Forrest closed his eyes. "Do you want to explain yourself, Mike? It wasn't accidental, was it?"

"No."

He waited for some explanation and, when it didn't come, he turned and studied the engineer. Krasnarov was staring at nothing, rubbing his hands back and forth, like he was washing them. Forrest reached across the gap that separated them and took him by the sleeve.

"I got to know, Mike. This is the biggest thing mankind has ever stumbled over and you erased the only clear evidence. Tell me it wasn't a whim. Tell me you had a reason. A damn good one. God knows, I can't imagine what that could be, but it would sure make me feel better knowing there was one."

"Without knowledge," Krasnarov told him with utter and terrible sincerity, "there can still be hope."

Forrest released the sleeve and stared at the Russian. He rubbed his face with both hands. "God, what will Deep Space say?" *What would van Huyten say?* Here was the evidence she had been looking for and . . . it wasn't "here" any more. He started to push away from the table. "I better make a report."

There was no change in Krasnarov's expression. "Don't bother. There are no longer any prints—and it will be eighteen years before anyone can go back to see if there are others. I deny I ever saw any footprints. I invented a 'tall tale' out of boredom and you believed it."

Forrest felt like crying. "You were making a joke? Jesus Christ, Mike. No one in the world would believe *that.*"

Hours later, Nacho discovered him in the solitude of the forward observation blister. The viewport had darkened to mute the sun's searing brightness and, consequently, much of the heavens had faded from view. There was still enough to stir the heart, though; and one point of light was brighter than all the rest.

There was nothing to match a Russian, Forrest thought as he contemplated the heavens, when it came to gloom. They had raised it to an art form. Next to a Russian, the Preacher was a cock-eyed optimist. Yet, you couldn't ask for stauncher friends when you had it to do.

Damn Krasnarov.

Nacho drifted up close behind him. "It is your watch, friend."

"In a minute. In a minute. That sure is a sight, isn't it?"

The Brazilian laid a hand on his shoulder. He said nothing for a long while, drinking in the stars in silence. "Out there, somewhere," he said at last, "they came out of those bright, distant stars. Not from anywhere in our system, or we would have met before now."

Forrest didn't bother asking who "they" were? "Unless they're long gone," Forrest said. " 'As a flower, he flourishes. Then the wind passes over and he is gone, and his place knows him no more.' I mean, what was the solar system like way back when? Maybe there are Martian cities sandblasted to nubs, like ol' Nineveh. Or Venusian ones crushed and melted like Sodom and Gomorrah." How could he tell Mendes what Krasnarov had done with a few careless sweeps of a foot?

No, not careless. Krasnarov had been very careful indeed.

Nacho shook his head. "No. I believe they are still out there," he said. "Waiting for us to join them. You, my friend, are too gloomy."

Forrest laughed aloud at that. The Brazilian wouldn't know gloom if it stood up on its hind legs and bit him in the nose. And if Mike had read far too much into a few puzzling scraps of data, why, so had Nacho. Nacho's certainty did not need a set of footprints.

"When I was a kid," Forrest said suddenly, "I was a big fan of westerns. I ate 'em up. Louis L'Amour. Zane Grey.

The Cowboy and the Cossack—I ought to get Mike a copy of that one. But I remember this one scene, where a tough guy is confronting the hero and the tough guy says, 'I'm a big man where I come from.' And you know what the hero says?''

Nacho shook his head. Forrest turned back to face the universe.

'' 'You're not where you come from.' ''

Nacho said, ''I don't understand.''

Forrest didn't respond. He didn't understand, either; but he could sense, a little, the darkness that lay over Krasnarov's heart.

12.

Silent Night

The jump ship touched down at Pegasus Field just as the sun was painting the sky above the mountains with brilliant bands of purple and orange. When Flaco stepped across the gangway onto the elevated bus, his breath came in great bursts of cotton. Well, it was coming onto the Nativity. Even the Southwest cooled off when winter came.

Inside, Pegasus Central was strictly utilitarian. There was a check-in desk and a waiting area. A poster on the wall warned him in English and Spanish not to go out on the landing field unescorted. A few Pegasus people were hanging out, probably waiting to service the ship; but there was no one in the holding area. *Sikorsky* would not be ready to lift the other half of Green Crew for another three days.

Ossa & Pelion had set up a table in the large conference room to process the returning trainees. Flaco lined up with the others. There were four lines, one labelled M–P. Flaco wondered if they would have his paperwork under ''Mercado'' or ''Gonsalves.'' You never could tell with Anglos. In a corner of the room, a tall cactus in a big clay pot had been decorated with Christmas ornaments. Just above the threshold of hearing, the music system was playing mariachi carols with a doo-wap beat. Flaco shook his head. Mexicanos were weird.

"Name?" The man behind the table was brusque, but not impatient.

"Eddie Mercado."

The man did some things on his computer screen and nodded. "Run your card through the reader." he said. "Thank you." More ticky-ticky on the keyboard. The man had a thin, Anglo face and prominent teeth. Horn-rimmed glasses. Flaco wondered if he was one of the Uncle Waldo crew. The clerk indicated a monitor. "Your account balance appears on the small screen to your right. Read it over and see if everything is right."

" 'S okay, man."

The clerk looked at him. "You verified the arithmetic, just like that?"

"Hey, when it comes to pay stubs, everybody's a mathematician."

The clerk grunted. "Ain't that the truth . . . You going to be staying in the New York area while you're down?"

"With my wife."

The man wasn't interested in his love life. "The screen has a list of O&P jobs available around there. You're entitled to two weeks R and R to get your land legs back; then report to the site of your choosing."

Flaco studied the list. "I gotta pick one of these?"

"If you want to stay in the City. You want to go somewhere else, we got other lists. O&P doesn't pay people to sit on their butts waiting for the next lift."

Flaco refrained from pointing out that sitting on his butt was exactly what O&P paid the clerk to do. It never paid to piss off the guy who accessed your payroll file. "What's this job here? New Jersey Transit/LANTA line extension."

The clerk noodled a file off the hyperstack and a window opened on Flaco's screen. "Says here, New Jersey Transit, the Lehigh and Northampton Transit Authority and the Delaware River Joint Bridge Commission are fixing the old Jersey Central line. Plan is to run high-speed rail service between the City and the new jump port west of Allentown.

O&P is prime contractor. Site's an hour's drive west of the City."

"You from back there yourself, man?"

The clerk looked surprised. "Bayonne. How'd you know? I thought I ditched the accent years ago."

"You called it 'the City.'"

The clerk laughed. "Yeah. Like it's the only one. The company runs a one-car shuttle for New York area workers out of Penn Station five-thirty each morning, snow or sun. You interested?"

Flaco shrugged. "Sure. Put me down."

A few more flourishes on the keyboard and the printer buzzed. The clerk handed him a pocket folder and a printout. "Here's your job authorization and your plane ticket, Sky Harbor to LaGuardia. Next bus leaves in half an hour. Good luck."

Sepp Bauer and Henry Littlebear were waiting for him in the lobby. A few minutes later Tonio Portales joined them. The Cuban was all smiles. "You guys feel like you got weights on your ankles, too?"

Sepp nodded. "A good t'ing dey made us exercise each day. Wit' a giant rubber band, yet."

"Any you guys sign up for the Chicago Sportsplex project?" There were headshakes all round. It turned out none of them had signed up for the same groundside work.

"So," said Littlebear. "Guess we won't see each other till February."

"If we made the cut," Flaco said.

"Aw, I wouldn't worry about that," the Mohawk said. "O&P has too much money in us already to scratch us off the list."

"Dey might keep us," Sepp pointed out, "but keep us groundside."

"With the dust bunnies," said Flaco, and they all laughed.

They exchanged grips, and Flaco wondered as they lined up to board the shuttle bus, if he would see any of them again after tonight.

* * *

When Serafina met him at the airport this time, her mother was with her, hovering in the background like a duenna. Serafina greeted him with kisses and hugs, but they were noticably more restrained than before. Well, what woman acted wanton in front of her mother?

"Buenas dias, Mother Cruz," he said when Serafina had led him to her mother.

"It is a terrible time of the morning for my daughter to be about."

"I took the red-eye," Flaco explained. "I was anxious to get back."

Señora Cruz nodded, but made no other comment. "We will have dinner tonight. Your parents are coming over." She turned and led the way. Flaco exchanged a look with Serafina, who rolled her eyes and grinned at him. Her hand entwined his. "You get a proper welcome home later," she said, squeezing his hand. "After dinner."

Mama Cruz served *lechón asado* with side dishes of *mofongo* and pigeon peas with coriander seasoning. The barbequed pig was Puerto Rico's national dish, when Boricuans were in the mood to think of themselves as a nation. Flaco wondered if the woman had chosen it because this was a celebration or just to remind her Dominican guests that they were in El Barrio, and not the Heights.

Flaco's parents arrived at the Cruz apartment a half hour after Flaco. *Papita* looked older than Flaco remembered. Gray and drawn; but still slim: a collection of bones held together by gristle. Flaco embraced him and kissed his mother. "It is good to see you, boy," *Papita* said in his low, husky voice. "I have been taking care of your apartment. When do you plan to move back in?"

Flaco led him into the apartment, using the confusion of greetings to avoid answering the question. " 'Fina!" he called. "They're here! Did you have a good trip over, *Papita?*"

"Ah, the taxicab had a problem with his onboard. It told him to turn on 148th Street, which everyone knows is under

repair; so we went in circles for a while. I would not pay
him for the extra miles. He did not like that, so we argued.''

"Your father likes to argue with taximen," Flaco's mama
said. "It was less than a scruple of gold, old man."

Papita grinned. "I have no scruples."

"It sounds like the construction hasn't been loaded into
the citymap deebee," Flaco suggested.

"It makes no difference," Papita said. "In my day, the
taximen knew all the streets up here—" And he tapped
himself on the side of the head.

"Ah, the baby is beginning to show," Flaco's mother
cooed over her daughter-in-law and neatly stoppering her
husband's monologue on the decay of New York cabbies.
"He is due in May?"

"Yes, Mama Gonsalves. May sixteen."

Flaco's mother looked at him. "You take good care of
this baby," she said.

"Yes, Mama." He was twenty-two, almost twenty-three.
He was a man, with a man's job. He had made a son. And
yet, with his parents, he became a child again. Was it always
this way? Had *Papita* felt the same when they had gone to
visit Grandpapa? Felix Mercado had been no older than
Flaco when he had become a father. Had he felt as helpless
then as Flaco did now? He never spoke of such things. What
man did? And Flaco did not know how to ask him.

The meal was good. Felipa Cruz was a fine cook. But
there were many things Flaco had to swallow along with
the pig.

He told them about the construction work. He emphasized the strangeness. Everyone laughed at how the Red
Crew had stranded the newcomers in midair. He emphasized
the serene beauty of infinity and the many-colored sphere
that seemed to hover above them. Serafina sighed when he
told how he used to wait for New York to pass under the
station. He told them about the stern Rector, about Meat's
friendship and Rhys Pilov's strictness, about Tonio, Sepp,
Littlebear, and the others.

He did not tell them about Wendy McKenna's seduction,

or that he had nearly been beheaded by a swinging beam. That would only have complicated matters.

"How long will you be with my daughter this time, Eduardo?" Mama Cruz asked.

"Every possible minute," he answered, and was rewarded by his mother-in-law's blush and his father's guffaw. *Mamita* clucked her tongue and said, "Your place is by her side."

Flaco jabbed his fork into the barbecued pig. "I know that. But the work is not so far away. I can be home in less time than if I were in the Republic. Construction workers must travel if they are to find work. While I am dirtside, I will be working in New Jersey . . ."

"Flaco," said Serafina, "that is wonderful!"

" 'Dirtside,' " sniffed Felipa Cruz.

"What is this job in New Jersey?" his father asked.

"They are fixing the railroad so people can ride into New York from the new spaceport." *Papita* said, "Ah," and nodded his head wisely.

"Does this mean your work in space is done?" Mama Cruz asked.

Flaco hesitated. "A lot can happen," he said. "They will evaluate my performance. If it was good, they'll ask me back for the second half of the training."

"Then you don't *need* to go back," his mother-in-law insisted.

"You would rather that I failed?" He wondered if Serafina's mother did not want just that. What prophet did not long for the fulfillment of her prophesies?

"Flaco will not fail," Serafina said. Her hand squeezed his under the table.

"Oh, they'll ask him back, I am sure," Mama Cruz said in a voice that betrayed no such assurance. "But he needn't go back when asked. They let you keep this railroad job, no?"

Flaco could not lie. "Yes. I wouldn't lose my O&P job if I quit the project. They would put me on another project."

"Well, then." Mama Cruz spread her hands as if all was

settled. Even his own mother looked pleased.

"But I will not have it be said that José Eduardo Gonsalves y Mercado turned his back on a difficult task."

"No, son," his father shook his head. "Never quit. I raised no quitter. Still . . ." He, too, thought of space as "far away."

"And the money I earn will let Serafina and me buy a house."

"Yes," said Mama Cruz, "off in New Jersey, among the Anglos."

"Does the space work pay so well, then, son?"

Almost, he told his father what it paid, but then he thought that it was more than his father could make in several years of waiter work. Could he say that which would unman his father and make his labors trivial? "It pays well, Father," he said.

Felix Mercado licked his lips and nodded. "That is good," was all he said.

"Your son is due in May," Mama reminded him.

"I know that." Flaco fought hard to rein his temper. He had never spoken crossly to his mother. Not like his sisters had done. He had seen as a child how much that had wounded her. "The second turn is only three months. I will go back up in February and will be back down in May." Mamita looked doubtful.

"That is a long time to be away . . ."

"I know that, too. But sometimes we must sacrifice today to have a better tomorrow."

His father nodded, once, twice. "Yes, yes. That is true." He spoke as if to himself.

Mamita said, "I don't like it."

"I don't like it either, *Mamita*."

"With so many not liking it," Mama Cruz observed, "it's a wonder that it will happen."

It was Serafina's childhood room. The wallpaper was pale with pink and red flowers. A stuffed lamb nested among colorful, square pillows. The dresser was littered with cream and lotions, and the whole room smelled of powder. Tucked in the corner was a battered, old Pentium PC, the best a poor family could afford for surfing. Flaco closed the door behind him. He leaned back against it.

"They're gone," he said. "And your mother is watching television."

Serafina sat on her bed with her legs tucked up under her. She picked up the stuffed lamb and stroked it. "I was lonely," was all she said.

"Yeah. Me, too." He sat down beside her on the bed. "You had your family. I had no one."

"There was an accident on the station," she said. "I saw it on the news. They said there was some damage, but no one was hurt."

"No one was."

"Were you there when it happened?"

"No," he lied.

"Good. I don't know what I would do if anything happened to you."

He put his hand on the back of her neck and massaged gently. Serafina leaned into him. "You said little at dinner."

"You're my husband. I will not disagree with you in front of others."

"Only in private."

"You do what you gotta do, Eddie," she said in English. "I can see it. I can even agree with it." She stood up and laid the stuffed lamb aside. "But that doesn't help me not be scared." She went to the dresser and stood before it with her arms hugging herself tightly.

"That's only because it's new. You'll get used to it."

"And your absence? Will I get used to that, too?" She unfastened her blouse, button by button, lowered her arms and let the blouse slide off.

"No more than I ever will," Flaco answered. He stood, too. On the station, one saw women half-dressed from time to time. Tantalizing glimpses, sometimes staged, sometimes not. Once, he had even seen Millie Hess bare from the waist up, and that was something widely assumed to be unseeable by those still living. But this . . . Desire coursed though him; filled him up. Flaco placed his hands on Serafina's shoulders and let them slide down her arms and up her back. She arched her back like a cat.

He fumbled with the hooks on her bra, his fingers trembled so in their eagerness, but he got it off. Bending down, he kissed her in the curve between her neck and shoulder, then, as she twisted her head, on her throat. His arms enfolded her from behind, one hand cupping her breast, the other flat against her belly. Their lips met and her tongue probed his mouth. When they parted, he gasped for breath. "It's been so long," he said.

She placed a finger on his lips. "Hush. Mama does not play the television so loud."

Serafina undressed him with hands as eager as his own. Their breathing turned to hurried panting, broken now and then by stifled giggles when one of them made a noise a little too loud. Serafina backed against the dresser and Flaco went to his knees and kissed her on the belly, kissed his son, little Memo, placed his palms on either either side of the gentle swelling and caressed him, caressed her, travelled down to her thighs, around to her buttocks. Serafina curled her fingers in his hair, pulled his face against her, and made quiet, contented sounds.

When he stood again, they joined eagerly, handling each other with quick, impatient touches. Her arms wrapped around him, gripped his back. Her moist, warm lips pressed against him as he probed inside her with his tongue. Through the mist of her hair, Flaco saw her reflection in the mirror, watched his own hands caressing the sweet curve of her hips. They rocked together against the dresser and the dresser creaked, sparking another moment of half-guilty self-awareness; then they resumed, slowly and more gently, this time. In the mirror, Flaco saw the accusing stare of the stuffed lamb on the bed.

What sort of madman was he to give this up? He could bid onto the railroad job instead. He'd have to leave early in the morning and would not return until late in the evening, but he would be home each night. He would be with Serafina each night, and she with him.

All thought vanished eternally into feeling, and Flaco felt as if he were again in ziggy, floating weightless over the void. In his ears, like the distant cry of a bird, he could hear Serafina's exclamations. "Flaco, oh. Flaco." Over and over. Her body swelled against him with her breathing.

When he came to himself once more, Serafina gripped him fiercely around the waist and would not let him disengage. She rubbed the back of his leg with her foot. "You were gone too long," she said when he ceased his mock struggle against her embrace. "I have you close now. I will not release you."

"Never have I been held in a sweeter prison, nor by a kinder warden."

"You sound so romantic when you talk Castillian."

"And how do I sound when I talk Dominican?"

She kissed him. "Wild. And dangerous."

"An' when I talk English?"

"Mmm. Sexy."

They remained so, speaking nonsense to one another, telling each other how much they pleased, making promises, building futures. Presently—it may have been an hour or it may have been a few phantom moments—romance surrendered to passion once more.

It was a different sort of shuttle that took Flaco to his new job. No numbing, bone-shaking roar, no acceleration pressing you into your seat, no soaring, puking weightlessness. Just a gentle rattle-clack over rails whose path had been laid out a century and a half before. Once west of the Plainfields, the special car that Ossa & Pelion had chartered rolled through the farmlands of the Raritan Valley. Everything had a soft, subdued color. "The dawn's early light." Flaco saw a cow. A real cow, standing out in a field. Every now and then, a flash of morning light revealed a high-tech, chrome-and-glass business campus, all angles and geometry, hidden among the trees.

Past High Bridge, the tracks curved north around the end of Musconetcong Mountain and then down the Musconetcong Valley to the Delaware. The land here was different from what he was used to; different too from the arid splendor of the Southwest desert. It was rumpled; set on edge. Ridges and low hills rippled like the waves of a deep green sea. They were not high hills, but they were abrupt, rising almost like walls from the valley floors. Funny, that they seemed to have come so far, and yet High Bridge itself was only fifty miles from Columbus Circle. As the crow flies, his seatmate told him, if crows flew straight lines.

Flaco had no idea of the flying habits of crows. He was a city boy. Pigeons were more his style.

The tracks ran through the outskirts of Phillipsburg atop rocky ledges and massive stone trestles. The roads below ducked through tunnels carved from the living rock. From his window, Flaco noticed a party tent being erected at what looked like a banquet hall atop the hill; then the trees closed in again and blocked the view.

Rickety, wooden row houses lined narrow streets. Some houses were set on the sides of the hills, with tall, concrete footings propping them up and long, winding stairs leading from the street to the front doors. He saw other hillsides too shear for houses, but still with zigzagged stairs climbing their faces. Who on Earth would ever walk them?

The car slowed as it passed a foundry, where men were loading flatcars with beams of smoke and steel. Flaco craned his neck to see better. WARREN FOUNDRY, the sign read, A DIVISION OF WILSON ENTERPRISES. Flaco's seatmate tapped him and indicated the foundry with a jerk of his thumb. "That's where they fab the steel for the project. They got a yard engine brings the stuff over to the site." He was a dark-complexioned man in his midthirties who wore his straight, black hair in twin braids.

"Neighbors didn't object to putting it there?" Flaco asked.

"Nah. That foundry was there before they invented zoning. The town council counted the number of jobs and decided it was 'grandfathered' in. You heard of NIMBY? This was PIMBY. *Please*, in my backyard. Guys can live across the street and walk to work.'' He was silent a moment, before he added, ''My great-great-grandfather, he was a blacksmith there, a hundred and twenty years ago.''

''You're from around here? I took you for an Indian.''

His seatmate grinned. ''That's my mom's side of the family. *Her* great-great grandfather was shooting Confederates out in the Territory. Whups.'' He pointed ahead, out the window. ''There it is.''

The tracks ahead crossed the Delaware on a long steel trestle bridge, with the apparent intent of ramming directly into a sheer granite cliff. There was a cut in the cliff, though, and the tracks angled off to the right and crossed the mouth of a second river that cascaded over a low dam into the Delaware. Flaco saw a large, black iron bridge set atop two enormous stone piers.

''That's the bridge? It doesn't look in very good shape,'' Flaco allowed.

''It ain't, buddy. That's why we're here.''

When the car passed through the cut, Flaco could see that, except for the flat ground at the forks itself, both sides of the second river were lined with nearly vertical hills. He whistled. ''Is that where the tracks go?''

His companion nodded. ''Yeah. The deal is the Authority uses existing right-of-way for the high-speed line. Which means either the Jersey Central or the Lehigh Valley. I wouldn't worry, though. Those old engineers knew their shit. Their equipment couldn't deal with half the stuff we can handle nowadays, so they always laid out their routes along the easiest ground.''

Flaco studied the valley ahead. ''And that was the easiest route?''

''Word up, man. Easi*est*, not easy. There ain't no easy road.''

There was a God and he had a really bad sense of humor.

He proved it while Flaco and a half-dozen other new guys

were studying the plans for rebuilding and smoking the bridge, waiting for the boss to come and brief them. The trailer was a long one, done up in cheap plastic paneling that didn't try very hard to look like wood. Bulletin boards were thumbtacked like voodoo dolls. A long paper map lined one wall of the trailer, showing the route to be refurbished: the former Jersey Central tracks, from the bridge to the new spaceport north of Allentown. Another set of drawings showed the views and levels of the bridge. The tricky thing was that the railroad bridge crossed over an automobile bridge that happened to be the only connection between the north and south sides of the city. On the south side of the river a brick and stone railroad viaduct ran along the base of the cliffs. Another work crew was gathered there. Flaco nudged one of the other men.

"What's goin' on over there?"

The man looked out the window. "Damfino. Hey, Buck. You're from around here. What're they doing across the river?"

"Maglev demonstration project."

"What the hell's maglev?"

"Doncha read the magazines? That's where the train floats in the air wit' magnets. They're using the old Lehigh Valley line to test it out."

"Jeeze, how many railroads went through this one-horse burg?"

If Buck was offended by the slur on his hometown, he didn't show it. "Beats me. Four, maybe five."

"That many *railroads?*"

"Hey, railroads used to be a big deal."

The door opened again, and Flaco figured it had to be the crew boss; but when he looked around, he saw Bird Winfrey.

The Bird grinned when he saw Flaco. "Well, call me a liar if this isn't old home week. How's it going there, Chico?"

Flaco had given up correcting Bird a long time ago. It

constantly amazed him what other people found to be funny. "What's the word, Bird?"

Winfrey took a seat among the other new arrivals. "You just come in on the shuttle, right? I remember you said you were a New York boy."

"Tha's right. What about you?"

"Oh, I moved up from Philly. Took me an apartment up on the hill." He wiggled his thumb over his shoulder, but that didn't narrow it down. Flaco could see about six hills from the windows of the trailer. "Way I figure, if we get as much snow as we got last year, there'll be a lot of days we get to sit on our kiesters and goof. Not like those guys who took gigs in the sunny south." He turned and looked at the others. "Any you guys local? You get much snow up here?"

"Not much to speak of," said one man. "Though you gotta watch you don't break through the crust when you walk on it."

"Break though the crust?" said Bird.

"Remember Johnny Holzenbeck?" said a second man to the first. "Took the rescue squad a day and a half to find him after he broke through. Had to use those long poles they got to poke through the snow."

"Yeah," said the first. "Good thing Johnny had the good sense to dig him a breathing hole out."

"Oh, Johnny, he got a head on his shoulder. Needs bigger feet, though, if he's gonna go walking on top the snow."

The Bird covered his face with one of his broad hands. "Oh, Jesus, save me from comedians."

Later, Flaco went out to the rail yard to get a twenty footer for the support structure they were building underneath the old bridge. He waved the crane over and told the operator over his two-way to lower the tackle. Bird Winfrey popped up from the other side of the stack.

"What the hell you doing, Chico?"

"Fetching a twenty footer."

"Well, not that one, numb-nuts. Can't you see my mark?

It's got a void in it. Never should have left the billet mill, let alone the foundry.'' He came around the pile of steel and scowled at the offending member. ''Ah, damn. Someone dropped a crate right in front of it.'' He pulled a can of flourescent orange spray paint from his pouch and shook it. ''Sorry, Chic'. Not your fault.'' He sprayed broad Xs along the top face of the rail. ''Though, long as you're here, why'n'cha have Crane move this over to the reject pile?''

''Sure. Let me tell my boss.'' He whistled the tackle down. ''You know,'' he said while he fastened the chains, ''this 'Chico' business gets a little thin after a while.''

''Ah, I don't mean nothing by it. You oughta know that by now. It's like I call your buddy 'Fritz,' or the Russians, 'Ivan.' That way I don't have to remember so many names.''

''Not very friendly, though.''

''What would you know?'' Bird looked away for a moment. ''I have a hard time with names, that's all. I see people I know. I know I know 'em. I recognize their faces right off, but the name doesn't always come. Hell, it's probably a disease. Everything's a disease these days, right? Something or other syndrome—except I'd probably forget that name, too.'' He laughed and stepped away from the steel pile. Flaco called up the crane operator and told him to follow Bird's directions.

''My wife's Mexican, you know.'' Bird waved his arms, semaphore style. Flaco followed him.

''Didn't know you had a wife. Do you call her Chico, too?''

Bird laughed. ''Hell, no. I call her Chica.''

''And what does she call you?''

''Tonto, mostly.''

Flaco laughed. ''An' what does she think about you working up in space?''

''Oh, she's all for it. Says when I'm away she doesn't take me for granted and I don't get in her way so much.''

''Married long?''

''Thirteen years. I was a child bride. Both of us right out

of high school. They told us it wouldn't last. Hell, they might still be right about that. If it ain't forever, it 'didn't last,' right? Okay, it's your steel again.''

The crane had lowered the bad beam on Bird's reject stack. Flaco unfastened the rigging and told the crane to pull up and rotate back to the staging yard. ''You know my wife is expecting a baby,'' Flaco said.

Bird tugged off the thick canvas gloves he was wearing and wiped his forehead with the back of his hand. ''No fooling? Congratulations.''

''Yeah. In May. I was thinking . . . Maybe I shouldn't go back up, you know? Maybe I should stay down here with her.''

Bird shrugged. ''It's as good a reason as any,'' he said, batting the rolled-up gloves into his hand. ''As good a reason as any.''

The snow spattered against the window in a flurry of tiny sounds. Behind it, pushing it, the rush of the December wind. Flaco held the curtain aside and stared out Serafina's window. The night scene was all black and white. The cars lining the street were soft hummocks, buried beneath the blizzard. The streetlamps were spheres of white, reflecting off the snowflakes that whipped around them. On the sidewalk, a few lonely figures struggled in ankle-deep drifts. A battered old Range Rover crawled down 110th toward the park, leaving tracks quickly filled in. Flaco let the curtain fall shut as he heard Serafina enter the room.

''We need beer,'' he told her. ''Or wine. What kind of Nativity dinner is it gonna be without wine?''

''On a night like this? You're crazy.''

''It ain't that far. Just to the corner and back.''

She laid a hand on his arm. ''It can wait. Nativity's not till next week.''

He pulled away. ''I just need to get outside, is all. I'm goin' nuts cooped up like this.''

''Weatherman, he says it blows inland by Tuesday. It's what he calls a northeaster.''

He went to the trunk where he kept his clothes. The Cruz apartment was anything but spacious, especially with him living in with Serafina. Like a one-room flat. He felt like a visitor. He found his down-filled coat and threw it on. He stuffed gloves in the pocket. ''What you want from the store?'' he said.

''You made the right decision,'' she said.

Flaco stood with the ski-mask balaklava in his hands. He stretched it out, turning it the right way round. He knew she didn't mean the decision to go to the corner *bodega*. ''I don't know.''

''It's better for you to stay here.''

He turned and faced her. ''I'm all mixed up, angel. When I made my mind up to take the job, I felt like I belonged down here. When I decided to stay here, I feel like I should go back.''

''Flaco . . .''

''We need the money. Otherwise, we're stuck here.''

''I'm not 'stuck,' husband. My family lives here. My cousins. So does your family. You are the one who wants to leave.''

He looked at her. ''And if I do?''

''I'll go with you. But we can be happy here, too.''

He wondered if she meant that, or if she only thought she did because that way he wouldn't have to go back to LEO. How many people convinced themselves they were happy when it was only expedience? ''I'll be right back. The night air, it clears the mind.''

''It's *cold*, Flaco.''

''So when I come back in, I'll need you to warm me back up again.''

''Sherry, then. You can bring me sherry.''

Flaco grinned at her and tugged the knit cap over his head.

It was colder than he had thought it would be. The wind was in his face all the way down the block, coating his eyes and nose with sleet and ice. The ski mask he wore became hard and crusty where his breath passed through the fabric.

The drift on the pavement worked its way into his boots, soaking his socks. Halfway down the block, a wild gust of wind took his breath away and he turned his head. Almost, he turned back; but, the devil, he was halfway to the *bodega* already.

Old Pablo, who ran the store, started when Flaco entered; but Flaco pulled the ski mask down and said, "It's only me, Old One." He picked up a handbasket by the entrance.

Pablo shook his ancient head. "Ah, it is too wild a night for the *sinvergüenzas* to be about. But you startled me, Flaco. How is your beautiful wife?"

"Growing more beautiful every day," Flaco answered as he walked down the aisles, filling the basket. A six pack of *El Presidente*. Pretzels. Why in the name of the Virgin had he come out on a night like this? He picked up a gallon of milk, some *massa* and two cans of red beans—just so Pablo would not think he was crazy coming out for nothing at all. He almost forgot the sherry, turned back and plucked a bottle off the shelf. Pablo smiled as he registered the tally.

"Ah, it looks like a warm and cozy night tonight, eh, boy?"

No one could see him blush under the ski mask. "You know women when the child is coming."

Pablo laughed as he placed the sherry in the sack. "And I know men, too."

It was not so bad walking back. The wind was behind him, pushing him, so he seemed to walk with lighter steps. Around the streetlamps, the sleet in the air danced and swirled like flocks of distant, shining birds.

He almost tripped on the outstretched foot.

When he looked, he saw a small, black felt ankle boot protruding from the snow that had piled up against the anonymous cars. Flaco fell to his knees and set the grocery sack aside. He brushed the snow away with quick swipes. A bare leg with an ankle bracelet. A leather miniskirt and white fur jacket. The face . . .

Flaco paused and sat back on his heels. The face was washed out, colorless, as blanched as the snow itself. The ears and the tip of the nose were frostbitten. Ice rimmed the staring, vacant eyes; snow filled the open mouth and nostrils. Flaco had seen death before—of his friends, of his enemies—though usually it had come robed in red, not white. Death had run wet, not froze hard.

Her hair was straw, dark at the roots; and the thin, angular face was made broader and softer where it blended into the embedding snow. She looked like Serafina a little, but paler, thinner, whiter, bleached, and painted, with a hardness around the mouth and eyes that Serafina would never have.

"So that's where the bitch wound up."

Flaco had heard no footsteps coming up behind him. He looked over his shoulder and saw a short man in a thick, ankle-length coat and a popular lumberjack "goofball" hat. His hands were stuffed deep in his pockets and sleet painted the side of his coat. "I been looking all up and down the barrio. Goddamn."

"Was she your—" he hesitated barely a second—"girl-friend?"

The man laughed. "No, but you might say she was my 'employee of the month.' She had gold between her legs, man." He shook his head. "Now she got nothing."

"I'm sorry for your loss," said Flaco.

"Loss? What do you know? Where'm I gonna find another bitch could turn like she did? What she doin' out here, anyway. Waiting for you? You a john of hers?"

Flaco shook his head. "I only just found her."

The pimp looked at the frozen face. "I sunk a lot in that stupid hole, and this is the way she pays me back." Abruptly, he lashed out and kicked the body. "You. Stupid. Cunt." Snow flew and the body slid away from the car it had been sitting against and slumped into the drift. "God. Damn."

Flaco swung his grocery bag as he rose and caught the man on the side of the head. He staggered and slipped in the snow. "What the fuck?" His right hand came out of his coat pocket and a knife gleamed silver in the winter night. Flaco swung again and the blade sliced the bag open.

The groceries scattered in the snow. The sherry bottle, marvelously intact, landed at Flaco's feet. He stepped under the pimp's swipe and scooped the bottle up. Without breaking stride, he smashed it against the lamppost and turned and caught the man's wrist with the broken neck. The pimp howled and dropped the knife. When he doubled over, clenching the wrist with his left hand, Flaco cut him across the face.

He shrieked like a woman and both hands went to his eyes. Flaco grabbed him by the lapels and pulled him hard into the lamppost. "You got no right," he told the man. "You gave her the pearls and she was so damned happy that she didn't care shit about anything. Not the snow and not the cold and not the sleep when it finally took her."

"I can't see," the man blubbered. "You blinded me!"

"I shoulda cut you down at the other end."

"She was just a hole, man. What do you care? Oh, God. Oh, God." ¨

Flaco rammed the man's head into the lamppost again and his knees bucked and he fell to the reddened snow. Blood streamed from his broken nose and froze on his lips. "That's what she *was*," Flaco told him. "That's not what she coulda been."

"Oh, God, don't hurt me any more." The words were slurred by broken teeth, by lips split and broken.

"You thought you were tough as long as you could kick women." Flaco threw the shard of the bottle as hard as he could across the street. He watched it arc and vanish into the thick-layered snow. He bent over the grovelling man. "I won't hurt you no more. I can't answer for God."

He turned away and stood frozen for a moment. His hand twitched and his knees began to shake. His breath was ragged streamers in the winter air.

"We don't need his kind here."

Flaco saw the old man from the *bodega*, shivering in his store apron, with a shotgun cradled in his arms. He stepped over to the moaning man and spit in his face. Then he lifted his shotgun and broke open the breech, covering it against the howling snow.

Flaco looked around at the scattered groceries. The bag of pretzels was smashed. The *El Presidente* had vanished into the snow. He stooped and began to gather the cans of red beans. "Get back inside, Old One. You'll die of the cold."

The *bodeguero* waded through the snow toward the corner. He paused and looked back. "It was a man in a ski mask who bought the groceries. He was a big man, perhaps two hundred pounds. I did not know him."

Flaco watched the man walk away. "Thank you," he said. The old man shrugged. "I know what he was," he said with a gesture toward the fallen pimp. "And I know what you and Serafina are. I will not throw the good after the bad. And as for what you know about street fighting, I will not ask what you once were."

Back once more in the Cruz apartment, Flaco studied his down jacket for any sign of blood before he hung it in the closet. He checked his pants, too, and his gloves and cap. The cap, he discovered had been sliced at the scalp line, but when he placed his hand to his forehead, it came away clean. The gloves, he bundled into a plastic bag and stuffed them deep inside the kitchen trash.

Serafina emerged from their room, dressed in woolen pajamas and rubbing sleep from her eyes. "Flaco? What took so long? I fell asleep."

Flaco glanced at his mother-in-law's bedroom door. "The snow was too bad," he whispered. "I walked the other way around the block to stay out of the wind, but it was too deep. I was slipping and sliding. So I gave up and came back." He followed her into their room.

"You're shivering," she said.

"It was very cold."

"Your clothes are wet. Take them off this minute! Hush, I will get a towel and rub you dry."

Flaco began unfastening his shirt buttons. "Ah, I should have gone walking in the snow sooner."

Serafina giggled. A moment later, she returned with the towel. Flaco was already stripped. He wrapped his arms around her and she swallowed a shriek. "Flaco! You're as cold as ice."

"Warm me, then."

She snuggled against him, wrapping the towel around the both of them. "You're trembling still."

Slowly, her heat sank into him, and feeling returned to his tingling limbs. The numbness began to leave him. He began to hurt.

"It wasn't the cold," he said, but softly.

"What did you say?"

"Nothing." He held her in arms of steel. Serafina was life. Serafina was hope. Serafina was an oasis of light and warmth, surrounded by a desert of forgotten lives and nameless bodies lying on hopeless streets. In the distance, muffled by the snow, a police siren broke the stillness of the night.

13.

The Ghosts in the Machinations

A bright spark of light in the heavens, growing brighter and brighter until it casts shadows. A searing, purple line scarring her retinas. A fountain of earth and water tossed skyward by a playful god-child. Soot and ash and dirt filling the air, blotting out the sun forever.

Mariesa stood dumbstruck on the patio behind Silverpond while a boiling cloud of dust and vapors, black and evil, writhed skyward from the place where North Orange had been. *Too late. We were too late, after all.* A sound, a roar, the Devil's laughter, as the tower of smoke climbed toward the tropopause, where the top anviled out and lightnings played across its angry face.

And then: a rain of debris striking her—rocks, clumps of earth, pieces of buildings—leaving welts, beating her onto flagstones that rippled from the breaking of long-forgotten faults. Harriet stepped onto the patio, tugging on a pair of white cotton gloves. *Really, Mariesa, why are you rolling about on the ground like that?*

I'm sorry, Mother. But it was the end of civilization. A few rules could be relaxed.

The last shard of sunlight fled as the dust clouds overwhelmed the sky. Harriet faded into shadows. Cold gripped the world and Mariesa began to shiver as she crawled toward the shelter of Silverpond. Barry stood in the doorway, shaking his head. He smiled ruefully. *Looks like you were right all along.* He bent over and stretched out a hand. *Let me help you.*

No, not *his* hand.

But she took it anyway. Seized by the wrist, pulled easily, light as a feather, into the building, she landed *effacée* in front of Ned DuBois. He cocked his head and grinned with half his mouth. *I guess it's too late now*, he said.

Endless night enveloped her, bored into her, and she began to shake uncontrollably. Ned whirled his flight jacket over her shoulders. She pressed herself against his solid, hard muscles; wrapped her arms around his neck and kissed him fiercely, attacking him with her tongue. *I always wanted to fuck you*, she said.

It's your dice; start shaking.

They were naked and lying on the floor and he was riding her, moving in time with the shuddering earth while she gripped his firm, hard buttocks with both her hands, pulling him into her. She felt herself building, building, until . . .

The impact shockwave reached them, lifted them, and tossed them, still coupled, across the meadow, up the flanks of the mountain. As they coasted through the caressing air, Ned morphed. His face melted and ran, changed, changed back. He was Ned, he was Barry, he was Wayne, he was Belinda. For a brief moment, he was even Piet. Finally, he was Harriet, stroking her face and making soothing sounds as they spun toward the cratered earth far below.

"What's wrong, dear?" Harriet asked. Mariesa turned and buried her face in her pillow. She could feel Harriet's fingers in her hair, combing it. "You had a nightmare."

Mariesa pressed her face deeper into the feathery softness. She embraced the pillow in her arms, hugged it to her. "I know. I know, I know, I know." Thank God it hadn't lasted. The last part—alone in the dark and the cold—she could never bear.

"There, dear. It was only a dream."

Mariesa emerged from the pillow, propped herself up on her forearms and let her head hang. "Only a dream . . ."

That part with Ned was new. Such brazen behavior, even in a dream! Did she want Ned that badly? She had found him intriguing, but she had never *consciously* lusted after him. He had gone back to his wife—had given up FarTrip to stay with her—and Mariesa had hardly spoken to the man in the last few years. Whatever might have been now could never be. "Only a dream," she said bitterly. "What do you know?"

"Very little, I am sure. I only know that my little girl is frightened."

Mariesa rolled on her side to face Harriet. Her mother was sitting on the bedside, wrapped in a Japanese-style robe all bright cherry and snow. Her face, in contrast, was gray and worn; her lips, pale. She looked old. Sleep was the great betrayer. "Your little girl," Mariesa said. Harriet pursed her lips.

"Always," she said. "'Some fates cannot be fled, nor burdens ever lifted.'"

Unless it was not Ned. Unless Ned was only a convenient image tossed up at random by her subconscious. But an image meaning . . . what? "I can take care of myself, Mother."

"Certainly, but why should you have to?" Harriet brushed a curl from Mariesa's forehead and Mariesa stopped herself from brushing it back. "You're working yourself into a breakdown, you know."

"It's only until May. I'll vacation after May. We'll go to Prague together in June." She didn't know why she said that. She could imagine nothing more numbing than Prague in June with Mother.

"I don't know what could be so important. All those White House calls. Trips hither and yon. Comings and goings. Why are you meeting here? Why not at your office?" Harriet fussed with Mariesa, smoothing the covers, rubbing her shoulders.

"Piet was in my dream," Mariesa said.

Harriet paused in her ministrations; she settled back on the edge of the bed. A noncommittal "ah" escaped her lips, and she tugged at the end of the sheet. When it seemed the silence would go on forever, Harriet spoke. "He was drunk. In the hallway, all these doors look the same. Nothing happened."

"He was always drunk. Every day of my life that I remember."

"Not always. It only seemed that way, because those occasions were more . . . dramatic."

"Dramatic. Oh, God." Mariesa turned away again, and lay with her head resting on the pillow. She stared at the sitting area, the vanity. What time was it anyway? The curtained windows were dark. Outside the dull glow of distant city lights showed above the treetops.

"He cared about you. He never wanted to hurt you."

"Oh, he was a good-hearted drunk, he was."

Harriet stiffened. "He had his reasons. Sober, he and Willem would argue. Drunk . . . Well, they argued when he was drunk, too, but at least then he didn't care. Willem found fault with everything he ever did. Piet was a good man in the clubs or on the tour. Good with a joke, or conversation. He was fun to be with. He knew the theater and liked acting folk. He would have made a damn fine playboy, but your grandfather insisted he learn the business. He didn't like it, and it showed; but he *tried,* though that didn't show so well. If Willem had chosen Christiaan or even Beatrice, instead of Piet, things might have turned out very different."

Uncle Chris would have been a stolid, unimaginative steward; Aunt Bee would have lost it all. What a choice Gramper had been faced with, when he looked for an heir among his offspring.

" 'Might have makes no never minds.' "

"Eh? What?"

"Something Belinda used to say."

Harriet stood. "I'll let you get your sleep now. It's early yet." She gathered her housecoat around herself and pushed off the bed. Her limp, Mariesa saw, watching her progress toward the door, was more pronounced.

"Keith McReynolds," Mariesa said suddenly. Harriet paused at the door and gave her a cautious look.

"What?"

"What you quoted earlier:

> *Some fates cannot be fled;*
> *Nor burdens ever lifted,*
> *So long as love is ours to hold,*
> *And hearts and minds are gifted.*

"That was from one of Keith's poems. 'The Penalties of Love.' I never knew you read his poems."

Harriet looked uncomfortable. "Some of them," she admitted.

Mariesa sighed and reclined once more on her pillow. "He was a dear old man."

"Yes," Harriet said. "He was."

"He was like a father to me."

"Yes," Harriet said. "He was."

It was all a matter of making lists. It was all a matter of drawing lines. And when they were done, there would be those within the lines and those without; and so, you had to be careful where you stood when the circle was closed.

"Who can we trust?" asked Dolores Pitchlynn. She had her own copy of the list. She had her own opinions. The sunroom at Silverpond was long and narrow, with a glass wall that arched up to form half the ceiling. Through the glass, Mariesa could see the flank of Skunktown Mountain and, above it, clouds that were "black with December snows unshed." The furniture was light wickerwork, altogether out of tune with the bleak, wintry scene outdoors. It looked like a white Christmas in the offing.

"Who can we trust—*and* who has need-to-know?" added Duckworth, the Air Force liaison. "That's a shorter list." He was a slim, dark-featured man of thirty-two. Short, and with the impatience and subtle belligerence that short men sometimes used to compensate. He smoldered with an intensity born of righteousness. A mere captain, though, and a bit old to be one; so perhaps that intensity told against him. This project would be Duckworth's big chance for oak leaves, Mariesa thought; and very likely, he knew it, too. She hoped that would not cloud his judgment.

Mariesa picked up her stylus. "Let's just go down the list," she said, activating the IR links that connected their personal note-puters.

"Steve Matthias," Dolores read the first name on the list with a curious twist to her voice.

"Who's he?" Duckworth asked.

"One of our opponents," Dolores said. Mariesa frowned and pursed her lips and did not quite look at Dolores.

"Dolores means that Steve is against the project."

"And he's too clever by half," said Dolores. "Ex-military intelligence. He discovered Prometheus on his own and invited himself onto the team." The president of Pegasus spoke matter-of-factly, but Mariesa detected an edge in her tone. Well, Steve had ruffled more than a few feathers on the Steering Committee—the more so because he took no pains to hide his ambition—and that scandalized the others on the team, who did.

"You think he would suss this out, too?" the captain asked. He was tapping his screen with his stylus, calling up poppers. "Not much time between green flag and task completion. Is he *that* clever?"

"He doesn't have to be," said Mariesa. "He's the Prometheus program manager and we plan to co-opt assets and redirect tasks on the Prometheus schedule. That will accelarate some threads and delay others. Think of a spider sitting in the center of a web. He'll know. He can't help but know."

Duckworth placed the stylus between his lips and thought a moment. "Okay," he said at last. "Three things." He used the stylus to tally on his fingers. "A: Do we need him? B: Can you convince him? C: If not, can we neutralize him?"

Mariesa leaned over the table. "A," she replied. "Yes,

at least we need his silence. B: Not a chance. C: Are you seriously proposing to assassinate one of my presidents?''

Duckworth blinked and pulled away from her. ''Jesus, no. Where do you get your ideas? From Hollywood? You said he was ex-military.'' He tapped his screen again with his stylus. ''My dossier says he's a reservist. If all you need is his silence, he can be activated and placed under orders.'' He studied the screen, rapping the stylus against his teeth until Mariesa wanted to scream, leap across the table, and grab the instrument from him. People with tics got under her skin.

''It says here, he's a Jew.''

Frostily: ''So?''

''So, the Jews in the Balkans have been getting the short end of things, like always. You hear the joke? This guy's walking down a road in Thrace when a soldier stops him and asks his religion. Well, if he says Muslim and the soldier's Greek or Serb, he's dead. But if he says Orthodox, and the soldier's a Turk, he's just as dead. So he says, 'I'm a Jew.' Well, the soldier thinks this over for a moment, then asks: 'Okay. But are you a Muslim Jew or an Orthodox Christian Jew?''' Duckworth chuckled.

''I don't find that funny,'' Mariesa said.

The laugh vanished. ''Yeah, macabre funny, maybe. When God's on your side, no one's *allowed* to be neutral. All I'm saying is your man, Matthias, may have no reason to support *Steel Rain,* but maybe he has reason to keep quiet about it.'' He worked his stylus and a note—*Recall to active duty???*—showed up on all three cliputers, via the IR bonds that linked them. ''Next name.''

Mariesa hesitated only a moment before her eyes dropped to the list. ''Christiaan van Huyten, Argonaut Labs.'' She looked up. ''Chris ought to be onboard. Someone needs to deal with Lucifer. That's either him or Will Gregorson, or both.''

''Lucifer's *your* problem,'' Duckworth said. ''But if you can't bring him around, don't clue him in on *Steel Rain.* That goes for Gregorson, too.''

They went down the list. João Pessoa was out. He'd been against the proposal from the start and, as a Brazilian, was suspect to Duckworth. Dolores scored his name off with peculiar satisfaction. "We don't need an offshore loophole this time," she said. Dolores had argued against the Brazilian scenario from the beginning, claiming that the Planks could be designed and built at Pegasus in spite of everything. Hearts and minds could be changed. Deals could have been made; politicians bought. Maybe she had been right; but something about her attitude reminded Mariesa of Nixon or Clinton compiling their enemies lists. Payback time for long-nursed grievances.

Khan Gagrat and John E. Redman were unenthusiastic about *Steel Rain*, but they would put shoulder to wheel and juggle the dollars and the laws. They were yeomen; they were in. Correy and Wallace were supporters, but could bring nothing to the table. They were out. "This isn't a fan club," Duckworth said, "it's a functional project team. No one is in unless they pull an oar."

"Ham Pye is in, then. He owns the oars." Nothing could happen on orbit without Ham's construction people knowing. It was his schedule they were diddling.

"Agreed," said Duckworth, "but no one below him. There are too many damn odínists in his construction crew."

The project manager would have to know. Christensen or Bensalem or Jackson or Tiny Larsen, whichever crew was up when the equipment was installed. "What's an odínist?" she asked. "Someone who worships a one-eyed god?"

Duckworth's puzzlement was genuine. "What? No. 'Odín' is Russian for 'one'. An odínist is a Russian who wants to reassemble the old Soviet Union—the Slavic parts, for sure; and maybe a few odds and ends, just to tidy up around the edges."

"A lot of Russians feel that way."

"Sure, but odínists don't believe that the Ukranians or the Lithuanians have any say in the matter." He held his hands up. "Word is Moscow will stay mum on this op. But the odínists think Moscow is sissy. I'm just saying this mustn't go below the top level at Ossa & Pelion. Who's next on your list?''

"Belinda Karr." Even saying the name aloud, she could feel the slice of the knife across her heart.

"Assessment?"

A dear friend. A dreamer. A lover of children. A hand to hold onto when decisions come hard.

"A no brainer," said Dolores. "Dead set against, and no need to know." Mariesa parted her lips, but Dolores was ready. "No question, Mariesa. I have nothing against Belinda, but even if she *could* be convinced, Mentor has no contribution to make. She's out."

Duckworth glanced from one to the other, but said nothing. After a silence that was longer than it should have been, Mariesa crossed the name off the list.

After they had hammered out a rough schedule of activities and Duckworth had departed, Mariesa and Dolores retired to the library, where Sykes met them with a perfect Manhattan and a Margarita. The library was a large, dark-paneled room lined with floor-to-ceiling bookshelves and furnished with high, comfortable chairs. There was a faint whiff of ancient pipe tobaccos, even these many years after Gramper's death. One bay window, in an alcove framed by two of the high-back chairs, opened on the same vista as the sun room. You could sit in those two chairs, as she and Barry often had, and never quite face each other.

"Francis says that dinner will be ready in half an hour," Sykes told them.

"Your butler makes a fine Margarita," Dolores said when they were alone. "Or do you keep a bartender somewhere?"

"No," said Mariesa. "Sykes is a man of parts. To replace him, I would need a half-dozen others."

"I don't keep servants. Anything needs doing, my hands do it."

Her ranch hands, she meant; but a glance showed that the

woman herself was no stranger to manual labor. Dolores raised her glass. "Here's to *Steel Rain*," she said.

"To Lucifer," Mariesa replied.

Dolores took a generous sip. "That's not a good name. You ought to pick something more auspicious."

"It means 'Light-bringer.' " But Dolores was right. Images of fallen angels. The Father of Lies. Her enemies would have a field day. A demon's name might be well for a battlefield weapon, but not for a power generator that might someday double as an asteroid defense. *Michael*, she thought. The loyal angel. The Defender of Heaven.

"At least things are moving now," Dolores said.

Mariesa gazed out the bay window at the naked forest and the lowering sky. "Yes, but in which direction?"

"You got everything you wanted. Rent for the facilities. Compensation for Ham Pye's redesign work . . . A head start on long-range power transmission . . ."

Everything she wanted. Mariesa shook her head. "I don't like picking who is in and who is out."

Dolores's laugh was short and sharp. "No? How did you organize Prometheus? I don't recollect Brad Zimmerman or Jimmy Undershot at any of our meetings." Mariesa turned and faced her.

"That was different. We chose people back then because they believed. Is there anyone on today's list who is not passively acquiescent, lukewarm, or mercenary?"

"You sound like those are pejoratives." Mariesa looked at her.

"Are they not?"

"It depends." Dolores smiled in bitter triumph, but looked to the side. "Do you want to accomplish a goal, or do you want to stroke one another?"

Mariesa gazed into the other alcove, the one to the left of the doorway, where she had once kept Gramper's big floor globe. She had marked it up during her freshman year with circles showing where meteors had struck. Black rings everywhere. She could remember Gramper's harsh remonstrances; his refusal to listen to her fears. She could see Barry standing there with a drink in his hand, spinning the globe—in the wrong direction—trying to puzzle out its riddle.

"Always the Goal," she said into her Manhattan glass. "Always the Goal."

Christiaan van Huyten was a tall, lanky man and certainly had the advantage over her in the arms and legs, for all that she herself was tall for a woman. In most regards, that did not matter, but on the tennis courts it made him an unbeatable adversary. The winter that had brought chill to the forests of New Jersey had brought temperance to the deserts of Santa Fe and made a match on Chris's clay court something other than an invitation to a stroke.

The least he could do, Mariesa thought as she watched him lope after her return, is make it look hard. She backpedaled to the baseline, trying to anticipate where his return would come. Left court, she decided; close to the net.

Her judgment was sound; her legs, less so. She started forward in anticipation, but barely made it in time; and his next return was a hard spike in the opposite court that might as well have been in Arizona for all her chance to reach it. "Game and match," Chris announced.

Grateful for the reprieve, Mariesa crossed to the sideline, where she plumped down on the wooden bench. Chris joined her and tossed her a bottle of water from the cooler. "Drink up," he told her. "You've lost more liquid than you think."

Her clothes were barely damp, but that was a consequence of the dryness of the air. *It's a dry heat,* New Mexicans liked to say—as if that excused the rotisserie they called a climate. She drank the water gratefully. Darby handed them towels and Mariesa draped hers around her neck. Chris inserted his racquet into a vice and snugged the screws.

"So," she said, mopping at her face with the towel. "How goes the photovoltaic research?"

Chris glanced at her, handed both racquets to Darby, and

straddled the bench facing her. "I thought this was my birthday."

"Oh, well. You know."

He grinned. "Business never stops. But, really, the situation tomorrow will be remarkably like that today. Relax, Riesey. This is not a short-term project."

"According to your most recent reports, you haven't choosen the PV materials to be used on the solar power stations."

Chris sighed and capitulated. "The amorphous silicon and copper indium diselinide are the leading contenders," he said, "but we can't rule any of them out yet. Thin-film PV is inherently more radiation-tolerant and can be manufactured on lightweight substrates to reduce the lift-up cost to the solar power satellites. We've been using CID receivers for the Helios demo project for the last year and a half, and they seem to be holding up well."

"What about manufacturing costs?"

Chris shrugged and rose. "Let's get back. Marianne is waiting on us. Darby, let her know we're on our way." The butler nodded and left with the racquets tucked under one arm.

"You haven't answered my question," Mariesa pointed out as they followed after.

"Because I can't." Did she detect a note of exasperation in his voice? "EarthSafe Solar goes on-line in two months. They'll supply supplemental power to the southern California grid during peak load times. If the pilot project is successful, additional 500 kW ground-based stations will be built over the next few years, and the growing demand for PV modules will push their manufacturing costs down the learning curve into a regime we can live with. Until then . . ." He stopped walking. "Look, Riesey. There's no rush on this. The first SPS isn't bracketted for nearly twenty years."

"I don't want to wait nineteen years for a progress report." She would be an old woman by then, in her late-sixties; but still young enough to hold the helm, still able to hold the course. The van Huytens were long-lived stock—barring cutlass, train wreck, or jealous husband. Or drink.

Chris gave her an irritated look. "You won't have to wait that long."

He did not understand her anxiety. He did not know she had plans for those SPSs that went beyond power generation. Mariesa shook her head. "I'm sorry, Chris. I never meant to imply that. But you know what the issue is. The SPS program sits on four legs, but the work on the other three will be meaningless if ground-based solar plants do not fasten on a PV technology that space-based stations can also use."

Chris listened with a patient look on his face. "The Crusades direct EarthSafe, not us," he reminded her, "but 'Japan-America Friends of Solar' invested enough in the project to have a voice on their board. So Arthur Kondo is nudging them toward materials compatible with our long-range plans."

"I just don't like a key thread being outside my immediate control," Mariesa said.

"I know." Chris turned and resumed his progress toward the house. "But we don't have to run the show, as long as we can harvest the fruits. VHI's purse strings will only stretch so far. Kick-starting the Plank program on our own was an awful gamble."

Mariesa laid a hand on his arm stopping him. "Chris, how long have you run Argonaut?"

"Twenty years."

"Longer than I've been chairman." Chris nodded but said nothing. They climbed the low, flat stairs toward the house in silence. After a few steps, she broke the silence. "Have I done a good job?"

If the question surprised him, he did not show it. "I can't fault your stewardship."

"But you would have done things differently, if Gramper had put you in charge, instead."

"That was never in the cards, was it? You grew up in

his house. He hardly ever saw me. You were special to him. I saw that a long time ago.''

"Nevertheless . . .''

He shrugged. "Oh, sure, some things, of course. Some things, I think *you* would do differently, if you could hit Reset and replay the game. I doubt I would ever have conceived of Prometheus on my own. What a cat's cradle of interlocking projects!''

She spared him a wan smile. "You were a hard sell.''

"I wasn't about to allocate funds just because Keith liked to read science fiction. But Keith was a damn fine accountant, too. A better one than Khan, if I may say so. He wasn't all numbers. And he knew how to package them better.''

A short man, she remembered. With a perpetual smile and a red bow tie and calm, high-pitched voice. "I always treasured his advice.''

Chris was silent a moment. "So did I. I think we miss his voice more than we may realize. But . . .'' He gathered himself. "He's the one who convinced me that the solar power satellites were doable. He showed how to create separate, profitable ventures with achievable ROIs for each of those 'four legs.' Inexpensive orbital transport—through the Plank program; power beaming, from Torch and Helios and FarTrip; on-orbit construction capabilities, courtesy of LEO; and space-survivable photovoltaics developed and proven in ground-based stations.'' He shook his head. "By 2029, when ground-based solar saturates and utilities start looking for continuous-output solar to produce *base load* power, the infrastructure will all be proven off-the-shelf technologies; and the step up to solar power satellites will be a small, low-risk investment. The beauty of it is that each step can be profitable in itself. Khan can track money like Dan'l Boone and round it up and brand it like Charlie Goodnight, but I don't think he would ever have created the bootstrap financing and 'staging' corporations that Keith came up with.''

"He was a poet, too. Keith was.'' They had reached the broad patio that surrounded Chris's sprawling home. Marianne saw them through the sliding glass doors from the kitchen and waved. Mariesa walked to the stone balustrade that overlooked the drop from the mesa into the canyonlands. Below her, the winding courses of occasional rivers cut through brilliant sandstones on their way to vanished oceans. In the distance, the Sangre de Christo mountains marked Colorado. "He was a poet," she said again. "He knew how to dream."

Chris came to her side. "I always thought you were in love with him."

She looked at him, startled into laughter. "In love? With Keith? What a notion!"

Chris leaned on the balustrade and studied the play of sunlight on the canyon walls opposite. "He never married. Nor did you, until after he died."

"Chris, I never felt the slightest physical attraction for Keith."

"I don't think I suggested that."

"He was simply a treasured advisor."

"He was more than that."

"Yes, all right, he was more than that. But—"

"What would he have said about the president's attempt to co-opt our project?"

Mariesa stood away from the canyon view. She would not quite face Chris. "It's a shame we can't ask him."

"Do you know what I think? I think he would do a cost-benefit analysis and he'd find that—"

"Don't hide behind ghosts, Chris. Don't put your words on his lips."

Chris shoved his hands into the pockets of his tennis shorts. "We should shower before dinner."

"Yes."

He sighed. "We put a lot of sweat into organizing LEO, Riesey. Why risk the dissension with our foreign partners? I know what John E. says, but why take the chance? We're businesspeople. We should tend our own fig garden and let the politicians play god in the Balkans."

"That was my first impulse, too."

"This isn't an impulse. I've thought it out. It's all cost and no benefit. What do we get out of giving in?"

"Valerie Kloch doesn't shut us down. I think that may count as a benefit."

"She can't do it. There are too many heavyweights on our side."

"Like you said, Chris. Why risk it?"

He shook his head. "Look past the immediate crisis, Riesey. You were always the one with the long-term outlook. What happens next time if we knuckle under this time? 'If once you have paid him the Dane-geld, you *never* get rid of the Dane.' If we do anything, we should drag it into the open and fight it out."

"I told you about the laser Dolores and I saw."

"What about it? Sure, it would leapfrog us a couple generations on the power-beaming leg; but power beaming's not the critical path. I'd love to have my boys and girls take that cannon apart—if you can get it without any strings—and put it back together right. If the Argonauts can't whomp up something over the next five years that's twice as good as Lucifer and *not* usable as a weapon, I'll resign."

A power laser that could not be used as a weapon would be of no use at all. Mariesa bit down hard on the words before she spoke them. If Chris saw no urgency on accelerating the Phase VII primary thread, how would he ever see the urgency in an asteroid shield? He would do his cost-benefit analysis, and he would laugh. There was no point even in broaching the subject.

Urgency, impact and trend. Those were the three criteria for prioritizing decisions. NEOs loaded very high on impact—a grotesque pun, there!—but hardly registered on urgency.

And that left trend, a far more troubling question.

And the funny thing was that on this one issue she knew precisely what Keith MacReynolds's ghost would say.

Mariesa craved solitude while she worked. She wanted a cocoon of silence within which she could concentrate without stray noises or voices to distract her. She could insulate herself somewhat at the office; but even there, Zhou Hui would sometimes intrude with a query. The Roost was better. She could, if she wished it, cut herself off entirely from the rest of the world. The first lift for *Steel Rain* was set for March—in Air Force shells—but might slip to April, according to Ham Pye's workups.

But isolation would be *so* antisocial at this time of year, with Christmas approaching and preparations to be made. The tree was going up in the ballroom under Harriet's careful directions. Sykes, Armando, and Roy did the actual work, and were adept enough to follow or ignore the directions as need be, and so the erection went well enough. Mariesa, who had set up at a table in the parlor where she could watch the proceedings through the wide, arched doorway, was not sure what spirit her nearby presence was supposed to enhance; but Mummy had been insistent, and it *was* Christmas coming on.

Miss Whitmore proceeded past the table with her arms full of boxes. Decorations for the tree. Mariesa wondered what motif Mother had chosen this year. Every year was thematic and color coordinated according to some arcana that only Harriet was privy to.

It was a tall tree—nine feet from base to tip—but the ballroom was high-ceilinged. Harriet had positioned it in front of the mirrors, directly between the portraits of old Christiaan III in his gray beard and frock coat and Albert Henry in his powdered wig. Both had shepherded the van Huyten fortune through troublesome times: the crisis of 1873, when the country had teetered on the brink of class war, and the crisis of 1785, when the country teetered on the brink of dissolution. Mariesa wondered if her own portrait would someday grace the walls of the mansion—and who would be living here when it did. With a sudden, intense pang, she remembered that it would be no descendent of her own. She turned in her chair so she could not see the Christmas tree. Christmas was a feast for children, and there were no children at Silverpond.

The telephone rang and Sykes abandoned the tree to answer it. A moment later, he was at Mariesa's side. "The call is for you," he murmured.

"Who is it?"

"A young woman."

Mariesa looked carefully at the butler. "Is it . . . ?"

"I couldn't say, miss. She did not give a name."

Mariesa took the call in the library, hesitating a moment before lifting the receiver. "This is Mariesa van Huyten."

"I just called to let you know. I'm putting together a Christmas present for you, but it won't be ready in time." It was Styx's voice, all right.

"A present? How thoughtful . . ."

"Yeah, just for you; *and you won't like it one bit.*"

"Roberta—"

But the line was dead.

Mariesa cradled the receiver slowly. What possessed the woman to call and taunt her like this? Did she define her entire life by a single disappointment in high school? What a sad life, if its voyage were impeded by an anchor fixed in the mud of adolescence. If Mariesa van Huyten was such an abomination in her eyes, why not simply cease all contact? Why keep picking at it? Mariesa might accept the loss of Styx's affection more easily had it meant loss of contact as well. She glanced at the read-out on the phone set and saw that the call had come from the same Washington number as the others. A public phone. Would Roberta linger there? Her finger hovered over the call-back button. Perhaps it would be best to have it out. To end it, once and for all.

Hesitation is headsman to the deed. She turned away without doing anything.

Sykes waited in the parlor. "If the young lady calls again . . . ?" he asked.

"I'll still take the call."

When she returned to the ballroom, she saw that Harriet had selected an Old-Fashioned Christmas as her theme. Roy, the groom and groundskeeper, balanced on a tall stepladder while Armando passed him the ornaments from the trays that Miss Whitmore had laid out. Harriet stood by, supervising their placement. A little higher. More to the left. Papier-mâché angels and children. Small, cunning figurines of carolers. All very Currier and Ives. Mariesa brushed at her cheeks with her sleeve. They were tears of sentiment, she told herself. Brought on by the season.

The scene beyond the window was one of crystaline beauty. Gleaming snow, melted and refrozen into shiny-smooth crust, shrouded the parkland along the river. The river itself was frozen into sparkling filagrees—except farther upstream under the footbridge, where Spokane Falls remained defiantly liquid. Beyond the park, office windows glittered like ice. Everything, bright with reflected sunlight. But it was a winter sun. It shined without melting.

Mariesa studied the vista in silence. Of the modestly tall buildings that comprised the downtown, there was little to remark. The anonymous look of urban mid-America. At first glance, who could tell Topeka from Des Moines from Spokane? You had to get closer to sense their individuality, to find that each was deliciously different. She could see what looked like a clock tower—probably the university—and another structure that looked like a giant maypole. She turned away from the window as Belinda hung up the telephone.

"They said the airport will be open by tomorrow morning," Belinda said. Mariesa folded her arms across her chest and nodded. "I hope you like the suite," Belinda went on. "The hotels fill up pretty quick when the airport shuts down."

"Yes. Yes, it has a marvelous view."

"Oh, you should be here in the spring, for the Lilac Festival," Belinda said. "Or during the Royal Fireworks. I like Spokane. It's a quiet town, away from the hectic bustle of Seattle and Portland."

Hectic bustle? Mariesa, who lived a helicopter hop from Manhattan, made no response other than a companionable nod. Belinda's voice had held a note of forced cheerfulness, as if she didn't quite know what to do or say. There was something indefinably awkward in this delayed parting. Memories of the past; expectations of the future.

"It looks like a scene from an old science fiction pulp," Mariesa said, returning her gaze to the scene outside. Second-floor "skywalks" crisscrossed the streets below. Within them, people moved in comfortable shirtsleeves from building to building, despite the sub-zero weather. There were few destinations in the downtown that required going out of doors. On the frozen river, brightly clad skaters proved that some still dared the cold.

Belinda played with the necklace of shells and beads that dangled from her throat. "Our skywalks have been around for ages," she said. "They keep growing when new buildings go up or old ones get rennovated. In a way, the whole town has become a single, interconnected structure; an arcology designed by 'Topsy.' The zippers are new, though; within the past two years."

Mariesa had been startled on the way to the hotel from the parking garage to find battery-powered AGVs cruising the skywalks and intrabuilding commons. Automatically Guided Vehicles had been used in manufacturing plants for decades to transport parts and assemblies. Why not people? "They don't get in the way of the pedestrians, do they?"

Belinda shook her head. "Avoidance sensors. The carts stop when an unprogrammed obstacle is in their way. There's a fine for deliberately standing in the path of one, but you know what kids are like."

"Some things don't change," Mariesa said, turning back to the city view.

"And some things do." There was a sadness in Belinda's voice, but Mariesa didn't ask her what she meant. In the window, Belinda's reflection hovered like a ghost in a ghostly hotel room. Mariesa watched her run a finger back and forth across the telephone.

"Why are they called 'zippers'?" Mariesa asked. Neutral topics were best. With them, you could simulate a conversation.

The ghost-Belinda looked up. "Originally, they were supposed to 'zip on over' when you ran your transit card through the pylon reader; and 'zip' you to whatever destination you entered. The bar codes on the routing pylons tell them where to turn and when to stop. But they were slowed up after opponents spread scare stories of runaway AGVs mowing down defenseless women and children." She laughed without humor.

"It's an interesting system," Mariesa commented. "I wonder why it hasn't spread."

"Minneapolis is experimenting with a pilot program. Calgary is thinking about it. The problem is, you need a multiply connected skywalk system to make it work, and that's a big investment. If you like, we'll take a zipper later—over to Patsy Clark's Mansion. I'll treat you to their Duckling Amaretto."

Mariesa turned away from the window and fetched her briefcase from the chair where she had dropped it earlier. A typical, upscale hotel suite, decorated with simple, pleasant furniture. A sitting room with sofa, chair, microwave kitchenette, and table. A separate bedroom. Anonymous, worn, inoffensive. Not a place to spend too much life. She set the briefcase on the broad, blond-wood table and extracted several folders. "Yes," she said. "If you like."

The silence of hesitation. Mariesa looked at Belinda a moment before the woman spoke.

"Mariesa . . . ?"

"What?"

"Why are you avoiding me?"

Mariesa laughed. "Avoiding you?" She waved a hand around the suite. "We're trapped in downtown Spokane together. That is hardly avoidance." She would not quite lock eyes with Belinda.

"Circumstances. If the sudden freeze hadn't grounded all the planes, where would you be right now?"

Halfway to Phoenix . . . "Chris was planning to test his MHD engine tomorrow. The Chang-Diaz drive. He asked me to be there." *What do you get when you create a plasma inside a magnetic bottle, but the bottle won't seal at one end? Initial answer: a failed fusion experiment. Creative answer: an "immaterial" rocket engine with a specific impulse of thirty thousand. Talk about good gas mileage . . .*

"You seem to spend all your time with Dolores and Hamilton Pye, these days."

Mariesa touched the folders she had pulled from her briefcase. "Perhaps we can spend the evening reviewing the dossiers on the children from this years's baseline evaluation. Some of them seem very promising. Jacinta Rosario. Welton Kammerman. Sanjiv Chetnani—"

"There are other ways we could spend the evening."

"Belinda, you have always said that I should take more of an interest in the children."

"Did you know that whenever you're stressed you grow excessively grammatical?"

Mariesa picked up the folders and stuffed them back in her briefcase. "If you do not wish to discuss these—"

"Mariesa, I always thought we had a special bond between us."

The briefcase closed with loud snaps. Mariesa laid it flat on the table, squaring it against the edges. A special bond? She remembered long evenings snuggled together with creme sherry and a starry sky. The two of them had spent many hours shaping school curricula, discussing pros and cons, hammering out presentations. If Wallace and Correy had helped her see what the future must be, and Keith had discovered how to finance it, it was Belinda who had shown her how to people it. What use wonders, if no one wondered? *Hope is the most precious gift,* she had said one time in the sunroom at Silverpond, long after the sun was fled, when the night was old and they had slumped together on the divan, too tired to make their way upstairs. *To take away hope is the cruelest theft of all. Children will bounce back from anything short of that.* Mariesa could remember that evening with the same crystaline clarity as the icy afternoon now outside the hotel windows. The sight of the night-blackened windows; the sounds of nocturnal creatures waiting for dawn. Belinda in her khaki shorts and top.

"Well, yes," she said. "There is. A bond." She smoothed her skirt, tugged her jacket. "Perhaps I should change out of this business suit," she added quickly. "Unless your restaurant enforces a dress code . . . ?"

Belinda snorted. "In the West?"

Mariesa carried her travel bag into the bedroom, where she laid it on the bed. Belinda followed and sat on the other side of the bed. Mariesa noticed how stiffly she moved; how visibly pleased she was to take the weight off her legs. How that weakness must distress a woman like Belinda!

Mariesa unfolded the suit bag and examined her choices. Not a wide range. She had packed only for a three-day trip, Spokane and Phoenix. "The navy slacks," Belinda told her. "And the white blouse with the edging. What is that, Russian styling? It's very becoming."

"Thank you. It's by Nina Simyonovna. Do you know her?"

" 'Simyonna'? Only by reputation, I'm afraid. When do *I* ever get to St. Petersburg?"

Mariesa laid out the selection on the bed. She removed her jacket and undid the bow on her blouse. "I could take you with me on my next visit. Rukhavishnikov wants to discuss the Motorola contract for upgrading their Iridium repeaters."

"You wear clothing well," Belinda said. "I've always envied that. You could have been a model."

Mariesa took a hanger from the closet and draped her blouse over it. She looked at Belinda while she hung it on the closet rod. Belinda was dressed casually, in jeans and a partly unbuttoned, blue denim blouse whose sleeves were rolled halfway up her arms. The brightly colored Indian beadwork around her throat contrasted with the dull blue. "Do you? But I'm so plain-featured. And as for my chin—"

"Grace matters. The ugly duckling became a swan."

She unzipped her dress skirt and let it drop to the floor. "Well, modelling is hardly the highest calling for a woman in any event." She gave Belinda a sardonic smile. "I prefer being a role model to being a clothes model." She turned to face the closet door and adjusted her bra straps and straightened her hose in the full-length mirror there.

"I see you're keeping in trim," Belinda said.

Mariesa had always been thin, but *pace* Belinda, it was hardly a model's body that she saw. More flesh than bone. . . . Gravity had not won the war yet, but it was winning battles here and there. Though, on the wrong side of fifty as she was, she was lucky to be still in the fight. "I try to keep active," she said. "Tennis. Riding."

"The hotel has a health club. Would you like to work out and go to dinner after?"

There was more in her voice than casual suggestion. There was need. And fear. Was Belinda, too, searching for the threads of their friendship? She turned and faced the older woman. "I have been neglecting you of late, haven't I?"

Belinda's eyes dropped. "I've been feeling 'marginalized.' Prometheus's school thread has taken a back seat. FarTrip. Helios. Torch. LEO. Especially LEO. Not much room among all that hardware for a few children."

Mariesa crossed the room and sat beside her on the bed. "It's like breathing, Belinda. It's absolutely vital, but it's easy to forget you're doing it." She placed a hand over Belinda's. "And what you're doing—you and the others who followed your lead—it's as essential as breathing itself. Without the children, Prometheus cannot last beyond our lifetimes." She felt the momentary twitch in Belinda's hand and hastened to add, "And Prometheus, in turn, gives the children a frontier, an inspiration."

Belinda squeezed her hand. "You and I were the dreamers," she said. "With the others, it was more a fascination with the technology or with the money to be made. Gadgets and abstractions. We all wanted to build a future, but ours was the only one with people in it."

"There was Keith," Mariesa said.

Belinda nodded. "Ah, yes. The third dreamer."

"And Barry."

"You knew him more intimately than I did; so I won't argue with you. Still, you and I are the only ones left, aren't we? 'Dream Your Way Ahead.' Right? That was Mentor's motto. The future begins with a dream, and determination."

It was more than a motto, Mariesa thought. It was the literal truth. Though the dream was, in fact, a nightmare; and it had propelled her from decision to decision, like a cork bobbing in a flowing river. Through the bedroom window, she could see in the distance the crashing waters of Spokane Falls.

The ornamental garden and hedge maze behind Silverpond was not a place that Mariesa often sought. It was Harriet's domain. The design, the placement, the trimming and pruning, all of it spoke of her mother's earthbound preoccupations. Indeed, from her vantage point by the fountain of Hyacinth, Mariesa could see Harriet on her hands and knees attending to a new grafting at the far end of the gravel path. "They must all be made ready for the spring," Harriet had said earlier. It was so like Mother to want to tidy up Nature.

The February winds were chill where they played off the flank of Skunktown Mountain. Through the skeleton trees, she could just make out the dark speck of the gazebo at the crest. She and Barry had made love up there for the first time. And that was where he had shown her the most awful pictures. It was where he had thrown himself on his sword. Mariesa gathered her sweater close around her neck. February was the impatient time of year. The stasis of winter was ending; the gaudy extravagance of spring not yet begun. "Tears Like Ice." Hadn't that been the title of one of Roberta's poems? Who knew better how to eulogize sorrow than that poor, unhappy child.

Should she have given the girl happiness? *Could* she have given her happiness? Had that gift ever been within her power?

Probably not. Styx had pursued sorrow the way moths sought flame. She had created an ideal Mariesa; and now reviled the real one for not measuring up. Lord knew, Phil Albright had his flaws, too. What would happen when Roberta found them out?

Mariesa looked back toward Silverpond. Up there, on the roof walk, she had studied the stars with Belinda. And up there, Ned DuBois had thrown his sheepskin flight jacket around her shivering frame.

Mariesa circled the fountain "widdershins," running her hand along the smooth concrete of the rim, hearing her shoes crunch on the gravel underneath. She and Barry had spent an hour here looking at stars, evoking navigators and romantics. That had been early on, at a party she had thrown for "Belinda's Kids." She had hardly known him then. She hardly knew him now.

And Styx used to go off into the hedge maze, looking for solitude in odd pockets and cul de sacs within the winding shrubs. It was an odd effect of the deepening twilight, but she had the momentary conviction that, if she ventured deep enough into the enfolding shrubbery, she would find the girl still there, contemplating.

She shook herself. It was a foolish notion. That girl no longer existed. She would no more return to Silverpond than—

William, her child, had he ever been born, would be two and a half years old now. Staggering along on new-found legs, arms held high, laughing and "speaking in tongues" as he puzzled out the mysteries of speech. She had the momentary sensation that something small and soft had gripped her by the forefinger of her right hand, but it was only a curious trick of the wind.

Perhaps she ought to sell Silverpond and set herself up in one of the smaller places she owned. Perhaps she could live at the lodge. But, no; winters there would be impossible. Yet, she did not think she could live here much longer, in a house so empty and yet so full of ghosts.

14.

Descent

The courier was Tani Pandya, which meant that Jimmy was sending two messages. The first message was on the disk Tani brought with her: information skimmed off of Mariesa van Huyten's own personal home equipment. The second was more subtle. Tani still hung out with Jimmy Poole. That knowledge disturbed Roberta more than Mr. Ear did.

Tani held out a padded brown envelope. "I'm supposed to give you this," she said.

Hey, deja vu city! Roberta was standing on the flagstoned porch in front of Silverpond and the Rich Lady was handing her a large manila envelope. *Take this. I had intended only to show you its contents, but you may take it and decide for yourself what to do about it.* And Roberta pulled a sheet out at random and saw that it was a bank statement on a secret account that Simon Fell had kept. *Why are you giving me this?* But the answer was obvious. To break up the Crusades by driving a wedge between Simon and Phil.

"Are you going to take it or not?" Tani asked.

Roberta shook off the past and took the envelope—it was a disk packet. The bulk was from the padding, not from bundles of photocopies—and Tani turned to go. Roberta hesitated a moment, then asked her inside. "Just for a few minutes, if you have the time." Tani caught her lip between her big beaver teeth, but nodded and stepped over the threshold.

Roberta-that-was had refused a similar invitation that sultry July evening two and a half years ago. Perhaps if it had been a damp cold, slushy, knee boot and down coat, Washington D.C. kind of day she would have thought twice. And maybe all that Tani wanted when she kicked her boots clean and stepped into the hallway was a few moments of dry warmth. She hung her coat and scarf on one of the pegs behind the door and stuffed her knit cap down a coat sleeve. She put her boots on the rack and followed Roberta in her stockinged feet.

Tani had been there, too, that day at Silverpond. Roberta had brought her there to confront Azim and, while Azim and Tani had gone off by themselves to get things straight between them, the Rich Lady had handed over that hurtful envelope. No good deed goes unpunished.

The living room was halfway to tidied up. Phil was coming over tomorrow, and Roberta liked her place to be presentable. If Tani was too high post for the piles of magazines and soon-to-be-folded laundry that was her problem. "Would you like something warm to drink?" she asked. "Tea? Or a toddy?"

"Chocolate, if you have it?" Tani stood with her hands clasped behind her back and moved, as if by gravitational force, toward the bookshelves that lined the long wall of the living room. Roberta ducked into the kitchen, where she found a squashed packet of powdered chocolate in the back of her "anything drawer." She emptied it into a mug and then filled the mug with near-boiling water from the red faucet on her bottled water stand. She made herself a cup of peach tea the same way.

Returning to the living room, she saw that Tani had picked up the copy of *Taj Mahal* from the stand by the big chair. If Tani noticed where the bookmark was inserted, she said nothing, but replaced the book and accepted the chocolate.

"It's a great book," Roberta said as they took seats; she on the chair, Tani on the sofa.

"Everyone says so."

"Are you working on another?"

Tani took a cautious sip of chocolate. "Everyone expects me to."

"That's an odd way to put it."

Tani shrugged. "*Taj Mahal* simply poured out. You must know how that is, Roberta. When the story just *has* to come out, and all you do is sit at the keyboard and . . . transcribe. It took me less than a year to write. But in another sense, it took me a lifetime. I don't have another lifetime for another book."

"You're only twenty-six. Wait awhile. There's more life coming."

"Beans," Tani agreed, with what Roberta thought was an inward smile. "A lot waiting to be experienced."

Awkward silence, broken by the sounds of mugs on tabletops. By the muffled sound of the traffic on Pennsylvania. By the shrieks of children squeezing out their last moment of play in the melting snow. The tea was still hot and had the sweetness of peaches underlying the bitter tannin. Tani finished her drink. "I should be going."

Roberta stood with her. "No, wait. Do you want to have dinner?"

"You're just being polite."

"Do you have other plans? Are you staying in town, or are you flying out somewhere tonight?"

"It doesn't matter. You're not comfortable having me around. The last time we had drinks together, we quarreled."

"That was months ago. I was tired and bitchy from my book tour."

"You barely spoke with me at the reunion."

"I had . . . A lot on my plate that night."

Tani hesitated. She looked at Roberta. "Jimmy told me that you didn't want him to take me out. You tried to talk him out of it." Then her face clouded over and she made a sudden, restrained, angry gesture that took Roberta by surprise. "What did I ever do to you? You don't have to make others unhappy, just because you are!" Tani's anger was a glowing charcoal in a brass brazier. Not for her, either fireworks or cold iron.

And it was wrong, Roberta thought. That wasn't what she had had in mind, at all. "I was trying to protect you."

"I already have a mother." Tani walked to the clothes rack and picked up her boots, but she paused with them in her hands.

"Did he hurt you?" Roberta asked. "I was afraid he'd hurt you."

Tani looked down at her boot and rubbed the side. "No, he treated me like a princess, like I was the most precious thing in his life."

"It was an act. He just wanted a fuck. He just wanted to know what it felt like."

Tani threw her head back and laughed. "And you think I didn't?" She dropped the boots and turned on Roberta. "Oh, Lord, Styx! Do you think that *I* made no decisions? Why do you assume that *he* was using *me?*"

Roberta the Poet, the sculptress of words, could find no words. She fell back on cliché—easily available, always servicable. "But, Tani, you could do so much better!"

A twist crossed Tani's lips. "What do you mean? I could seduce some young 'Krish' or 'Dal' who'd make lots of babies on me while he built up his practice or his store and bought me nose studs and saris so I would *never* forget that I didn't belong here? Or maybe let some terminally serious lit critter hump me so he could show his friends how really liberal he is by *doing me the favor* of sticking his white magic wand inside me? is that what you mean by 'doing better'?"

Roberta stood rooted to the floor by her chair. "God, no. But those aren't your only choices."

"No, they're not. But the thing is, the choice is mine, not yours. I used to think you were doing me a kindness when you forced me to confront Azim; but you were just getting a kick out of moving people around, weren't you?''

"No. It wasn't like that," Roberta pleaded. "You were wasting away in that convenience store, and . . ."

"And you decided my life ought to be different."

Oh, God, it was exactly like that. Roberta looked away. "Well . . ."

"Well, you were right. And I *will* always be grateful for what you did. But I've got wings now. I can fly on my own. Jimmy doesn't make messes on the floor, and he's so damn happy getting straddled that he really doesn't care about . . . conventional notions of beauty."

"But . . . What do *you* get out of it?"

"Is that important to you?"

"I need to understand."

"Okay, Roberta, if it's that important. The first thing I get out of it is some pretty damn-good sex without any complicated relationship. Jimmy's awkward and inexperienced, but he *is* a fast learner and I get to train him. And his equipment's in good shape. Never been used, you might say."

"It doesn't sound very romantic." Not very romantic? It sounded like mutual masturbation.

"Romance is something people invent so they don't have to admit to using each other."

"Oh, God, Tani. I never thought of *you* as so cynical."

"No, I'm the innocent and naive one, right?"

Almost, Roberta could not ask the next question; but she did, because she could not stand not knowing. Tani had shown her a pit, and she had to know if the pit had a bottom. "What's the second thing you get out of letting Jimmy pork you?" she asked, and even she could hear the bitterness in her voice. She thought again about what she and Phil had between them and, God, she was grateful.

Tani reached out and crooked a finger around one of the coat hooks behind the door. Her answer was surprisingly gentle, given the provocation in the question. "Do you know what it's like to hit it so big with your first book? A real high, right? Major ego-boo. But you know what? Deep down inside, your stomach is a secret little knot, because . . . What happens with book two?'' She slipped her foot into the boot and pulled it up. ''No matter how good it is, if it's not as good as the first, it's a failure.''

''That's not always true. Cliff Johns puts out a new Mark Hardware story every year and the public gobbles them up, but no one claims that his latest is as good as his first.''

Tani's smile was a subdued one. ''And they keep getting bigger and bigger, because he's so damn rich and successful no editor dares correct his drafts any more. Well, they say everyone has one good book in them . . . but insists on writing five.'' She pulled on the second boot. ''But *Mark Hardware* was good. Half a parody and half a serious look at the conflict between mercenary and idealist in the heart of a soldier-of-fortune. But Johns just keeps him going now, long after the real story is over. The critics stopped taking him seriously long ago; but more importantly, he did, too. *I don't want that to be me.*''

''Then, don't write another book. Do something else with your life.''

''But don't you see the trap? *I* have to know if the first one was a fluke. I have to know if it was my talent, or just a happy coincidence of time and the zeitgeist.''

''And Jimmy Poole will help you do that?''

''I told you. I poured my entire life into *Taj Mahal*. There is nothing left to cobble into another. With Jimmy, I can create a new life, live new experiences. Jimmy can be raw material.''

Roberta shook her head. ''That's cold.'' And she almost felt sorry for *Jimmy* in the exchange. ''If you don't feel anything, there'll be no feeling on the page. What made *Taj Mahal* work was the genuineness of its feelings.''

Tani took her coat off the wall and put it on. She pulled the knit cap low over her head. ''Roberta, how would you know?''

Some of the sandbags that Tani had dropped on Roberta's heart must have been there still the next evening, because

Phil asked far more often than usual about her tranquility. Obsessed with making her happy (and *there,* Tanuja Pandya, scoffer-at-romance!), he inquired after it with earnest persistence. Roberta assured him that she was cheerful with his company, contented with his loving. Dinner was delicious (she hardly tasted it). His latest plans were clever and right on (she barely heard them). His caresses sent thrills of ecstacy through her (she scarcely felt them).

"You seem distracted," he said as they lay together amid the rumpled sheets. His hand travelled down her side and around the curve of her hip onto her thigh. "Who's clipped my Robin's wings?"

There weren't many names you could pull out of "Roberta." Ellis Harwood had proven that! But there was something about the way Phil said *robin* that created a tingle deep within her. She was his "sweet delight," his "honey jar." He was her "bear." Absurd sobriquets, not fit for the ears of others and not to be lightly used; yet, in this one room, precious to hear.

"It's nothing," she told him. She let her fingertips dance through the hair on his chest and down across his belly to his groin. He was an older man—though she never said so—and, as the Bard had said (and before him, the Evangelist and the Emperor): If it were done, 'twere best done quickly. That was something they acknowledged. He was an honest man, and not obsessed with his wand like some macho bullshitter. But it was not something they discussed openly. Society placed too much baggage on the subject. There was a *man* inside that body, even if the too, too solid flesh did melt a little sooner than it ought. By trial and error, they had come to an unspoken accommodation, cultivating patience and foreplay; finding in the end an ecstacy unknown to those who plunged too quickly. She had once thought Vaclav and Karel superior lovers; men who put the boy, Emmett, to shame. And yet, lying beside Phil in her own quiet room, she knew them for the callow youths they were. *We were so earnest then,* she thought, contemplating her time in Prague. So impatient.

And yet, when the time came, you struck while the iron glowed.

She knew the moment from his pulse and from the tempo of his breath. Rolling atop him, she guided him, enveloped him, embraced him. "Oh," he said, and he sucked in his breath. His hands stroked her flanks, rode up, found her nipples. This time, his touch did send its signals through her and she shivered. "My robin redbreast," he said. At one time, the flush that tinted her upper body when she was aroused had embarrassed her; now it was erotic and she flaunted it with pride. "Fly away with me."

He talked a lot when he made love, while she was mostly silent, or whispered carnal thoughts in his ear. They both eschewed a darkened room—they had nothing to be ashamed of—but they kept the shades drawn. Exhibitionism was as bad as prudery and stemmed from the same defect of character. And if, when the moment had come and gone, they pulled the sheets and blankets up close, it was less against the sight of naked flesh than a deference to the January camped outside the bedroom walls.

"You seemed melancholy earlier," Phil said after they had snuggled wordlessly for a time. "Something was gnawing at you." Phil was more attuned with her feelings than any man she had ever known.

"Oh . . . Just that people aren't always what you think they are."

"They wouldn't be people otherwise, would they?"

"It's just that you think you know someone, and then you find out you don't know them at all."

Phil became very quiet. "Anyone in particular?" he asked.

"No, just in general."

"Because if it's that letter Simon sent me . . ."

In fact, she had been so upset over Tani that she had forgotten. "Phil," she said, "you and Simon were friends for thirty years. He had to leave the Crusades, but why should you break off all contact?"

He lay on his side and propped his head up with his hand. "Suppose you tell me . . ."

"Okay. It probably would have been the smart thing to do, what with Simon's push-the-envelope tactics. But you're not the sort to sacrifice friendship on the altar of . . . expediency."

"You know I don't agree with a lot of what Simon does—the ecotage, the phone threats, the direct harrassment. What does he get out of it? A newsbyte of the Direct Action Faction screaming at women in fur coats; or the spray paint on St. Patrick's Cathedral; or the this-could-have-been-a-bomb bricks mailed to big-time polluters. Antics like that put the whole Movement in a bad light. And maybe . . ." This he said more thoughtfully. "Maybe I *ought* to speak out against them more often."

"He certainly makes our positions look more reasonable."

Phill turned and pushed himself to a sitting position. "Hmm. Good cop/bad cop . . . You think that's what Simon and I are up to? Sorry. No collusion. But we aim at the same targets. When Simon goes over the top and we don't, *of course* people see that we're more reasonable. We *are*."

"And his suggestion about putting a lawyer on that industrial accident case?"

Phil snorted. "Simon's no fool. He knows 'direct action' has limits. It doesn't win lawsuits—at least not since trial-by-combat was dropped." He grinned and she couldn't help laughing. "So he alerts me to cases he comes across where Crusades's tactics *would* pay off."

"And does it work the other way? Do you alert him?"

"No," said Phil Albright. "Of course not, Robin." He opened his arms and Roberta slid within them. There was comfort in that circle, enclosed in strong but loving arms.

The butcher paper on Roberta's office wall looked like a dozen mad copy editors had had at it. The original block/affinity diagram had been supplemented with colored sticky notes, with mark-ups and annotations in blue and green and red. The damn thing had metastasized! Roberta paced back and forth in front of the diagram, studying it, trying to comprehend its totality. The picture was coming clearer, but it was still not clear what it was a picture of.

She had lots of data, thanks to Jimmy. But data was not information until it had been organized. Some order or pattern had to be found; and that was where the danger lay, because the eagerness to find a pattern may lead to imposing one. Any random collection of facts could be built into a conspiracy theory—and often was. But facts were like bricks; you could stack them into different shapes. The Latin root of *fact* meant "to build or make."

To squeeze meaning out of the jumble, Roberta had prepared several summaries, which had spread across other sheets hung on the remaining walls, crowding out photographs of friends and nature, evicting Phil's "Secret Admirer" Valentine card along with the corkboard it had hung on. Each summarized the data in a different way. "Always look at the situation from more than one angle," Onwuka Egbo had told Styx during the Dark Ages at Witherspoon High.

She shook her head in annoyance even as she studied the timeline summary. Problem-solving. Latin roots. Little shards of Mentor still rattling in her brain like broken glass. They'd done a good job—Fast, Egbo, Glendower, and the others teachers—or as good a job as they could manage, given the zeitgeist of the late nineties. She could admit that, privately. Witherspoon had been, along with a sergeant's guard of other private, charter, and public schools, a light shining in the darkness. Why had they spoiled it with their hidden agendas?

She brushed her eyes with her shirtsleeve and scowled at the timeline, willing it to make sense. Then she ran both hands through her hair. "Okay. Let's try a scenario," she said aloud. Talking helped, even when there was no one to talk to. "July of nine, the Rich Lady visits the White House and Donaldson asks her if he can pretty please borrow her space station so he can threaten the world. Or else she tells him she has a phat weapons platform and would he like to put some death on it. Then she does nothing about it for almost four months.'' Carefully worded memos, pro and con, referring to ''the Donaldson initiative.'' Contingency studies authorized. (And presumably carried out, though none had dropped into Jimmy's net.) ''Why? And what is the White House Weasel up to meanwhile?''

That last question she couldn't answer. Jimmy had drawn the line at hacking the White House. Jimmy wouldn't know a scruple if it weighed a pound, but risk management was second nature. After all, he was *already* getting laid; what more did he need?

''Okay. It was Donaldson's proposal, and she wasn't sure at first if she wanted a piece of it.'' That fit the data. (Thank you, Mentor Academies, for teaching me always to bludgeon my theories with a fistful of facts. . . .) That project had been simmering for a long time, so it was hard to call van Huyten the instigator, as much as she would have liked to.

So there must have been arguments at high levels within VHI. She had laid those out; she could even guess at what the sides had been. ''Then, starting in late November,'' she continued, ''a flurry of events on the LEO project over and above the normal engineering activity.'' Tasks deferred; Plank lifts rescheduled. Engineering Design Change Notices. ''Points-in-space'' simulations. Some sadistic streak had driven Jimmy Poole to gloss one memo, half of which consisted of partial differential equations, with the single word: *Aha!*

So the decision had evidently been made, but what sort of leverage did that give Roberta Carson? Spill the beans? But to whom? VHI officers? You couldn't incite people by telling them something they already knew. The public? They'd get pissed at Donaldson, if they got pissed at all. And while that might be fine as far as stopping the Death Star went, it did nothing to humble Mariesa van Huyten. It had to be the Rich Lady's own hubris that brought her low.

She remembered that her official project was to learn enough about Donaldson's Star Wars project to scuttle it.

For the first time she began to wonder whether she would find any lever at all to topple van Huyten.

Roberta sighed and began making notes to feed Jimmy for his next fishing expedition. Who was this Duckworth character who had shown up in a couple of recent memos? And, okay-Jimmy-you-win, what was so "Aha" about those equations? What was "Steel Rain," beside the title of a popular goofball song? It sounded like a project title the couple of times it had surfaced in memos. And what was its connection with *Michael?* Why the sudden flurry of VHI activity after November? It might be nothing more than a bloated organization finally overcoming inertia, but there might have been some triggering event. Maybe a key retirement; maybe a government nudge. Something in the news. There had been some FarTrip contacts in the week before, including a personal visit by Mariesa van Huyten to FarTrip headquarters. Was there a connection there?

She wrote the queries to a disk and encrypted them to her private key, and then reencrypted that using a special key that Jimmy had given her. She would E-mail the corpse from a public terminal in the branch library across town to a drop that Jimmy had created in a Net node. Hey, paranoia was catching. And (goddamn you, Jimmy) if the romp blew now, it'd catch Tani, too.

Roberta moved on to a second summary, a hurricane chart with "the Rich Lady" in a box in the center and the other players arranged in a constellation around her. For each memo, she had drawn arrows from sender to receivers. Occasionally, as Jimmy had taught her to recognize, the router codes indicated nodes that had been *blocked* from the distribution and she had laboriously correlated those with individual names. Mind-numbing work, but the devil is in the details. Oh, yes, indeed. And no one had ever promised it would be easy. Or even that it wouldn't be boring.

Buried in that jumble—in that "hurricane" web of communications—was the power structure at VHI. In-groups and out-groups. Who told whom what, and who was out of the loop . . . She already had the *official* organization charts, but there were always unofficial relationships. Power often short-circuited the official flow.

Funny. Roberta had always thought of Big Business as a sort of black box, monolithic and hierarchial; but tiptoeing through the corporate tulips for the past few months had revealed a more complex reality of faction and clique, noise, personal agendas, and just plain fubar. The Rich Lady was almost like Phil in that regard: less an autocrat than a ring-master. Someone who ruled only so long as she led.

Try to make sense of a plate of spaghetti. She had drawn it cumulatively and the name-nodes had turned out not to be optimally arranged. (That was VHI-speak for lines that crisscrossed and looped all the way around to the other side.) Sooner or later, everyone talked to everyone else. She ought to redraw the diagram and arrange the nodes to shorten the lines and minimize the crisscrossing. Maybe focus on a smaller cut set, like the LEO-related activity since November.

Life was like a picture puzzle, where you never had all the pieces, and those you had never fit exactly right. Sometimes, there were extra pieces that didn't even belong. Even when there was a picture, you could wonder whether you only saw what you wanted to see.

Jimmy Poole couldn't just be clever. He had to let you know how clever.

Roberta was surfing the movie load-down on the television. She knew the film she wanted to see, but she didn't know the title, which meant she didn't know the file number. She knew it had been about Dorothy Day and that it had been the screen debut of Jillian Brunet. But the Divine Jillian had been only a child extra at the time, so adding her name to the search parameters actually slowed the spider down. Roberta had entered <Dorothy Day, Catholic Workers, and 1990–1999> but the search was glacial; nearly a minute had gone by.

Then the waited-for words: Search Object Found. Then: Loading.

But what showed up on her television was not a μCD download from the cable film repository, but a laughing face that looked remarkably like Max Headroom. Not exactly; it was more like President Donaldson with a buzz cut. And it kept changing. But he had the same manic, postmodern tics. "Hey, hey," he said, looking out from the television screen. "He-he-he-he-he-he-hey there, Styxy. You alone? Alone? Alone?" A flashing placard gave a phone number. *Lonely?* it read. *For a good time call now.*

Roberta aimed the channel wand at the set. She was sorely tempted to nine the transmission. This intrusion was only slightly less alarming than the time he had called her on a public phone in a concourse at Washington National Airport. She had just used the phone to call Phil, and Jimmy's construct, Mr. Ear, scanning the 202 area code for her phone card, ran CallBack as soon as she hung up. *You can't do that!* she had told him. *You mean I* shouldn't *do it,* he had explained.

Sometimes the weenie scared her. The boy had no principles. Even Mariesa van Huyten, she had to admit to herself, had principles, wrongheaded as they were. And, to be even more honest, not all of them and not entirely. Or that other piece of work, Bullock. At least you could see where he was coming from. He wanted to be safe, warm and cozy. (God, how he held forth over dessert at that Neo banquet last October!) But not Jimmy. He took no stand—not for, not against, not anything. It was all the game to him. It was the accomplishing, not the accomplishment, that mattered; and that made him unpredictable, because who knew what he would see as a challenge? "Mr. Ear" gave him the ability to conduct blackmail on a massive scale. What would happen when he realized that, and he needed money?

But she sighed and signalled telephone mode to the set and triggered the number Jimmy had posted. *How could he be sure I was really alone?* she wondered. How would he know she wasn't setting him up?

Because if she turned Jimmy in, not only would she kamikaze, but she'd take down Tani as well.

Jimmy couldn't have been *that* clever, could he, the night he took Tani home? He'd just been eager to get porked. And yet, he was quite capable of whacking two birds with one stone.

The Max Headroom icon spoke. "Hello? Earth calling Morticia? You there? He-he-he-hey?"

"You sound more like Fred Flintstone than Max Headroom," Roberta said.

"Picky-picky. Don't ralph time. The Cracker isn't the only goon trolling the Bell. Governments, corporations, interest groups, freelancers . . . You'd be surprised who's trying to listen in to what and sell it to whom. Make it short and make it sweet, or 'crypt it all to hell.'"

"Now who's wasting time?"

"So listen and learn." Max suddenly condensed into a flat sheet and flew away into infinity. The screen showed outer space. A legend scrolled. *A long time ago in a galaxy far, far away* . . . A shot of an observatory. An astronomer turns to another and says, "What do you make of that, Professor?" Men in arctic clothing cluster around a radio set and the man with the mike says, "Keep watching the skies. Keep watching the skies." A shot from a TV movie: a meteorite strikes a small resort town. Montage: a forest of felled trees; a satellite view of the Aral Sea; false color shots of Jupiter geysering from comet strikes. A barrage of images, repeating, reappearing, tiling the screen, overlapping, until, in the dead center, a bird's eye view of Meteor Crater, Arizona.

"Very postmodern," Roberta told the screen, "but I'm New Art. What's the authorial intent?"

"Gaw." It was never Jimmy's unaltered voice that she heard. It was always filtered, overlaid, modulated. But she always knew when he was speaking direct. "Lit crit." Max Headroom reappeared making the antivampire cross with its disembodied forefingers. "But no time for play. This is serious weenie. I've been going through the data Crackman sent you."

Roberta pursed her lips. "I thought it was up to me to

make sense of it,'' she said sarcastically. She didn't bother with the fiction that "Crackman" was doing the outlaw hack.

"It is, herb. You paid for a trawl; not for analysis. Am I going to give you data when I don't know the information content? 'Silly Wabbit.' ''

Roberta made a wasted gesture. The screen was not two-way. "So what gives? You called to spill. Make a mess.''

"You wanted to know why you-know-who made a deal with you-know-whom." Max's words were out of synch with his lips, of course. "It was toy for toy. It looks like a battle laser is going upstairs. Code name . . . Lucifer! Trumpets, and a black-and-white André Doré engraving of Satan appeared and vanished. Your friend wants it to burn meteors.''

Or Donaldson wants to burn cities? Women and children? What kind of mind thinks like that? And what kind of mind enables it? "Meteors,'' she said.

"Yeah, it looks like she was spooked by that business on Calhoun's Rock.''

"Calhoun's Rock? What was that?''

"Don't you pay any attention? Hello? The alien inscriptions . . . ?''

"Oh, that. I figured it was just Deep Space goosing more funding. Like that Martian 'fossils.' ''

"What it is,'' said Jimmy. "I dug a little on my own tick. No invoice. And it looks like this has been a bee in her pantyhose for a long time—''

"Yeah, I know. Barry Fast told me—''

"The lady does not want to be knocked on the head by anything large and fast—''

"—and *that's* why she's going along with Donaldson?

"—and I can't say it's high on my list of favorite things, either.''

Roberta paused. "You're not serious, are you?''

A dinosaur segment from Disney's *Fantasia* flashed. "Dunno, Morticia. Ask Barney. Your friend's in Sky Watch. Maybe she knows something. Maybe *it's on its way!*

Or maybe she knew the Big D was going to get what he wanted. He's the president of the U.S. of fucking-A, after all. So if she was going to get screwed, she might as well lie back and get something out of it.''

A disgusting metaphor. Not that it fazed Jimmy either-or. And she could not imagine the Rich Lady as passive. Donaldson might think he was using her, but she was just as certainly using him. What surprised her was the hard-headed managers around her buying in to such a flakey reason.

The laser must have a secondary purpose, she thought. Something more practical. Then—like a meteor impact itself—the thought struck her.

The others don't know about her real reason . . . !

"Crackman," she said, paranoia being catching, "I know you didn't mean it, but you've been a big help." Then she did wand the TV off and retreat to her office, where she studied the affinity diagram into the wee hours of the morning.

Ellis Harwood shrugged into his winter coat and looped the scarf around his throat. He picked up his gloves. "I'll walk you to the metro stop, Bertie," he said. "That's enough crusading for the day."

Roberta pretended to be engrossed in her spreadsheet (which took a lot of pretending). "Thanks, Ellis," she said, "but I've got to get this finished. Then I have a meeting with Phil."

Ellis glanced at the empty office and shrugged. "No rest for the wicked," he agreed cheerfully. "Just be careful when you do leave. It's wet, dark, and freezing out there." As he reached for the knob, the door opened inward, nearly catching him, and Isaac Kohl staggered in, holding himself upright with the same door.

"Jeez!" he said. "Hey, Ellis. Be careful where you step. It's freezing over." Phil Albright followed Isaac inside. He shook the sleet from his *chapka* and brushed at his coat sleeves.

"Phil," said Ellis, "when you get the time, we need to talk about the *New York News* strike."

Phil nodded. "As soon as this War Powers Act is done with," he promised as he hung his coat on the coat tree. "Thanks for waiting, Roberta. Isaac, we'll use my office."

Ellis looked from Phil to Roberta to Isaac. "You're in this meeting, too?" he asked.

"I've been analyzing sleezy poll data. Roberta's been tracking amendments."

Ellis shrugged again and looked at Phil. "I'm not so sure that Donaldson and the humanitarians are wrong on this one, Phil. It's an awful mess. Even the good guys are fascists."

"There are no good guys, Ellis."

"Yeah, I suppose the pacifists have a point, too. I just hate to see you dealing with Anson and that crowd, Phil."

Albright smiled. "The Constitutional War Powers Reinforcement Act has diverse support."

Harwood laughed. "Libertarians opposed to any foreign entanglements; liberals wary of anything military; conservatives who take the eleventh clause of Section 8 far too literally. That's not just 'diverse,' Phil, it's forbidden by Leviticus."

Roberta and Phil laughed; Isaac said, "I don't get it."

Phil said, "The old labels are losing meaning, Ellis. 'The times, they are a-changing.' "

"That doesn't mean I have to like it. Muddying up the terms of discourse, Phil. But I suppose any debate where MacNab and his American Party are on the other side puts us with the angels." He put a hand to the door. "You won't forget what I said about the *News* strike, will you? I'd hate to see the country's biggest city become a one-newspaper town."

Professor Harwood was okay, Roberta reflected, but he was behind the curve. New York City had at least a dozen "newspoppers" on the Web, three of them of professional quality. But if it wasn't printed with paste on the shredded corpses of trees, Ellis didn't recognize it as a newspaper.

Phil was of the older generation, too, but Phil was wired in. The future seldom caught him by surprise, and it *never* passed him by unnoticed.

After Phil had personally made them all a pot of coffee and they had settled around the meeting table in his office, Roberta asked them how things were going on the Hill.

"Maintaining," Phil said. "Isaac managed to soothe over Ganner and Wolfe. The poll had them spooked. Three-to-two in favor of intervention. They thought if they bucked Donaldson on this, their constituents wouldn't punch their meal ticket next time."

"Never mind conscience and principal," said Roberta.

"Oh," Phil was generous, "senators are supposed to represent their states. I can't fault someone too much for going along with what their employers think."

"Or what they think they think," said Isaac. "I showed them the actual poll questions and pointed out how the lead-up questions prepared the respondents to answer 'yes' on the key points. 'Do you approve or disapprove of the massacres of civilians in the Balkans?' " he quoted. "Jeez, some of it was so blatant, I can only guess they never expected anyone to see the actual questions."

" 'Friends, Romans, and countrymen,' " said Roberta.

"That's the idea."

"Well," said Phil, raising his coffee to his lips and sipping. "As John Wayne would have said, we rounded up a few strays that'd been spooked. Not a bad day's work."

"What I don't get is what Donaldson gets out of a loaded poll," said Roberta.

Phil gestured with his cup. "Simple. One, he convinces the public that he's at the head of their parade; and two, he gets some of the opposition to roll over."

"Like they almost did," said Isaac.

"Polls can *create* reality as well as reflect it. Our press conference will be at three tomorrow. That gives the newsgroups time to post for the evening surf. Oh, and TV, too, of course. Robbie, why don't you knock me up five minutes of byte. Isaac can feed you factoids. You know what to say and how to say it.''

''You can huff and puff and blow their house down,'' Roberta said. ''Senator Egan jumped ship today.''

Phil raised his eyebrows. He set his cup on the table and sat upright. ''That doesn't sound like Senator Partyhack to me,'' he said. ''What happened? There was no noise on the Hill.''

''Jill Noyce, Senator Navrati's aide, told me. Egan proposed an amendment *strengthening* the language in the bill.''

Phil and Isaac traded glances. ''Really? What was the language?''

Roberta closed her eyes and concentrated. ''Uh, 'no ground forces within the national boundaries; no naval units within the five-mile limits; no fighters, bombers, or reconnaissance planes overflying the territory of any belligerent state.' ''

Phil scratched his head. ''That pretty much seals it up.''

Isaac shook his head. ''No, it doesn't. There's no prohibition topside.''

Roberta scowled. ''Sure there is. No planes . . . Oh. Shit.''

''Star Wars,'' Phil guessed.

Isaac nodded. ''Sounds like Donaldson's lapdog pretending to bite his master's hand while he digs a loophole.''

''Word games,'' said Roberta.

Phil pursed his lips. ''No. If only specific kinds of overflights were prohibited, he stays within the letter of the law. He might plan to go against the *intent* of the law, but in this country laws restrict what you can do, not what you can think. So they can do anything they want to Donaldson afterwards, except charge him. Do you two want to fill me in on your special project? It sounds like it might be relevant.''

Isaac waved a hand. ''Go ahead, Robbie. I just helped software it. You did all the gold panning.''

Roberta took a deep breath. She looked at Isaac, then at

Phil. "I haven't said anything up till now, because I wasn't sure what I had. A great big haystack of data that might contain a few needles of information. I bounced a few notions off Isaac earlier, and . . . Well, what it looks like is that Donaldson tried twisting VHI's arm to put his Star Wars weapon—they call it *Steel Rain*—on the LEO Station. VHI dragged its heels for a couple of months, then gave the go-ahead in November. VHI got a laser, supposedly to test long-range power beaming, but actually to shoot down asteroids."

"Shoot down . . . ?" Now Phil looked definitely puzzled. "Why would VHI care about that? I don't see a big ROI."

"Unless the asteroid's headed for us," Isaac Kohl said, thoughtfully. "I've read about the possibility." Phil shook his head.

"Defense is the government's job. Maybe it should be done, but what's *VHI*'s motive? They won't shoot unless we pay them? How do they make money out of that?"

Roberta could barely restrain Styx. "That's the beauty of it. VHI doesn't even know it's committed." She wriggled in her chair. It was delicious, absolutely delicious, and this was the first chance she'd had to share the knowledge. "It's just Mariesa van Huyten and a few others. A couple of them went along for the government contracts they got out of it, or to kiss ass with the boss; but the Rich Lady herself is just whack on the subject of asteroids. It's a phobia of hers."

Phil frowned and tugged his lower lip. "And Donaldson knew that and used it to leverage her?"

"No. As far as I can tell, he used the ordinary threats. Like exercising eminent domain, or slipping the SecTrans's leash."

"I heard rumors from Liberty Party leaders that Donaldson was leaning on 'major contributors,'" he said thoughtfully. "Now, he's maneuvered them—and me!—into approving a bill whose language specifically gives him a loophole to use space-based weapons. Damn, he's clever.

He should have stayed on Wall Street. At least there you can get arrested for pulling a fast one.''

"Should I put this into the press release?" Roberta asked. "Or do you want to do a separate one on this?"

"Robbie," said Phil. "I'm very serious. Could you and Isaac get in trouble over this?"

"Uh, you'd have to say a whistle-blower tipped you off." Isaac looked at her and shook his head.

"Oh, great. Fucking great."

"You're clear, Isaac."

"Robbie, I'm not going to say anything about this, and neither are you two; not even to the Cadre. For now," he added, holding up a hand to forstall Styx's objection. "Number one reason: If there are any tracks that need hiding—not that there are, of course—appropriate action can be taken. And number two: I want Donaldson with his hand in the cookie jar. If we holler foul now, he can abort the operation and claim it never existed. Let's wait until the equipment is installed. He can't deny it then. The station construction crew will be our witnesses. Agreed? Good."

"What I don't understand," Isaac said, "is Donaldson's motives. Why is he doing this in the first place? He spent his whole first term not doing anything stupid."

"Maybe," said Phil, "he didn't want to be remembered as 'the president who didn't do anything stupid.' "

"Boy," said Styx, popping out of her box, "he sure got his wish."

Asteroids. An obsession of hers, Barry Fast had said. Yet, Poole's datalanche had been oddly restrained on that topic. E-mail exchanged with other members in SkyWatch; a database containing scores of orbits; a sim program that would not run on Roberta's puny machine—all of it very earnest in the way amateurs had of out-serious-ing the professionals. Either van Huyten never confided her fears to her computer, or she never confided them at all. Maybe Barry Fast's were the only ears she had whispered them into.

The popular articles on asteroids that Roberta read for

insight were in various degrees alarmed, complacent, and academic. A few showed how existing craters would look superimposed over a big city. (New York was the favorite target, and she wondered at the hidden animus that implied.) But how did you evaluate a risk like that? A miniscule chance, but a massive payoff. If a world-killer asteroid came along once in sixty-five million years and the population of the Earth was seven billion, then on the average 107 people died each year from asteroid strikes. That's how the Crusades calculated other risks—power lines, homelessness, food additives—but in this context, it sounded crazy.

"She *feels* that risk," Barry Fast had said. "It gives her nightmares."

Roberta hit the bricks. The Smithsonian. The New York Museum of Natural History. Hayden Planetarium. The Franklin Institute. Telephone and peephone calls placed to observatories and museums beyond the reach of mass transit. Experts were a dime a dozen. You could have held a garage sale on opinions.

"Like Dante's Inferno," one expert told her when she went to ask him about it. "A six-mile-diameter asteroid, striking near Chixculub, on the Yucatan, and . . . *adios, señor dinosaur*. The heat was so intense that the world's forests caught fire. Global wildfires . . . Soot and charcoal at the K/T boundary layer show that as much as a quarter of the world's plant life burned . . ."

"A global wildfire," another expert at another institution commented, "would have boiled a lot of lakes—*boiled* them!—and the rain of organic and inorganic debris would have choked most of the others. When the bacteria went to work on the organic debris, man! It would have depleted all the oxygen in the water. So why didn't *fish* 'go the way of the dinosaur?' If anything, they prospered."

"Impact winter," said a third expert. "All that dust thrown up would produce extreme cold. Not in the oceans, of course. Huge heat reservoirs, there. That's why the fish survived. But on the continents, our models predict subfreezing temperatures for as long as six months. The Big Chill . . .''

"Subfreezing temperatures would affect ectothermic tetrapods the most . . . Oh, excuse me. 'Cold-blooded' is the common term. Not exactly accurate, but . . . Turtles and crocodilians cannot tolerate freezing at all, and frogs and salamanders go into torpor only because of seasonal cues which would not have been present in an impact scenario. Yet, over 75 percent of turtle and crocodilian species survived the K/T event. And *all* the frogs and salamanders. Every loving mother's son of 'em . . .''

"The tremendous energy of the impact would have compounded atmospheric oxygen and nitrogen into nitric acid. And sulfur dioxide vaporized from the rocks would combine with water vapor and oxygen to create sulfuric acid. You think we got acid rain problems today . . . ?''

"But aquatic vertebrates would be most impacted by an acid rain scenario, and their K/T survival rates are among the best . . .''

"All sunlight cut off. Photosynthesis shuts down. Plants die. Herbivores die. Carnivores die. It's the domino theory of mass extinction.''

"But, Miss Carson, the K/T extinctions are confined to only a very few groups. The two orders of *Dinosauria* were the most dramatic, but the *Elasmobranchii*, *Metatheria*, and *Squamata* also saw significant die-offs. Most other groups came through fine. In fact, the striking thing about the extinctions is the way some groups were almost wiped out while other groups were barely touched.''

". . . worldwide iridium layer a certain sign of extraterrestrial impact . . .''

* * *

". . . worldwide iridium layer a certain sign of extensive vulcanism. The Deccan Traps . . ."

". . . dinosaurs were dying off long before the K/T boundary. There are fewer and fewer fossils the closer you . . ."

". . . because they never looked close enough. When the terminal layers are sampled in greater detail, we find fossils all the way up to the boundary, when they suddenly vanish . . ."

"Even dinosaurs did *not* 'go the way of the dinosaur.' Birds are saurischian dinosaurs plus another sixty-five million years of evolution. Tweety Bird is a closer relative of Tyranosaurus rex than a crocodile is. So one answer to the question of why the dinosaurs vanished is . . . They didn't!"

". . . very much overrated. Survival across the K/T is only a slightly smaller percent of genera than between the early and middle Paleocene or between the mid-Campanian and the late Maastrichtian. It's only the loss of the dinosaurs that makes it seem like a big deal. . . ."

". . . environmental stresses. Marine regression of the intracontinental seas reduced coastal habitat at the same time that the breakup of Pangaea was reducing continental habitat sizes . . ."

". . . agnostic, myself. *Was* there a contemporaneous worldwide extinction at all? Our entire knowledge of K/T extinctions comes from a single area of the world: the interior of the western U.S., especially western Montana. The only place in the world, if you will, where we have 'before-and-after photographs.' The Uzbekistani sequence, where ungulate mammals seem to appear *before* the dinosaurs' demise, is far less clear. There were dinosaur fossils, including eggs and articulated skeletons, *above* the K/T boundary layer in the southeast China sequence; but that could be a reworking of older fossils through erosion and redeposit. Still, it does make you wonder . . .''

"The Earth took *bigger* hits than Chixculub during the age of the dinosaurs. Why didn't *they* cause mass extinctions?"

"Sometimes I just shake my head. Dante's Inferno? Give me a break. Personally, I don't give a shit if a big rock nined the dinos or if that was only the *coup de grace* coming on top of habitat depletion. You know why, Miss Carson? *Because I'm not a dinosaur.* Except in the eyes of some of my colleagues . . . Heh-heh-heh. I don't care what the 'death star' may or may not have done to Barney and his friends sixty-five megs ago. I care what *another* one may do to *us, tomorrow.* Even a relatively small bugger would screw us royally. . . .''

"The odds? Slim to none. At least for a big honker. The Earth has been 'sweeping' this region of space for billions of years. I doubt there are very many intersectors out there any more . . .''

". . . called NEOs. Near Earth Objects. I can give you a list, if you want. No, none of them have impacting orbits, but the orbits can be perturbed by Mars or other bodies. Chaos theory, you know. Poincaré showed that orbital mechanics is ultimately chaotic. One of our amateur associates— you've heard of Mariesa van Huyten, surely!—she and her study group have identified ten asteroids that appear to have changed orbits over the last two decades. . . .''

"The odds? Hard to say. Remember Shoemaker-Levy, the comet that jackhammered Jupiter? Well, medieval chronicles report five successive bright flares from behind the moon on 18 June 1178. Probably the strike that made the Giordano Bruno crater. I'd say it was damn good luck that the moon was in the way that day, wouldn't you?"

* * *

The sky over Washington, D.C., was mostly overcast and the cloud cover reflected the lights from the monuments and the government district. Everything looked like the inside of a large room, lit by indirect lighting. It was hard to know that there *was* a sky, let alone what it looked like. Roberta took the Blue Line to L'Enfant Plaza and changed over to the Green, which she rode all the way to the end at, appropriately enough, Greenbelt, Maryland. The overcast here was patchy. One swatch of clouds glowed ghostly white from the shrouded moon. In a few places, stars could be seen. She found a bench in a small park, away from the lights of the metro station and the highway, and sat there with her knees tucked under her chin.

Toward midnight, the cloud cover began to break up like a moth-eaten curtain, revealing the black abyss behind it. Roberta contemplated the sky like she used to do at Silverpond. People looking at the sky saw only a backdrop with white lights sprinkled on it. They saw a painting, a theater set. Deep down inside, they still believed in crystal spheres. But those two stars, beside each other . . . One was probably millions of miles farther away, right? (Millions? Maybe billions . . . ? Those weren't even numbers. You couldn't feel them.) She picked one of the two stars at random and willed herself to see it as *behind* and not *beside*; willed herself to see a *vista* and not a painted backdrop. And suddenly, as if by sheer force of will, the sky took on infinite depth and she was looking *up* into a pit.

It was just for an instant, like in those optical illusions where the drawing of the old hag becomes a drawing of a young woman. It was just for an instant that she looked *up* into an endless *down*. She sucked in her breath and held it, as if that would hold the moment.

A streak crossed the sky and vanished. *Make a wish.*

I wish . . .

That things had turned out differently. But *which* things, she wasn't sure. That her mother had been closer; that van

Huyten had not been a cold-hearted manipulator; that she had had real friends in high school; that. . . .

Wishes vanished into a bottomless pit. There was no one up there listening, anyway.

Another streak. This one lasted longer, though it still vanished before reaching the black line of treetops at the edge of the park. A bigger one, that. The bigger they were, the longer they burned when they fell. Mariesa van Huyten was a lot bigger and a lot higher up than Simon Fell. She would make quite a flaming streak when she was brought to Earth . . .

A third streak. This one went in a different direction.

The Siberian Meteor of 1947 had scattered one hundred tons of nickel-iron over its crater field, one of the astronomers had told her. The biggest fragment weighed two tons. She thought about a hundred tons of rock coming down on Washington. She tried to make it feel real. What would it look like? How big was a hundred tons anyway? Would you even be able to see it coming? Or would it break up into smaller pieces before it hit? She shook her head. She couldn't imagine it. She had no referrents; and, lacking referrents, she felt no fear.

A lot of people would die if something like that did happen. But a lot of people died from hurricanes and earthquakes and floods and volcanoes; and those were a lot more likely. If you wanted to be afraid, there were more credible bogeymen than asteroids. The Big LA Quake would hit a lot sooner than the Big Rock from the Sky.

Roberta hopped off the park bench and started back toward the train station. It was a chilly night and she jammed her hands deep into the pockets of her windbreaker. Her breath made glowing clouds of steam in the air. Another shooting star caught her eye. She wondered if that was unusual. How many did you usually see in an hour? Maybe it was a meteor shower. They happened at certain times of the year, one of the astronomers had told her, when the Earth swept through the debris of old, dead comets.

A couple tons a year. She had forgotten the figure already, but she'd been told that meteorites added a couple of tons a year to the Earth's mass. The Earth was young yet; still growing. She grew by taking whatever hits the universe threw at her and plowing right along. Chance collisions with rogue bodies.

Yeah. A lot of people grew the same way. It was how you grew up.

15.

Otterwise

The train was full of suits.

Aurora Ballistic Transport ran a special two-car train out of Penn Station early Monday morning bound for Allentown Spaceport. Most of those who handed their tickets to the security guard were duded up in three-pieces and long cashmere overcoats with silk scarves. They looked askance at Flaco, and no wonder. A jump-ticket to Aomori or Woomera or Jo-burg, that was no-fooling-around money. Flaco, dressed in blue coveralls and weather jacket, didn't look·to have that sort of travel budget, but Flaco flashed his Green Crew badge and the conductor nodded him aboard.

One of the cars was a club car and most of the suits headed straight there to numb themselves for the upcoming trip. They poured the liquor down their throats, laughing in voices a pitch too high, pretending that their guts weren't knotted up and their bowels ready to let go. The pursuit of money could drive men to do many things against their wishes and fears. Leap atop a tower of flame halfway into space and back? Flaco wondered if the first commercial air travelers had felt the same dread. A few businessmen seemed more relaxed; and those, Flaco judged, like himself, had made such trips before. A single such experience was enough to mark them; and later today, many of the same men now growing insensibly drunk in apprehension would chat smoothly of the experience and mock the trembling first-timers boarding the return flight. Flaco tossed his duffel in the overhead rack and slouched by the window in one of the triple seats. He pulled his O&P baseball cap low over his eyes. Currents of nervous chatter drifted in from the club car.

Oh, yeah, a herd of dust bunnies, for sure. Probably hurl, come ziggy, high over the Pacific. Land in the Rising Sun with ralph all over their pinstripes.

A tapping at the window, and Flaco lifted his cap to see Serafina waving frantically. The security guard must have let her come down on the platform, after all. No. He saw the man behind 'Fina, standing with his hands behind his back, trying to look both stern and pleased with himself at the same time. Flaco smiled and pressed his hand against the glass. He saved a smile for the guard, too, who gave him a thumbs-up gesture in return. Serafina, looking so much more solemn, pressed her hand against the other side and they touched each other through the glass.

I do not understand why you must go back, her eyes said.

"It's better you don't," he whispered to her.

Her lips said, "I love you," in exaggerated pantomime and he repeated the pledge to her.

Someone on the platform must have hollered, because 'Fina looked down the tracks and then stepped away from the train. There was a hiss and the doors closed just as a man and woman danced aboard, laughing. They both wore long, dark overcoats and dragged small, compact suitcases with wheels on the bottom. "See?" said the man. "I told you they would wait for us." Flaco placed his accent as Russian, though it was not as thick as some he had heard aboard LEO.

"They had no choice," the woman answered, "but they did not like it. They nearly took my ass off with their door."

Flaco did not like it when women talked crudely, but the comment could not help but draw his eye to the body part in question. It was a fine example and it would have been a shame for the closing door to have taken it. The woman was of the man's height and her hair was cropped short like a man's, so that it resembled a skullcap. A whitened scar on her right temple was a streak of lightning through the stubble of her hair. "Let's sit here, Valery," the woman said. The two of them took seats across the aisle from Flaco.

The train jerked and then rolled smoothly out of the terminal toward the tunnels. Flaco waved to Serafina, who was trying to pace the train without running. One of the businessmen returned from the club car balancing a drink in a plastic cup and sank down next to Flaco.

'Fina pulled up short at the end of the platform and she passed from sight. Flaco sighed and slouched in his seat.

The man with the drink pointed out the window. "Was that your other?"

Flaco said, "My other what?"

"You know. Your significant other. Your live-in, your girlfriend." His breath smelled of gin.

"My wife."

The man grunted sourly and finished his drink. "People live too long to make lifelong committments." He looked at his drink a moment and scowled, as if remembering.

"That was your generation," Flaco said. "Things are different now."

"Yeah?" The man gave him an appraising stare. "See me in ten years, and we'll see."

"I make a promise; I keep it."

The man stuck his plastic cup in the seat pocket in front of him. Then he leaned back and folded his arms. "Right. You tell me you never had something you wanted to do—that you *needed* to do—that *she* didn't want. Or maybe the other way around—I'm no chauvinist. Tell me you never heard different drummers."

Flaco pulled his cap down. "Ain't none of your business, *'mano*."

The man grunted and his lips curled in sad triumph. "Yeah, I thought so."

* * *

The express ducked underground a few miles south of the spaceport and coasted up to a sublevel platform that was still under construction. Only about half the walls were tiled; everything else was exposed wiring and ducts and trusses. Flaco and the other passengers made their way past black-and-yellow-striped barriers to the escalator leading to Security Screen.

The departure area at ground level was a buzz of confusion. Passengers, "starcaps," ticket clerks, news reporters, building security, TV camera crews, all jostling and mixing. People searching for check-in counters in new and unfamiliar surroundings. People picking up or dropping off, questioning, photographing, or just standing around gawking. Rodneys wearing doid bands on their foreheads circulated through the crowd interviewing anyone who would hold still, and chasing a few who would not. A pack of them had encircled a tall, elegantly dressed woman, pinning her with rapid-fire questions and a lightning storm of flashes.

Check-in was a spacious gallery, long but not very deep, and at first gave the odd impression of being set in the open air. Enormous windows and pixwalls recreated a panorama of the surrounding countryside where the walls should have been. Cornfields, freshly plowed and black with turned earth. The highway to the south with its crawl of traffic. The mountain ridge on the north, distant and tinged a strange shade of blue—a wall across the horizon, notched here and there by the wind. Out front a band of people stood waving signs and handing out leaflets. The outside had been invited inside by transparency and transmission.

There were only four check-in counters. Federal Express, on the left, was freight only. Next to that, Aurora passengers lined up fifty deep for the Aomori flight—the port's inaugural lift—and that was where the rodneys and the other newsers concentrated their efforts. The Northwest counter was unmanned, but a poster behind it proudly announced its premier flight for March 12: Allentown to Prague, connecting to Woomera, "The Gateway to ANZonesia." Pegasus was at the far right. Its flight board listed Phoenix and Nairobi, "with connections to Mir and LEO."

There were only a handful of people in line at Pegasus. One of them was a Green Crewman Flaco knew slightly. He supposed the others were Gold Crew, or had other business in Phoenix unrelated to LEO. When he reached the head of the line, he ran his O&P card through the scanner, keyed in his private encryption, and rested his chin on the FaceMaker, which agreed he was José Eduardo Gonsalves y Mercado, O&P rigger—or else one of maybe two other people on the planet who had the same face. Sepp had tried to explain one time about resolving images into "orthogonal eigenfaces," each of which represented a unique combination of "face-factors," but Flaco didn't get it and he didn't think Sepp knew much beyond what he had read in popular magazines. Cerberus Security had posted a million dollar reward for the first person who could fool a FaceMaker. Yung Okiwara, Hollywood's "man of a million faces," made a well-publicized attempt about every other month, but the word was that Cerberus itself was backing him for the publicity.

"Bird Winfrey check in yet?" he asked the clerk.

"Half hour ago." A stylus waved in the air, indicating several possible directions. "Check out the restaurant or the lounge."

The short odds were on the bar, and Flaco found the man sitting on a stool in "the Distlefink Room" with a tall mug of Kuebler's ale in front of him. Bird saw him and grinned. "Hey, Pancho," he said, raising the glass.

"Hey, Tonto."

"Give my compadre here a tall one. Chico, this here's my wife, Rosie. She come up from Philly to make sure I really leave." The Bird's wife was a short woman with dark, broad Indio features. Flaco introduced himself and when his beer arrived the three of them retreated to one of the mezzanine tables that overlooked the check-in desks.

The lounge was nearly deserted. Everyone was in the main lobby, where the action was. Maybe hoping to catch a glimpse of somebody famous here for the riboon-cutting, or maybe just hoping to be doid-background on the evening news. A few tables away, over Bird's shoulder, a thin, dark-clad woman watched the crowds below with a twisted smile. She had straight, black hair, cropped just below the ear, and wore a navy jacket, unzipped. Either she had no makeup on or she favored the new style that affected a natural look.

The far side of the lounge was a pixwall of the landing field, where a jumpship was riding its tug out to the apron. The remaining walls were lined with gaily painted disks in a variety of abstract patterns. Hex signs, Bird told him. The strange-looking bird in the large disk over the bar was a distlefink, and Flaco deferred to Winfrey's knowledge of birds, real or mythical.

"I thought you told me you were going to stay with your lady," he said to Flaco. "What's her name?"

"Serafina."

"That is a pretty name," said Rosie.

"You had a fight and she threw you out . . ."

"It's too complicated to explain."

"Women are always too complicated to explain," Bird said. "Rosie here's as simple as they come, and even she's too complicated for me."

"Listen to *el tonto*," Rosie said in Spanish. Bird laughed and slapped his thigh. He lifted his beer in toast and shouted, "Here's to the otters! We do what we gotta!"

Flaco answered. "There ain't no easy lift!"

Mugs clanked and beer disappeared. The dark-haired woman glanced curiously in their direction. Bird was a strange sort, Flaco reflected. Not exactly friendly, and his humor was often cruel and barbed; yet not a bad sort of man to know, once you were past his guard.

Bird pointed to the pixwall at the far end of the lounge. "That our ship, you think?" Flaco shrugged.

"Can't read the RS from here . . ." He got the bartender's attention and twirled his finger around the table to indicate another round. The bartender nodded her understanding.

"That is *Princess Shakhovskaya*," someone behind him

said. Flaco turned and saw the pale-haired woman from the train. "Allentown to Aomori. Are you lifting in her?"

"Nah," said Bird. "Flaco and me, we're on the second flight, *John Hambleton,* switching to the *Harriet Quimby* in Phoenix."

"Oho," said the woman. "*Quimby?* Then you will be working on LEO?"

"Been there; done that," said Bird. "Goin' back for the T-shirt."

"Sit down, please," Rosie said.

The woman introduced herself as Katya and said she was waiting for her husband. Up close, Flaco saw that she was an older woman, perhaps in her forties. The scar on her temple tended to disappear when the light struck it, which gave it an odd, flickering appearance as she turned her head one way or another. "How far along is the station now?" Katya asked after she had settled in.

"Number Five oughta be in line by now," Bird said, "which means the Hub is done, except for dressing the insides. Plan is to make the Hub an operational ziggyhab before Spokin' and Spinnin'."

"You said that," Flaco told him, "just like the Deacon clears his plans with you." The bartender set the fresh drinks on the table and Flaco handed her a twenty. "See what the woman over there by the window wants. Our treat."

"Excuse me," said Katya, "but what is 'ziggyhab'?"

"ZG habitat," Flaco explained. "Zero-g . . ."

Her smile was distant and amused. "Zero-g, I know, a little; but you call it 'ziggy'? Ha . . . !" She waved, and the smile became for a moment radiant. "Valery! Over here!" She had unsealed her overcoat and the motion pulled the front open. Flaco saw an Aurora purple jumpsuit and a name tag reading *Volkovna.* So Katya must be on *Shakhovskaya*'s crew. No wonder the train could not leave New York without her!

Her companion, too, wore an Aurora uniform. He carried a bottle of mineral water in each hand and handed one to

Katya when he sat down. Introductions ran around the table. The bartender reappeared with Flaco's change.

"The lady said thanks, but no thanks."

Flaco shrugged and pocketed the change. A glance showed the woman still absorbed by the media circus on the floor. "Who is that?" Valery asked, nodding toward the lone woman.

"We don't know," Flaco said. "Someone waiting for the Aomori flight, I guess."

"Ah. That explains it. I saw her face as I passed by, and she looked very unhappy. Her first flight, perhaps."

Katya rose from her seat. "I will talk to her."

Flaco nudged Bird. "Come on. Let's go cheer the lady up. Remember how spooked we were on *our* first lift?"

Bird snorted. "I remember how spooked *you* were." But he followed anyway.

Flaco arrived in time to hear the black-haired woman say, "No, I'm *not* riding on any damned spaceplane. And neither should you. It's too dangerous." She reached into the pocket of her jacket and pulled out some brochures. "Here. Read these." The brochure featured computer drawings of Planks in various stages of destruction. In one, a flaming jumpship plunged toward New York City. Another showed unsuited passengers sucked out into the void of space. A third was a ship exploding on takeoff. On the back side was the morgue photo of Anselmo Takeuchi with a detailed clinical description of the effects of decompression. Katya Volkovna scowled. "What is this?"

"Just a little public service information that VHI would like to keep quiet. You put corporate greed and megabucks on one side of the scale and public safety on the other side and we all know which weighs more. This restores some balance."

Katya shoved the brochure back to the woman. "Whoever gave you these," she said, "told you lies. No ships have exploded or crashed."

"No, that's just it." The woman leaned forward intently.

"It hasn't happened *yet*. But it *could* happen. Remember the *Georges Chaves* accident?"

"Nah," said Bird. "I wasn't there."

"Hard landing, right?" said Flaco. He stuffed his pamphlet into a pocket of his coveralls.

"People were hurt," the woman insisted.

"*Da,*" said Katya. "Five people hurt. And the pilot won a scar across the temple. Landing gear pneumatics failed and the legs telescoped instead of cushioning. But on the day *Georges Chaves* landed hard, an elephant broke loose at the St. Louis zoo and trampled its handler. A truck driver in Smolensk dumped his load without looking and smothered his partner under a load of gravel. Five people were killed in a chain collision on the autobahn outside of Leipzig. I have looked up these things, because . . ." She paused and seemed annoyed with herself. "Because it was important. What did you have in mind that is *not* dangerous?" She didn't wait for an answer, but turned on her heel and strode back to her husband and the two of them left the lounge. Bird chuckled and shook his head. His fingers toyed with his beard. "Sure clocked her."

The dark-clad woman made an exasperated sound. "I guess I was wasting my time."

"Guess so," said Bird. "She's flying the *Princess Shakhovskaya* in an hour or two."

"If you're not lifting," said Flaco, "what are you doing here?"

"Is that any of your business?"

"No."

"I'm here to see someone. Is that all right with you?"

Flaco spread his hands. " 'S all right with me. How 'bout you, Bird?"

"I got no objections," said the Bird.

The woman looked at them. "I'm acting bitchy, right?"

"We won' bother you no more, miss," said Flaco. "We jus' thought you were scared about the lift, you know. Since we been up already . . ." He turned to go.

"Wait." She laid a hand on Flaco's sleeve. "That's right.

I heard you talking earlier. Do you two work on the space station?''

Bird nodded. "Couldn't build it without ol' Chico an' me.''

"They told me there'd probably be a few of you people passing through here today. Would you mind if I ask you a few questions?''

Bird and Flaco exchanged glances. Bird said, "It'll cost you three beers." He waved Rosie to join them. "We're easy, *and* we're cheap."

Flaco chose the seat across the table. "Did you really mean what you said earlier? About Planks not being safe?''

The woman hesitated, then responded more cautiously than before. "I think it's an issue that needs a lot more study than it's been given.'' Rosie arrived with their Kueblers and passed them around. "But I wanted to ask you about the space station.''

And you don't want to anger us like you angered the Aurora pilot. Flaco considered the woman; tried to gauge her. "What do you want to know . . . Miss . . . ?'' he asked. From the way she looked at him, some of the suspicion he felt must have shown in his voice.

"Roberta. Call me Roberta. Nothing proprietary. I'm not, like, an industrial spy or anything. I'm a poet.''

Flaco snorted, but Bird raised his eyebrows and looked at the woman with new respect. " 'Words that ring in patterned sound,' " he quoted, " 'That echo in our heart.' "

She seemed surprised and a little pleased. "Do you know who wrote that?''

Flaco interrupted, pointing to the departure area below, "Looks like they're heading for the ribbon-cutting.'' And quick as that, Roberta turned away from them and stared down at the milling throng. Like a hawk, Flaco thought, searching for rabbits. A crowd of news-doiders parted and for a moment, the tall, thin woman Flaco had noticed earlier could be seen flanked by the husband-wife Aurora pilots. Posing for pictures. Evidently someone of importance. A movement must have caught her eye, for she looked up at the mezzanine.

Roberta pulled back quickly, leaving only Flaco on view. The tall woman frowned, then a doider's question took her attention and the whole entourage resumed their slow procession toward the gate.

"All I wanted to know," Roberta said, as if the odd, momentary distraction had never happened, "is whether you've noticed anything strange or unusual on the space station."

Bird laughed. "I dunno. Hey, Chico, you notice anything strange or unusual? Besides your pal, Tonio, that is . . ."

"I never notice anything familiar and usual when I'm ziggy. 'S all different, y'know."

"Bean word," said the Bird.

"No," Roberta explained. "I mean, like secret goings-on. New stuff they won't tell you about. Have they put any part of the station off-limits, or anything?"

Bird said, "Nah. They couldn't if they tried."

Flaco said, "You're looking for some big scandal so you can trash the space station, aren't you?"

"It's not that, exactly . . ."

" 'Cause, I don't go against my employer . . ."

"Cump'ny man!" said Bird, pumping a fist. Flaco turned to him.

"I take their money; I owe 'em my loyalty."

The woman, Roberta, leaned across the table. "And what if they do something *wrong?*"

"Everybody makes mistakes. That don't mean nothing."

"No. I mean they deliberately do something immoral."

"Then . . . I quit and I don' take their money no more." He crossed his arms. "Nothin' worse, take a man's money and then turn on him."

"So, it's all money to you."

Flaco scowled. "What do you know about it?" he said. "Sure, they pay me t' go up there. Pay me real good. That ship out there?" He pointed toward the north wall of the lounge, where the *Shakhovskaya* stood tall in midfield. He wasn't flying on the *Princess,* but he didn't mean that ship in particular. "That's my ticket out. Outta the Heights, man. Out of a dead end." Flaco blinked as the double meaning of what he had just said sank in. A dead end. Yeah, like Diego and Chino. Like that woman in the snowbank. He shivered and wished that the Kueblers was stronger than it was.

"Well," said the woman, "You may think you're being loyal to your bosses, but maybe you owe some loyalty to the rest of us, too."

Flaco scowled. "What do you mean?"

"Just remember what I said. There's a lot of people underneath you. They'll depend on you to speak up."

"Speak up," said Bird. "About what?"

"Have you heard any talk about 'Steel Rain'?"

Flaco laughed. "I wish I could get 'em to *stop.* 'S all anybody's singing these days. Worse 'n—what was it?— 'Polka Nails,' a couple years back. Worse'n the 'Macarena' when I was a kid."

"Do me a favor . . ." She reached into her purse and pulled out two business cards. "If you ever hear about 'Steel Rain' and it *isn't* hardball goof, let me know about it."

The card read ROBERTA CARSON, and gave a public encryption key and E-dress. Flaco stuck the card in his pocket. "Maybe."

Carson stood to go. "That's all I ask."

After she was gone, Bird sighed. "Why'd you chase her off, Chico? She was good for at least two more rounds."

Rosie gazed down over the rail as Roberta Carson hurried across the ticket lobby toward the front doors. "She was worried about something, I think."

"Was she?" Bird asked. "What?"

Rosie shook her head. "I don't think she knows."

Bird ordered another round and stared into the dark red ale. "She's right, you know. Whatever her name was. Sooner or later, people gonna die."

Flaco studied his own glass. "People gonna die anyway.'' The foam was like a cloud; you could see faces in it.

Bird tipped his glass to him. ''Word.''

''What'd she mean, anyway, about 'Steel Rain'?''

Bird shrugged. ''Means she listens to hardball goof. You know: ' . . . tears like iron rust my eyes/Steel rain falling from the skies/But I ain't gonna bow my head . . .' ''

''Not my kinda music, *'mano*.'' But she hadn't meant the song. It was something else, and she didn't want to tell them. Or else Rosie was right, and she didn't even know herself.

''Hey,'' said Bird. ''Remember that lady pilot was here before? You know who that was?'' Flaco shook his head. He had read her name tag, but had forgotten.

''That was Katya Volkov, the one they used to call the Ice Angel. And her husband, Johnny Danger.''

Flaco looked at him. ''Johnny Danger?''

''If you were a guy named Valery, what would you call yourself? They were two of the pilots who tested the original Planks down in Brazil, along with Calhoun and Krasnarov and 'The Man Who'.''

''I thought you had a hard time with names.''

Bird tipped his glass to his lips and set it down. ''Yeah, well. Some names get remembered.''

Flaco grunted, thinking again of the drawings in the pamphlet, thinking of the suit seals that were all that stood between him and Anselmo Takeuchi. Thinking of a Plank ship heading down, out of control, like a meteor, like ''steel rain.'' Maybe that's what the woman had meant. Ballistic flight paths didn't cross over New York; but if you were on board, it wouldn't matter if you cratered here in a Pennsylvania cow pasture or right in Central Park. He wondered what those drunken, crap-your-pants businessmen in the club car would say if they knew they were being flown to Japan by a man who called himself Johnny Danger.

Later, when the ribbon cutting was over and the media had dispersed, the tall woman Flaco had noticed earlier appeared at the entrance to the lounge. Her hair was shot with gray and her face was drawn, but her clothes were perfectly tailored and could not have looked more expensive if they had been sewn from dollar bills. The smile on her face died by degrees as she looked from table to table. Finally, she seemed to shrink a little, and turned and left without a word. Flaco remembered that the Carson woman had said she'd come to the jump port to *see* someone. She hadn't said she'd come to be seen.

When the *Harriet Quimby* stopped at Mir, the thickset black scientist that Flaco had met earlier came aboard cradling a satchel like it was his first-born son. The scientist noticed Flaco and Flaco could see the wheels turn behind the man's eyes. "You've been down," the man said. "Now you're coming back up."

"Yeah, Hobie, right?"

"Yeah, that's right." Hobart opened a locker a few seats down from Flaco.

"What you got there, Doc?" Flaco asked him.

"Oh, just some wafers I made. Superconducting ceramics."

Sepp Bauer, sitting on Flaco's right, said, "I have heard of dese t'ings."

Tonio, another seat over, said, "Sepp, you've heard of everything."

"What the hell is a superconductor?" Bird asked. "Sounds like a comic book hero who runs a train."

"Oh," said Dr. Hobart, "it's a phase some materials go into when they're cold enough. They carry a current, but no voltage—because there's no resistance."

Bird shrugged. "If you say so, Jackson."

"The opposite of a woman," Tonio said. "The colder they are, the more they resist."

Sepp shook his head. "It is a scientific matter," he chided them. Tonio and the others hooted at him, but Flaco said, "What do these superconductors look like?"

"J-just little squares. Metal-ceramic." Hobart cracked open his case and showed them rows and rows of bright, glittering squares stacked in padded holders like slides for a projector. "I create a mixture of vapor fractions and let it grow into a crystal in microgravity. I use an IBM atom-nudger to get everything lined up right."

Hobie pulled a wafer out by the edges, like it was a μCD, and held it to his eyes, turning it this way and that. It caught the light and sparkled like a star. "Three months ago, I drew some wire from one of these," he said. "Just a foot or so, you know, for an experiment? I laid a couple milliamps on it, then I disconnected the fuel cell. The current kept going because none of the energy was lost to resistance."

Sepp pulled on his chin. "You keep a current in the circuit without a battery?" He shook his head in wonder. "For how long?"

Hobart shrugged. "Don't know. Still going. Maybe forever."

"But you gotta keep it cold, right?" Flaco said. He didn't want Doc to think Sepp was the only one in the gang who was smart. "You said it gets superconducting when it's cold enough, so when it gets warm . . ."

The scientist nodded. "The effect turns off like that—" He snapped his fingers. "That's a problem dust-side; keeping things cold enough. 'Cause we're not talking refrigerator cold, you know. This next batch, that's growing right now, I'll be back up in three months to harvest it. That batch ought to be real beans, if my calculations are right." Flaco thought he spoke like a man whose calculations weren't often wrong. What was it like to be a man like that, to rig thoughts instead of steel? Dr. Hobart was not much older than Flaco; yet he *seemed* much older, almost like science automatically put years on your age.

"But in outer space," Hobart went on thoughtfully as he stowed his sample case into a locker and settled into an acceleration couch, "keeping things cold is easy. All you need is a good shadow."

"Surely," said Sepp, "it cannot be so simple as that."

"Details," said Hobart. "That's why God invented engineers."

* * *

The crew quarters in Module Two, the one they had named after Anselmo Takeuchi, seemed oddly homelike to Flaco as he stowed his duffelbag in his old locker. The crazy, upside-down dormitory where sleeping racks circled the room and you could lie on your back and look up at people lying on their back looking up at you. The space-filling tables of the cafeteria, where you could eat every which way. Gold Crew veterans and Green Crew trainees darting about like fish in an aquarium. Uncle Waldo lurking in mobile and sessile pods and in the guts of every terminal. The focus and determination of men with a mission.

There was no ''welcome aboard'' party this time around. Green Crew already knew the wheres and whats and most of the hows. The Rector was not aboard; the cadaverous DeWitt Christensen with his unruly mop of straw-colored hair was site manager this turn. By all accounts, Christensen was more easy-going than Wesley Bensalem on matters outside the work schedule, but then it was hard to imagine a stricter man than the Deacon.

Flaco felt more relaxed here than he had groundside, and he could not quite understand why. Partly, it may have been ziggy. It was luxurious to float about unattached to anything—and that message could have made its way through his muscles to his brain, easing his mind. But it had to be more. After all, he'd felt plenty tense on his first lift! Nor could it be the easy cameraderie of casual partners. He had his *panas* dirtside, too. It might only be that the invitation to complete the on-orbit training meant that he was finally accepted; that the testing and the training, while never complete, was no longer intended to weed him out. He was with the wheat now, not the chaff. He could think of his bunk as *his* bunk, and not simply as one that he occupied for the time being.

Uncle Waldo announced that *Harriet Quimby* would drop in fifteen minutes. Shortly after, a small swarm of men passed through the dormitory on their way to the space dock in Module One. One of them was Nellie Hess, reputedly the prime candidate for Madonnahood if a virgin birth was ever needed for the Second Coming. The last holdovers from Red Crew were dropping after their six-month stint. A man detached himself from the group and sailed over to Flaco's bunk. It was Rhys Pilov.

"Looks like you made it back," the lead rigger said.

Flaco knew it was at least in part on his mentor's say-so that he had been put on the regular crew, but he couldn't help think that Pilov sounded disappointed. "Yeah," Flaco answered. "You can't keep a good man down."

"Number Five's already in place," Pilov told him. "You guys have a special job coming up. Some sort of module lifting on a Shuttle flight for attachment to Number Four."

"We'll handle it," Flaco said.

"I know you will, otter. Gold Crew's onboard to hold your hand." With that he toed off toward the aft manlock. Flaco watched him go for a moment, then turned his attention back to stowing his things. He stuffed a bag full of socks—carefully paired and balled together the way Sepp had taught him—into a compartment in his locker. He closed the door and paused thoughtfully. He'd been wrong. He hadn't been fully accepted until just now.

Time was quicksilver on LEO Station. The tighter it was grasped, the faster it ran off. Time was eaten broiled, baked, and stewed; it was eaten raw. Number Four was dressed out: manlocks bored between Four and Five; bulkheads muscled into place; pipes and conduits laid amid the sparkle of μwave welding torches. The air was harsh with fumes: acrid sparks of flowing metal, pungent jellies and lubricants, fifty-four sweating bodies, trays of nuked muck bolted down in the caf. It rang with the clamor of smoked metal seating, fasteners banging home, instructions and orders shouted in "Orbital English" and casual chatter in a babel of tongues.

Endeavor lifted hard, dumping a prefab module into an orbit above its nominal flight ceiling; and a tasty morsel of a Pegasus pilot named Alexandra Feathershaft flew the tug down with a couple of Gold Crew riggers and Uncle Waldo to boost it up to the site. Two days later, the orbits synched and they brought the module into position against the Earth-side surface of Number Four. His own assignment was the less exciting task of prepping Number Five. Uncle Waldo told him not to sweat the small stuff; and when Chase Coughlin, the Punk Pilot of the Spaceways, brought up a bumboat, he said that the Hub was definitely shaping up. You couldn't prove that by Flaco, but he didn't have the right perspective for it.

It wasn't all work. In some ways the crew put as much ingenuity into play; sometimes more. One sleep shift, Bird Winfrey managed to paint a bull's-eye on Red Hawkins's bald head without waking the man; and the Australian had gone the whole next day before twigging. Jimmy Schorr, the Gold Crewman Flaco had met during the ground trials, rigged a pool table in the center of the aft bay of Number Two. Since ricocheting balls were the last thing anyone wanted inside the weightless sleeping habitat, the whole thing was encased in a clear SPP box with small holes drilled around the edges to accommodate a cue stick. The balls contained embedded iron pellets and were racked by means of magnets. When Christensen saw it, he shook his head, but took no official notice. Flaco wondered what the Rector would say when the rotation brought him up again.

When the special module had been successfully installed, Gold Crew held a *vyecherinka* in the caf and invited Green Crew. It was not a proper party, Tonio grumbled to Flaco: there was no booze and too few women. Flaco told him Wendy McKenna alone was enough woman for half the crew. He also told him to stop carrying an electromagnet in his pocket when he played pool because the others were beginning to puzzle over the startling trajectories some of the balls were taking. Tonio pouted the way he always did when one of his little scams had been found out, but when Flaco saw him later, he was relaxed and smiling and slot-dancing with McKenna.

The music came from the oddest orchestra Flaco had ever heard. There were recordings a-plenty in the databanks; but something in the human heart craved live music, and the High Flying Ziggyphonic Orchestra and Bounce Band was one of a kind. Rhythm came from Mohmat Senkou's djembe and a variety of metal sheets and tubes that Delight Jackson had cut and tuned himself and which he played with a pair of three-quarter wooden dowels. A couple of guys had brought up harmonicas; Wendy McKenna had shipped a piccolo flute; and Gold Crewman Cormac McDermot had himself a tin whistle. There was a concertina, two ocarinas, a pair of maracas, and a jaw harp—anything small enough to stuff into a duffel bag without overmassing had found its way aboard. Other instruments had been fabricated on-site from bits and scraps and odds and ends. Red Hawkins fashioned something he called a didgeridoo out of length of two-inch pipe and a few nozzle fittings; and others had created instruments stringed and blown and struck to which no earthly name could be given.

It was amazing enough to imagine that such a rag-tag could play anything approaching music; it was nothing short of astonishing to hear them play old-time heavy metal.

The older men formed a mosh pit—or whatever you called one of those when it was three-dimensional. A mosh space? They stripped to the waist and clambered along the trellis of stays and hawsers into the center where, as far as Flaco could tell, they spent the next half hour playing rugby. They collided and ricocheted and used the trellis to rebound into the center. When the band switched to goofball, the moshers all shoved fingers down their throats, making gagging sounds, but they vacated the dance stere to the younger crowd with only a minimum of hassle. Flaco neither played nor danced, though he enjoyed music—Delight and some of the other Islanders managed to slip in a little merengue and salsa. The merengue on an ocarina? What would the old men say? But the highlight of the party was little Conchita Ferrer, who danced a *bamba*.

It was like no bamba Flaco had ever seen. A Senegalese *djembe* was not a *bamba* drum and Delight Jackson had no *fua* sticks. And without gravity, the faster steps were not possible. Still, it was an astonishing thing, and soon the men were clapping time and cheering the dancer on as she and the drummers traded rhythmic challenges. Conchita, a robot repair mechanic from Ponce, was a dusky jewel of a Boricuan. She played against the rhythms that Delight and Mohmat gave her, throwing them back at the drummers, making her moves in half-time to the beat because she had to make allowances for the slow grace of weightlessness. She twisted among the guidelines and trellises, bouncing from them like the moshers had done, though with far more grace. She spun and somersaulted and shook her shoulders, controlling her rotations with tucks and extensions of her arms and legs, changing her direction by touching or swinging on a guideline. It was not so much a dance as a strange blend of gymnastics, ballet, ice skating, and swimming. Yet, it worked. Flaco shouted and whistled with the others.

Afterwards, everybody tried to dance—though the results were a great deal less aesthetic. Some of the men formed a conga line and bounced around the cafeteria like a snake. It soon broke up into a string tumbling individuals that Jimmy Schorr likened to the Shoemaker-Levy comet when a dozen or so welders and riggers impacted on Red Hawkins one after the other.

"Yeah," said one of the Gold Crew riggers as Jimmy, Flaco, and their companions turned away from the spectacle to resume their conversation, "but I can't figure out what the hell it's supposed to be. The inside is just a honeycomb of cylindrical cavities. What goes in 'em?"

Jimmy shrugged. "Science experiments. Spy cameras. Environmental sensors. Who cares? Maybe it's a humidor for some honking big cigars. We just build the space; we don't rent it."

Gennady Belislav grunted. "I am not liking it. It is too secret."

"Sure," Jimmy laughed, "not like in Russia."

Belislav shook his head.

"I don't like that, either. My brother, the colonel,

said . . .'' His voice trailed off and he looked away, trading a glance with one of the other Russians.

''What about the connections and circuitry?'' Flaco asked. The others looked at him.

If Gold Crew had a motto, it was WE'RE THE GOLD CREW, AND YOU'RE NOT. They'd been the first up, and a lot of what Flaco had been taught, they had had to work out for themselves. They had lived aboard cramped Planks and a *Salyut* module for months before they got Number Two functioning and could move into more spacious quarters. Blue Crew they regarded as a parent did a promising child, but everyone else was Johnny-Vanka-and-Juanito-come-lately. As a Green Crewman, Flaco was very nearly below their notice—but for Jimmy's sake, they tolerated him.

''On the P&Ws, the module is almost self-contained,'' Belislav said. ''Just a wire harness to be brought inside through a port.''

''I don't like breeching the hull,'' said another man. ''I don't care what they say about the seals. That's just one more microleaker.''

''You mean, the new module does not draw on our power cells?'' Flaco asked and the Russian shook his head.

''Ah, waddaya care about micros? *We* won't be living up here.''

''So the inserts—whatever they are—must contain their own power sources.''

''Just means they have to bring up replacement air more often. Adds to operating cost.''

''*Shto znayet tvoi brat'*, Gennady Kirilovitch?''

A pair of Ukrainians started a cossack dance, doing their strange, squatting kicks in midair. The Westerners and the Latins clapped time for them, but the ''moskaly'' Russians just shook their heads. Two of them nearby traded glances and one held up a forefinger, a gesture the other repeated. Belislav frowned at the exchange and said, ''*Tozhe mnogo uzhe krovoprolitye—*'' The first man shrugged and replied, ''*Zabichai nikogda, ser,*'' again holding up a forefinger.

Flaco figured it was the Russian equivalent of ''yo'

mama!'' because Belislav flushed, twisted away, and kicked off.

The way Flaco reconstructed it afterwards, this is what happened.

Conchita Ferrer was fixing a snail in 4-B, which was under pressure with everyone working shirtsleeve. A conduit-laying robot was malfing, not laying down the molded circuit in its wake—the ''slime trail of the electric snail'' is what the crew called it—and someone hollered for maintenance. Conchita was diagnosing the fault when she noticed that the snail's shell was growing warm and, curious, she placed her hand flat on it.

That was when the microwave welding beam broke through the partition from the other side.

The snail's innards and shell resisted the beam for a fraction of a second and the flesh-and-blood of Conchita's hand not at all. The beam burned a hole through her palm and out the back, cauterizing it and numbing it at the same time.

Flaco was forward in Number Five, which was still unpressurized, when he heard the uproar on the all-suit channel. The men around him began lowering their tools and looking around. A few, including Flaco, had the presence of mind to check for structural pieces in motion before allowing themselves to be distracted. Jimmy Schorr, the rigging leadman, listened on the management channel for a moment, then beckoned.

''Hey, Flaco, we got a problem. They need you back in Four-B.''

''What's happening, 'mano?'' Flaco fastened down his work and squirted his way aft toward the manlock that led into Four without waiting for an answer.

''They're beating the living shit out of that buddy of yours, Portales.''

The airlock seemed to take forever to cycle. Flaco pushed through the inner door before it had opened fully. At first, he was confused because the bay was empty; but then he remembered that Jimmy had said B, so Flaco flexed off on the lock door and sailed through the unfinished space to the bull's-eye that led aft. He didn't bother unfastening his helmet; there was no time.

A brawl in weightlessness is an utter chaos. Every swing, every kick, sends both parties caroming off bulkheads, equipment, other brawlers. Men grappled up, down, and sideways. One man, having missed on a roundhouse right, was spinning like a top. It was impossible to tell who was on what side—or even if there were sides.

But Flaco had seen street fights before and his eye picked out the action. Three groups, he saw. The largest by far was trying to get a piece of Tonio, who danced nimbly from point to point, dodging his attackers or fending them off. A second group were defending him, or at least trying to keep his attackers away. Sepp and Tiny were with them. The third group was trying to separate the first two.

For the moment, Flaco was the only one in a power suit, which meant he was armored against any blows and had mobility the others lacked. His compressed air jets gave him speed and momentum. He opened a channel to Jimmy. "It's a mess back here. We need the cops."

He took aim and launched himself at Tonio, plowing through the crowd, bumping people aside. His path wobbled from the impacts but he corrected and came at his friend. He was not yet as expert in suithandling as the more senior hands, but there was an Artificial Stupid that took care of the details.

The Cuban didn't recognize him and tried to bounce out of the way, but Flaco grabbed him in a bear hug and continued through the crowd and out the other side. He could hear the shouts—feel them, actually, through the vibration of his helmet visor. Inchoate sounds, from which he could make out no words. Flaco saw a space between two partitions—destined someday to be a locker or a storage bin. He changed his suit vector and went straight into it.

There was no time for any fancy flip-over-and-brake maneuver. The impact jarred him and must have knocked the wind out of Tonio, because the man went limp. Flaco seized the edge of the partition and turned himself around, making himself a door between Tonio and the angry mob.

Bird Winfrey was the first man to smash into him and Flaco wished fleetingly that he had the build of that football player-turned-scientist, Dr. Hobart. Somebody realized that pushing Flaco wouldn't work—just make a tighter cork to protect Tonio—so they went to pull. Men flailed at him, grabbed his arms. Flaco kept his hold and they only succeeded in pulling themselves in, rather than Flaco out.

And then the manlock to Number Three popped open and DeWitt Christensen entered with half a dozen gang bosses and leads at the same time that Jimmy Schorr led five more suited riggers back from Five.

There was Hell to pay, and Hell levied tax, besides.

Christensen had to admit that Flaco had done the right thing. So had Red Hawkins and a few others who had tried to break things up. But he also had to admit that the situation was nasty. Conchita Ferrer was in bad shape. In shock, dosed with pain killers and seditives. She was due to go down on one of the escape pods, a new-model *Soyuz* capsule. No one had studied how weightless conditions might affect surgery, and no one was inclined to lift a doctor to do the experiment.

Tonio Portales was in much better shape, though you wouldn't know it to look at him. His lip was split wide open and both his eyes were black. There were cuts on his cheek and bruises on his chest and back. He was conscious, but looked like he wished he wasn't.

Christensen ought to have had a desk to sit behind and look severe from. And a carpet to call people in on. But that wouldn't work here, and to some extent *dignidad* suffered. The project manager had a chair—one of the pilot couches salvaged from the *Glenn Curtis* after that ship's unauthorized visit to the moon. But Christensen had the disconcerting habit of drifting out of the seat.

"All right, Taras," he told the welding boss. "I'll grant you that Ferrer should not have been behind a panel when welding was taking place on the other side. That was her negligence and her compensation will be proportionately reduced.''

Bird Winfrey and Tiny Littlebear, both of whom had been present when the accident happened, voiced a protest, but Christensen held up a hand. "Negligence has its price. What good are safety rules if people learn they can violate them and not pay a penalty?"

"I would say," said Littlebear, "that having a hole drilled through your hand is penalty enough."

Christensen winced. "Yes. I know she was popular—astonishingly so for a woman who insisted on her chastity. Or maybe not so astonishing. What we obtain too cheaply we esteem too lightly—and Adrian tells me that she was his second-best mechanic. But how does that translate into an obligation on others to pay for injuries she brought in part on herself? Never mind. The accident wasn't wholly her fault. Yes, Taras, I know you want to defend your welder; but the fact is, he was supposed to be welding, *not* cutting. So I want to know. Was he given incorrect instructions, or did he fail to follow them?"

Kutuzov looked around the control room. At Tonio; at Tiny and Bird and the other witnesses; at the mechanics boss, Adrian Whitlauer; at Flaco. He cleared his throat. "The work order was to weld," he admitted. Christensen did not smile.

"Don't look so glum, Taras. That lets you and Uncle Waldo off the hook, at least."

Kutuzov grimaced. "I was not worried about myself. A young woman has been maimed and a young man must live with it. I would rather it had been an error in the printout."

"Then O&P would be at fault, and O&P had deep pockets, right? Never mind. I'm not interested in who pays. I'm not a lawyer. I'm interested in *how the damn hell it happened;* so I can make it not happen ever again! You! Portales! Why did you cut through the partition?"

Tonio licked his lips and looked from face to face, searching for allies. Flaco did not see much sympathy for him in the room—Sepp, Tiny, and Kutuzov. Mostly hostility—and just a touch of triumph in Bird's face. From Christensen, Flaco saw only impatience.

"Well," said Tonio. "I did'n' know I was cutting until it was too late. You know how everything is under a clamshell, right? So you can't really see what you're doing, except through the viewport. And then what you see is mostly sparks. And you know how the UHT trigger has these two positions—halfway for weld, all the way for cut? Well, tha's dangerous, man! Usually, you can tell by feel, but sometimes not; an' this time . . ." Tonio covered his face with his hands. "This time . . . Oh, *mierda*!"

Flaco reached out and laid his hand on Tonio's shoulder, but the Cuban shrugged it off.

Christensen folded his hands as if praying and tucked them under his lip. "Waldo?"

"Yeah, boss?" The voice came from a grill over the manager's console after the usual delay.

"Have there been any other accidents involving trigger positions on the welders' UHT?"

"Half a sec." There was a pause, long enough to take several breaths, not long enough to look Tonio in the eye. "Here we go. Corrective Action Log shows three other instances. One of them was 'weld instead of cut,' but it was the same mechanism. No irreparable damage in any of the priors. Corrective action in all three instances was 'refresher training in trigger feel.' "

Christensen groaned. "I don't even want to know if any of those were on my watch."

"None of them escalated high enough to get your attention," Waldo said. "Or Wesley Bensalem or Tiny Larsen."

"That's great comfort. Tell Señorita Ferrer."

"I got more," Uncle Waldo volunteered and, grim-faced, Christensen said go ahead. "This failure mode was identified during Process FMEA and given a double-H. High probability of occurring and high potential impact."

"And nothing was done?"

"The Universal Hand Tool was Ukranian design. I'd

guess there was some politics behind it. Somebody signed off on the design in exchange for Russian and Ukranian participation.''

"Oh, just great." Christensen fell silent and scowled at a space a foot in front of him. Flaco and the others waited. It was like most accidents, Flaco decided. It was no one thing that made it happen. It was a design that had a potential for error—and what design did not? And it was a momentary lapse of care on the one part and a neglect of the safety rules on the other. Flaco felt sorry for Tonio, twice as sorry for Conchita.

Finally, Christensen unfolded his hands. "Waldo? I want the trigger redesigned. Either a two-trigger arrangement, or have the positions notched, or have indicator lights showing status. I don't care how; I care what. That's why we feed engineers. I won't take any more units with the old design, and I want the old units retrofitted ASAP. Run this past Bensalem and the other crew chiefs, too, before sending it to Ham. Got that?''

Waldo acknowledged and the project manager turned his attention to the people surrounding him. "Taras, you know what to do with your welders. We can't stop work while we wait for new units. I want your leads to double-check everybody on their turn.''

"You want me to take my best men off a gun and have them babysit.''

"Just do it. It's only a patch until we get new units. Adrian, you and the other supervisors, I want you to pound safety into everyone's pointy little head. Show 'em the pictures of her hand if you think that will make an impression. I don't want pussyfooting—hell, being too hesitant can cause accidents, too—but I want diligence and attentiveness. *Be aware,* people! Okay, that's it.''

Bird Winfrey pointed at Tonio. "What about him?''

"Are you the new PM, Winfrey? No? Then that's not your problem. Mercado, wait here. Portales, wait outside.''

Flaco didn't know why the site boss wanted to see him and he ran over the whole incident in his mind, trying to decide if he had screwed up somewhere. When he was alone with Christensen, the boss ran a hand through his sparse, straw hair and sighed. "You always know something will happen," he said. "I've never been on a job yet where no accidents went down. You? No, I didn't think so. You just hope they're minor. You hope you get through them. Mercado, you did okay, today. You showed initiative and you showed intelligence. That's an unbeatable combination, because either one without the other is shit. You understand me? We'll be keeping an eye on you. A little more seasoning and, who knows?"

Flaco swallowed. He bobbed his head. "Thanks."

"Oh, don't thank me. You ever get to be a boss in *this* organization, you'll have plenty of opportunity to cuss my ghost. Because there won't be a day goes by you don't worry over the men and women you lead. You think your partner is upset? Imagine Taras or the crew lead thinking *now* of all the things they could have done *then* to prevent what happened. You can go. Think about what I said. And send Portales in on your way out."

As project manager, Christensen had the luxury of a private office, but there was no wall or bulkhead insulated enough to block the sound of a royal ass-chewing. Flaco waited outside and tried not to listen to the blistering. As far as Flaco could tell, the project manager used no obscenities, but just the tone of voice made Flaco want to cringe. When Tonio emerged, he was white as a sheet. He gave Flaco a sickly grin.

"He says I am to be more careful in the future."

Flaco let the understatement go. "He's not sending you down?"

"No. There is no point. There are no bumboats scheduled until May, when our rotation will be up. I am not worth the cost"—Tonio stopped, and looked away—"not worth the cost of a special lift."

Flaco took him by the upper arm. "Tonio," he said, "one thing I must know. Have you been 'brushing your teeth' too much?"

The Cuban held a hand up, palm out. "No, Flaco, I swear on my mother. I have never used it before reporting for work."

Flaco followed him aft toward Number Two—and who knew what sort of reception from his mates? He wondered if Tonio had told him the truth about not using the pearl. Granted, the UHT's design was weak, yet it was just the sort of accident a pearler might have. The *carefree* attitude that the pearl induced led always to a *careless* one. If not this time, then the next.

Under pearl, a man forgot his cares for a time, but their return as the drug wore off was more keenly felt. The answer was always more pearl, more often. Tonio was slipping down a steep slope. Flaco knew he should do something, but what? He *owed* Tonio. Tonio had saved him from the runaway beam. Now he had to save Tonio. Pearl was not so sudden and direct a threat as the beam had been. Pearl killed slowly; it killed "carelessly." But in the end you were still dead. He would try again to talk with Tonio.

Flaco kneaded his forehead. Sometimes he wished Tonio had not saved his life. It would have made everything so much easier. What sort of price would the friendship someday extract from him? What sort of man must he become to pay it?

INTERLUDE:

Going Down That Road Feelin' Bad, Lord, Lord

It was an odd sort of garden that Forrest tended, and the plants that sprouted in it were strange and wonderful things. Tall and wispy and thin as ballerinas, undeterred by anything so mundane as gravity, the plants basked under a bank of sun-simulating lamps in a zeolite soil of time-release capsules: Mustard plants and spider plants—and tomato plants yielding the most outrageous fruit Forrest had ever seen. Like horses or dogs, some of the plants were for work and some were for show. The working plants helped the scrubbers remove carbon dioxide from the air or provided the occasional fresh fruit or veggie for the weary spaceman's diet. It was a meager harvest, but it fed the soul as much as it did the body. The "show" plants were there because the folks back in the rubber room wanted to know how they would flourish in weightlessness. After all, Mir, LEO, and the other habitats planned for Low Earth Orbit would eventually have to feed themselves. Frontiers were settled by farmers, not by explorers.

"Upload complete, boys," said the sultry A/S. Krasnarov, at the nearby chess board, growled and set a piece down with greater force than needed. Forrest spoke for the audio pickups.

"Intercom. On. Nacho, old buddy, anything interesting or amusing in this week's mail?"

"Just scrolling the index, friend," the loudspeaker announced. Nacho was sitting watch back in *Bullard*. "Let's see . . . We have a newspaper. Another newspaper. Software patch from Technical for that malf in the Number Three PVA positioning motor. Ah, my geological journal! A magazine. Upgrades on the lock cycle and 'fresher control programs. A message from Ned DuBois. Um, it says, 'Punxsutawney Phil saw his shadow,' whatever that means."

Forrest made a theatrical groan. "Six more weeks of winter. I thought it looked mighty punk outside." Nacho whooped and Forrest raised his eyebrows. "You like winter, son?"

"No, No. But I have the confirmation from the Earth of that analysis I sent them. I was right. It was amino acids."

"Good for you." Forrest had gone through all the predeparture briefings on asteroids and meteors; so he knew it was not unheard of to find organic chemicals—including amino acids—in meteors. In fact, some folks said how the "building blocks of life" had been created first in outer space and then dropped into Earth's chemical "soup" by meteor bombardment. That struck Forrest as a helluva way to run an airline, but the Almighty hadn't tapped him for the design review team.

"Two of the acids are not among those used by Earthly life. Do you know what that could mean?"

Forrest raised an eye to Krasnarov, who remained hunched over the chessboard as if he had not heard. "Could mean a lot of things, I guess," he said.

"They could be a biological spoor of the Visitors."

"Might be; might not. There are thousands of amino acids, even on Earth, that nobody uses." Again, it seemed oddly inefficient; and he wondered for a moment whether you could construct a viable life-form using those "extra" amino acids. How would a critter like that fit into the ol' food chain? Nacho agreed, reluctantly, and signed off the intercom. Forrest turned to Krasnarov. "You didn't say anything."

Krasnarov's hand hovered over a white bishop, hesitated, swooped on a knight and shifted it. Then he turned the board around and faced the other side. He looked up at Forrest only for a moment. "Why bother?" he asked.

"I only asked . . ."

"Let him dream." Krasnarov advanced a red pawn, threatening White Queen. He grunted, as if the move had taken him by surprise, and turned the board around again. Forrest shook his head.

"I still think we ought to tell him about the footprints."

"I never saw them."

Forrest pressed his lips together. "Have it your way."

Krasnarov looked up from the game. "If I can live with knowledge, he can live with hope." The Russian cupped his chin in both hands and contemplated the board.

A month and a half had passed since Krasnarov had blurted out his confession. Forrest had encrypted a personal report to van Huyten, laying out the situation as straight as he could; but so far there had been no reply beyond a terse acknowledgment of receipt on the bounceback. A news release by Deep Space on the "remote possibility of alien visitors" had been greeted in equal parts by ridicule, skepticism, speculation, and blind acceptance. The typical mix of human responses. How long would it be, Forrest wondered, before some "prophet" translated the inscriptions and started a new religion? Not long, he decided. The human capacity for self-delusion was unlimited.

Forrest sighed and returned his attention to the garden. He noted the pH level of the zeolite pseudo-soil in tray 27. Then he took a handful of dwarf wheat and stuck a ruler behind it to measure its growth. He entered the data in the system. Funny. He had never imagined that mankind's first encounter with alien life would involve evidence eons old, or that the only certainty would be deliberately wiped out. He wondered if Krasnarov was right, and that it was better to live in ignorance, imagining yourself in the lead, than it was to live with the knowledge that you were millennia behind.

Well, it was like Len Chandler had sung, back in the '60s. That funky old folk-bluesman had sung a lot of truth, from "Keep on Keepin' On" to "Feet-first Baby," but one stanza, which Forrest had forgotten until coming across the file in the μCD library had brought finally into focus the nagging, formless confusion that bothered him ever since they had left the Rock. It was a paraphrase of Ella Wilcox's "Winds of Fate":

> *One ship sails east; another sails west.*
> *While the very same breezes blow.*
> *It's the set of the sail and not the gale*
> *That bids us where to go.*

And so, too, the asteroid had blown the three of them in very different directions. They could see and smell and hear and taste and touch the same reality, yet in the end sail entirely different courses. Forrest had posted the quote on the console above the reclaim monitor. Krasnarov and Mendes had both read it, but he didn't think either one had recognized in it their own situation.

The crisis came unannounced, as crises always did. Forrest, relaxing in *Bullard*'s command chair on the second watch, was mounting an armored assault on a citadel holding the key to the enemy's heartland when the monkey gibbered and shrieked like a whole troop of baboons. Forrest came suddenly alert and slapped the alarm cutoff, blanked the game board without saving it, and called up the diagnostics.

Step One: Identify the problem. His eyes danced around the dials—permanent dials in the console; special-purpose "virtual dials" displayed on the monitors by the A/S. "Locator malfunction. Number three photovoltaic array positioning motor," said the Voice. "Overload. Malfunction in receiver dish. Connection with Earth broken. Attempting to reestablish link . . . Connection with Earth still broken."

"Damn." Forrest thought briskly. First things first. *Step Two: Make it stop.* According to the 3-D sim, the PV array was trying to imitate a pretzel—something neither God nor man ever intended. Forrest punched the power cutoff and the sim froze into a blinking icon.

Forrest paused and took a breath. Okay, he thought. *Analyze the situation*. Problems had three features: urgency, impact, and trend. What was the size and shape of this particular monkey?

First question: Urgency? Did anything need doing *now?* Shutting down the PVA had left them without external power or communications—but Forrest didn't feel very talkative at the moment, and the power handoff to the fuel cells had kicked in automatically, so the urgency was not immediate. He began to relax, but only a little.

Second question: Impact? When you stepped in it, you always wanted to know how much you had on your shoe. What were the consequences of the failure? Power link first; then the receiver dish. A part of Forrest's mind marveled, even as he called up the information. This scenario wasn't one they'd simmed in training; yet, somehow, he knew exactly what to do. You couldn't rehearse every problem, but you could rehearse problem solving. "Failure modes and effect analysis," he ordered. "System: *Power reception.* Subsystem: *PVA positioning motor.* Failure mode: *Will not locate.* Perform."

"Analyzing, lover-boy." Lights twinkled. "Clarification. Intermittent fault or complete failure."

A glance at the last readout from the PVA was all he needed. "Complete."

"Analyzing . . ."

A FMEA layout appeared on a side monitor, with "PVA positioning motor failure—complete" in the topic box. Effects began to appear at microsecond intervals and Forrest read the line items as they scrolled up. The design engineers had traced the consequences of every conceivable failure (and of more than a few that weren't) and assigned each one a neat little probability. According to the diagnostic readouts, a four-hundred-dollar relay had given up its life to save a five-penny fuse. Forrest shook his head. Good ol'

Murphy always came through, didn't he? The FMEA had assigned that line item a low prob, so there was no work-around in the troubleshooting manual—and wasn't that the way it always happened. With the positioning motor screwed up, they couldn't plug into the Sun or Helios. So whatever was in the fuel cells now was *it* for the duration—a shade over three more months.

That was at the high end of the performance range, considering onboard power usage; but well within the envelope. *As long as we don't run the batteries down.* There had been stretches during the voyage when Helios had been too weak to replenish the cells, but up to now they had always had the Sun available—a kilowatt and a half per square meter, twenty-four hours a day. More than enough to run the ship *and* decompose the water from the fuel cells back into hydrogen and oxygen for another go-round. The sun was an electrical socket the size of a dime powered by a utility that never shut down.

Third question: Trend? Forrest studied projections over the next three months and slowly, slowly, ice began to form in his stomach.

"How bad is it?"

Forrest jumped at the question. He looked down and saw Nacho in the tunnel opening. "Bad enough," he said.

The Brazilian nodded grimly. "The monkey chattered all over the ship. I figured that was the general alarm."

"Where's Mike?"

"Sleeping. I don't think the alert woke him."

"Get him."

Nacho disappeared and Forrest turned back to the readouts.

Three months was well within the range of the fuel cells, *if* they were fully charged to begin with. But two of them were halfway down their cycle and none of the others were topped off. The wobble in the PVA positioning motor that had pestered them for a few weeks had reduced the amount of sunpower harvested, resulting in greater drain and slower replenishment during the Long Orbit. At current usage, there was only enough onboard power for two months and twenty-nine days. Systems would start to shut down with two weeks still to go before docking at LEO.

Two weeks was not long compared to a year's voyage; but it was damn-all too far without light, heat, or air. Forrest wasn't afraid of the dark, and he could bundle up warm when he had to; but he didn't think he could hold his breath that long.

Step Three: Interim action. Could they work a patch in the meantime? Maybe repair the positioning motor and restore the shorted-out circuits. They carried some spare parts, and materials and drawings to fab others. Forrest noted that as a possibility. *Have to inspect the damaged array and see what's shaking.* There was plenty of slush hydrogen and LOX in the fuel tanks. Could they jerry-rig a fuel cell out of that? A honking big fuel cell, the size of a ship. But they'd need that fuel to get into Clarke Orbit when they reached Earth. Otherwise, they'd skip off the upper atmosphere like a stone tossed across a pond.

They couldn't even tap Earthside experts to brainstorm a workaround. When the main array went down, the cascade had blown their comm link, too.

"Fault tree," he ordered the A/S. "Develop."

Another screen cleared and Forrest glared at the diagram that came up from the ship's library, daring it to make the bad news worse. The designers had chased down the possible roots of every failure. Engineers could be a royal pain, but sometimes they paid their freight.

The fault tree developed on two major branches. Hardware malfunction. Software malfunction. *Scratch the software malf. We installed the patch on that last week.*

Or did we?

Deep Space had ascribed the PVA wobble to a mechanical glitch. The software patch had been intended to work around it and avoid the need for EVA. Working with sudden intuition, Forrest's fingers danced on the armrest keypad, calling up the ship's log.

He ran the log back to Groundhog Day. Nacho had received the patch in the upload and flagged it next watch for the engineer's attention. But on Mike's watch . . .

Nothing. No installation.

And nothing since then, either. Without the workaround, the original mechanical problem had grown worse, eventually triggering the final failure. Forrest smacked the console with the flat of his hand. He composed a macro on the armrest keypad and sent it to fetch the array's virtual "black box," which kept a seventy-two-hour running data log.

Nacho reemerged from the passageway with Krasnarov in tow.

And Forrest turned on him. "You goddamned son of a bitch!"

Krasnarov turned a dark red. He turned to the panels. "What have you done now?" he demanded.

"It ain't me, good buddy. Drag your carcass over here and check it out." The copilot pulled himself into the second chair, gave Forrest a brief scowl, and studied the data Forrest had laid out. Slowly, his color darkened further and his fists clenched into balls.

"Not possible," he said, so softly Forrest wasn't sure he was meant to hear.

"Looks like ol' Senhor Machine finally missed a stroke," Forrest observed and Krasnarov turned an ugly glare on him.

"Is this another of your little jokes, Calhoun?"

"Some things even I don't find very funny."

Krasnarov stiffened. "Leave the cabin," he ordered through clenched teeth.

Forrest looked at his sleeves. "Say, did I forget to wear the T-shirt with the four stripes?"

"Leave!" Then, more urgently, "Quickly."

Forrest gave him a funny look, then shrugged. "Let's go, Nacho. See what we can power down in *Salyut,* just in case." He unseated and hovered by the tunnel entrance until the geologist had left. Krasnarov did not move so much as a jaw muscle, but remained fixated on the panel readouts. Forrest opened his mouth. "Mike . . ."

"Go."

Forrest ducked into the transfer tunnel. Nacho was waiting at the far end. His face was all a knot.

"He grew careless," Nacho said with a snarl in his voice.

Forrest could feel the souress in his belly. The crunch was a long ways off, but a man can spot the sidewalk as he falls past the eighty-ninth floor, for all the good it did. "Yeah. But you and me, we just assumed he done his job. I shouldn't have ragged on him just now. I even talked to him about his slacking off, and then *I never checked up on him*. It's my fault, too, damn it."

"No, it was his fault, not yours."

Forrest smacked a fist into an open palm. "Yeah. Well, maybe I just figured out what it means to be the captain. Come on. Let's see what we can do without, if push comes to shove." Though, there wasn't a kilo on board that hadn't been justified; and if push ever did come to shove, no way could they get out and push or shove the ship any faster. . . .

"You shouldn't have left him back there alone."

Forrest shook his head. "Call it a command decision."

They had gotten halfway through the checklist of *Salyut* subsystems, marking them priority one, two, and three, when Krasnarov called from *Bullard.* "Captain to the bridge, please."

Forrest looked up at the call. He handed Nacho the cliputer. "Here, finish the inventory."

"Should I come with—"

"I'll call you." Forrest kicked off and returned to *Bullard*'s command deck, where he found Krasnarov still snapped into the copilot's seat. He would not look directly at Forrest.

"I have uploaded and installed the software patch, but have still not achieved function," he announced. "I suspect the mechanical malf that the patch was supposed to correct has now caused further hardware damage on the array itself. There may be bent or twisted struts. And an electrical short, since some sensors and controls on that circuit are also out or functioning below nominal."

"It's not a crime, you know," Forrest said.

Krasnarov paused, face hung low in front of the screens. "What is not?"

"To cry."

Krasnarov faced him and Forrest saw that the Iron Mike was in critical danger of rusting around the optical input devices. "Crying is for weaklings," the Russian said. Forrest couldn't tell if he was stating a conviction of his own or repeating an admonition from childhood.

"I guess it is," said Forrest, "but that don't mean the rest of us can't indulge ourselves, too. It's just a question of how often—and over what."

Krasnarov shook his head. "What do you know?"

"I cried like a little kid when my pa died." Of course, he'd only *been* a kid at the time, but why complicate the discussion? "Look, you let your depression get the best of you. You blew off a few jobs. Anyone can make a mistake."

"But not anyone should."

"Jesus, you live in a hard world."

"Yes. One where mistakes can kill."

"Can't argue with you there, Mike. Which brings me to the next topic. You're our engineer. You know this ship inside out. Is there anything we can do?"

"Other than cry over our mistakes?" Krasnarov shook his head. "I don't know." Unbuckling his harness, he floated free. "I must inspect the damage."

"No doid view or diagnostics available?"

Krasnarov looked at him. "I must see for myself what I have done."

As he turned away, Forrest blurted, "Your father must have been one strict, unforgiving son of a bitch."

Krasnarov stopped and turned and gave him a thin, spitless smile. He laughed, once. "In actual fact, Alexei Fyodorvitch was hopelessly disorganized and never planned one minute beyond the present. He explored for LukOil, so he was gone sometimes for weeks. When he was returning, his paycheck is already spent in Siberian boom towns. Not on drink or women or gambling but squandered on small impulses and trivial presents for my sisters and me. When he was making mistakes, he would apologize over and over. It would be then that he was drinking cheap vodka and weeping over an unappreciative world.'' The smile melted like hoarfrost. ''I have his face. Nothing else.'' He turned and passed through the manlock into the ward room.

Forrest watched after him. ''Nothing else,'' he murmured. ''Not even a trivial, worthless present . . .''

It took two hours to get Mike outside. The ship had been returned to normal pressure and nitrogen, so he had to prebreathe to purge the N_2 before suiting up and reducing pressure. Since the regs said that someone else had to be on standby, Forrest decompressed right along with him. Someday, someone would have to go EVA in a hurry, get the bends, and die. Or someone would come up with a space suit that could flex easily even while pressured up to Earthnormal. Or they'd fly the whole mission with a low-pressure, pure-oxy atmosphere.

When Mike was finally ready and all the seals had been double-checked, Forrest grabbed him suddenly by the arm. A half-forgotten dream, weirdly reversed, flashed before his eyes.

''You are planning to come back in again, aren't you?''

Krasnarov just looked at him and pried the hand from his sleeve.

''How's he doing?'' Forrest asked Nacho. The suits were good for EVAsions of up to seven hours, and there was no way this particular task should take near that long; but it wasn't the spec limits on the equipment that had Forrest worried. He was all duded up himself, except for gloves and being plugged into the ship's power, ready to EVAde if anything went down outside. Yet if Mike planned on taking the Long Walk, there was no way Forrest would ever catch him. Cold equations. A man on a one-way trip could spend his SPU's compressed gas a lot more profligately than a man contemplating a return leg.

The geologist looked away from the screens. "He's retrieved the tool kit from the outside locker and has moved around to the PVA. It's hard to see what he is doing. The closest doid view is from seven meters. Everything closer burned out when the positioning motor shorted. It looks like he's just standing there, staring at the equipment."

Krasnarov spoke over the radio. "I have called up the drawing on my visor screen and magnified them to actual size. If I superimpose the drawing over the actual subassemblies, I can detect physical damage more easily. Calhoun?"

"Yassuh." Forrest was evidently an engineering assistant now. "What do you need?" Everytime he spoke he had to take the prebreathing tube out. He felt like he was smoking a waterpipe.

"Run electrical system diagnostic. The recorders have sufficient short-term memory to cover the time of the malf. See if you can discover the failure origin." Forrest glanced at Nacho.

"That PVA black box I asked for up yet?" *Step Four: Diagnose the Cause.*

Nacho checked the active files and nodded. "I'll put her on screen G."

Forrest kicked over to the designated screen, which was "heads up" between the forward viewports and the "sunroof" viewports. He anchored himself by gripping the back of the copilot's seat with both hands. "Take it back to just before the failure and run it on slow-mo."

A sim of the PVA appeared on the screen, flanked by data boxes listing XYZ position, array angle, signal strength, time, and other stats. As the digital clock scrolled, the sim shifted and fidgeted. Forrest stared as if the force of his eyeballs could make the puppy behave.

"I have identified damaged components," he heard Krasnarov's voice announce. "Downloading part numbers into engineer's log."

The PVA sim suddenly jerked to one side, then returned

gradually to nominal. Forrest scowled. *What the hell?* It looked as if the jerk had taken place in zero time, which was not possible. While he pondered the problem, it happened again, then twice more.

"Hey, Nach', run it back a couple of deltas and come forward one delta at a time." The geologist nodded and the screen blinked and restored.

Each delta-T increment was only a microsecond, the intervals at which sensor data had been logged for possible later analysis. The screen blinked and Forrest noticed that the signal strength on the array had dropped. There was no corresponding change in either X, Y, or Z, which was damn peculiar. The signal strength continued to drop across the next couple of increments—still without any apparent change in the array's position. Then, over the very next interval, the array jerked to a new position. He had Nacho run the sim back and forth until he was satisfied. That much traverse in one microsecond? Gross mechanical parts just weren't that fast.

The other instances, studied one by one, were similar. A slowly weakening signal without any change in the array position, followed by an instantaneous position change in the X-coordinate. After that, normal recovery of signal and position. All except on the final event, when all the readouts suddenly went to nines and the screen blacked. The last frame showed complete signal loss.

Forrest scowled and rested his chin on the back of the copilot's headrest, contemplating what he had seen.

"What is it?" Nacho asked.

"Not sure. When do two wrongs make a right?"

"Please?"

"What do two impossibles add up to?" Loss of signal without position change plus instantaneous position change equaled . . . What? Forrest closed his eyes and imagined that he *was* the PVA. *I'm looking at the Sun. How do I lose signal without turning my head?* Sun growing weaker? Eyes film over? Problem with the transducer or the amplifier? *No, that wouldn't account for the weird position changes.* Space dust coating the cells? PV degradation? *No, I recovered my sight each time but the last.* Mentally, he tried to turn his head without turning his head.

It wouldn't work, unless he had two heads.

"That's it!" he shouted.

Nacho said, "What?"

"Whoever said 'two heads are better than one' didn't know shit."

"I don't understand."

"Look here." Forrest pulled himself down into Krasnarov's seat and played with the keypad, replaying the sim. "See how the signal gets weaker, even though the array isn't moving?" The Brazilian nodded slowly. "Well, that was because it grew a second head, a virtual array, so to speak. The real array, the mechanism, *was* moving—that wobble we were seeing earlier—but at some point, the position sensor developed an intermittent malf, so it didn't detect the wobble. Far as the sensors knew, the array was straight arrow. The command-and-control A/S *didn't know* the array had wobbled off target, but it was detecting a weaker signal; so . . ."

"It boosted the amplifier to compensate," Nacho guessed.

"That's a big ten-four, good buddy. Then when the sensor kicked in again, the "ghost" vanished and the A/S suddenly noticed that its head was cocked. It brought everything back on target and reduced the gain. Well, that wobble was getting progressively worse, and the last one put the array completely off the Sun. The signal dropped to zero, but the A/S was convinced it was still looking at the Sun and boosted sensitivity to the max, trying to pick up the signal. The sensor kicked in again, the array corrected position, and—bango—direct sunlight at maximum amplification. Overload. After that, the array went totally spazz."

"Krasnarov thinks that if he repairs the structural members it will restore performance."

Forrest shook his head. "Not with the position sensor malfing. We'll need a new sensor, probably some other electronics. . . . Check the inventory. See what we have on board. If we're lucky, we can plug-and-replace with spares, or maybe fab something out of components.''

Nacho hesitated a moment before asking, ''And if we're not lucky?''

Forrest did not answer and, after another moment, Nacho turned away to do as he'd been told.

Krasnarov cycled inside two hours later. He carried a bent strut with him, which he lobbed to Forrest. It coasted across the cabin, spinning like an ice dancer, and Forrest snatched it when it reached him. He glanced at the bent metal, then at Krasnarov.

''What am I looking at?''

The Russian broke the seal on his helmet and lifted it off his head. His face was flushed and a sheen of sweat coated his broad forehead. He unfastened the straps of the Snoopy cap. ''Micrometeor strikes,'' he said with a nod toward the strut. ''I counted at least a score of them in the vicinity of the array.''

Forrest found the small blemish near one end of the strut: a tiny crater, no greater than a zit. Krasnarov must have eyes like a hawk to have found it. ''Damage?''

Krasnarov mopped his forehead with a kerchief. ''Mostly cosmetic,'' Krasnarov said. ''A load of 'birdshot' seems to have glanced off our hull. These orbits are dirty. Gravel-sized debris, knocked loose from 1991JW and nudged by the passing of the Earth. Some of the photocells on the array are damaged, but not enough to impair efficiency. One strike, however, seems to have damaged the X-axis position sensor.''

Forrest rubbed his cheek. ''Come over here and look at this.'' Krasnarov swam over and Forrest reran the PVA black box sims for him. The engineer grunted softly at the first ''impossible event,'' and pursed his lips intently as the others followed.

''Yes, I see,'' he said at the end. ''The wobble in the motor was amplified by the sensor failure.''

"You know what that means, good buddy?"

Krasnarov shrugged.

"It means it wasn't your fault. The software patch wouldn't have fixed this anyway."

The look Krasnarov gave him was honestly puzzled. "Why would you think that matters?"

The rest was only hard work. They replaced wiring and circuitry when they had spare parts; worked around when they didn't. Forrest and Krasnarov took turns doing repairs EVA while Nacho fabbed structural members to replace those bent by the PVA's uncontrolled oscillations. Nacho became a fair-to-middling machinist in a very short time, but there is nothing like a death sentence to focus the mind. The position sensor was irreplaceable, but they could rig the array for manual targeting. Not good enough to hold the microwave beam from Helios, but good enough to hold the Sun. If they could keep the array running long enough to recharge the depleted fuel cells, they would have enough onboard battery power to reach Earth still breathing.

There was collateral damage, too. The overload had fried the comm, a control computer, and a μ CD-ROM. But Forrest postponed worry over communications until the power situation was in hand. Silence, they could survive.

It was an oddly protracted emergency. With two months' reserve in the power cells, there was time to consider things; and you couldn't live forever balanced on the knife edge of urgency. Forrest trimmed the duty list to the bare essentials: life support and the like, but the crisis did not mean that other duties could be ignored. It seemed strange to tend the air filters when death lurked in the background. Yet, the routine served another purpose by injecting a note of normalcy into their day.

Through it all, Nacho worked with furious concern and Forrest with grim determination. Half a dozen times the Brazilian asked how it was going and half a dozen times Forrest told him things were looking up. After a while, Nacho figured it out and stopped asking.

Krasnarov, with the lion's share of the work, performed with stoic fatalism. Forrest never found an error in the Russian's work—and he did check—but he never found evidence that the Russian cared whether they succeeded or not. The only thing that seemed to matter to him was that, having made a serious error, he would make no more. He spent his off-hours in his sleeping bag staring at nothing, or at the chess table, where he pursued endless, elaborate problems.

The background noise of hums and beeps and clicks were subdued, almost subliminal. Krasnarov's chessmen made sharp taps as he moved them around. It was important to relax, Forrest knew. Tension and impatience could kill through haste. It was an injunction he had had to enforce on Nacho several times. Yet, Krasnarov's nonchalance seemed almost too natural.

"We couldn't pull this off without you," Forrest told him.

Krasnarov made no reply. The Red Knight dodged a White Rook.

"I mean, I know a spot of engineering, but I could never have worked out that business with the control logics."

White Rook chased Red Knight. The board swiveled again. Krasnarov was in his end-game. Each side had only one piece to guard its King.

"It would take me twice as long to do the structural repairs. I don't think Nacho is up to that sort of EVA work."

The Red Knight dodged the White Rook again. Forrest frowned. After a few more moves he saw that Krasnarov was stalemated, repeating the same sequence of moves over and over. "If one of you doesn't give in soon, you'll just keep going 'round and 'round."

Krasnarov's smile was just this side of manic. "Yes," he said. "But which one?"

When the day came that they powered up the array, Krasnarov did not even come to the control deck to watch. His absence bothered Forrest in a way that he could not quite define, but he could not let it distract him from the business at hand. He went through the checklist with Nacho, verifying each circuit and function. Nacho's hand shook as he scrolled down the list on the copilot's screen. His voice quavered as he called out items. Forrest wanted to tell him not to worry, but how could you enforce an order like that?

"What if it doesn't work?" Nacho asked suddenly.

Forrest ran his finger across the track-pad in the armrest and moved the cursor over the activation "button." Forrest didn't look at him. "Then we'll try something else."

"Or give up?"

"That's not an option."

"It was a joke."

Forrest turned his head and took in the other man's sickly grin. He reached across and punched the Brazilian lightly on the shoulder. "Yeah." Then he pressed the screen button.

Krasnarov was zipped up in his sleeping bag when Forrest came back to tell him the news. His eyes barely flickered when Forrest swam up to him, would not lock when Forrest looked down at him. Forrest put a hand on his shoulder.

"Mike, I thought you'd want to know. The repairs worked. Comm's still out, of course, and we have to keep the array Sun-locked manually; but it's pulling power now. In another couple days—if we're frugal on usage—we'll have all the onboard battery power we need and we can stop worrying."

Krasnarov didn't blink. He nodded slowly. "Yes."

Forrest turned and kicked off. At the entrance to the smaller module, he turned and looked back. Mike was staring at the opposite wall, humming some sort of Russian tune in a minor key. Except for the rhythm, it almost sounded like the blues.

Back on Fernando de Noronha, back when they had been young and handsome and the world lay at their feet, even then Krasnarov had never been exactly Mr. Jolly. Hell, the man had more "gravity" than a black hole. The other pilots had joked about Krasnarov's seriousness, but they had been inspired, too, a little. Krasnarov had pushed the envelope with the best of them, taking his chances with cold-eyed precision and pulling it back before it could sour. The Iron Mike had flown the bird when no one knew shit. His was the first butt to hang out over the edge. He had taken *Nesterov* up when everyone *knew* there was a malf somewhere. And later, on that suborbital, Krasnarov had flown with his lips pulled back in a fierce grin. Perhaps his heart had sung with the hum of a finely tuned machine, but it had sung.

Abruptly, Forrest propelled himself abruptly toward the transfer tunnel.

On the command deck, Nacho was concentrating on the PVA monitor, every muscle in his body carved from marble. "Relax," Forrest ordered as he exited the transfer tunnel. "If it drifts, we'll get a warning and crank it back until the sun is in the crosshairs again."

Nacho unlocked slowly, almost by effort. "I feel betrayed," he said.

Forrest started. Betrayed? Yes. It was just the right word to use. He settled into the command chair.

"Our ship worked so well for so long," Nacho said, "I began to accept it as flawless."

"Yeah. It's easy to forget we're in a little tin can in a honking big ocean. The system is ninety-nine-point-nine percent reliable, but the trip is a hundred percent long."

"I don't think I will feel safe again until I am down on Earth."

"Son, don't you ever think you're safe there, either." They weren't any of them safe, anywhere; not from themselves. *Jesus, pull up the flaps on that sleeping bag and tie them and it might as well be a body bag.* He rubbed his hands up and down the arms of his chair. What was Nacho Mendes doing sitting in the copilot's seat? It wasn't right.

Some time later, the monitor gibbered softly. "Ookook," like a monkey. "Ook-ook." Nacho turned to the targeting controls and began to nudge the vernier on the monitor screen with his power glove.

With sudden, angry motions, Forrest tore open his arm-rest keypad and stabbed on the buttons. Nacho looked at him. "What are you doing?"

Forrest entered the virtual control panel for the alert sounds and found the monkey. He dragged it into the trash, along with the foghorn and Humphrey Bogart and the sex-pot add-ons to the A/S vocals and a half dozen other comic sounds. He set the alert indicator to the "beep" and the problem indicator to the "klaxon." Then he closed up the panel and sat there for most of the rest of the shift with his fists clenched into balls on the arms of his chair, fighting back tears.

16.

Tangled Webs

The pixcreens filled the boardroom wall opposite the chairman's seat. They were affixed on both sides of the doorway and the upper tier flanked the portrait of Henryk van Huyten. Sometimes, when face time was impossible, interface time made do; and her presidents and other advisors reported by teleconference. Chris van Huyten's call had been routed to the screen just to Henryk's right; and his scowl, so like Henryk's unsmiling glare, accentuated his resemblance to the family's founder. Nearly four hundred years separated the two men, yet they could have been father and son. Henryk was the swarthier and looked older, though he had, in fact, been only thirty-five when Lastmann captured him on canvas. The aging oils had darkened over the centuries, and had picked up a patina of soot when the old mansion at Rensselaer had burned down in the 1870s. The Vandyke beard added years that Chris's clean-shaven chin did not. Yet, Chris had the edge on him by almost two decades.

"I don't like it," he said. "*Torch* was my project, not Will's."

A subsonic rumble drew Mariesa's attention to the other screen, to the left of the portrait, where Werewolf Gregorson sat in his Cleveland office. Gregorson's desk, as always, was littered with eviscerated equipment: wiring, circuit boards, chips and chassis, as if a bomb had gone off in Radio Shack. Will had the soul of a techie. His company flourished because Mariesa had annexed its business functions—and because Will was a very good techie, indeed. "I don't like it, either, Chris," the man grumbled.

"I've tried to explain," Mariesa insisted. "*Michael* depends on *Lucifer,* which is a classified government project. The RFP was confidential, at the Pentagon's insistence; and when the bid was awarded to Werewolf Electronics, they set strict limits on need-to-know. I don't care for it myself, but there it is."

"Nobody likes it," Chris commented sarcastically, "but it's happening." He rubbed his chin; looked to the side for a moment. His lips settled briefly into a thin line and he shook his head. "Converting a battle laser into a power laser sounds like a task for the Argonauts. That's all I'm saying."

"Converting a battle laser into a power laser *without* compromising government secrets," Mariesa said. *Or my own,* she added to herself. Even Werewolf did not yet know about the *Steel Rain* side to the operation. He would have to be told eventually; but not until he had embraced the Tar Baby.

"Werewolf built *Torch*," Gregorson pointed out. "And the equatorial laser stations. *Michael* is just *Torch* on steroids."

Chris shook his head again. "Linear extrapolation. We don't *know* what the correlations look like beyond the envelope we've tested. Yes, Will, I know what theory says; but theory says bumble bees can't fly. Every theory has built-in assumptions; and some are so built-in we don't know we're making them. That's why R&D is important."

"I'm not arguing, Chris," Werewolf said, "but my hands are tied." His eyes shifted and Mariesa knew he was looking at her on his other monitor. *God, Will, I'm sorry for putting you in this spot. But you did not have to bite the apple I offered you.* It could be that the Werewolf was as angry over discovering the limits of his principles as he was over anything else.

Chris ran a hand through his hair. "All right. You say it's a matter of clearances and need-to-know. I say it's a matter of business missions and capabilities. We're not supposed to step on each other's turf without some courtesies. Suppose I give you a list of my top laser and power beam people, with their security ratings and histories. You pick one or ten or however many you want, and run them past that liaison officer of yours. Whoever makes the cut, I'll loan to Werewolf for the duration of the project. If detaching this gadget from its classified matrix is such touchy surgery, I've got people who can split hairs and keep their mouths shut."

Mariesa hesitated. It was a reasonable offer—*if* what she had told Chris had been the whole truth. But that *Michael* was the price for—and the cover for—*Steel Rain* was not on the table. Before she could say anything to put Chris off, Gregorson spoke.

"That sounds like a dandy idea, Chris. That should satisfy the Pentagon and—" again the shift of the eyes— "other parties, and still keep Werewolf-Argonaut teamwork alive. What do you say, Mariesa?"

That was the penalty of not filling him in, either. Based on what Will thought he knew, Chris's offer seemed entirely reasonable. Well, she would have to take it up with Duckworth. There must be ways of making it work. Will would have to involve some of his Werewolves, anyway. If some of those people were on loan from Argonaut, it only complicated things slightly. They would have to watch the conduit so that information on *Steel Rain* did not leak back to Argonaut prematurely. And that probably meant keeping Will, if not in the dark, at least in the gray a little while longer. "We'll discuss the matter with the Pentagon," she said, which was as far as she could commit herself. Mariesa let her eyes drop from the pixcreens to the computer inset in the teak, boardroom table. "Meanwhile, gentlemen, the purpose of this meeting. Ms. Sridharan has informed me that negotiations with the government of India have bogged down. Are there sites in Bhutan or Nepal that we can consider for construction of the Himalaya laser or should we drop the project and consider alternatives?''

Chris grunted assent, but Mariesa could tell he was still not satisfied. Even if the *matter* was confidential, the mere existence of the contract ought not have been. At the very least, he should have been told. He was, after all, her cousin and, were anything ever to happen to her, her likely successor. Yet, he had made crystal clear his opposition to Donaldson's proposal, and not even dangling *Lucifer* before his eyes had budged him. She wondered if *Michael* had stirred any suspicions. Did he see it as a payment, and if so, did he wonder what—and who—had been bought?

Gene Wilson kept a home near Kemps Bay overlooking Tongue of the Ocean. From the broad, open, flagstoned patio in the back you could see the ships dancing with the waves. All sorts of ships, from small personal sunrays to schooners rigged fore-and-aft, sloops and ketches sliding atop the swells, sails a mix of gaudy colors or white like snow upon the waters. Motor vessels zigzagged impudently among them. In the distance, a cruise ship wound its way through the deeper channel. A warm Caribbean breeze stirred the beryl waters and carressed Mariesa's hair. She lifted a hand half-consciously to hold it in place.

''You do yourself well, Gene,'' she said. While she watched, a schooner luffed up and the weather leech of her mainsail feathered. ''Do you sail?''

Gene Wilson approached with a drink of unlikely color, as gaudy as any spinnaker on the water below. Enough impaled fruit floated in the wide-mouth hurricane glass to ward off a bout of scurvy. ''Time to time,'' he said. ''When I have the time.''

Mariesa tasted the drink and found it sweet and cloying. Maybe it was her Dutch ancestry, the no-nonsense, down-to-business, Reformed Church Protestantism that Gramper had practiced, but she felt that if you were going to drink, you should not, by God, pretty it up.

''How is it?'' asked Wilson.

"Delicious," she said.

"Are you enjoying the sun, you and . . . ?"

"Wayne Coper. We were childhood friends."

Wilson nodded. "I see."

She laid a hand on his arm. "Oh, he escorts me sometimes. But we have no ties on each other."

"Ah." Wilson visibly relaxed and Mariesa wondered what shenanigans Wayne had been up to in Moxey Town. The doorbell rang and Wilson set his drink down. "Excuse me."

Mariesa studied Tongue of the Ocean while she waited. A laid-back, mellow life, here. 'Vejj,' they said now. Lounge in the sand, sport in the water, kick in the clubs after dark. It would drive her crazy after the third day. How could Gene take it, she wondered? He was an entrepeneur who, like Werewolf, had started in the proverbial garage. Men like that had to *learn* relaxation; they did not come by it naturally.

The breeze freshened and shifted a point, catching her short, white skirt and raising the pleats immodestly. She turned away from the wind and toward the house just as Wilson returned with a second guest.

Ed Bullock.

Bullock's mouth was small and overred for a man's to begin with; but it seemed to shrink to a pinpoint when he saw Mariesa. He wore white duck trousers and canvas shoes and a long-waisted blue blazer with a red kerchief. "Well," he said, taking in Mariesa, "if you're thinking of a career in matchmaking, Wilson, I wouldn't quit your day job."

"Sit down and relax, Ed, and I'll fix you a drink."

"Whiskey sour."

Wilson smiled. "You're in the Islands, friend."

When he had gone, Mariesa said, "Gene decides what we drink." She held up her own glass. Bullock shrugged.

"Why this meeting?"

Mariesa shook her head. "It's Gene's show. He asked me to come down. 'A matter of mutual interest.' I didn't know you would be here."

Wilson reappeared with a third fruity concoction, which Bullock took with an expression of uncertainty. "Anyone else coming we don't know about?"

Wilson took a position near the rail. "No, just us three. Bill, Pete, and some of the others wanted to be here—whether for a weekend in the sun or to enjoy your peerless company, I don't know—but I had things to say that I don't want them to hear. They told me I can speak for them. You don't believe me, you're free to call 'em up and ask." He gestured to the portable phone lying on the umbrella-shaded table.

"Them," said Mariesa. "Boeing-McDonnell-Douglas; Lockheed-Martin. Who else?"

"The usual suspects," Wilson said. "Kelly, Artemis, Northwest, Santa Fe Ground and Space, Phoenix, Motorola . . ."

Bullock swirled his drink. "Sounds like you've been a busy boy, Wilson."

"Oh, I've talked to a lot of players this past month."

"All right," Bullock allowed. "You contain multitudes. You speak with many voices. What does the Greek Chorus have to say?"

Mariesa crossed the patio to sit under the umbrella, out of the sun. The table was glass and white iron, with pits of corrosion at the seams and joints. She placed her drink on the glass and leaned back in the canvas sling chair so that she was entirely shaded. Wilson stood by the rail braced on one elbow with Tongue of the Ocean behind him. "Just this: We're calling a truce between you two."

"Gene," said Mariesa, "I was not the—" But Wilson held a hand up to forestall her comments.

"It doesn't matter, Riesey. Matters have gone far enough and we want to rope them in before anything irreversible happens. This last little go around—I'm talking about the nonsense with the Power Beam Bill, Ed—it pissed a lot of third parties."

"I was the target, Gene," Mariesa pointed out, "not the shooter."

Bullock said, "I don't suppose it would matter to you if power beams really did damage the atmosphere."

Wilson snorted. "I don't think it matters to *you*. It was just a handy excuse. The fact is that half of Motorola's repeaters would be useless without ground-based microwave power. They'd have to redesign them with onboard power plants at twice the cost. And Artemis is looking toward Very High Power beams for its lunar mines. The same goes for LEO Station. Do you know what happens to LEO's P&L projections if we can't use ground-based power lasers? No, of course, you do. That's why you tried to pull the plug. Well, a lot of people have Very Serious Money at stake."

"And the others?" Bullock asked.

"They're all in the game. If satelites become more expensive, there'll be fewer of them launched and that hurts the Earth-to-Orbit carriers. The fractional ballistic folks figure they'll be next on your list. And the shipbuilders like Boeing and Pegasus depend on the ballistic and orbital carriers for orders. We're all on the Big Raft, Ed. You swing an oar at one of us, you swing an oar at all."

Bullock did not seem daunted. He saluted Wilson with his drink. "Maybe the Big Raft is headed the wrong direction. That might be a waterfall you think you hear, and not a roar of approval. A lot of us prefer good management to dog-eat-dog. Everything in order; each of us tending our own plot."

"Who's going to parcel out the plots, Ed? Are you that anxious to be the glove on the government's fist?"

"Conjure up some other bogeyman, Wilson. You've dealt with the government. I have." He glanced at Mariesa. "And even your friend here has been dropping in on a lot of interesting people lately. The government isn't some alien thing plunked down among us. *We* are the government. We hire them every two, four, or six years. So why not work together? Why not an alliance between business and government—and academia and labor—to rationalize the economy and get everyone working *cooperatively* for the common good rather than *competitively* for themselves?

You only get music if everyone plays together under a director. Anything else is noise.''

"Who gets the baton? Never mind. I didn't ask you here to argue fascism.''

"No," said Bullock, "you brought me here so you and your corporate buddies could threaten and bully me. Well, I have some 'buddies,' too; and I wonder if some of the voices in that chorus you're speaking for might be singing a little less loudly than the others.''

Wilson narrowed his eyes. "Meaning?''

Bullock tilted his glass back, and set it down empty on the concrete rail. "Meaning, I'm a troublemaker; so some folks might want me to shut up, even if they like the song I'm singing. Not everyone on your 'raft' would be upset if noise gave way to music.''

Wilson nodded. "No, I suppose not. Surrender is cheaper than struggle—in the short run. Eternal vigilance always was the price.''

"Will there be anything else?''

Mariesa spoke. "You won't convince him, Gene. It's personal. He's channeling his uncle's ghost.''

Bullock pulled his kerchief from his breast pocket and dabbed his lips. "You could ask for worse mentors.''

Wilson sighed. "I'd hoped to avoid this, but . . .''

Bullock looked at his watch. "But what? My wife is waiting for me at the hotel. We've booked a schooner for a private cruise down the Banks. A *very* private cruise." He lifted an eyebrow, as if he expected the people with whom he had just been bickering to savor the innuendo.

"It has come to my attention," Wilson said slowly, "that your uncle sponsored the missile attack on my Antisana ram accelerator eight years ago, an attack in which three of my men were killed—and in which two score *could* have been killed if the pipeline had fireballed.''

Bullock turned and looked at Mariesa for a moment. "Rumors," he said. "That was years ago, and, unfortunately, my uncle can no longer respond to your slurs.''

Wilson waved a hand back and forth. "Ed, Ed, do you

have any idea how many different scenarios I've heard about that attack—from Shining Path to the CIA? No, this tip came from a steady and reliable source; and when I dug into it, I found enough corroboration to satisfy me. Cyrus Attwood was responsible; and you were his right-hand man and designated successor. You can't claim you were just a bystander.''

''Did *she* put you up to this?''

Wilson shook his head. ''Mariesa didn't know why I set this meeting up any more than you did. Think of me as representing neutral third parties.'' He ignored Bullock's derisive grunt. ''All right, *I'm* not neutral. I'm pissed. And I get pissed again every time I think about what happened.''

Bullock's lips thinned almost to vanishing. ''And your point is?''

''Lay off or I spread the word around.''

''That 'word' has been spread for years by my enemies.''

''But not by *me*, and not with anything like proof. I think a lot more people will pay a lot more attention if I do. And even some of your 'buddies' may wonder if the same thing could happen to them if you disapprove of one of *their* business deals.''

Bullock thrust his hands into his pants pockets and rocked for a moment on his heels. ''Can you spell libel?''

''Ed, I don't want to do it. I want to . . .'' His mouth twisted into a half-smile. ''. . . tend my own plot of ground. But your attacks on Mariesa are beginning to seriously annoy me—and a lot of others. So, you tend your garden; we'll tend ours.''

Bullock made a face. ''Until I have no garden left because you have sucked up all the investment capital and shot it into outer space.''

''Then join us on the raft. The pie's not that small, and it's growing. There are opportunities for everyone.''

''I'm particular about who I raft with. But about the other matter . . . I'll think about it. Thank you for your gracious hospitality, your gracious drink, and your even more gracious threats. It's always a joy to know what sort of men I deal with.''

Wilson walked Bullock to the door. Mariesa stayed behind and stared out across the sapphire sea. Waves were barely visible from this angle. A calm sea and a steady wind. The big schooner had taken the weather gauge from a smaller one-master, whose sails had gone slack in consequence and whose master could be seen shaking a fist at the larger vessel. A gull cried—oddly in synch with the shaking fist.

Wilson reappeared with two more hurricane glasses. He set them on the patio table and joined Mariesa under the shade. "I hate that twerp," he said without preamble. "He knew. He can't pretend he didn't know. But he thinks he's saving the goddamn world from economic chaos, and that justifies everything he does.''

"If he truly believes he is saving the world," Mariesa said, "I would hate to think he'd give anything less than his best efforts.''

Wilson lifted his glass. "Yeah." A slow swallow. He did not quite put the glass down again. "But, you know, the world can stand with a few less saviors. They always wind up trying to save you from yourself. Me, I just play with oddball technologies and try to make a few bucks here and there. I'm an entrepeneur. If my next project goes belly up, I'm in the soup lines. Bullock can go broke, and he'd *still* be rich." He grimaced and looked at Mariesa. "No offense.''

"None taken." She pushed her drink aside a few inches. "And thank you for taking my part.''

"Oh, I wasn't sticking up for *you*. I was sticking up for *me*. And you're not entirely blameless. Some odd reversals have hit the Attwood fortune in recent years. Tell me you haven't tossed a few rocks at his window to get his attention." He stirred the slush of his drink with the straw. "And how long have you been sitting on this Attwood information? Two years? Three? Don't you think I should have been told?''

She did not bother with denial. "It would have hurt others. Third parties."

"Who? No one was involved in the incident but Attwood, the Crusades people he bribed, and my ram staff. And last time I looked, Phil Albright's Crusades was no better a friend than Bullock."

"Albright at least has principles."

A shrug. "That only means you can't talk him into seeing reason. I don't see why you're defending him."

"I have my reasons."

Wilson fell into a thoughtful silence. "Yes, your cousin Norbert thought there was something odd between you and Albright."

Mariesa nodded at the confirmation. "It was Norbert, then."

"Yes, he told me that Albright claimed to have documents proving Attwood's involvement in attacking my ram; and both Bullock and Albright's young protégé gave you the evil eye over it. So, it sounds to me like those documents came courtesy of Mariesa van Huyten."

"Do you really want to know everything, Gene? I suppose Chisholm could reconstruct . . ."

"Oh, hell." Wilson scowled into his drink. "Just stop waving red flags in Eddie's face, okay. All scores are even; all weregeld paid. The *Thing* has spoken."

"Is that what the consortium has become now? The new *Althing*?"

A sudden breeze toppled the glass that Bullock had left on the wall edging the patio and it rolled off to shatter on the flagstones. Wilson grimaced as he turned that way. "I suppose I should send him the bill for that, too." When he faced Mariesa again, he changed the subject. "Rumor has it that you and J. Clement are as thick as thieves at a session of Congress. Bullock asked me at the door whether I'd heard anything about you and the president becoming allies. I think it worried him."

Mariesa dismissed the implicit question. "Bullock thinks

that all power flows from Washington. So any hint of a Washington connection . . .''

Wilson interrupted. ''Are you allies?''

''Donaldson has no allies, only partners of convenience.''

''Yet the administration helped stomp all over Bullock's pet bill in Congress last month. And I had *way* too easy a time with government files, confirming what Norbert told me. Well, it looks like interesting times, as the turtle said pulling his head inside his shell. Just one question, Riesey. Is there anything rolling down hill that *I* need to know about?''

Mariesa assured him that the hillside was clear, but Gene did not seem to listen too carefully. He swirled the slush in his glass. ''I'll take your word for now, Riesey; but that Greek chorus, as Ed called it? We can sing more songs than one.''

Mariesa was in the sitting room reading *Taj Mahal* when Harriet entered. Nestled in the soft barrel chair by the windows, she was so engrossed in the book that she barely registered her mother's presence. *Taj Mahal* had sat on the shelf for some time before, pasting the umpteenth rave review into her scrapbook, Mariesa realized that she hadn't actually read it herself. Who had time for casual reading? Now, moved by tears and pity, she found it difficult to put down, and scheduled time each day to read a section. Autobiographical without being autobiography, parts of it hurt and parts of it made her want to weep. How much of Tanuja Pandya lived in the character ''Chandra'' was hard to say. Mariesa hoped it was not as much as she feared. Tani had always seemed the most ordinary of Belinda's kids. Had she actually taken drugs to stay awake while she crammed thirty hours into a day? Had she ever really pondered suicide?

Imprisoned in a convenience store by her father's dream. Mariesa had always thought of dreams as liberating, but Tani had shown they could confine, as well. Each character in the novel struggled within the tomb of someone's dream—or delusion. Usually another's, but often enough their own.

She closed the book, marking the place with her finger, and paused in thought. Suddenly, she became aware that Harriet sat at the table waiting patiently to be noticed.

"Mother," she said, "you startled me."

"Is it true?" Harriet asked without preamble.

"Is what true?"

"That you've been seeing Wayne Coper. Lillian Beckwith saw you together in the Caribbean last week."

Harriet's dreams had confined the young Mariesa. The endless search for suitable men, the continual round of arrangements. Young Wayne had only been the first of them. Obedient and defiant, she had at last chosen a man—but one of whom her mother profoundly disapproved. Some whispered that she had taken up with Barry only to put an end to the endless matchmaking. Perhaps it was even true. She had never settled that question in her own mind; had never dared pursue it too closely. "Casually," she said.

"And never a word to me. Apparently *everyone* knew. Even Norbert knew—and that man doesn't even know what his equipment is for."

"Mother!"

Harriet shook her head. "Wayne is entirely unsuitable for you."

It took a moment for the remark to sink in. At first, Mariesa could not believe she had heard it; then she threw back her head and laughed. "After all these years?"

Harriet never cracked; nor did she need Mariesa to explain the comment. "As a boy, he had a great deal of promise. But he's been divorced twice. What does that say about his reliability?"

"His first wife cheated on him," Mariesa said—though she didn't know why she felt compelled to defend Wayne, of all people, to Harriet, of all people.

"They were *both* catting around, according to Pru Scales—and she ought to know, if you know what I mean.

I don't mean one cheated and the other retaliated. I mean they both did on their own.''

Mariesa found her bookmark and set it in place. She laid the book on her lap. ''I don't see that it matters, anyway. We're just good friends. Marriage is the farthest thing from either of our minds.''

Harriet sighed and looked away. ''You're right. It doesn't much matter any more.''

''It never did.''

Steve Matthias gave his report with sullen correctness. In his early sixties, Steve cut his hair short and dyed the gray parts. He was on the cutting edge of hair fashion, he liked to say. He had worn it short all his life and only now was the world catching up with him. He was a careful and methodical man. His division—Thor Machine Tools—produced consistently ahead of the industry. So when Prometheus had grown too large for her personal oversight and Mariesa had looked for a program manager to coordinate the multitude of projects, Steve Matthias had been in place.

And a clever man, too. He had deduced the existence of Prometheus in the early days, when it had still been a closely held secret, and had, in effect, invited himself aboard and positioned himself for the coordinator's job that he had foreseen. Brainy and ambitious, a combination Mariesa usually approved of, he had always been a consistent supporter of her programs among the divisional presidents and later on Prometheus itself. But Mariesa was never entirely sure whether his support came from conviction, expedience, or design. Steve looked out for Steve. And that made it all the more disturbing when his demeanor bordered so closely on insolence.

''The lift finally goes up this month,'' he said, ''in a fleet of four Air Force Planks. We had to do a bit of juggling on the bumboat schedule to fit them in. The cover story is that they're bringing up the big laser to field test orbit-to-moon power transmission. That should fool your board, at least for now. And we can say that the communications blackout and the Army personnel are because *Michael* uses classified technology. . . .''

''It does, Steve,'' she pointed out quietly. Her office windows faced north, toward First Watchung Mountain, and everything in the room had a soft and uncertain look in the morning light. She normally took divisional and project reports comfortably seated in the low, leather chairs by the windows and with a service of coffee and tea brought up. But Steve had gone to her desk and had sat in the chair there, as if deliberately marking himself as a subordinate.

''The truth,'' he said, ''and nothing but the truth. But not the whole truth. It's better that way. Omission is much more effective than an outright lie.''

''I don't care for the 'spin' you're giving this, Steve.''

''That's *Captain* Steve. Hey, I'm on your team on this, right? Because if I'm not, there's always the UCMJ and a court-martial.''

''You object to *Steel Rain?*''

He closed the briefing folder. ''Damn straight. I said so from the beginning. LEO isn't designed to be the Death Star. I don't know who's been feeding you comfort, or why, but this could create serious ill feelings.''

It already had, if Steve Matthias, corporate mercenary, could be upset over a matter of principle with retirement only single digits in the future. Correy Wilcox had once called him a ''managerial prostitute.'' Yet she could not help but remember a story Steve had told her years ago: how he had quit his first job cold when a VP told him to sit on some quality improvement ideas that would have made a rival look good. ''It's not quite as bad as all that,'' she protested. ''It's one small installation.''

''No? How big is a camel's nose? Ah, never mind. That's not what upsets me.'' He hesitated.

''What does upset you?'' Mariesa asked. She sat almost rigidly in her chair, unsure whether leaning forward on her desk or back in her chair would give the wrong message.

Steve drummed his fist on the the desk where he sat. He

was beginning to feel the discomfort of the seat, Mariesa could tell. She waited for him to make up his mind.

Steve shoved himself to his feet and stepped to the windows, where he stood with his arms crossed, facing the outside world. "I'm a student of history," he said at last. "Did I ever tell you that? I don't know. It's not something I go on about in management retreats."

"History?"

He turned, his arms still folded. "Yeah. A thorough understanding of history is a better grounding for an executive than all the economic models and three-letter acronyms ever invented. Let others major in finance or marketing. I *hire* those people."

"I thought history was open to interpretation; that you can learn almost any lesson you wanted by what you read into the facts."

"That's right. And that's the first thing you learn from a 'thorough understanding of history.' The facts look different to everyone involved—or uninvolved. Though the uninvolved usually have a wider range of opinions," he added sardonically. "I call it the Rashomon Principle. It's something every executive needs to know—and take into account. But I was thinking of something else. Ferdinand of Austria and Maximilian of Bavaria during the Thirty Years' War."

Mariesa shook her head. "Can you explain without a lecture?" she asked.

Steve unfolded his arms and stuffed his hands in his pockets. He grunted. "All right. Let's say you have these two dudes: Ferdy Hapsburg and Max Wittelsbach. Ferdy is the head of the Holy Roman Empire, but he 'reigns,' he doesn't 'rule.' There's a mare's nest of laws and customs and all what-have-you called 'the German Liberties' that put limits on what he can do. Okay, so in a nutshell, Ferdy wants to 'rule'—without any messy Diet or Electoral College or princely veto; and Max wants to preserve the German Liberties intact. You can see the problem, right?"

Mariesa nodded, uncertain what the man was getting at. "Go on."

''It's a little more complicated, because Ferdy also wants to think that he never breaks his word, so he gets very, very clever in how he sets things up; and Max wants to advance his family's fortunes, so he's, ah, open to opportunities. Then along comes a crisis, a revolt in . . . Well, it doesn't really matter what it was. Just that Ferdy starts 'ruling,' and Max lends him the help he needs.''

Mariesa blinked. The story was not going where she had anticipated. ''Whatever for?''

''Three things: he actually agreed with Ferdy about crushing the revolt; second, he thought that if Ferdy owed his success to the support of Max and his friends, it would preserve the German Liberties; and third, Ferdy gave Max a big-time title and position.''

Now Mariesa did lean back in her chair. She folded her hands into a steeple under her chin. ''I see. And what came of it in the end?''

Steve shrugged and he picked up his briefcase. ''The empire collapsed,'' he said briefly and turned to go.

When he reached the door, Mariesa spoke. ''It was a good story, Max. I'll think about it.''

Steve paused with his hand on the knob and looked at her with a sad smile. He nodded without speaking, then left.

Of all the people Mariesa expected to see walk into her office, Barry Fast was not even on the list of possibles. ''Discovery School,'' Zhou Hui had announced, and *Discovery School,* it read on Mariesa's agenda screen. Perhaps if she had taken time earlier to review the background file she would have seen his name as principal; though what she would have done if she had, even she did not know.

Nor did she know what moved her to suggest taking their meeting off-site, save that it had been a long and stressful day and she and Barry had once made a custom of dining out. How easily the old paradigms resurfaced! If Barry was surprised by the suggestion, he did not show it, but quickly proposed the Black Forest Inn. Strudel and spätzl were not exactly what Mariesa had had in mind for an early dinner, but she went along with it. Barry offered to drive, but she had a car brought around so they could discuss his business en route without the distraction of negotiating the traffic.

Barry had never much cared for wealth, she remembered as he settled into the back of the limo. Even though the car was not luxurious by her standards—no television, no bar, no padded swivel seats—she caught a brief look of disdain on his face. The reverse snobbery of the middle class. Barry considered himself above all that; but was, she thought, afraid of being seduced. How he supposed she would conduct business while driving herself in an ordinary car she did not know.

"So, Barry," she said as the limo pulled down the broad driveway and around the pond in the center of the VHI campus. "What brings you here?" The building itself was an unremarkable glass box, cruciform in shape and surrounded by acres of grass and trees. March had come in with a lion's breath and all trace of snow and ice had fled. Buds had appeared on the trees and the brown lawn had begun to darken. The goose flock that had established itself in the pond had not yet returned from the Carolinas— though their annual reappearance had become something of a corporate holiday and marked the return also of the outdoor joggers and the breaktime picnickers.

"What ever happened to Laurence Sprague?" Barry asked with a nod toward Louis, the driver; and there was something very Barry-esque in the way he first asked about people he had known.

"Laurence retired," she told him. "He still runs the business—Louis works for him—but he no longer drives himself." She thought for a moment, then added, "Though, of course, he still does drive himself."

Barry turned toward her, but the puzzled look turned quickly to the chuckle she had learned once to treasure. "Yeah, Laurence always was a go-get-'em kind of guy, wasn't he? How's the rest of the gang getting on?"

They chatted for a few pleasant miles, while the limo sought out Interstate 80, and they tried to pretend that there had never been either intimacy or estrangement. Keep Barry at arm's length and you reduced his power to hurt. The minuet of manners enabled them to dance around the issues that lay between them. Mariesa filled him in on Belinda and John E. and the others he had known back when he had moved in the Inner Circle, and he responded with polite queries and comments. She wondered if he ever missed those days. There had always been an element of the climber in Barry's approach to life. She did not notice until afterwards that they had driven right past the hill where Piet's sanitarium had been.

Ultimately, there was the reason for his visit.

"Shannon, Tchatika, and I have some students at Discovery School that we want you to look at." He had brought a folder with him of student records and evaluations. She took it without opening it and Barry looked uncertain. "That is, if you and Belinda still do that. Pick likely kids to encourage."

"We do, but why not give these right to Belinda? She and her staff at Spokane run the program."

"Ah . . . Well, Discovery School isn't part of Mentor. We're an independent charter school. Maybe you don't remember the setup."

As close as he would ever come to saying that it had been a practice Mariesa had funded just to keep him in teaching after his marriage had made further employment at Mentor impossible. The gesture had been kindly meant, and by all accounts he had been reasonably successful in it; yet she could see now how it might have seemed condescending. She opened the folder and glanced at the contents. Alonzo Sulbertson. Dobie Weston. Cheela Jackson. Only names. Only "pixures." And yet, how full of hope and cheer they seemed! They lived in a milieu far more oppressive than had the kids at Witherspoon, yet she saw none of the sulleness and ennui that had marked that first class. Was it the neighborhood or the teacher? Or was it only that it was ten years later, and times and people and children change? "I'll give these to Belinda," she said.

"Thank you. Discovery doesn't operate a high school, and our kids go on to Mollie Pitcher; but I'd like to make sure . . ."

"Have you spoken to Paul and Maria about them?"

"Yes, of course."

"Well, then. That's settled."

The conversation petered out into a silence broken only by the soft hiss of the tires on the road and the occasional sound of another car passing them. There were other questions she thought to ask, but did not know how to ask them. Shannon Morgenthaler was one of his partners in Discovery. Was she still his partner in other ways? Unbidden, photographs long-trampled in the mud atop Skunktown Mountain rose pristine and glossy in her mind. Bodies clasped together. Legs wrapping, hands caressing, lips seeking. She could feel the flush at the base of her throat. More distressingly, she could feel other emotions as well. You could explain it however you wanted—Pavlovian conditioning—but whatever else Barry had been, he had been an accomplished lover.

"Have you seen any of your old students from Witherspoon lately?" she asked, breaking the silence. That was a safe topic, or at least a safer one.

Barry nodded. "Meat Tucker, a couple of times. And Karen Chong called when she had her baby. I ran into Cheng-I Yeh over in New York. He was in town for a symposium and I treated him to dinner. And, oh. Hold on to your hat. Last September, just after school started, Roberta Carson dropped in."

She turned and looked at him. "Roberta?"

"Yeah, right out of the clear blue sky."

"Ah. How was she?"

Barry laughed. "As full of piss and vinegar as always. I couldn't figure out why she came. At first, I thought she was trying to dig up dirt on Discovery."

"On Discovery? Why?"

"Hard to tell with that crowd. Some of 'em—not all of them, by any means—seem just as upset when you do the right thing for the wrong reasons as when you do the wrong thing. Maybe she was on the prod because you financed Discovery . . . No, wait.'' He squinted and looked far off, shook his head. ''No, she didn't know you gave me the seed money. So, maybe she really did want to hash over old times and see how her old teacher was getting on.''

Louis had reached the Stanhope exit and Mariesa could hear the ticking of the turn signal. Oddly, though they were only a little higher here than in Wessex County, there was yet no sign of spring. Barren yellow poplar and white oak commingled with evergreen red spruce on the hillsides of Second Watchung Mountain. No hint of flowers or buds. Mariesa stared out the window. ''Did she mention me?''

''What?''

She turned. ''Roberta. Did she say anything about me?''

Barry shrugged with his hands. ''A little. Mostly the same old rap about brainwashing the kids into space cadets. I told her she misjudged you. I told her you really did want to save the world.''

''Oh, did you now?''

He frowned and rubbed his hands together, placed them on his knees. A handful of heartbeats went by. ''Yes,'' he said. ''The asteroid business . . .''

Instantly wary, she responded. ''You told her that?''

''You still have that dream. The one where you—''

''Yes.'' Her nod was almost a jerk.

He fell silent while the car negotiated a bend in the road. ''Look . . .'' He stopped and shook his head. ''Never mind.''

''No, tell me.'' She started to lay a hand on his arm, but drew it back and it fell by her side. ''You think I am a lunatic.''

''No, not that, but . . . Have you ever thought about seeing someone about—about—''

''About my delusion?'' Reaching up, she took hold of the car strap, clenching it hard, so that her nails bit into the soft base of her thumb.

''About your dream. About your . . . Riesey, knowledge

is one thing. Hell, I know there's a chance we might get hit someday. Maybe even a monster hit. I read the material you gave me. But I'm also pretty sure a big rock isn't going to pop New York City any time in the next half hour. So I don't understand your—''

''Of course, you don't understand,'' she said through clenched teeth. ''No one does. *But I saw one!*''

''I know, Riesey. I know. You told me the story.'' He did not quite lean over and pat her head, the patronizing bastard.

''Do not call me that.'' He had not seen that awful streak of light. He did not know how close the world had already come. He did not know the world was living on borrowed time.

''But, Mariesa, thousands of people see bolides every year without being gripped by paralyzing fear afterwards.''

''Then they are fools who do not realize what they have seen.''

''Or else it wasn't the Firestar that really frightened you.''

''Oh, thank you, Sigmund Freud.''

They rode the rest of the way in silence. When the car pulled into the parking lot at the Black Forest, neither made a move to unlatch their door. Late afternoon sunshine was a ruddy stain seen through the ragged, naked branches of the trees. Shadows were long and sharp, grasping like hands across the parking lot. ''I guess there's not much point to dinner,'' Barry said at last.

Louis opened the door for Mariesa. She turned to him. ''We've changed our—''

Barry interrupted. ''But where's poor Louis going to eat?'' he asked, ''after dragging us out here?''

She exchanged a look with her ex-husband. She hadn't even thought of Louis, but he had. She turned to the driver. ''You do not—You don't mind eating in the lounge while we discuss business, do you? We'll be along presently. Be a dear and arrange for a table? Thank you.''

When the driver had gone, Barry said quietly, ''Change of heart?''

"As long as we're here." She hesitated, rubbed the seat cushion with her knuckles. "Barry, I know you said what you did because you are . . . because you're genuinely concerned about me. I've enough reasons to be angry with you that I don't have to pick foolish ones."

"Thank you. I think."

"Some days I ask myself, 'Why does it obsess me so?' I don't know the answer. It's just something that wells up out of . . . Oh, not 'nowhere,' I suppose; but I don't know where. And yet, my fear, as unreasonable as it might have been, may be justified, after all."

He frowned, and looked suddenly worried. "Justified? You don't mean you've spotted . . . ?"

"No, not quite that. Only troubling, and it may be that I'm reading something that isn't actually written. Because of that fear. I haven't even told the others in SkyWatch. And it may have led me to make a terrible misjudgment."

"Do you want to tell me about it?"

"I can't tell you some things. I suppose I shouldn't tell you anything." Barry waited patiently while she tugged at the hem of her jacket. "But . . . You were like Keith in a lot of ways. He said so himself. You always knew how to listen."

"That's why God invented ears," he said. "Two of them, and only one mouth."

The laugh that dug from her was perfunctory, but enough to lighten her mood a little. "Barry, I think something is happening to the asteroids."

"Something . . . What?"

"Some of them have moved into orbits that bring them closer to Earth. SkyWatch started noticing them about two or three years ago. We didn't realize, at first. We thought we had screwed up some observations. When we began sharing and sifting our database, we found more and more instances . . ."

"No usual explanations?"

"Gravity tugs from Jupiter or Mars . . . ? No, they can't account for the pattern. Then, last November, some of the

FarTrip scientists told me that they thought Calhoun's Rock had been altered by alien visitors.''

He nodded. "I read about that in the paper. But it's not a proven fact, is it?"

"If we wait for a proven fact, Barry, we may wait too long. On the one hand, asteroids have been shifting in their orbits. On the other hand, at least one asteroid has evidence of tampering. And I thought, 'Dear God, someone is throwing rocks at us.' ''

Barry looked away, out the window. "Jesus," he said. But when he looked back, he had his old grin in place. "If they're throwing pitches, they'd never make the Cleveland Indians, let alone the San Juan Conquistadors."

It was hard to take jokes on a subject like that. She said grimly, "It is just as well they haven't found the strike zone yet."

Barry grunted. "What possible reason—"

"It's hard to see a benevolent purpose behind throwing rocks," she said. "But even if there were . . . Orbital dynamics is a chaotic system. Poincaré proved that long ago. The n-body problem. Gravitational tugs. Collisions and ricochets. Over a period of tens of thousands of years, asteroid orbits are impossible to predict. So even if the original intentions were somehow benign, we cannot depend on them after so many years."

"Mariesa . . ." She could see that his face was distorted with some internal struggle. "Is this just you, or do others think the same way?"

She shook her head and did not answer. Had anyone put the two pieces together: FarTrip and SkyWatch? *Would* anyone put them together? And would anyone draw the conclusion she had drawn? Did she even dare suggest the idea? Maybe there were a hundred others as convinced as she was; and each one fearing ridicule or worse. "I don't know," she said. "I don't know if *I'm* right. I only know that if I am and we do nothing, we could be in for a . . . for a 'royal screwing'—by accident or by design."

"Mariesa. Riesey. Did Keith ever tell you why he joined Prometheus?"

Worry chased fear across his face. "To save the world," she said, though she knew somehow that was not true.

"He told me. He gave me a . . . a 'briefing.' I guess you'd say, toward the end, when he knew it was only a matter of time. He made me promise something, and I failed him."

She laid her hand on his arm and leaned across the seat to him. She did not speak.

His eyes were shrouded. "He didn't want to save the world. He only wanted to save you."

17.

Bugle Call

Waldo was in the dark, and that worried Flaco. After all, Uncle was—quite literally—plugged in and whatever skinny there was, he, she, or it usually had it straight. But there were four ships rising toward co-orbit with LEO Construction Site and the off-site crew was just as puzzled as the otters.

"Maybe it's just an unusually big lift," Tonio suggested.

Waldo was tracking the ships with the doids on the Earth-side hull and had relayed the image to the pixcreen in the crew quarters in Number Two. Four shapes, far below, slowly pulling ahead of the station. It was hard to track them against the night beneath them, but Waldo had enhanced the image. Grainy and false-color. You could tell they were Planks by their shape, but not much else. Flaco and the other off-duty otters were watching and speculating, and the module hummed with a half-dozen conversations.

"I don't know," said Tiny Littlebear, scratching his head. "They got something real big to lift, they use the Shuttle and some O/Ts, right?"

"Not 'big,' " said Sepp, "but maybe 'many.' "

Tonio looked at him. "What does that mean?"

Sepp shrugged.

Bird Winfrey floated past. He paused and looked at the screen and at Flaco and the others. "You guys are nuts," he decided. "None of you know squat, but you think if you throw guesses at each other, you'll learn something." He laughed and Tonio stuck his chin out.

"Yeah, *ailo?* What do *you* think they are?" He waved a thumb at the pixcreen.

"I don't *think,* asshole; I *know.*"

"You do?" "What are they?" "How'd ya find out?" "Tell us."

Bird grinned. "They're four Planks rising into low orbit. Anything more than that and I'd be guessin', just like you. *You* don't know. *Waldo* don't know. *Christensen* don't know—unless he does, and he ain't saying. They'll rendez' in a couple of loops—*if* they keep coming—and *then* we'll know. But it could be flight exercises, or the ERT heading toward some Earthside rescue mission."

"I know what they're bringing," Flaco said softly. "Trouble."

Bird tugged at his steel-wool beard and regarded Flaco. "Why you say that, Chico?"

Flaco shrugged and didn't answer. He didn't know why he felt that way. Maybe it was the very absence of rumors. There had been no whispers on a grapevine that was usually chock with "I heard" and "heads-up." Down on the Street, it always got real quiet just before something big went down.

The four ships vanished around the eastern limb of the Earth, into a blaze of sunrise lurking just behind the horizon. "There they go," someone said, and sighs gusted from a dozen lips.

"Dey'll be back," said Sepp, in a voice that sounded so much like an old Schwartzenegger line that everyone cracked up. Sepp bore the laughter with stoic dignity. He was right, too, Flaco knew. The ships would reappear over the western limb before LEO had made another circuit. Unless the flock *was* heading for somewhere on Earth, but Flaco didn't believe that. Those ships had been steadily climbing over the past three loops, which didn't make sense if they were heading Earth-to-Earth. And there were only three destinations in this part of town: Mir, LEO, and Wilson Enterprises's SpaceLab III.

"Yeah?" said Tonio. "I bet they're bringing whatever goes into that module Gold Crew attached to Number Four."

"Or else," added Sepp, "what attaches to the 'faces we built onto Number Four's starside outer hull."

"That's what I said," Flaco told them. "Trouble."

Flaco was outside on the hull when the strange Planks finally rendezvoused four hours later. He was wearing one of the special suits where the helmet visor could act like a pixcreen. You could bring up data and schematics and put them in a popper window off to the side, so all you had to do was turn your head to check them out. Or you could put them in see-through mode and superimpose the drawing over the actual work. Flaco was doing the final checkout on the fixturing for whatever was going to be installed on the starside of Number Four. When he had satisfied himself that the clearances and true positions off the datum were within the print tolerances, he used his personal key to enter his approval. His signature appeared in the approval box, and Flaco contemplated that for a moment before he logged off. Hell of a thing. That was his say-so that the assembly was okay; and if it failed, it was his butt in the slinger. Who said promotion had no downside? He was a lead rigger now, but all it meant was he had more responsibilities and headaches than before.

He gazed out at the stars. Maybe they were putting in a telescope. There were, sure enough, stars to look at. Fiercely bright, numbering in the millions; *enough stars to cast his shadow* when the work floods were off. On a sudden impulse, he held his arms out wide, embracing them. Golden Saturn sat in his left hand; brilliant Jupiter, in his right. Mars was a ruby setting behind the curve of Earth, just out of reach. Only Mercury and Venus were missing, lurking on the far side of the sun.

He lowered his arms and looked around, in case anyone

hàd seen him. Maybe it was another powerscreen they were going to install here. Though facing starside like it did, how would it catch the beam from Helios Light?

"Flaco?" It was a woman's voice, and for a moment he didn't recognize it.

"What is it?"

"Nothing. Just dropped by to see what you were up to."

"Oh . . . Hey. Leilah, right?"

"Yeah." She sounded pleased. "Leilah. You don't know how tired I get of being called Waldo all the time. It's so herbie. 'Where's Waldo?' 'Everywhere!' Every bunny cracks that joke, like I haven't heard it a million times already. Sometimes, I feel like . . . Well, never mind. I called to ask you a favor. Your boss'll be bringing everyone in pretty soon."

Flaco grunted. "Soon's I tell him job's done."

"No, this is from Earth. I just saw the upload. How often does the groundside program manager tell the skyside boss when to call his outsiders in?"

"You sure about that?"

"Word."

"Strange . . ."

"It must be the rendez'," Leilah said. "They don't want anyone outside when those Planks close. Gotta be."

"How come?" Flaco wondered. "Secrecy's not O&P style."

"Yeah, that's what I said. So I thought, maybe you can go around the hull and get a look for me. They should be on close approach soon."

"Use the doids, so we all can see."

"Can't. They've been shut off. The whole aft Earthside quadrant's black. Official explanation is it's a software malf at Waldo Central. But one of our consultants got curious and hacked around, and he found it was a management decision. The orders came down from so high up, the memo left a crater on Hamilton Pye's hard drive. So I figured . . . You're out there, and, well, maybe you could just go take a personal peek."

Flaco pondered the request. If they wanted the crew inside and the doids shut off, it meant they didn't want anyone eyeballing the approach. So would he get in trouble if he peeked? Nuts. If they wanted him not to look, they should have told him not to look instead of playing cute.

Nobody else on the hull took any special notice as he strolled around the barrel of Number Four. He walked carefully, flexing his feet to work the boot magnets the way he'd been taught. He was supposed to use his lifeline, too, but most otters didn't bother unless they were working in one spot. Too much hassle to reel it in and out as you shifted position.

"You were stargazing, weren't you?" Leilah's voice asked. "Before. When I hailed you."

Flaco grunted. "Yeah," he admitted. "The doids on this side of the hull seem to be working," he added sourly.

"What's wrong?"

"Some of us don't like it when we don't know if we're being rodneyed or not."

"I'm sorry, Flaco. I'll cut off your circuit if you want. But usually we're in the loop because we're playing lifeguard. Not worth lifting a bonebag just for that; but if you ever do pull a levkin, you'll think it was phat stoopid that one of us was watching and could raise the alarm."

" 'Pull a levkin'?"

"You remember. Gregor Levkin, the Human Moon? From when him and Ned DuBois orbited the first Plank. It means, like, if you go sailing off into the Big Empty."

Flaco grunted. He wondered how slang like that got started. He had never heard anyone on Red *or* Gold Crew use that phrase. Maybe it was the sort of quip that only people safely groundside could make without wincing.

"All suits," announced Christensen's voice. "Secure your tasks and return to pressure. Acknowledge through your crew bosses."

Flaco listened until Selodkin, Murasaki, and the rest of his crew responded, then he tongued the command channel to Izzy Mac, the rigging boss. "Rigging crew acknowledges.'' Meanwhile, he kept walking. They had ordered him inside; they had not ordered him not to look. How could you defy an order you were never given?

"I like stargazing, too," Leilah said. "Sometimes, I plug into the starside doids and patch through to my virtchhat— you know, the helmet we wear when—"

"I know," Flaco said.

"Oh. But you can't know what it's like. I feel like . . . Like I'm LEO Station itself. That I'm sailing around with my back to the Earth and my face to forever. Like I'm, you know, free. Not cooped up with four walls and a teep set, never meeting anyone except by 'face, and always wondering when the doorbell rings if some old associate finally recognized my dad and came around for the payoff. I should move out. I really should."

"So why don't you?" He wasn't sure he knew what she was talking about, but he didn't mind listening to a woman's voice. He searched the sky. He ought to be able to see the Planks by now. He didn't have much time before they would expect him at the manlock.

"Then there wouldn't be anyone at home for dad. Mom died a couple years ago; and my sister, the Queen of Creation, baled out even before that. I guess she went to Hollywood to sleep with producers. Bitch."

"What's wrong with your dad? He sick, or something."

"Paralyzed. A bullet from an old friend after he turned State's evidence. Look, Flaco, I've said too much. I shouldn't have told you any of that, not even my name. It's just that I'm going herbies down here. I need to talk to *someone*."

Her voice twanged like a plucked string. A "Joisey" accent—North Jersey—practically a homegirl. Flaco could imagine her sitting in front of her teep set with her head encased in a full sensorium virtchhat, her hands and feet stuffed into boots and datagloves. 'Facing with images, touching icons. The few seconds on the bounceback emphasizing the wall of glass between her and the images.

Always alone, except for her father. "Why me?" he asked finally.

A puff of rocket vapor caught his eye, and suddenly, now that he knew where to look, the four Planks stood out against the night. Flaco kicked his visor to magnification and a close-up view appeared in a popper. He caught his breath.

"Because you keep your word when you give it. I saw when that McKenna woman tried to slut you. I was running an inventory control mobile across the bay. You could have screwed her there in the air lock and your wife would never have known. No one would have known."

"Except Uncle Waldo," he said sharply. "And me." Flaco kicked in his suit spews and took the shortcut to the manlock, where the last of the riggers was just going in. He rose above the hull and guided himself forward, away from the dock and the approaching ships. He was a satellite now himself, just like that Levkin. A free-standing, rocket-propelled orbiter circling the Earth. Only the presence of LEO Station just beneath his dangling boots preserved the illusion that he was riding *on* something, rather than falling along *with* something. An exhilirating feeling, cut short when he touched down by the lock.

"I guess you didn't get a glimpse after all," said Leilah.

Flaco almost didn't answer her. A peeping tom, catching glimpses. Watching him. Seeing that he had *wanted* to do McKenna. Lithe, strong, supple Wendy McKenna. Arms like wire that could bind you tight. Eager. Hungry as any man months away from home. He might have done it, had she been less direct. A few touches with her delicate fingers in the right places might have been enough, and he would have burst out and into her, and lost his honor.

With Uncle Waldo watching all the while.

"I saw 'em," he snapped. The green light on the panel beside the manlock hatch told him the lock was ready for another cycle, and he passed the bar code on his sleeve across the scanner so they would know that everyone scanned out was back in. "Air Force bars on all four."

* * *

Flaco didn't have a chance to tell Tonio or the others about the Planks. He felt the vibration of the first ship docking while he was still shucking his hard suit in the prep bay; and by the time he had joined the others in Number One and located his friends, the visitors were already coming aboard. They wore night black jumpsuits bearing the silhouette of a howling wolf against a white disk. That had to be a VHI company, though he didn't recognize the logo. He closed his mouth and took another look. Not a trace of Air Force blue. No badges; no wings. No sleeve stripes or shoulder pips.

The first was a burly man with wild hair and a beard that enveloped his entire face. He blinked as he looked around at his new surroundings and a pink smile split the bristles around his lips. He was about as unmilitary-looking as Flaco could imagine, and for a moment Flaco thought he had been mistaken about the emblems on the Planks. But behind him came a thinner man who seemed to have been hewed from granite. Close-cropped hair and steel gray eyes. He, too, looked around the bay; but where the first man had gawked, the second man assessed. Only the brief widening of his eyes betrayed any unease at the strange orientation of the receiving dock and the assembled otters floating at random angles.

More men—and a few women—emerged from the manlock and hovered around the lock looking distinctly queasy. All of them wore the black jumpsuits. Flaco kept quiet. He could read two languages and he didn't need anyone to spell this one out for him. Either VHI was using Air Force ships these days, or the Air Force didn't want to announce themselves. And if that were the case, Flaco was not about to volunteer the introductions.

There was a spot of blue among the black-clad newcomers and Flaco recognized Meat Tucker, wearing his O&P outfit. Meat saw him and kicked over with unconscious grace, tumbling like a trapeze artist in midflight so that he took the landing on his legs. He traded fives with Flaco and his friends. "Hey, Meat," Flaco said, "what you doing up again so soon?"

Meat flipped his hand. "Ah, they gave me a special exemption to the rotation rule. You guys are supposed to assemble and install a megawatt laser we brought along. Someone important must've noticed that I helped build the prototype down in Arizona, and that I have experience on LEO. So, here I am."

"A laser," said Sepp. "So that is what it is to be."

"Who's 'we'? The guys in black?" asked Tonio.

"Werewolf Electronics," Meat answered with just a moment's hesitation. "The guy with the bushy face is Werewolf Gregorson, himself. He brought along some of his laser techs, but they're not space-broken. We'll need a top crew for this, Flaco. Rigger, electricians, and all. You got any names you want to share, see me in about an hour, after I sit down with the big hats and brief Christensen."

Some of the newcomers gathered in a disorderly cluster around Werewolf; the others lined up behind the gray-eyed man. Flaco was pretty good at arithmetic, too. He could add two and two. The best place to hide trees was in a forest.

The gray-eyed man snapped something and the group with him set forth gingerly, pulling themselves along the guidelines. The otters moved in for the traditional welcome—looting the newcomers' duffel bags followed by the DuBois handshake—but no more than two or three had been tugged off the ropes and left dangling before the gray-eyed man—their officer, Flaco was sure—said something sharp to Christensen; and the O&P boss flushed a deep red and blew his whistle.

"No horseplay this time, otters," Christensen announced. "Leave the bunnies be." The other man said something else and Christensen replied loud enough that Flaco could hear. "They're bunnies, *Mr.* Duckworth, until they prove otherwise."

Flaco scratched his chin. If Duckworth wanted to pretend he and his men were not Air Force, that was fine by him, but a little more subtlety was called for. Ivan Selodkin and a few others, deprived of the expected fun, sprung off their guy lines and bounded toward the crew quarters. As they passed the crab-scuttling newcomers, Ivan said something in Russian and his companion laughed. Gregorson and the other blacksuits followed at a distance. Flaco was struck by how awkward and disjointed their movements were. Their legs tended to drift out of line as they pulled themselves along. A few of them had solved the problem by wrapping their legs around the line, like they were rope climbing.

"Dust bunnies, for sure," Tonio said.

"Word," said Bird Winfrey, so bemused by the sight that he accidently agreed with Tonio.

"It iss not good," said Sepp. "If they are to work on this laser, they must be not so clumsy. It will be up to us, my friends, both the laser to build and the bunnies to coddle."

Flaco laughed. "Listen to us. How long ago was it that we were dust bunnies?"

"Not like *those*," Tonio protested.

Sepp shook his head. "Hierüber," he said, "reift man schnell."

Later, when Flaco went to find Meat, he found that the briefing was still in progress, so he decided to hang around the admin module and review next week's rigging schedule. Erecting the laser was going to play holy hell with the PERT, and Flaco wanted to see what other jobs could be postponed or rearranged to make men available for the laser project. Van Huyten shelled out too much troy to have pipe fitters floating around idle because the rigger they needed was working on something else. Could be that someone already had everything figured, but the secrecy shrouding the new arrivals argued against it. Secrecy meant that the left hand hadn't been talking to the right.

The PERT A/S would be some help with the jigsaw puzzle; but the lead operators had not named the Critical Path Integrated Logistics neural net "CRAP PILE" for nothing. The Artificial Stupid considered each rigger to be an equal, interchangable "unit," but no way would Flaco plug Hirao Murasaki into a slot vacated by Ivan Selodkin without making other adjustments to compensate for their relative strengths and weaknesses. Flaco didn't have the final say on who would shift over to the laser installation. Izzy Mac was the Gold Crew rigging boss, but Izzy always listened to what his leads had to say.

Selodkin emerged from the radio shack, saw Flaco, and grunted a greeting. Selodkin was a man of few words. His stocky build and bullet head gave him the appearance of a surly fire hydrant, but he was friendly enough. "*Privyet,* Mercado," he said. "You are waiting to use the radio?"

The Consortium was generous with communications time. Having hauled collective rear ends five hundred klicks straight up, the least they could do was let the crew talk to their families as often as possible. In practice, with almost seventy men and women in the construction crew plus the Maintenance and Utilites Cadre, that meant once a week.

"Sure," Flaco lied, and felt a pang of guilt that he hadn't called Serafina yet this week. "How's it going, Selodkin?" Russians, he had discovered, did not consider it rude to call a man by his last name. A friend might call Selodkin "Ivan Pavlovich" or "Ivan Palich"—or even just "Palich"— with varying degrees of informality. A close friend might say, "Vanya"; and a *very* close friend, "Vanechka." If you wanted to be snotty, you called him "Vanka." You could tell a lot about where a Russian was coming from by how he greeted you.

"Oh, my wife," said Selodkin waving a hand in circles and wagging a thumb toward the radio shack—actually a small booth that could be closed for privacy. "She thinks I am *durak.* How you say, crazy."

Flaco clapped him on the back. "They all think that, Selodkin. And they're mostly right."

The Russian laughed and swam out of the room. Flaco entered the radio shack and closed the door, and floated there unmoving, staring at the equipment. It would be a little more than six weeks before Flaco went back down and Serafina would give birth. She was all a storm of emotion now, accusing him of abandoning her; herself, of being ugly and no longer desirable. Flaco did not know how to deal with that. For him, an emotion played a single theme. He knew joy from sorrow; and when one possessed him, the other was not to be found. Yet the last time they had talked, 'Fina had raged and cried and gushed and pleaded in a tempest of love and frustration that he could barely juggle. Joy and sorrow were all ajumble, and her words had both lashed and carressed him. All women grew thus, Flaco knew, as their time approached; yet, he could not help but think that if he were with her, she would bear things more calmly.

As he settled himself into the sling, but before he could activate the connection to Uncle Waldo, he heard voices outside. The briefing must have broken up, because Flaco recognized the voice of DeWitt Christensen.

"... but I don't have to like it."

"Imagine how much that bothers me." Flaco didn't know that voice, but supposed it was either Gregorson or the other man, Duckworth. "I said no Russians on my job, and that's what I meant."

"The important thing," said a rumbling bass—and *that* must have been the barrel-chested Gregorson. "The important thing is installing the laser ..."

"And keeping the construction on schedule," added Christensen.

"Yeah, profits before patriotism, right?"

"We'll let history judge who the patriots were, Duckworth."

"History's a whore, Gregorson. She goes to bed with the winners. How you can stand by when women and children are being slaughtered, cities bombarded, young men brutalized—"

"I thought that was your whole gig. Brutalize young men so they break things and kill people. I thought you guys'd be standing in line over in Belgrade or Athens or Ankara panting to be accredited observers."

A long icy silence followed. Flaco was frozen in place.

He couldn't leave the booth now, and he couldn't start talking without them hearing that he was in here. He held his breath, trying to be somewhere else.

"I'll pretend I didn't hear you say that, Gregorson; and maybe when you think about what you said, you'll pretend you didn't, too. People like you can *pose* all you want to, but *we're* the ones who know how it is. There isn't a man or woman among us who doesn't pray for peace every day, because it's *our* ass you'll hide behind when the crap hits the fan. ' . . . Between our loved homes and the war's desolation . . .' Keep that in mind. Meanwhile, we'll do what little we can to stop the barbarism and the butchery in the Balkans. Tonight, you can ask yourself what *you* did."

"I still don't like it," Gregorson rumbled.

Duckworth laughed. "Full circle, gentlemen. And I don't feel like another round. You've got the schedules and the deadlines. Now, 'Just Do It.' "

Even after the voices had died away, Flaco didn't move. He stayed in the booth for a long time, trying to sort things out in his mind.

Strangely, it was the disembodied Waldo, Leilah, who showed the most sympathy for his loneliness. Tonio only laughed and said, "You care too much about things you cannot touch." And Sepp seemed an atom, a man alone, who had left no one behind to long for. Bird Winfrey had the sad ability to compartmentalize his life. When he was on the job, he gave no thought to Rosie or Earth. As for Tiny Littlebear, he only shrugged and said, "When you've been married longer, you won't feel it so bad."

But Leilah understood separation; perhaps because she herself was separated from everything: the world, her work, her one-time friends; one step removed from everything but her invalid father.

"Hey, Flaco," Leilah whispered one night while Flaco vainly sought sleep. She spoke from a grille close by Flaco's head. It was part of the intercom system, but no place was closed to Uncle Waldo. "You awake?"

"Yes . . ."

"Feel like talking?"

Flaco had nothing better to do, so they talked a little bit about the job. About the upcoming baseball season. Nothing consequential. But it was pleasant just to lie there and listen.

"You have termites, you know."

"Termites. Little bugs that eat wood. Right?"

"Right, except sometimes they eat words. They're little A/S programs that cruise the comm channels snipping out bad words. We call them Mrs. Grundy."

"Bad words? You mean like . . ." And he said a bad word.

Leilah laughed. "No, not like that. When they put that new laser on the station. It's based on some classified stuff, so they put termites in your system so no one says anything accidently to their friends on the ground. Waldo think it's real herbie. What if the termites chop out something important because they mistake it for something classified?"

Leilah only knew about *Michael,* not the second installation. Flaco wondered what would happen if he mentioned Duckworth's toy, but decided against it. Why draw attention? "When did these termites go to work?" he asked.

"Right after they brought the laser up. I think it was the next day, but no one noticed until a message came down that looked like Swiss cheese." She laughed. "Some of us are working on bug spray. Not me, I'm just a teeper; but some Waldos are code dancers and stuff. I'm not bothering you, am I?"

"No. I like hearing your voice. You sound like Serafina, a little."

"Lonesome? I know about that."

"Yeah, I guess you do. You have a guy?"

The bounceback took a long time. "I used to have lots of guys," Leilah said at last. "Back in school. I used to think that was the answer to everything, you know. That I could have anything I wanted—security, position, wealth— if only I found the right boy and laid down on my back."

"I guess you were pretty."

"Any girl is pretty when she hikes her skirt up. But you know what I found out? You get more security when you stand up than when you lie down. You know what I mean? I still like to do it—not that I get much chance these days— but not for the same reasons. Not because I need someone to make promises that he never means to keep."

Flaco tilted his locker door open, and saw Serafina taped against the inside. A saucy pose, one Flaco himself had captured in Atlantic City. Serafina leaned back against a boardwalk post, with her arms in back of her head and her long, tanned legs braced into the hot sands of the beach. Her swimsuit, slung low around her hips, teased him. Her eyes looked boldly into the camera and her smile beckoned. They had been married then less than a week. "I make promises," he said, "I keep them."

"She must be very beautiful. Your Serafina."

"Her heart is beautiful." A heart had grown waspish lately, but that was only the chemistry grappling with her body. Snugged into his bunk-bag like a sack of groceries, Flaco could see the other men and women on his shift lining the cylindrical walls of the bay like human wallpaper, separated from one another by little partitions. He could look "down" into the boxes above him, on the far curve of the hull. In one cubicle, two figures writhed in one bag. Flaco looked away. An otter treasured his privacy, but learned not to insist on it. And others learned to grant the illusion of it when the need arose. He reached out and touched Serafina's cheek with his fingertip. Far above him, a muffled voice sighed, "Oh . . ."

"You must be lonely, too," Flaco said.

"Oh, I can put on my virtchhat and be with any guy you want to name. They got programs, you know. E-stars. Bodscans, some of them. You know—real guys, but cybercopied? And original morphs, too. Designer buff. Some of them are too good. A real guy always has a flaw somewhere. It's all audio-visual, though. Tactile, you have to supply yourself. And you don't get the smells and the tastes."

"It sounds . . ." He couldn't think of a word for how it

sounded. Horrible; and tempting, in a horrible way.

"It sounds lonely? It is. 'Cause there's no one on the other side, you know? It's just another way to play with yourself, but at least it leaves both hands free. Hey, Flaco, you have a virtchhat in your cube, doncha? Put it on and I'll show you."

Flaco unfastened his virtchhat from its niche and held it in his hands for a moment. He glanced across the bay, where pleasure fought ziggy and arms and legs alternated between caresses and handholds. Abruptly, Flaco pulled the set over his head and the goggles and earphones shut out the rest of the world. His finger found the activator and suddenly an endless, slowly swirling gray mist enveloped him.

"I'm on," he said. "Just wanna see what you're talking about. Tha's all."

"Sure. I know how it is. I'm uploading a visual to you now." Stereo earphones. Leilah's voice seemed to come from just beside him, as if she were lying with him in his cube.

The gray mist blinked and his eyescreens cleared to a bedroom. Three-dimensional, because the eyescreens were stereo. The decor was a little too plush; the colors a little too bold. Overdecorated, Flaco thought. Yet, taste varied. There were photographs on the dresser, little odds and ends lying around. A pair of panties had been thrown at a clothes hamper and missed. A pair of woman's shoes were tucked under the bed. It was virtchuality, but it was a real bedroom, too.

A woman appeared. No entry. The image swiped onto the scene. She was dressed plainly, in jeans and sweatshirt. Her black hair was pushed high up on her head, exposing a swan-like neck. Her nose was long and had an arch to it. Dark brows framed an oval face. She was three-dimensional, too. Very three-dimensional. "Do you like it?"

The voice was Leilah's. The image's lips moved in synch.

"Is that . . . You?"

"Do you mind?"

"No. I always wondered what you looked like."

The figure turned around—not quite like a real person. "Rotated" was the right word. "What do you think?"

"I think you don' need tricks to be pretty." If this was really Leilah, Flaco thought. If this was not some idealized virtch of the real woman. A mask she was presenting to Flaco, or even to herself. Everyone liked to pretend they were something more than what they were. Beauty, honor, swagger, knowledge. Whatever it was of themselves that they cupped most tightly in their hands they made bigger, bolder, or brighter when they showed themselves to others.

"Thank you." The Leilah-image reached up and its arms grasped the sweatshirt and tugged it up over its head to reveal the bare, perfect torso underneath. Smooth, unblemished skin curving from her shoulders to her hips. The figure rotated again and faced front. Flaco sucked in his breath.

"I don' think I should do this . . ."

"It's just a picture. Guys look at pictures all the time."

But the pictures hardly ever looked back. . . . Flaco closed his eyes and Serafina rose before him. Bold, dusky, modest, loving. "Serafina," he said.

"Tell me about her. What does she look like? Is she taller than me?"

"No, shorter. And her hair is longer. It flows to her shoulders like a black river."

"Like this?"

Flaco opened his eyes and saw that the Leilah image had morphed. The hair hung down now and the woman was shorter. Flaco swallowed. "Her nose is longer, but it don't have no hook in it."

"Hey, not everybody can be Italian, right?" And the nose straightened.

"Her eyes are brown, and they shine like the stars. Her chin . . . Your chin is sharper; hers is rounded. Yes, like that . . . But her mouth is wide and her lips full and soft. Ah . . . ," said Flaco, forgetting himself. "How I long to kiss those lips. . . ."

He told Leilah about Serafina, described her every intimacy; and his words sculpted the image. The face narrowed; the breasts shrank; the brows thinned. At her urging, Flaco used his dataglove and touched the image himself to show where the changes were needed. The feedback signals to his fingertips was not like touching flesh. The highlighting where he touched was not the rush of blood into the skin. But he could imagine that it was.

"Ah, my morning sun . . . ," he whispered. "How I ache to hold you. . . ."

"Oh, yes," whispered the voice in his ear.

Flaco stopped. He zeroed the glove cursor. "This . . . isn't right."

"Right? Two lonely people helping each other be less lonely isn't right? I can help you hold your love tonight. That isn't right? You can help me forget that I'm sitting in a closed little room with a helmet on my head, and not a friend that I can ever lie with; and that isn't right?"

Yeah, lonely. You couldn't have guys over with your father in the house listening, especially not with him hiding from the mob. And you couldn't go out and leave him, and you'd be scared of hiring a nurse—because who knew, right? So what did you do when the itch grew unbearable? Watch the otters do it? Sit in your chair and wet your lips and maybe touch yourself, maybe imagining it was *you* that guy was going into. Had she been *disappointed* that time in the air lock because Flaco kept his jumpsuit fastened?

The Leilah-Serafina figure moved to the bed and lay upon it. "It's not real, you know. Except what your mind makes real." It—she—caressed herself. An invitation. Was the morph, Flaco wondered, slaved to the real Leilah. Did she sit there naked in her teep set, but for her helmet and dataglove? What images was *she* looking at? Flaco flipped his goggles up and LEO Station crashed upon his senses. He stared around the habitat, seeking. "Ah. Ah. Ah," drifted from the rustling bodies across the bay. With his free hand, he reached for the privacy curtain that he could pull across the top of his cubicle.

"No," said Leilah through his earphones. "Please."

He knew what images Leilah saw now. Yet, why him? Why not the two across the bay? But even as he asked himself the question, he knew the answer. Watching was not intercourse. It was not the touch of a body that the woman below craved, but the touch of a voice. It was the Flesh made Word.

He flipped the goggles back in place and the strange neverland consumed him. The woman that was not quite Serafina, not quite Leilah, waited for him. Her lips parted in a hungry question. Flaco gloved the move icon in the toolbar above the frame and his point of view moved closer. He selected the body icon and gloved the waistband of the jeans. The fingertip pads in the dataglove tingled. He moved them experimentally, felt the hyperlink actuator feedback and crooked his forefinger. The waistband parted and the image wriggled free of its pants.

"Talk to me, Flaco. Tell me what you want . . ."

"My hands want to explore your thighs, caress your flanks, cup your breasts. My lips want to take you in. I want to press your softness into me and hear the music of your voice and smell the sweet perfume of your love."

". . . Flaco . . ."

Was it Serafina's voice? It might have been Serafina's voice.

And yet . . . He couldn't help but feel a pang for the lonely woman whose breathing now came heavy to his ears. Now a nun to circumstance, locked away in a convent of love and duty.

"Your body is wine for my eyes," he said—*but said for whose benefit?* "Never will there be another. No flesh for my flesh; no heart for my heart; no mind to stir my own. I can see you now in that dark, Atlantic City hotel room"—*and in microseconds the A/S had replaced the background with a nondescript room that might easily have been in that very hotel*—"your hands awkwardly placed, unable to hide, unwilling to reveal, suddenly shy for yourself—as if to give yourself was now a more serious thing, as if it would make our future a reality. As if the act, and not the words, would become our pledge. I am transfixed by the strange new sight of you and by my own glimpse of our future. I rise, reaching toward you. Our fingertips touch, and we stand linked at arms' length for long minutes, drinking in the sight of each other.''

''Oh, God . . . Oh . . .''

Flaco blew his breath out in a gust and opened his visor. The rustling movement across the bay had ceased. The gasps had stilled. Yes, that *was* Tonio's slot. Yes, that *was* Wendy McKenna emerging from his bag. Most of the lights in the sleeping cubicles were out, but a few burned where men read books or downloaded letters. They lit McKenna from odd angles when she emerged into the central core, where she closed the fasteners on her coverall.

''She is a lucky woman,'' Leilah said in a languid voice. ''She is lucky you love her so much.''

Flaco knew she didn't mean McKenna.

''I'm tired,'' Flaco said. ''We put up the laser's final section tomorrow.'' He wished Leilah would log off. He was suddenly reluctant to speak to her or to hear her voice. He felt absurdly guilty, as if he had lain with another woman. Yet he had spoken only of Serafina and had thought only of his love for her and the three weeks that still lay between them. What Leilah had been doing while listening, he neither knew, nor cared to know. The words had been a release, and he felt as he always felt when he arose from Serafina. He had broken no vows.

And yet he felt as if he had invented a new sort of unfaithfulness. What Wendy McKenna had not managed in the close confines of an air lock, Leilah had accomplished from five hundred kilometers away.

The blacksuits in Number Four fell silent and watched as Flaco led his crew through the bay, all but one technician who listened on a headset as she probed the guts of an open control panel with her wand. They had been doing that silent act every day since they had moved in last month, and Flaco thought it was very unneighborly. They still slept apart, in some stere-age they had co-opted in Number Three, but at least they didn't form a human screen in front of their work like they used to.

The "mystery fleet" had left some canisters tethered outside before departing. Duckworth had demanded riggers from Izzy to move them into Number Four, and Izzy had protested to Christensen and Christensen had protested to Program Management Earthside, and the word had come back from Hamilton Pye himself: *Give 'em what they want.*

So a whole cord of long cylindrical containers had been brought in at the dock and tugged through Number Two and Number Three, to much speculation on the part of the watching otters. If low profile had been the objective—and why else the secrecy?—the geography of LEO Station had defeated them. Only Number One had space doors large enough to admit the containers they had brought and only Number Four had enough pressurized work space. After the first "Parade of the Giant Cigarettes," Flaco had half expected Duckworth to demand a new set of space doors be cut into the fuselage of Number Four. Maybe he had, and someone finally just said no. So Duckworth's people did whatever it was they did to the cylinders in Number Four and then had to take them out again through Number One, while otters lined their route and Jimmy Schorr sang, "I Love a Parade."

The special module, according to the Gold Crew people who had ferried it up and installed it, was essentially a bundle of empty tubes just big enough to accept the containers. Selodkin likened it to a wasp nest, and the tubes, to wasps. Christensen passed on an "explanation" that the cylinders were experimental packages and the whole thing was an Earth Resource Monitoring Station, and there would be no more open speculation about it, thank you very much.

The whole arrangement reminded Flaco of loading cartridges into a revolver; but, if so, who on Earth was it aimed at? Everyone, possibly. The station made a complete orbit every hour. He thought of the woman he and Bird had met in Allentown jump port. *Secret goings-on. New stuff they won't tell you about.*

Flaco felt eyes on him as he led his crew past. It made him uncomfortable, but what was he to do? LEO was a string of sausages. His people had to pass this point to reach the laser work site. Ivan Selodkin glanced over his shoulder and muttered to no one in particular, "I wonder who they think they are fooling?"

Izzy Mac's real name was Isaac McDonald and he was a Jewish Scotsman—a combination that some said made him doubly stingy and others, doubly devout. Flaco had been on the receiving end of too many of those easy judgements to take them seriously. It was the man that owned the character. If Izzy was devout, it was because Izzy was devout, and not because his covenanting forefathers had scrabbled up rugged, mist-shrouded Highlands to praise their God, or because his mother's folk had climbed older hills farther away. And if Izzy was frugal, it was because a man who grew up with little except salt spray and herring nets learned to make do with less and counted himself wealthy with the difference.

Flaco liked Izzy. At thirty-five, he was one of the oldest men aboard LEO. He was a fair boss and an accommodating one. His tongue-lashings were legendary among the Gold Crew riggers, but he played no favorites and applied the same hard standards to himself; and he never held a man responsible for an error until he had first made damn certain that the man had, in fact, caused the error. Izzy held regular meetings with his leads at shift change, when they staked claim to an empty table in the caf and reviewed the status of the various jobs.

"Work on dressing Number Five is *way* behind," Jimmy Schorr pointed out one day, turning the screen on the laptop so the others could see the milestone chart. As second-shift straw boss, he often had to make independent decisions, and so functioned as Izzy's *segundo*. Gennady Belislav, the first-shift Gold Crew lead frowned and pulled at his lip as he studied it. Izzy Mac shrugged elaborately. "We canna do a thing aboot it," he said, with a sidelong glance at Meat Tucker.

Technically, Meat reported to Gregorson, not to Izzy. He was aboard only for the special project; but he was also a Red Crew lead and his project used Izzy's people, so as courtesy, Izzy had invited him to join the discussions. Meat took the hint and said, "It won't be too long a delay. I told you. The Werewolf people broke the whole thing down into modular subassemblies before we left. Most of the really delicate work has already been done. Sure, erection's going a little slower than the 'Wolf expected, but things always take longer up here. It's not as though we're using *all* your manpower, Izzy."

"It's the welding and electrical work that's holding things up," Jimmy volunteered. "Your boss" he meant Werewolf—"ordered three welds torn out and redone just yesterday. Sepp and Yaz were both pissed yellow, and my riggers had to hang around with their thumbs up their asses because the site wasn't ready for the next erection."

"Sepp Bauer and Genichi Yazaki are the two best outside men the welders have," Flaco observed. "I don't think nothin' is good enough for that hairy gringo."

"The 'Wolf's okay," Meat told him. "But this laser is his baby, and he wants everything perfect." He shook his head. "You think this is bad? You shoulda been with me when we built the first one, down in Arizona."

"I wonder what it's for," said Belislav. "It swivels from fifteen degrees to fifteen degrees, almost the whole starside sky."

"The big ones at Antisana and Kiliminjaro, down Earthside," Meat said, "goose satellites and transfer rockets. Maybe they want to see what a big one can do when they don't have to compensate for atmospheric scattering."

"Yeah," Jimmy admitted, "we can goose the moon every half orbit. I heard they want to sell power to Artemis Mines."

"Then why dinna they use a sun-synch—like Helios,

only bigger?'' said Izzy. "LEO spends half the day in shadow. No," he concluded, "someone has a different game in mind, and he's come up here to play it."

"And what of our other playmates," Belislav persisted. "What game are they playing, our American military friends?"

"Ye dinna know that they are . . ."

"Tcha! Izzy, I am neither stupid nor blind. The Great Superpower is throwing its weight around again."

"Now, wait a minute," said Jimmy. "You're talking about the U.S. of A. there."

"This station is international territory, by UN charter," Belislav insisted. "It bothers me, the secrecy. It bothers me that the secrecy is so ill-concealed; as if they do not care if we pierce their disguise. And . . . some of the men are bothered more than I am."

"Really? Like who?"

They turned at the new voice and saw Duckworth and one of his techs balancing microwaved meals in their hands. The Air Force officer contrived to look razor sharp even in baggy coveralls. He was still not fluid in his zero-g movements, but after a month on board he had at least grown less awkward. His mouth smiled; his eyes did not. Belislav raised both hands, palms up.

"Some who think the secrecy conceals something more sinister than the smug self-importance of a nation that can do whatever it pleases."

Duckworth's eyes narrowed. He wagged his thumb at his companion and she launched off to find a table. "I could take that the wrong way, you know."

"*Nichevo.*"

"But . . ." And Duckworth's mouth twitched. "Sometimes, when you're the only game in town, you have to do what you have to do, whether it pleases you or me or Great-Aunt Sophie. It's like they used to say, 'Who ya gonna call?' If we *could* do whatever we pleased, we sure as hell would be doing something other than this."

"I hear you, *'mano*," Flaço said. The man gave him a

quizzical look, but Flaco did not explain. Green Crew would be going down in May, along with those Golds whose six months were up. Flaco was counting days now, not weeks; but the days seemed to take longer, and there was a rumor that rotation would be postponed so the bumboat could co-ordinate with the return of FarTrip. Thinking about Serafina, he almost missed Duckworth's next question.

"There wouldn't be any *odinisti* among those men you mentioned, would there?"

Belislav shrugged. "Every *moskaly* is a little bit *soyusky*. Some dream; some wake up; some get out of bed."

Flaco did not understand, but the explanation evidently meant something to Duckworth, because the man nodded. "So. At least you can't object in principle to military men on board LEO, can you, Kirilovitch? That's assuming there are any."

"A man's clothing does not concern me so much as what he does when he puts it on."

Duckworth grunted. He flipped Belislav a mock salute and then, with only a little fumbling with his right foot, found purchase on a guy line and kicked off toward the table his tech had claimed.

The rigging bosses turned inward. Meat pursed his lips. "He just about came out and admitted it, didn't he?"

Flaco figured Meat was being a little cute himself. The Red Crew boss had to know whose ships had lifted him and the Werewolf people. Like, duh? Flaco said, "He's a man who knows his duty and does it." Belislav seemed intro-spective and said nothing.

Jimmy said, "What's an o-di-ni-ski?"

Berislav did not answer for a moment. He rubbed his palms together slowly, as if in thought, and stared at them. Then he said, slowly, "It is like in your country, there are southerners who will not forget that they were once a sep-arate country. In the Rodina, there are those who will not forget that we were once *not* separate countries." He looked up. "*Soyuz* means 'union' and *odin* means 'one.'" He held up his forefinger, a salute Flaco had seen around the station.

Flaco and the others nodded. Flaco said, "Selodkin was just a kid when that happened, but he talks about it all the time."

Izzy Mac frowned. "Should we keep an eye on these unionists? Do you think they might try to jimmy Duckworth's project?"

Belislav shook his head. "Most of them just dream about 'good old days' that never were so good. But most wake up; and some, as I told our friends, get on with life."

Jimmy Schorr looked at his watch. "Jeez, my shift is about to start. See you guys tomorrow." Meat, who ran second shift on the laser project, also pushed away from the table. Izzy Mac laid a hand on Belislav's arm to keep him from leaving, too, and said, "Gennady, what did Duckworth mean by that remark about uniforms?"

Belislav answered smoothly. "Years ago, I was a captain in Russian Army Intelligence."

"And now?"

A shrug. "And now I am a rigger."

Izzy rubbed his chin as he watched the Russian go off duty. He shook his head and looked at Flaco. "Och, and here I thought our biggest problems were a horny electrician and some smuggled pearl."

Flaco started, but would not look directly at Izzy. Did he know who had brought up the pearl? Should he warn Tonio? *Damn* the Cuban, if he had started dealing. "What's the bigger problem?"

The Scot waved a hand around the cafeteria. "There are too many folk up here to think none of them are serving two masters, but DeWitt thought he had all of them spotted."

Flaco blinked. "You mean, government spies?"

"Aye, on company property." Grimly, as if that were the greater sin.

"Why?"

Izzy looked at him with thoughtful eyes. His forefinger traced patterns on the table. "We're the high ground, Eddie. An' every man-jock down at the bottom of the well knows

it. Now maybe''—a glance across the room at Duckworth—
''someone has brought up a pile of rocks.''

Flaco looked away. An uneasy feeling stole over him. A
premonition. He remembered the conversation he had overheard that first day the Werewolf people had come aboard.
''What will happen now?''

Izzy Mac spread his hands, as if to say it was outside his
craft boundary. ''It depends, I would say, on who knows
and what they know or what they think they know.''

Flaco couldn't argue with that. And he thought that
maybe a few more people ought to know, so when he went
back to his cubicle, he searched among his possessions until
he found the card with the netdress that the woman in the
jump port had given him back in March.

INTERLUDE:

Tiptoe through the Termites

TO: Roberta
FROM: Eddie
SUBJECT: Remember me?

Hi. We met last March in the bar in Allentown Jump
port. You were real worried about jump-ship safety
and me and my buddy told you how it was okay and
we had some beers together before we had to leave
for the space station. You said you would like to hear
from me someday.

Well, I been thinking about you a lot lately and
wishing you were up here in orbit with me so you
could see all the stuff I see. Things people down·on
Earth they don't get to see, you know? We could talk
and maybe listen to that song you said you liked. You
know the one. You asked back then if I ever heard it
and I said no, but I heard it since then. There's some
guys up here they want to play it with heavy metal. I
think; but I don't think that's such a good idea, which
is why I'm telling you about it.

Don't write back. Somebody might read it and make
trouble for me because I'm writing to another woman.

Roberta read the E-mail again. A love letter? Oh, God.
She'd talked to those two space-riggers at Allentown that

one time; and now one of them's been in orbit long enough to have the hots for her bony bod. But why did he think "Steel Rain" was her favorite song; and why make a big deal about how he's heard it on the space station since then? Like he'd never heard it before. Right. Besides, she hadn't meant the song. She thought she had made that clear to the two men.

She'd gone to Allentown with the leafletting Crusaders because Isaac had told her it was her best bet to meet construction workers and ask them questions without going to Phoenix and maybe drawing attention. Well, she'd met a couple of construction workers, and she seemed to have drawn some attention anyway.

She wondered if Eddie was the fat, hairy one or the skinny, buff dude.

She kinda hoped it was Buff. Not that it mattered, but the last time she'd had a secret admirer it had been Jimmy Poole.

Though Hairy had known and recited a line from one of her poems, so . . .

The skinny guy had gone high postage, she remembered, when she asked about secret goings on. And she'd said . . .

Oh, God.
    She *had* made it clear.
    Eddie, whoever you are, I love you.

18.

Impact

The landscape around Argonaut's headquarters was unbearably brilliant with the sunlight off Nassau Bay winking like fallen stars and the anonymous glass windows of the building's facade reflecting the sparkles back. The air was warm and heavy with humidity, but had not yet reached the temperatures that turned Gulf Coast summers into a rotisserie. The car's onboard computer directed Roberta past the fast food joints and aerospace remoras that lined NASA Highway One and onto the long curving driveway that led to Argonaut. The sign portrayed a silhouette of an ancient galley: gracefully curved fore and stern posts, an eye on the prow, the hint of a ram under the waterline. She pulled into the visitor space closest to the door.

After turning the motor off, she sat behind the steering wheel for a few moments staring at the crackling sunlight, impatience and reluctance warring within her now that the time had come. She took her cliputer from her briefcase and scrolled through the documents once again, though by now she knew the contents nearly by heart. Jimmy Poole had personally verified the major points and covered all their tracks. They had spun scenarios to cover every possible interpretation of the data. Still she wondered: What if there was something they had both overlooked? Some harmless interpretation that Chris van Huyten would pull out of his hat at the last minute and make her feel like a total herbert.

She stuffed the cliputer back into the briefcase and closed it with a snap. She caught a brief glance of herself in the rearview mirror, and recalled that she had scanned the docs at least a dozen times during the flight into Hobby. *Why am I so nervous? It's all tied up in a pink ribbon.* And she could have E-mailed the materials anonymously. She needn't have come personally.

Roberta hestitated with her hand on the door handle. She had the oddest feeling. A *wyrd* feeling, in the oldest sense of the word. Not exactly *deja vu*, but something very much like it, as if this had all happened before. But she shook the feeling off, got out of the car, and strode resolutely toward the building.

Christiaan van Huyten was a harsher-looking version of Mariesa, Roberta thought. His face was more hard planes, contained fewer softer lines, and his eyes held none of the patience that the Rich Lady's often had. This was not the face of a dreamer, at least, not of the softer-edged dreams. His fancies were spec'ed and costed and, by damn, stayed within realistic tolerances. Which was not to say there were no laugh lines around his mouth or that he did not watch Roberta's approach with something approaching humor. When he rose to shake her hand, it was like a ladder unfolding.

He led her to a square of comfortable chairs arranged around a low table. The office was as severe and functional as any room Roberta had ever seen. Even the artwork. The one spot of whimsy was an engineering "blue-line" assembly drawing of a frog, labelled "Frog Prints." *Anal* was the first word that sprang to mind, but *organized* might be a fairer measure of the man. A band of windows behind his desk and along the wall beside the chairs revealed a panorama of the bay, on which sailboats tried the springtime weather. In the distance, a graceful bridge arced over the water to Kemah. "It was good of you to see me, dropping in unannounced like this," Roberta said as she eased into a seat.

Van Huyten nodded and settled across the table from her. "You made me curious, Miss Carson; and, in my line of work, I've learned to pursue the curious. 'Information that will make both of us uncomfortable,' you told my assistant."

Assistant . . . Nobody had "secretaries" any more. "I'm from the Peoples' Crusades."

A slow nod of the head and a steady, "Yes." No inflection, no sign of feelings or thought. *I'd like to see this guy at a poker table . . .*

"I know you don't approve of the work my organization does . . . ," she began. But van Huyten held up a hand to stop her.

"You don't know anything of the sort," he said. "Some of your crusades, I approve of whole heartedly; some of them, I approve the end, but not the means. And some of them are dangerous nonsense." A quick and genuinely amused curl of his lips. "Call it ideological triage. Don't paint with too broad a brush, and don't confuse me with your caricature of me."

Van Huyten had not raised his voice; yet Roberta felt herself flush. All the van Huytens had that snotty streak, all the more grating for the casualness with which it was used. Yet she wanted something from him, and verbal sparring was not the way to get it. Roberta looked at the envelope she held. Seven months of painstaking research by Jimmy Poole and herself. Evidences carefully tracked down, documented, downloaded, pieced together. Memos, databases, newsgroup clippings. It wasn't legal, but it was all true. The evidence showed how the Rich Lady had circumvented her own organization to cut a private deal with the president out of her own neurotic fears. Used the right way, this information would bring her down.

Roberta glanced at the stony-faced man sitting opposite her. Was she turning this over to the right person? She had formed an opinion of Christiaan van Huyten from public d-bases and reading the purloined memos. A bit of a prig, a stickler for the rules. A "Dutch uncle," both figuratively and literally. But what if family loyalty weighed most?

Roberta took a deep breath. She had rehearsed this speech many times. Now was not the time for stage fright. "Have you ever heard of a hacker named Crackman?"

Van Huyten's eyes narrowed slightly, but he gave nothing away. "Yes." No word of previous encounters; no hint that VHI had recently stumbled over Crackman's four-month-long encampment inside their system and chased him out. (As a parting shot, "Crackman" had sent a virus that placarded THE SCARLET PIMP STRIKES AGAIN on every terminal in the company.) Red faces all over VHI, and heads in Information Systems and Security rolling along the hallways like bowling balls.

"He sent this to Crusades Headquarters," Roberta said. She laid the envelope flat on the table, popped the flop from the cliputer and pushed both across to him. "Here. Take it and decide for yourself what to do about it." Van Huyten tracked the envelope with his eyes, but made no move to pick it up.

"What am I looking at?" he asked.

"Maybe you can tell me."

Van Huyten regarded her for a moment before he picked up the envelope and opened it. He pulled out a hardcopy and read it. Then another. The sides of his neck colored slightly, but his expression did not change. Methodically, he sampled and read through a half-dozen others. He stopped finally and looked at her. Roberta had to stop herself from sinking into the seat. "Why are you giving me this?" he said.

Roberta gave him the practiced half-truth. "A whistle-blower inside the government alerted the Crusades to Donaldson's Star Wars scheme. We were reviewing our options—to verify the warning, strategies to counter it if it proved true—when this package plopped into our laps."

"Information is property," he pointed out.

"Yeah. I know. And this is stolen property. That's why I'm returning it."

Van Huyten tapped his long, delicate fingers against the envelope. He cocked his head. "You still haven't told me why you're giving this to me." he said. "Aside from your civic duty," he added sardonically.

She leaned forward. "To stop Donaldson. He's been using VHI as a cat's-paw—taking advantage of your cousin's obsession. Why you? You're opposed to the project on principle, like we are; and you were deliberately cut out of the loop when your cousin sold out. So maybe this is one of those Crusades where we see eye-to-eye."

"I see you've read the material thoroughly."

"Well, we had to see who to return it to."

The smile was small, but genuine. "I can easily verify whether these are forgeries," he said, watching her to gauge her reaction.

"Good," Roberta said as positively as she could. "We were hoping you could. We didn't know how trustworthy this 'Crackman' person is. He might have serious weenie for Donaldson—or for VHI or the Crusades—and be setting any or all of us up."

Maybe that had been the reaction he'd been expecting. "I'll look into it," he said, placing the envelope back on the table.

It was a dismissal. He was certainly not going to confirm anything to her, nor carry tales out of school. He had shown little reaction—the whole family seemed to have been reared in stoicism—but Roberta did see a grimmer set to the line of his jaw. For a van Huyen, that was as good as a screaming rage. An old proverb popped into Roberta's mind—*You shoot your own dog*—and she was suddenly very glad she had never been a pet of Christiaan van Huyten. She stood up and he rose with her. "Don't take too long," she said, looking up into his face. "There was a secret Air Force flight to LEO late last month. A whistle-blower on board the station told us. Whatever's going down has already gone up."

He smiled again at her turn of phrase. "And if I simply 'sit on it'?"

Roberta shrugged. "Then it's your problem. The Crusades will get Donaldson, one way or another. What he's done will spill, sooner or later. You have to decide how deeply splattered you want VHI to be when it does."

Outside once more, Roberta settled behind the wheel of her rental. Before starting the engine, she checked her plane tickets, which were in her attaché with the second envelope. It was maybe a half hour to Hobby Airport, and the flight to Spokane did not leave for another three. Time enough for a quick supper along the way.

She watched the eateries along NASA Highway One. Every food known to mortal man was served along this stretch of road. The NASA CAFÉ sported an astronaut on a sign reading Authentic Middle Eastern Cuisine, though what astronauts had to do with halvah she didn't know. The sign that drew her in, though, was FRENCHY'S ITALIAN FOOD. You couldn't pass up something as postmodern as that.

Entering the restaurant—there was a sandwich side and a sit-down side, and she opted for the sandwich—Roberta passed a family trio coming out. A slim, hard-faced woman in jeans and checked shirt; a short, stocky, well-built man with steel-gray in his hair and a way of walking that was almost dancing; and a younger woman, maybe eighteen, who looked like a compromise between them. The man held the door for her, making the gesture with such self-mocking ostentation that Roberta gave him a second look.

Yeah, he was the sort of guy who got a lot of second looks from women, and fished for them when he didn't. Slim hips, tight buns, solid chest, and a spark of intelligence and humor behind his stolid, masculine eyes. A glance at his other was enough to show that, if Roberta wanted to fish these waters, they were guarded by barracudas. The guy was an old horizontal athlete, that was sure; but he was retired from the ring now.

"Thank you," she said.

"De nada," he answered with an easy smile.

Okay. Semiretired. Yet, there was something about him that was familiar, and it was more than his easy attitude.

Inside, she asked the counterman. "Say, wasn't that . . . ?" She let the question hang.

The counterman grinned. "That?" He pointed to the man, who was slipping into the most outrageous muscle car Roberta had ever seen. Gallons per mile, she thought. The woman took off her scarf and shook her hair out, the better for it to stream in the breeze. Behind them in the jumpseat, their daughter hunched over a book. "That," said the counterman, "is Ned DuBois. 'The Man Who.' He's going up later this month, so he came over to Boeing Outfitters to check his suit out. He lives just down the road in Clear Lake City."

Roberta had already learned more than she had asked for, so she interrupted to give her order before he got around to what shade of wallpaper graced the DuBois bathroom. She *had* met DuBois, she remembered. Years ago, when van Huyten threw a party after the rescue of his copilot, Levkin. That had been the very night when Styx had overheard Dr. Karr and the Rich Lady arguing and learned the wretched truth about Mentor Academies.

"I think I may hate you." And wasn't it something the way the past could rerun like an old file, randomly accessed? *Styx stepped out of the doorway from the darkened observatory after Dr. Karr had gone and into the Roost where Mariesa van Huyten stood alone. Styx held her arms stiff at her sides; balled her hands into fists. "I heard everything. I TRUSTED YOU!"*

The Rich Lady turned away. "You did not hear everything. You do not know everything." She often spoke that way, Roberta remembered. Did not. Do not. She always lost her contractions when she was stressed. Formality was the armor.

Rage was the lance.

"You're brainwashing us!"

"I would rather say that I have a vision to share."

"What right do you have to force that vision on us?"

"What right does anyone? Would you rather be fed visions of Hollywood and music videos and fashion statements? Or visions of doom and apocalyptic disaster? If I have fed you hope rather than banality or despair, is that so terrible?" She took a step forward with her arm held out, but Styx skipped away from her. The Rich Lady was so caught up in her plans and her visions that she had not even seen what the real betrayal had been, even though Styx had shouted it straight out:

"I thought you cared about me! I thought you were the only one who did!"

Slowly, Mariesa's hand dropped and hung limply by her side. "I do care about you, Styx."

Like a craftsman cares about his tools. *"You want to use me. You want to play with my head, so I'll write your poems instead of mine."*

The elevator hummed and the door slid open. Styx turned and bolted for the alcove, nearly colliding with Barry Fast as he stepped off, and she pounded the buttons with her fist until the door closed on her and the cage whisked her away.

"I said," the counterman repeated, "your sandwich is ready."

Roberta accepted the sandwich. "Sorry. I was daydreaming."

"It's a day for it," the counterman agreed.

And yet there had been a time when she had followed after Mariesa van Huyten like a hungry puppy. When she had sought out Silverpond at every chance. She recalled the time she had gone to Princeton University for the Young Poets panel. The first time she had learned that strangers saw promise in what she had done. She remembered trying to pretend that Beth was not really with her. She remembered how she had met the Rich Lady there and how they had drawn a circle around themselves that left her mother outside.

What poem do you plan to read? her mother had asked.

I don't know, said Styx. *I haven't decided.*

Is it one I've heard?

Stupid question. *No, I don't think so.*

I wish you would show me your poems more often, Roberta.

"I wish I had, too. . . ."

"What was that, miss? Did you want something else?"

Roberta looked up from her plate. "No," she said, "nothing else." At least, nothing that was on the menu here. Roberta shook her head. It was a day for strangeness. *Deja vŭ* and flashbacks. A day like those when the sky turned iron, just ahead of the breaking storm.

19.

Ejecta

May was a snowlike month—the blooms were all white: doll's eyes and devil's bit and foamflowers; mayapples peaking from under spreading leaves. The drive from Silverpond to VHI was a pleasant one, winding through forested, gently rolling hills; and Mariesa regretted those days like today, when circumstances forced her to forsake the woods for the skies and take the helicopter across Skunktown Mountain.

Her fingers sunk like talons into the armrests while Charlie Jim circled the VHI rooftop. He always made it a matter of pride to set his machine down in the exact center of the helipad's crosshairs; but Mariesa valued dispatch more than precision on aerial trips, and she was out onto the pad breathing hard and trying to recover her calm even before the blades had quite stopped turning. Somehow, a copter flight, buzzing mosquitolike above the treetops, unnerved her more than soaring beyond the clouds in a jetliner.

Zhou Hui was inside the rooftop waiting room. She rose as Mariesa entered. "Mr. Christiaan is in your office," she said. Mariesa barely nodded and strode right past her toward the elevator. *Mr. Christiaan . . .* Shades of the *Bounty*. She found no amusement in the comparison. Ms. Zhou scurried to keep up.

They rode down the elevator in silence. Zhou Hui asked

no questions, offered no comments. Privy to everything, betraying nothing, she was an enigma to Mariesa. Where did she stand on these issues? What did she think of her employer's activities? Did she even have opinions, or did her loyalty to her professions preclude any such considerations? Almost, Mariesa asked. Her lips parted with the words already on her tongue, but they closed around the question before it escaped. If loyalty masqued disinterest, it was better not to know.

As they entered the outer office, Zhou Hui said, "He flew in from Houston last night and asked to be put first on your agenda today. I saw to a tray of pastries and coffee."

"That was fine. Did he say what he wanted?"

Hui shook her head. "He said it was urgent and critical."

"Any clue?"

Zhou Hui's hesitation was momentary. "There has been considerable cyberactivity originating in the Argonaut system. Headquarters codes have been breached. Secure files have been downloaded from VHI to Houston and Santa Fe. A lot of cross talk between Argonaut and other divisions. It may"—only the slightest of pauses here—"have to do with the recent hacker problem."

Mariesa nodded, hesitated with her hand on the knob of her office door. She looked back. Chris had often dropped in on headquarters when affairs brought him East, but never unannouced, never so preemptorily. "No interruptions, Hui. You may need to clear my calendar." She did not wait for an acknowledgement, but put on her face and stepped into her sanctum.

Chris stood by the windows, viewing the spring mountainside. He stood stiffly, with his hands clasped behind his back. Mariesa saw that he had put on a charcoal-gray suit, a rare-enough event that it could not be marked down merely as a concession to East Coast sensibilities. The proprieties betrayed him: he had come on a somber mission. Coffee and pastries lay untouched on the silver tray beside him.

"Chris!" She glided toward him with an outstretched

hand. "Why didn't you tell me you were coming?"

He took her hand, but his returning smile was no more than polite. "I only made my mind up last night."

"Sit down, please. You look uncomfortable."

"I feel uncomfortable." Nevertheless, he sat. Erect, Mariesa noted. No crossing of the legs, no leaning back in the chair. A blind man could not fail to read the signals.

"Something is wrong," she said, feeling the answering tension grip her by the throat.

"A little bird paid me a visit two weeks ago and dumped a load of crap on my head."

Mariesa was not sure if that were meant for humor or not. Certainly nothing approaching humor had modulated his voice. She nodded, but made no reply.

"It didn't take my people too long to verify everything. I—" He stopped, looked unhappy, then grim, just before he glanced away and said in a voice loaded with despondency, "Jesus Christ, Riesey, what've you gotten us into?"

"I don't understand."

His mouth thinned into a disapproving line very much like cousin Norbert's. "Don't play games, Riesey. You went around the board and made a private deal with Donaldson."

She had been expecting something like this. Ever since the early morning call from Hui, the sense of foreboding had been growing within her. Not that the matter could have remained secret for long, but she had never given any thought as to what she might do when it finally came out. There were no studies on how the principals might react; no plans on how to deal with them. The step had been taken from the sheerest impulse, leaving her exposed on her blind side. "Oh," was all she said.

Chris did not even remark on her response. "The Steering Committee was opposed . . ."

"The Steering Committee was divided," rousing now to her own defense.

"Which is hardly a consensus for unilateral action."

"A decision was required and the committee was unable

to make one.'' Mariesa stood up and took herself to the windows. Pale wildflowers spotted by darker violet and red littered the forest floor and the meadow below where the trees broke off. Hickory and birch jostled red oak for the sunlight. Zhou Hui's voice whispered in her earclip. *I have examined his logs. His visitor was Roberta Carson from the Peoples' Crusades.* Mariesa wrapped her arms around herself against the hurt. ''It was a legitimate contract with the U.S. government,'' she said. ''The secrecy was a stipulation of that contract.''

''We used to have a phrase when you and I were young: 'Selling Out.' ''

''That was before we learned it meant, 'Growing Up.' ''

''Cynicism is too easy.''

''I had my reasons.''

''Oh, yes. I know that.''

She turned and faced him. ''Who was your 'little birdie,' Chris?''

''It doesn't matter. Truth is independent of the messenger.''

''Not always.''

''I verified everything.''

''Chris, even the truth can be a weapon. Not many of us are brought down by lies. It's the partial truths that do us in.''

''All right, if you must know. That hacker, 'Crackman,' who got into our system, downloaded a host of incriminating documents and mailed them to the Peoples' Crusades. Albright was smart enough to realize that he was in receipt of stolen goods, so he turned the package over to me.''

''*Albright* did.''

''He sent one of his people. Does it really matter?''

Mariesa sighed. ''I suppose not.'' She ran a knuckle across the soft leather of the chair back nearest her. ''I suppose not.''

''But Mariesa, I can't imagine that Albright wasn't also smart enough to read that material first. The Crusades already had wind of Donaldson's plans and were out to blow him off the water. My little birdie has at least given us a chance to set our house in order before it all hits the fan.''

Mariesa's smile was as much a grimace. ''Well, it's symmetric, at any rate.''

''I don't understand.''

''Never mind. Old wounds and old scores. Why have you come to see me?''

Chris's face lengthened. ''To see what we can salvage. If the Crusades are about to turn their guns on Donaldson, I'd rather we weren't standing right beside him. I've already spoken to some of the other presidents. There's a great deal of unhappiness.''

A monumental understatement, she was sure. ''No one likes to be left out of the loop. The danger to Consortium unity can be dealt with.''

Chris cut a hand through the air. ''The hell with the Consortium! What about VHI? João Pessoa wants to take Daedelus out entirely. He's already lined up Chilean money—maybe the Argentines, too—to buy out our shares.''

''We . . . don't need him. We have another aerospace company.''

''Oh, yes, and Dolores will wet herself when she hears. She's been trying to squeeze Daedelus out of the corporation for a long time.'' Chris looked disgusted. ''She played you like a Strad.''

''I had my own—''

''And what about Mentor? Do we have another educational services firm in reserve? Belinda may not be able to buy herself out, but she and her senior principals may jump ship. Each practice is independently owned, remember. Mentor itself only provides common standards and materials.''

''Belinda . . .'' She looked away again, gazed at the awakening hills, where the grasses and flowers bowed before spring breezes—a wave rippling across the meadow like the tide coming in off the bay. But a break with Belinda was inevitable. Mariesa had seen it coming long ago and had closed her eyes against the impact.

"You can't be so surprised," Chris said. "She and I had different reasons for opposing the venture, but we both opposed it from principle. Were you *trying* to force a break with her? Because you couldn't have done better if you had done it deliberately."

Her hands balled into fists. "You don't understand, Chris. You don't understand."

"Explain it to me, why don't you? I'm not entirely stupid." Anger, contempt, and—yes—pity roiled beneath the placid surface of his words. Mariesa looked into his eyes and recoiled.

She turned away and took a breath to calm herself. Somehow, imagining the confrontation to come, she had always expected a tearful Belinda, or a disgusted Werewolf, or a Steve Matthias in new possession of a spine. Never Chris, though; never family. Oh, Styx had aimed her dagger well!

She faced one of the photographs that adorned her office. Calhoun's Rock. A view from the west end, where that strange bore hole ran down its centerline. *And where are they now, Calhoun and the others?* Swallowed up in a sudden radio silence. Helios unable to lock on. A few weak signals that might have come from a damaged antenna. The whole world waited with straining ears for some word out of the darkness. Donaldson's hopes and fears and insecurities seemed suddenly trivial beside Calhoun and the others and what they may have discovered.

"Protection, Chris," she said in a steadier voice. "The world needs protection."

"What, from Balkan barbarians?"

She turned to face him, willed him to see. "No. I only *used* Donaldson. The real threat is from the sky. From rogue asteroids. There have been too many near misses, and they're growing too frequent. We need to be able to break them up *before* they strike. We need to learn to do that, and we may need to learn soon."

He stared back at her in silence, showing neither shock nor surprise. *He knew already,* she thought sadly. He knew already, and he had discounted the threat.

"So, you wagered the integrity of the station, the unity of the Consortium and VHI itself, *and* the stability of the United States government just to get a ray gun to shoot down rocks . . . ? Does that about sum it up?"

She struck the back of the chair with her fists. "No. It. Does. Not. Don't you see? The rest of it means nothing if the Earth is hit. There are disturbing trends . . ."

"Disturbing trends. Yes. On that, we're agreed. How much more would you be willing to barter on the counter of this obsession of yours?" He hesitated, and his long, thin fingers ran down the seam of the leather on his chair. "The Family Trust is meeting on the sixteenth."

She jerked as if slapped and stood with her arms dangling by her sides. "That soon? No, please, Chris. None of our cousins has any imagination. I need you to stand by me."

He shook his head implacably, like the tolling of a bell. "I cannot countenance placing weapons on a civilian facility."

It was already too late for that. She wondered if Chris knew that, too. Mariesa closed her eyes and opened them to the peace of inevitabilty. After all, what could Chris do, evict Duckworth? Give back the laser? It was a done deal. She had four days before the family met; and in four days, who knew what could happen?

"I do not belief," Sepp Bauer said, "dat dey want to stop us from calling the Earth." He nodded sagely and Henry Littlebear grunted. Flaco said, "Must be the padlock and the guard on the radio booth that fooled me, *'mano.*"

Selodkin glowered and Tonio smiled, but neither responded. The five of them clustered around a dining cube in the mess hall, discussing, like everyone else, the station's sudden change in status. Duckworth had received a coded message that sent him, Werewolf, and Christensen to huddle in Christensen's office; and when they emerged, the station was under martial law. Someone Earthside had spilled some premature beans, Duckworth said, and all messages in or out of the station were temporarily subject to censorship.

Just temporary, Duckworth assured everyone. But Flaco had the icy feeling in his heart that Rotation Day would be postponed, not just until the return of FarTrip on the fifteenth, but just "until." The smile and the bitter humor he showed his friends disguised the turmoil he felt. Guilliermo might be born before Flaco hit dust again!

Littlebear shook his head. "Bad enough when they had those—what'd y' call 'em, Flaco?—Yeah, those termites censoring our mail. Now we gotta give Duckworth prerecorded messages, and he screens 'em. Yeah, I know Christensen said we should cooperate. But, hell, we can't even talk with Uncle-fucking-Waldo." He raised his voice. "Isn't that right, Uncle?" There was no answer, and the Mohawk grinned without humor. "Sure sounds like they don't want us talking to the bunnies."

Sepp wagged a finger back and forth. "No, no, no," he said. They hunched forward over the table so they could hear one another over the hubbub of the other conversations. "Since two months, anyone here could haff called the dustball and chatted about our new installations. Dey are no secrets. *What* they are iss secrets, but *dat* they are iss not."

Littlebear rumbled. "All right, smart guy . . . Why can't we yack?"

Sepp shrugged. Selodkin spoke up. "Our German friend wants us to guess. But is obvious why. Is so people on *Earth* are not speaking to *us*."

Flaco glanced at his segundo. Ivan Selodkin clenched and unclenched his fist, though never quite enough to squeeze the juice from his drinking bulb. He wondered if the Russian knew he was doing that. Selodkin's gaze was fixed on something a foot in front of his eyes. Something unpleasant, to judge by his expression. "You mean," Flaco said, "they know something down there that we don't."

Tonio roused himself. "Who cares?" he asked lightly. "Long as we do our jobs, right?" Selodkin looked across the table, focusing on the Cuban without losing the look of unpleasantness.

"What could Dusty know that we don't?" Littlebear

asked. "Like Sepp said, we *know* about the installation; and it's not too hard to guess that it's a weapon of some sort. And not too hard to guess what part of the world needs a swat back of the head."

"Orthodox countries, you mean," Selodkin said in a low voice.

"You don't *know* that," Littlebear pointed out. "You have no proof." Sepp rapped the table with triumphant knuckles.

"Dot's chust what I wass saying," he proclaimed. "We are up here *guessing*. Down below, dey *know*. Someone spilled beans."

"That's a couple billion folks in on the secret, then," Tonio said in a querulous tone. "Why can't they let us in on it, too?"

Selodkin pushed away from the table. "So is making no trouble *here*, where is no room for trouble."

"Ivan Palitch!" That was Gennady Belislav, the Gold Crew lead rigger, sitting at another table with Izzy Mac and Meat Tucker. *"Davaitye govorit', tovarish!"*

Selodkin made a chopping motion with his hand. *"Uzhe slyshkom mnogo slova, 'gospodin'."*

"Vanya . . ." Belislav hesitated a moment. *"Khudoi mir luchshe dobroi ssory."*

Selodkin's laugh was a bark. *"Nye vsegda, gospodin. Nye vsegda."*

Flaco bit his lips. The crews were forming into cliques and the use of national languages was only one symptom. It had started with Duckworth's arrival, and the latest development would only accelerate the process. He looked over his shoulder at Duckworth and the other bosses. Gregorson's face was cherry red and he and the Air Force man were almost nose-to-nose. ". . . and that includes VH-fucking-I," Flaco heard Duckworth say through the curtain of sound.

If Duckworth thought he could keep things normal, he was *loco* in the *coco*. But Flaco sensed that the Air Force man wasn't sure what he was doing either. The message had caught him by surprise, too, and he was improvising. He'd been sent up to install a piece of equipment and safeguard it; and now, like it or not, he was in charge of the whole *chingao* station. If Flaco didn't hate his guts for postponing rotation, he might even feel sorry for him.

Sepp watched Selodkin go with a frown on his massive brows. He shook his head. "Vanya iss wrong," he said. "*No* place is there no room for 'no trouble.' "

"What if 'Memo is born before Duckworth lets us go?" Flaco said.

Tonio laid a hand on Flaco's arm. "You shouldn't let it worry you, Flaco. People worry too much."

To get away from the angry hubbub on board the station, Flaco sought solitude in an empty bin in the warehouse module. Four big Seebeck motors had been stored there, but they had been installed on the Lunar power laser the week before and the slot was empty until the next shipment. Uncle Waldo had an eyeball in there, as he did in all bins; but since the space was known to be empty, Flaco didn't think he would peek. Weak illumination reached into the shadowed recess from the brightly lit "marshalling yard" in the center of the module—a narrow shaft of light that wriggled between the bulkhead panels and the struts—but the darkness suited him and he did not turn on the bin lights.

Flaco tucked his knees under his chin and wrapped his arms around them. Almost, he felt like he was floating atop the rolling waves off New Jersey. The sounds were all different, though. Hisses and hums instead of the slapping waves and the shrieking gulls and children, and Serafina's voice on the other float. They had almost drifted out to sea that day—the lifeguards had to holler them back in—and they both got a nasty sunburn. Up here, the sun would not burn you. It would fry you deeper than La Cabana's *pollo frito*.

Serafina had been right, all along and, worse yet, her mother had been right. His place had always been by his wife's side; not up here. He should have stayed on O&P's

railroad project. There'd been talk that the whole line would
be converted to maglev. A lot of rigging work there, for
sure. Years of employment, same as up here; and if it was
not safer than orbital work—heavy construction was never
safe, anywhere—the funeral, at least, would be closer to
home.

"Hey, Chico."

Flaco grunted at the interruption. "What's the word,
Bird?"

"Wish I knew; but they never tell me anything."

Bird Winfrey pulled himself into the storage bay. Floating
in the light, he looked like a jigsaw-puzzle man. The spiderweb shadows of the struts and guy wires crisscrossed his
body, severing arms and legs and head into disconnected
fragments of a human being. The eyes looked around. The
mouth spoke. "Nice little hideaway you got here."

Flaco sighed and uncurled. "It was."

"Ah, don't worry. I ain't gonna hang around." The NDT
technician tugged on his wiry beard. "If I was gonna hole
up in a dark, little hole like this, it wouldn't be with you,
amigo, no offense." He hooked a leg around a strut to keep
from drifting. "Jesus, you know what I hate worst about
free fall? You can't fucking sit down, that's what. You can't
just drop your butt into a seat; you have to *push* yourself
into it. And then, if you don't watch it, you drift right back
out." He let out a long, slow breath; cracked his knuckles.
"Been looking for you," he said casually.

Flaco considered that. "Yeah?"

"Yeah. Me and some of the others . . . We've been wondering where you stand."

"Standing needs as much work as sitting, up here."

"You know what I mean. Duckworth and this martial
law crap. Some of the guys, they're saying we should grab
the Plank when it comes tomorrow and take it down to
Earth."

Flaco snorted. "Sure. Who's gonna fly it?"

"They think they can force the pilot to cooperate."

"Ned DuBois?" Flaco didn't even bother to ridicule the notion.

Bird shrugged. "Didn't say it would work. Doesn't mean they won't try." Bird hesitated a moment. "They asked me to ask you about it. That's why I'm here."

"Ask me?"

"Yeah, they all know about your baby and all. They think it sucks. The delay, not the baby. So if you wanna come along . . ."

Flaco covered his face with his hands. *"Jesús, María . . .* I don't believe this, man."

"It's just an option. If Serafina's still important to you."

Flaco studied Bird's expression. "You better be careful, *cholo,* when you pick your next words."

Bird hesitated, squinted into the darkness where Flaco drifted. He passed the back of his hand across his lips. "I wish I could see your eyes, little brother. Sometimes, I see your eyes, I think: Bird, that kid can be dangerous if he lets himself."

"You could see if you come closer . . ." Flaco suggested. He flexed his legs against the bulkhead, ready to spring if Bird gave him reason.

The tech nodded. "Yeah. Look, I didn't mean it the way you think. It's just they thought you'd want the chance."

Flaco untensed. What was he doing, looking for a fight with Bird? The tension on board was getting to him, too. "A chance? Bird, I'd jump out of this can with a hankie for a parachute if I thought it would get me to Serafina's side. But it won't; so I don't. I'm not anxious to *leave here;* I'm anxious to *get there.* You understand the difference?"

"All right, I'll let 'em know."

"You keep sayin' 'them,' *'mano,* but I keep hearin' 'we.' "

Bird smiled crookedly. "Do I look that nuts? I don't gotta be no where, no time. Duckworth can't keep us up here forever. Spaceman's Protective Act. I figure I can wait."

"Then, who's planning . . . ?"

Bird shook his head. "You think I know? It was Uncle Waldo asked me to ask you."

"Uncle Waldo's in on it?" Somehow, that bothered Flaco more than a few guys going stir-crazy.

"Some of him, anyway. The idea is, if DuBois won't cooperate, Waldo can mouse into the Plank's system and run the autopilot landing sequence."

Flaco pondered that bit of news. If the Bird had the word, the attempt just might have a chance of success. Enough of a chance? But even if they did succeed, and he made it to Serafina's side in time, afterwards he would only get to see his son on visiting days. If Leavenworth had visiting days. Spacejacking. A whole new crime. They'd invent a whole new punishment. "I can't go against Christensen," he said at last.

"I know."

"You don't know nothing. If I do something stupid and lose my job, then *what was the point of me coming up here in the first place?* I gotta think about next year and the year after that; not just next week." Next week, he would be a father. It still felt distant, like a story he'd been told, not an in-your-face reality. He rubbed his temples with his fingertips. There was a time he never thought to the next day, and the only thing that mattered was what was going down now. "I can't take a man's money, then work against him."

"Sure. A cowboy 'rides for the brand.' But that doesn't mean he gotta like it; and you and me, we can't just ride into the sunset and sign on with another outfit. Duckworth said, 'Frog,' and Christensen—or Christensen's bosses— said, 'Ribbit.' You'd just as soon play the merengue on Duckworth's bones for keeping you away from Serafina, but the company rolled over on you." He looked away and worked his lips silently for a moment. "Ah, hell, Flaco, we're supposed to be building a space station, you 'n' me. That's what I signed on for; not to 'save democracy.' Most of the places they send the kids to never had it in the first place; so why's it any of our business?" Bird grimaced and shook his head. He moved out of the light, so that, he, too, was floating in the shadows, almost side by side with Flaco. Neither one spoke for a long time. After a while he said, "Hey, Chico. We had some good times on that railroad job, didn't we? How many bars did that town have?"

Flaco told him they'd had good times.

"You went across that bridge when you came out to the jump port. How'd it feel to you? Good work, right?"

Flaco told him it was good work.

"That's the way it should be. Men doing good work. Men getting things done. Like that Calhoun dude said up on the Rock. 'Let's get to work.' None of this politics crap. Just gets in the way. An honest day's work, a few beers, and go home to your woman, right?"

"I think it's all my fault, *'mano.'*" Flaco said it before he even knew he was thinking it. Winfrey blinked at him.

"What's your fault, Chic'?"

"This. Everything." Flaco waved an arm around, which put him into a slow counterspin that he stopped on a brace. "Remember that woman at the jump port? Remember how she said something about we owe loyalties to everyone, not just our bosses. I think she knew something was going down, but she didn't know what it was."

Bird looked into the darkness. " 'Steel rain of sorrows/ Trouble in my life . . .' Yeah, could be, brother. But what's that got to do with . . . ?"

"The first day Duckworth was up here, I was in the radio shack to call Serafina, and I heard 'em talking—Duckworth and them—and it was all about they were putting a weapon on board and the VHI bosses didn't like it." Flaco avoided Bird's eyes. "I didn't know what to do, and I sure didn't know who to ask. But things kept happening and people kept talking about it, so . . . So last month I dropped a message to the netdress she gave us."

Bird groaned. "Oh, man . . ." He shook his head. "So you figure she musta done something about it 'cause some-one dusty spilled the beans and now we're sealed up tighter than Millie Hess's underpants."

Flaco rubbed his face with his hands. "I change my orbit

just 'cause I bump into some *bomba* in a jump port. And this is what happens.''

Bird nodded and began to turn away. ''Look, if it means anything to you, and just between you and me, I think you did the right thing. Dropping the word, I mean.'' He pushed himself away and floated toward the entrance to the bin, where he stopped. ''I'll leave you be, now. But don't take too long making up your mind, little brother. Trouble's brewing, and it ain't decaf. Too many guys don't like what's happened. If things break, you won't be able to stand aside. You'll have to stand somewhere.''

Flaco shrugged. ''I stand with my friends.''

''Yeah?'' Bird shook his head, and he might have been talking to himself when he answered. ''What if your friends aren't all standing together?''

Flaco was awakened, not by the whisper in his ear, but by the urgent hand shaking his shoulder. He had been dreaming of Serafina, hovering in the sky above her childbed, watching on as she struggled alone in the room. Where are the doctors? he wanted to cry. Where are the nurses? But his tongue was impotent. He tried to reach for her, but the farther his arms extended, the farther she seemed to recede. As she receded, snow fell in the hospital room, blanketing her bed, covering her body, and slowly she grew still and her skin turned blue. When he turned away from that awful sight, Tonio Portales was with him. The Cubano pressed a handful of pearls into his hand. ''You will feel better, if you don't care.''

His eyes snapped open and he stared into the face of Red Hawkins. It was station night and the lights were turned to dim, though here and there in the personal cubicles that lined the cylidrical walls, a small reading light or video screen burned, like stars in an artificial sky. The gleam off the Australian's bald pate was enough to identify him. ''Wake up, dammit,'' the man said in a hard voice, just above a whisper.

Flaco siezed Hawkins's wrist and stilled the hand. "I'm awake," he said. "Now tell me why."

Red wrenched his hand free. "Selodkin's on *your* crew. Maybe he'll listen to you."

Flaco shook his head. The sleep was still on him. "What're you talkin' about, *'mano?*"

"Selodkin and his mates are off to wreck Duckworth's toy."

Flaco said, "*Mierda!* That *hijo de zorra!* He could blow us all up." Flaco unhooked his sleep tether. A part of him wanted to curl back into sleep and let Duckworth take care of his own toys, but better to be up and about than to return to that awful dream. "Where is he now?" he asked in the same pressing whisper.

"Tool crib. He ain't stupid. He ain't about to whack away with hammers on something that might blow up."

"Tool crib? How'd he get in without a work order?"

"How d'you think, mate? Uncle Waldo let him in."

That made no sense. Waldo had thrown in with the would-be highjack-ers . . . But, no. He was still groggy. It was easy to forget that Waldo was not a single person. His name was Legion. He was scattered among who knew how many telecommuting sites down Earthside. At least one— the woman, Leilah—worked out of her home. Had one of him found a way to bypass Duckworth's censors? Flaco pushed out of his cubicle. Beyond Hawkins floated three others: Wendy McKenna, Tiny Littlebear, and an NDT technician named Long. "Who's with Selodkin?"

"Korloff, Dazhvilli, maybe two, three others. All Russkies. No. Murasaki's with them, too. That's how Delight Jackson and I overheard. They had to tell Muri in English, and me and Delight were sitting two tables away. Hawkins thought for a moment and looked around the nearly sleeping bay. "Doesn't mean there aren't others in here who know and are cheering them on. Hard to fart in this place without everyone getting a sniff."

Silently, Flaco agreed that an unusual number of otters seemed to be awake at this hour. Like they were waiting for something to happen. "Sounds like you don't approve of cheerleaders." He slipped his feet into a pair of stick-fabric slippers.

Hawkins pantomimed spitting. "I don't like freeloaders. You believe in something, you get off yer ass and work it. And speaking of getting off it, we're wastin' time, mate."

Flaco kicked out of his cubicle. Like the others, he was dressed in singlet and shorts. A bunch of guys in their underwear. . . . *Don't we look dangerous.* Well, McKenna, maybe. *The right to bare arms . . .* And bare legs, too. The shape of her nipples pressed into the singlet. He suddenly realized that, in his dream, Serafina had worn McKenna's body, and he deliberately averted his eyes. "Anyone tell Christensen?" Flaco whispered. They might be outnumbered when they caught up with Selodkin.

Tiny grunted. "We keep management out."

"But—"

Hawkins cut short his protest with a harsh whisper. "We already decided, Pancho. I don't cut a fart for Duckworth or his missiles or your U.S. of A. throwing its bleeding weight around. I just don't want the station busted up—because that's all that keeps the air in here where I can breathe it, farts and all. We keep this between us; give Ivan a chance to back down without official notice. He's a good man. You know that. He wouldn't be doing this if Duckworth hadn't come up."

They set off with Hawkins in the lead and Flaco bringing up the rear. Since McKenna was right in front of him, it was a very fine rear to bring up, and for all Flaco's good intentions, he could not avoid staring at it. They tacked toward the forward manlock, single file, bouncing from the Bay Three starside bulkhead to the Number Two ring strut, to the temporary center brace. A few of the men lying awake watched them. Some called out questions in low, cautious voices. Perhaps they had chosen sides and were not sure which one this was. One man, evidently drawing a conclusion from McKenna's presence, indicated his willingness to dock with her and Flaco said, "It isn't that sort of gang bang, *'mano*." And the man whispered, "Oh, Jesus."

"Sit tight," Flaco told him. "We'll handle it."

McKenna waited for him at the manlock. "You ever a gang-banger, Flaco? You know the kind I mean. On the streets."

A line of perspiration gleamed on her lip. Her breath came more rapidly than her exertion so far could account for. Flaco was keenly aware of the way her breasts moved under her singlet, of the smooth, dark legs that dangled from the cuffs of her shorts. The dull, reddish night lights created a flush across her brow and cheeks. Her tongue darted in and out, moistening her lips. She was scared about the confrontation. Flaco knew the signs. Clotario had come close to tears while they waited in the alley for Diego's killers, and Flaco himself had felt balanced on a tightrope over an endless chasm. He touched McKenna on the arm. "Don't worry. They won't fight. What Selodkin plans, it depends on speed and silence. All we have to do is show up."

McKenna's smile was fleeting. "That sounds reasonable, Flaco. I just hope Vanya sees it that way and . . . Damn. I can't get any purchase. Give me a push, would you?"

Flaco placed his hand against her seat and shoved her toward the manlock, checking his backwards motion against a cross-brace spar; then he followed after, only to collide with her on the other side, where everyone was huddled. Tiny Littlebear gripped him by the arm and indicated silence. Hawkins placed a finger to his lips then pointed out into the mess-hall bay.

The mess was as dark as the barracks, but there were three men scattered among the eating cubes. "There's Delight," Hawkins whispered. "Can you make out the other two?"

Flaco squinted into the darkness. Jackson, another NDT tech, was virtually indistinguishable from the shadows he sat among. If he noticed the little group by the manlock, he gave no sign. "That's Tonio Portales by the dispenser," Flaco said. "He'd join us. He's a good man."

"Bloody hell he is," Hawkins whispered back. "He's ditzed half the time. Looks like he's ditzed right now; so he wouldn't know if a flock of kangaroos bounced right across his table. . . . Who's the third dingo? I recognize him, but . . ."

"Gennady Belislav," Flaco told him. "My opposite number on Gold Crew."

"He Russian or Ukrainian?"

"Russian; but I don't think he gets along with Ivan." They were leaning close, whispering in each other's ear, while Tiny, Wendy, and Nigel Long waited.

"He's an older guy," Hawkins pointed out. "Cautious. You think he'd go roust Christensen?"

Flaco wondered if Christensen might not know already. How many of Waldo's eyes had they—and Selodkin's people—already floated past? It was station-night, but some Waldos worked the off-shift. They might still be on-duty, even though work on the project had been temporarily suspended. And who knew? Some of them just might like peeping. . . .

Though, if other Waldos had raised an alarm, it was a remarkably silent one.

Hawkins signalled Jackson and pointed to Belislav. The black man nodded and floated silently to where the Russian sat. "Lonely night, eh?" Flaco heard him say. "When's de mon gonna start work again?"

While the Jamaican kept Belislav distracted, Flaco and the others coasted through the mess hall behind him, one after the other, silent as space-drift, straight and true toward the forward manlock. Flaco, bringing up the rear again, held his breath until they had all passed through into the intertank module. Nigel Long opened his mouth to say something, but Hawkins clapped a hand over it. "Hard part's coming," he whispered. "Bosses' quarters—Duckworth's gang dosses there—then the control center. Someone from M&U will be standing watch there."

"Sleeping watch," said Tiny.

"Whatever. We can't take the chance." They passed

through the lock into the next tank. Once in the "back porch," among the storage lockers, they relaxed a little. "We slip through 3-B one at a time," Hawkins said. "Absolute quiet. Then, Wendy, you go in the control center and distract whoever's there."

McKenna had been nibbling on her lower lip, which gave her rounded face a bunnylike appearance. She frowned. "Distract how?"

Hawkins's eyes caressed her sweat-stained undershirt. "You'll think of something."

The electrician stiffened. "Hey, what do you think I am?" No one answered her. Tiny coughed. Flaco dropped his eyes. "You sons of bitches," she said bitterly. "Hey, I do it because I *like* it—like a guy." A glance at Flaco. "Like most guys. Whoring's when you do it for some other reason."

"Look," said Tiny, "maybe . . ."

"Just distract the bastard, Wendy," said Hawkins. "No one said you gotta fuck him. If Selodkin manages to blow up the station with some boneheaded stunt, no one will care if you whored or not."

"But—" Her mouth settled into a grim line. "All right. But what if he's gay?"

Nigel Long spoke softly. "Then I go in first." He and Wendy locked eyes for a moment; then she sighed. "Okay. Let's go."

"One at a time, remember," Hawkins cautioned them. He took Flaco by the arm and held him back. "When we get to 4-C, where Selodkin and them are, you take over. See if you can talk sense to the crazy bastard."

"And if not?"

Hawkins released him, clapped him on the back. "That's why Tiny's here."

After the anxiety of the build-up, it was an anticlimax to reach the control center and find that the watch had been neatly bound hand-and-foot with duct tape and blindfolds. There were two of them, Flaco noted—an M&U man to monitor the station alarms and an Air Force man to guard the radio booth—so Wendy would have had her hands full, so to speak. Flaco could not tell who they were, with their mouths stopped up by tape and a pair of shorts pulled over their heads. He checked to make sure they could both breathe. Hawkins hissed.

"Leave them. No alarms till we get this settled." Flaco kicked off the niner spar and shinnied out the starside catline to join the others.

"The radio's been busted into," he told Hawkins.

"Yeah. I saw. Let's go."

The ready room and the tool crib in the forward bays of Number Three were deserted. This would have been off-shift in any case, but the sight of the darkened and sealed lockers saddened Flaco. It was like a house in which all the furniture had been draped with dust covers. He missed the bustling activity, the sense that they were actually accomplishing things. The stalemate could not last forever. Duckworth would have to act—perhaps prematurely?

It suddenly occurred to him that postponing rotation was not meant to keep them on board the station. If Sepp was right, there were no secrets they could take down that Earthside did not already know. Duckworth could send Golds and Greens down in the bumboat with no problem; it was the thought of bringing Blue Crew *up* that bothered him. They would be coming up with all the information, rumors, arguments, and general hoo-hah circulating on Earth. The Air Force man was playing for time, just trying to keep a lid on things until his bosses slipped his leash. After that, it wouldn't matter who came and went.

But that meant that Duckworth only needed to keep the M&U grays on board, not the O&P construction crew! All he needed was Maintenance and Utilities to keep the station going. He could send Flaco and the other otters downside *tomorrow!* Had Duckworth or his superiors considered that? Or did they have their own distractions? Whatever shit was going down on Old Dusty—whatever those gaps in Serafina's last message had meant—it seemed to consume Duckworth's attention, and Flaco had sensed an emotion very close to panic the last time he had encountered the Air Force man.

It was such an insight that Flaco blundered directly into Tiny and Nigel when they stopped at the manlock leading to Number Four. But when Flaco tried to explain to the others, Hawkins said, "We haven't time for that, mate. You're on. Talk to that crazy Russki. He's putting us all in danger." Red pushed Flaco toward the intertank connection. "If you need our help, just holler—"

" 'Sant' Iago!' "

Hawkins gave him a funny look. "I don't give a shit what you holler. You can holler 'Santa Claus' for all I care. Quit dawdling." But it was Red who stopped him one more time, with a hand on Flaco's bicep. "Good luck, mate."

Flaco nodded. "Yeah." He took hold of the rim of the manlock and pulled himself through.

If Flaco had been in charge of wrecking Duckworth's toy, he would have posted a man just inside Number Four to act as a lookout. It was an obvious choke point. Any interference had to pass through one at a time. But either Selodkin was confident that speed and surprise would carry the day or he had simply never thought of it. Well, how many otters had ever planned an ambush?

It took a moment to adjust to the view. Number Four had not been fully dressed when the Air Force had co-opted one of the bays, so temporary lights had been placed where the work crews had been. Only the Air Force installation was lit, so the view was like the interior of a vast, dim cave. The pool of light where Selodkin and his allies worked was an oasis that threw gray shadows throughout the remainder of the tank. Flaco could make out the ring frames that marked the bays, the rack of mobiles that Uncle Waldo used, and, less distinctly, the control console for Werewolf's laser farther forward. Both control consoles had the look of jerry-rigging, but the laser controls, at least, had been tested. At the long range, Artemis Mines had reported signal acquisition; at the short range—and by accident—one of the leftover intertanks in the outside marshalling yard had been sliced in two. Whether Duckworth had tested his own toy, Flaco could not say.

One of Selodkin's friends was poking inside the Air Force control panel. Flaco thought it was Grigor Dazhvilli, who was an electrician. Murasaki and Korloff struggled with a fourth man, wrapping tape around his ankles and wrists. Probably one of Duckworth's techs left on guard. Though it was dark enough in the tank for Selodkin to have approached unseen, Flaco thought it likely that the man had fallen asleep. It was not as if Duckworth had brought along any Special Forces or even Military Police.

Selodkin himself kept watch, but he was floating in a well-lit globe of light staring into the darkness. Flaco shook his head. *First* you turn out the lights; *then* you lift the window shade . . . Selodkin would see nothing.

They were not very far along, Flaco saw. Dazhvilli had only gotten as far as the cover plates. At least they were going after the controls and not the weapons themselves. Since there was unlikely to be a circuit that would trigger the warheads before launch, poking around inside the panel without schematics was unlikely to cause an onboard explosion. That stole some of the urgency from Flaco's heart, and he watched them a little while longer. The need to deal with the watch and with the Air Force guards had delayed the saboteurs. So Flaco might be able to stop them before any real damage had been done.

The question was, did Flaco *want* to stop them. O&P had said not to interfere with Duckworth; it had not told him to go out of his way to prevent others from interfering. Selodkin was breaking orders, not Eddie Mercado; and if Eddie Mercado returned to his cubicle and his dreams of Serafina, he would not be breaking company policy. He had no instructions from Izzy Mac to guard Duckworth's toy.

That device stood between him and Serafina. Render it inoperative, and Duckworth would no longer have cause to hold Green Crew on board. On the other hand, he might be so outraged over the sabotage that he'd keep them up here forever for interrogation.

It would be easier if he had his *panas* with him. A man always knew where he stood when he stood with his friends. Yet there were Ivan Selodkin and Hirao Murasaki on one side and Tiny Littlebear and Wendy McKenna on the other. And Red Hawkins—though Flaco was not sure how Red counted in the constellation of his friends and companions. Bird, it seemed, had consciously stood aside; and perhaps Sepp's detachment extended to this as well. As for Tonio, the Cuban was digging a great hole in his heart and pulling the dirt in on top of him.

What was he doing here, in the middle of station-night, contemplating the ambush of a group of saboteurs he half-agreed with? He ought to be sitting vigil with Tonio in the mess bay, tugging his friend back into the world of those who cared. Or he ought to be in Christensen's office laying everything on the desk of someone with the authority to act. The real danger was not the sabotage of a control panel, but the unilateral action of men without authority. The station was too small and too fragile a thing to tolerate anarchy— or vigilantism—in its ranks.

And it might be the best thing he could do for Tonio was to have him remanded for treatment before his carelessness grew worse. To stop accepting his excuses. To stop—what was the word?—enabling. And yet, what man can turn over his friend and still look at himself in the mirror when he shaved? If Selodkin was not so close a friend as Tonio, he and Murasaki were still members of Flaco's crew and Flaco was responsible for them. He would handle this himself; call on Red and Tiny if needed.

Like the control room watch, the guard at the panel had been hoodwinked with his own undershorts. So Selodkin must still hope to keep identities secret. Turning on the lights; bringing in witnesses—witnesses who would remain silent, if need be—that would be all that was needed. And quickly, too, before restless sleep brought Christensen or Izzy Mac or Adrian Whitlauer on the scene.

Flaco flexed off from the 3-4 manlock bulkhead and sailed gently and silently forward. He chose a route that took him eastward along the northern quarter of the hull. By chance, and because the equipment they were jimmying was installed on the earthside quarter, Selodkin's people were aligned so that north was "above" them and even after several months in space, few Greens glanced routinely in that direction. Selodkin, in particular, expected that if anyone did approach from Number Three, they would come straight out of the west.

Selodkin, brightly lit in the globe cast by the work lamp, frowned when Flaco toed off and peered into what was for him utter blackness. Perhaps he had seen a hint of motion in the shadows. Flaco reached the A-B ring frame and changed course with a hard tug of the arm. Another flex of the knees against the ring frame and he shot eastward, straight and true to the B-C ring frame, where he stopped himself. He hovered "above" Selodkin like a falcon and waited for his moment.

It came when Dazhvilli, inserting his probe in the wrong place, touched a live wire. He cursed in Russian and held his one hand in the other. Selodkin turned and asked him a question. It suddenly occurred to Flaco as he glided gently toward them, that while there might be no circuit that could detonate the weapons before they had been launched, there was surely a circuit for launching them, and a foolish move on Grigor's part might send death hurtling down on unsuspecting victims. And while the odds sided with a harmless dump in the seas that covered three-quarters of Old Dusty, Washington Heights and El Barrio were no less likely an impact zone than any other randomly chosen spot on Earth.

His slippers touched the earthside longitudinal guideline and he brought himself to a halt in the midst of Selodkin's little group, like an acrobat landing feetfirst on the tightrope. The e-side long line was knotted at intervals, so that bunnies like Duckworth's people could haul themselves back and forth to their worksite. A similar line had been paid out starside for Werewolf's crew to work on the laser. Otherwise, and except for some partial installation of bulkheads, Number Four was empty space.

Flaco's move had been so graceful and so silent that it was a moment or two before Selodkin realized there was another man in their midst. When he did, he jerked and shouted, *Bozhe moi!* The jerk put him into a tumble. Flaco put a hand on his forearm. "Ivan Palitch," he said. "I don't suppose you have a work order for this?"

Perhaps it was the unexpectedness of the question, but Selodkin laughed. "No, Mercado. I cut my own orders this time."

Hirao Murasaki let go of the now-quiet guard. "We take orders from people of Earth," he said.

"I don't remember seeing the People in the org chart, Hirao. Don't use them as an excuse for your own decision. Grigor! Hold off. Without the schematics, you're working blind. You could give yourself a nasty shock."

"I will be taking that chance." He turned with a needle-nose pliers to attack the panel once more.

"You haven't even found the power source, Grigor, or you would have cut that right off. And that means you could spark a short that might actually launch those things. Have you thought about that?"

"It's a risk," Selodkin admitted. "But we will take it."

"But will the People take it? Did you ask them? They're the ones underneath us."

Murasaki frowned. "He has a point, Vanya. With the board still live . . ."

"Minutku!" said Dazhvilli. "Budu nakhodit . . . I will be finding it, the power source."

"What nonsense is this?" demanded Korloff, who had remained mute to this point. He held up his forefinger. "Odin vsegda," he said.

"How will this unite your country?" Flaco asked Selodkin.

It was Korloff who answered. "The world will see that Slav comes to Slav. That all Slavs must band together, whether Moskaly, Ukrainsky, Belarussky, or Yugoslavsky. We are one nation under God."

The unexpectedness of the phrase made Flaco laugh, for

it was used in the States to describe the coming together of many peoples, not the homogeneity of one; but Korloff took the laugh as a slur and, with a cry of rage, launched himself at Flaco.

Flaco evaded the grasping arms, but the impact sent him spinning like a top. Dazhvilli abandoned his needle-nose pliers and came at him from the other side. Murasaki backed off toward the hull—brawling with his crew boss not having been his intention. Selodkin, too, closed in on Flaco, but he seemed anxious to separate the combatants. "Mercado nye vrag," he said. "Stop fighting, *p'zhalst'*. We draw attention."

But it was too late for such caution, because Henry Littlebear collided with them like an avalanche and that was something that concentrated their attention fast. There was no room for debate and Selodkin found himself committed by circumstance.

Flaco saw all this in flashes, as he spun helplessly. A chance leg—he thought it was Hawkins, but it might have been anyone's—caught his outstretched arm and enabled him to check his motion; though the bay continued to spin even after he had stopped. He was going to boot for the first time since his maiden lift.

Something hard struck him a glancing blow on the head and he saw flashes of colored light. Twisting, he saw Uncle Waldo "playing football"—one of the soccer-ball-sized mobile units the off-site crew used for inspection. Flaco put a hand to his temple and it came away wet. Waldo braked with a few bursts of compressed air, reversed course, and came straight toward him. Whoever was riding the mobile was playing for keeps: an inspection probe had extended from the sphere's body and while it might not be honed to a point, with enough mass and velocity it would puncture him easily enough.

Flaco grabbed the long line and waited. He was upside down now with respect to the others. When Waldo was nearly on him, he yanked hard on the rope and pulled himself aside. Waldo hurtled through the space Flaco had just vacated, changing course only after Flaco's moves reached the operator's teep set. Too late. The sphere struck the hull and crumpled. When its air jets fired again, it moved erratically. Flaco blew his breath out.

And sucked it back in when he saw another Waldo detach from the rack and turn toward him. A piece of advice Rhys Pilov had given him suddenly surfaced. *You shouldn't get Uncle Waldo mad at you. He's everywhere.* Selodkin's off-site ally had just "changed horses."

This mobile was more oblate and extended a set of shears, a more deadly lance than the inspection probe had been. Flaco tried the trick with the rope again, but this time Uncle Waldo anticipated the move, and Flaco avoided a nasty wound only because he curled up into a ball. The mobile grazed him on the side of the head and down the back, but failed to drive home the shears. Flaco crouched on the long line and sprang off, hoping to reach the shadows outside the range of the work lamps.

But once launched, he saw that he had made an error, perhaps a fatal one. Until he reached the starside longitudinal, he could no longer maneuver, no longer alter his trajectory; and Uncle Waldo could see in the dark.

It made sense. Why waste light when you could build night vision into your unit? The Waldos kept working even after lights out. Hell, some worked 'round the clock on the outer hull in conditions a lot tougher than simple darkness. It took Waldo's A/S only a moment to calculate Flaco's trajectory and plot an interception, and Flaco watched helplessly as it launched itself across the bay. He didn't need an A/S to see that it would strike him well before he reached starside.

Perhaps, depending on fine details, he could tuck in at the last moment—though he suspected that Uncle had aimed at his center of mass. Perhaps, too, he could grab hold or deflect it with his hands—though, again, Waldo had teeped the mobile's lights out and he would not see it until it was right on him. Without much hope—only that the puncture would not prove fatal—Flaco readied himself.

Hands pawed his ankles, slipped, then seized hold. Flaco cried out as he and his tackler swung around their mutual center of gravity. In the dark, Flaco lost all orientation. It was as if he was still and the lighted area around the weapons console revolved around him in polar orbit. A moment later, he heard a dull, meaty sound and a cry of pain; and a moment further still before he was sure it was not his own.

When Jimmy Poole threw an info-feast, he always saved something for *lagniappe*. How long he had possessed the nugget of information, Roberta did not know; but that he had deliberately witheld it for later, she was dead certain. There was something very juvenile in the gesture, a childish delight in pulling a fast one that seemed to define Jimmy's personality. At first, Roberta refused to believe it; but Jimmy never *lied*. He might not tell the whole truth—and sometimes that lack would do for a lie—but it was part of his shtick, part of his own self-deception, that he was always *literally* honest.

How did she hold her emotions in while she rode the metro to Crusades headquarters? It seemed at times, when the train stood too long on one station or another, that she would explode. And yet, when her stop came, she sat in a daze and missed it and had to take the return train from the next station down the line.

Union Station was all abuzz. People clustered around the televisions in the bistro and restaurant; the public terminals booths had waiting lines. In some, several people had crowded together to check out I-Net newsgroups—a show of racial, age, and gender integration that the old town seldom experienced. Even the taxi drivers were bent over their radios, each the center of a cluster of listeners, and not one a fare.

Styx was too agitated to take a cab. She had to walk it out. She downloaded a hardcopy newspaper from the dispenser by the front of the station, but only glanced at the headlines as she strode down F Street.

Star Wars on LEO Station:

FOURTH DAY OF CRISIS

Bill of Impeachment Introduced

Farther down the page was a sidebar:

VHI PROVIDES THE FACILITIES

—But for a Price

No! thought Styx, crumpling the hardcopy and trashcanning it at the next corner. *That just makes her look venal and greedy.* It was the wrong take. It was her lunatic delusion with meteors that had driven her to it. The rent was just her accountant's way of salvaging something from the situation. Mariesa van Huyten, Roberta was sure, would have done it for free.

Free, plus a big, honking laser.

She spared a glance at the sky as she walked. Could meteors fall during the day, she wondered or only at night? During the day, wouldn't they be coming from the direction of the sun, which was like rolling "uphill" in gravity terms. It irritated her that that fragment of Mentor propaganda had stuck in her mind; and it irritated her more that she didn't know the answer. She nearly collided with a senior citizen at the corner and apologized.

"Get your head out of the clouds, young woman," the gerry-boomer told her.

"Yeah, whatever," Styx said. And *when* would that generation stop lecturing? They had lectured their elders when they were kids, and they were lecturing their juniors, now that they were old. Phil was a Boomer, of course; but Phil was different.

Wasn't he?

The hubbub at headquarters was no different from that in Union Station, just smaller in scale. Someone had begun posting headlines—presumably faxed in—from papers around the country. Most of the Crusaders were staffing the phones. Calls were pouring in. "The Crusaders feel that Donaldson has overstepped his . . ." "No, we don't know what sort of weapon. We've heard it's some kind of super-laser, but . . ." "It's up to the House to indict, but we believe . . ." "Yes, thank you very much. Every dollar helps the cause . . ." "I'm sorry you feel that way, but macho posturing is not . . ." Isaac Kohl could spare her no more than a grin and a thumbs-up. As Roberta crossed the room toward Phil's office, Ellis Harwood emerged from the coffee alcove with a steaming mug in his hand. He had shucked his signature tweed jacket, and his polo shirt was unbuttoned at the collar, providing a glimpse of grizzled chest hairs. His mug shifted hands, and he held his right out to Roberta.

"Good work, Bertie. Phil told me you and Ike put together the right cross we laid on King Log's choppers."

Roberta smiled for him. "We all do our part, Woody."

Harwood's smile faltered briefly at the unexpected nickname. Ellis was okay—and no one stayed on top of workers' issues like he did—but for all of his "muscular progressivism" and "little guy simpatico," his idea of his own nickname was "Dr. Harwood." He probably didn't mean to condescend; it was just something that came naturally. You had to learn to shrug it off—like Dottie's humorlessness and Isaac's nerdiness—and accept him for his good points.

"Donaldson will resign rather than face impeachment," Ellis predicted. "Which will make Rutell president. Donaldson talked progressive, but the guy never *did* anything. Rutell's on our side. Out with King Log; in with King Stork!" He raised his mug in salute and took a sip of coffee.

"Is Phil in?" Roberta asked with a nod toward the closed office doors. She wondered if Ellis had ever read the fable of King Log and King Stork and what had happened to the frogs after they had traded the one for the other. Another flash of irritation. They had read Aesop back at dear old Witherspoon, as part of the "cultural heritage" package.

Was she the only one in the room who understood how ironic Ellis's declaration was?

Phil was on the phone when Roberta stuck her head inside the door, but he waved her in while he talked. "Yes, Senator. I understand. But it's still a clear circumvention of the *intent* of the Constitutional War Powers Reinforcement Act." Roberta found a seat and pulled it up close to the desk. She clenched her hands on her knees and sucked in her lower lip. Phil gave her a questioning look, but kept up his conversation. "Certainly, there's a loophole—thanks to you. And we'll make sure the people know *that*, too. I'm sorry you feel that way, Senator. Yes, the action was within the *letter* of the law, but maybe we shouldn't go by the letter of the law so much as the spirit." Phil listened briefly and suddenly laughed. "Yes, the spirit does move in mysterious ways. Good-bye, Senator." As he hung up, he shook his head. "Good old Senator Partyhack. Always ready to take a bullet for Donaldson." His smile faded as he studied Roberta's face. "What's wrong, Robbie?"

"I found out why Donaldson was so insistent about putting those weapons on LEO." She couldn't quite look Phil in the eyes, afraid of what she might see there.

Phil folded his hands and said quietly, "And why was that?"

"Deputy Assistant Security Advisor Barton Hughes put the bug in his ear; and Assistant Secretary Lillian Debroccio kept telling him how it would assure his place in history. Between them, they sold Donaldson and then helped him convince State and Defense." She hesitated and focused on the engraved writing set on Phil's desk. "Both Hughes and Debroccio are auxiliary Crusaders."

"I—see. And do you think they—we—instigated the whole affair?" Phil spoke slowly, as if he, too, were afraid of the answer.

"Did we? Don't lie to me, Phil. I can tell if you lie to me." She locked eyes with him, at last. Daring him; defying him.

"Yes," he said. "You could. I'm sure of it. You and I . . . Oh, Robbie . . ." He shook his head.

"Yes." Then, more firmly, "Yes. Our people in the administration and the party pushed the idea on him. No, Robbie, don't turn away. I couldn't take it if you turned away from me."

Roberta looked back at him, though again avoiding his eyes. She could feel something building within her; she could hear Styx raging in her box. "Why?" she said in a voice that sounded unnaturally calm to her.

"Why? To get Donaldson out and Blaise Rutell in. Blaise is more in line with our thinking, but we didn't want to contest the nomination and maybe throw the last election to some clone of Jim Champion. Donaldson had the party regulars locked up, anyway. But once he was reelected, we didn't need him anymore. There were no handy scandals to trumpet, so . . ."

"So you trumped one up." The words were painful and poignant at the same time. She didn't want to believe them. She wanted Phil to tell her she was wrong.

"You can't con an honest man. Donaldson really did put that weapon up there, and Mariesa van Huyten really helped him do it."

"Call it entrapment, then. You can paint the old whore, but you can't make her pretty."

"Robbie . . ." He rubbed his forhead with his fingers. "Oh, God, I didn't want this to happen. I didn't even think Donaldson would go for it when Simon sugges—" He stopped and bit his lip.

But she ignored him and concentrated on the knife in her heart. "You never let me in on it. You never told me what the real plan was. Why? Because you thought I was too honest?"

"I didn't like it, either; but something had to be done to stop the country's drift. There was no leadership in Washington; no vision of the direction this country ought to take! Just an aimless, benign neglect. Sometimes, to reach important goals, we're forced to take shortcuts, to downplay any doubts we might have, to simplify the issues; even to take measures we find personally distasteful. It's a choice— sometimes—between being rigidly honest and being effective. It's not the methods that matter, but the goals. We each have to find a *balance*—"

"Now you sound like *her*."

He rose from his seat and came around the desk. His hands reached for hers. "I didn't want to hurt you."

She refused his hands, rose ramrod straight from her own chair. "You mean you didn't want me to find out how you were *using* me!" Her voice rose in pitch, and Phil winced. His face was sharp, the pain on it cut both ways.

"Robbie, don't let this ruin everything."

"Oh, don't worry, Macchiavelli. You get what you set out to get. Too many other people are twisted up in this scheme for me to blow the whistle."

"I didn't mean the Crusades, Robbie. I meant us."

She looked at him; at his dark, teddy-bear face, tightened by anguish. She had to fight the urge to wrap him in her arms and comfort him. She had to press the memory of his tender caresses and sweet lips deep down into the shadows, where she couldn't feel them. "Us?" she said. "*Us?* Why, you're just another old man who can't keep his dick up long enough to matter." She spun away from him and yanked open the door to his office, stepping out among the still-ebulent Crusaders. Dottie Wheeler, sitting at the desk closest to the office, smirked at her. "Lover's quarrel?" she asked sweetly.

She told Dottie where she could go and what she could do when she got there. Then she pushed her way through the celebrating volunteers to the front door, where she stepped outside into a springtime bright with flowers and singing birds.

20.

Steel Rain

RS47 *Louis Bleriot* latched onto west-end spacelock of LEO Station at 0640 hours, 13 May 2010, and if any of the otters reflected upon its lateness or their own delayed rotation Earthside, they kept those thoughts to themselves. There were other matters to occupy them—like the hoorah in Number Four a few hours earlier. A runaway mobile unit had smashed into the Air Force control console and badly injured welder Antonio Portales. A few satisfied smiles broke through here and there among the staff and crew assembled for the welcome. Twice blessed! Not only had Duckworth gotten his comeuppance; but there had been ill-feeling toward Portales ever since the incident with Conchita Ferrer, and some felt that by stopping the runaway mobile with his own body, Portales had finally done sufficient expiation.

Some might have suspected that there was more to the story than that, but those thoughts, too, were left unspoken. After all, Werewolf Gregorson and Meat Tucker—napping in Number Four after a long, tedious shift fine-tuning the lunar laser—had seen the whole thing. And Gennady Belislav, who had been reviewing schedule changes in the caf', had come in near the end and backed up their story.

As to the cause of the runaway module, Kiril Korloff, Hirao Murasaki, and a few others had been severely reprimanded. Pranking two of Duckworth's people by way of "making a statement," they had hoodwinked the men with undershorts, bound and gagged them and plugged their ears, and stripped them naked for their captain to find later. Unfortunately, Staff Sergeant Dvorkin had put up a struggle, in the course of which the mobile had first been damaged, then activated. Christensen had assured Duckworth that the men would be heavily fined.

Flaco, of course, knew better, as did the others who had been caught up in the affair; but they had been cautioned to keep their lips sealed. Werewolf chewed them all royal— saboteur *and* vigilante—once he and Meat had sorted everyone out; and Christensen, fetched by Belislav, had pounded the cover story into their heads. Even the sullen Korloff had agreed that an open breech with their unwelcome guests could still be avoided; and Selodkin, who had hoped to carry out the entire hack in secret, breathed a not-so-secret sigh of relief. Flaco had to admit that it was a damn good cover story for having been made up on the spot, especially when Werewolf himself had delivered the *coup de grace* to the control panel using the now-disabled module. Stripping the two techs and decorating them with Day-Glo in several interesting and hard-to-scrub places was a stroke of genius that provided a believable, if not entirely blameless, explanation for the binding and gagging.

It was maybe a little too pat and complete to have been made up so quickly—because when Flaco paused at the 3-4 manlock, the last of the otters to leave the scene, he had glanced over his shoulder and caught Gregorson, Christensen, Belislav, and Tucker trading high-fives.

Christensen arranged a formal welcome for DuBois. The otters lined up by crew and craft, Golds on the starside of 1-B and Greens on the e-side. Each had been given a kerchief in his crew color to wear around his neck. Because only half of Green Crew was on board—the second lift was waiting out the unexplained delay below—the M&U station cadre in their gray "Roaring Lion" coveralls, the black-clad Werewolves, and the handful of Blues who had come up before the embargo were ranged with the Greens, as were a scattering of Mac-Dac, Energia, and other non-VHI personnel. Crew bosses floated in front, toeing their mark on the longitudinal guide lines. Leads were ranged behind them, one at each of the circumferentials; and behind them were the masters and journeymen of each craft.

It all sounded very well-organized and Flaco thought they would have made a splendid display if only construction workers had had the least notion of order and discipline. But the kerchiefs were worn in a variety of ways—Boy Scout style, bib-style, drawn up "outlaw" style over the mouth and nose, as headbands, or *babushkas,* or just stuffed into hip pockets. And the orderly lines of journeymen tended to break up into chattering knots as the otters exchanged news and rumors and jokes. Adrian Whitlauer tried to keep his mechanics in something approaching order, but Izzy Mac, Taras Kutuzov, and the other chiefs hardly bothered. Someone on Gold Crew had contrived a rubber ball— at least, a sphere of some sort of elastic material—and it traveled back and forth across the bay in a somewhat haphazard game of catch. The LEO Grays, who worked their own rotation independent of O&P, had solemnly arranged themselves in a single row, alternately heads up and heads down, as befitted a gang of computer geeks and techies.

Only Duckworth's people, arrayed with severe precision at the east end of the bay, looked out of place. So much so that, after studying the gathering, Duckworth issued a sardonic, "At ease." They still wore the black Werewolf jumpsuits they had come up in, having brought no uniforms of their own. The false colors irritated Flaco. It was the triumph of pretense over pride. He suspected that Duckworth was equally bothered. Whatever else, the man had pride in his own service, and the need for at least the pretense of a pretense accounted in some measure for the man's overbearing attitude. Lacking the symbols of his authority, he replaced them with autocracy, reminding Flaco of an accommodating, street-smart patrolman he had known in the

Heights who had become an overbearing bully when a promotion to detective took him out of uniform.

Flaco's glance took in Werewolf Gregorson, who looked impossibly smug. The man had never approved of Duckworth's presence, Flaco knew. Had he taken advantage of Selodkin's raid, or even surreptitiously instigated it? Certainly O&P's top people on the scene had colluded in the cover-up. The lunar laser had come up on the same lift as the Air Force, but the two projects were separate and one had simply been a cover for the other.

Yet Duckworth, hovering a few feet east of Gregorson, did not look entirely unhappy. In fact, he might have looked smug himself. Maybe that meant the panel hadn't been wrecked as badly as everyone hoped, or maybe it meant that Duckworth himself was relieved at its destruction.

It was odd, Flaco thought, as he turned his attention to the front and let his thoughts wander. It was odd how everyone's hopes and plans collided off of one another, like the balls in Jimmy Schorr's ziggy pool game. All the while he was making his plans with Serafina, others were making their own: the Air Force and its plan to end the Balkan War, Gregorson's plan to power the lunar laser, DuBois's plan to welcome his old comrades home. They had all bounced off each other, one way or another; and they had not all stopped spinning, even yet.

There was another great clang, then a hiss as the locks on the station and the ship opened and the pressures equalized. All eyes turned toward the A-B interlock.

The demigod who pushed through looked very much like an ordinary man. Short and square-built, with powerful shoulders but dainty hips and feet. Hair cropped impatiently short. Eyes of gray-green that darted around the assembly, assessing them.

The otters, whose casual chatter had filled 1-B with a continual murmur, fell quiet. Flaco could almost see the wavefront of silence pass along the Gold ranks on the opposite side. This was "The Man Who." The Man Who first reached orbit in an SSTO. The Man Who saved Gregor

Levkin, the Human Moon. The Man Who played chicken with the *flocker* autopilot program. The Man Who flew the impossible Skopje rescue mission. He wore the brown jumpsuit of Daedelus Aerospace, and sported the winged sun emblem; but the cuffs had a lot more fillagree than the usual four captain's rings. Flaco wasn't sure what job titles Daedelus used. Was DuBois a "chief pilot"? An "admiral"? A "sky marshall"? Or was he simply "DuBois," and Daedelus was too awed to give him a uniform with ordinary insignia.

DuBois paused just inside 1-B as he contemplated the silent ranks of otters. Flaco saw a rueful smile curl his lips. What was it like to be a "Legend in Your Own Time," Flaco wondered? It couldn't be very casual, that was certain; and maybe the adulation grew less welcome over time. But that Eddie Mercado would never know from personal experience was even more certain.

Christensen advanced to meet DuBois and welcome him aboard with a few well-chosen words that Flaco tuned out. Someone started to clap, and pretty soon everyone was clapping, a sound like rolling thunder. And then, to Flaco's horror, someone across the way in Gold Crew threw that damn rubber ball straight across, on a trajectory that passed right between Christensen and DuBois.

But it didn't make it. DuBois's hand struck like a snake and snared the ball in midflight. The applause died away as the otters realized what had happened and there was a hush while DuBois contemplated his prize. Even the sound of breathing vanished. Had they just offended The Man Who? Christensen glared into the innocent-looking ranks of Gold Crew trying to identify the culprit.

Then DuBois grinned and launched the ball toward Green Crew, pretty much on its original trajectory. And that meant it came to Flaco, who caught it. When he hesitated, DuBois bowstringed off the 1-B/a southern traverse, launching himself down the length of the tank with one hand outstretched and Flaco grinned and threw the ball after him. DuBois caught it, jackknifed so he now flew feet-first, and relayed the ball toward the Golds. Jimmy Schorr sprang out and swatted the ball in midflight so that it bounced off the ring-frame toward the Greens. And that, pretty much, was how DuBois became The Man Who invented ziggy bounceball.

For a certified demi-god, Ned DuBois was pretty good folks. He didn't mind hanging out with the otters, sucking the inevitable juice bulbs and exchanging tales. DuBois was close-lipped on Earthside affairs, a promise he'd made to get permission to lift; but he dropped enough hints of heavy political shit hitting lots of fans to satisfy the curious without violating any oaths.

Meanwhile there wasn't much else to do but wait and watch Jimmy Schorr and Flaco play for the Gold-Green championship in ziggy pool. The work schedule was wrecked, the crews couldn't rotate until the embargo was lifted, and *Louis Bleriot* wouldn't drop until FarTrip arrived.

"We've been getting some weak signals from *Bullard*," DuBois told them, "so we know they're still alive." He watched while Flaco studied the balls in Jimmy Schorr's pool box. Jimmy had somehow given the cue ball such a spin and bounceback that it sat smack in the middle of the ricocheting balls, like a sun in the center of a maniac solar system. Flaco wondered if Jimmy had done that on purpose, or if it was just dumb luck. "What was it that happened to them?" Flaco said. "Last we heard, communication was lost." He jackknifed to study the situation from the other side, but the balls didn't look any better from that angle.

"Today," suggested Jimmy Schorr. "Today."

"Don't rush me."

"That's not clear," Leland Hobart said, "but we think they hit some gravel." *Bleriot* had stopped at Mir on the way to pick up Doc and his glittering harvest of superconductors. Now, he was stuck on LEO with everyone else.

"Gravel?" said Gladys Winchell. "In outer space?" Flaco frowned at the protective screen of colliding balls. Anyone who waited for the balls to come to rest before taking a shot was a weenie. Besides, house rules said that if another ball struck the cue ball first, that was his shot. On the other hand, the other house rule said that he couldn't touch any other ball before the cue ball, and that included balls in motion accidently hitting his cue stick.

"Sure, Schatz," said Sepp Bauer. "In space, it gives much gravel." Gladys Winchell did not like terms of endearment, at least not from men; but it was hard not to like Sepp. "How come?" she said.

On the other side of the barracks bay, Delight Jackson was singing. He had a fine, rolling baritone, amply complemented by Wendy McKenna's contralto and by Silvestre Pono and a few others. Cormac McDermot accompanied them with his tin whistle.

Farewell and good-bye to you, old LEO Station.
Farewell and good-bye to you, otters and friends.
Rotation Day's coming; we're dropping down Earthside;
And maybe we'll not see each other again.

"I forfeit my turn," Flaco announced. Jimmy started, looked surprised for a moment, then frowned and studied the situation himself.

"Smart move, Chico," said Bird Winfrey.

"Can he do that?" Hobart asked the crowd of watchers.

"Any move is legal the first time you try it," Bird explained. "House rule. But if Jimmy tries the same move, he's just a weenie." Jimmy Schorr saluted him absently, using one finger. Delight Jackson's group hit their chorus and a few others joined in.

We'll party and roar like the otters we are.
We'll fly and we'll soar o'er all the world wide,
Until we strike air on our last braking orbit.
From LEO to Phoenix is three hundred miles!

"Nice tune," said DuBois, sparing the singers a glance.

"Delight is buff for folk songs," Bird said. "But he's a bad drum-meister when it comes to mosh or goof."

"'Bad' meaning . . . ?"

"Stoopid."

DuBois nodded, as if understanding.

"What about the gravel?" Gladys asked again.

"Ah. Well . . . Calhoun's Rock doesn't have much gravity," DuBois said. "So when another rock collides with it and knocks debris loose—"

"A lot of it," finished Sepp, "doesn't settle back down."

"That's right," said DuBois, unmiffed at the interruption. "It goes into co-orbit with the Rock, where it gets tugged this way and that by Jupiter, Mars, and the Earth-Moon and winds up in nearby orbits."

"And that's what they hit . . ." said Gladys. "Okay. I wasn't sure. It seemed so unlikely, but I guess you'd have to expect a lot of junk in that neighborhood."

The seven ball bounced off the side of the pool box and struck the cue ball on the rebound, sending it out of the pack. Jimmy Schorr expressed his grave disappointment with a single, well-chosen word. Flaco grinned. Delight Jackson sang:

We cast our ship loose when we pass over Greenwich
And de-orbit boost till we brake into air.
We opened the scram-jets when we crossed the jet stream
And right to Sky Harbor we flew straight and fair.
Oh, we'll party and roar . . .

Duckworth wriggled his way through the otters and tapped DuBois on the shoulder. "A word with you, Captain." DuBois looked at him.

"What about, *Captain*?"

Duckworth looked over the crowd. "In private?"

The Man Who assumed an innocent air. "Is it about that ship we spotted on the way up?"

The surrounding otters fell suddenly silent, then erupted into a babel of sounds. What ship? Was the rotation boat coming? Flaco heart beat faster. Delight Jackson broke off his song with the rotation boat going Max-Q over the Pacific. Duckworth winced, but saw that surrender was the best course. Or perhaps he had seen how far secrecy got him in the tightly knit orbital community. "Yes, the ship. Who was it?"

"I told Christensen everything already."

"Tell me."

DuBois looked at him for a long time, and Duckworth actually shrank a little from the gaze. Still, it was a question that wanted answering. "Tell us," Flaco suggested, and he was supported by a chorus of seconds. DuBois glanced his way, then nodded.

"Okay. Not much to tell, though. We picked up a trace on another orbiter during our climb. Very tight radar footprint; no visual. Well, maybe a visual. Some stars were occluded. On the next pass, we couldn't find it."

"No markings?" asked Duckworth.

"I'm not sure I saw the *ship*; I'm damn sure I didn't see markings. If the glimpse we had was accurate, it's above and ahead of LEO; so you're catching up to it."

"What does Space Traffic Control say?"

DuBois shook his head. "Nairobi STC picked it up, too, but they don't have a flight plan on file. There aren't enough groundside stations to cover the whole sky—it's mostly Indian country up here—so if you don't post your position by radio . . ."

"Meaning the ship is silent?"

"I got a glimpse. I told Nairobi. Nairobi was puzzled. That's all I know. How come you guys didn't see it lift? Nairobi figures you guys were line-o'-sight when she lifted."

"When was that?"

"About five, six hours ago."

Duckworth's mouth thinned into a line. "The control room watchman was 'tied up' at the time."

"Well, it's probably a test flight on some new hardware. Pentagon, maybe. Or Ariane. Proprietary. That's why they're flying black. If they were coming to visit, they would have been here by now."

* * *

DuBois was a smart man, but he was wrong about the mystery ship. The watch raised the ship above the eastern horizon at 17:42 when the station's faster orbit caught up. Flaco was visiting Tonio in the clinic in 3-E when Bolislav Drozd found him. "Hey, dude," the watchman said. "Ship approaching from the east on intercept. Number Four isn't wired, yet, and I need Christensen right away. Shoot forward and tell him. I don't want to leave my post." The Gray turned on a traverse line and shot back toward 3-C without waiting to see if Flaco had obeyed him. Flaco shrugged and squeezed Tonio on the bicep. "Gotta go, *'mano.* Be right back."

Tonio gripped his wrist. "Don't leave me," he whispered. "What if something happens? Oh, God." He groaned as Flaco pried his fingers loose.

"Nothin's gonna happen," he told the Cuban.

"That ship could miss docking and hit us . . ."

"No way."

"Flaco, I need to brush my teeth . . ."

"DuBois lifted three doctors. They're supposed to check those FarTrip guys when they get here tomorrow. But until then, you got the best doctor/patient ratio in the world."

"But they won't give me what I need . . ."

Flaco opened the curtain and kicked away. The drapery did not exactly partition the clinic from the rest of 3-E, but it did provide a patina of privacy. Flaco nodded to the three doctors, who were grouped around the biomonitors. The senior physician, a long, serious woman named Marshall, returned the nod.

He found Christensen consulting with Werewolf and Meat Tucker at the laser site in 4-D and sent him aft. Flaco followed. The Air Force people in 4-B looked unreasonably cheerful. Flaco did not look at them as he passed by.

Back in 3-E, Dr. Marshall stopped him and took him aside. The other two, Plekhev and Do Campo, pretended not to listen. "Your friend," said Doctor Marshall with a nod to the curtain, "he sucks pearls, doesn't he?"

Flaco glanced e-ward. The bay was over four man-length's wide—four fathoms, some of the otters said—and just over two deep, bulkhead to bulkhead, but it was not all that difficult to overhear things that were said. "I wouldn't know about that."

"He exhibits the classic symptoms," the doctor insisted. "A record of careless mistakes on the job and bouts of intense scrupulosity."

"Hey, then you turn him in, *'mana*. He's my friend."

"Then you ought to look out for him a little better. The substance is natural and easily metabolized. No chemical test in the world can prove it was taken."

"I guess you got a problem, then."

"No!" And the physician's eyes were both stern and sad as they bored into Flaco. "*He* has a problem. And so does anyone who has to depend on him."

Flaco looked away. "He saved my life. Twice."

"I never said he was a bad person . . ."

"What do you know about it?"

"I know this: I've told Chistensen what I suspect; and your boss can have Portales's belongings searched—or simply act on the suspicion. The Orbital Safety and Health Act gives him pretty wide discretion. If his *friends* know anything that can help expedite the matter, they ought to speak up."

The doctor might have said more, but Christensen's voice came over the repeater. "Mercado, you still in 3-E? Go fetch Werewolf and"—the hesitation was slight—"Duckworth. Muy pronto, amigo."

"Sí, padrón." Flaco welcomed the excuse to break off the conversation and he hurried—no, he fled—to the forward tank. The doctor's act was like a slap in the face. He had been "flaco," a weakling, after all. He had accepted Tonio's excuses, believed his lies. A man under pearl became carefree, but on his braking orbit all his banished fears came crashing back; almost as if fear and worry could not be banished, but only postponed and accumulated. So a man who one day makes a mistake because he does not care to do it right, may do so another day because he fears doing it wrong. In the end, too much postponed too long could smash a man, the weight of troubles like the rubble of a collapsing building crushing him into endless uncaring.

Loyalty had played him false. For months, he had done nothing while Tonio's dependence worsened, telling himself that he was "standing by his friend" when he was only "standing by." Now the doctor had relieved Flaco of the decision, had lifted the whole, terrible weight from his soul. He could *help* Tonio, now. See that he got the right treatment. He could pay the debt he owed. Christensen might not think to look inside the toothpaste. Yet Flaco felt no relief. When another man had depended on him he had not acted. What sort of friendship had that been?

Flaco contacted Werewolf and Duckworth and escorted them to the control center. When he passed the clinic, he pretended that he, too, had been summoned to the control room, and so avoided speaking with the doctor.

Christensen waited in the control center with DuBois and Drozd. Werewolf said, "What's up? The kid told us there's a ship coming."

Duckworth said, "Wait," and wagged a thumb at Flaco. "Out."

Werewolf snorted. "Why? You think you can keep *this* secret, too? How long before they board us?"

"How the hell would I know?" Duckworth snapped.

"It's your ship, isn't it? Reinforcements . . . ?"

"The hell it is!"

Christensen held up a hand before the two could squabble. "Mercado, stick around."

Duckworth held his ground. "You need a reminder that we're still under martial law?"

Christensen scratched behind his ear. "Gee, I dunno, Captain. Do you want him spreading stories right now, or later? Waldo, you there?"

Duckworth opened his mouth, then closed it again. Before he could think to say something, Christensen told Drozd to fill everyone in, and the watchman told them that the station was rapidly overtaking a Lock-Mar cruiser bearing no identifiable RS number and making no signals. The cruiser was flying bass-ackwards, using its main engines to brake into co-orbit with LEO. "Uncle Waldo projects docking at the east end spacelock at perigee."

"That's a tough maneuver," DuBois said. "He'll have to rotate first."

Waldo answered his page. "Yes, boss?" Flaco recognized the voice as Leilah's.

"Keep an eye on the approaching ship and let us know if anything changes. Keep a channel open, but encrypted. Use code dancing. I don't know who might be listening, and I'd rather not find out the hard way."

"Is it the same ship you saw during your ascent?" Duckworth asked DuBois.

The pilot shrugged. "How many ships are up here flying dark? I'd say it was real likely."

Duckworth tapped his teeth with his thumbnail. "What do they want?" he wondered aloud.

Werewolf rumbled. "I'd say it was that can of worms VHI was forced to bolt onto Number Four. That's 'real likely,' too."

Duckworth did not even turn his head to look at the avionics man. "Hardly 'forced.' Your Consortium board voted to allow the installation."

"After you were already up here. And half the board abstained. Abstention is hardly—"

"It damn well is when you know what has to be done but hometown politics won't swallow a Yea."

Christensen barely raised his voice. "Gentlemen, if we can keep the politics to a dull roar? What's done is done. We need to decide what to *do*." He looked at the clock on the control panel. "And we need to decide within forty-five minutes. After that, it won't matter."

Flaco spoke up. "Maybe I *should* go back to the other guys. So they can get ready."

Christensen looked at him. "Ready? For what?"

Duckworth spoke as if to a child. "To repel boarders."

The tone evidently annoyed Werewolf, who said, "With what? Cutlasses? Pistols would turn these tanks into collanders. Which it doesn't matter because we don't have pistols *or* cutlasses on board."

"You can seal the spacelock."

Drozd said, "No, sir, we can't. Any lock can be cycled by a man outside."

"Oh, *that's* secure," the Air Force man commented acidly.

Drozd colored. "This isn't a neighborhood where you want to be caught outside without your housekeys. And no one ever expected burglars . . ."

"Put a welder on it, then. . . ."

"We ought to get some guys into suits," said Flaco. Christensen looked at him.

"Why?"

"What if they're not planning to board?"

Werewolf squeezed his eyes shut. "Oh, Jesus!"

"If they're planning an attack," DuBois pointed out, "we ought to get everyone on *Bleriot*. One good shot— placed just right—and they can plow right down the length of this station. Rake us from stem to stern. These ETs aren't exactly armor plate."

Christensen looked at DuBois for a long heartbeat, then said sharply, "Intercom!"

"Acknowledged . . ." Flaco had seldom heard the A/S's voice. It was not a channel he used very often, not being on Maintenance and Utilities. It sounded oddly like a natural voice, but one that was not identifiably male or female. "Contact. All craft head and section chiefs. Message. Confidential. Begin. Assemble crews and board the Plank at the west end dock in an orderly fashion. Be quick, but avoid panic. Time limit, thirty minutes. Possible attack; possible boarding to seize weapons system. Volunteers to don suits without prebreathing in case of breech. Message ends."

"Acknowledged. Sending." The voice was even, without emotions to be affected. Flaco found it oddly comforting. He knew it was a synthetic voice, but the lack of panic was soothing. Christensen looked at the others. "All right. Assuming the bogie means to board or attack when the orbits converge at perigee . . . what can we do to defend the station?" He made no move, either to the ready room or the space dock.

"How fast," asked Werewolf, "can we detach and jettison the—"

"The hell you will!" said Duckworth. "Not without direct orders from the president of the United States!"

"If that man is still president when we get back down. If we jettison your crap, they won't have a *reason* to attack."

"I could have you arrested!"

DuBois shook his head. "You're assuming too much, Will. We don't have the time, and I doubt the bogie would believe us. And for all I know, they're bringing up their own weapons for mounting."

Christensen said, "Being a Dane, what your president wants matters less to me than what the Consortium board wants. Unfortunately, *they* wanted us to cooperate. None of that does us any good before we reach perigee. I asked what we—Bolislav, you handle the calls, and don't let anyone in here except crew chiefs—I asked what we can do. Eddie, you might as well get back to the dock with the others."

Flaco hesitated. If the bogie attacked, *Bleriot* would cut loose and drop. And even if there was no attack, how would they ever get all those orbit-weary otters out of the ship again without crowbars and tackle? He'd be back on Earth tonight. He leapt for the e-side long line and gave himself a tug.

"Eddie?" It was Christensen's voice.

"Suits are this way," Flaco said as he coasted toward 3-D and the ready room. Sometimes you had to do the right thing even when it hurt. Or maybe especially when it hurt.

He had his long johns on and had attached the electrical harness to the upper torso when Sepp Bauer entered the ready room through the bunny hole from the central corridor. The welder looked around at the racked suits and kicked toward one of the larger ones. Flaco snapped the connector into place. "What kept you?"

"Dere is not enuff suits for everyone on board," his *pana* explained. "So we had to draw straws."

Meat Tucker emerged next and, like Flaco, picked one of the six suits that lined the inner bulkhead of the donut-shaped room. These were for lead operators. The outer bulkhead contained thirty-six standard suits when all the racks were full. Three suits, side by side, ran fore and aft. Fourteen such triplets ran head-to-toe around the outer bulkhead, except where the spacelock itself was located.

Jimmy Schorr followed with two other Golds. Tiny Littlebear made the complete circuit of the room before he found another suit as big as the ones he and Sepp used. Bird Winfrey naturally complained. "We're all gonna get the bends. You know that, don't you?" and Red Hawkins pulled the O_2 mask off his face long enough to say that depended on how much prebreathing he got in, so quit yapping. Most of the others were too busy prepping to bother with chatter. Magda Würm groaned when the diagnostic on her cooling system reported a malf. She would have put the suit on anyway, but Jimmy Schorr ordered her back to the *Bleriot*.

You couldn't put a space suit on in haste. There were too many things to make sure of. Flaco skipped the snack bar, but filled the drinking bag to its full two-thirds liter. There was no way of knowing how long he might have to wear the thing. He connected the "Snoopy" cap to the electrical harness and let it float in the air above the torso. "Hey, Sepp," he called. "I need the anti-fogger for my helment visor." As he snagged the squirt can—Sepp's lob was high—he saw the inner door to the spacelock and was struck by the sudden fancy of the intruder ship blowing it off and sucking them all out into space half-dressed. Spinning like little fans, their harnesses twinkling in the lights of the marshalling yard . . .

Flaco suddenly grabbed his Snoopy cap and pulled it on.

He pulled the throat mike into place and flipped it on. "Watch, this is Mercado. Lemme talk to the Big Guy."

"Christensen's a little preoccupied," Drozd told him. "This important?"

"Uhh. I'll get back to you. Patch me through to Waldo." After a moment, he said, "Leilah?"

"Yeah. Who's that? Flaco? Where are you? Wait a minute; lemme get an eye. Okay. I can see you. What do you want. Make it real quick, though. Recife STC just went offline. Might be a coincidence, but now nobody in Space Traffic Control can see you until you hit Nairobi airspace."

"Quick question. You're tapped into the reference database? Do Lock-Mar cruisers sight on stars to fix their position on close approach? This is important, Leilah."

"Hey, sport. Just for you." He could hear her subvocalizing as she entered search strings on another channel. Navigation. Stellar position. Lockheed-Martin Orbital Cruiser. Close approach. "Here it comes. Do you want anything beyond a yes? Because if you do . . ."

"No, you did good. Look, do you know a scientist named Leland Hobart? He came over in the Plank from Mir, and . . ."

"Hobie the Doorman? He's up there? Oh, wow! That's so bean!"

Flaco started to ask how she knew Hobart, but decided Memory Lane could wait awhile. "He's probably onboard the Plank by now. Could you tell him to . . ."

"I can't see inside the Plank. Lemme just holler."

Meat Tucker tugged on Flaco's sleeve. "What's going on, Flaco? Why'd you stop dressing?"

Flaco looked at him. "Hey, Meat, you knew that scientist Hobart back in high school, didn't you? Yeah, that's what he told me back on my first lift. You, him, and that pilot, Chase. Did you ever know a girl named Leilah?"

Meat stared as if Flaco had grown a second head. Well, it was an odd sort of chitchat, under the circumstances. "Yeah," he said after a moment. "Why?"

"Nothing. Look, you remember the problem we had

bringing in Number Four back during Red Shift? Remember how the A/S got confused because the reflection from the welding debris messed up its nav comp? Well, your pal, Hobie, has a whole suitcase full of little reflectors . . .''

Hobie did not want to part with his little reflectors. ''It took me months to grow these things,'' he protested, but Meat and Flaco talked him into bringing them up to 3-D. Jimmy Schorr tugged his lip and wondered if they oughtn't clear things with Christensen first, but Flaco said Christensen had too many problems already. Meat cycled the inner door of the 3-D spacelock and pulled it open. Hobart hesitated a moment, then yanked open his sample case and tossed the shining wafers into the lock. ''I h-hope this works,'' he said. ''Otherwise, I'm s . . . ending you the b . . . bill for the gallium.''

Meat cycled the lock without evacuating the air. When the outer door opened, the air pressure spit the wafers into space. Hobart sighed. ''I spent months on those things,'' he said again.

Flaco didn't weep for him. ''Yeah, well, I spent months on this thing,'' he said, striking the bulkhead with his fist. ''You can rebuild your shit a lot easier.''

''Tucker!'' hollered a voice from the passageway. ''To the laser! Let's go!''

''Right away, Wolf.'' Meat paused long enough to trade fives with Hobie, then dived head first into the bunny hole. Flaco hesitated, and Jimmy Schorr said, ''You helped rig that thing. Maybe you oughta go with him. It's not as though we have assigned battle stations on this rig. It's a damn construction site, not a battleship. Look, Flaco, we'll stand by at the manlocks in case . . . You know. In case we need to operate them by hand.''

''Yeah, in case it's vacuum on the other side. I know.'' He pulled himself toward the bunny hole. Red Hawkins pulled his breathing mask off for a moment. ''Yer okay, mate.''

* * *

Tonio was still in the clinic when Flaco passed by, although the three doctors were bundling him onto a stretcher. Flaco glanced at the clock and wanted to tell then not to bother. Everything would be decided within the next ten minutes. "Take good care of my *pana,*" he said. "If they shoot at Number Four and miss, they'll hit here."

The doctors ignored him, which was just as well, because what could they do about it?

Duckworth's people were in 4-B. They had removed the damaged control panel *in toto,* revealing underneath a second entire control panel. *He knew,* Flaco thought as he passed through. Duckworth knew someone would try to smash the controls and had placed a dummy panel over the active controls. He must have planned it that way from the beginning. No wonder Grigor Dazhvilli had been unable to find the power source . . . Flaco didn't know whether to be outraged at the deception, to be disappointed at the result, or to admire the cleverness.

No time for that now. He told the suitless techs to haul butt back to Number One. If the approaching ship shot birdies at this installation, the tank would rupture and spill them into space. "Thanks," said one of the techs without looking up. "We would never have figured that out."

Flaco paused, hanging onto the e-side long line with his left hand. "You guys really think you're doing the right thing, don't you?" The tech snorted and turned around.

"No, we're just willing to die for things we don't believe in." One of the others said, "Dude."

"No, I meant . . ."

"Sure, I know. But did you ever see a mass grave dug up? Ever see women who've been raped by twenty or more 'men'; or a kid who's been swung by the heels and his head smashed up against a wall?" He shoved two fingers at his throat. "Those bastards deserve anything we dump on their heads."

There was no point in arguing. If two gangs wanted to fight, the cops couldn't stop them forever. But maybe that didn't mean the cops shouldn't try. "Could be you're right," Flaco said.

"Program's running," one of the others said.

The tech started to turn away. "Yeah. And, thanks. Way I heard it, was you who busted up that soyuski 'prank.' "

Flaco had been ordered not to talk about it, but he shrugged. "Wasn't for you. Was for the station."

"Whatever. I don't care *why* you did it." To his companions, he said, "You guys can cut out now. No point all of us sitting here waiting to die." He saw Flaco's look and held up a fist with a cord running back to the panel. "Deadman's switch," he explained. He studied the instrument silently for a moment; then said, "Hell, we weren't ever supposed to use this thing. This rig was just supposed to bring 'em to the table." He shook his head. "But I'll be damned if I let those killers take it out without swatting 'em back."

Flaco kicked off to 4-D, where Gregorson and Meat Tucker waited. Gregorson wore a head set with the microphone folded up, but did not have a suit on. Sepp Bauer was fastening a lifeline around Werewolf's waist. "You better get out of here, too," Flaco warned Gregorson. "Meat and I can handle this." But a glance at the control panels and he knew he lied. He could take the structure apart and put it back together blindfolded, but he had no idea how to handle the electronics.

Meat shrugged. "I tried to tell him . . ."

"Shove it," said Werewolf, as he datagloved settings on the virtual control panel. Pointers on slide gauges moved up and down with his finger. "This is what I do." The icon of the microwave mast tilted toward horizontal. It could depress, Flaco recalled, to fifteen degrees. Werewolf pondered the settings. "Lucifer's target acquisition A/S is still in place," he told them. "But we need to tutor it." He rubbed his beard and scowled at the readouts.

"Fifteen degrees from horizontal," Meat reported. "Tracking smooth."

Sepp Bauer finished with the belt spool. "Now" he said.

"I take the free end and bitt it in 3-F. We have to, Tiny and I, we pull you in as fast as we can before we seal the interlock." Werewolf licked his lips, swallowed, and nodded. "Yeah," he said.

After Sepp departed, Werewolf said, "Look, they'll probably try to dock with us; but if not, they'll come starside, past the laser. The weapons system is on the earthside hull, but if they brake below us, they'll drop into a faster orbit and start falling ahead of us. If they go starside, *we* pull past *them,* and they get another docking opportunity at the west end." He paused and scowled at the controls. "I hope this is just a false alarm, and there's some harmless explanation; but . . ." He shook his head. "Ah, the hell with it." He flipped the throat-mike down. "Control, this is Laser. Position?"

Flaco could hear the response over his lead operator's circuit. "Estimate one minute," said Drozd. "Bandit is having trouble locking on. Attitude engines firing erratically. Someone dumped a whole shitload of reflectors out the 4-D spacelock, and it seems to be confusing their navcomp." Flaco and Meat grinned at each other and exchanged fives. Werewolf noticed and grunted.

"Okay, Meat," he said. "You're power. When I say sizzle, you give us the juice. Up is more power; down is less. Watch that indicator, right there. No, to your left. That's it. Keep that in the green zone. Yellow is okay for a short time. Red means you're overloading. Okay?"

Meat nodded.

"Good. And you . . ."

"Flaco."

"Flaco, you're tracking. Use that joystick. You okay with that?"

Flaco shrugged. How many arcade games had he played when he was a kid? A million?

"Keep the crosshairs on your target. The A/S will learn and hold position once you press that button; but if you want to shift to a different target, you have to do that yourself by jerking the joystick. I'll monitor systems . . ."

"Wolf," said Meat, "you explained things. Now bug out."

Gregorson shook his head. "Not everything's A/S, yet. Half this shit is jerry-rigged. Hell, the controls ought to be slaved into the main office. But the Artemis trials weren't scheduled until next month . . ."

". . . *LEO Station, calling LEO Station.*" The voice came over the management channel. Flaco saw from how Meat cocked his head and Werewolf put a hand to the earflap of his Snoopy cap that they had heard it, too. "*Please be evacuating your second tank from east. You have allowed placement of weapon of mass destruction on your premises, contrary to international law and wishes of all Earth peoples.*"

Christensen's voice: "This station is private property. You are in tresspass—" Meat looked at Flaco. "Oh, *that*'ll scare them off . . ."

"—and the weapons system in question has been already been disabled."

"*I cannot take your word for that. We intend to fire missile to destroy outlaw installation. We do not want loss of life. Please evacuate target tank.*"

"And if we don't?"

A pause, and the voice was heavy with sorrow. "*Then we must fire, regardless, before orbits diverge.*"

"There is other, valuable property in that location that cannot be moved . . ."

"*Too bad.*"

Abruptly, DuBois's voice broke in on the channel. "Levkin? Levkin, is that you?"

"Ship rising over the hull," Werewolf reported. "Get ready."

"*Ned? You are aboard? Ah . . . To meet again after all this time . . .*"

"Those Lock-Mar cruisers aren't designed with missile launchers," Werewolf said. "And I doubt they jerry-rigged outboards on the hull; so . . ."

"Levkin call off the attack. There are innocent people up here."

". . . so they must have carried the missiles as cargo, which means they have to open the cargo bays and . . ."

"Who is on side of angels now, old friend?"

". . . and stage the missiles in co-orbit for launching. Yes, I can see them on the visuals. They have three of them out of the bay already. Weren't waiting for an answer, I guess. There are six space suits servicing them. . . . Look at 'em . . ."

"Levkin, two wrongs don't make a right. Stay cool. Congress'll make the president pull the crows off the station . . ."

"Look at 'em bug out. Christ, those birds are ready to fly. They must have been prepping them since their last burn."

"We cannot depend on your government to . . ."

"Flaco, see if you can lock onto the missiles and fry them. Don't hit the people, if you can help it."

Flaco shot a glance at Werewolf. The man had bit through his own lip and spots of blood floated in the air. Meat, to his right, looked suddenly grim. *If you can help it . . .* Flaco was suddenly aware of two things: first, that this was no arcade game; and second, that Werewolf had deliberately split the aiming and the firing of the laser between him and Meat—so that one aimed without firing, while the other fired without aiming. Flaco nudged the joystick over the first missile, centering the crosshairs on the propellant tank; then he pressed the button that told the A/S to retain that target.

"Levkin, you should have lifted with me, to welcome Forrest and Mike back. Not this."

"Ah . . . Tell Mishka and Forrest I salute them when you see them."

"I'm asking you as my friend . . ."

"I am not in command of this police action, Ned. I am only the pilot . . ."

"The bird is turning. That one. Number two. They're launching that one first!"

Flaco saw and shifted the joystick to target the center missile.

"I'm asking you as my friend, Don't do this!"

"*I must.*"

"Kill the bird before they light it. Shift to the second one right away."

"Don't fire."

"*I am sorry, my friend.*"

"Meat, power up!"

The station went dark, as the laser sucked up all the available power from the sunscreens and fuel cells. Everything happened in a blur. Werewolf had told them that the laser had been designed to kill tanks. The missile did not have that sort of armor plating. The first bird, caught as it fired, ruptured along the side of its oxydizer tank and pinwheeled off, spewing a plume of furiously boiling gasses. Flaco saw it only from the corner of his eye because he shifted his joystick toward the next missile. The crosshairs passed over one of the space-suited figures, which appeared to spasm, then float still. He did not let himself think about it but centered on the next bird. Werewolf called out something about power drain. Meat hollered, "Reducing power."

Flaco guessed wrong. The laser sliced open the second missile, but it was the third one that launched. The laser's beam, invisible except where it ignited particles of space dust, passed through the exploding remnants of the second missile and struck the cruiser itself. Flaco tugged on the joystick to bring the crosshairs to bear on the rapidly approaching third missile and hit the lock-on button. But his timing was off and the laser locked onto the cruiser, burning a hole in its aft propellant tank and drawing a fiery gash across its fuselage. A brilliant light erupted inside the ship and flared out through the portholes. Welds blew and seams ruptured. Flaco heard DuBois cry out, "Levkin!" Then he tugged on the joystick and relocated the approaching missile and the laser locked on and the nose glowed cherry red and it was too late.

21.

There Is a Balm in Gilead

Mariesa van Huyten stood in the foyer of Silverpond, waiting for Harriet. She had dressed lightly, in spring colors, as befitted May; but the cut of the suit was strictly business. The early morning sunlight, sliced and diced by the prisms set in the thick wooden front door, scattered dancing colors across the floor tiles. Gazing through door glass, she had an insect's-eye view of the world—a host of replicated images, so that there seemed not one pond at the base of the hill but scores, all subtly different in shade and hue. From different positions in the foyer, certain of the images would suddenly invert. The world turned upside down. It was an odd door, a quirky door; one of the few ways in which Willem van Huyten had allowed playfulness to show through the no-nonsense crust that had accreted around his soul.

The tilework was another. Everything in the foyer was arranged in strict geometric symmetry: the arch, the vases in their niches, the chandelier overhead. You could prove theorems from Euclid with this foyer. Yet, the tiles on the floor, like the prismatic windows in the door, seemed to have been scattered, willy-nilly. Hidden among the green and brown terra cotta was a maze. Not many had noticed it. Harriet never had. Sykes had had it pointed out to him. Barry alone of those who crossed her threshold had noticed it. Noticed it, and solved it. Perhaps that playfulness in his own heart had been his attraction to her. Perhaps that was why she had married him.

Sykes appeared, silent and dutiful as always, and murmured that Harriet would be down presently. Absently, she acknowledged the message as she traced the path of the brown tiles with the toe of her shoe. Barry had shown her the solution to the maze, years ago during their courtship. (Or what had turned out to have been their courtship, to everyone's amazement, her own and Barry's included.) Yet, somehow, she had forgotten. The child Mariesa had scampered and skipped through the maze, searching for years for the solution. Now she struggled in vain to recall it.

A discreet cough drew her attention to her butler. Sykes stood by, just to the left of the vase, which he resembled in overall shape. He had lost weight in the past year, so that his clothing and his skin seemed a looser fit than before. Yet, he dressed impeccably, as always. The cut of his jacket, though tailored to the modern taste, was irrefutably formal. Though was that the style or the wearer that projected that image? Mariesa sometimes wondered whether Sykes had adopted a calm, imperturbable demeanor in consequence of his employment, or whether he was naturally so inclined and had gravitated toward a career of personal service because of it. Was he consciously playing a role, or was he type-cast? ''Yes, Sykes. What is it?''

''The staff has asked me, miss, to convey their best wishes. For today's meeting.''

''Did they? That was thoughtful. Tell them that I thank—Tell them, 'Thanks a lot.' I appreciate it.'' Still Sykes hesitated. ''Is there more?''

The man looked decidedly uncomfortable. What the cues were, Mariesa could not rightly say, for the face and posture changed little, if at all. And yet, she definitely sensed a hesitation in him. ''Come on, Ed,'' she said. '' 'Let it all hang out.' ''

Perhaps it was the unexpectedness of the colloquialism, but Sykes grinned. His smile was a pleasant thing that brightened his face. It was not the sort of smile that one put on for politeness. It was not painted on. It was more as if a curtain had been pulled aside to reveal a smile that had always been there. "Okay, miss," he said. "How long have I worked for you now?"

Surprised at the question, not sure where it was leading, she paused to tally the years. She realized as she did so that she barely knew Sykes outside his role. He liked to read romance novels (of all things) and he had never married. Perhaps also, and partly this justified her ignorance, he was a solitary man. "Thirty years," she said at last, surprised at the total. "Counting the time you were Gramper's driver."

He nodded, as if she had passed a test. "Thirty years," he repeated. "And I might add, an enjoyable thirty years. I've seen a lot of characters come in and out of here. Punk kids to ex-presidents. It hasn't always been easy, but it's always been interesting."

He's building up to a resignation, Mariesa thought—and the thought was so alien and startling that she nearly burst into tears.

"What I mean to say, miss, is that I sincerely hope everything turns out for the best today."

"Why, Ed!" On sudden impulse, as if the dread had been a lid holding her down, she stepped toward him and kissed him on the cheek. Sykes appeared first startled, then pleased, then appreciative. When his smile vanished again behind its screen—on hearing the footsteps of the approaching Harriet—it did not vanish utterly, for in Mariesa's eye its memory lingered on his face.

Harriet was all bustle. She strode into the foyer tugging on a pair of white gloves. Harriet was a rock in the seas of change. It had been years and years since white gloves in springtime had been mandatory; but in her youth, Harriet had learned how a lady ought to dress and she would not change. Such customs were not followed for any reason, she had argued during one of their interminably silly wrangles (young Mariesa had called mannerisms "hypocritical") but following them *is* the reason. To do is to be. Zen from mid-fifties finishing schools. And yet Mariesa now wondered how much of the reaction against fashion had itself been mere fashion. *My dear, anyone who is* any*one is burning their bra this season.* . . . There had been mannerism and conformity among the young, too; nor had hypocricy been banished—only one sort substituted for another.

"Louis is waiting, Mummy," she said.

"Let him wait," Harriet replied. "He's paid by the hour." She faced the mirror behind the vase on her side of the foyer and straightened the bow in her blouse—a few deliberate and unnecessary motions, as if delay was their purpose and not their consequence.

"I cannot afford to be late."

"Bosh. They cannot start without you."

"It would make a bad impression."

Harriet turned away from the mirror and regarded her with a steely eye. "Your cousins formed their impressions of you a very long time ago. What you say or do today will make no difference in *that*."

"But it may affect their vote on the chairmanship. If I am late, and consequently appear haughty or indifferent—"

"Don't speak such nonsense. You have your shares and mine. Tom Longworth will support anything 'the grand-daughter of Willem' does and your Aunt Wilhemina thinks President Donaldson walks on water. And of course, you can always count on Chris, and he votes his father's proxies. Have you forgotten how to do arithmetic, darling?"

Mariesa kept silence. Cousin Brittany had called the meeting, but Chris had instigated it. Mariesa had not yet found the courage to tell her mother how badly she had "screwed the pooch."

The old test pilots' phrase reminded her of Ned DuBois and his broad shoulders and knowing ways. Would she have been happier, she wondered, throwing all this up and living as his mistress? (She could *not* imagine being his wife.) Never mind its impossibility. She could never have done that any more than he could have become a kept man. But build a parallel world with a different Mariesa, living in a split-level, gossiping across the fence, shepherding kids in a minivan, discretely entertaining her occasional, wild-man, fly-boy lover. Imagine a Mariesa who had never looked through a telescope, who had never seen an asteroid or a proxy, and wouldn't know a balance sheet from a PERT. Would such a Mariesa have been happier, or only oblivious?

"Come, dear," said Harriet; and Mariesa came to herself to find Harriet already out the door. She took a step forward and paused, because she found herself standing in the middle of the maze and had forgotten the way out.

Brittany van Huyten-Armitage was spare and slight. She sported an everlasting tan, hard-won on scores of high-price golf courses, and a jaded look, hard-won on scores of high-price mattresses. She dressed to impress. There was always some article of jewelry or clothing on display for no other purpose than to incite admiration or envy or (depending on her purposes) lust. She fancied herself a Power, wielding the third largest block of voting stock on the Van Huyten Trust (which in turn wielded the largest block of VHI stock), so that she could make-or-break without ever the need to involve herself in the work of the corporation. A Woman of Means did not grub like an employee in the marketplace or the office (let alone in the shop) but deferred such labor to her "man of business" (or, possibly, her "woman of business"), becoming no more immersed in day-to-day affairs than to decide on whom to bestow that role and on how to spend the dividends.

Perhaps, Mariesa thought, as she studied her cousin across the board room table, perhaps she was being a trifle judgmental. By her own lights, Britt did the Right Thing. Self-indulgence came naturally, and she was no more to blame for enjoying it than a cat sleeping in a sunbeam. She was no more and no less a social butterfly than any number of acquaintances in her circle. Yet, it irritated Mariesa when someone in the stadium crowd presumed to judge the work of the gladiators in the pit. That thrust was a little weak. You could have moved faster with the net and trident. Matters always seemed simpler when viewed from the detached and unresponsible bleacher seats than from the blood and the sand. In some ways, Mariesa felt closer to Ed Bullock than to her own cousin.

Though sometimes, in retrospect, matters seemed different, even to the gladiators themselves.

Aunt Wilhemina, who by reason of age held place of honor at the foot of the table, just under the portrait of old Henryk, spoke in a quavering voice. She had been the middle of the three siblings—Willem, Wilhemina, and Wilfrid—though the only one of that generation still living. Gramper had always joked that his father, Conrad, had stopped at three legitimate children only because he could think of no more names beginning with Wil—. A link to the past, Aunt Wilhemina was a living symbol of a heritage that stretched back to the days of the Thirty Years' War and Dutch Independence. When she was gone, Mariesa wondered, would the sense of family unity go with her? Or was that something already vanished?

"I think," Aunt Wilhemina said, so faintly that the others had to strain to hear her, "that young Mariesa did the right thing. We *ought* to support our president."

Tom Longworth, one of the few stockholders who were not family, nodded. Norbert looked thoughtful, but unconvinced. Chris looked both unhappy and unmoved. Harriet spoke up. "And I say that we ought to support *our* president."

A slight change of emphasis, a slight shift in the subject. Strange to think that Harriet was one of her few allies in the room. Mariesa could recall so many years of antagonism and manipulation, of sly and subtle head games, of opposition and obstruction on every personal front, that it startled her when mother stood by her. And yet was that so bizarre? True, they had been at loggerheads over so much, but Harriet had always been motivated by What Was Best for Riesey.

I will decide that myself, Mummy, thank you very much. But thank you, too, for wanting it.

"Family solidarity is all well and good," said Pauline. "We should show outsiders a united face. But should we gather on the quarterdeck singing 'Nearer, My God, to Thee' when the ship is in danger of sinking."

Chris sat to Mariesa's left, as Harriet sat to her right. He spoke up through fingers held prayerlike to his lips. "The ship is in no danger of sinking," he said. "But to extend the metaphor, she has taken on a great deal of water and the seas are rather choppy." The laughter that greeted this was restrained and self-conscious. Pauline, and her mother Beatrice, were the sort who wavered between complacency and panic. Binomial thinkers, they could imagine no middle ground. Thank God, Gramper had bypassed his own treasured daughter when he sought an heir. Yet, might that not have kindled a spark of envy that Beatrice had passed on? Mariesa caught her lip between her teeth. *That* was paranoid thinking. Chris and his father had the same reasons for jealousy, but . . . She turned her head slightly to look at him.

Could Chris have harbored such thoughts all these years without her awareness? Brittany certainly did. Every now and then, Mariesa caught Britt casting triumphant glances at her brother—which meant she knew how the second largest block of stock would vote today. But Mariesa saw nothing but turmoil in Chris's eyes.

No, Mother, I haven't forgotten my arithmetic. Today's vote of confidence would be a close-run thing, very different from the times when Chris and she stood together with their respective parents' proxies and Aunt Wilhemina's backing. This time, half a dozen smaller blocks held the balance. Altogether too much depended on cousins like Norbert and Pauline, whose minds and lives were as distant from VHI affairs as Pluto was from the sun.

"As I see it," Brittany told the other stockholders, "the present CEO is much too likely to risk our trust fund on, well, speculative ventures. VHI is overextended. We ought to pull out of the riskier positions and stick with sounder investments.''

Mariesa spoke up for very nearly the first time at the meeting. It was unseemly for her to defend herself too vigorously. Custom demanded that she not appear to hunger for the job. ''Which ventures are those?'' she asked softly.

Brittany turned to her with a look of ingenuous surprise. ''Why, the LEO Consortium, for one. If it wasn't a boondoggle on its face, events earlier this morning have made it one.''

''The station defended itself successfully,'' she pointed out. *But at what a price! At what a price . . .*

''A defense that would have been unnecessary, if you hadn't placed weapons on board in violation of international treaties.''

''Nonsense,'' said Aunt Wilhemina. ''Little Riesey did the patriotic thing.''

Mariesa sat stiffly in her chair. ''*I* did not place any weapons on board. The government of the United States did. I only rented the space—and under pressure, I might add. If anyone broke a treaty, it was Donaldson.''

Chris shook his head. '' 'That dog won't hunt,' Riesey. Donaldson was just an excuse you used to put a laser on board. Jesus, if you'd done it because you *believed* in Donaldson's notions, that'd be one thing . . .''

''Chris,'' said Pauline, ''I wish you'd not use profanity.''

Chris sent a puzzled look toward the far end of the table. ''. . . or if your arm had been twisted so bad it fell off. But it was this asteroid delusion of yours . . .''

''It's not a delusion,'' said Tom Longworth. ''The risk is real, though maybe''—with an embarrassed avoidance of Mariesa's gaze—''a little overstated.''

''The repair costs on the space station push Break-Even Day even farther into the future,'' said Brittany. ''And now that the station has been shown to be vulnerable, additional costs must be sunk into defense against future terrorists. And who will rent space on what has become prime military ground? It might be best to bail out now. We may never see a return on that investment.''

A silent ripple passed down both sides of the table. Mutters of agreement, a few words of caution. No one, Mariesa noted, spoke out in favor of pushing on. Norbert leaned forward across the table and the others fell silent.

Norbert was the only cousin present wearing a three-piece suit. He was Old Boston personified. A throwback to the days before the arrival of the brawling Irish. Deliberately so, Mariesa suspected. He cultivated a staid, proper fustiness—at least in his public life. (His private life might be something else altogether; though Mariesa had trouble imagining whips and leather.) Not only did he not "let it all hang out," as Brittany had commented cattily at Wilfrid's funeral years ago, "but he probably didn't have all that much to hang out in the first place." However, when Norbert spoke, his serious mien dictated that he be taken just as seriously.

"I think Brittany may be right," he said. "We should keep our positions in ballistic transport and in aeroshell construction. Those are proven technologies, and Aurora and Pegasus have the potential to become the American Airlines and the Boeing of the twenty-first century. But the other ventures . . . Space platforms. Power satellites . . .'' He shook his head. "Too risky. And there is insufficient demand.''

"The demand will grow," Chris said quietly. "Energy without groundside pollution . . . There will be a market. I've seen the projections. The venture has potential in the billions.''

"And what if the projections are wrong?''

Chris spread his hands. "Norbert, the stock market could crash and wipe out safe and stodgy blue chips, too. I can remember when SSTOs and ballistic ships were outrageous notions, too. Yet we took a chance on them.''

Norbert pursed his lips. "Then let others take the risks now. We took our big chance.''

"That's not so important, Norbert," Brittany said.

"What's important"—and, oh, what a sly, sidelong glance!—"is that the new CEO make those decisions on a hard-headed, businesslike basis."

They took a refreshment break before voting. Dagda Catering had set up coffee and petits fours in the larger meeting room down the hall from the boardroom. The stockholders gathered there and engaged in soft conversation with one another. Few, Mariesa noted wryly, approached her. Tom Longworth, whose father (a close childhood friend of Gramper) had run Vulcan Steel for many years, assured her of his support; but he voted only two percent of the shares. So, while grateful, Mariesa was not overwhelmed. Aunt Wilhemina, enthroned in her wheelchair near the windows, smiled brightly in her direction. But the looks she caught from Norbert were guarded; and those from Beatrice, Pauline, and Brittany were positively gleeful.

Mariesa stood by herself and sipped a cup of tepid tea while she weighed her chances. This was worse than when word of Prometheus had originally leaked out, back in '99. At least then she'd had Chris on her side and her company presidents firmly in line. Covertly, she watched Chris circulate, chatting, shaking hands. He spoke for a while with his father, Christiaan, Sr., and then made his way across the room to her. Mariesa pretended she had not been watching him.

"Mariesa," he said in a low voice, "we need to talk." Without waiting for a response, he took her by the elbow and guided her into a corner away from the others. But when they were alone, he stood silent, clenching and unclenching his hands.

"You said we needed to talk," she suggested.

Chris gave her a troubled glance. "You were right," he said. "About the others. They really don't understand the importance of the Prometheus projects. Norbert had business training, but it's all financial. He had no grasp of hardware, spin-off, seed technology, or the need for patience. I swear: Aunt Wilhemina has more grasp of the long-term—

and less use for it, I'm sorry to say—than all of them put together.''

"What are you trying to say?"

He took a deep breath and studied the side of First Watchung Mountain, where the noontime sun warmed the lawn surrounding VHI. It was a Friday. Mariesa could see some of the staff outside, jogging or eating their lunches on the tables under the trees. She wondered if they had any notion what was happening in the boardroom; or whether, knowing, they cared. Chris shoved his hands in his pants. "I think we may be stuck with you."

"What?"

He turned from the window. "I think we may need to keep you at the conn. No one else has the vision for the future."

"You . . . don't sound very happy."

"Should I? What you did was wrong, and wrong on several levels. Donaldson's plan was bad in the egg—elect a man president and right away he thinks he's a geopolitical master strategist—but even if his plan had been sound, the way you went about it was wrong." He pulled a hand from his pocket and pointed a finger at her. "VHI is not your personal playtoy, Mariesa. It's a collaborative effort. Tens of thousands of people—from you and me in the boardrooms all the way up to the lab tech and the welder and the payroll clerk—working together on common goals. We may set the policies and the strategic plans—and there are often good reasons for maintaining confidentiality—but don't distort the whole structure for your personal fears." He grimaced and lowered the finger. He turned toward the window once more and crossed his arms. "Look at me, the 'Dutch uncle.' "

"It is more than just my 'personal fears,' Chris. Did you read the package of materials I sent you? About the asteroids?"

"I skimmed it."

"Something's wrong with the asteroids, Chris. More and

more of them are coming toward us. Some of them have had to change course to do it.''

He hesitated. ''I agree the data is puzzling.''

''Not puzzling. Frightening. If it was just random chance, then maybe I am just a crazy old woman, worried about something that will never happen. But if someone came around our neighborhood an eon ago and fitted out some asteroids with engines—''

Chris shook his head. ''You're adding two and two and getting two hundred.'' He paused, scowled, and added, ''Maybe.''

''Those gigawatt lasers we were planning . . . They can do more than beam power. They can be turned outward to defend us.''

His eyebrows climbed. ''I began to suspect something like that after *Michael* . . . But, Riesey, do you really think you can disintegrate a nickle-iron asteroid with a blow-torch?''

The laugh was short. ''What sort of odds do you give on building orbital platforms with nuclear-tipped missiles? Microwave lasers would give us *some* protection. Boil . . . Sublimate part of the rock and it would act like a jet and move it off course. I am not entirely whack, you know.''

Chris tugged his lip. ''No. Not entirely. I read the memo from Dr. Blessing and the FarTrip Alien Task Force. Look, it's something we can talk about, okay?''

She laid a hand on his arm. ''Promise me you'll keep the option open when you build the SPS platforms. Promise me that you'll study the situation.''

''When *I* build them?''

''You could.''

He laughed, once and bitterly. ''Maybe. I can execute the vision. And I'd do damn well. But, don't you see? I'd be beholden to the others. To Sis and Aunt Beatrice and the rest. And they would . . . Not be looking at any night skies. Even if the night skies *were* falling on them. On the other hand''—he looked over his shoulder at her—''if I vote my shares to retain you—my shares and Dad's—then *you* would be beholden to *me*. I'd expect a greater role in matters, and I'd expect to be consulted on all majors decisions, certainly as much as you consult Khan and Redman.''

Mariesa laid her teacup on a nearby tray. ''I see. You would do that out of pragmatism.''

He nodded. ''Yes. Out of pragmatism.''

She looked at the rest of the room. ''They're going back in,'' she said. ''Time for the moment of truth.''

Chris offered his arm. ''I'll escort you.''

She almost told him she could damn well walk by herself; but the gesture was well-intended and he had, after all, offered to escort her in much more important ways.

Mariesa did not even keep a tally of the votes as they ayes and nays rumbled like a train wreck up the table toward her. Norbert, acting as secretary for the trust, would do that. He had placed half-glasses on his nose and, were it not for the computer screens and keyboards set in and under the table, she would have half-expected to see him pull out a pen knife and cut a fresh point on his quill. Aunt Wilhemina, as expected, voted ''Aye'' on the issue of retaining the current CEO. So did Longworth and two of the more distant cousins. But the big hits were the blocks that Gramper had apportioned among his three children and four grandchildren and the block that had gone through Wilfrid to Norbert. Mariesa remembered the advice that Gramper had once given her. *A chairman must deal from a position of strength, so I am giving you the largest block of shares. But a chairman must also learn to build bridges, so it is not a majority.*

An old man with lively eyes and a long, stringy, white beard. *You old pirate*, she thought. Gramper had held absolute control. His brother and sister and more distant relations combined could never have outvoted him. Why he had settled his own legacy in another fashion had always puzzled her. Though perhaps he had learned the hard way the pitfalls of absolute control.

Norbert. Beatrice. Pauline. Brittany . . . Each voted their shares to put Chris in her place. Each time, Mariesa glanced covertly at Chris and saw the subtle twist of emotions that played there. Harriet, when asked her decision, favored the trustees with twisted smile. "Do you honestly expect a mother to vote against her own daughter?" Mariesa, who had expected Harriet to do exactly that on more than one previous occasion, refrained from any comment or outward show.

Then, quickly, before Chris could speak, and before she herself could entertain second thoughts, she interrupted the smooth flow. "I vote my shares in favor of Christiaan van Huyten, Jr., for chairman of the Van Huyten Trust and Van Huyten Industries." Then she stood and turned to the astonished president of Argonaut Labs and extended her hand. "Congratulations, Chris. I know you'll carry out the vision we set, together, for the company, and I wish you the best of luck. Though I do hope you'll consult with me from time to time." Dumbly, Chris rose and took her hand. He placed a smile on his face and spoke through the teeth.

"Riesey, what on earth do you think you're doing?"

Harriet seemed equally shocked, though her face also betrayed a certain relief. Mariesa sat down again and glanced at her screen. "Norbert, you can close your jaw and enter the vote. You heard correctly."

It was hard to tell if Norbert heard her or not. Voices arose like a swarm of bees. Questions, demands, congratulations aimed at Chris. A few supporters berated her for having thrown in the towel. Brittany seemed nonplussed, as if unsure she had won a victory. Mariesa only closed her eyes and leaned back in her chair, ignoring them all. The hubbub faded to a distant murmur, the words in a gentle blur. She felt suddenly weightless, as light as a feather, uncertain which way the wind would blow her, and no longer caring very much, either.

Mariesa left immediately after the vote. She told Harriet and Chris to stay for the planned lunch but insisted that she herself needed some time alone. Chris, God bless him, ran interference all the way to the elevator; though she could tell that he struggled with his own questions. Crossing the atrium at the center of the ground floor, she exchanged greetings with several managers she knew by sight. Some of them gave her puzzled looks, and she realized that she was damn near skipping.

Outside the front door, milling reporters shouted questions at her. She let them shout over each other and said only that Norbert Wainwright-van Huyten had kept the tally and they ought to direct their questions to him after lunch. Although it was obvious that she would divulge nothing, the reporters insisted on pelting her with even more questions. The early news downloads would no doubt report that lack of information as the lead story. These days, half the news was about the news itself. She passed through the press by main force and with the help of a few courteous men and women, and when she reached the other side, there, leaning back against a battered old Datsun parked along the curb, was Styx.

There she is, Roberta thought as she watched the Rich Lady waltz down the steps from the VHI building. Darth Vader's Castle, they called it at the Crusades. The Rich Lady looked frazzled, but almost cheerful and wasn't that a kick in the head? Did that mean she had won the board fight? Styx leaned back against her car to steady herself. All of the rottenness and betrayal she had endured. It would mean nothing if the Rich Lady won anyway.

Their eyes met and Roberta fought to maintain a steady gaze. The Ray-Ban look. She pretended she had shades on; that she could see the world without being seen. Van Huyten came toward her, toady reporters clearing the way for her like goddamn courtiers. When the "richest woman in North America" halted before her, Roberta Carson, who was not even the richest woman on her block, deigned to notice. "Oh, hi there," she said with a deliberately phony pleasantness.

"Roberta," Mariesa said, "were you waiting for me?"

"Nah, I was just hanging."

"Would you mind terribly if I begged a ride back to Silverpond from you? I would like to have Louis stay and wait for Harriet."

Roberta shrugged casually. "Yah. Sure. Whatever."

A few minutes later, they were locked inside the Datsun. Van Huyten sat in the shotgun seat and not, as Styx had half-expected, in the back. Well, it took a real good imagination to pretend the Datsun was a limo. She paused a moment before starting the engine, toying with the notion of acting blasé as all hell. But, ultimately, she had to know.

"So," she said with casual cattiness, "How'd it go?"

The Rich Lady tugged at her sleeve and straightened her jacket under the seat belt. A long hesitation. A glance out the side window. "I've been replaced."

"Yeah?" Roberta feigned shock and astonishment. She twisted the key. "Gee whiz. That's too bad."

A cloud covered the May sunshine and the car sped through sudden shadow. "It may be," van Huyten said. "It may be too bad."

"I bet you fought tooth and nail to keep the job."

Van Huyten shot her a curious glance and studied her expression. Styx, glanced at the road ahead, at her passenger, at the road again. "Yes," said the Rich Lady. "Of course, I did. But in the end, the vote was unanimous."

Roberta tried to put a triumphant smile on her face. "Down. In. Flames," she said. The smile wouldn't stay, however. Funny. She had looked forward to this day for so long, but it was not as bright a day as she had expected. Who was there to share her triumph with?

"What's wrong, dear?"

"There's nothing wrong!" But the tone was sharp, the words abrupt; and they gave the lie to what she said.

"You can talk about it if you—"

"There's nothing to talk about! You're the one who's been stomped on, not me."

"I ... see." A long mile passed in silence and the road veered upward toward the low gap through Skunktown Mountain. The rundown scatter of buildings called Skunktown Furnace fell behind them, the road made an abrupt bend, and the trees closed in on both sides. Their bursting branches meeting overhead formed a canopy over the road. The highway settled into a sort of green gloaming. It was under just this sort of fey lighting, Roberta thought, that one saw the legendary ghosts of north Jersey—the White Preacher, the Hairy Hand.

"I've always enjoyed this section of the trip," van Huyten said. "It's so relaxing."

It certainly must be, Roberta thought. She had never heard the Rich Lady sound so natural and relaxed. That wasn't right, somehow. She had just had all her toys taken away from her. She ought to be raging against the injustice, not accepting it so stoically. "What?" Roberta said. "Trees and birds? I thought you were more the spaceship type."

"Spaceships can be beautiful, too; but they never brought me comfort. They were a means, not an end. The trees, on the other hand . . ." And she ran a finger across the side window, as if she were touching the greenery. "Why, they are infinitely renewing and, so, infinitely reassuring. You could cut every one of these trees down—the oak, the spruce, the hemlock, the birch—and in a hundred years, there would be another forest here."

"A hundred years," said Styx. "A long time to wait."

"Not if you're a tree."

Caught by surprise, Roberta laughed, a sound she had not heard in the three days since she had stormed out of Crusades headquarters. But just the memory of that last encounter with Phil was enough to snuff the laughter out. The sudden quiet earned her a curious look from van Huyten, a curiosity which Roberta refrained from satisfying. Phil's deviousness was none of her damn business.

At the top of the gap, they drove through a cut with sheer stone sides, almost as if they were passing through the battlements of a great fortress. The rock face on the left had frost on it—an astonishing thing to see on a bright May day!—but that side of the cut lay in perpetual shadow. The right-hand wall had a seep of water running down it: a glistening curtain that seemed to writhe even as it seemed to lie still. The Rich Lady studied the running water in silence. Then, turning again to face the front, she said, "How many times have I ridden through this cut and I never realized . . . That must be the wellspring for Runamuck Creek, the one that flows through Silverpond."

Roberta shrugged. She drove down the far side of Skunktown Mountain into the village of Hamm's Corner—a somewhat more prosperous-looking 'burb than Skunktown Furnace; but then, which would you rather put on your return address? "A few inches the other way," the Rich Lady said, "and the water would drain off into the coastal plain and there would be no Silverpond, at all."

Roberta could stand it no longer. She had played this scene out in her mind many times, but the Rich Lady wasn't following the script. "Who'd they name chairman?"

Van Huyten started, as if woken from a dream. "Oh. Chris, of course. There was no other possibility, if we were to keep it in the family."

"Chris," Roberta said. She nodded. "He'll do okay. He's honest."

"If that was intended as a cut—"

"Of course, it was. How can I see blood on the floor if I don't cut?"

Instead of snapping back, van Huyten answered softly. "Did he hurt you so badly?"

"I don't know what you're talking about."

The Rich Lady hesitated, then pointed. "Slow down and turn right, up ahead."

A rocky, dirt track led off the paved highway and into a copse of trees. A sign read OFFICIAL USE ONLY. "Here? But . . ."

"It's the back entrance to the estate."

"Oh."

Another few moments of silence; then the Rich Lady spoke in a distant voice. "People are never quite as good as we want them to be," she said. "I've found that out the hard way. But when they fail to measure up, does the problem lay in the measure or in our expectations?''

Roberta slowed the Datsun to negotiate a particularly ugly rock on the right side of the track. The car tilted alarmingly and she used her concentration to avoid a response. Was van Huyten probing at her relationship with Phil, or was she pondering her own relationship? It was hard to tell. She had spoken almost to herself.

"You'll stay for lunch, won't you?'' the Rich Lady said. For once, it sounded more like a request than a command.

Styx tucked her chin up. "Why should I?'' But her objection was not as strong as she might have made it; and so, fifteen minutes later, she found herself in the sunroom of a house she swore she would never set foot in again, with a tray of small sandwiches in front of her and a tureen of light consommé. The sun had fallen past noon and the slopes of the mountain behind the estate had blurred into a kind of blue-green mist that gave the entire scene a surreal quality. Hydrocarbon vapors, van Huyten told her. Drawn from the trees by sunlight to combine with nitrogen oxides in the air. Roberta refused to let the scientific names spoil the beauty of it. Somewhere, on the other side of that ridge of mist and rock, her mother lay buried. The mountain was like a wall between them.

"Chris will do a good job,'' van Huyten said, when the conversation had wandered back from trees and poetry and astronomy to the events of the last few days. "I've made a frightful mess, I'm afraid; but he's the man to clean it up.''

Roberta took a sandwich. It was filled with some awful pimento spread, and the crusts had been cut off the bread. Why did they do that? And what happened to the unused crusts? "He impressed me,'' finishing the sandwich in two small bites.

Van Huyten smiled a quirky smile. "I'll tell him that when I see him next.''

Roberta flushed. "I meant . . .''

"Yes, I know. I have confidence in him, too; perhaps more than he has in himself. He's smart enough to look at the data; he's smart enough to listen to advice. He'll grow in the job.''

Van Huyten was drinking tea, a beverage that gave Roberta the shudders. Somewhere or other, Sykes the butler had located a cache of colas. Styx imagined a wine cellar of sorts, with racks of aluminum cans, turned at intervals. Ah, Pepsi '98, a rare vintage. ''What will you do now?'' she asked the Rich Lady. She had intended the question as a taunt, but it came out somehow as genuine interest.

She did not find out, because Sykes announced that Harriet had returned, bringing Christiaan with him. Christiaan followed on his heels. The tall, lanky man with the granite humor in his eyes. He was two steps into the sunroom, demanding to know what the hell Riesey was playing at when he noticed Roberta. He looked at her and Roberta had the momentary fancy that she was being weighed and assayed. ''You,'' he said.

Roberta stood and extended her hand. ''So nice to meet you again,'' she said.

Chris turned to Mariesa. ''She's the one who brought me Crackman's package.''

''Yes,'' said the Rich Lady. ''I know.''

Roberta puzzled over that admission as she resumed her seat. *She knew?* And still she had ridden home with her and chatted like they were old friends. Did she know that Roberta had *instigated* the package? Perhaps not. Jimmy played things close to his chest. Not that the little weenie wouldn't snitch just for the amusement factor, but snitching would have exposed Tani Pandya and himself, as well.

''Ask her to step outside for a few minutes,'' Chris said. ''There are some things we need to discuss.''

''Roberta?''

''I'd rather stay,'' Styx said boldly. This was the payoff. The big confrontation. She'd rather not be offstage when it happened.

''It might be better if you—''

But Chris had lost patience. ''I want to know why you rolled over today, Riesey. I told you I would back you. I would have handled Sis and the others. Why did you throw your votes to me?''

"Chris . . .''

But Styx was already out of her seat. "You what? *You voted yourself out?*''

Chris did not seem to question her right to ask impertinent questions. He folded his arms and said, "That's exactly what she did. She might as well have resigned.''

It wasn't fair. It made her whole revenge a charade. Roberta felt the familiar shaking in her bones. "Why did you do that? Why?''

Mariesa rose from her chair and walked to the window, where she stared at the drifting mist. "I did it for you, Chris.''

The tall man unfolded his arms. He scowled. "What?''

"For you. I screwed up and I screwed up badly. We don't know yet how bad the damage to the station was. But even if it hadn't come to violence, I was still wrong. You knew that, but you would have backed me anyway. For mere pragmatism.''

"And what's wrong with pragmatism?''

She turned her back to the window and stood with her arms stiffly at her sides. "It's what brought me to where I am today. Stick to principles, Chris. Those are your anchors. Pragmatism sets you adrift. You forget that justice lies in the means and not in the ends.''

Roberta said, "But . . .'' Mariesa shook her head. There were tears in her eyes. Styx had waited a long time to see those tears, and now all she wanted to do was cry along with her. "Phil doesn't say that. He says if the goal is big enough—''

"Phil disappointed you, didn't he?''

Rage. Deny. Close close the lid. But she said only, "Yes.'' Then, more loudly. "Yes. You might as well know. It was some of his allies who goaded Donaldson into . . . what he did.''

Chris struck his palm with a fist. "A setup! I knew it.''

Mariesa nodded. She came to Roberta's side and placed

a hand on her arm. "But Phil isn't a bad man. He's only been sucked into the same trap as I have. That if the goal is big enough, it justifies any act. Carry that reasoning far enough and I could burn you at the stake—*if* I can save your immortal soul by doing it." A pause, then she asked. "Do you still love him?"

Reflexive anger snapped her head around. "What business is it of yours?"

Mariesa released her arm. "Why, none, to be sure. But that was a question I should have asked myself a few years ago, and I never did. I don't want you to make the same mistake."

Styx looked her boldly in the eye. "You mean, kicking Mr. Fast out?"

"No. I mean never grappling with what lay between us. I dismissed the problem. I didn't resolve it." She raised her head and said with ill-concealed impatience. "Yes, Mother?"

Harriet stood in the doorway with a cell phone in her hand. "It's Mr. Pye. He says it's important."

Mariesa made a little sigh. "Chris, you take it. It's your job now." Then again, more softly, "It's your job now."

Chris van Huyten said nothing, but held out his hand for the phone. Harriet gave it to him, looked over the tableau in the room, then turned and walked away.

"Yes, Ham, this is Chris. No, she can't. What did you say?" He placed a hand over the mouthpiece. "He says the Emergency Response Flock landed successfully at Phoenix. They brought back most of the construction crew."

Mariesa closed her eyes. "Thank you."

"Are you sure of that, Ham? No mistake? Oh, sweet Jesus! Riesey, Will Gregorson is dead. He was in the module the missile ripped open and he wasn't wearing a suit. There were two or three others who were sucked out with him.

The Rich Lady shoved the back of her hand into her mouth. "Will?" she said. "Oh, God. Oh, God, and it was my fault." She pushed Roberta aside and bolted from the room. Roberta staggered and half-fell into the long sofa. Chris turned away with the phone to his face, speaking low and urgently. Then he turned, snapping the phone shut.

"Tell Mariesa . . . No. Tell Harriet that I apologize for leaving so abruptly, but I've got to deal with this. Sykes!" He left the sunroom in brisk strides. "Sykes, tell Louis I'm ready to leave now."

And Roberta was left alone in the room. She looked at the phone in her hand, saw that it was powered off, then set it down on the table. She walked around the room, looking at the decorations and the furnishings without actually seeing them. Distantly, she heard a car door slam. Silence enveloped her, broken only by the echo of remembered voices and the ticking of a great clock somewhere nearby.

The Rich Lady wasn't coming back.

Well, it wasn't the first time she'd been abandoned. Time to pack Roberta-the-Activist into her own little box and wait to see what version emerged next. She headed for the front door. Sykes would have her car brought around. Whenever something needed doing, it was Sykes who did it. Why would a man like that spend his life as a servant? He was "administrative assistant" to the bone. He ought to be running a large office.

She passed through the ballroom, where the ghosts of her high school classmates scampered and posed for that reception so many years ago. She paused a moment and checked out the old, dead dudes in the portraits, remembering how daunting they had been to the kids who had gathered for the reception. Old, dead dudes in boiled shirts and tux; old, dead dudes in high starched collars; old, dead dudes in powdered wigs. That last one had been dead longer than anyone, she guessed.

Would the Rich Lady hang here someday? she wondered. This rogues gallery could use a woman's touch, that was sure.

That was Mariesa's grandfather, there on the end. Willem. The one she called Gramper. He was a wizened old dude with a stringy beard and a smile that Styx was sure would be a cackle if portraits came with sound. He looked *satisfied,* Roberta thought. He looked goddamn happy hanging there among that grim and dignified crew. He was a man who had complete control, used it, and loved using it. Roberta wondered if he still used it, even after all these years in the grave. "I don't know why," she told the portrait, "but somehow I think this is all your fault."

The ballroom was dark. The portrait did not answer. Roberta hunched in a little on herself and left the room. What was it like, she wondered, to have so many others looking over your shoulder? It wasn't right for the dead to rule the living.

In the entry hall, she wondered how you went around summoning Sykes. A pentagram drawn on the tiles? Styx would have just walked around the house hollering Sykesy! But Roberta had a modicum of dignity. She grunted. The tiles formed a maze. How peculiar! It was so unexpected that she was still puzzling over it, taking careful steps from one to another of the green tiles, when she heard a gasp behind her.

Turning, she saw Harriet Gorley van Huyten with a large book tucked under her arm. She looked at Roberta with widened eyes. "My goodness," she said. "Riesey used to do that when she was younger. Tip-toe around the foyer. I have no idea why. You looked just like her just now, when I stepped in."

"Your nephew had to leave in a hurry," Roberta said. "There was an emergency of some sort."

Harriet's smile was a perfect echo of Willem's. "Better him than Riesey."

"The R——Mariesa seemed pretty upset, too." Will Gregorson . . . Was that the electronics guru, Werewolf? Had to be. She remembered meeting the man once, down in Washington. She and Phil on one side; Mariesa, her head lawyer, and this werewolf on the other side. That was when they were all finding out how Attwood was playing them against each other. She remembered him as gruff and ill-mannered. His death meant nothing to her. Other people, closer to her, had died. "I was looking for Sykes to find my car."

Harriet nodded. "I will tell him, if you like. But first, come with me."

Puzzled, she followed the older woman to the dining room. *What, is she inviting me to dinner?* But all she did was place the book on the table and invite her to sit. "I thought you might like to read this."

She looked at the book, looked at Harriet, then shrugged and pulled out a chair. If this was the price of a cab, so be it. She hoped it wasn't the Great American Novel that the old bat had been scribbling in purple-tinted ink for the last thirty years and wanted the Well-Known Poet to read.

It was a scrapbook, she saw when she opened it. It was full of news clippings, download printouts, photographs . . . All arranged in a severe and geometric precision against a grid of faint, silver hairlines.

There was Chase Coughlin, in Pegasus red; and Meat Tucker in O&P blue.

There was Azim Thomas in his Marine Corps uniform, with the blue-starred ribbon around his neck.

There was a scientific paper, *"Toward a Periodic Table of Superconducting Ceramic Compounds,"* by Leland Hobart.

There was the book jacket for Tani's *Taj Mahal* and clippings of her reviews.

There was a photograph of Azim, looking both in-your-face and pleased as punch, flanked by Chase and an especially goofy Jimmy Poole under a headline: "HERO OF SKOPJE" HAD HELP FROM CLASSMATES.

And there, too, were all of her poetry book covers. The publicity shot that Emmett Alexix sent out to all the newsgroups. Copies of reviews and interviews. Accounts of her book tour. A gossip column linking her and Phil. Even, God help her, a reproduction of the nude painting Vaclav had done of her ironing clothes for the cover of *Uncommonly Commonplace*. Roberta looked up and turned to face

Harriet. Her eyes felt hot and she brushed them with the back of her hand.

"Why?" She stopped, and choked back reflexive anger. "Why is she doing this?"

"I'm sure I don't know," Harriet said. "But it's very important to her. I don't know what reason she gave Chris and the others for the gesture she made at today's meeting, but it was not the true one. Or at any rate, not the only true one."

"And what was the true reason?" she asked. She turned another scrapbook page. A news photo of Roberta and Tani at *The Tattered Cover* in Denver last winter. There was something wrong here. It should have been Beth keeping this scrapbook, at least the parts about her daughter. It should have been Beth showing it, half-shy, half-bragging, to her friends, chuckling in pleased disapproval over the nude painting. But her mother was dead, and if she had ever kept a scrapbook on her daughter, it was lost in the rain-soaked ruins of a bulldozed house. "What was the true reason?"

Harriet studied the book over Roberta's shoulder and made clucking sounds in her throat. "I don't understand everything my daughter does. She has always been a puzzlement to me. Yes, and a vexation, too, at times. But there are certain things I do understand, even if she herself does not. One is that she thought she was saving the world. And the other is that regaining your friendship proved, in the end, to matter more."

"My friendship?"

"Yours . . . and others."

Roberta shook her head. "Why?"

"I never understood why you hated her so. Granted, she can be trying, but . . ."

"She betrayed me." Even to hear it, it sounded melo-dramatic; and the words lacked the conviction they once had had.

"I suppose she did. But if she meant nothing to you, why should her betrayal matter so much?"

"Because . . ." But she had no answer to that one. The page showed her and Mariesa and Phil Albright sitting around a dining table at that charity benefit in New York. Someone had gone around doiding all the tables, she remembered, and selling the images. Bullock was there, too, with his Stepford Wife, and that *weird* cousin, Norbert, who looked like a dried prune, only not so lively. Everyone was looking at the doider, except Phil and Mariesa. Somehow, Roberta had wound up between them and they were exchanging a glance over her head. Not looking directly at each other, and Roberta wasn't sure if their eyes read challenge or respect or a little of both.

It looks like a damned family portrait . . .

Yeah. A dysfunctional family, with Mommy and Daddy fighting over the kid.

Phil or Mariesa, two would-be saviors of the world.

Pick one.

Neither.

Both.

And wouldn't *that* be a neat trick.

Life was full of contradictions. She didn't need a new mother; and if Phil was her father, who was that she'd been sleeping with? Oedipus sex? She started to close the scrapbook, but paused a moment. "Harriet?"

"Yes, dear?"

"Could you make a copy of this pixure and send it to me? I'll give you my address."

"I am not sure of many things, but that we have your address on file I am absolutely confident."

Roberta produced a week smile and sighed. "Thanks."

"If you care to wait in the foyer, I will send Sykes along presently."

In the entry hall, she was surprised to see how late it had gotten. The sun was low in the sky and the multiple images of the pond had taken on a peculiar, flat, silvery appearance. *I'll call Phil in the morning and we'll have it out.* The Rich Lady had been right about that. Don't just run away. Settle things first; then run away, if that's what still makes sense.

She brushed at her cheeks with her sleeve, but they remained wet.

Sykes made his appearance. Duded up, as always, he mananged to bow by simply inclining his head. "Mrs. van Huyten said you would have instructions for me."

"She didn't tell you what sort of instructions?"

"No, miss."

Roberta turned and left the foyer. She strode to the elevator just inside and to the right. "Mariesa has had some terrible news, and she does not want to be disturbed for any reason. I will call you when she is ready for supper."

Sykes bowed again. "I understand."

Roberta gave him a fleeting smile and stepped inside the elevator, where she pressed the button for the Roost.

When Flaco hobbled inside the waiting room at the end of the hall, Clotario leapt to his feet. He stood there for a moment with his mouth hanging open; then he broke into a smile. "Flaco, my friend!" They embraced and Flaco staggered. "They told me you had been thrown into space! Yes," Flaco said. "But I was wearing my suit, and my strobe lights told my friends where to find me. I remember nothing of it," He grimaced. "And I should be grateful for that."

Clotario seized him by the arms and led him, half-supporting him, to a seat. Flaco was glad for the help. His legs felt weak. It must be the gravity. The waiting room contained chairs of many designs and degrees of padding. Almost as if the hospital had been furnished from every garage sale in the Heights.

"I watched over Serafina, as you asked," Clotario told him, not without a strain of anxiety.

Flaco slapped him on the shoulder. "You did well, friend. How is she?"

Clotario nodded. "She could not be better. Flaco, we watched on the news. Serafina and I. They say you are a hero."

Flaco shook his head. "Not I. There were other men, better men. Some of them died."

"The astronaut, Levkin. We heard that, also. But he was a bandit."

"He thought he was doing the right thing. So did the man who dropped death on the soldiers in the Balkans. When he died, his weapon fired."

"But soldiers are paid to die."

Flaco shrugged. "Yet, who knows what will come of it? There will be conferences and diplomats will meet; and the Congress will pass laws and make treaties." He pushed himself upright and Clotario handed him his canes. "It's none of my concern."

Clotario followed him into the hallway and pointed him in the right direction. "What will you do now?"

"Go back," Flaco told him after a brief glance upward. "To finish what we started."

"Ah. And once it is finished?"

Flaco shrugged. "I don't know. Build another."

Clotario grinned and clapped him on the shoulder. "This is her room. I will wait where you found me."

"Maybe you will wait a long time."

Clotario laughed and left him standing there on legs of water. He reached for the door handle and paused.

Inside the room, a baby cried. It sounded like all the years to come.

Epilogue:

15 May 2010, Low Earth Orbit

Forrest entered *Salyut* for a last inspection before the braking burn that would put them into Clarke Orbit. Everything was buttoned up tight. The only loose object was Mike Krasnarov, who floated zipped into his sleeping bag at the end of a short tether. Beyond him, Earth filled the aperture of the observation blister. Bright white and blue, three-quarter full. Forrest entered the code that buttoned up the shield and the view vanished.

Forrest shook Krasnarov by the shoulder. "Wake up, Mike. We're counting down the checklist for the braking burn." The Russian grunted softly in his sleep and twisted, sending his sleeping bag into a slow turn. "Mike."

Krasnarov's eyes remained closed, but Forrest could feel the man come awake, and see it in the way his loosely floating limbs became suddenly still. "We're about to enter Earth orbit. We're home."

Mike Krasnarov opened one eye. "You can handle it." He closed the eye and turned away. Forrest shook the shoulder; this time more roughly.

"Damn it, get up there! I'm not moving from this spot until you come with me."

There was no reaction from the Russian. Forrest turned and slammed a fist hammerlike on the nearest cabinet.

"Mike, I can't handle it without you. No, listen to me. You will, by God, listen to me this one time!"

His outburst having gained him attention, Forrest suddenly found himself at a loss for words. He rubbed his hand across the Nomex fabric that covered the inner walls. He looked away from Krasnarov. "You were always numero uno, buddy. The one with the pants creased and the shoes shined, who checked and double-checked and measured the risks with a vernier—and then pushed the envelope anyway. We all knew it. Even Ned. We measured ourselves against you. Like you were some human Jo-block, traceable to the Bureau of goddamned National Standards. I could get away with being 'Cowboy' Calhoun because *Senhor Machine was always there*. I could always depend on you; because you were always dependable."

"But no longer," Krasnarov whispered.

"If you mean I can depend on myself now, the answer's yes—and you can, too. If you mean you're no longer dependable; well . . . That's something you have to answer yourself."

Krasnarov rolled in his sleeping bag and the rotation turned him away from Forrest.

"All right, have it your way. But if I were you, I'd be hanging onto something almighty hard when the big engines let go." He kicked off, hard, toward the frustum that led to the smaller module.

Back on the control deck, Nacho was working the copilot's seat. He looked up at Forrest's arrival. "Is he coming?"

Forrest didn't answer, but buckled himself into the command chair, where he sat for a moment glaring at the screens and readouts. He slapped the main armrest button with the heel of his hand to activate his controls. "Countdown status?"

"He was a hard, brittle man. He was bound to break."

"Countdown status!" Forrest snapped.

Nacho hesitated, then reported in neutral tones. "I have taken bearings on three global positioning satellites. The vector is in your course correction computer. I hope the numbers are correct.''

"Considering that the alternative is that we skip off the upper atmosphere like a stone off a lake, I hope so, too.''

"Do you think there's any—''

"There's always a chance. We been spilling V ever since we left the Rock, but we are still going almighty fast. Five klicks a second isn't exactly lollygagging. So, yeah, if the main engines don't light, we could—''

Nacho shivered. "Ever since the power system failed, I have lost my faith in the technology that sustains us.''

Forrest reached out and toggled the switches that activated the attitude thrusters. "Son, don't you ever lose faith.'' He turned on the intercom. "This is your captain speaking, Mike. We are beginning our initial descent into Earth. Get your ass back here before the main burn or hang on *really, really* tight. Braking burn in fifteen.''

Forrest pushed back in his chair and concentrated on the countdown clock, now blinking.

There were still five minutes left when Mike Krasnarov emerged from the transfer tunnel. He looked a little ragged and his coveralls were wrinkled and baggy, but his hair and mustaches were brushed and combed. He gave Forrest a sketchy salute. "Engineer reporting for duty.''

Forrest nodded. "Take the copilot's seat, son. Nacho . . . ?''

"I can sit in the back,'' Mike said. Nacho hesitated with one hand on his buckle, and Forrest said, "It wasn't a suggestion.'' Nacho yanked the harness open and squirmed out of the seat to his usual spot in the back.

"You did a good job filling in, Nacho,'' Forrest said.

"I do my job,'' the Brazilian replied.

"Once we're in Clarke Orbit, Mike, I want you to set the burn to bring us down on final approach Low Orbit.''

"No!'' said Nacho.

"Hard to do,'' Krasnarov offered, "without STC clearance or contact with LEO.''

Such considerations would never have given the Iron Mike a moment's pause. "Hell, son, we didn't have any of that when we closed in on the Rock, either. Comm is still out—at least the receiver is—but that don't make us invisible. They can track us and see we're heading for LEO Station. Folks down there'll be ready for us. We just need to keep an eye on the radar and visuals and a light touch on the attitude jets. You can do it in your sleep, Mike."

Mike didn't answer, but bent over his keyboard. Forrest was surprised at the empty feeling that caused, at how badly he missed the confidence of Mr. Perfect.

"I ever tell you about the time I was out jogging in the high desert?" he asked, when they had settled into their seats and waited with one eye on the countdown clock. No one answered. "I was down at Edwards doing a little flight test for MacDac. Ned, he was there, too. I think that was when we first met. Anyhow, I was out jogging, like I said, when this mother comes along in a little red sports car and damn near runs me off the road. Flipped me the bird as he went past."

Mike grunted and gave him a quizzical look. "What did you do?"

"Memorized his plates, just in case opportunity knocked later on. But it didn't matter. I just kept right on jogging, choking in this guy's dust for another half mile or so. Then I come around the bend, and there he is, off in the ditch on the left; and, man, is he cussing and kicking that 'chine of his. Me, I waved as I jogged past, and I didn't use any more fingers than he did."

Nacho laughed, and Forrest gave Mike Krasnarov a sidelong glance. "You never know what you might see wrecked on the side of the road, as long as you keep going down that road."

Low Earth Orbit. Home at last.

That was a funny thought. It was maybe the first time that any Earthling had felt "home" without actually being on the planet itself. But what did another three hundred miles mean after the distance FarTrip had already traveled? Forrest had the ephemeris integrated into their orbit. "I estimate we close with the LEO site in another hour," he told Krasnarov. The Russian pursed his lips.

"What is our delta-V, relative to the station?"

Forrest fed him the figures. "Looks like an apogee burn on the next orbit."

"Still no radio contact," Nacho reported. "They have to know we're coming. Our transmitter is working. Even if the targeting logic is fried, we should be close enough for our receiver to pick up nondirectional broadcasts."

"Maybe they don't want to broadcast," Forrest suggested. Still, it was damn funny. He felt like he was entering a darkened room full of people keeping a desperate silence. Any moment now, Deep Space would come leaping out, yelling, "Surprise!"

They had completed a quarter orbit at two-ten when their viewports flashed.

It was a brief glare, almost like a flashbulb, and Forrest resisted the impulse to jerk a nonexistent steering wheel; because the flash reminded him of nothing else but an oncoming driver flipping his brights at him.

"What the hell . . . ?"

A second flash, and then a third. Then a strobelike winking, flashing off their fuselage and viewports, off the micron dust and vapors their ship exhaled, off the monitors slaved to the outside doid array. A flickering light show.

Krasnarov scowled. "Burn in five," he announced.

"Are we under attack?" Nacho wondered.

Forrest quickly checked their sensors. Nothing had overloaded. If the flashing lights were some kind of attack, the energy wasn't near enough to damage their EM systems, let alone their vessel. Still, free-fall ballistics meant they could not easily dodge anything thrown at them. Duration could make up for a lot in the intensity department.

Suddenly, Nacho laughed. "It's code," he said. "The Morse code. Someone knows our receivers are malfed, so they flash a light in our eyes."

Forrest grunted. "One honking big flashlight, then—" He stopped. "Helios Light," he said. "I'll be damned. They must have shifted frequency from microwave to visible light to get our attention. Do you read code, Nach?"

"No," the Brazilian said. "I learned it once for amateur radio, but that was many years ago. All I remember is SOS."

"Jesus," Forrest laughed, "I hope they're not sending us *that* message. We're the ones need help."

"Actually," said Nacho slowly, after a moment's concentration, "they are. SOS." Forrest twisted in his seat. He wanted to ask if that was a joke, but one look at the Brazilian settled that.

"Nacho, check out the µCD library. There's an encyclopedia in there. It's gotta have a Morse code entry. The cockpit recorder has a complete record of this light show. See if the A/S can whack out a translation. Mike, start recomputing the burns we need for LEO rendezvous." Forrest shook his head. Message by Helio-graph. What was next, wig-wag flags? Throwing rocks to get our attention? He couldn't help laughing, which earned him a sardonic smile from Mike—as if Senhor Machine had followed his silent reasoning.

It took another half orbit before Nacho and the A/S puzzled it out.

<<FarTrip (the flickering lights had spelled out). NairobiSTC. Hld orbit. Do not cls w/LEO. Rpt: do not cls. Maintain orbit hld. Ackn. Yr xmitter OK. Wlcm hm.>>

"Tell 'em we get the message," Forrest said when Nacho finished reading the message. "No resource crunch for now, but we'd rather not spend another month on board."

Forrest rubbed his chin. He looked at Krasnarov. "What do you suppose it is?"

Mike shrugged. Nacho said, "Habitat comes into doid range in another forty-five minutes."

Forrest waited out the time. LEO was below them, so it would approach from the rear, which meant the front doid view since they were flying engines-forward. He shook his head. Space travel was hell on adjectives.

Their orbit crossed the terminator and they plunged into the Earth's shadow. The night below was clear, with only a few high, wispy clouds to block the view. The cities of Europe ran together like a river of light, from the Atlantic to the Eastern plains. If he held his hand up, he could catch them all in its span. Forrest sighed. "All the cities of the world," he said. No one asked him what he meant. No one spoke for a long time.

"Image," Nacho said at last, just before orbital sunrise, "in LEO's calculated location."

"Main view screen," Forrest ordered. "Maximum magnification."

A fuzzy blur appeared on the main screen. Forrest could make out several external tanks linked like a string of pearls, and what looked like three more co-orbiting a little farther away. "Computer," he said, "Main screen. Image. Enhance."

A ripple went through the picture, then another; and the image clarified.

"*Sancta Maria,*" Nacho breathed. He pushed himself between Forrest and Mike, closer to the screen. "What happened?"

A damn good question, Forrest thought as he studied the image. One of LEO's ETs was open to space, a gaping hole of rent metal in its side. *Dear Lord,* he prayed, *don't let that be the crew's quarters.* Nearby, what he had thought was another external tank turned out to be a modified Lock-Mar cruiser. Derelict, by the looks of things: no running lights, cockpit darkened, and tumbling slightly. It had no logo or RS-number, either, which was decidedly odd and against STC regulations. As the ship rolled, blackened paint and metal and long searing scars came into view.

LEO passed below them and began to pull ahead and no one aboard *Bullard* said anything.

Finally, Nacho spoke. "This is not the same world we left."

Forrest shook his head. "We aren't the same men who left it."

TOR
BOOKS The Best in Science Fiction

LIEGE-KILLER • Christopher Hinz

"*Liege-Killer* is a genuine page-turner, beautifully written and exciting from start to finish....Don't miss it."—*Locus*

HARVEST OF STARS • Poul Anderson

"A true masterpiece. An important work—not just of science fiction but of contemporary literature. Visionary and beautifully written, elegiac and transcendent, *Harvest of Stars* is the brightest star in Poul Anderson's constellation."

—Keith Ferrell, editor, *Omni*

FIREDANCE • Steven Barnes

SF adventure in 21st century California—by the co-author of *Beowulf's Children*.

ASH OCK • Christopher Hinz

"A well-handled science fiction thriller."—*Kirkus Reviews*

CALDÉ OF THE LONG SUN • Gene Wolfe

The third volume in the critically-acclaimed Book of the Long Sun. "Dazzling."—*The New York Times*

OF TANGIBLE GHOSTS • L.E. Modesitt, Jr.

Ingenious alternate universe SF from the author of the *Recluce* fantasy series.

THE SHATTERED SPHERE • Roger MacBride Allen

The second book of the Hunted Earth continues the thrilling story that began in *The Ring of Charon*, a daringly original hard science fiction novel.

THE PRICE OF THE STARS • Debra Doyle and James D. Macdonald

Book One of the Mageworlds—the breakneck SF epic of the most brawling family in the human galaxy!